Best Wishes!
John C. McMillan

THE LION
&
THE HARP

THE LION
&
THE HARP

John C. McMillan

www.ivyhousebooks.com

PUBLISHED BY IVY HOUSE PUBLISHING GROUP
5122 Bur Oak Circle, Raleigh, NC 27612
United States of America
919-782-0281
www.ivyhousebooks.com

ISBN: 1-57197-398-2
Library of Congress Control Number: 2003095468

Copyright © 2004 John C. McMillan
All rights reserved, which includes the right to reproduce this book or portions
thereof in any form whatsoever except as provided by
the U.S. Copyright Law.

Printed in the United States of America

*To my dear wife, Angie
and in memory of my wonderful parents,
with love and gratitude.*

Introduction

Colonel Iain Cameron had departed the safari base camp in Mozambique fourteen days earlier under the anonymity of a family emergency. The reason behind his leaving was clouded. Now he was back, and the nature of the emergency remained obfuscated within a dense fog of partial explanations. Iain's partner—and extremely close friend—Toby Drake had an extreme curiosity. Appreciating the fact that family emergencies were usually of a medical nature, Drake anticipated some explanation—like meningitis or a car accident—affecting some member of the Cameron clan. Also compounding Toby's inquisitiveness were the abrasions and bruises on the left side of his compatriot's face and a still-bandaged ear. "Slipping on a moss-covered rock and landing on a bramble bush," seemed an implausible explanation.

Sometime between the second and third sundowners—a euphemistic expression for safari evening cocktails—Drake began to speculate on the possibility that there could be a connection to the murderous Camp Invasion, which had occurred the preceding year. Nonetheless, he was restrained from further conjecture and never gave any consideration to broaching the question directly. After all, Toby realized that Iain Alexander Cameron had been—and to a considerable extent always would be—a military man. Though Drake didn't have any military experience, apart from running gun battles with Mau Mau insurgents back in the early 1950s, he was of the mind that military was equated with secret operations. Thus, Toby wouldn't attempt to stir any sleeping dogs—far better to leave them lie.

Certainly, Iain Alexander Cameron had been a military man, Scots Guards, retired—and holder of the Victoria Cross—the highest honor the British empire could bestow. Drake, like any other observer, who saw Cameron sitting in a camp chair with bronze skin showing from the margins of khaki safari garb and wearing a braided elephant hair bracelet on his right wrist, would realize that he appeared as the quintessential African hunter. Central casting would be hard-pressed to produce a more splendid example. However, underlying the analysis was a sense of the soldier—totally permeating his persona. Indeed, though his closest friends called him "Iain," clients would invariably refer to him as "Colonel." Certainly, the appellation suited him like a perfectly tailored dress uniform on a tall, slender, but muscular man.

After the third sundowner had gone down smoothly, Toby Drake abandoned all his speculations regarding Cameron's recent absence and switched his mind to matters of business. On the following day, new clients would be arriving in late morning on Safari Air, under the capable control of pilot Archie Andrus. Toby had already assigned—to himself—a pair of Texans whom he knew well from past safaris. After topping off Cameron's glass of Lagavulin single-malt whiskey, Drake smiled, saying, "You—old fellow—have the man and wife from Vermont to guide. Incidentally, she has a severe phobia regarding reptiles, so do your best to assiduously avoid them."

Cameron cocked his head and assembled his face in a dour expression, for which he was famous, and replied. "Once again; you have set me up—Toby. You know that's about as easy as eluding the sight of 'Ladies of the Night' in SoHo. Hopefully, we will avoid repetition of the appearance of a giant black mamba poking its head through the hole in the seat of the latrine! As I recall, your client, Mrs. Gilchrest, having confronted such an apparition, became incontinent and nearly in need of cardiopulmonary resuscitation." Toby pouted, then replied, "I did kill the snake didn't I?" Iain broke into a smile saying "Oh yes! But you riddled the latrine in the process as I recall."

"Humph! It was time to move it anyway," was Toby's rejoinder.

After completion of business, the two men were finally in their cots. In separate tents, Iain and Toby were left to ponder events. Again, Drake started to wonder what Cameron had been up to during his absence. However, his conjecture was short-lived, as the ethanol—recently embraced—quickly subdued his consciousness, though for Cameron, it was different, as the memory of recent events was very vivid. Also, African plains were not quiet places at night. Even though the great cats of Africa pad along soundlessly, a lion's roar or a leopard's snarl draw rapt attention from even the most experienced listener. Added to this were the raucous barks of the jackals and hyenas, plus all the startled sounds of their potential prey, whose nighttime tranquility was disturbed. Although aware of the sounds, Colonel Cameron's fully engaged mind was nonetheless capable of sublimating all such distractions.

For Iain, with his eyes closed to extinguish the soft, ivory incandescence of a full African moon playing on the canvas above him, mental images soon replaced actual ones. First appeared an island—more like a massive rock—jutting from the cold reaches of the eastern Atlantic, like the barnacled snout of a gigantic whale breaking the surface of a tempestuous sea. Such was the Isle of Skellig Michael. What had transpired there was fully known only to him. However, it could be surmised by the Irish fisherman who brought him there and later took him away. Cameron's restless mind rebelled at the violence that had occurred there and sought out gentler thoughts.

On the darkened stage of Iain's mind, Claire's face appeared. In memory, the image was always the one of the time she accepted his marriage proposal. Softly, Iain whispered. "Oh Claire! My dearest." How he would have loved to embrace her, but Iain knew that would never reoccur in this world. Imagery would have to suffice. Years together as man and wife had passed so swiftly. "I miss you

Claire," he whispered once again. Then, Iain added, "Have you come to help me—and set my mind straight—as you always did?" As if in answer to his behest, he began to imagine a parade ground. His long years in the military made that readily possible, as Passing in Review was an ancient tradition for nearly all armies. Soon, Iain envisioned himself on the Reviewing Stand with Claire at his side. Nearby stood his father, the general, and his mother, Mary. Also, one of his three sons and various beloved of kith and kin, who were now all deceased. They were all of the age at which Iain remembered them best, and all were smiling.

Soon, seemingly, sound swept into the silence, which Iain had previously imposed. Phantom pipers entered the drill field from the left. Kilts were swirling, and pipes skirling to the insistence of the accompanying drums. Immediately, he recognized their march, and Cameron began to recite the lyrics of:

March No More My Highland Laddie
See the tall grass so proudly waving
Like their banners of long ago,
With their heads held high while proudly marching,
Marching onward to meet the foe.
March no more my Highland Laddie,
For there is peace now, where once was war,
Sleep in peace—my Highland Laddie,
Sleep in peace now the battle's o'er!

Next came a full platoon, most smartly uniformed in Scots Guard's tartan, while some wore camouflage jungle fatigues. All were perfect in alignment and cadence. Iain recognized them all—for they were his men killed in the line of duty. All were free of the signs of death, mutilation, and suffering, which they bore when their spirits left this world. Then, as their CO shouted, "Eyes right," their heads turned, and each face bore a smile. Geordie MacCallum, Iain's dearest friend, was in command, as would be expected. How young he looked with hair still of fiery red; whereas Iain realized that he was alone in manifesting signs of age. Cameron saluted and called them by name. Interspersed within the ranks were several wee brown men; their size belying their prowess. They were his Gurkhas! "Why—Oh God! Did you take them and leave me here?" Iain murmured. However, because he knew that God never chose to disclose in this life, he realized there would be no answer now.

As the review continued, coming behind was a proud pack of fine dogs prancing in formation, as sharp as the soldiers preceding them. Iain noted the great tawny dog in front was Simba. Also, he knew all the rest by name. Again, Iain saluted smartly, as they all looked his way and responded with happy, wagging tails.

Suddenly, Cameron became aware that the music of the phantom pipers was still audible but changing. Now, he heard the somber notes of the "Minstrel Boy." Irish, it was, not Scottish! Appearing next was a jaunty, tall, muscular figure—surely a son of old Eire. Michael J. "Mickey" Manion-Moynihan was the mysterious man. Shunning protocol, the single figure dressed in civilian attire stopped in front of the Reviewing Stand and threw his best version of a military salute. This was accompanied by a broad smile; one that only an Irishman could produce, Iain smiled back and returned the salute—just as the image vanished. Soon, all the other visages were gone, except for that of Claire. She smiled—ever so sweetly—and seemed to say, "Have I helped make things right for you. Iain my love?" Then she was gone.

Colonel Cameron lay awake for some time, deep in thought. What had transpired in his life was a story he would like to tell. Consequently, Iain decided he would record it. *Perhaps, this would be a futile gesture,* he thought. *Then, again, some day a future generation might accept the lessons of history—and avoid repeating it!* Finally, sleep came, and by morning Cameron had reverted to his usual self, sometimes dour, sometimes smiling. However, as always, he was quick in repartee and dry humor, frequently spiced with just a touch of acerbity.

In the ensuing months, entertaining clients during evening hours with tall tales did not consume all of Colonel Cameron's time. Therefore, when alone in the privacy of his tent, he began to compose a narrative, which included much of his own life so far. Also, moved by his encounter with Michael Manion-Moynihan, Iain considered it only fair to devote a considerable portion to his memory. Many of the details originated in a diary, which he had found in Mickey's backpack Thus, the story—part fiction and part historical biography—would encompass the struggle of two countries arising from a common Celtic heritage and personified by two individuals. For the future novel, no better title came to Cameron's mind than *The Lion and the Harp*.

CHAPTER ONE

They were but a few months past graduation from the Royal Military Academy at Sandhurst. As of yet, there had been no call to arms. Second lieutenants Iain Alexander Cameron and George "Geordie" Edward MacCallum, of Her Majesty's Scots Guards, were the newest of the new. Their inaction was generating mental morbidity. Had they wasted those hellish years at Sandhurst just so they could muster for parade duties? Hell, if there were no chance to fight in a real war, even a billet in the British zone of Berlin would be welcome over this. How many nights could you spend in the Officers' Mess trying to act enraptured by everyone else's war stories, some of which were real and a few no doubt apocryphal?

Iain and Geordie were soulmates—simpatico to a degree rarely encountered. They were closer than the majority of brothers, at least those whose kinship (or lack thereof) they had experienced. There existed only two major differences in their lives. Iain was Roman Catholic, while Geordie was Church of England. Both were solidly though not profoundly religious. Neither had the slightest interest in or intolerance to the other's faith. While Iain had no steady lady friend, currently Geordie was engaged to a debutante of excellent pedigree; her name was Elizabeth Monteith. MacCallum was madly in love, or thought he was, and Elizabeth appeared similarly disposed, at least in public. However, the young lady and her family treated Iain with practiced polite disdain and, try as he might, it was difficult not to reciprocate.

Elizabeth's parents had a London townhouse that was quite splendid, and certainly a mecca for Geordie, who sought to include Iain's presence on frequent occasions. Second Lieutenant MacCallum seemed oblivious to the fact Cameron felt less welcome than a chimney sweep—but loathed to tell him. As far as Iain was concerned, the Monteiths were best known for their treachery in capturing William Wallace and handing him over to King Edward "Longshanks" and his torturers. He sometimes mused that if he had the reputation of Braveheart that Miss Monteith would gladly hand him over to the present monarch, assuming of course that Elizabeth II would have any interest at this time in history. As for his own love life, Iain had to be content with blind dates almost invariably disastrous—foisted on him by well-meaning senior officers' wives. These dear ladies seemed to have an inexhaustible supply of maidens, who had so far failed to generate even a spark of allurement on Iain's behalf. His always gentlemanly demeanor and feigned interest was frequently misinterpreted as genuine admiration. Thus, he had numerous requests for second social encounters. The majority of these he parried with kind and acceptable excuses, such as the need to assume the duties of a sick friend. There was, of course, Alexis Cochran in Aberfeldy—far north of the Roman Emperor Hadrian's Wall—but her responses to his letters were lacking in frequency and diminishing in ardor.

Both young men had been excellent students at Sandhurst. Iain's academic accomplishments resulted from long hours of disciplined study. Geordie was the salutatorian of their class and certainly could have been valedictorian. However, he assiduously avoided the distinction for two reasons. While he was a most gifted scholar, with the classic retention of the photographic mind, he would still have to exert slightly more studious effort to excel over Alexander Pitt Pembroke III—the genius martinet—who would most assuredly reign in first place. As Cadet Commander, one spent numerous hours in odious duties, such as guiding dignitaries about the institution, and Geordie would have none of that. Second, it would cut into the time he could devote to sports, and these Geordie excelled in and loved. Comparatively, MacCallum was smaller in stature than Iain, with his hair—a resplendent red—in contrast to the sandy locks of the latter. Whatever the sport—soccer, rugby, boxing, cricket, or fencing—Geordie was the warrior and dancer. His swift, extremely coordinated movements almost invariably left the opponent flat-footed and dazzled. Cameron might not have quite the speed or allusiveness, but he had strength and size. There was really no need to dance around an opponent if he could be demolished instead. Playing on opposite teams in a scrimmage, they were a wonder to watch—contrasting in strength and style but equal in determination. On the same team, they were a devastating duo.

It was 13 August 1948, one month past Black Friday, when units of the Scots

Guards had been sent from the peacekeeping forces in Greece off to the Malay Peninsula, where guerrilla warfare had broken out between the Malayan People's Anti-British Army and British forces. The former consisted primarily of Chinese Communist insurgents, and the latter were Malayan constabulary, plus a few elements of the British army. Iain was recumbent on his back with a weapons manual lying face down on his chest. He was contemplating whether he should dine at the Officers' Mess or cajole one of his peers into venturing out for fish and chips plus a few pints of Guinness stout. Geordie was off to the Old Vic, squiring Miss Monteith to a gala social event. There was no knock on the door. Suddenly, it just flew open, and Major Buchanan burst into the room. As Iain made a valiant effort to spring off his bed and assume an attitude of attention, his superior flipped a heavy envelope in his direction. "You have orders to Malay, Cameron! You had best get your ass in gear, pack your kit, and send a press gang out to find your red-headed buddy. The two of you are flying out at 0600 tomorrow!" Then, the door closed. Major Buchanan was gone.

Iain was bewildered, elated, and then bewildered all over again. He grabbed for a duffel bag, dropped it, and then reached for a phone. He must call his parents and advise them. Could he do this? Bloody hell—it wasn't some sort of top-secret operation covered by secrecy imposed by any War Power Act, or was it? Besides that, his father was a general, not some spook employed by the KGB. Wouldn't that make a difference? He ended up with the duffel bag in one hand, the phone in the other. Next, he packed the phone in the bag—apart from the protruding cord. Organized thought finally prevailed, and a call was made to his parents.

There was the rousing encouragement that Iain expected from the old soldier, and the cautious admonitions that would rightly come from a father. Underneath, he could feel the concern of a father for a son, who would be far away—in danger—and beyond his power to protect. Mother was like many Catholic mothers, choking back the tears, invoking guardian angels, patron saints, Jesus, Mary, and Joseph. There were promises of rosaries to be said, candles to be lit, and masses to be offered—all for her son, who was and would always remain her little boy.

Iain's exuberance was dampened by the call but not extinguished. His packing was complete when the door opened again without a knock. It was Geordie! The flaming red hair was heading in all directions, and it appeared only the roots were constraining it from flying off altogether. His face was flushed, and the freckles were thus subdued in prominence. A double scimitar of a passionate red hue festooned the margins of his mouth, no doubt the farewell kiss from Elizabeth Monteith. A resounding burp gave issue to the unmistakable aroma of stale champagne. Obviously, the two Sergeants he had dispatched to locate MacCallurn had done their duty. However, Iain realized he would have to pack for Geordie, who would be fortunate if he were in good enough shape to assemble his thoughts and dress in proper uniform by take-off time, as transport was waiting.

The venerable Dakota—Her Majesty's version of the American Douglas DC-3—was a slow but very dependable flyer. Given the relatively short range of the plane, the navigator, router, and the Foreign Office had of necessity to be magicians to get this old bird from England to Malay. Fortunately, there remained a sufficient number of bastions of the empire—augmented by present and former allies—to supply all the landing fields necessary for such a lengthy flight. Considering a cruising speed near 170 mph, a 1,000-mile range, and the need for the pilots to rest, it became a long and tedious journey. The crew and other passengers were bewildered—but entertained—by their two erstwhile plane mates, for Cameron and MacCallum seemed to think that every landing and take-off was as adventurous as the previous one. All their food was exotic and the scenery spectacular.

Iain and Geordie chatted away every waking hour, and many hours that others would consider best devoted to sleep. Who would see battle first? Who would get the first kill? Were there medals and promotions to be attained? Now they would have war stories to place in competition with their senior officers; their subalterns of the future—and to shyly share with the ladies though in a somewhat sterilized version. There were many discussions in regard to the fabled sloe-eyed, dark-skinned beauties of Malay. Some of their fellow travelers began to feel they were trapped in an aluminum capsule—with two modem Sinbads—whose imagined adventures were nearly as outrageous as those of the original mythical sailor.

On many occasions during their journey, the Dakota seemed as though it might fold its wings in flight and plummet earthward—in a fashion not dissimilar to a grouse paralyzed by a column of shotgun pellets. There were segments along the route where topography demanded the plane claw its way to the highest serviceable altitude. On occasion, either one or both motors developed paroxysms rather akin to the wheezing, labored breathing of an asthmatic in extremis. Despite their coughing and dysrhythmia, neither engine died, to the great relief of all on board. Transfusions of oil, fuel, and lubricants were administered, and spare parts were installed at many of their multiple stops. Once again, the bedraggled phoenix would arise from the ashes or dust of the most recent aerodrome where it had sought refuge. At last, the plane's tired old tires contacted the runway surface at the Royal Air Force base in the outskirts of Port Swettenham. Here was Malay!

Upon exiting the aircraft, the two would-be gallant warriors were assaulted by the blinding glare of the noonday sun. The deepest squint they could produce was incapable of diffusing the blinding light, and they involuntarily indulged their eyes by raising their hands in hopes of sparing their retinas from the cauterizing light of the searing sun. Simultaneously, both felt as though they were irrevocably encased in an impenetrable cocoon of sweltering, hellish, humid air. Every one of the innumerable apocrine glands each man possessed immediately released every drop of perspiration at their disposal. The clean and pressed uniforms they had recently donned—despite the rigors of dressing within the confines of Galloping Gertie—were soon limp and sadly stained. Iain and Geordie felt as if they had just emerged from a shower of someone else's stale sweat. The level of discomfiture increased as heat from the tarmac seared the plantar aspects of their feet, which found little shielding from the thin soles of their spit-shined dress oxfords.

Iain and Geordie quickly reconnoitered the area as best they could, and not a single sloe-eyed beauty was anywhere in sight. A dour, ramrod-straight Sergeant was partially visible in the blinding light. He was at attention as best they could tell. It was a strange apparition to see a shimmering soldier enveloped in heat waves. The dull thud of boot heels, descending on a hard surface in the classic cadence, alerted them to the fact that they had closed their eyes to shield them from the glare, and no doubt their faces were screwed up in a great grimace. The Sergeant was not as dour as they might have guessed from their limited visage. Under better conditions, a very obvious smirk would have been easily perceived. A booming voice snapped out: "Sirs! Welcome to Malay, gentlemen. Sergeant Purdey at your service!" Purdey did not say "poor bastards," which remained a silent part of his greeting. "The Private will grab your gear. Transport is straight ahead."

The Sergeant directed them to the rear of a much abused, beat-up Land Rover. There was no top to serve as a shelter from the sun. Both Iain and Geordie thought that getting the vehicle rolling might at least generate a cooling breeze. Shortly, they learned that it only sufficed to drive the heat to a deeper level. Once under way, the Sergeant turned to address them. His head was maintained in a fixed position, and there was a mounted .30-caliber Browning machine gun intervening. Thus, it became necessary for the two Second Lieutenants to assume awkward positions to see Sergeant Purdey's face. Viewing his mouth seemed necessary in the faint hope of adding some meaning to the words rendered barely audible over the roar of the engine and the concomitant road noise. They did make out "Its bloody hot here gentlemen! You'll welcome the rain—until you spend a couple nights sleeping in it." Iain was about to say, "We don't mind the heat, Sergeant" when he thought how ludicrous that would sound coming from a person constantly wiping his brow and wearing a uniform sporting only a few square inches of dry material.

More bumpy, lurching miles passed, and Purdey turned once more. "We didn't run into any land mines on the way down gentlemen. I doubt the bastards had time to plant any after we went by. We should have smooth sailing—so to speak—on the way home. There's always the chance we could run into an ambush of course. In that event, you gentlemen might wish to make use of the Browning. As you can see, there's a belt in place, so it's quite ready to go." He didn't add, "I hope you point it in the proper direction." He took the chance of assuming that even Second Lieutenants would have the savvy not to shoot him in the head.

An hour later, the Rover slowed and a quarter mile of straight road lay beyond. The Sergeant scanned the area with his binoculars, and it appeared clear. "Go ahead Smitty" were his words to the driver, and the Rover headed slowly for a small clearing on the left side of the road. "We'll stop here for a moment sirs. You may wish to take a leak. I've a couple of canteens, and you can wet your whistles as well." Sergeant Purdey and the driver walked off a few paces and relieved themselves. Their Lee Enfield carbines accompanied both. Geordie whispered, "Do you need to go?" Iain brought the canteen he had half emptied down from his lips and passed it to his friend. "Not me," he answered. "The way I am sweating there is no need to piss. Besides I would just as soon hug my sweetheart here in case the bad guys show up." Iain ran his hand down the Browning's receiver. "I suppose I'm to feed the beast, while you have all the fun mowing them down," retorted Geordie—fingering the belt of the .30-caliber cartridges.

As he returned to the Rover, Sergeant Purdey was aware Second Lieutenant Cameron was studying him, and the old soldier sensed the Lieutenant possessed a keen sense of discernment. He smiled. "You've noticed the limp, Lieutenant, and probably the grimace when I put my right foot down. I got winged with a 7.7 a month ago. Still hurts like hell, but it's much better than it was. The surgeon said I should thank God—and Sir Alexander Fleming—for penicillin, or I'd probably be named peg-legged Purdey. You've also noticed the jaundice, sir. Most of us have it—though the tan skin sort of hides it. Has to do with the mosquitoes, malaria, and the medicine. You add Malay, and you have the 4-M's. A discerning eye is help out here, Lieutenant—maintain it. It will serve you well."

The Rover finally bounced its way beneath a sign that indicated they arrived at Battalion Headquarters, Scots Guards Kuala Kubu Bahru. It was in the northern part of the Malay state of Selanger. Sergeant Purdey deposited them in front of the Headquarters Building and informed them that he would see to their gear, as he knew where they would be billeted. He saluted smartly and drove away. Their return salutes were perfection, now being free of the blinding sun. It was near dusk when they ascended the HQ stairs.

Once inside, they again exchanged salutes with the Sergeant at the Duty Desk and were ushered into the presence of Lieutenant Colonel Fraser, where further salutes took place. They produced their orders and then returned to an attitude of attention. "At ease, Lieutenants," were the Colonel's only words before he completed his study of their papers. This afforded time for Iain and Geordie to study the imposing row of campaign ribbons festooning the officer's uniform, which indicated many years of service in far-flung areas, plus an imposing number of awards. Their superior was deeply tanned with his jaw set and features chiseled. It was further noted that he had a long, livid scar on his left cheek. The lobe of his left ear was missing, and the left fourth and fifth fingers were also in absentia.

"I'll make it short and sweet, gentlemen," the Colonel gave as his preamble. "You have been assigned—or perhaps consigned would be a better word—to a hellhole, where there is a high casualty rate from wounds and sickness. You will receive two weeks of indoctrination here, which we trust will keep you alive and hopefully your men alive as well. Following that, you will be sent further out in the bush. There you will receive a couple more weeks training under the supervision of an experienced officer. If you make the grade, you'll be given your own platoon. If you make mistakes and survive, you'll get a proper ass chewing and one more chance. Should you not survive, we'll do our best to bury you. The Command Sergeant will show you to your assigned temporary quarters, field uniforms, and small arms. Maps and manuals will be available to you. Classes will commence at 0600 tomorrow. One last thing: I'm aware that you are the sons of distinguished field officers. That fact will bring you absolutely no favoritism. However, I know your fathers. I've served under them, and I hope—for their sakes—that you make it through with distinguished records. That will be all."

By the time they were able to pronounce Kuala Kubu Bahru—with the regimentally accepted inflections—the two-week indoctrination had passed. Now they were at least acclimated to a modest degree, and the dosage regimen for the antimalarials was down pat. Iain was starting to tan; however, there was less hope for the fair-skinned, red-headed Geordie unless all his freckles were to coalesce. They had endured all the jokes about the new kids on the block. Approval came from some, friendship from a few. Once again, Sergeant Purdey came to fetch them. He could sense they were fitting in, and they were good lads. Soon, they were on their way to join a company of Scots Guards in the area of Batu Arang.

As he drove his charges to their new post, Sergeant Purdey could sense a subtle change in the pair. Gone was the wild-eyed wonderment. They had more keen, alert expressions, and their eyes swept the road and jungle, just as his did. He noted the unusual personal armament of the larger, sandy-haired one. Sergeant Benson, the armorer, had been keeping the other NCOs posted on how Second Lieutenant Cameron had pestered him incessantly until he was able to produce the American-made arms and ammunition from a storehouse in Kuala Lumpur.

Chapter Two

    Captain Richards, the Company Commander, was the welcoming officer at Batu Arang. His Bravo Company utilized the buildings of an old abandoned coal mine, the only one in Malay, as their headquarters. He was friendly but not effusive. There was every reason to suspect that he was a solid professional, an officer from whom much could be learned. Later came the introductions to the other Lieutenants: Herrick, Carpenter, and Jones. The former two Lieutenants were to take them in tow and infuse them with as much savvy as possible. In ten to fourteen days, their teachers would transfer to Kojang in the south of Malay. There was much to acquaint oneself with in these few short days.

    As far as the enlisted men of Batu Arang were concerned, newly arrived Second Lieutenants were walking death warrants. Sure as bloody hell, they would become unglued when the firing started. Conversely, they could be cursed by having some foolish Custer complex, which would easily overcome their sense of caution and thus lead to some blind charge. This would only increase the number of widow's pensions back home. They usually ended such discussions with "Well, that's what we have bloody Sergeants for—right lads."

    On the first night in what was euphemistically called the BOQ, both Iain and Geordie were feverishly studying additional material they had received from their CO, Captain Richards. Between pages, there were frequent swipes at mosquitoes, who seemed to penetrate their netting with the same ease the German U boats entered Scapa Flow. "Oh shit," exclaimed Geordie. Iain cocked an eye and answered in a desultory manner, "Just a month away from the Monteith Manor, and you are back into the barracks vernacular, I see." He had been aware that his friend's language had become quite clerical since he had become enamored with the Barracuda, Iain's private appellation for the outwardly charming but inwardly devious Elizabeth Monteith. Iain quickly recounted to himself that it must be the gorgeous shock of auburn hair and the diamond blue eyes. Geordie could only appreciate that they were sensuous, not sinister. It couldn't be her personality that would lead him to the altar.

"What has led you back to excremental verbiage my friend?" Iain inquired of Geordie, setting his own to be studied material momentarily aside.

"It's all these bloody letters Iain. We're fighting a war against acronyms. Our forebears went to battle against Zulus, Fuzzy Wuzzies, Krauts, Frogs, Chinks, Afghanis, Russkies, Turks, and even Yanks. We, as I read this, are expected to expend our ammunition to slay the MCP (Malayan Communist Party), KMT (Communist Kuomintang), and the MPABA (Malan Peoples Anti-British Army) who stole all their weapons from the MPAJA (Malayan Peoples Anti-Japanese Army. For good measure, there is the WKT (Wah Kee Tong) and the NYCP (Nan Yang Communist Party)."

Iain replied "For God sakes, Geordie, throw that garbage in the latrine and study the maps! At least you will know where you are when an alphabet attacks. They are all one form or another of Commie bastards, so you can classify them all as CBs and end your anguish." Geordie reached for his map.

In the ensuing two weeks, they learned much and suffered not a little. Both were subject to sharp criticism, given in a seething whisper from their tutoring senior Lieutenants out of earshot of their men. They were introduced to punji sticks and booby traps—just split seconds before they would have fatally discovered them on their own. There were a few small engagements. They had seen the elephant—an anachronistic expression for first combat—and they had remained firm. However, wounds and death within their ranks were starting to become familiar.

The field of operation for Bravo Company was a very small part of Malay. The gourd-shaped peninsula projected itself into the waters, which bathed its shores. Anchored to the Asian continent by its attachment to Thailand, its bulbous extreme lies close to the Equator, abutting the Malaccan Straits. The South China Sea and its appurtenance, the Gulf of Thailand, washed the eastern flank. Westerly was the Andaman Sea, which derived from the Indian Ocean and formed the southern extreme of the Bay of Bengal.

There were swaying palms and white sandy beaches, which the two friends never really saw, for Bravo Company's habitat was in the great primordial jungle. It seemed impenetrable from the outside—and inescapable from the inside. They were locked in an inferno, despite the fact they were usually denied the rays of the sun, which seemed incapable of penetrating the green canopy formed by the limbs, leaves, and vines of the massive trees towering above them. From the air, it was a giant green cloak, which carpeted the sides of the mountains that ran like a dinosaur's spine from north to south in the centrum of Malay! In the floor of this morass, they shared this space with tigers, flying foxes, bears, elephants, monkeys, and even Komodo dragons. At least thirty species of snakes were known to slither in this pestilent place. Many had venom no less lethal than a fragmenting grenade. Myriad leeches sought one's blood, giving parasites, infections, and anemia in return. What blood remained was poisoned by the swarming, omnipresent mosquitoes, which gladly traded their plasmodia for the victim's erythrocytes.

God did not leave Malay devoid of beauty, as it was for all intents and purposes a divinely designed greenhouse. Though extremely inhospitable to humans, it was a splendid repository for flowers of the most vibrant colors and the sweetest scents. Interspersed between the bamboo and giant ferns were orchids, bougainvillea, wild hibiscus, frangipani blossoms, and tulip trees.

Hundreds of species of butterflies provided a moving mosaic, exhibiting exquisite patterns and perfect pastels. Parrots and other species of birds abounded, their polychromation being almost pyrotechnic in display. These were all glorious marvels to the nature lover, naturalist, ornithologist, and lepidopterist. For the soldier, they were just one more distraction or another hiding place for his adversary.

Iain and Geordie did see a considerable number of Malay aborigines—who were short, brown, and not a particularly handsome people. The ethnic Chinese inhabitants were not noticeably different from members of the same race anywhere else in the world apart from the fact that this particular group would like to kill them! The sloe-eyed, dark-skinned beauties did exist—just like the white sand beaches and swaying palms. As far as Iain and Geordie were concerned, they were as elusive as sirens, valkyries, and amazons.

It was now the end of Second Lieutenants Cameron and MacCallum's first month at Batu Arang. Their immediate predecessors, Lieutenants Herrick and Carpenter had departed for other assignments. Iain and Geordie had gained at least a modicum of skill at leadership and guerrilla warfare, and it would increase exponentially with each week's survival.

The men of Bravo Platoon were starting to become comfortable with their new leader—Second Lieutenant Iain Cameron. They were good lads. not really distinguishable from all the jocks who marched and fought from Sterling to Sebastopol. They would march to the gates of hell with Sergeant Major Sandy MacPhee in the lead, and they were getting enough confidence to go at least halfway with Iain. MacPhee was a stalwart, fatherly figure. He was strongly disposed toward his new commander, and indeed, he realized his sentiments were becoming paternal. He would sometimes say to himself, "You are a lucky man, Lieutenant Cameron. You have a General for your real father, and a Sergeant Major for a surrogate." He had no sons of his own. MacPhee realized that Iain's upbringing had finely honed his skills as a hunter, and Sandhurst had made him a soldier. It was a fine pairing that would serve the platoon well.

Sergeant Francis Findlay of Alpha Platoon was just as pleased with Second Lieutenant George MacCallum. His officer was more outgoing than MacPhee's. He certainly maintained discipline and let you know who was in command, though he did it in a friendly manner, which the lads appreciated. The men often joked, "The Lieutenant can chew you out—but in the end you feel good about it and convince yourself you really deserved it." They also said, "The Lieutenant could run you past the point of exhaustion, and it sometimes feels like you are having a good time."

In the early weeks, Alpha and Bravo Platoons were involved in independent operations. On occasions, there had been minor engagements with the Chinese guerrillas. Both platoons had a few members who sustained wounds, and each had a single fatality. They had enjoyed at least moderate success—indicated by the number of enemy killed, wounded, and captured. Alpha and Bravo Platoons were doing their part in building up the body count, as London now demanded, and Washington, D.C., would do the same in a bigger war some decades later.

On return to camp at Batu Arang, there was little in the way of diversion and entertainment apart from what could be conjured up on one's own. They had great facility and resourcefulness in that regard. Their happier moments were joyous and somewhat rowdy experiences. Geordie had somehow managed to transport his bagpipes to this alien land. He played them well, and his repertoire was considerable. Iain possessed a booming baritone of good quality. Captain Richards had a great bass. First Lieutenant Jeremy McIntyre and Second Lieutenant Benjamin Jones couldn't sing worth a damn, but when their efforts were mixed in with the drone of the pipes, they blended in reasonably well. Additionally, they sounded even better following consumption of a generous ration of the spicy Malaccan gin—or the occasional extreme treat of genuine Scotch whiskey. Given the rather relaxed nature of the small encampment, the enlisted men were usually invited to participate. Between officers and enlisted, some talented dancer could always be recruited. Such was the revelry on a Sunday night; the night before Alpha and Bravo Platoons were to go on their first combined mission. This was to be a sort of pincer's movement to the summit of Mountain 06. It was reported that a relatively large band of Chinese insurgents were active in that locale.

Sleep did not come readily for either Iain or Geordie that night. Each wondered how well they would comport themselves in their first joint operation. When dawn arrived, the surge of adrenaline they both experienced fully erased any vestige of fatigue. Their men were inspected and their own gear and armament fully checked. The two troop lorries departed at precisely the hour intended. Geordie's platoon would dismount first and Iain's would follow two miles after. Cameron gave his friend a thumbs-up salute as his lorry passed, thus causing a second thumb to rise in response. They both wondered what their reunion would bring. Neither questioned that one would occur.

When Iain's platoon came to their point of deployment, they disembarked and fanned out quickly. Two hours later, they had encountered not a single sign of hostility. It was time for a rest—and replenishment of all the fluids that flowed from their pores in response to the heat of the green furnace in which they would live or die!

Iain dumped his depleted self against the trunk of a huge tree. His legs sprawled akimbo until they gradually spread out, each seeking a defile between the massive gnarled roots, which were proportionate to the immense tree they supported. Thus sprawled, there was a modest measure of comfort for the body. For those of his men not assigned as pickets about their perimeter, there was also rest for the mind, as they rapidly became adjusted to their surroundings. Such was the mode of escape, which sustained fighting men throughout centuries of conflict.

Each and every one of Iain's senses persisted in a state of full alert. Though the mind drifted, the eyes still scanned for motion or aberrations of color. The ears searched for sounds that were in any way foreign to this particular environment—including those noises distinct to the men of his platoon scattered about him. Even the olfactory system could on occasion warn one of something alien. Iain mused momentarily on what a mixed blessing it would be to have a sense of smell like his beloved Labrador retrievers. Then, he laughed inwardly as he wondered if the aroma of himself and his men—overlong in dirty, dank, sweaty uniforms—would be overpowering. Cameron answered his own question by recalling the fact that his dear dogs never seemed disturbed by their own stench after a long and happy thrash and roll in a mass of sheep dung. That led him to recall the retort of Samuel Johnson to his fellow stagecoach passenger, who adamantly stated to the very odiferous Johnson "Sir, you smell," to which came the pointed reply "No, sir, you smell, and I stink!"

Shortly, it was time to move on. Sergeant Major Sandy MacPhee was attentively arousing those who had sought sanctuary in sleep. This was deftly done, following a protocol of long experience, for he knew that for those who would awaken in silence the nudge of a boot toe would always suffice. However, there were a few who startled readily. Their nap ended when a hand was placed across the mouth, and a thumb—in the ribs—recalled them rapidly to the state of alert with no opportunity to create a sound.

Iain quietly reslung the Model 97 Winchester 12-gauge trench gun over his shoulder. The Thompson .45-caliber machine gun he clenched in his left hand. A 9mm Browning Hi power rested in its holster—hard against his right hip—while the dirk with its twelve-inch blade rode in its scabbard slightly astern of the Browning. Two extra magazines of 9mm ammunition for the Browning on his left flank at least provided some counterbalance to the load. The other officers of the Scots Guards frequently chided him about his choice of weapons. It was always pointed out that the venerable Thompson was also the choice of the Yank mobsters. Everyone seemed to be aware of the fact that when the Winchester trench gun with its sawed-off barrel was introduced in France during World War I, it was considered inhumane. For a time, there was talk of banning its use as nonchivalrous—and a rather diabolical weapon of war. Iain became known as "Machine Gun Kelly," but he took no umbrage at this. A master of repartee, even at the tender age of twenty-two, Cameron would smile most gregariously and thank them for at least selecting a Celtic name, rather than addressing him as Frank Nitti or Al Capone.

Iain would advise his detractors that if indeed they did have any illustrious ancestors, who might have fought for the empire on either land or sea, they should be cognizant of their use of grapeshot. Furthermore, the twelve pellets or balls in the standard 12-gauge load was no different than grapeshot—except to the extent that the cannon from which it spewed forth was held in his hands rather than mounted on a cumbersome carriage. Besides that, chaps who would go about cauterizing the lungs of the poor bastards on the other side with chlorine gas—or twisting a bayonet in their liver—would do well not to be queasy about someone imparting a speedy and merciful demise on the wings of twelve lead balls.

With his cherished weapons in place and grenades and spare magazines properly positioned, Iain placed himself at the head of his platoon—and started their forward advance in a single file. Flankers were used to the extent the terrain and foliage would permit. It was not customary for the platoon leader to be at the head. However, Iain had quickly become attuned to jungle warfare. Furthermore, he was an extraordinary hunter and possessed in full measure all the qualities that could be attributed to the human predator. His men readily sensed this and greatly appreciated their Lieutenant's abilities. The Sergeant Major—Sandy MacPhee—remained in the platoon's center, marking the progress of the column, coordinating and deploying his flankers, and remaining ever mindful of any sign or signal of the enemy—or other form of danger—with a skill equal to that of his Lieutenant.

Iain maintained a steady pace commensurate with the safety and endurance of his men and the need for extreme caution. They were progressing upward on Ridge 107. A rocky spine located on the south side of a deep canyon, it culminated in an apex on the summit of a mountain referred to as 06 on his map. The other spine leading to the top was 106, and it was being climbed by Alpha Platoon under MacCallum's command. It was expected that Iain's Bravo Platoon would meet up with Alpha by nightfall. They would camp overnight and return to base via the canyon tomorrow, God willing. Those were the plans and objectives of Operation Zulu. It was nice for the cartographers and tacticians, Second Lieutenant Cameron mused. It was one thing to conjure up numbers for stick pins to place on topographical features—and then dream up catchy names for the actual missions; all in the comfort and safely of Headquarters. Here, it was just exhausting to those in pursuance—in this place and at this time—of someone else's madcap scheme, and arbitrary numbers in pursuit of an illusionary enemy! Whether it was 106, 107 or 5,555—there was the same umbrella of trees, bushes, vines, snakes, and leeches. The mosquitoes were not only loathsome; they could be lethal.

The pace upward continued unabated. The rendezvous and darkness barely two and a half hours away. Iain's eyes were constantly sweeping. Bent blades of grass, a broken stem or frond, or a displaced rock could herald the presence of the enemy. However, the progress of his platoon did produce some sound. They were men wearing boots, and they were passing through underbrush. One had to consider this as a sonic overlay from which you subtracted all the other sounds, like the call or flight of birds, the movement of animals big and small, even the menacing roar of a tiger fearful for her cubs. Last, there was the sound of other humans—the enemy. Those were here to kill you. It was generally said that "in the Malay jungle, you oft can see but twenty-five feet ahead." An invasive step into anyone of those twenty-five feet—or the thousands that lay beyond—could be one's last.

Bravo Platoon pushed on for another hour at a glacial pace in Iain's mind. Then, his ever vigilant eyes perceived a color and motion alien to what belonged in that particular space. He became aware of the acceleration of his heart—the emergence of cold sweat—and the rising of the hackles on the nape of his neck. How similar it was to the primordial response of the wolf on alert. Instinct, allied with intellect, instantaneously warned him that the visualized motion came from one man's hand signaling to another off to his left. Given the limitation of visibility, the second enemy was in all probability within ten feet of the signal maker. In a millisecond of fluid motion, the Thompson muzzle was aligned, the safety released, and the trigger depressed. The submachine gun responded with roaring release of its deadly fusillade. As the barrel traversed to the right, it produced a twelve-foot-long swath of mangled foliage. The jungle became alive with sound—as scores of birds fled their perches—seeking safety from the terrifying noise so swiftly introduced into their sanctuary. However, no human sounds emerged from the ravished thicket.

Sergeant Major MacPhee was instantly at Iain's side. His Lee Enfield Mark IV was pointed warily in the direction of danger. The pair advanced in a stealthy, extremely cautious fashion. Iain had been very accurate in his assessment of the enemy position, as well as in his marksmanship. The first body was that of a Chinese insurgent, who had betrayed his position with the hand signal. Two of the steel-jacketed bullets had caught him near the center of his chest, shredding his heart and exploding his spinal column. A grenade was clenched in his right hand with the pin still in place. There were two more bodies. One was near the ten-foot distance from the first, as Iain's instinct had predicted. The third lay sprawled in between. Both bore evidence of head wounds. Their rifles were deployed in a ready position, caressed by the closed fingers of their lifeless hands.

Corporal Thorburn came forward rapidly to search the uniforms of the Chinese, in hopes of finding maps that might be useful. Unfortunately, written papers were of no immediate help, as they had no personnel in the field who could interpret the Chinese characters. That task could be accomplished at Headquarters, so everything was retained.

The Lieutenant and the Sergeant Major were discussing the action in hushed tones when the Sergeant Major became aware that the rifle—carried by the probable leader of the trio—was unlike any they had encountered in Malay to date. It was a total departure from the Japanese 7.7mm Arisaka, which the Communists had in large numbers, resulting from the insurgents availing themselves of thousands of abandoned Japanese weapons following the defeat of the Imperial Army. Both Iain and Sandy MacPhee were small arms experts—and immediately aware that this was a 7.62 x 25-caliber PPSH-41. The stubby cartridge was the same as that of the Russian .30-caliber Tokarev pistol, and only about one third the length of the venerable .303 Lee Enfield. However, its punch was devastatingly potent—especially coupled with its ability to be fired in a fully automatic mode. The weapon's thirty-five-shot magazine—curved like a steel banana—could be emptied in less time than it took a Scots Guard to fire his bolt-action rifle twice. Equipped with a drum magazine, the number of rounds available was nearly doubled. This added a chilly dimension to this dirty little war. They would return this weapon to Headquarters for evaluation. Meanwhile, the two Arisakas were destroyed. The grenades and ammunition of the guerrillas were buried, and the bodies were left to decompose.

At this time, every member of Bravo Platoon with an attentive ear became aware of a steady pattern of gunfire from the opposing Ridge 106. It was the route of Alpha Platoon—Geordie's platoon—and generally in a line with their position, except on the opposite side. Alpha was in a serious firefight, as was evident from the numerous reports of detonated rounds, which drifted across the deep chasm that separated them. The educated ear was capable of distinguishing the resonant roar of the British 303 from the sharper crack of the Arisaka. Also, staccato bursts—no doubt from the PPSH 41s were repeatedly audible—in the deadly struggle between Alpha and their adversaries.

"Oh, dear Jesus, protect Geordie and his men," gasped Iain inwardly. The same prayer was reflected on the faces of his men. How he wished there were some way that he could hurl his way across the chasm and come to their aid. However, prudence demanded they continue up the ridge, then descend on the opposite side. Immediately, they moved out—at as fast a pace as their endurance would allow, driven to the extreme by their desire to aid their comrades.

Fifteen excruciating minutes into the forced march, they became aware of silence. The cacophony of gunfire from the opposing ridge had ceased, and the silence was devastating. They knew that the explanation lay in the completion of the engagement. It wasn't a rugby match where you retired to the locker room to nurse your bruises. Here the winners walked, limped, or crawled away; some were supported by their comrades, if any were capable of aiding them. Iain could only hope and pray that such was the situation of Alpha Platoon. He would not let himself dwell on the alternative.

Bravo Platoon attained the mountain crest, scarce moments before day's end. There was no sign of Geordie or elements of his platoon. One could rationalize this based on the fact that Alpha Platoon's pace would be agonizingly slow, given the extreme probability of wounded among them. Certainly, they could have chosen to remain at the battle site, knowing Bravo Platoon should reach them before noon of the following day.

As the men of Bravo dropped to the ground in the small clearing where they would spend the night, it was evident to Iain that even Sergeant Major MacPhee was dead on his feet. He was calling up his last bastion of reserve energy, just to post his pickets and pass out the order of the watch. *Men like Sandy are the spirits of every British Regiment,* thought Iain. *Such a man will perform his duty until his soul leaves his body. They will do so—even if it is necessary to crawl from one man to the other—all the while holding their guts in place lest they expire from a gaping abdominal wound.*

When it was determined that their position was made as secure as possible, Iain's body and brain totally crashed. He knew that the entire troop must obtain sufficient rest to enable them to strike out at first light. Iain would relieve the Sergeant Major from his watch at 0100 hours. Four hours of sleep would revive him, he was sure. "Oh God!—Why can't we leave now?" was the question that he repeatedly asked himself. *Sure—plow blindly through the bloody, black jungle and impale yourself on a punji stick—or blow your leg off on a land mine. That would do Geordie a hell of a lot of good. I'm trapped here until dawn—damn it!* he thought. In his frustration, Iain turned to prayer, for he knew God is a great ally to man when they run short of options. Iain made his apologies to his Creator. "I'm sorry—dear God! Why didn't I call upon you earlier? Forgive me Lord! Please save Geordie and his men." Just as few men pray without any doubt as to how God will respond, for added success, Iain decided to call on the Blessed Virgin, mother of Jesus. He recalled a prayer of his youth, the Memorare. He had been neglectful of it as of late. The big tough soldier had placed too much reliance on his own skills. It was easy to forget one must rely on God for one's very next heartbeat, and all those that followed. He quietly began. "Remember, Oh most gracious Virgin Mary—that never was it known—that anyone who fled to thy protection, implored thy help or sought thy intercession was left unaided—"

When the prayer was complete, Iain called up from memory reserve the time when he was ten. He had called on Mary to save his ancient Labrador retriever—Rory—whose temporal existence was drawing to a close at age fifteen. On the side, he also invoked the help of St. Francis of Assisi, the patron saint of animals. Surely, these supplications would save his beloved pet. They did not, and he was devastated as only a child can be. After the burial in the little pet cemetery on the estate, he had hurled himself on the ground and cried out in despair "Prayers are no good! Mary and the saints just don't care." Then, he found himself hoisted from the ground by his father's large hand, and he fully expected a stern rebuke. With a degree of tenderness that he had not expected, his father's words followed: "You know—Laddie—all of our prayers are answered, but it is quite human not to always like the answer you get. God created Rory, and he was God's to call home when He determined it was time. God allowed him a long life—a wonderful home—and all the hunting adventures that a dog could wish for—complete with a loving master. No doubt, God—in His infinite knowledge and wisdom—knew that given more time Rory might suffer some horrible sickness ending in terrible shape. So, why don't we thank God instead of railing at him? Besides, I think God planned for you to have a fine Labrador puppy, and that will make Rory happy knowing there will be a new wagging tail to fill the hollow he has left. Besides that, Iain, Rory will be waiting for you at the Rainbow Bridge right next to a pack of lovable hounds that are awaiting me." Shortly, upon return to the manor house, his father produced the poem, which read:

The Rainbow Bridge (Inspired by a Norse legend)

By the edge of a woods, at the foot of a hill,
Is a lush, green meadow where time stands still.
Where the friends of man and women do run,
When their time on Earth is over and done
For here, between this world and the next,
Is a place where each beloved creature finds rest.
On this golden land, they wait and they play,
Till the Rainbow Bridge they cross over one day.

No more do they suffer, in pain or in sadness,
For here they are whole, their lives filled with gladness,
Their limbs are restored, their health renewed,
Their bodies have healed, with strength imbued.

They romp through the grass, without even a care,
Until one day they start, and sniff the air.
All ears prick forward, eyes dart front and back,
Then all of a sudden, one breaks from the pack.

For just at that instant, their eyes have met,
Together again, both person and pet.
So they run to each other, these friends from long past,
The time of their parting is over at last.

The sadness they felt while they were apart,
Has turned into joy Once more in each heart.
They embrace with a Love that will last forever
And then, side-by-side, they cross over . . . together!

After the third reading, the page was dotted with tears, but his father's words and those of the poem brought peace to his rendered heart. This was Iain's last thought before surrendering himself to total oblivion—his mind and body too far exhausted to allow even a dream.

The predawn birdcalls softly saluted the very first rays of sunlight, which pinkened the eastern sky and imbued the distant crags with the softest of purplish hue. The boy was gone; the soldier had returned. The soldier vowed to God that "He would do all he could for his friend and yet is prepared to accept His Will." Weapons were checked, rounds were chambered, and they were on their way. Second Lieutenant Iain Cameron was in the lead!

Despite the urgency, which they all shared, the advance was slowly cautious and measured as before. One hour out, Iain repeatedly mimicked the cry of the cockatoo. This was one he had mastered in the same way that he could call the great gray Canadian goose; the mallard duck, or imitate to perfection the "go back" call of the Scottish red grouse. Geordie knew it well—and would respond in kind if he were near. However, there was never a response. A mile further ahead, Iain's olfactory sense was assaulted by the stench of flesh in a state of early decay. Iain was aware that putrecine, the by-product of that process, has an indelible odor extremely offensive to humans, and they were enveloped in it! Slightly further on, their ears became attuned to the drone of insects. Alpha Platoon must lie ahead. They were not victorious. They had not survived!

Apart from Sergeant Major Sandy MacPhee, there were no previous experiences that would have prepared the men of Bravo Platoon for what they saw. Even under the necessity of rigidly imposed silence, there were grunted curses and prayers. Iain softly sighed, "Oh—dear Jesus every man of Alpha Platoon is dead!" Then, the next sounds were those of uncontrollable retching, which emanated from the sight of so many bodies that lie scattered helter skelter. They had been stripped of their weapons and any article of use or value. Many were mutilated; all showed wounds of varying magnitude. Steeling himself to a degree, which he didn't even know he possessed, Iain began to search for Geordie. Then, he recalled that his foremost duty was to care for the living in his command! Quietly, Iain conferred with MacPhee, and a perimeter was established. The capable Sergeant Major made sure it consisted of those most severely affected by this vision from Hell. He knew that it would be impossible to transport the bodies at this time. Rapid burial—after identification where possible—was the only alternative they could employ.

Iain had no sooner made his orders clear than he became aware of a bamboo pole—to which a sign had been attached! The sign—in crudely lettered English—seared his mind like nothing he ever had, or would, encounter. "A present for you Scots—running dogs for your Imperial British. This pile of dung is your Lieutenant." It was signed in Chinese character letters. Iain looked down. The pole had been inserted into a mound of flesh composed of large hunks of Geordie's body, which had been hacked to pieces. Sergeant Major MacPhee's firm arm anchored Iain's sagging shoulders, and he sighed, "Even bloody Edward was kind enough to leave William Wallace in five recognizable pieces! Go elsewhere, lad, and I'll attend to things here." Iain replied, "Thank you Sandy, but he was my friend—my brother—and it's my duty." The moment was such that proper military titles were not called for, and MacPhee answered, "I knew you would feel that way, Iain. God give you the strength, lad." Then, the Sergeant

Major wiped a single tear away from his leathery cheek, cleared his nose, and walked away, knowing this young man was as stalwart as any of the Scot's heroes who had preceded him!

Summoning all the strength at his command, Iain took his razor-sharp dirk and cut two locks of red hair from such parts of Geordie's head as he could find. These he carefully placed in the pocket of his jacket. Then, prodding about with the tip of the dirk, he uncovered Geordie's dear heart. This was torn in places, though relatively intact. Iain wrapped it carefully, and placed it in his pack. He thought of Robert the Bruce, King of Ancient Scotland, whose heart was carried to the Holy Land, fulfilling in a sense a pledge to lead a Crusade, which he could not keep.

Geordie's heart would return to Scotland—that he vowed! The other remnants, he buried personally in the center of his fallen comrades.

Iain cleansed his hands as best he could, then sought out Sergeant Major MacPhee. "Sergeant, keep the men on vigil, and then walk with me while we scour this area," he said. Their search produced innumerable spent cartridge cases. A large number were from Geordie's 9mm caliber Sterling machine pistol, which indicated to Iain that his friend had gone down late and must have sent a goodly number of the enemy to the Hell they deserved! Dozens of empty .303 hulls were present in the area surrounding the bodies of Geordie's platoon. Off on both sides paralleling Alpha's route of advance were numerous clusters of empty brass, recognizable as having been ejected from a large number of Arisakas and several PPSH—41 submachine guns. Hundreds were of 7.7mm caliber from the Arisakas. Additionally, the smaller cartridge cases of 7.62 x .25 ejected from the PPSH-41s were discernible in small piles—paralleling the trail Geordie and his men had been following. A short distance from the ambush site lay the decapitated bodies of Geordie's flankers—thus explaining that they were killed by stealth and by one accomplished at doing so! This would explain why Geordie's platoon had no warning of what they would soon encounter. The Sergeant Major signaled several of the men and indicated there were further bodies for burial. Also, there were numerous pools of blood along the line of ambush, and bloody trails leading off into the jungle, so Cameron knew that the insurgents had paid a dear price for their victory. However, it was a foregone conclusion that their leaders didn't give a damn! In several small, clear but muddy areas, Iain discerned a boot print. He knew the rank and file of the insurgents generally wore sandals and some were even barefoot. The design on the heel print was sharply defined. *An officer,* thought Iain, *and I'll wager my life that the whore's son came from China—to give some leadership to these mongrel bastards!*

A brief conference was held between the Lieutenant and Sergeant Major. Emotion was a pervasive force, and the desire for revenge was rampant. However, prudence prevailed. They agreed that to charge blindly after their enemy could well be a fool's errand. They had sufficient time to have covered many miles since yesterday's encounter, or the enemy could have set up a new ambush that Bravo Platoon might well stumble into, given their physical depletion and present psychological state. A return to base was the reasonable course.

Assembling his small force, apart from the pickets, Second Lieutenant Cameron presided at the gravesite ritual. His voice was strained with the words passing resolutely outward. Though his mouth was open, the jaw was fixed. Although the eyes were moist, no tear was allowed passage down the cheek. The service, by necessity, was brief. However, the words permeated the very souls of those assembled. Then, they departed this sorriest of scenes with Iain again in the lead. He remained ever mindful of dangers, which might lie ahead. Nonetheless, his mind became cognizant of that Pibroch—sad to play: "There was a Soldier, a Scottish Soldier . . ." Geordie's heart would return to those "green, green hills of home."

Each man knew that he would remember this hideous scene for all his days. Also, loss of a platoon might be of little moment to politicians and people in general. However, for the jocks of Bravo Platoon, it was tantamount to loosing your brother of the here and now! Such was the spirit and bond derived from sharing life, death, and the simple little pleasures, which so infrequently came to the men in the jungle of Malay. Consequently, it was not a moment to be shared with others in the future. No!—you locked this in your heart—and never let it go. Some would have only a short time for the recollection, because they would in due time join the ranks of the fallen. There would be a similar service someday for them, but their participation would be inert. For those who did return to home and loved ones, they did remember to a man.

All hoped that the bodies of their fallen comrades would someday be unearthed and returned home. However, that hope would remain unfulfilled.

Upon entering their home base, the bone-weary soldiers of Bravo Platoon sought sleep and solitude. Their fighting spirit would reignite on some future day. For now, they thought that only the deepest level of somnolence would purge their fears, replenish their bodies and their spirits! For Second Lieutenant Iain Cameron and Sergeant Major Sandy MacPhee, debriefing was their fate. After all they had endured, it was psychological torture, but their duty nonetheless. "How the hell did this happen?" was an oft-repeated query. However, Iain's fellow officers—though few in number—were supportive in a fashion that only another soldier who had witnessed a similar event could manifest. After the platoon grilling passed and recommendations were made, a bottle of single-malt was passed around freely. However, before collapsing in his own cot, Iain sought out the armorer. There was need for a wee welded kist in which to carry Geordie's heart home to Scotland—from whence it came and where it belonged.

Chapter Three

In the weeks succeeding the annihilation of Geordie's platoon, Iain molded his devastation into determination. Of course, there were the obligatory letters to write. The missive to Geordie's fiancée, Elizabeth Monteith, was resplendent, though no doubt redundant with words describing at what height of esteem Geordie had held her always. Iain even thought it would be an act of extreme kindness to lie and tell her that his dearest friend and her beloved was still alive when they came upon him, and that he had whispered with his dying breath, "Tell Elizabeth that my love for her will be eternal." In the end, Iain forsook this bit of well-meaning duplicity. Nonetheless, he did try and convey in every way that he could conceive how much Geordie idolized her. "His love was constant, and it sustained him throughout the desperate circumstances encountered here—a half-world away from his one true love." Iain spared Elizabeth the grim details surrounding Geordie's actual last agonizing moments. He could not bring himself to personalize the letter in any fashion on his own behalf.

The letter to General Sir George Edward MacCallurn and Geordie's mother was a commission that seemed to bleed the very essence from his soul. Again, he could not divulge the exact nature of Geordie's mutilation. Previously, he had advised his own father of the circumstances in a personal letter safe from his own mother's eyes. The elder Cameron would advise Geordie's father in a way acceptable to old soldiers, who having survived their own mortal dangers must in this case face the fact that his son had died and thus steel himself to accepting the way of its occurrence. In the letter to the MacCallums, Iain was very high in his praises of Geordie and his soldierly qualities, his devotion to his men, and the reciprocity of their devotion to him. All of this was done without embellishment. The fine words were direct from the heart—free of any ornamentation—and they were true.

In the personal letter to both his parents, Iain tried admirably to place the best possible face on the horrendous occurrence. His words, he knew, would provide little comfort from the claws of fear, which would rip his mother's resolve—turning every waking moment into anguishing apprehension and twisting her dreams into nightmarish scene. "You can't make a convincing argument regarding your own safety when your dearest friend has been destroyed a scant three miles from where you stood." Iain did his best. It could be said of him throughout his life that he always did his best. Finally, after sustained effort, the letters of condolences were written. The sorrow and devastation they represented would always bob as unsinkable flotsam in the wake of the rest of his life. However, massive waves that descended and crashed the bow of the ship of life in which Cameron sailed on his mortal journey were yet to be conquered. They represented the rest of Iain's war. He vowed it to be an indomitable voyage.

In the days when Alpha Platoon was being reconstituted, Iain's Bravo Platoon—acting either independently or in concert with Charlie Platoon—was constantly on the move. However, it seemed they always arrived a few hours late, so they were unable to avert the heinous depravations of the Communist units. There developed an easily perceived pattern of death and destruction perpetuated by one particular insurgent unit, which for the most part, operated in company strength. Frequently identified in the grotesque remains of their assaults on the homes of local rubber plantation owners, was the heel imprint of the Chinese boot!

Apart from evidence of wear, it was a nearly immutable indication that Geordie's killer was also the source of this despoliation. They had captured a sufficient number of guerrillas and had ample testimony from the rare Malay aboriginals, who survived these satanic raids, to know that their enemy was indeed mainline Chinese! He was extremely well steeped in warfare, having experienced and survived many combat encounters with the Japanese and subsequently the Chinese Nationalists. His formal appellation was Major Chin Shin Yee. He was a graduate of Wampo, the Chinese Military Academy. It was alleged that he was an aficionado and master of Chinese martial arts. Some testified to the fact that he had appropriated a samurai sword from a high-ranking Japanese officer, whom he had slain, and that he had become deadly in its use. Major Yee's sobriquet was "the Serpent"—a name both fitting and well deserved!

News of an attack on the home of a rubber plantation owner reached Company Headquarters via shortwave radio, and Iain's platoon deployed immediately. They had the obvious advantage of a connecting road of reasonable surface and adequate width. With the usual circumstances inherent in a nonhostile state of affairs, it was a twenty-minute trip. Multiplying minutes by number of possible land mines substantially altered the equation. Depending on your personal timidity factor and desire to spare one's men and self, a Commander could invoke prudence and justify a one-day jaunt. Iain had his own means of solving the weighty equations of timely arrival and suicide. They drove with the highest level of alert and perception, arriving alive in thirty minutes with racing pulses and maximum adrenaline levels.

On arrival, the sight that greeted Bravo Platoon was a scene of total devastation and savage carnage. Those of the workers who had chosen not to join the Communist guerrillas now lay grotesquely sprawled in the same places they had once occupied as living and erect human beings. Their last agonized grimaces were now fixed in their faces. Those bodies, whose mortal existence was not terminated swiftly by the bullets impacting their flesh, bore the unmistakable wounds of multiple bayoneting, or grotesque deformity deriving from the brutal bludgeoning of the thin calvarium that once encased their brains. The planter's home and all the buildings had been torched. Blackened pyres, still smoldering, offered the only evidence of what might previously have existed.

To the left of the burned-out shell of the planter's abode was a sight that even Dante Aligheri would probably have excluded as being too obscene to describe to his readers! In a small semicircle, formed around a once beautiful tulip tree, lay what must certainly be the bodies of the planter's two children and wife. The little girl and boy had been decapitated. The small heads lay beside the bodies, which had at one time supported their smiling countenances. Those same dear faces—eyes agape—now stared blankly toward heaven, a refuge to which they had certainly already gone. The wife and mother's body was fixed by rigor mortis and tightly coiled in the classic fetal position. Her outstretched arms appeared to try and return the gravid uterus to its rightful place within her eviscerated abdomen, but in vain. Central in the drama was the immolated body of the planter. On inspection of the charred remains, it was evident that his hands had been nailed to the tree above his head. Then, his body had been tightly lashed to the tree's trunk with barbed wire. Little was left to the imagination, and there was no question that he was thus affixed to be witness to the execution of his family. Someone had gone to great lengths to ensure that the planter would be in excruciating pain, as he struggled in some vain hope of saving them. Nearby, a petrol can lay tipped and empty. Off to the side immediately adjacent to the container were telltale heel prints. Surely, the Serpent had directed every facet of this satanic scene!

Iain tore his tam from atop his head and hurled it at the ground. He seemed further infuriated that the Balmoral didn't penetrate the earthy crust. As he kicked violently at the inert crumbled cloth, he hissed through clenched teeth, "That dirty, fornicating son of a whore!" His men had gown used to their Lieutenant's own peculiar form of invective; however, they remained puzzled as to the reason he employed this grammatically correct but anachronistic form of barracks banter. Iain, of course, knew that he did this due to his father's example—coupled with the parent's admonition when he left for Sandhurst: "You may become a soldier, but you should be a gentleman! Remember, lad, I'll tolerate no foul mouth in my presence. If you must—in an extreme case of agitation—employ a word descriptive of coitus, then use the proper term. Also, in referring to parentage, remember a bitch is a dog, and no good dog would have a son of a type to which you would apply that label. A whore is a 'whore,' and the meaning is universally understood. Lastly, there will be no reference to such topics in the presence of ladies. To do so will land you on your backside if ever done in my presence. I'm still quite capable of positioning you thus," said his father. The look that accompanied the words left little doubt that his elder had full confidence in his ability to do just that. Thus, the expressions had become an inseparable part of Iain's lexicon, given the proper audience. Additionally, there was a certain satisfaction to be gained in the selection of words, which allowed one a decided roll of the r's commensurate with Highland speech. Such a pleasure was not to be found in the much more commonly used terms.

After retrieving his headgear, Iain dusted it sharply against his thigh. "We're not cavalry charging to the rescue, damn it Geordie! We are bloody gravediggers. We might as well turn our arms in to the Quartermaster and draw shovels." To a considerable degree, his words were true. Successes were few; the number of enemies killed or captured were small. Shortly thereafter, they undertook a most thorough search for booby traps. Pickets had been placed on arrival. Now, there was need for graves. Iain and Sergeant Major MacPhee found a suitable spot, and the grim task began.

As Lieutenant Cameron started to return to his vehicle to have access to the radio, he noted the body of a large dog, whose tawny color stood out in at least moderate contrast with the foliage in which it was lying. "Poor old fellow," he said in muted tones, more to himself than the fallen canine. "At least, they didn't take you away for dinner. The Chinese are quite fond of dog meat, you know. I suspect you must be the planter's pet, so we will find you a spot close to him." As he bent to pick up the dog, he became cognizant of a slight respiratory motion. Then, the lid of the uppermost eye opened, and an extremely weak effort was made to initiate a snarl. Considerable blood was puddled near the dog's hindquarters. Also, the adjacent foliage was stippled with blood droplets characteristic of those expelled from a pulsating artery. No sign of persistent arterial flow was present, and Iain assumed that as the dog's pressure dropped to shock level, the punctured artery with its elastic walls finally contracted and sealed itself. Only a very slow ooze of the darker venous blood persisted. He dressed the wound as best he could, then placed the animal in his Rover. Hopefully, the dog would survive, and that would please him. Iain thought, *Oh God, how much nicer it would be if it were all the people, or at least the children, had survived!*

Upon return to camp, Lieutenant Cameron proceeded to report to Captain Richards, while the good Sergeant Major went off to find a medic to treat the wounded dog. Fortunately, since there were no human casualties, the poor beast would not have to wait his turn in some type of man-canine triage system. Meanwhile, the Commanding Officer greeted the reporting Lieutenant Cameron. "Another tough day, Lieutenant, according to your radio message."

"The bastards have us chasing our tails as always," Cameron replied.

"Sit down, Iain." Captain Richards motioned toward a chair. Opening a bottom desk drawer, he produced a partially filled bottle of Lagavulin single-malt Scotch whiskey. "I think there is sufficient 'Usquabah' left to settle our souls for a moment. Besides, there is an event worth a wee celebration! Some stodgy old band of WW II campaigners has decided to award you with a promotion. Congratulations, First Lieutenant Iain Alexander Cameron." They clicked their glasses and savored the golden brown liquid treasure. Such was its rarity in Malay that each precious drop was left to be absorbed by the tongue, rather than swallowed. To quaff it would be an inexcusable gaffe!

Captain Richards explained his newly conceived tactical concepts to Iain. He let Cameron know that he wished to experiment with various plans and tactics. They should seek and destroy the Serpent and his troops. Iain would remain in command of his own platoon, but a second platoon would be frequently placed under his leadership when deemed advisable. Then, other strategies were discussed. Consequently, it seemed to both that they might be heading in a direction that would prove rewarding.

In the ensuing three weeks, they were sorely tried. On frequent forays afield, the Serpent and his company of marauders was never encountered. Iain, usually in command of one platoon and sometimes two, was easily the most successful in finding small groups of guerrillas and killing or capturing them. In between missions, Lieutenant Cameron and Sergeant Major MacPhee kept training the men, and honing their ability to move stealthily—and perceive even the most inconspicuous signs of the enemies' presence.

Consequently, Iain had little time to devote to the dog he had saved. However, thanks to the care of their Medic, the beast was starting to recover. Cameron had correctly recognized the male canine as a Rhodesian Ridgeback. The dog's size, color, and absolute characteristic of a raised column of hair along its spine rendered this self-evident. This breed was well suited to the habitat of the country from which the dog derived its name, but Malay was a far cry from the arid plains of that part of Africa. "I suppose," Iain addressed the dog, "that a few of your ancestors were brought to this hellhole—and were tough enough to survive! You got all the good genes, old fellow." Lacking any knowledge of the animal's real name, Iain decided to call him Simba. The dog became gradually accustomed to this address, as he did to having his ears rubbed and tummy patted by his new master.

A few days after becoming ambulatory on three legs, Simba's demeanor suddenly changed. Gone were the soft eyes and weakly sagging tail. Suddenly, his eyes became fierce, and his upper lip was rolled in a snarl exaggerating the gleaming white fangs! Simba made every effort to launch himself in a three-legged charge despite his debilitated condition. Iain carefully grabbed the dog's collar, alert to the fact the dog might turn on him. Such was not the case, for the animal's attention was drawn to something outside. Restraining Simba, Iain opened the door of his quarters and was immediately aware that all the dog's attention and hostility was directed toward a small column of Chinese prisoners, who were being loaded on a lorry for transit to an internment camp.

Being a hunter and having a great knowledge of dogs, Cameron was immediately aware that Simba had easily detected the scent of the Chinese and had made the connection between the scent and the pain he had suffered. As hounds chase the stag and fox, driven by commands from their olfactory systems, it occurred to Iain that Simba could just as easily locate their common enemy. Of course, Iain was acutely aware that an undisciplined dog could ruin a hunt. In the past, he had gone afield with other hunters and had witnessed their half-trained, unchecked canines scattering birds in all directions—far ahead and totally out of range. Such a happening in a sporting event could be a matter of extreme frustration. However, if a bark or charge betrayed your position while stalking an armed enemy, disaster would surely follow. As always, Cameron never seemed to want for a plan to suit a situation, and soon one was sure to evolve.

In the weeks following, Iain utilized every available moment to train Simba. To further his purpose, he recruited one of the Chinese prisoners. Through the interpreter, this former hostile, Wai Chan, had made a convincing argument that he was a defector from Communist ideology. He pleaded that he had been forced to join the guerrillas' movement under the threat of execution and had taken pains to deliberately miss hitting anyone on the English side. His hopes had been that he would have the good fortune to stay alive long enough to defect. Probing deep into his soulful slanted eyes and divining his body language, Lieutenant Cameron and Captain Richards had decided to gamble on Wai Chan and place him on trustee status. Given the hapless soul's surname, Iain elected to dub him Charlie. Charlie Chan was the Oriental equivalent of Sir Arthur Conan Doyle's Sherlock Holmes, and one of Iain's favorites, along with other readers and moviegoers, who were enraptured by the lore and lure of the mythical crime fighters.

The translator, despite all his skill and Confucian patience, experienced extreme adversity in educating Charlie to his new duties as the quarry in a dog-training program. Seemingly, the Chinese defector had great difficulty in comprehending that the plan was not intended to utilize him as dog meat, and that Lieutenant Cameron had no wish for him to experience a premature reunion with his honorable ancestors. So, the first drills required the reluctant Charlie to simply walk across a portion of the campground, while Iain restrained Simba on a very stout leash. Fortunately, the dog had been restored to quadrapedal status by this time, and he was a very eager participant in stark contrast to Wai Chan's reluctance. The Oriental bolted on the first three occasions, leading Iain to wonder if he also should be on a leash. Meanwhile, Simba's response was one of totally unrequited savagery. The vicious snarls and barks were of sufficient amplitude that Iain was forced to distance the exercise further from the camp.

In time, utilizing all the guile at his command, coupled with treats, affection, and stern admonition—where applicable—Simba began to make progress. The dog was totally devoted to Iain and was thus able to sublimate his fury in return for the affection of his beloved new master. In time, Simba learned to go on point when he detected the scent of the hapless Charlie. The reflex positioning—in the pointing stance—was totally unobtrusive and absolutely quiet. However, the part of the training that Simba craved, even more than his daily rations and periodic treats, was the chance to attack! This was done in complete stealth—and only at his master's command. In time, even the well-padded Charlie, frequently fortified with rice wine, began to enjoy this part of the barbarians' strange game. Finally, the Rhodesian Ridgeback was ready for his first field trial.

Human members of Iain's platoon were also the subjects of intensive drill. Results were impressive, and the London-cherished body counts were increasing. Officers and men of the other units in this small command were impressed! There were requests to participate in his training, so that they also could benefit from his background, and Cameron's newly developed expertise in jungle warfare. They were warmly received. Morale was high, and there were greater expectations—on the behalf of each—that they were gaining an edge on the enemy—one that might permit them to someday return to the embrace of their loved ones whole in body.

Two other occurrences came along that were fortuitous and most beneficial pieces to help solve the puzzle of victory and survival for the men of the company. Iain had been ordered to go to Kuala Lumpur to supervise a detail, which would pick up needed supplies for his company. It was his fabulous good fortune to locate several cases of American M-2 .30-caliber carbines stored well-preserved in protective coats of cosmoline. Better still, there was a goodly supply of the appropriate ammunition protected from the heat and humidity by sealed metal canisters. The Supply Sergeant had gradually given in to Lieutenant Cameron's very convincing argument and friendly banter. This treasure of Yankee largess was conveyed to his lorry.

At the office of personnel, Iain was able to claim six new enlisted men that would be welcome replacements for his companies' casualties. However, it was only by the greatest of good fortune that he happened to see three Gurkha enlisted men sitting quietly on a bench in an adjacent room. Much like a young sports car buff, spying a showroom exhibition's shiny Aston Martin or Jaguar roadster, Cameron knew they were something that he had to have—young lads from the hills of Nepal with faces of brown, appearing disarmingly innocent. These Gurkhas were far smaller than his Highland jocks, but then, so were cobras. Each Gurkha carried a kukri, their legendary killing knife, in a scabbard hung from his belt. As fangs were to the deadly cobra, so was the kukri to the Gurkha! Cameron knew that historically these men were not of the Nepalese warrior castes, but their exploits in many wars left no one in doubt that they were proud warriors in every connotation of the word.

Iain Cameron had sat beside or astride his father's or grandfather's knee on hundreds of occasions. Those that stood out most firmly in his mind were the ones where other old soldiers were present, and the subject was war. Rare was the time when some old soldiers' tales did not include Gurkhas! He knew that you could spell the title at least eight different ways. However, regardless of the spelling, the pronunciation seemed always the same. Gurkha was said to mean "cow protection" in Nepalese, and indeed, many of them did just that. Then, there were the chosen ones, who came each year to the places of recruitment—such as Pokhara, 210 km from Kathmandu—where they sought out the Gala Wallahs or "recruiters."

Iain remembered that anthropologists claimed the Gurkhas were of Mongolian descent, and, certainly, their eyes would give credence to this belief. Surely, no Mongol who rode with Genghis Khan or Tamerlane was anymore stalwart than these, their descendents. Remembering from all the stories that he had heard as a child, First Lieutenant Iain Cameron had retained only five words of Gurkha—which he now repeated—"Kaphar hunnu bhanda marnu ramro," or "It is better to die than be a coward!" Such was the motto of these men, and he became determined to have some fight at his side. "Just in case I should live to be an old soldier, what would it be like not to have a Gurkha story of my own?" he wondered. Cameron's mind could be astonishingly agile when necessity called. All one needed was guts, guile and a gullible ear. Iain had the first two, and now it was time to test the Sergeant on the third.

When the noncom in charge of the desk handed him the completed paperwork, Iain studied it carefully. Then, he suddenly exclaimed, "Where the hell are my three Gurkhas?" The Sergeant was both startled and befuddled. "Beg your pardon, Lieutenant, but I have no indication that any of the Gurkhas were to be assigned to your unit. The only ones I have on my roster are to the best of my knowledge to be sent to join a larger unit of Gurkhas down south. I'm just awaiting the proper paperwork, which should be here any day now." Iain drew himself up to his full six feet, three inches and stated in a loud and most authoritative manner, "Sergeant—am I to assume that you are completely ignorant of 'Operation Kukri?' Good heavens man! This has been talked about for weeks! What the bloody hell is going on? Every company in the field is to be assigned three to four Gurkhas. I've driven down here expecting three Gurkhas, and I intend to get them!"

The NCO stammered, was going to object and seek an opinion from a superior, when he noted that the Lieutenant was now leaning over him with clenched fists resting on the anterior rim of his desk. He flinched from the officer's malevolent glare and cold, hard eyes. "Well, Sergeant, I'm waiting!" shot toward him, through the clenched teeth that filled the space between the curled lips. The sergeant glanced about nervously, regained the papers, and dutifully assigned three Gurkhas to the Lieutenant's unit. "Sorry about that, sir," exclaimed the flustered man.

"It's been hell here, Lieutenant, sixteen-hour days, and all the heat. I do recall hearing about 'Operation Kukri,' and I'm pleased to have the opportunity to fill your quota."

"Good man!" said Iain, now smiling.

Cameron quickly gathered his new charges into a lorry and sped away. The Gurkhas came willingly, only too happy to escape the confines of the humid office. They did wonder why the officer had not called them by name. Perhaps, he just had trouble with the pronunciation. Simultaneously, it dawned on Iain that he had taken charge of three souls, and he hadn't had the foggiest notion of who they were—except that they were Gurkhas! He quickly studied the roster to correct the situation.

Iain's innovative tactics were having a telling effect on nearly every member of the Scots Guard unit. Majorities of the men were now eager to find and destroy the enemy, and they had confidence that the outcome would favor them—and it did. Conversely, because of the Scots' success, the Communist forces experienced a reciprocal diminution in morale. With increasing frequency, individuals or even small groups would simply fade into the jungle. Each recorded departure would leave Comrade Yee in a state of incredible wrath! For any captured deserter, the magnitude of their chastisement could only lead to a desperate desire to die, rather than endure another second of the Serpent's sadistic vengeance. To a degree, Major Yee relished a deserter's return. The screams of the condemned were an aphrodisiac, their death extreme gratification.

Yee's perversions did in no way detract from his guile, as he devoted long hours in an effort to analyze the reasons behind his dwindling success and increasing losses. He knew, of course, that a majority of the surviving rubber plantation owners had fled to enclaves of safety near Kuala Lumpur, and a few had deserted Malay entirely, deciding to repatriate themselves to their countries of origin. A few of the staunchest planters remained. Holdings were now quite fortified and reinforced by members of the Malay constabulary. Despite this increase in his enemy's vigilance and strength, he still enjoyed considerable success in exterminating them by virtue of his tactical superiority in numbers, firepower, and planning. Though it was far more fulfilling to kill the capitalistic dogs, he could still take a measure of pleasure in driving the others away. Both alternatives would lead to the ultimate victory, which was to change Malay to a completely Communist state.

Yee was readily able to discern that the only real impediment to the completion of his task were the Scots Guards. Though Major Yee still relished the annihilation of the entire platoon led by the red-haired officer, his rapture was diminished by the knowledge that the Scots Guards Company had been brought back up to strength and something had changed to greatly increase their elan and success. Based on the intelligence his spies had been able to garner, the Serpent thought it highly possible that the metamorphosis he had come to appreciate was strongly related to the barbarian giant, who led one of the other platoons. Yes—this man and his unit must be the next British sacrifice! With great relish, the Serpent conjured up mental images of all the various ways he could kill the Scottish officer and his subordinates. Perhaps, he might even have one of his agents deliver the Lieutenant's head to the Governor's Mansion on one of their gala party nights! The Serpent smiled very malevolently, as he polished the exquisite blade of his katana with the obligatory silk cloth. "You will have more Scot's blood to savor—and soon—my love," were his whispered words to the sword. "I'll spin my web and set my trap!"

Meanwhile, Iain's purloined Gurkhas had become an instant success at Batu Arang. In the three weeks since their misappropriation, there had been no demands for their return or blatant threats of court martial. "Perhaps," Iain mused, "Operation Kukri has become an updated version of the Emperor's Clothes!" Cameron had discovered that two of his Gurkhas—Kulbir Ghale and

Lalbahadur Ghale—were brothers, twins to be exact, and Tulbabahur Thapa was a slightly older first cousin. Proper pronunciation of the names could be a problem, so each was assigned a nickname. Kulbir became "Cool Beer," while Lalbahadur was assigned "Lullaby," and Tulbabahur became "Tully." The Gurkhas did not find this in any way denigrating, but rather considered their new names as signs of inclusion if not endearment. Real camaraderie and mutual respect quickly replaced their initial aloofness. They embraced and were embraced. On patrol, they were diligent and vigilant. So stealthy were the Gurkhas that the Chinese sentries' first awareness of their presence might be the indefinable sensation of a razor-sharp kulri transecting their necks.

Simba was an equal success and a delight to his master and the men of the unit, including Cool Beer, Lullaby, and Tully. While all benefited from the dog's prowess, only Iain possessed his absolute loyalty and attention. The Rhodesian Ridgeback was able to recognize a Chinese scent at sometimes unbelievable distances, thus alerting the unit to their presence and providing ample time to deploy in ambush or attack the unwitting enemy. At a little ceremony attended by all at the encampment, Simba was presented with a new collar resplendent with Sergeant's stripes. "You're the four-legged equivalent of Gunga Din, old boy," said Iain while rubbing the ears of the dog. "It's a pity old Rudyard Kipling isn't still around. He could do wonders writing a proper poem about you." Simba wagged his tail and placed a front paw on his sitting master's knee. His eyes were shining brown arcs, overfilled with admiration. Some things a dog can do to show his love and devotion transcend the need for words, and do, indeed, leave them unnecessary. At that exact moment in time, neither man nor beast, could be aware of what a test they would be put to in the very near future.

Iain, like his adversary, Major Yee, was quietly formulating plans that would place them in the same place at the same time. The Serpent owed a debt to humanity for all of his evil depredations, and the young First Lieutenant was resolute in his resolve to obtain revenge in full measure for the death of Geordie. Also, officers and men of the company were becoming increasingly aware of a new weapon that Iain had taken to carrying, as did his ancestors. The weapon—obvious to any Scot—was a basket-hilted broadsword. This was no parade weapon of ceremonial salute, for it was meant to be a purveyor of death. They accepted its presence and speculated on its purpose. Many guessed correctly.

Chapter Four

✥ ✥ ✥

Emanating from a single source, the drone from the motor of a distant plane is a lonely sound. The wings and body of the patrolling craft dipped and rose in response to the wind and thermals 1,500 feet above Mountain 06. The aged aircraft for the most part followed a grid pattern of search. However, deviation occurred at intervals when the pilot had a perception of a finding, which stood out as an anomaly in the expanse of green-carpeted landscape. Then, the airplane would fly in a lazy circle, mimicking a hawk that had caught sight of some minor movement indicating the presence of a lesser bird or rodent that might provide its protein source for the day and fuel to inaugurate its flight on the morrow. Such was the occurrence on the morning of 1 May 1949.

Prior days had provided no sightings of significance. This day was different. Thin wisps of smoke curled skyward from the very crest of Mountain 06. It was a pattern to be expected from multiple cooking fires and was surely worthy of further investigation. Consequently, the pilot nosed the small aircraft down and proceeded into a loose, lazy spiral that would allow for maximum degree of surveillance. "Could be anyone," intoned the aviator. "Doubt it," replied the observer, who added, "I'll radio it in! Maybe the lads at Headquarters know where the little brown fellows are camping out—and preparing a fine monkey stew."

The Radio Operator from Intelligence replied, "They had no information regarding any natives being in that particular region, but who the hell can keep track of them!" "Go in for a closer look around," was the next command, which the two-man crew of the plane received. They responded and were now down on the deck, which was basically flying 100 feet on the heavenly side of the tree tops. On pass number three, coming in over a miniscule clearing, they spotted three men with raised rifles, which were quickly put into action. A single bullet hole appeared in the left wing! However, the airmen felt free of the assumed symptoms of gun shot wounds, and a quick palpation of accessible body parts produced no telltale crimson smear on their hands. These were the kind of negative findings for which they could be grateful. Furthermore, their aircraft responded promptly in compliance to their urgent desire to escape. When rapid breathing had subsided to a level commensurate with intelligent conversation, they radioed in their discovery. Over the crackling radio came the response, "Are you sure they're Chinese?"

"Bloody hell," replied the pilot. "I'm no flying anthropologist! If some bugger down in the bushes is trying to put a bullet up my bung, you can draw your own conclusions!"

There was sufficient concurrence at Headquarters to generate a command to scramble a couple of Spitfires; each one was outfitted with a brace of 250 pounds. The fighter-bombers honed in on the preferred target and delivered the deadly canisters with precision, then followed up with saturation strafing before expending their final rounds. The Spitfire pilots were unable to confirm any return fire from the devastated site.

All information was communicated to Captain Richards at Company A, Batu Arang, and it was being disseminated in his briefing to the other officers. When the known information had been conveyed to his subalterns, the Captain presented a brief outline for his plan of conceived action. First Lieutenant Cameron's platoon, in conjunction with the reconstructed Alpha Platoon, would depart at first light and proceed to the summit of 06. They would search the area that the fighter bombers had just hit and thus determine the degree of success that was presumed to have resulted from the bombardment of the insurgent campsite. The Captain felt they would be in sufficient force to readily handle any surviving guerrillas.

Iain's hand was elevated when C.O. Richards had reached the point of the obligatory query as to whether or not there were questions or comments. The C.O. pointed to Cameron, who said, "The discovery of campfires when none have been observed before puzzles me sir! As best I know, the Chinese are much more given to eating a little rice and dried fish during the day. That wouldn't be cooked. Also, the obvious appearance of the three shooters in the tiny clearing. Most soldiers with any sense would douse the fires and remain hidden. Then, the spotters in the plane might come to the conclusion that the sighting was illusory. I hope that all our presumptions are true! However, somewhere down deep in my gut I wonder if this was orchestrated. At any rate, it's time to seek out the Serpent! We cannot play Blind Man's Bluff with the bastard any longer!" Pulses quickened and hollowness invaded the solar plexuses of some. All nodded in accord.

Predictably, Sergeant Major Sandy MacPhee had his platoon ready for inspection a full thirty minutes before departure. First Lieutenant Iain Cameron performed the ritual in a most thorough manner. Every single item to be carried and needed while afield was determined to be operative in the case of weapons or full in respect to canteens and ammunition pouches. Second Lieutenant Jim Douglas did the same for his unit.

At the end of the routine, Iain addressed both groups. "I have every reason to believe we will see action before we return. Whatever happens to us out there will never be heralded as was 'The Thin Red Streak Tipped with a Line of Steel' at the Heights of Balaclava; the Square at Quatre Bras; the Plains of Abraham, The Somme, El Alemain or Normandy. We are but a tiny group in a dirty little war! Those who survive—and God willing it will be all—will recall what occurs in the next forty-eight hours, and that is most important to us after all. What we do today or tomorrow will not save the world, but it can save you and the lad who marches by your side. I have the utmost faith in you, and your fight to avenge our fallen comrades. God bless you!" Then, Iain saluted sharply, held his position, and let his gaze press on the resolute eyes of every man. Turning, Lieutenant Cameron saluted his Captain. After the right hands were brought down, they enmeshed in a handclasp. The strength of the grip—and the message delivered by their eyes—alleviated the need for any words apart from "Good hunting Iain!" and "Thank you, Captain!" Lieutenant Cameron handed the Captain a letter addressed to his parents. In it was conveyed the love and gratitude Iain might never be able to tell them in any other way. Most of his men had entrusted similar missives to those who remained in camp.

Soon, troop-filled lorries lumbered off as the first streaks of sunlight called the jungle to life, heralding a newborn day. Simba sensed the coming of a chaotic event—much like a dog senses an earthquake well before the tremor starts. He was curled on the lorry floor with his muzzle on Iain's boot. There was no sign of skittishness, but Simba did not sleep.

"The Serpent" and his men had returned to the area so recently devastated by the RAF Spitfires. They had suffered no casualties since the area had been immediately evacuated following the clever ruse perpetrated for the benefit of the crew of the observation plane. Major Chin Shin Yee congratulated himself on the fact that the "feckless fools" had so eagerly succumbed to his clever stratagem. His ebullience was further fueled by his certainty that the policy promulgated by the senile eunuchs of Whitehall would prompt a reconnaissance mission—for the purpose of producing a body count—to justify their hopeless attempts at quelling the insurgency and thwarting ultimate Communist victory. Indeed—there would be a body count! It would consist of every man they sent against him. If his success continued, and Major Yee had supreme confidence that it would, the sobbing mothers of Britain would wail and clamor until Parliament would be only too pleased to withdraw their forces. This was, indeed, a cowardly lion! Perhaps, they should adopt the pig as their national symbol, as a pig is content to be immobilized and placed live on a spit!

Major Yee was certain the Scots would come to his trap up one of the two ridges they had previously utilized. He felt there was a high probability they would avoid passing by the graves of their slain compatriots, as this would be loathsome to them. Nonetheless, he would deploy his force in such a way as to ensure their destruction regardless which route they attempted. For this purpose, it was the Serpent's plan to strategically place several guards on either side of both trails. They would lie in stealth until the enemy had passed. Any flankers used by the Scots would be killed quietly by his very talented, noiseless assassins! As soon as the last man of the enemy column had entered the trap, then his men would close in behind them. A considerable number of the enemy should be cut down in the initial fusillade. Major Yee would lead the charge of his main body of soldiers in a head-on assault, which would destroy any enemy left standing. The unit he positioned on the ridge, not used by the opposing force could now converge on the scene of slaughter.

Several times, the Serpent had rehearsed the action, and his men had performed flawlessly. They were no doubt spurred on by his tirades as to what fate any comrade might suffer should he be found to be lacking in soldierly qualities. Far better to be killed by gunfire than to be impaled on a bamboo spear. Major Yee was a devoted reader of sadistic lore, and Vlad—the real Romanian king of the fourteenth century and the model for the fictional Count Dracula—was one of his esteemed heroes. He would now wait—with great anticipation—the coming of his foe. He was confident it would be in the late afternoon.

Meanwhile, in his planning, First Lieutenant Iain Cameron had decided to avoid either of the ridges previously used. There was no squeamishness or cowardice responsible for his decision. He selected Ridge 105 for two reasons. This ridge extended to the summit of Mountain 06 and the distance would be longer; however, the slope was more gradual. The decreased severity of the climb would result in less fatigue for his men—an important factor if they were suddenly engaged in battle. Second, he had every reason to believe "the Serpent" would deploy in relation to the two previously climbed ridges, thus making it mush easier for a company of enemy soldiers to be concentrated for maximum effect.

Vegetation present on the ridge now to be climbed was in no way dissimilar to the others. Therefore, speed and stealth were most easily produced in a single column, rather than a widely spread out movement. As in the past, Iain would lead Bravo Platoon, this time with Simba at his side. Sergeant Major MacPhee would bind the column together from his central position. Two of his Gurkhas—in this case the twins Kulbar (Cool Beer) Ghale and Lalbador (Lullaby) Ghale—would flank his position in the column lead. Alpha Platoon, led by 2nd Lt. Douglas, would remain in the rear. There were many times when the Gurkhas wouldn't be visible, and they were invariably "damned quiet." For the purpose of communication, reliance was placed on birdcalls, which had been endlessly practiced until perfection was achieved. Besides Iain, the three Gurkhas and Sergeant Major MacPhee, Second Lieutenant Jim Douglas of Alpha Platoon and his Sergeant Jerry Turpin had all become proficient members of "the Singers" as the others dubbed them. Nonetheless, the other men, who were nonsingers, were well attuned to the meaning of the songs. Iain reckoned that the culmination of their ascent would occur at about 1730 hours leaving a reasonable span of daylight remaining, since they were approaching the time of the Summer Solstice. They would also allow for a one-half hour rest period, during which they could take on some sustenance.

As the platoon climb continued, every appropriate sense of each man was at the height of alert. Simba, of course, enjoyed considerable advantage over the human members of the force. However, that was a gift of his nature, against which they could only strive to compete. By the time they stopped for rest, no hostile force had been encountered. Still, any hope of relaxation was scarce among the recumbent men. They were still relatively fresh, so the instant collapse produced by utter exhaustion was not reflexively produced. Danger occupied the minds and actions of some, and a ration of water was necessary for all. Many thought how damned nice it would be to have a cigarette, but the urge was quelled by the knowledge that the smoke from cigarettes might be easily detected, resulting in the betrayal of their presence.

Iain's time was largely occupied by the need to conference with his Sergeant Major, Lieutenant Dawson, and Sergeant Turpin. Meanwhile, the steadfast Gurkhas maintained their flank positions. He did find time to share part of his meal with Simba, and he positioned one broad hand on the nape of the dog's neck. The placement allowed him to caress the back of both of Simba's ears—thumb on one side—and the remaining digits on the other. Then, it was time to move out. As they proceeded, there were none among the men who weren't sure that they would be in the middle of hell before day's end. However, that was a topic they knew not to dwell on. Also, there were others—besides Lieutenant Cameron—who said a prayer.

Through breaks in the dense foliage, the summit of Mountain 106 could—

on occasion—be partially visualized. Furthermore, the grade of the slope that the soldiers were ascending was starting to flatten. Consequently, Iain slowed their progress by a preordained signal. Suddenly Simba halted abruptly! His nostrils flared as his upper lip curled and elevated in small, spasmodic movements with the nose bobbing in synchrony. As Simba's muzzle elevated, the ridge hairs of his back became stiffly erect, while his tail formed a rigid crescent. Immediately, Iain was aware that what breeze he could perceive was coming from the South; the area that he expected "the Serpent" led Communists to occupy. Then, Simba turned his head in that direction, as his olfactory system conveyed its discovery to his brain.

Now Cameron was sure! The insurgents were within 200 yards, and the approach of his force had so far been undetected. Iain commenced his signals. The perfectly reproduced call of the macaw was audible to all and meaningful to his units, while no cause for alarm to his enemies. Members of both platoons began the stealthiest approach conceivable. As they advanced, the column began to widen, and as a result they should be able to maneuver into a much wider column for their assault. Tulbadahur (Tully) Thapa, who had been repositioned on the far extreme of the right flank, due to the terrain, was the first to kill. A single guerrilla was hidden at the base of a tree. Obviously, he was meant to guard the approach to the main Chinese force and silently slay any forward advancing scouts. The insurgent was reasonably watchful, but not sufficiently alert. He surrendered his life to the curved Kukri blade. Given the position of the cut, his death was instantaneous and soundless.

All the men in Iain's command were swiftly and silently deployed in a flank, which was broadened at multiple points by the addition of a single man in a second row. This was done to create at least a modicum of depth—in hope of preventing a gap—which might occur from casualties, thus minimizing the creation of a breakthrough point. Then, Simba's collar was deftly removed to allow the dog liberty of initiating an attack, as determined by his instinctive response to any situation that might arise.

Now, Cameron's two platoons had secured the high ground above the Chinese, which was an advantage, except for the fact that balance was rendered precarious for some of his troops. Their planted knees were anchored lower than their connected feet—where the slope was most angled. The altered center of gravity left some in danger of pitching forward. This happened to Private Whalen, just before Iain gave the signal to commence firing! Whalen's mishap created sufficient sound to alert some of the Chinese, who rapidly turned to determine the cause of the broken silence. Iain's response was immediate, and the enfilading fire of Alpha and Bravo Platoons erupted. Staccato reports of the MI .30-caliber carbines—on full automatic—dominated the cacophony of the battle. Nonetheless, they could still hear the punctuating heavy muzzle blasts and rolling reports of the Lee Enfields. These occurred at intervals commensurate with the abilities of those working the bolt actions at a furious pace. Considerable numbers of the Chinese fell to the first fusillade. However, those remaining still constituted a formidable force outnumbering the Scots Guards by at least two to one—and they started to organize and generate return fire.

Bursts from Iain's Thompson were focused on numerous insurgents with devastating results. The nearly one-half-inch diameter projectiles had shredded a number of the enemy's bodies before the first 50-shot drum was emptied. As he jettisoned the exhausted magazine and slammed a fresh one into position, Iain perceived a screaming voice from deep in the enemy ranks. This was not the wail of a wounded man but a shrill command! Such an order could be for either attack or withdrawal. However, the instantaneous advance of the insurgent force excluded the latter. It had to be the Serpent exhorting his men to charge forward—and crush their assailants or perish in the effort. Immediately, the contents of Iain's second magazine erupted with singular fury—cutting down a number of charging Communists. "Hold steady, lads, we'll carry the day!" he cried. Cameron's shout penetrated the deafening noise of the battle, which was made all the more violent by the addition of the return fire of the 7.7-mm Arisaka rifles and the PPSH-41 submachine guns. Some of the Chinese fire was effective, as was devastatingly indicated by the writhing or inert bodies of some of his men. Still, the Chinese advanced. Though it was basically a suicide charge, there could be enough of them reaching his position to overwhelm them.

As the battle continued, in one or two areas along Lieutenant Cameron's thin line, the enemy combatants had approached to a point where hand-to-hand combat became the only means for survival. Also, the barrel of Iain's Thompson had become so hot that the weapon's wooden forearm was beginning to smolder. Then, the bolt remained open when the last round was exhausted. Immediately, he ripped the strap-slung Winchester 97 "Trench Gun" from off his shoulder—just in time to level the muzzle into the face of a screaming Communist. The twelve lead balls had barely time to separate before they penetrated the enemy's face and exploded his head. There was just time to whirl and fire again. Fortunately, Cameron knew that a more rapid firing rate could be achieved using the Winchester if one held the trigger down, so he furiously worked the bolt with forward and aft motion of the gun's forearm. Consequently, the second load of buckshot hit another Chinese in the shoulder, crudely amputating the man's entire right front quarter and producing a great grout of blood gushing from the shredded axillary artery. The enemy fell at Cameron's feet, writhing in terminal agony. His shotgun erupted three more times before expending its deadly cargo. Each thunderous explosion eradicated one more charging foe. Unfortunately, the fearsome weapon did not lend itself well to rapid reloading under conditions of extreme urgency and deadly peril. So, for Cameron, there was no alternative but to discard it in favor of the Browning pistol.

As Iain ripped the side arm from its holster, he had a split second to scrutinize his surroundings. Simba had an insurgent on the ground. He had gone for the man's left wrist, which was the one supporting his rifle's forearm. The dog's powerful jaws—and penetrating fangs—had ripped through skin, muscle and bone! His dangling hand was a useless flail. With his right hand, the insurgent tried in vain to free himself from the dog's deadly grasp. Immediately, Iain aimed his pistol at the man's head when Simba was out of the line of fire. A single bullet entered his brain from the outer margin of his left orbit. He quivered and died. Simba sought other prey.

Shortly thereafter, Iain sensed a slowing of the Chinese charge. "Oh dear God—let it end in our victory," was the silent scream that reverberated within his sensorium. For Lieutenant Cameron, there was ample evidence that his own men were being decimated—despite the savage defense which was gradually annihilating the charging Communists. He gasped as he saw Sergeant Major Sandy MacPhee grimace in great anguish, as he dropped his rifle and clutched at his upper right thigh in the area of the hip joint. A wisp of smoke arose from his uniform in the area of the entry wound. The red-hot projectile had actually ignited the cloth in its passage, though gushing blood extinguished the smoldering material almost instantaneously.

Sergeant MacPhee dropped to his knees, striving to hold himself upright with his free left arm. Then, a live grenade landed just in front of him! Part of the time before detonation had already been used up by the burning fuse. Iain leaped toward the fallen Sergeant and threw himself at the deadly explosive device. His hurling body smashed into MacPhee, sending him sprawling in agony. As Cameron's own body landed on the Sergeant, his cupped hand curled around the grenade. Then a sweeping arm propelled it up and away before it exploded! While the result was life saving, it did not prevent injury. A searing pain tore through Iain's face and right eye—attended by a blinding flash—and was followed by utter blackness in that visual field. The grenade had exploded close enough so that one jagged fragment found the edge of his orbit and coursed diagonally downward—cutting into the eye—before incising his right cheek.

Iain sat upright—severely dazed. Suddenly, another Communist bayonet-tipped rifle was directed toward his chest—and only a scant few feet from plunging the naked steel into his heart. Amazingly, a tawny blur erupted into the peripheral vision of Iain's intact left eye. This time, Simba went for the throat. The muscled ninety-pound mass of the dog struck like a wrecking ball.

His fangs tore into the soft flesh, which offered scant protection for the man's carotid arteries, which bore a life-sustaining flow of oxygenated blood to the brain. Dropping his rifle, the man collapsed at Cameron's feet.

Iain staggered upright, his senses rapidly clearing. There was still gunfire; however, it was ebbing rapidly. Remaining fire seemed to be coming almost entirely from his men. Lieutenant Cameron had little time to ponder possible victory, for his left eye perceived a vision from hell. Twenty feet away was the charging Serpent! The gleaming blade of a katana sword was discernible high in the air above his right shoulder. Both of Major Yee's hands were clasped iron-hard around the sword's hilt. His loathsome face wore a demonic mask!

Instantly, Cameron grasped for the hilt of his own sword. The basket-hilted weapon, with two razor-sharp edges, had been positioned vertically and deployed in a scabbard, which rested between his shoulder blades. It was slung in the same fashion as the great two-handed broadsword carried into war by his ancestors.

Iain had his weapon firmly in hand when the gleaming blade of the katana arched downward toward him. He successfully parried the strike intended to kill him. Obviously, it would be a battle to the death! The mystic steel from the forges of Kyoto versus the finest from the smiths of Sheffield. Iain's weapon had been his grandfather's. Never meant for the parade ground, both edges were razor sharp—as was the point. The weapon was meant to kill, either by slash or thrust. George Patton III, a fine swordsman in his own right, had once claimed the Scottish broadsword to be the finest weapon of its type ever developed. The Serpent's katana had once belonged to a samurai of the Edo era. However, the history of each weapon was now irrelevant. This moment was to be the moment of death for one of the combatants.

Little time was needed for Iain to determine that the Serpent was an excellent swordsman who handled his weapon with extreme skill. Lieutenant Cameron was thankful for the hundreds of hours he had spent perfecting his superiority, both at Sandhurst and during summers at the Ecole Militaire in Paris. The singing blades clashed over and over. Fortunately, despite the loss of his eye, Iain was not depleted in strength by any significant injury to his body. Physically, he was more powerful than Major Yee, and when the Chinese had to parry one of Iain's downward strokes, the reverberations emanating from his own tightly held sword was having a devastating effect on his hand and arm.

As Major Yee's strength ebbed, a deep-seated fear arose within the butcher's mind. He must end this very soon. The Scot remained unscathed as a result of this duel, while the Serpent had suffered a deep gash in his right thigh, which was sapping his strength due to blood loss. Therefore, it was thwarting his precise movements due to his legs' lagging response. He coiled and reconciled himself to one final gamble. At the instant Iain parried his last blow and held his quivering sword at bay, the Serpent lashed out with his left leg in a classic Tai Chi maneuver, intending to smash his opponent's knee cap. Too late, he beheld the blade of a dirk held in the Scot's left hand.

The sandy-haired giant had removed the second weapon from its scabbard a millisecond earlier. The dirk's tip plunged deeply into the calf muscles of the Serpent's thrusting leg. He reflexively pulled away, and for one horrendous instant, the Serpent stood awkwardly footed, totally off-guard. War cries that burst forth from Wallace's lungs so many years ago resounding from the walls of Sterling Castle were in no way greater than Iain's. The primordial scream, which all that remained conscious heard, was "Geordie!" For the Serpent, it totally obliterated the sound of the broadsword's blade, as it whispered through the air before cleaving his body, passing from the base of his neck on the left side through to his axilla on the right.

Some of the Communists fled the battle scene after the death of their leader. The majority of the Communist company was dead or wounded. They had paid a very dear price. Six gallant men of the Scots Guards had been killed and twelve wounded. Fortunately, in varying degrees, there were sufficient men who had come through unscathed to carry the wounded to a point of rescue, although ultimately three of the wounded did not survive despite every attempt to save them. However, nonambulatory Sergeant Major MacPhee did come out alive, though his soldiering days were over.

As Iain sat among the carnage—prior to their moving out—he knew that his eye was devastated. *Well—one can get along better with one eye than one leg,* he thought. *I'm a hell of a lot better off than many of my lads who died this day!* Lieutenant Cameron was about to stand when he felt something warm and wet on his right cheek. The sensation was from Simba's tongue "So, you have come to lick my wounds—just like your ancestors did for Lazarus. You're a good soldier—Sergeant Simba!"

Later, on arrival at Camp Batu Arang, the medic rapidly triaged the wounded and rendered what care he might, given his limited abilities and supplies. One more Scots Guard had perished from his wounds during transit. Unhesitatingly, Captain Richards ordered the wounded to be further evacuated to the nearest hospital, which might possess a competent surgical staff and a proper operating theater. This would be Kuala Lumpur. Cameron and several of the men were walking wounded. The rest were consigned to litters.

Iain sought out Sergeant MacPhee and found him near a lorry. He was next in line to be lifted aboard. "We've not much time, Sandy" he said, discarding the use of rank given the circumstances. The Sergeant Major's pain had been partially ameliorated by a generous injection of morphine. However, given the nature of the man, he had not as yet released himself to the embrace of Morpheus, the Roman god of sleep for whom the drug was named. Sandy's jaw was set and the muscles taught. A Media Luna of slender radiating tiny groves converged on the outer canthus of either eye. It was a corona, symbolic of pain or distress. A patina of fine sweat stood out on his face, conveying a glistening sheen to the once deeply tanned skin, which now exhibited a grayish cast due to his shocky condition.

"First Lieutenant Iain Alexander Cameron, would you mind, Sir, if this beat-up, old soldier squeezed your hand with what strength he has left." Then he added "Thank you—laddie—from the bottom of my heart for taking such a great risk to save me, and thank you for my Molly! She'll be planting a kiss on your bonnie cheek if she ever catches sight of you. God never graced us with a fine lad of our own, but now I'm sure He waited and gave me one on loan when I needed him most. I'll keep pestering the Holy Ones to save your eye, lad!" Their tightly clamped hands sealed the bond, which had been growing these past months. "God bless you, Sandy," said Iain as the litter was lifted up. "God willing, you haven't seen the last of me," were his final words.

After giving encouragement to the rest of the wounded men, Lieutenant Cameron turned and saw Captain Richards and the three other officers of his unit—standing in a tight-knit cluster—about the Rover, which would take him away. Again, the handshakes and expressive eyes conveyed meanings, which most men never put in words. Verbally, the other officers swore to remain in touch. Two of them did. The other two were denied the joy of reunion, as their lives were later lost in Malay. For, as Joyce Kilmer said, "They were never to love or laugh again, nor taste the Summertime."

Lieutenant Jeremy McIntyre held Simba, who strained against the leash with his face portraying "a hang-dog expression." The beloved canine, a hero in his own right, was a perfect portrait embodying the characteristics so deftly described by these words. While a dog is said not to possess an intellect, all that were present knew Simba must be cognizant of his master's imminent departure and the sorrowful separation, which would occur. Iain bent and kissed Simba on the head and squeezed his ears. Then, he quickly straightened, came to attention, and saluted the other officers. They were aware of the single tear coursing down his cheek below the unbandaged eye. No exception was taken at the sight of the saline droplet, as they were preoccupied holding their own in check.

Cameron mounted the Rover and fixed his gaze ahead. In the peripheral field of the good eye, he beheld the covered bodies, which were the earthly remains of his comrades, who had made the extreme sacrifice, on an obscure mountaintop called 06. Lieutenant Cameron gave them a final salute. Simultaneously, recalling the poignant words of Alexander Sanguinetti, "The Warrior merely carries the sword on behalf of others. His task is a lonely one, for the warrior still agrees to die for the mistakes of others!" Then, Iain wished that he could get Jesus to say to them, as he did to the good thief Dismas, who hung on the cross by his side on the hill of Calvary, "This day you shall be with me in Paradise!" Iain asked the Divine Savior for the favor. However, Cameron knew that he would not know the answer this side of eternity.

Iain's drooping right hand fell on the wrapped bundle that held the Scottish broadsword and the katana—mute and inert reminders of Malay—and all it had wrought in his life. Close by was the wee kisk holding Geordie's heart. Meanwhile, the roaring Rover engine muffled the pleading whines of Simba, who strained against the leash held taught in his new handler's hand. However, it did not obliterate the mournful howls, which followed until the ensuing 500 yards had been crossed.

As the traversed miles increased, Iain found himself somberly reflecting on his own fate. Was there anything remaining of his ravaged right eye to be salvaged? Once again, Kipling came to his mind. "For it's Tommy this and Tommy that—and chuck him out the brute—but he's the hero of his country when the guns begin to shoot!" Would his men, like those returning from the Crimea, be soon forgotten by the politicians and populace—anxious to compromise? Would yet another piece of the Empire, purchased by the lives and blood of all the Tommys and Jocks who responded to their country's call, be discarded? Then Iain recalled verbatim the words of Major General Boucher, the Supreme British Commander of the Malay Campaign: "I've had experience fighting red terrorism in Greece and India, and I can tell you this is by far the easiest problem I have ever tackled." "I do not share your sentiments, Sir!" Iain said to himself.

In Kuala Lumpur, there was an ophthalmologist who possessed reasonable skills. He did his best to close the ragged wound in Iain's cornea following the debridement procedure. Every suitable, available topical and systemic antibiotic was given to the maximum dosage. The infection subsided but did not resolve. Then, in forty-eight hours, Iain was on his way to Bombay, where there were better facilities and more experienced eye surgeons.

After arrival, Cameron had to steel himself with every dressing change. However, with the bandage removed, there was never a glimmer of light, which might be a harbinger of the return of his vision. For the good left eye, staring at the red, swollen right eye and the purulent drainage that issued forth was like watching the death throes of one's own twin.

In Bombay, the lead ophthalmologic surgeon explained that given the exigencies arising as the result of the unresponsive process in his eye, it was necessary to remove the diseased orb. Also, described was the possibility of sympathetic ophthalmitis—a condition whereby blindness could occur in the good eye secondary to the process in the other. Iain listened to the explanation, outwardly devoid of emotion. When the surgeon paused and sought approbation, he expected denial of the seriousness of the situation and a plea for more time, but the response he heard was "Then do it!"

CHAPTER FIVE

❈ ❈ ❈

On his first post-operation day, Iain sat alone in a sequestered area in the beautiful Memorial Hospital garden. The good nurse, a Sister as they were called, was prone to favor him with a surfeit of cold lemonade, and when dinnertime approached, Sister Prentice took pains to fortify it with a generous dose of Bombay gin. However, on day two, he received a mild scolding from the gin purveyor. "Come now, Lieutenant Cameron—why are you not resting in the shade? Are you just another bloody Englishman out in the mid-day sun?"

"No, Sister. I'm a bloody Scot! We're forever denied real sunshine in the Highlands, so I'm here to obtain my full ration, which I'll not receive if I were to defer to shrewish demands!" Then, a wee smile came hard on the heels of his words. The mind was healing, as was the body, and Sister Prentice was pleased.

On post-operative day three, Iain was walking about the garden, now dressed in his uniform. Sister Prentice approached him, and the smile on her face was uncontrived. "You have a visitor Lieutenant Cameron. May we bring him out here to see you? "Him" seemed disproportionately emphasized, but Iain paid it no special heed.

"Who is it?" asked Cameron.

"I'm quite sorry Lieutenant, but I didn't really catch his name. However, I can assure you that he seems most anxious to see you!"

"Please bring him out," replied the puzzled patient.

Then, Sister Prentice waved her arm at someone concealed behind a bush. That person appeared and was being dragged in the wake of a large tawny dog. It was Simba! All of his former training and discipline was erased by the magnitude of the moment. Ending his charge with a great leap, the pet imparted his full force in the middle of his master's chest. When both were finally able to contain their exuberance, Iain became aware of a note attached to Simba's collar. It read: "Iain—this bloody beast has not eaten since you left! We convened a court-martial, found him guilty, and sentenced him to spend the rest of his days with you! It was the happiest sentence I ever gave. Hopefully, he will find you before he starves. Good fortune and God speed from us all." It was signed "Jim Richards."

Two days later, dog and master were airborne. Iain would go to London or Edinburgh for reconstructive surgery. The airplane Crew Chief agreed to accept the furry passenger only if the Lieutenant would perform any clean-up during the long journey. There was no argument. However, the innocent fantasies, which had invigorated the two young warriors-to-be on their way to Malay, now lay like a thick cover of dust on some ancient unread tome. Dear Geordie was dead, and the only true relic of his existence Iain had packed in his kit. He was grateful for the kindness shown by the plane's crew, but it was becoming increasingly more difficult to continue being a bon vivant. When left alone in the aft section of the aircraft, Iain sometimes found himself clinging to Simba—like a lost little boy. Perhaps that was what he was becoming, he thought somberly. As Cameron dwelled on his situation, he tottered on the brink of morosity—and was not far from despondency. It became ever so much easier to wish it were himself who was dead!

When considering the reunion with his parents, they seemed to take on the aura of strangers. Could he embrace Geordie's mother and father? *Here I am—General Sir George and Lady MacCallum. I'm the lucky one! Your son is decomposing in a shallow grave, but I made it back. I even brought you a hank of hair, and his heart is all sealed up in this wonderful wee kist. It was terribly nice of me, don't you think? Why don't we ask God why I won the prize?*

Reflecting on this last irreverent thought, Iain suddenly became repulsed by his own morbid monomania. Immediately, the inner fire of the real Iain Alexander Cameron was reignited. Yes, indeed, God had allowed all of this to happen in this exact way. There was a purpose to it that God alone knew, and which he—the survivor—must accept. Iain knew that seen in a philosophical light, there are no accidents. All that occurs to us has a purpose. *I'll probably never know what it is,* he thought. *But, I'll try to give meaning to the rest of my life. It's the least I can do in thanksgiving to the God who spared it!*

True to his promise, the lost little boy became transfigured into the realistic young man, who strode erect and proud, down the ramp of the plane that brought him home. Simba was pleased that his master seemed more himself. He was also perplexed by all the new scents, which were imposed on his nostrils.

Iain's parents met his plane. All their character traits were displayed without any deviation from what he had expected. His father saluted, for that was the nature of the man. Then, he stood aside while mother claimed her son. She was a soldier's wife and a soldier's mother. While the tears flowed freely, there was never a hint of hysteria. They kissed, and then, she embraced him and held him ever so tight. Father finally had his turn. He looked on his son, and no eyes ever conveyed more love and pride. A serious bear hug followed. The casual observer of the reunion likely missed the maneuver whereby the General unobtrusively cleared his throat, sniffled, and wiped at his eye before formality resumed. They would have easily perceived the love and sense of relief in the tear-stained countenance of the mother. Next, Simba was introduced, and there was no mistaking the happiness conveyed by an abundantly wagging tail. Then, it was off to home, an intimate family dinner, and a very long and loving discussion, which would extend well into the wee hours of the following day.

Iain's reunion with his parents went extremely well. They were not at all the remote strangers he had needlessly feared. Rather, they were an extremely wonderful mother and father—ever so loving toward their son and profoundly grateful to God for his return. Iain's parents reported that his older sister, Jane, was now in Crete with her husband, who was a career diplomat. They had recently been blessed with a baby girl. Iain cocked the brow of his one good eye when informed of the bairn's name. He had never been endeared of the appellation of Penelope. Iain assumed his parents were of like mind, as it was presented in reserved tones, indicating a lack of enthusiasm on their behalf. "It does seem to be a favorite name for a girl in Percy's family," said his mother, accompanying the words with a wan smile. "I believe a close relative is a Penelope, and she is a duchess," his mother added.

"Nothing more than a mania for alliteration, as far as I'm concerned," replied his father. "Perceval Paul Pembroke, my son-in-law, and now a granddaughter whom I shall ever be forced to call Penelope Patricia! If the next child is a male, I may boycott the baptism." Iain laughed, while his mother produced a mild frown, and his father looked quite smug.

Iain's younger sister, Annie, chimed in, "Is that why you never called me Caroline, Corinne, or Cynthia, Father?" Annie's chessy-cat grin was not squelched by the General's frown.

Young Miss Cameron had grand plans for her brother. She was sure all the fair maidens would be totally smitten by her handsome sibling. How sad it was that only one could be his wife. The rest would languish in heartbreak. Some might resign themselves to a convent! Annie stopped short of suggesting suicide. Iain was amused. Indeed, his little sister had achieved the silly season of her life, where hopeless romanticism and absolute altruism provided an impenetrable barrier to common sense, he thought. "I won't be much of a Prince Charming, my dear little sister—until they patch me up. So, please keep the little lovebirds on their perches. Besides, for all you know, some utterly beautiful Malay maiden may show up any day now to claim me!" The winking left eye alerted his parents to his mischievous banter. Annie missed the signal—and looked utterly aghast.

Iain was off to hospital early the next day. Fortunately, Simba had recognized Iain's father to be somehow an extension of his master. He was not happy to see Iain depart, but he resigned himself, somehow sensing that he was not ever really to be abandoned.

After Lieutenant Cameron's arrival at the hospital, a thorough examination of his mutilated right eye was undertaken by the senior surgeon in the Ophthalmology Service. The tissues all looked quite good. The surgeon said, "Lieutenant, you're fortunate that the doctor in Bombay did such a fine job. There doesn't seem to be any residual infection. The extraocular muscles, the ones that make your eye move, all appear to be intact. If there is no nerve damage of consequence, then a prosthetic eye could move just like the other. We will also get some of the reconstructive chaps to remove the scar running through the lid and cheek, then, follow up with a fine plastic repair."

The surgeon continued. "You can plan on staying around here for a couple of weeks, then we will set you free. I'll see you before surgery. Some technicians will be in to visit you shortly. We need to get measurements of your orbit and match the color of the good eye, so everything will be as imperceptible as we can make it. All sounds worse than it is, Lieutenant. I like to compare it to getting some dentures. Match them up with the teeth that are left and re-create the perfect smile."

Iain took umbrage with the analogy. *Bloody hell,* he thought. *You can chew with false teeth. If you don't have any teeth, you can drink soup. What do you get out of a damn glass eye?!* These thoughts Iain didn't verbalize. His only response was, "That's a good way to think about it, Sir."

The measurements and color matching proceeded with alacrity, for which Iain was quite thankful. With the ophthalmologist's blessing and the fortunate loan of an idle staff car, young Cameron decided it was a propitious time to call on Geordie's parents and Elizabeth Monteith, Geordie's presumably grieving former fiancée. He felt it was both a duty as well as a privilege because no one else in the world was better positioned to convey Geordie's love or speak so appraisingly of his devotion to duty and exalt his qualities as an officer. Also, Iain could describe the devotion and loyalty of his men, and relate the respect he was given by his peers. The task was made infinitely easier by virtue of the fact that everything he could say would be true. There would be no need for contriving.

Iain's first phone call was to the home of Geordie's parents. They lived in a very handsome estate on the banks of the River Tay, close by Dunkeld. A wave of nostalgia passed on Cameron, as he recalled all the magnificent hours he had spent with his friend angling for the river's prized fish and shooting driven birds from stands spread among the trees and bracken-covered hillsides.

When he phoned, the housekeeper put Iain through immediately to the General. "Yes—we would like to see you, Iain! We look forward to it, and we would be most appreciative if you could arrive for dinner and stay the night." Iain most graciously accepted and gave the elderly gentleman an arrival time that he knew could be achieved without difficulty. He knew Sir George was a stickler for punctuality, despite the reason for his visit. Next, Cameron tried to ring up the Monteith Estate to determine whether Elizabeth was there or in London. However, the line seemed to be perpetually busy, prompting his decision to proceed north without further delay.

Airntully, the Monteith Highland home, was just off the A-9, a short distance south of Dunkeld. Lieutenant Cameron decided he would stop for a moment, determine her presence, and request a time on the following day when he might visit with her. This seemed an appropriate course of action and would use up some of the spare moments Iain had allotted himself prior to his timely arrival at Dunkeld. So the two lockets containing Geordie's hair were carefully placed in a tunic pocket. They were sufficiently small as to be quite inconspicuous. He elected to leave the kisk, as it seemed far better to broach the topic and ascertain the General's wishes rather than simply produce it and provoke an awkward scene.

Time passed quickly after crossing the Firth of Forth Bridge, and soon Iain was in Perth. Noting a flower shop along his route of passage, he decided to stop and purchase a proper bouquet for Elizabeth Monteith and Lady MacCallum. If Miss Monteith were at the country home, the receipt of flowers prior to his planned visit the following day might somehow soften the circumstances attendant on the discussion of Geordie's death. Not much later, Iain noted the appropriate side road and a short distance further, he entered the long driveway to the manor house.

An Aston Martin was parked near the entry door, though sufficiently removed to be out of line of sight. Two occupants were ensconced in a single seat and enveloped in an obvious all-encompassing embrace complete with a kiss, which unmistakingly was meant to convey the depths of passion they held for each other. One of the occupants was Elizabeth Monteith. Beholding the perfidious performance, it took all of Iain's force of will to stop from smashing the Staff Car into the rear of the resplendent roadster. Tires squealed, as he slammed on he brakes. Iain threw open his door and in a swift motion applied the hand brake. Then, for some unexplainable reason, Cameron grasped the bouquet in his hand.

Meanwhile, the cuddling couple, having already abruptly terminated all sensual contact, as they sensed an impending crash, were further terrified by the rapid approach of a towering man, black patch over one eye with a livid red scar arising from top and bottom margins. Elizabeth was just able to shriek out "Iain Cameron," before the thrown bouquet hit her full on the bosom. The despoiled flowers finally came to rest, as they rolled onto her lap. They partially obscured the meretricious appearance of a considerably exposed thigh, brought to view by the elevated hem of her skirt.

Finally able to speak out a few words, Elizabeth's pale blond, mustached lover declared, "I say! Who do you think you are? What sort of a boor are you—to come upon us in this manner! I happen to be the Earl of Dunmore, and your attack upon the person of Miss Monteith will be protested to the highest rank of the Army and to the Prime Minister, if necessary." This only served to infuriate Iain!

No avenging angel ever gave more the appearance of being a messenger sent to convey your soul to hell. In a commanding voice, which would drive any slacker to immediate duty, Iain hammered out, "Elizabeth Monteith—your fervidity in the face of Geordie's death is beyond my comprehension! I had come to present you with a locket of Geordie's hair, but I can see that you are attracted to Little Lord Fauntleroy's mustache. You never did deserve Geordie! You do deserve the philandering bastard beside you. As for you, Sir, it is a pity that dueling was outlawed. How I would love to demand satisfaction from you! However, if you have the manliness to step from your car, I will undertake to achieve what satisfaction I can from beating the hell out of you!" The Earl slid down in his seat, eyes affixed on the medallion-encrusted horn mounted in the center of his steering wheel.

Elizabeth cowered in her seat with face flushed and head down. However, she gave no reply. Iain continued, "Your actions do not run counter to my opinion of you, Sir!" These were Iain's final words before returning to his car and driving off. Cameron knew he needed to compose himself before seeing the MacCallums—and that was what he did.

As Iain approached the door of Auchtar House, General Sir George and Lady MacCallurn emerged. His arrival was personalized by their presence, rather than by formal admission by a servant. The old officer was in civilian attire, but still appeared quite resplendent in Harris tweeds, tattersall shirt, ascot, and mirror-polished boots. Also, the Lady of the Manor was elegantly coifed and beautifully attired in a chiffon dress of a dusty rose hue. There being no need for salutes, the General grasped Iain's hand in a vice-like grip "Welcome, Iain! You honor us in your coming!" He placed his arm around Cameron's shoulders and steered him toward the entry. Geordie's mother ran her soft fingers tenderly over his eye patch and traced the sutured scar on his cheek, before bestowing a kiss to the same wounded area. Her streaming tears obviated the need for words.

Once inside, composure had come to all. The servant took Iain's Glengarry cap, then proceeded to attend to his luggage and park his car. The trio proceeded to the study in silence. Once inside, the door was closed. Then, the General directed Iain to a chair close by one selected by his wife. "I think you could use a wee measure of claret, Margaret," said her husband. "For Iain and I, it will be a couple of stiff tots of single-malt, with more to follow as the evening goes by." He handed Iain a snifter of exquisite Edinburgh crystal, containing a generous allotment of the celebrated MacCallum blend of single-malt whiskey. The golden brown liquid was best enjoyed by vision, taste, and smell in a fine glass. Scots considered it superior to any cognac. While he had no business interest in the distillery, the General savored the brand for its name, as much as its taste.

Seating himself across from Iain and his wife, thus constituting a small circle, Sir George took a generous sip of his prized libation, then said "Well, laddie, tell me all about it and bare every detail that comes to mind! We want you to share with us every experience, thought and word that you and Geordie shared!"

So, Iain began his tale. Geordie's mother and father sat enraptured. Questions were asked, and Lady MacCallum's eyes frequently glistened with tears, which were released down her cheeks—on many occasions. Her fine linen handkerchief was well dampened as the story unfolded. The narration and his audience of two carried the topic of Geordie and Malay through the dinner, with all the delectable courses and fine accompanying wines. The spirits were somberly sipped, and the topic discussed kept them free of any alcohol-induced loquacity.

Following their meal, the three once again retired to the study. Further libations were proffered and accepted, as all were aware they were drawing to the end of the narrative that would describe Geordie's death. Iain hesitated, and his hosts were well aware of his reluctance to enter on the discussion of the last horrid event. Breaking the silence, the old soldier said calmly, "This will be hard on you, Iain, and we deeply appreciate your need to try and spare us the grim details. I know the condition of dear Geordie's body when you came upon it, and I've shared the sordid facts with Margaret. We have both accepted the tragedy. Perhaps it was made easier in some ways by the horrible misfortune, that befell us early in life. I spent three years of hell in the First World War. My older brother was killed in France early on; his body forever entombed in the muck of Flanders. Margaret's father went down with his ship, and his grave is the North Atlantic. Her brother's Spitfire—with him aboard—lies at the bottom of the Channel. Your forthright recounting of the events will bring us more solace than devastation, so please continue."

Iain recounted the event to the last detail, then he presented the locket to Geordie's mother. She opened it slowly and kissed the soft red curl. The General broke the silence by saying, "Your father told me about the kisk containing Geordie's heart, Iain. I suppose there are many who would consider it a morbid topic. However, you have done us the greatest service possible by bringing this part of Geordie home. We'll plan a fitting memorial with burial in the family plot here at Auchtar. The kisk will be placed between where Margaret and I will be buried, and I'd be honored if you would command the Honor Guard for the service."

"The honor would be all mine, Sir George," was Iain's solemn reply.

"Well," said the General. "We have exorcised all the demons regarding Geordie. While there are differences in our religious beliefs, we still surely believe in heaven, and we are equally positive Geordie exists there now in pure happiness, as he awaits our joining him. So, sleep well, Laddie, you've surgery to prepare for soon."

Iain did have a restful night. When he departed in the morning, his hosts stood in the driveway waving their good-byes and signifying their gratitude. Iain could not miss noticing the gold locket clutched tightly in the mother's loving hand.

Iain drove back down the A-9 at a slower pace than his journey north on the preceding day. It was late spring in the Highlands, and the mist for which Scotland was renowned was much in evidence. The sun was making feeble attempts to break through and provide some warmth and brighter light, but was thwarted by the scudding gray clouds, propelled in a southwest direction by cold winds blowing in from across the North Sea. Seeing the wet heather and appreciating the diminution in the vibrancy of its purple flowers wrought by inability to capture the sunbeams left Iain in a gloomy mood.

Of course, it hadn't helped to drive by the road to the Monteith Manor. "Damn it," Cameron said aloud. Then, in silence, Iain castigated himself for teetering on depression and commanded his mind to seek a different topic. *Grouse! That's it! Grouse and heather are inseparable. They hide in it—nest in it—and feed exclusively upon it. Is there a good hatch of the Scottish Red Grouse chicks this year?* He hadn't asked his father, but then, there were far more important matters to discuss. Iain's next mental image was that of the wee grouse, wet, cold, shuddering, and probably dying in the rain and cold. "Bloody hell!" he exclaimed "Am I incapable of a cheery thought? I'll look up Sandy MacPhee. He must be back by now—could even be in the same hospital! I'll tell him about Simba." The concept of locating his Sergeant and cheering him up—if needed—had a reciprocal effect on Iain's psyche. Soon, he was singing Bobby Burn's immortal "Coming through the Rye!" The weather outside remained the same, but his personal black cloud had been propelled away by the warming wind of his kindled spirit!

Arriving at the hospital, an orderly escorted First Lieutenant Iain Cameron to a sparse, small but private room in the Officer's Section of the Military Hospital. The aromas were foreign, medicinal, and at least mildly offensive. A barless prison was the way it struck him. Cameron positioned the single chair to permit room for his legs. Was he supposed to sit and wait—or get into bed? This was a Gordian knot he had not foreseen.

His dilemma was resolved by the appearance of Sister Carlisle, who swept into the room and offered him a folded piece of cloth. "Well now, Lieutenant Cameron, we aren't going catatonic, are we? Let's get out of that uniform and into your gown. We don't operate on fully dressed patients here. Of course, you know that. You're just bashful!" She laughed generously at what she perceived to be uproariously humorous. Iain scowled, but accepted the folded cloth, assuming it was the gown in which he was expected to vest himself. He stood holding the unwanted article and gave Sister Carlisle the "I desire privacy" look. She interpreted it correctly and turned to leave. However, she was unable to depart without a quip: "You remind me of a lad facing a dose of castor oil, Lieutenant! It's always alluring to encounter a modest man. Yet, I find it strange that a man wearing a kilt would have reservations about such a nice gown." She smiled broadly and took her leave, closing the door quietly behind her.

"Bloody Sassenach," fumed Iain, using the ancient Celtic term for the previously despised English. He disrobed and folded his uniform components carefully. There was no indication of proper hangers. Then, he determined the top of the gown was signified by what seemed to be an aperture, which would encircle his neck. This decision was confirmed by the presence of adjacent sleeves. Two free edges had a series of slender ties. *Do they go in the front or back?* He correctly decided it was far better to opt for increased cover for the part of his anatomy most likely to be presented to the public, and he so vested himself. Given his proportions, Iain soon discovered that his hospital garb was absurdly short. Furthermore, he did not possess the range of motion in his arms to fasten it. Fuming, he extracted his arms from the sleeves—and rotated the back to the front—making it possible to secure the ties.

This created a new dilemma. If he secured the closure tightly enough to make the gown's edges approximate, he could still rotate it around to its slot in the rear orientation, but he couldn't get his arms back in the openings. "Merde," he hissed—using the French expression, which didn't seem quite as vulgar as the Anglo Saxon equivalent. Iain had not heard the door open, so he was puzzled as to the possible source of what was unequivocally a soft, feminine snicker.

The voice that followed the giggle was sweet and lilting with a Highland accent. "May I help you, Lieutenant Cameron? I presume that's who you are, though I can't see you with the gown over your head." Just then, it dawned on Iain—given the brevity of the garment—that if his head was covered, more personal area might be exposed! With considerable effort, he did manage to pull the flimsy covering to a more modest level; however, now his arms were pinned inside. He had succeeded only in enveloping himself in the imprisoning cocoon. Iain felt totally ridiculous! His level of ire was mounting at a meteoric rate, and he was on the brink of freeing his trapped arms, as a desperate measure, which he was sure would rend the flimsy cloth but obtain his release. At the exact second he was to start his large, muscular arms in a lateral direction; an inner warning system aborted the synapses. He stopped, now realizing that a shredded gown would cover nothing!

"Thank you for your concern, Miss, Sister, Nurse—or whoever you are. But just go away and leave me alone! I'm quite capable of handling this situation."

The unseen woman's voice replied, "If you said that to a superior officer appraising you in a tactical situation, you would be relieved of command. Lieutenant. Now don't be such an oaf! My duty is to care for patients, and that includes you. I certainly don't want you strangling yourself on my shift." Her deft hands loosened the ties, and she proceeded to open the back of the gown widely. "I trust you can find the sleeves, Lieutenant! As soon as you do, I promise I will close it all up in proper fashion as your sense of modesty obviously dictates. Furthermore, your secret is safe with me. Not a single soul in your regiment will ever know that you were rescued from ignominious defeat and total exposure by a frail woman!"

Iain was about to launch a stem rebuttal commencing with "Bloody Hell" when he caught his first real glimpse of the young lady who saved a gentleman in distress. She was remarkably beautiful. Spun golden hair magnificently framed an angelic face, gorgeously highlighted by a stunning pair of sapphire blue eyes. Also, ruby red lips—in the form of twin cupid bows—and a porcelain complexion with a soft pink rose petal gracing each cheek. Her nose was artistry, and the sweetest dimples were tucked in either cheek. Her figure was no less resplendent. Though visualizing her was a source of aesthetic delight, he could appreciate there was a great deal of warmth underneath, as well as a vast reserve of inner strength and intelligence. Iain finally found words, but he could do no better than "thank you for helping me."

"It has been my pleasure—as well as my duty, Lieutenant Cameron. Perhaps you would feel more at ease in bed with the covers pulled up." Then, she added, "Incidentally, you will be in my care for at least a part of the time you are here. My name is Claire Campbell, since you didn't inquire."

Among his faults was one Iain would never admit. He had always regarded his sense of humor as being a bit dry though very witty, while—in truth—it frequently bordered on the acerbic. He blurted out, "A Campbell, are you?! One of my mother's ancestors was slain at Glencoe by a treacherous Campbell. I don't suppose he was kith or kin of yours."

The nurse's countenance became decidedly less angelic. The blue eyes looked more like blue flames, and the roses in her cheeks became red embers, while cupid's bow now formed a most resolute pout, appearing as though they were in the process of launching arrows. Her voice was strong when she said. "I think I have given you all the help you deserve, Lieutenant!"

Iain started to say, "Are you without any sense of humor, Miss Campbell?" but the room was void of anyone but himself.

Iain was left to his own devices, which in a room devoid of radio or reading material, meant personal reflection. Thoughts of the impending surgery, his parents, Geordie and his parents, the treachery of Elizabeth Monteith, Malay and his men, and Simba were all addressed. His cognitive power was at times disrupted by a recurring distraction, who was blonde and five foot seven. "Bloody hell!" was the silent proclamation, which he issued every time Miss Campbell's apparition materialized.

Cameron found himself indulging in drawing up a balance sheet on the comely young lady, and he took some perverse pleasure in trying to place her almost exclusively in the negative column. However, he became distraught when a debate started to arise between opposing neurons in his brain. *Would I ask her for a date?* said one area of cerebration. *Would you blame a beautiful young lady for something some ancestor did two hundred years ago?* came the retort. The second round went like this: *She is probably committed to some fop like Elizabeth Monteith's sleazy Don Juan, the Earl of Eros, or whatever the hell his name was!* This challenge was also countered by the apologetic defender, who replied, *She doesn't have a ring—does she? No sense of humor,* was the next selection of his inner inquisition. *Don't forget, your own dear mother has been hurt by your self-styled humor, old fellow,* said the defense counsel, and so it went.

Realizing his reflection on the condition and whereabouts of Sergeant MacPhee had been sidetracked by this inane game, Iain scowled and in so doing produced a very sardonic expression. The timing was most unfortunate as it coincided exactly with the entry of Claire Campbell. She could only assume the horrific image was meant for her, as Lieutenant Cameron had not seen or tasted the dinner she was delivering. Claire's demeanor instantly went from ice cold to absolute zero, but her professionalism stayed her hands from dumping the tray in the most gratifying place rather than the bedside table. "This is your last meal until after surgery, Lieutenant! I suggest you eat it if you can recover from the look you seem to have developed!" Again, Claire Campbell completed her egress well ahead of his response.

Round three occurred coincident with the hospital's determination of bedtime. Sister Campbell entered with a tiny paper cup, containing a sedative capsule in one hand and a glass of water in the other. Her degree of reservation bordered on absolute rigidity, but she was still perfectly professional. "Your doctor ordered a sedative for you, Lieutenant Cameron. This will help you to get a good night's sleep prior to your surgery."

Iain had resolved to be nonconfrontational. With a hint of cheer and a wan smile, he responded, "No need. I'm able to sleep under any circumstances. But thank you anyway."

Claire Campbell, who had come prepared to do battle launched her attack. "Are you so concerned that a treacherous Campbell will slay you in your sleep, Lieutenant? Or perhaps you are like the great Cameron of Lochiel, who when camped with his sons in a blizzard observed one of them fashioning a pillow of snow. Thus, supposedly, the great Lochiel kicked it out from under his poor son's head, saying, 'Are you so womanly that you need a pillow!' Could you please tell me, Lieutenant, which of my suppositions are correct?" The graceful hand extended the cup; the firm voice proclaimed, "Take it!" Iain complied, and she disappeared.

Cameron's surgery and his post-operative course were for the most part free of significant events—except one. He suffered no pain of consequence, and the angry red scars were replaced with a fine line of closure sealed with numerous tiny sutures. His newly acquired prosthetic glass eye was somewhat sluggish in movement, but he was advised that was secondary to edema of the extraocular muscles, which would clear in time. It was disconcerting to look in the mirror and see the strange foreign body looking back at him while knowing it saw nothing!

The only occurrence that did trouble Iain was actually a nonoccurrence. No Sister Cameron appeared. He could easily brave another confrontation, just to have the opportunity to gaze on her. Sister Carlisle was her old officious self, bordering on homely, and of sufficient age to have been his mother. The younger nurses were pert and reasonably attractive, but not in Miss Campbell's league. He finally inquired of Sister Carlisle as to what had become of Sister Campbell, couching his inquiry in such a way as to avoid any suggestion of romantic interest. "Sister Campbell is on emergency leave, Lieutenant. Her dear mother is in hospital in Oban, as a result of a ruptured gallbladder. Touch and go for a while, but I understand she seems to be turning the corner. Miss Campbell should be back here next week, but you'll be gone. Is there any message you want me to give her?"

"Uhh—no, nothing special," replied Iain.

Lieutenant Cameron was discharged the following day, and he was exuberant when his parents came to pick him up. Claire Campbell was, for the moment, relegated to a deep recess in his mind. Before entering the family car, Iain stowed his overnight bag in the boot of the Jaguar, oblivious of a small package that had been placed in his valise. Happily, he looked forward to two weeks of leave before reporting back to Regimental Headquarters in London. Then it would be determined if he was fit to continue his duties and in what capacity. So he filled the interlude by spending many wonderful days with his family.

Simba was overjoyed to see him. Iain's reunion with the lovable dog reminded him to caution his father that the new family pet had an extremely strong aversion to Chinese people, and it was probably prudent that the ethnicity of Simba's sense of smell never be tested again. Unfortunately, the Rhodesian Ridgeback possessed no thought process that would enlighten him to the point he could distinguish a cook or laundry man, who were very decent human beings, and very different from those Chinese that were mortal enemies. Utilizing his free time, after several inquiries, Sergeant Major MacPhee was located at his cottage in Moneymeede, just outside of Aberdeen. Following a series of surgeries, he had been furloughed home with his shattered leg in a cast. Amputation would probably prove unnecessary unless osteomyelitis supervened. The orthopedic surgeons were hopeful that the nearly irreparable limb would at least serve as a suitable stanchion permitting standing and limited ambulation. He was currently on crutches. Hopefully, a sturdy walking stick would suffice for the future. Sandy and Iain embraced with a genuine sincerity peculiar to those that had fought side by side and managed to survive. Further emotion was added to the occasion by the intrusion of Molly MacPhee, who as the Sergeant predicted, bestowed a very warm kiss of gratitude on the Lieutenant's cheek.

Hours of heart-warming conversation passed quickly, and it was time for Cameron to take his leave. "Sandy, I know how much you love the Guards, and I wish for the entire world you could go for the full thirty years. We both know that the damaged leg rules that out. I want to tell you my parents and I would be delighted if you would consider a position at Caperkaille. The billet involves a responsible job, a good wage, and a fine cottage that comes with it."

Molly MacPhee's face became aglow, and she knotted the front of her apron with her callused fingers. She was about to exclaim "Oh! Lieutenant Cameron, that's indeed wonderful, and we can't thank you enough," however, she was preempted by the Sergeant's sober response. "We are grateful to you and the General, Sir, but I have my pension, and I'm afraid I would feel like a charity case. I hope you understand, Lieutenant."

In response, Cameron became official, his voice commanding, "Sergeant Major MacPhee! This position was not offered out of charity. Rather, it's a selfish request from someone who strives to obtain the most loyal, competent man for a tough job. If you're that man, then I expect you to volunteer!"

The Sergeant's gray eyes met Iain's blue ones hard-on. Then, "Aye, sir, you have your volunteer, or volunteers be the better word! Molly and I will report for duty as soon as possible, sir!" A happy-hearted Iain departed, leaving two happier hearts embracing inside the cottage.

Iain's spirit had been lifted by his visit with the MacPhees. Consequently, he looked forward to the following day's ceremony for Geordie. Perhaps, there is a no more solemn, stirring service than the ceremony attendant on the burial of a Scots Guard who gave his life in battle in the service of his regiment, Queen, and country. The fact that Second Lieutenant George Edward MacCallum was the son of a Lieutenant General did add to the splendor, as the assemblage included many officers of the highest rank, representing all the Highland Regiments. Also, a goodly section of British Units of land, sea, and air as well as the Irish Guards were present. Soft shafts of sunlight often penetrated the giant puffs of gray, tinted cumulus clouds, and—when this did occur—all the tartans present were highlighted in magnificent display! Bright reflections from sword hilts, dirks, cap badges, and buckles burst from the ranks of those present, momentarily dazzling the eye of the observer. Pleated kilts swayed softly at the behest of a caressing wind, which also enlivened fur of the bearskin shakos worn by many.

Such was the scene of solemn gravity that came into Iain's view from his preeminent position in the funeral cortege slowly progressing from the Manor House to the small private cemetery on the estate grounds. First Lieutenant Iain Cameron was immediately behind the caisson bringing Geordie's casket. For the purpose of the service, the kisk containing Geordie's sacred relic had been placed inside a larger burial case, which had been solemnly cloaked with the flag for which he died. The Color Guard—bearing Regimental Standards, as well as those of Scotland and England—were well forward as custom dictated.

Iain's good left eye, when fixed forward, could easily catch the rippling red Rampant Lion proudly erect in a vibrant yellow banner. The massed pipes and drums—with the latter enshrouded in black—were playing the Scottish Funeral March. The dirge was a somber melody but absolutely appropriate to the circumstance and mood of all assembled. A rider-less black stallion, bearing an empty saddle with boots reversed in the stirrups, slowly pranced in cadence with the drumbeat of the slow march. Behind the caisson marched the pallbearers, Geordie's father, and other uniformed relatives.

Iain's gaze frequently rested on the vertical blade of the Scottish broadsword, held rigidly upright in the steel grasp of his right hand. This was the blade that had avenged his friend! How appropriate that it now honors him! Standing stiffly at attention throughout the service, Iain's mind drifted away from the words prescribed by the Episcopal rite as well as those giving their speeches of praise and condolence. He had his own silent eulogy for Geordie, which his mind numbly recorded. However, his return to reality was prompted by the pipes' and drums' rendition of "Tunes of Glory." The lyrics cascaded on his sensorium.

> *March no more, my Highland Laddie*
> *March no more now the battle's o'er*
> *Sleep in peace, my Highland Laddie*
> *Sleep in peace now and forever more!*

Then Iain reflected on a stanza of Kilmer's "Rouge Bouquet," which was written to honor fellow members of another army in another war. Yet still the poet's epic verse was so fitting to this time, this place, and Geordie! Substituting the singular for the plural, he recited the words to himself:

> *Now over his grave abrupt and clear—three volleys ring,*
> *And perhaps his brave young spirit—hears the bugle sing,*
> *Go to sleep—go to sleep!*
> *Danger's past, now at last—go to sleep.*

Iain presented the folded flag to Geordie's mother. Hers was the saddest face he had ever beheld, but flint was present there, damming up all tears and stemming the quiver in her lips. They would be released to flow in private. His salute to General Sir George was given. The old soldier stood desolate, though resolute, and returned in kind. Once his about-face was complete, Cameron led the Honor Guard away, stopping once to present the farewell salute to Geordie.

Chapter Six

Two days after Geordie's funeral, it was time to return to duty, or so Iain hoped, not knowing for certain if there would be further opportunity for a one-eyed First Lieutenant. He busied himself packing, frequently but fondly interrupted by a soldier's mother, fretting over whether or not her son was including all he would surely need. *Where was my small case? Bloody hell! Did I leave it at the hospital?* His recall was blank. *Who was the saint of lost articles? The one he always invoked as a small boy—whether it was for a lost puppy, or the allowance he placed in a secret hiding place—then promptly forgot. St. Jude—he's the one! No, he's the one in charge of the impossible, and a lost case doesn't fit that category. Ah ha! It's St Anthony!* "Come on, St Anthony—give me a clue," was his mildly irreverent prayer. St. Anthony—possibly prompted by St. Jude—piqued his memory. "It's in the boot of father's car," he recalled. St. Anthony did not receive the thanks he deserved, but such was frequently the case.

Iain retrieved the valise, returned to his room, took out the shirt and other items. Underneath the last article removed was a small package, carefully gift wrapped with a card neatly written by a graceful hand. The message read "To Lt. Iain Alexander Cameron—a peace offering," and was signed "Best Wishes, Claire Campbell." Inside was a can of soup—Campbell's Soup! It was tomato!

On the following morning, Iain was up early. He completed the packing of his automobile with a flourish. The sports car was a vintage Austin Healy—on loan from his father until such time as he was able to purchase a car for himself. His father had that "Don't wait too long" look when he surrendered the ignition keys. Iain's parents bid him adieu, and the scion of this particular band of the Cameron clan was off again. Iain glanced back and saw Simba—hang-dog expression again, but the gnarled hand of another Cameron kneading his left ear helped remove some of the sting from another separation from his master.

The Austin Healey, gaining release from the garage in which it usually remained incarcerated, responded to the freedom of the A-9. In a short time, it was halted in the parking lot, adjacent to the ward to which Sister Campbell was assigned. Would she be there? wondered Iain. He approached the Nurses' Station, cognizant of a pounding heart.

She was there! Claire's face bore a puzzled expression, as she beheld the appearance of the approaching officer. His face was flushed, the expression one of bewilderment. Given her clinical acumen, she was immediately concerned that he was ill, possibly a post-operative infection. "Are you ill, Lieutenant?" she said with obvious concern.

"It has been referred to in those words, Miss Campbell, but I really think my problem is. . . . No, that's not right. It really isn't a problem! Well—it's just that—well . . . I think I'm in love with you, crazy as it may seem."

"I don't think it's crazy at all, Lieutenant. I think it's rather cute, but rather sudden." Her beautiful smile erased any doubt of insincerity or mockery.

Claire requested a short break from her superior, then turned to Iain and said, "Perhaps, we can go outside for a moment." She led the way and once outdoors, she turned and faced him. "I'm very happy you stopped to see me, Lieutenant Cameron," she responded.

"Please call me Iain," he replied.

"If you call me Claire," she responded.

"Aye, that's a deal I can accept," he declared. "I can't stay long, Claire. I'm on my way to London to rejoin the Regiment. I just felt I had to see you!"

"What brought that on?" she said with a smile. "Tomato soup, that's what did it. Are you going with anyone Claire? If not, I would like ever so much to call—and come to see you when I can."

"That would be very nice," was her reply.

The next few seconds were spent just looking at one another. Then, hands finally found their opposites, and there was a gentle squeeze by both. "Iain, I must get back to the ward," she said with a sigh.

"I know, and I must leave," he replied. Then, the little squeeze of their hands grew tighter. Iain bent his head, intending to bestow a kiss. Claire's closed eyes and pursing lips informed him it would be welcome, and it was returned. "I'll ring you up tomorrow," he said.

"That might be easier if you had my number," was her smiling response. She wrote the number on a slip of paper and pressed it into his hand. "You've made me very happy, Iain. Now go and drive very safe. I'm already sure I like you enough to worry about you." They kissed again, and Iain was gone.

The other Sisters on the ward seemed puzzled by the change in Sister Campbell. They felt it strange to talk cogently with an alert person, who at the same time seemed to be in a sublime state! This was not usually found among the nursing personnel on the post-surgical ward.

Cameron was late arriving in London. Heavy traffic along the route had materially increased his driving time. However, he bore it all in good humor since he traveled with a happy heart. Without significant problems, Lieutenant Cameron located the Bachelor Officers Quarters, which he would utilize. After checking in, Iain was assigned a room and proceeded to impart on it some reflection of his own persona. Family pictures and a few from Malay were displayed. A photo of Geordie had a commanding position atop a dresser, while mother's, father's, and sister's photos occupied equal prominence on the top of a small desk. They were stationed just to the left of the only truly decorative item present. Though others might deem it entirely curious, Iain had no compunction about placing the red-and-white Campbell's soup can in a most conspicuous place.

In regard to the service facilities, the government-imposed austerity was never in absentia, consequently there was no private phone in his room, a disconcerting deprivation from his initial stay. A pay phone in the hallway was the only viable alternative Fortunately, Iain was heavily armed with a multitude of ten-pence coins, which he quickly loaded into the coffer of the greedy phone. The sacred slip of paper with Claire's number entrusted to him the preceding day was held at the proper focal distance by a slightly tremulous hand.

Was she there? Had Claire reconsidered, and decided he was a dolt and a boor after all? Iain's level of doubt was rising with each successive ring. After seven rings, a very soft and sweet "hello" dispersed all the black clouds obscuring his horizon of hopeful optimism. The second "hello" was also soft, but somewhat quizzical; no doubt due to the lack of response to the first. "Hello, Claire—Iain here! Iain Cameron. I talked with you yesterday."

"Yes, Iain, I know. You didn't have to give your last name. I really don't have so many Iain's calling that I can't figure out which one it might be," she said laughingly.

"I'm pretty relieved by that revelation," he replied.

Claire continued "I assume you arrived safely and found your quarters. Are they decent enough? Did they give you an assignment yet?" Such was her query. Iain gave clear answers to all and was about to tell Claire that he missed her very much and how anxious he was to see her when the phone went dead!

Iain had glaringly underestimated the time and had already exhausted his supply of coins. "Bloody hell! Will she think I hung up on her?" He pummeled the hapless phone with his right fist, while digging furiously in his pocket with the contralateral hand. Fruition finally overcame frustration, as he pumped the fresh supply of coins into the receptacle. "Claire, it's Iain again. The bloody phone went dead!" Using the military terminology with which he was accustomed, he exclaimed, "I've reloaded. I miss you! Would you be comfortable with me writing you every day?"

"Yes, Iain, but that might be very difficult for you with an officer's busy schedule. Also, I'm not a terribly good correspondent, and I can't promise answers."

"Claire, you needn't answer them all. I would be very happy if you would just try and read them."

"Aye, I can surely do that," she promised. "Your letters will be quite welcome, and they are much less expensive than a call. We Campbells are a wee bit penurious, in addition to other proclivities, and I doubt a Lieutenant's stipend can support a large phone bill. I'd hate to see you drummed out of the Guards as a hapless debtor. You'll keep me very happy with our letters, and a short call once a week or so."

As they were exchanging their good-byes, Iain was about to say "I love you, Claire." He stopped short of that, recalling that you didn't shoot at an uncertain target. This early on, the possibility of true, lasting romance fit that description. This very first call was over. Though he had blurted out the words at the hospital and still felt that way, it was really too much, too soon to repeat. Surely, it was a satisfactory start, and a good foundation on which to build. Time was still left in his day for the first in a very long series of letters to Claire.

On the following morning, Iain was scheduled to report to the Commanding Office at 0800. He arose to a bright June day that was quite pleasant by London standards. His mood reflected the warmth of the late spring sun, which had awakened the neighboring birds a good three hours earlier. *How different the robins, wrens and warblers sang by comparison to the raucous avian chatter so common to Malay*, he thought. A last glimpse in the mirror assured Cameron that his uniform, as well as his person, was meticulous in appearance, save for the small dressing that hid and protected the sutures closing his reconstructed shrapnel scar. "I must remember the stitches are due out tomorrow," were the last words to himself before departing his quarters.

Lieutenant Cameron's objective was the office of Lieutenant Colonel Edward Thorburn, O.B.E. and the current Commanding Officer. His arrival time was precisely 0753 hours. For reasons only Cameron could fathom, he always arrived seven minutes early when reporting to a superior. Given the rigid regimen prevailing in the formal atmosphere of Regimental Headquarters, it always seemed to Cameron that the Duty Sergeant—defending the outer precinct of the Commandant's inner circle—would compulsively spend at least three minutes shuffling through and examining appointment schedules, copies of orders, and so on. Then, the Sergeant would indulge in some seemingly mindless banter generated to exhaust the remaining minutes before he was formally ushered into the office. Today's experiences once more proved his thesis.

"First Lieutenant Iain Alexander Cameron reporting for duty, Sir!" His voice was strong, his figure imposing, and the salute perfection. Thornburn's return salute was perfunctory, as was frequently the case of those that were elevated in rank. However, his smile was broad and genuine. "Welcome to Regimental Headquarters, Captain, it is a pleasure to have you join us at least for a while." Blue eyes behind the desk were studiously evaluating Iain's face in an effort to ascertain whether or not the reference to Captain had registered. Even a face of someone standing at attention can generate a quizzical expression. So it was with Iain. The Colonel knew that no Lieutenant would be so bold as to correct a senior officer. They would simply assume he made a mistake or it was news too good to be true. The former was highly probable, the latter an extreme rarity in the British Army.

"Please be at ease and take a chair," said the Colonel with a broad smile still present. "This is good news, Cameron, which I am sure you will be happy to hear. Addressing you as Captain was not a bobble on my behalf. You have very definitely been advanced to that rank. However elated you may feel upon hearing this news may prove inconsequential compared to what follows. Surely, it would seem, Captain, that based on the testimony of the men in your platoon, and especially that of Sergeant Major MacPhee, you have been recommended for the Victoria Cross!"

Iain was nonplussed. This was such an honor—but did he deserve it? Colonel Thornburn continued. "Captain Cameron, I have an inkling of your thoughts at this moment. If you had broken into a broad grin or let out an exclamation, I would be concerned. You are thinking that you didn't do anything anyone else wouldn't do, or there was no bravery involved. You just acted out of reflex. I'm proud to say I shared those same feelings when I received my V.C. in '43. Rest assured, Captain, that a lot of good men made this decision and that you do merit it. Set aside all doubts and accept the honor you deserve." Thorburn strode around his desk to bestow a very hardy handshake of congratulations.

"Captain, you are detailed to take the rest of the day off. I'm sure you will want to ring up your father, the General, and your mother to share the news. Oh, yes, I'm certain a brand-new Captain will be more than happy to supply the habitués of the Officer's Mess with a few salutary rounds of good Scotch whiskey. Happy hour begins at 1800 hours! Contact Major Wilson in Administration tomorrow. He will see to giving you a temporary post. You are dismissed, Captain." This time, the Colonel's salute was just as crisp and perfect as the Captain's.

Iain deferred calling his parents until the following evening. His sojourn at the Officer's Mess with all the attendant celebration had induced a level of inebriation that he hoped was mild. However, he appreciated the fact that ethanol, even of Highland origin and mellowed with great care for twelve long years, did render judgment fallible, resulting in predictable self-deceit on behalf of the imbiber. Discussing a promotion and the magnificent honor of the medal with anyone, much less his parents, should surely not be conducted with slurred speech and disjointed sentences. Iain did pen his letter to Claire, but only after midnight and four cups of coffee when he was satisfied that he was reasonably rational.

On he following morning, quite alert despite the proceeding night's revelry, Iain reported to Major Wilson. "Ah, yes, Cameron—I hear you put in a bloody good show over in Malay, Captain," said the Major, taking note of Iain's freshly acquired insignia of rank. "Just the man we need to flesh out our new training manual. We've set aside an office for you—a bit of a box actually—but big enough to put some of your experiences and suggestions into words for the edification of those we'll be deploying in the future. You can utilize any of the young ladies from the Secretary Pool or Sergeant Mackay for assistance or procurement of supplies. Please check in with me every two or three days so I can stay abreast of your progress."

"Fine, Sir, I'll get right on it!" were Cameron's words of assurance.

Sergeant Mackay deposited the new Captain in the cubbyhole that would serve as his office. Though even less commodious than the hospital room from which he was so recently paroled, it would suffice. Iain picked up a pen and applied its tip to the waiting tablet. After five minutes, he had produced a crude cartoon of a Rhodesian Ridgeback. The word "Simba" was written in several places and printed in several others. "A tough job without a dog that can point out Chinese soldiers, not pheasants." That was underlined several times. "Fantastic start," he said to himself. Then, Iain arose, crumpled up the paper, and dropped it in the hallway receptacle, having none of his own in the sparse office. *Certainly hope they burn the trash,* he thought. *Imagine the damage to National Security if a spy was to latch on to that.*

"I need copies of all your recent training manuals, Sergeant," were his words to Mackay.

"Yes, Sir, give me fifteen minutes, and I'll give you everything we have." True to his word, the Sergeant produced a small stack within the promised time.

Well before lunch, Iain had ascertained what constituted an interesting and informative manual and plunged into an outline for producing one, hand-written though very legible. Consequently, by the end of duty day, Cameron had accomplished much, and more important, he was satisfied with the results. Then, after a quick dinner devoid of Scotch whiskey or other spirits, he placed a call to his parents. Iain's father was elated by his disclosures. Mother was more reserved, as she knew such things could lead to new adventures and dangers for one she loved so dearly. His mother's concerns were based on thirty years of experience with her first love, Iain's father.

Sensing Iain's reluctance to freely discuss the upcoming reception of the Victoria Cross, his father decided on a preemptory strike. "Laddie—I know what you are thinking, and how you feel about the Victoria Cross. First off, you are concerned that you don't deserve it. Then, you are abhorred by the possibility that you won't be able to live up to it. I have a few medals of my own. However, I've never forgotten there are hundreds of fine, brave men—buried or blown to bits on battlefields all over the world—who deserved the honor more than I. For reasons known only to God, the medals came my way. Long ago, I decided that I would accept them as a form of honor to those other men, and I would never defile them, as it would dishonor all those unnamed true heroes. I know you will do the same."

Iain thanked his father and assured him that he would proudly carry out his tradition, for the old soldier had the same medal bestowed on him back when it was known as the Queen's Cross. Also, General Cameron had many more medals, including those of other countries allied to England in the two great wars. To his mother, Iain gave temporary restraint from worry. He advised her that he was to be assigned to a desk—free from any harm worse than writer's cramp.

Finally reconciled to the honor he was to receive, Iain placed a telephone call to Claire. She answered on the third ring. Her "hello" was as sweet as it had been on his initial call. "Claire, it's Iain. The one and only Iain!" He had remembered her remonstration in the initial call. "I've somewhat exciting news, and there is no one else I would rather share it with than you!"

"That sounds intriguing. Iain. Please don't keep me guessing."

In response, Iain revealed his promotion to Captain and laughingly suggested he could now afford longer and more frequent phone calls.

As a comeback, Claire humorously chided him about being a spendthrift. Then, she ended with a question "Is there more you are holding back?"

"That's the way it is supposed to be with the best part. It always comes last," was his rejoinder. "Claire, I've been selected to receive the Victoria Cross. The ceremony is set for the first of July at our Headquarters in London. Queen

Elizabeth will be making the presentation. Her Majesty is in fact, the Colonel-in-Chief of the Scots Guards. Of course, it's an honorary title. She has never led anyone into battle and, obviously, she never had to seek promotion to ascend to the highest rank. In all humility, I don't think I deserve it, but my father has made a cogent argument for me to accept it. In addition, one would be considered an ungrateful scoundrel were he to decline. Is there any way you could come to the ceremony, Claire? This would mean the world to me—if you could."

"Oh, Iain! I'm so happy for you, and yes I would be honored to attend, but since I was gone during my mother's illness, they may be unwilling to grant me any further leave."

Iain spent the rest of the time allotted by his deposited ten-pence coins making convincing arguments in hopes of luring her to London for this, his finest hour. Claire indicated she would do all in her power to obtain the necessary time away—but could make no promises. "Oh! Claire, please try hard," he said.

Suddenly, Iain was aware that some of his early unbridled enthusiasm was ebbing, as he became aware that circumstances might render him bereft of her presence on this most important of days. He never gave pause to the thought that the most auspicious day of his life was the day he merited the medal, rather than the day he was to receive it.

"Call me next weekend, Iain. I will know by then. I am so happy for you and your parents. Thank you for your letters. They are very nice, and I enjoy them."

"I enjoy sending them," he said, stopping short of adding any terms of endearment. "I miss you, Claire! I'll call you next week."

"I miss you too, Iain." Then, the connection was broken.

Claire readied herself for bed. Although it was early, she had spent an exhausting day. She hoped sleep would come rapidly. However, reality told her that wouldn't happen. She had come to realize she was very deeply interested in Iain Cameron, though she wasn't about to admit she might be in love. *You can't love anyone you've only known for a few weeks,* was the first of her self-proclamations. *Would I really recognize love?* she wondered. *I love my parents, but that's different from loving a man—who could be a husband! I thought I was in love with Jimmy Hendry that summer when I was seventeen, but that was an adolescent fantasy.*

Claire pummeled her pillow, then rolled onto her back. She ended up wide-eyed and staring at a dull light, which had come from outside and gained access through a deficient shade and ended up on the ceiling of her darkened room. *You want to be in love, Claire Campbell,* she nearly said aloud, *however, you are afraid of the consequences!* She had approached the possibility of that condition from almost a clinical perspective since the time Iain had stopped by to see her. Softly,

Claire murmured, "You make the diagnosis, and then you determine if there is a remedy."

Given her acumen, Claire had taken it upon herself to learn more about the young man's family. His father was a General, and they had a fine estate with all the trappings and social connections. What did Claire Campbell have? A decent education, a profession. and two wonderful parents. Her list ended there. If he survived, Iain would rise in rank, as his father had. He was handsome with a plentitude of fine characteristics! This man would be considered a splendid catch for dozens of debutantes, whose fathers graced the House of Lords. Her father was a sweet, generous, honest, and wonderful owner of an antiquated hotel.

In her mind, Claire could picture Iain's parents looking aghast at the prospect of his inviting this Cinderella to attend the award ceremony. If they had him alone, how quickly might they convince him to drop this silly infatuation in favor of any of a dozen beauties from fine families, which were of his own class. Her fine coach would indeed be a pumpkin, and the horses would revert to mice. There was no glass slipper or fairy princess in her story. She had best come to reality and accept bitter disappointment now, rather than face devastation later. Sleep finally came to Claire Campbell. Two small patches of moisture were present on her pillow, remnants of the tears deposited there.

Chapter Seven

⊠ ⊠ ⊠

In the following four days, Iain devoted himself enthusiastically to the Malay Manual. Corrections and suggestions given by Major Wilson were accepted with genuine gratitude. The man was easy to work with, extremely knowledgeable, and proficient in the matter of manual production. He had been a warrior. Now Wilson was consigned to administration. This was the results of the loss of half of his right lung when he intercepted the lethal messenger from an 8mm round sent his way by a Wermacht Corporal. A degree of dyspnea was tolerable at Headquarters but unacceptable at or near the front lines.

Iain could not help but contemplate the possibility of a similar fate. Would a one-eyed Captain be of any more value than a short-winded Major? They might show consideration until retirement age arrived. However, when it came to promotion, the officer with a handicap would sooner or later realize he had no more rungs on his ladder.

Fortunately, Wilson had a wonderful way with words, and his new disciple was quick to discern this and develop his own skills. Furthermore, the Major had a consummate ability with time allotment and beneficial disruptions. Whenever he sensed tedium or tension, it became the propitious moment for tea, an anecdote, or war story generally spiced with good humor and self-depredation. Rows of ribbons on Major Wilson's chest would have supported a good deal of bravado, though none came forth. Iain recognized a fine role model and mentor. Therefore, he had a great desire to inculcate this man's traits in himself.

Late on the fourth evening, following the extension of his invitation to Claire, Iain was writing again, extolling the joy of seeing her. He did not stop to contemplate that his repetitive endearments were giving new meaning to the old canard, "Second verse, same as the first—isn't any better and isn't any worse." Like all those who were in love, thought they were in love, or were simply energized by the concept of love, he was driven only by emotion.

Suddenly, Iain set his pen aside, as he conjured up a vision of Claire emerging from the train. He was astute enough to realize that she wouldn't have an auto, so the train was the logical means of conveyance. There he would be, peering over the heads of other passengers until he caught sight of her. "Claire! Over here!" She would hear his voice, scan the crowd, and immediately recognize the waving bouquet held high above the heads of those intervening. Claire would smile, wave, and even possibly throw a kiss. Pushing through the throng, they would meet and embrace. Finally, freeing themselves from the melee, they would rush to his car and . . . and then what? Heretofore, Iain had very little need to consider the pragmatic aspects of propriety, but now they hit him head-on, and he was suddenly jolted by the collision. Mores were still quite Victorian in 1949! Of course, it was a misnomer, since few of the royals were hampered in their pursuits or conquests by the rigid rules of conduct imposed in the former Queen's name.

"Bloody hell!" was Iain's standard invective in the face of stress or a disquieting situation, and it erupted from his lips. "I just can't drop Claire off at a hotel! That would look nearly as bad as bringing her here. What would she think? What would her parents think?" Iain stopped short of contemplating what her parents would think, as he was fully preinformed in that respect. Other ugly images invaded Cameron's thoughts. He sensed that he was surrounded, his situation hopeless! To fight on with this battle plan could be disastrous! Surrender could be considerably worse. Furthermore, Iain—being a man and especially a man committed to wearing a prescribed uniform—had never bothered to give any thought as to whether or not Claire possessed a suitable wardrobe or funds to secure one for such an event.

At the same time, although eight hours by car or train to the north, two delicate, firm hands opened the most recent of Iain's letters and presented it for perusal by her blue eyes. The message pleased Claire, as it indicated his persistent interest in her. She had been aware of all the problems that would arise over going to London, well before Iain had completed last week's call. It was all a fairy tale, but one with too many poisoned apples and witches spells for her to overcome. She would just tell him there was no way for her to get the time off. That was a white lie, of course, because she had already received the supervisor's approval on condition she worked a double shift this week. Claire had made the request early on—when enthusiasm held sway over doubt. However, doubt was now fully in command, and the only open course was realism. She would tell Iain that she couldn't attend. If that ruined their relationship, then so be it! The finality of her decision at least provided her with a degree of comfort. It was a relief, just not having to worry about facing his parents, who might consider her an opportunist, a gold-digger out to capture their son—a son she could barely know.

Meanwhile, since his father always played golf on Friday afternoon, regardless of the weather and providing it wasn't hunting season, Iain decided it was the opportune time to confide in mother. His rationalization was that if you have a serious medical problem, you sought the finest specialist in that field. He had a special problem and knew a specialist best qualified to handle it. "Mother, I've got a problem, and I need help—your help!" Iain explained all that had transpired and did the best he could to try and put his feelings for Claire—and her presumed feelings for him—into perspective. His mother was finely tuned to all that he said, and a reasonable approach to a solution was beginning to formulate even before the call was completed. Mary Cameron promised to see what she could do. Of course, there was the caveat that—depending on the young woman's true disposition—a mother could make matters worse. However, if so, it might be for the best. Her final words were:

"Nothing happens by accident Iain! If the lass is to have a further place in your life, and if is a big word in the case of someone you have known for so short a time, then this will be only the first of the hurdles you both must cross. Say a prayer that it all works out."

Another call was placed a short time later. "Miss Campbell, this is Mary Cameron. I am Iain's mother. He called to tell us some of the nice things you did for him in hospital, and that he had invited you to come to London for the ceremony. I'm afraid he is much like his father and apart from war and hunting, they have no concept of logistics—especially for a lady! I know there is a question about getting the time off, so I hope I'm not premature. However, if you were to be free, we could surely stop on the way to London. You could ride with us, though I must warn you, Iain's father can't be long without a cigar, and the fumes are sometimes overpowering. In addition, my sister Jane has a flat in London, and I know she would welcome a guest. You can think it over and let me know. I would be happy to call your mother. if you like. and explain that we would be responsible for you."

Superficially, the call was all a polite invitation. However, it was also a test administered by a woman who knew women. It was extremely unlikely that an opportunistic young woman would volunteer to spend hours in the company of an elderly couple, especially if one were belching forth clouds of cigar smoke. That would be a real test for an opportunist. The same held true for staying at her sister's flat—and the possible phone call to her parents. If she agreed to all the provisions, there was a high probability she was really a nice young lady. In the event she said she couldn't come, she was either telling the truth or she couldn't abide the conditions and would await some future opportunity to snare her son. Mary Cameron would cross that bridge when she came to it. Being a woman, she knew a wardrobe could be a problem for Claire Campbell. Also, Mary knew that she had not always been affluent, and a resourceful lass could find a spare quid or two, remake an old dress, or borrow from a friend.

Claire pronounced her thanks for Mrs. Cameron's entire offer. She was still uncertain as to whether to go. Claire found the invitation appealing but decided not to commit herself without further thought. "May I call you on Saturday, Mrs. Cameron? I will know for certain by then. You needn't call my parents, for I know that if I am able to go and tell them who is watching out for me, they will certainly be agreeable."

Mary Cameron smiled, as she replaced the receiver. "The lass has a sincere enough voice—and she passed the first test!" Those were the words that she murmured while nodding her head.

A day later, Sister Campbell's nursing instincts suddenly began to rise. Now, it became obvious to her that she was guilty of temporizing. On numerous occasions in the past, there were examples of doctors confronting an acutely ill patient and supplying them with supportive care, then advising the relatives that it was better to let nature take its course, as intervention might be fatal. Other surgeons decided quickly that it was far better to do something, even if in the end it did not produce the desired affect. You saved some, you lost some—and you lived with the outcome. Cinderella—if that were what she was—would attend the ball, and she would rely on grace and ingenuity, while lacking any semblance of a magic wand.

Claire decided that there was time to resurrect and refurbish the dress she wore for her graduation from Nursing School. Depletion of her little treasure of pound notes to purchase a proper suit and at least a bare minimum of accoutrements for her Spartan wardrobe would also be necessary. Yes, she would look more than proper. Her appearance would be attractive. True, twenty quid had been saved for her art supplies, and it was a great sacrifice to devote it all to this project. Nonetheless, if this would help find a man that she could love, respect, and perhaps sometime marry, then the brushes and canvases could wait. A passionately pursued hobby might end up being her solace in spinsterhood if she were to squander what seemed to be a very wonderful opportunity in the here and now!

Claire knew that Iain would be calling the following evening, so she should get back to his mother soon. She felt there was something very reassuring in Mary Cameron's voice and words, which she recognized as being quite similar to her own mother. Perhaps that had influenced her decision far more than she realized. Her call was placed and answered by a voice she did not recognize. Claire hesitated for a second, then came to the conclusion that she had no doubt reached the maid. This was a situation to which she was not accustomed. However, she continued.

"This is Claire Campbell. May I speak with Mrs. Cameron, please?"

"Just a moment, Miss Campbell," was the reply. Shortly after, she heard "Yes, Claire, this is Mary Cameron." Iain's mother had purposely used the young lady's given name in hopes of putting her at ease.

"I shall be able to go to the ceremony for Iain, Mrs. Cameron. I would like to accept your very generous offer of a lift, as well as the possibility of staying with your sister, if that is still all right?"

"Certainly, it is still quite fine, Claire. In fact, I'm looking forward to meeting you."

Mary Cameron's remark was more than casual curiosity. However, Iain's mother's intonation gave no indication for analysis. Mrs. Cameron continued. "We should be coming through Edinburgh fairly early on Friday, Claire. Iain's father—though retired—hasn't been able to free himself from the notion you should always attack at dawn. Being a nurse, I'm sure you are quite capable of coping with early rising. I've milked a few cows in my day, so I am prepared for his early reveilles, thank heaven! Well, Claire, I'm pleased, and I'll ring you up next Thursday evening to give you all the details."

"Thank you so much, Mrs. Cameron. I'm really appreciative!"

Their conversation ended, the two women were now free to analyze. Claire was pleased that Iain's mother had mentioned cows. She assumed rightly that the General's wife was letting her know of her middle-class heritage, and it was something they shared. Again, Mary Cameron congratulated herself that Claire had seemed a young woman of merit. The nurse had accepted her offer most graciously. *Middle-class she might be, but you've never lost sight of your own origins—Mary Cameron—or Mary Frazier as it used to be. My John was able to discern there was something special in the Head Gamekeeper's daughter.* As the name of her husband came to mind, she was reminded that she had to put the proper spin on her little game. The good General hadn't the foggiest notion that he would be conveying Claire Campbell to London and return. She smiled, looking forward to the challenge!

Iain's weekend telephone call was one of the happiest experiences that had come his way recently. Claire would be attending! Better yet, the young lady, now the center of his interest, seemed quite taken by his mother. Their conversation had gone well, with no hint whatsoever she had taken umbrage to the insertion of Mary Cameron into their relationship. Concentration on the Malay

Manual became more difficult until he decided that plunging himself into the project would make the time between now and Claire's arrival pass more quickly. So it was that Major Wilson was quite astonished with the progress made. He would have been even more amazed if he were fully cognizant of the competing focus, which assailed Captain Cameron's thoughts.

Meanwhile, Mary Cameron was sufficiently versed in the art of warfare, having endured countless hours of dinner talk discussion between several generations of the Guardians of the Empire. In fact, she had a passing knowledge of all the recommended tactics of Sun Tzu, the storied warrior and writer of ancient China, plus those of the more contemporary German general and statesman Von Klausevuitz. These were certainly not the usual reading for a woman. However, since she had been a lady consigned to bed because of a threatened miscarriage, Mary had to have some diversion. Having made her way through all the classics deemed most appropriate for the fair sex, she began to relish a change of pace and found it in these two volumes in her husband's study. She recalled that the most successful attack was one that was unsuspected, and one could anticipate victory, especially if the opponent was preoccupied.

Mary chose her opportunity when Iain's father was both unsuspecting and preoccupied. Dinner was over. The General was firmly ensconced in his favorite chair; a double dram of single-malt in easy access, with a fresh Corona lightly clenched between his teeth. He had just received the newly printed catalog from James Purdey and Sons. General Cameron was poring over the pictures of the splendid double-barrel shotguns portrayed, for which they were famous throughout the shooting world.

Mary Cameron had learned early that a man, and certainly her husband, having become enraptured by what he was reading could carry on a conversation without ever hearing a word you said. This was the proper time to launch her offensive. "Did I tell you that there is a young nurse, a friend of Iain's, whom we are going to pick up in Edinburgh on the way to London?" His smile widened, as he tuned the page, perceived yet another beautiful gun and started to contrive how he could rationalize the expenditure for purchasing it, in addition, to convincing his wife it was an excellent investment. "Oh! Yes—yes," he replied, having no concept of the implication.

Mary took note of the "yes, yes of courses," and "certainly," in addition to the occasional grunt. Also, she noted the fact he was becoming more involved and no doubt scheming more with each passing page. In a louder voice, she suddenly said, "Then, it's all right with you?"

"Yes, of course, why wouldn't it be?" There was a pause, and the frown that developed knitted his bushy gray eyebrows more closely together. "What is it that's all right, Mary?"

"As usual, John, you haven't heard a word I said. I guess you are more interested in that silly gun catalog than what your wife has to say!"

"Of course, I heard what you said," he replied, with some defiance accompanying the words.

"All right, what did I say?" was her parrying sentence.

"Ah! Something about giving someone a ride—I think."

Based on myriad similar past experiences, Mary now knew he would be defensive, somewhat contrite, and agreeable to accept what he had clearly consented to do when he was mesmerized by the intriguing catalog. "I'll repeat it one more time—in hopes I can get through to you," Mary asserted. "There is a young nurse, Claire Campbell, who took care of Iain in the hospital. He has invited this young lady to London for the ceremony. I told Miss Campbell we would be happy to have her ride along with us." Then the drawing end of the smoldering Corona was deeply dented by the General's clamping jaws.

The frown was hard fixed on General Cameron's face, as he raised piercing blue eyes from the subject of his intense interest to confront the now smiling countenance of his wife. "Bloody hell! Who is this Claire, or whatever her name is?! How did she find her way into our lives anyway? I never heard Iain even mention any such person—much less say he was engaged!"

"He's not betrothed John! Iain is just interested in and indebted to her. I personally think it was very nice of him—and I for one am quite willing to put myself out a bit if I can be of accommodation to our son." General John Alexander Cameron knew the skirmish was lost! Thus, there was no hope of returning to the Purdey Catalog short of total surrender. He nodded his head and produced a half-smile. Mary recognized a white flag when she saw one. Her return smile gave the General leave to relight the cigar, refill his glass, and return to his reading. The foremost tactician in the Cameron household had never failed when she relied on Sun Tzu!

Chapter Eight

※ ※ ※

The Nurses Residence was a scene of frantic activity ever since news of Claire's forthcoming weekend adventure had surfaced. Now preparations were well under way. Given her gracious nature, winning ways, and readily proffered friendship, there were few of her peers who did not hold her in high esteem. Consequently, these young ladies were eager and anxious to reciprocate for all the fine things Claire had done for them. They seized on the opportunity to help. The result was that she ended up with nearly a dozen surrogate fairy godmothers. Willing hands and talented fingers replaced magic wands to revamp the old graduation dress, so it would be completely compatible with the current trends of beau monde. Dorothy just happened to have a rather stunning hat, which would be absolutely complementary. Lois came up with a valise that she had inherited from a well-traveled and affluent aunt. Then, there was Rosemary's purse—and so it went. Claire promised to care for all the borrowed, collected finery and thanked each one profusely.

Momentarily mentally absenting herself from the hectic preparations and feminine chatter, Claire came to the realization that she had neglected to do something on which all her plans and preparations hanged. "How could I have possibly forgotten my parents?" She had to tell them, no ask if it was all right for her to go. She thought it would be very easy to simply do it and say nothing. There being very little chance her father and mother would ever be the wiser. *No—I won't live a lie,* Claire decided. *If worse comes to worse, I could go against their will. It's better to be defiant than deceptive. Perhaps, I should have let Mrs. Campbell call after all,* she thought, but that opportunity was past, for yesterdays are never subject to recall.

Seeing what some other young women did in reference to personal behavior, Claire sometimes felt as though she belonged in another century. Even if this was the twentieth century, her standards were not subject to change, regardless of the date or someone else's mores. She would call home immediately. Father would be either at the reception desk or at his office at the White Herron Inn—a hotel that he long managed and now proudly owned. Claire experienced neither temerity nor timidity, as the dial tone gave way to the ring. She believed that if you are someone doing the right thing, there is no need to seek relief in either of these emotions.

"Father, it's Claire."

"Yes, dear, what can your old father do for you, lassie?"

Perhaps, she should have asked to speak to mother first, she thought. No—her parents were a team, and she could confide in one as well as the other. "Well, father, I'm kind of in a quandary. It's my fault, I know, and I'm late in calling, but I need to square it up with you and mother."

Angus Campbell was a protective, loving father, but he was worldly. No matter how much he trusted his daughter, his mind started to pounce on conclusions—ranging all the way up to deeds nefarious—when he heard Claire's rather disjointed opening. He thought, *My God!—has she done something serious enough to be discharged from the hospital? She's pregnant—that's it!* Doing his utmost to bring his wildest imaginary fears to rest, Angus Campbell blurted out, "Tell me! Mother and I will stand behind you. We'll see it through together." Suddenly, Angus thought he might detect a heart palpitation with the last promise, as he had no comprehension of what horrible circumstances there were to confront.

Claire was a bit bewildered by her father's parental pronouncements. She really hadn't even begun to describe the problem, and already she could sense alarm on the part of her father.

Claire's succinct description of her dilemma was laudanum to the wrenching, emotional pain that her father had just endured. In the end, he was so relieved by what he heard that he gave his permission conditionally. She could explain all to her mother, and he felt certain she would agree. Rachael Campbell was located. The phone was transferred, and her father went in search of a good dram or two, easily procured from the hotel bar.

Mrs. Campbell didn't jump to the same conclusion as her spouse, nor was she as quick to grant permission. Claire was reprimanded for being impulsive, derelict in not discussing it earlier, and leaving her prone to the question of impropriety. Following a lengthy inquisition, in which Mrs. Campbell made every effort to assure herself that her beloved child wouldn't be considered a hussy or tart, her mother finally saw fit to extend her accord. A lengthy list of admonitions accompanied the permission. Then, Claire returned to the beehive of activity. Her friend Pamela was waiting, with pincushion in hand, for one more fitting of the remodeled dress. By consensus, it had been decided that a bit more décolletage might be in order.

Four Cameron and one Campbell were getting ready for the great day, all in their own way, as dictated by mindset and the exigencies of the occasion. Iain had succumbed entirely to the joy of Claire's coming. The imposed limitation on phone calls had been breached. Now, there was at least one call on each remaining night. Temporarily reduced to a distraction, the Malay Manual was hardly added to during these days. Major Wilson assumed it was the medal. He was unaware of Claire. General Cameron had his finest dress uniform and all other necessary accoutrements meticulously packed. Mary Cameron's valise was as yet unfilled, as she wrestled with the dilemma of women—pink, ivory, pale blue, or fuchsia. The General was of no assistance, as he was sequestered in the gun room. As for Annie, the younger daughter still at home, she was suffering from her own wardrobe dementia and spent considerably more time seeking advice than rendering it.

Claire was least distracted of all, not by desire but by duty. Daydreaming could cause inattention, and that would produce complications for her patients. She was far too conscientious to allow that to occur. The thrill must wait the coming day. Mrs. Cameron had called saying the General's declared ETA was 0730 the next day. This acronym and the military time designation were explained. Again, the two ladies expressed happiness at having the opportunity to meet.

Friday dawned at last. The old campaigner Major General Cameron had not waited for the intrusion of the sun. His internal timing mechanism was nearly as precise as that found at Greenwich. Without any need of mechanical devices, he could arouse himself from the deepest somnolent state and be ready to confront any emergency presented by a newborn day. Since retirement, emergencies were exiguous, which he often regretted. Nevertheless, when provoked, he could turn a trifle to titanic—and such was his course of action at departure hour minus ten minutes. Bereft of the swagger stick, which he carried for many years, General Cameron repeatedly slapped his hand to his thigh in frustration. Several times, he approached the tires of his automobile intent on delivering a savage kick, only to restrain himself at the decisive moment, realizing the damage he might do to the gleaming polish on the toe of his Wellington.

At 0537 hours, the old war horse, with hands on hips, stance erect, and jaw jutting, exclaimed to the car, "You couldn't get a woman to be punctual if you were prodding her with a bayonet!" General Cameron heard no sound, but he did detect the aroma of Mary Cameron's favorite fragrance. Turning, he was prepared for a stiff rebuttal, with one eyebrow arched high above its mate. Instead of an acerbic response, he was greeted with a sweet spousal smile, and the softly spoken "John, darling, your wife and daughter are now ready to proceed."

A moment earlier, he had considered them in the same category as a flagging infantry unit who had not thrown themselves over the parapet following the cessation of the artillery barrage, when hearing the command to charge! However, now he was placated.

Conversation in the southbound car was the usual banter—centered on reckless drivers, slow traffic, and any changes that had occurred in a village they were passing through. Also, there were the questions necessary to assure themselves that they had not forgotten anything. The General was behind the wheel and in command of his Jaguar sedan. Mary Cameron was alongside, giving suggestions when to pass. Annie was in the back seat and was slated to share it with Claire Campbell at such time as they took her in charge.

As he passed a road side sign indicating a distance of fifty miles to Edinburgh, General Cameron decided it was time to gather more intelligence on the young lady. This was a briefing he had assiduously avoided since the subject had first been foisted on him a week before. For that purpose, he cocked his head toward Mary, who was his G-2 or Intelligence Officer on such matters. "Mary, dear, can you provide me with any information on this Miss—what's her name?—that we are to collect in Edinburgh?"

Mary replied "Miss what's her name is Miss Claire Campbell, as I've said many times before. Really, John, you sometimes amaze me! Surely, a person who can remember the names of every officer, and most of the noncoms in a regiment, should not be rendered memory less by one young lady!"

"All right! She's Claire Campbell. How did she manage to infiltrate our family?" was his responsive query.

"Well, she was one of Iain's nurses. Apparently, he was very much impressed by her concern and the care she gave him. I presume there is also some element of attraction, but—being a man—you should surely know more about that than I do," she said, with an accompanying smirk.

"Good heavens! He was only there a few days, and I doubt she was on twenty-four-hour shifts! It strikes me as odd behavior to go to this length for someone who should be more in the role of a passing acquaintance."

Annie, anxious to expound on the matter, with all the wisdom which seventeen years of worldly experience could provide, chimed in, "Daddy, don't be a fuddy duddy. I've read all sorts of splendid romances that started out with a single glance. Love can be that way!"

"Annie, when we return home, please remind me to check your reading material. It does seem you need a bit more emphasis on theology and less on love." General Cameron noted his daughter's modest blush and pursed lips in the rearview mirror, and he was assured she would have little more to say on that subject.

After a suitable pause, General Cameron groped for a Cuban cigar, passed it to Mary, who had a cutter in her purse based on long experience. After cutting off the end so it would draw, she lit it and passed the cigar back to her husband. "Mother, how disgusting," was Annie's outburst.

Her mother turned to confront her detractor. "Annie, I only light your father's cigar when it's a matter of safety! I don't do it in public, and I have no intention of smoking one myself. If you are such an expert on romance, you should realize that such things are done just to please the one you love. Besides, it's much better than chewing rawhide—like the female American Indians did for their husbands!"

Annie sighed, rolled her eyes, and then started giggling. "What's so humorous?" asked her father. "I just happened to think how funny it would be if Claire Campbell saw mother lighting your cigar," was his daughter's reply. With that, they all started laughing.

Having coaxed a little extra speed from the Jaguar, the elder Cameron was perfectly punctual arriving at the nurse's quarters, in which the center of his son's interest abided. Mary observed a sudden increased bounce in his step as he approached the door of Miss Campbell's domicile. After ringing the bell, his posture was relaxed and his anticipatory smile warm. Someone—unseen from the car—beckoned him inside. Then after a few moments, the door reopened, and a very beautiful young lady emerged, shepherded by the General, who was also serving as the porter for Claire's valise. At the car, introductions were made and salutations exchanged. Though the trip to London was long by the standards of the day, it was far from tedious. A typical saying, applicable on rare occasions, was "After a few minutes talking with her, I felt I had known her all my life!" So it was for the four of them.

London was not achieved until relatively late. Auntie Jane was awaiting their arrival at her flat in the Kennsington district. She was pleased that at last Claire was delivered safely to her door. The young woman impressed her in both appearance and demeanor. Aunt Jane felt it was easy to make her feel at home, especially since her guest obviously committed herself to consuming the proffered late-night repast with gusto, though quite ladylike in degree. The elder Camerons, with Annie in tow, took their leave quickly, inasmuch as the General wanted to check into the Savoy as soon as possible. The fact that Aunt Jane was abstemious and borderline Temperance League played a part, as there was no such prohibitions at his favorite hotel.

General Cameron had even projected his anticipation beyond the nightcap into a vision of venison carved at the table, a specialty of the Savoy Grille, which he would consume in sublime ecstasy on the following night. Recalling all the fantastic feasts dating back to the time it was called the Ritz Grill honoring Caesar Ritz, the manager, he stopped just short of salivating.

Soon, the travelers were all accounted for and tucked in for the night. However, the blissful sleep of one was shattered, just past midnight. When the noisy phone was answered, it emitted the voice of a perplexed, somewhat irritated young man who proclaimed, he had been waiting for hours, and it would have been nice to be informed as to what was taking place! General Cameron in hushed but firm tones told the Captain that it had been a long drive. They were safe and had been asleep. Furthermore, Miss Campbell was in the protective custody of Aunt Jane and had been fully provisioned with delectable food and was, in all probability, now ensconced in one of his sister-in-law's celebrated feather beds. "Now, Iain, put your mind to rest and get some sleep. We'll see you around 1000 hours, if your mother and sister muster in timely fashion."

"Just one more thing—" but Iain had no chance to continue. Further discussion would have been between him and the dial tone.

On the following morning, Iain also planned his arrival at 1000 hours. Precisely at that time, the dark green Jaguar, now serving as the General's charger, turned through the Headquarters' gate from Birdcage Lane. His father tethered the twelve-cylinder steed in the space reserved solely for those of highest rank, and he was first to dismount. Vice-like clasp of hands between father and son occurred. Misting of eyes said all that was needed but still did not stanch a short verbal exchange. "I love you, father."

"I love you, too, laddie, and my heart is filled with pride!"

Then, Iain deftly moved to his mother's door. Though his hand was grasping the handle, his eye was focused on Claire, as were hers on him. The millisecond of recognition was sufficient to evoke warm smiles on each face.

On Mary Cameron's emergence, she was warmly embraced and kissed by her son. The embrace was of sufficient duration to allow his mother to recall how the hugs had evolved all the years since Iain was born. She remembered the first little hug when she held him in her arms, and he placed his tiny arms about her neck. This memory was just as vivid as the nearly bone breaking one bestowed now. Iain kissed her and pronounced his love to her, as he had with his father. "My golden boy," she softly said. "Oh! How much I love my golden boy!"

Aunt Jane and Annie received a generous hug and kiss. Though it wasn't really possible for the memory of one sound of mind to significantly dissipate in two weeks time, Iain was certain that his had, as he now beheld Claire

Campbell. He recalled her beauty and physical attributes, but now he was overwhelmed. The hand that grasped her arm in assistance telegraphed his feelings. Both knew propriety, especially in light of the audience, demanded a gentle clasp of hands and an innocent peck on the cheek. Consequently, the norms of their society were dutifully followed. Eyes conversed silently and described deeper feelings. Much can be said by silent eyes, and they provided all the discourse needed.

Having a little over an hour to spend prior to the commencement of the ceremony, it was decided that a fast tour of the grounds was in order. This was done largely for the benefit of Claire since she was the only stranger to the premise. However, familiarity having bred no contempt in the others, it was in a very real sense a going home. Aunt Jane's husband, Lieutenant Colonel William "Jack" MacIntyre, had served in the Guards until his death in World War II. Lieutenant Colonel MacIntyre had led his headquarters unit against a trio of Tiger Tanks, which were in the vanguard of a Panzer Division.

Iain was very content to have the older trio and sister at the front of their little column. Claire walked on his right, following the custom of chivalry dictated by the position in which the gentleman's sword was hung. Her left arm was gently enthroned on his right, and tenderly affixed by Iain's much larger hand. Ears were tuned to the General's very comprehensive narrative, as well as to the responses of Mary Cameron and Aunt Jane. Claire and Iain partook, but their participation was punctuated by little messages, not shared by the others. They took the form of a squeeze of the hands, warm smiles, and on several occasions a subtle wink. After one of the latter, Claire regained her professional aplomb and noted that her escort's surgical scars were well healed. Also knowing the right eye was glass, Claire observed it did nothing to detract from the loving expressions coming from his face.

The time for the ceremony was soon at hand. The four ladies were escorted to the gallery where they would occupy a place of honor. General Cameron would act as a temporary Aid de Camp to the Queen, who was to make the presentation. Then, Iain joined his unit for the entry parade. All were in readiness! The ceremony began at precisely the hour ordained.

Pipes and drums of the Scots Guards were not as yet in sight when the drone of the pipes and the rhythmic beat of the drums were audible, and quickly mounting in magnitude. Bagpipes of Scotland were regarded as instruments of war as well as music. No one who heard them remained free of emotion. In a battle situation, they impelled the Scot to wildly charge, while instilling fear in the foe and an overwhelming urge to flee. On all other occasions, bagpipes adapt perfectly to the mood of the Scottish listener—as they did now. Whether at a procession or gravesite service, it is only with the greatest restraint that tears do not flow unabashedly. Those observing the ceremony realized somewhat paradoxically that tears are not strangers—even on happy occasions, such as the one about to commence.

First, there was a wee shiver and a tingle arising in the nape of the neck. Then, in those endowed with the chromosomal attributes of the Highlanders, the eyes began to glisten while the nostrils moistened. Claire Campbell and the vast majority of those present were rapidly expressing these programmed symptoms as the splendid sound drew near. An explosion of emotion occurred as the pipes and drums entered the esplanade. As their ears strained to capture every haunting note and drum concussion, their eyes became entranced and enthralled by the brilliant profusion of color. They seemed mesmerized by the motions perceived.

More than 200 pleated kilts—comprised of eight yards of heavy Saxony cloth brilliantly imbued with the red, yellow, and black of the Royal Stewart Tartan—swayed in unison. Red and white diced hose with red garter flashes contrasted starkly with the black tunics, though the latter were strongly embellished with gold piping, medals, and battle ribbons. Ebony handled Sgian Dubhs projected from the roll of the hose on the outer side of each right leg, starkly silhouetted against the flesh of the knee. Silver mounted dirks swung from the belted waists of the officers and Pipe Major moving in rhythm with the basket-hilted broadswords suspended on the contralateral side.

Mary Cameron glanced at Claire. Therein, she recognized all the emotional impact she had hoped to see. Certainly, it was the same as hers. Something they were sharing and perhaps meant to share in the future. She reached over and squeezed the young woman's hand, and the two turned faces mirrored the exact same expression.

Pipes and drums were playing "Garb of the Old Gaul"—a traditional slow march—as Iain entered the esplanade with his battalion. When the proper position was obtained, the band joined them in a splendid rendition of "God Save the Queen." The music was all the more memorable by virtue of her actual presence. "Rule Britannia" followed, and then came "A Man's a Man for All That," which was the prelude to the Commanding Officer's orders.

Lieutenant Colonel Moray read the citation; his voice strong and clear. Little echoes emanating from the adjacent stone buildings seemed to embellish his words and add measure to the meaning. On command, Captain Iain Alexander Cameron paced forward. The pride he felt was balanced by humility, which should be experienced by anyone joining the list of gallant men who had been his predecessors in receiving this most noble award! Captain Cameron's salute was directed to Elizabeth II, the Colonel in Chief. However, in his mind, Iain could imagine it passing beyond her and all those assembled to be conveyed by some warrior angel—to the spirits of those heroes—many of whom were honored posthumously.

Responding to the disparity in height, Iain—who had been standing straight and tall with face firmly fixed—gracefully bowed, thus making it possible for the diminutive monarch to properly place the ribbon-suspended medal around his neck. General Cameron, who had been given the honor of being her temporary aide, accorded Queen Elizabeth some assistance. All the pride, memories, and emotions of the moment were richly displayed on the fine features of the older man's countenance. Then, the Queen took Captain Cameron's hand in hers, and added her personal words of congratulation conveyed in the company of a heartfelt and endearing smile. Those softly spoken words were not conveyed beyond the three but did evoke reciprocal response in the faces of son and father.

On return to his formation, the pipes, drums, and band broke out in a stirring rendition of a favorite of World War II, fresh in the memory of those gathered. As the music for "Ee're No Twa Tae Bide Awa," wafted from the courtyard, the assemblage spontaneously found their voices in unison and the lyrics emerged. The pageantry of the swaying kilts and horsehair sporrans of the proud battalion, marching in perfectly matched measured steps, was repeated once again as the unit passed in review. Then they withdrew from the esplanade to the tune of "Scotland the Brave." The ceremony was complete, but the memories embellished in the minds of many would be preserved well beyond this generation. However, due to his wounds, Sergeant Major Sandy MacPhee attended only in spirit.

After the ceremony, a reception was to follow, and Iain rendezvoused with his family and Claire. However, the formal receiving line was limited to Captain Cameron, his parents, and the dignitaries present, so Claire and Annie were placed in the care of Aunt Jane. General Cameron was certain his sister-in-law would preserve Annie from the ruination resulting from imbibing champagne, while being permissive enough to allow Claire to partake. In the receiving line were Her Majesty Elizabeth II, Commanding Officer Lieutenant Colonel Moray and his wife, Captain Iain Alexander Cameron, and Major General and Mrs. John Alexander Cameron.

Queen Elizabeth was quite gracious in her conversation with her fellow participants, for which they were most appreciative. Most of the guests approaching the line were anxious to meet their monarch in person. For a few, it was an old routine, though still one of great importance. All were anxious to congratulate Captain Cameron.

Claire, in the company of Annie and Aunt Jane, found herself in the tail of the serpentine queue that had formed. The sight of many young women preceding her was carefully captured by Claire's watchful eyes. She dutifully noted all of their studied caricatures and propriety on confronting Her Majesty. Face to face with Iain, they seemed to morph into varying versions of coquettish femme fatales. Sensuous smiles, batting of over-mascaraed eyelashes, parting lips, provocative movements, and overly long hand clasping—frequently enforced with a secondary squeeze of the hand—were repeated ad nauseum. Obvious to Claire was the fact Iain was considered a splendid prize—and one that some of these well-bred young ladies were set on acquiring.

Claire—far from free of jealousy—was spurred to anger, and then, to determination. Though her initial impulse was to withdraw from the reception line, pleading a need to visit the ladies' room, she now found that she was actually moving ahead of Annie and Aunt Jane. Claire had convinced herself she was riding to Captain Cameron's rescue, and the sooner the better! Furthermore, in all probability this was her only chance to meet the Queen. She would not lose this opportunity, nor would she deny her friends the knowledge that all the work they had done on her dress and the articles they had loaned, would not be observed by Elizabeth II. As Claire moved resolutely forward, she was suddenly seized with the knowledge that she had never learned to curtsey. Fortunately, she was a quick study, and the graceful gesture presented to Her Majesty was unsurpassed that day.

Finally, Claire achieved her primary goal. Iain was still trying to free his hand from a seductress immediately in front of her. Finally, completing that feat, though not as yet having turned his head, Captain Cameron became aware of a hand that was soft and small but seemingly possessed strength well beyond its size. As he turned to see who this might be, he heard "I'm Miss Claire Campbell, Captain Cameron, and I wish to offer my congratulations!"

Iain looked her straight in the eye and said, "Aye, Miss Campbell, I recognize you, and I thank you for your congratulations, but I would request something more." He bent forward and kissed her gently on the cheek. The demon of jealousy was exorcised, and a happy young lady completed her passage through the line.

Later, by the standards of the glutton, gourmand, or gourmet, the epicurean feast presented by the ever attentive, refined, and disciplined staff of the Savoy Grille was unequaled—and the ambience, as always, was splendid! The General and the Captain—still resplendent in their dress tartan attire—stood out from the tuxedo-clad patrons, as would peacocks in a cluster of penguins. The ladies of the party, though not as ostentatious, were the subjects of admiring or envious glances. Noteworthy was the fact Claire's dress—the product of the Nurses Quarters haute couture—was quite up to holding its own.

General Cameron possessed exquisite taste in all things edible and potable.

While knowledgeable about and conversant with the fine wines of the world, his personal taste began and ended with the letter M. In light of that proclivity, the party was freely indulged with Meursault and Margaux. Even Aunt Jane—after proclaiming that wine could be considered a tonic rather than an intoxicant—was noted to indulge! This did not go unnoticed as she had a sufficient measure of "tonic" to render her somewhat tipsy.

General Cameron and Iain opted for the venison, and the maitre d'hôtel, being well aware of the Officers' capacities, indicated to the server that double rations were in order. While his generosity would subtract from the establishment's profits, he knew it would add substantially to the gratuity! Meanwhile, the ladies indulged in more feminine fare with good appetites and considerable delight.

After the feast was consumed and plates removed, it was time for single-malt and Coronas for the gentlemen, and a fine sherry for the ladies, apart from Aunt Jane, who dozed off intermittently. Both father and son took advantage of the fine dance band and led the ladies to the polished floor on a rotating basis—though Iain's rotation was a bit skewed—as it went Claire, Mother, Claire, Aunt Jane, Claire, Annie, Claire. Then, as all good things do, the evening came to a close.

Iain was designated to drive Aunt Jane to her flat along with Claire. Then, he would return to the BOQ. On the following morning, Sunday, the route would be reversed, and Claire would be returned to the Savoy at noon to join Iain's parents and sister for their drive back to Scotland. The General cautioned Iain to be very careful with Bobiecka. He knew the remonstration would cause his son to frown and shake his head, not only in regard to the needless warning but also in consternation over his father's eccentricity over naming his car after El Cid's favorite and famous warhorse. General Cameron delighted in minutiae militaire. Bobiecka always got a rise from someone, and this time Claire took the bait. "Who is Bobiecka?" she asked. "Oh! I've named my car after Rodrigo de Vivar's horse," replied the smiling elder Cameron. Naturally, it followed that when one's curiosity was piqued, another question was mandated, and Miss Campbell was delighted to find out that Rodrigo de Vivar was better known as El Cid! All of this was to the annoyance of the family, but a delight for the General.

When the front steps of Aunt Jane's flat was reached, the dear lady bolted for the door, unlocked it, and threw the following words over her shoulder, "I'm going to run in and start some tea Claire dear! Join me when you can." After one of the most wonderful days in their lives, now it seemed fitting the evening should end in some moments of privacy. They exchanged their feelings regarding the events that had transpired. Their embrace was prolonged and the proffered kisses enrapturing. "Until tomorrow Claire!"

"Yes! Until tomorrow, Iain." Her fingers slid slowly from his and, then, he was gone.

Over tea, Claire and Aunt Jane exchanged their pleasantries. Then, because the hour was late, it was time to retire. "Will eight o'clock Mass be fine for you, Claire?" asked the older woman. Claire was struck and befuddled by the word *mass*. She had always thought in terms of "church service," as commonly employed by Protestants. Quickly, Aunt Jane registered Claire's quizzical expression and added, "There are also Presbyterian and Anglican services very nearby and at a good time Claire. I can drop you off and pick you up before Iain comes."

"The Anglican would be fine, if it's not an inconvenience," replied Claire with a hint of despair finding its way on to her finely featured face. No suggestion of reluctance was present on behalf of Mrs. MacIntyre, although each had suddenly come to realize that they were on opposite sides of the Reformation.

"Fine it is, my dear," replied the widow. "I'll wake you at seven." Then, they both retired.

Sleep came quickly to Auntie Jane, as an aftereffect of the tonic However, it was quite tardy in enveloping Claire, who struggled with a new barrier against the feelings she was developing toward Iain Cameron. *Perhaps, this one would prove insurmountable,* she thought.

On the next morning, the young lady who was becoming the target of his affections seemed slightly distant to Iain on the way over to the rendezvous with his parents at the Savoy, but he ascribed it to fatigue. His own exuberance unstilted, as he talked enthusiastically about the possibility of seeing her in Edinburgh in two weeks. At their parting, Claire was filled with turmoil. However, the part of her that was falling in love carried the day, and none perceived any suggestion of inner struggle or response contrary to the occasion. Soon, Bobiecka was given his head and charged northward. Iain returned to his soldier's life, a very happy man!

Chapter Nine

Across the Irish Sea, a career of a different sort was about to be launched. This career also had elements of patriotism—and violence—as well as love. Mickey Manion would march to a different drummer, but he was no less resolute in his convictions. Mickey's future would be determined by people and events, which hardened his resolve starting with "Get off your stinking Provo arse and up on your feet Manion. It's time to try and wash the Provo stink off you. This will be your last bath at Her Majesty's expense, you maggot! You'll be leaving our tender care in three days. How we hate to see you go. But, a piece of work like you'll be back, unless the SAS shoots you full of holes. You Taig bastard! We'd like to see that, but sure it would be sad for us not to be able to beat you to death on your next stay here at the Maze. We came close this time, Bucko, but, we'll get the job done sooner or later!"

Such was the banter of the three prison guards who came to lead Michael "Mickey" Brendan Manion to the weekly shave and shower at Northern Ireland's most notorious prison. Surviving a stay at the Maze helped establish the bona fides of the majority of the Irish Republican Army Volunteers. If one wished to draw up a long list of quintessential attributes needed to epitomize the perfect soldier in the Oglaigh na h Eireann, the Gaelic term for the IRA, they would be describing Mickey.

Manion's four years in prison came as a result of his participation in a pub bombing in Ulster in spring 1945. He had gone with his friend Jerry Noonan to place the explosive-laden car outside the pub frequented by known members of the Royal Ulster Constabulary. Having arrived well before opening time, no passersby were observed. Noonan was the older and more experienced at twenty-one years of age and four years older than Manion. "Move on down to the corner, Mickey. I'll set the timer, then we'll move our asses out of here! This place should be crawling with Prods by six P.M. Sure n'it will be nice to know you and I will have sent a good numbers of the fookers to Hell." Manion was nearly forty yards away when he was struck by the shock wave!

The bomb, which his associate was arming, had detonated prematurely. This was a fact of life in the IRA since many in the ranks were not professional bombers, thus resulting in a significant number of mortalities. That day, it was Jerry Noonan's turn to join the list of self-destructed martyrs. Mickey staggered to his feet; somehow he must save Jerry! That was the driving force behind the neophyte's decision to return to the devastated pub. Given the absolute destruction of the car and similar condition of the front of the bomb's target, he should have been aware that his friend would have been reduced to tiny shreds of tissue, un-recognizable as part of the body they used to comprise. Manion was still struggling through the destroyed pub, tearing through debris and shouting his friend's name, when the Royal Ulster Constabulary arrived. Blood was coming from both external auditory canals, as a result of his ruptured eardrums. However, despite the bleeding and Manion's shock-like state, a very generous "resisting arrest" beating was rendered before he was shackled and thrown into the police van.

After arrival at Police Headquarters, Manion was given a cursory examination by a police surgeon and pronounced fit for interrogation. During this time, he lost track of the blows, kicks, and excruciating applications of cattle prods. However, Mickey was made of superior protein, and he never broke. Insults hurled at his tormentors only resulted in further beatings, but he kept it up until his lips were too swollen to permit the passage of audible words. "There's no point in killing the Taig bastard! Throw the fooker in a cell, so he can heal up for the trial," were the final words of the interrogating senior officer.

His trial received little publicity. He was provided a legal defender with virtually nothing to argue on his client's behalf. Testimony alleged that the defendant had defiantly admitted participation and cursed his inquisitors, in addition threatening more bombings at first opportunity. Those words had been clearly recorded. However, the sounds of blows, threats, and taunts were not audible on the evidence tape submitted by the police. Manion's case had been assigned to Judge Collins of Her Majesty's Court. The Barrister, presenting Manion's case was pleased because Judge Collins was a Catholic. "Michael, if there is any hope of clemency, you'll get it from him!" The magistrate was considered a "fine Gael," an Irish Catholic politically conservative and opposed to the IRA. However, the four-year sentence to be served at the Maze did not strike Manion as any act of clemency.

Somehow, Mickey had survived the four years of incarceration. However, the guards were particularly malevolent toward prisoners who didn't betray the Cause, and Manion was frequently left in his cell more dead than alive. Therefore, his sanity and physical survival were the result primarily of his all-consuming desire for revenge. In and out of consciousness, the message imprinted on his sensorium was always, "Someday I'll kill them all. It will be slow, and I'll take pleasure in doing it!" He had long since committed to memory the names and faces of his tormentors. They would be found and made to pay a terrible price.

Following his shower, the prisoner was allowed to shave. In the four years of his captivity, the sparse beard of his late teens had become black as coal, full, and even. Mickey's beard was truly bristling and a complement to the thick, black brows and wavy hair of matching hue. Every muscle above his waist was full and heavily sculpted. When not debilitated by beatings, he had started a regimen of workouts in his cell, which consisted of every means of making a muscle or muscle group contract. His image in the mirror gave Mickey every assurance of just how successful he had been! Heavy knots were present on many ribs at sites of bony callous formation signifying that healing of the guard-induced fractures had taken place.

Any facial vestige of his youth had been erased. Yes, he was handsome. Scars at sites where the truncheons and boots had burst his skin had healed well, leaving only thin white lines barely discernible through the stubble. However, overall it was a tormented face, and even an attempt to smile did little to ameliorate the bitterness there. While Manion's eyes were bright and shining and of a brilliant dark blue, the hooded lids and fixed margins of the canthi prohibited any sign of what might be considered merriment.

As much as he prided himself from the waist up, Manion loathed his legs. They had resisted all his attempts to hypertrophy the muscles. In addition, he was bow-legged. How he had hated the soccer matches when his legs were in view, and the subject of "bird legs!" taunting, which he so abhorred. Anyone guilty of mouthing such an insult had to face Manion's oversized fists and forearms after the match. His hands were now a size twelve and the wrists some ten inches in circumference. They were formidable weapons, very unlikely to be harmed, as they smashed the much more delicate bones of a face. Mickey had the perfect build of the enforcer, and he knew his attributes would be in great demand on release. That would be a start for Mickey Manion, "the Volunteer," but his intention was to beat his way to the top.

Manion's four years as inmate of the Maze were over as he passed through the gate on day 1,461. Even on discharge, his guards presented him with a tawdry, threadbare suit that was several sizes too small. Also, they shorted him on the Queen's Allowance and chose rather to throw some coins at his feet, thus presenting him as an ignorant, groveling spectacle. As he passed out of the gate, Mickey wondered what he should do and where he should go. His father, Jimmy, had died two years ago from the Poteen-induced ravages to his vital organs. As the cirrhosis shrunk his liver, the veins of his esophagus became extremely varicose, and one day ruptured, bringing a quick end to his shabby forty years of existence. Mother had gone first, finally succumbing to the "red snappers." Tubercle bacilli had cavitated her lungs for three long consumptive years before invading her systemically and routing all resistance in a short forty-eight hours.

Mickey's little brother, Sean, had been crushed beneath the wheel of a rich Protestant's Bentley, and little sister Maureen was never able to receive the care she needed for her meningitis. The Bloody Brit bastards had much to answer for—and he would see that they did. His stupid parents had never embraced the Republican cause, as they seemed content to praise God's will, and accept whatever shit the English saw fit to throw their way. Well, that wasn't for him. Manion hadn't set foot in a church since his First Holy Communion, and he never would again.

"I'll walk to Bayside," he said to himself, thinking it would be good to walk the miles after four years of lock-up. His pace accelerated, as his enthusiasm grew. However, Manion didn't notice the plain Morris sedan that was slowly following him a block or so behind.

Ten minutes later, Manion had picked up his full head of steam. He began to revel in the fact that he was moving away from the Maze with his pathway free from walls, fences, and guards that had restrained his movements the past four years. A deep, satisfying breath—free of prison odors—was repeated over and over. Each succeeding one proving more elating than that just exhaled.

Suddenly, engine noise intruded on his reverie, and the sound of tires as they neared the curb raised the first sign of alarm. Mickey faced the car as the rear doors opened, allowing two very large, burly figures to impose their presence on him. "We'll be taking you for a little ride Mickey, me bucko! Get your ass in the rear—and spare yourself some trouble!"

Manion was not intimidated. He faced his adversaries and said defiantly, "You can take your ride and stuff it up your ass!" A blackjack was now easily visible in the massive right hand of the first goon, and the threat behind it made all the more real as he rhythmically tapped it hard against the palm of his left.

"Suit yourself, Mickey darlin'! You can ride in one piece or get tossed in the boot with a bleeding head!"

Meanwhile, the other goon was proceeding to Manion's left side with a heavy truncheon carried at the ready. No need for further invective was needed, as it was now very obvious to the two heavyweights that he wasn't going to go down easy. Truncheon raised high, the goon on the left charged. He was expecting Manion to raise his arms to ward off the blow, so his eyes were intent on the young man's upper extremities and the intended target, Mickey's head! However, reality of the heel of his victim's heavy shoe, smashing into his patella with great force, caused the brute to scream out in anguish. His kneecap had fragmented and dislocated. Furthermore, the damage did not end, for there remained sufficient force in the devastating kick to thrust the assailant's knee inward while his foot remained fixed. When the massively muscled, top-heavy man lurched sideways, all of his weight and the force generated by his movement was directed to his knee. The cruciate ligaments were shredded and lateral meniscuses torn asunder.

Manion had no time to exult in victory because before the first of his vanquished foes had hit the ground, the second thug was hard on him. But in the fraction of a second he had before the heavy sap struck him, Mickey was able to twist his torso and turn his head. The blow, which would have surely cold-cocked or even possibly killed him, instead struck on the back of his heavily muscled left shoulder. The pain was intense, and Mickey's entire upper extremity went numb. Had it not been for his ability to commandeer his physiology, a skill derived from dozens of prison yard fights, Mickey would have become shocky. Force of the blow from his right fist was reduced; however, it was sufficient to severely traumatize the cartilage and surrounding tissue protecting his opponent's larynx. The man became wild-eyed, as he clutched his neck and fought for sufficient oxygen flow to pass through his swollen, constricted airway.

"You can stop now, Mickey Manion! You've shown yourself to be the better man me bucko! But, I'll not have ye killing off two of the best enforcers in Belfast. Ya know lad, you could have just got in me car like you were asked. I'll give you a break this time as I need to get me lads to hospital. You can accept the invitation of Frank McGann to ride along and talk some business, or I can stiff you here and now!" Mickey saw the revolver in the hand of the well-dressed man and decided to comply. The bore at the muzzle was of a generous diameter, and McGann seemed quite comfortable and confident in the use of the weapon.

Manion was quite sure this man, who was obviously in charge of things, was

IRA and fairly high up the ladder. "If he had been with the Ulster Defense Association, then I'd be dead by now," he concluded.

Big Frank, as he was known, called to the driver. A small, weasel-faced man emerged. He, along with Mickey, was ordered to assist the injured goons into the back seat. Jocko's breathing was extremely labored, and Tom was unable to bear weight on his leg. Still, both were capable of casting most malevolent looks in Mickey's direction. Big Frank suggested to Seamus, the driver, that he deliver the wounded to the nearest hospital where they were least liable to ask a lot of questions.

After depositing the pair of thugs to hospital, McGann informed Manion that if he were interested, they would go somewhere quiet for a chat. This would be his last chance to bow out. Beyond this moment, there was no quitting! He was in for the long haul, which, simply put, was for the rest of his life, however long that might be.

"Count me in, Frank," Manion said without hesitation.

"I'll do that, boyo, but, don't forget, it's 'Mister McGann' to you until the day I shake your hand. In the meantime, put on this hood. Trust is earned and comes slowly with us, Mickey!"

The car moved along for what he estimated to be fifteen to twenty minutes before Manion sensed it was being housed in a garage. After being led up two flights of stairs, he was pushed into a chair and the hood removed. The room was large, very well appointed, and richly paneled in a dark mahogany. McGann approached with a whiskey glass well topped off in hand. "Before we talk Manion, go through that door and get a bloody shower! You look and smell like a fookin' tinker. Seamus will find you something decent to wear, and we can burn that gallows garb they gave you at the Maze."

Fifteen minutes later, Mickey emerged, and Big Frank was pleased at the transformation. "Manion, I'll cut right to the chase. We have our eyes and ears at the Maze, and you had a fine report. You were a Volunteer four years ago but not a very clever one. You should be a damn sight tougher and smarter now. Are you still with the Cause, Mickey, or did the Brits beat the fire out of you? I'm always in need of a good man to handle some of the jobs that come up. Since you seem to have put Jocko and Tom out of commission for a time, I'll need you sooner than I had planned. Seamus will find you a room, and here is a five-punt note to put in your pocket. Here—I'll pour you a drink of good Bushmills to seal our agreement."

"I gladly accept, Mr. McGann, but I want no whiskey," replied Mickey.

"You aren't one of those pious, fookin' Pioneers, are you, Mickey?"

"No sir! I got an aversion to it—seeing my Da drink himself to death."

"That's fine, me bucko, to each his own. Well then, Mickey, until tomorrow!"

Big Frank did not extend his hand. As Seamus was leading Mickey away, McGann called out, "Don't forget to burn that fookin' tinker suit."

"Yes, sir!" Manion replied; however, he smiled a sinister smile, which no one saw. He had other plans for the suit, but they would have to wait until the proper time arrived.

Chapter Ten

Manion saw little of Big Frank McGann in the ensuing months. However, it was through the office of the IRA Chief that he secured a position at a pub owned and operated by Con Hogan, a very dependable Provo and a Cell Leader. Con's Blarney Stone was an inauspicious watering hole for the neighborhood drinkers, but also a magnet that drew in a fair parcel of Republican Volunteers. Manion was designated both bartender and bouncer. He relished the latter but detested the former. Dispensing Guinness or other potables to those overly happy or dismally depressed, loquacious or sullenly quiet had no appeal. To the contrary, they were an abject reminder of his Da and all the nights of his childhood when he experienced the mood swings, while remaining in hope his father would quickly reach the level when anesthesia occurred.

Belligerent drunks Manion could appreciate, as they would often as not give him an excuse to level them with a solid right. His only responsibilities, consistent with desire to prove himself as "a Volunteer," largely revolved around his ability to recognize persons of importance and direct them to the back room with a furtive nod of the head.

Mickey's dreary little room on the back side, upper floor of a dilapidated rooming house—a few blocks away from the Blarney Stone—was a stultifying refuge at best. Mrs. Conaty, the landlady, was both crone and harridan. Her appearance he could tolerate, but the shrewish scolding to attend church and save his soul was to be avoided at all costs. A single decoration in his squalid room hung above the old iron bed. This was a small, tarnished plaque that proclaimed "Life springs from death—and from the graves of the patriot dead spring living nations." A famous Republican slogan, it was meant to spur the Irish Freedom Fighter to acts of glory! For Mickey, it served only as a bitter reminder that he was at best a quasi-Volunteer, far from being a soldier, and light years from being the leader he had dreamed of being all those nights at the Maze.

"Well, I'll bide me time and, sooner or later, they'll see I've got what it takes," Manion said to himself, as he once again shifted his mood from disconsolate to optimistic! "Just save me shillings—and get out of this dung heap!" Thereupon, surveying his modest accumulation of punt notes and coins, Manion decided a few small additions to his meager wardrobe were in order. This decision buoyed his mood and helped quell the frustration that haunted him.

Con Hogan was a fine judge of men, particularly the type that one could rely on in the dangerous black operations for which his Bravo Cell was best known. He had taken notice of everything about Manion, while leaving him thinking he was entirely unnoticed. In his early forties now, Con had risen rapidly through Provo Ranks. A wrestler's physique made his nickname, "The Bull," a natural. Though some gray had emerged along his temples, it was barely evident as a border marking the transition zone between his pale, still freckled skin and the shock of carrot-red hair, which—though close cropped—remained his crowning glory.

Hogan had decided it was time. He liked everything about Manion. The young man was dependable, and although you could sense his frustration in performing his menial tasks, he had continued to do them very well. There would be little you could teach Mickey in regard to the use of his fists and feet, and few in Ireland could best him in a brawl. These talents were fine in themselves. However, if Manion were to become the weapon that he was capable of being in the long fight against British oppression, then he had to be honed just like turning a fine piece of tempered steel into a superb sword blade. Yes, it was time for Manion to become a soldier and make his contribution to securing Republican Victory in the "Troubles," as the Irish called their 400-year war of attrition with the Brits.

At half-past nine in the morning, Hogan sauntered through the front door of the Blarney Stone. Seeing Mickey behind the bar polishing glasses, he called out, "Mickey, lad, put down your towel. Hennessey will be filling in for you today. I need you to take a ride with me."

Mickey was puzzled, yet eager for the diversion. He whipped off the apron, sprang into the back room, then emerged with cap and coat. The closest thing to a smile that he could manage was followed by, "I'm all set, Mr. Hogan!"

Hogan's car was outside with a fellow by the name of Jerry Clancy at the wheel. Manion knew from his weeks of observation that Jerry was near the top of the cell—probably only one step below Hogan. As they passed through the outskirts of Belfast, the conversation revolved about the ordinary. For them, this included all forms of vulgarity—directed toward any sign of British or UDA forces—as well as young women who might be long of leg, prominently busted, or showing a provocative degree of gluteal motion in their gaits. Beautiful or sensuous faces were likewise included in the ribald commentary.

When they had finally cleared the last of Belfast's environs and only countryside lay open before them, Manion's thought reverted to that single time in his past life when he had left the city. The occasion was to attend the ordination of a cousin in Sligo. Also, it was memorable as one of the few times his father had been sober for more than a day or two. *I'm quite the urban gentleman,* he thought to himself, reflecting on the fact he hadn't even seen much of Belfast, apart from the time he stole a bicycle and rode as far afield as he could each day. Bitterness replaced this relatively happy recollection when he remembered riding the purloined bicycle into a very Protestant area. Mickey had the hell beaten out of him by a gang of Protestant teenagers out to teach a wandering Fenian a brutal lesson. However, Manion's reverie was broken when Clancy accelerated in the open area with a clear road ahead.

Simultaneously, Hogan's words issued forth from the back seat. "Mickey, you are probably wondering what's up, so I'll let you know what we're about. This is no picnic we're headed for, and sure it's not some bloody, fookin bird-watching expedition. I'm convinced you want to do your bit for the Cause, and it's a training expedition we're going on. I'm in no need of hot-headed hot shot—all talk and no brains or balls!" Hogan continued on. "What I must have is pros. I think I can make you a damn good one! If not, I'll just stiff you, and I won't be the worse off—except for the wasted time."

Soon, they cleared the checkpoint between Ulster and the Republic. Hogan passed easily as a respectable squire, and the other two were considered hired hands by the nonconfrontational border guards.

Clancy headed for Ballyshannon, a small hamlet on Galway Bay. On reaching the outskirts, he turned right and was soon in the driveway of a large farmhouse. Greetings were exchanged with the farmer and his wife, and all partook in a generous and delectable lunch. Then it was time for work.

Hogan was as good a preceptor as the Provos could provide. Fortunately, the road in from the highway was wide enough to serve as a training ground to teach Manion how to properly handle a car. Also, two hours were given in firearm instruction. Hogan was a stickler for safety, at least for all those on his side of the Troubles. No details were spared in teaching his disciples regarding proper gun handling, cleaning, and takedown. However, firing lessons were a long way off. The Provo officer's approach to automobiles was no different. Many weeks would pass before his student came anywhere near to mastering the complexities of a controlled skid and looping a Brody to escape a pursuing vehicle. Furthermore, more time passed before Manion grasped the rudiments of forcing another car over a cliff, or the gentle art of vehicular homicide applied to a pedestrian target. The pupil was eager and apt; the professor pleased.

Border crossing guards saw much of the frequently traveling squire and his two attendants in the ensuing months. Finally, Hogan determined that it was graduation time! Mickey was now a better wheelman than Clancy. He had mastered all the weapons in the Provo's ragtag arsenal, including a variety of American guns—such as Colt and Smith and Wesson, in addition to the .455 British Webley revolvers. Some semi-automatic pistols, such as the Colt, Luger, and the Broomhandled Mauser became part of his repertoire. At a distance, Manion had become a formidable sharpshooter with the 303 Lee Enfield and 8mm Mauser rifle, and he was first-class with the Bren gun. Consequently, there was no need to return with any frequency to the back roads and ravines at Ballyshannon, which had allowed them to conduct their clandestine training in stealth. Any return would be for refresher courses only.

Now that Manion's training days were over, the border guards would always wonder if the squire's business had hit a downturn. As for Mickey, he knew days of fulfillment were coming soon. His first assignment as a real soldier was just around the bend, and he had found a more commodious living space to which he moved the plaque that read, "Life springs from death and from the graves of the patriot dead springs living nations." Mrs. Conaty, the hated harridan of the old rooming house was history, and Bernadette O'Neil was soon to come into his life.

"You need a night out and a bit of brisket to put more meat on your bones, boyo," snapped Con Hogan to a perspiring Mickey Manion, who had been hard pressed to keep abreast of the drinkers' demands at the Blarney Stone. Business was unusually brisk due to a mysterious fire at Flaherty's Pub, which was just down the street. In IRA circles, it was well known that it was the work of the UDA. Hogan was already planning revenge on behalf of old Flaherty, but he jokingly told his inner circle that he "should probably send the Prods a thank-you note for all the added revenue that they had provided." Also, Hogan had stationed three of his better men to guard the Blarney Stone during hours of closure. This IRA Cell Leader was not the type who would brook a visit to his premises by arsonists, bombers, or shooters.

When Hogan produced a pair of substitute bartenders to go along with his invitation, Mickey needed no further inducement to divest his apron, roll down his sleeves, and don his cap. They cleared their way through the crowd, exited the premises, and immediately noticed the waiting car driven as usual by the ubiquitous Jerry Clancy. Then, it was only a short drive to Brennans, the only place in Bogside that could qualify as somewhere near first class.

"You'll find some proper good eats here, boyo, so dig in and don't spare the fork!" Con's testimony was accompanied by an energetic poke in Mickey's side. "If we Irish had a system like the Frog Tire Company, we could give old Brennans a four- or five-shamrock rating!" Manion had not the foggiest notion of Michelin and their fabled guide, but he made the assumption that Hogan's words were indicative of a fine place with food to match. Brennan met the trio and escorted them to a corner table—discreetly situated in the dining room's rear section.

The IRA generals were quite adept at mimicking the actions of Wild Bill Hickock and most Mafia dons in regard to seating arrangements. In addition, it was not fortuitous that they were in intimate proximity to an exit fire door, close to the men's room, which featured a window leading to the alley.

"I'll be sending you over three double shots of Bushmills for such fine gentlemen as yourselves. Sure'an it should make you more likely to be ordering from the fine fare on the menu."

"Just make it two Brennan, me bucko," replied Hogan. "This lad here is a practicing Pioneer, though he never really took the holy pledge. Fix him up with an orange squash with no hint of the devil alcohol in it! Sure'an if you're in the company of saints you keep them free from any temptations!" Hogan, Brennan, and Clancy laughed heartily, and Manion displayed only a mirthless smile.

Manion had learned his lessons well under the tutelage of the good nuns at the parochial school he had attended. Also, his scholarship during the few years he was able to study under the Christian brothers had been excellent. As a result, he had voraciously devoured all the material at the Maze library to which he had access. Mickey was a rough-cut stone—no question of that—but polishing does wonders, and all he needed was a generous buffing.

Manion had never held a menu like the one now residing between his fingers. To him, it was a culinary Book of Kells. He marveled that there were people who dined this way as a matter of course, while he was like Kim, Kipling's street urchin and one of the idols of his childhood fantasies! As Mickey's eyes shifted from one delectable dish to another, he wondered if rank in the Provos brought relative wealth, or if substance were prerequisite to rank? Obviously, Hogan and Frank McGann had the trappings of the upper class. "I've got my start," he reflected. "I'm just a bloody cork waiting to pop up to the top!"

Hogan's next sentence tore Mickey's mind from the menu. "Speaking of sin and temptations, get a load of this!" Manion's attention was drawn in the direction that seemed to hold the fascination of his boss and Clancy. The approaching waitress could be best described as statuesque. Tall by Irish standards, she was very lissome indeed! At a distance, she carried herself with a degree of assurance certainly rare in a waitress. She seemed very much aware that she provoked attention, expected it, and enjoyed it! Her uniform was modest, but her figure and size of the garment relative to her obvious attributes tended to leave the initial impression very much open to question.

This young woman's hair was glorious. Wavy locks of richest auburn with an iridescent sheen hung to her waist. Seemingly her skin was opalescent, apart from the softest of rose hue in her cheeks. The tip of her nose had the slightest hint of a pug, which in her case seemed to add to her beauty. Detracting not a bit, her full lips were rather petulant, beautifully formed, and exquisitely painted. Finally, arched auburn brows perfectly matching magnificent tresses formed an infinitely fine awning for each eye. Though none of the three men could have defined dichromia, all three became quite aware that one beautiful eye was green and the other blue!

The two older men let their fantasies revert to reality; however, the transition was delayed for Mickey. Both Hogan and Clancy took note of the fact that Manion seemed to be forever ordering side dishes or refills, each reorder leading to a reappearance of the fair lass. Finally, even Manion had gone far past gluttony, and it was time to leave. For reasons he could not comprehend, Mickey gave way to a compulsion to grasp her hand, as she deftly placed the dinner bill on the table. Immediately dropping the check, the waitress ripped her hand away. Then, the look she gave the errant young man was one of maximum disdain—bordering on loathing—and she held it for several seconds. Mickey felt devastated and was about to avert his eyes, when suddenly her face softened ever so slightly, and she winked the green eye. Then she was gone.

Hogan was ready to leave. There was business to conduct and plans for an assassination to go over in the quiet rear seat of a parked car. Mickey was bewildered. Would he ever see the beauty again? At least, he was able to obtain her name from the affable proprietor.

Manion had no hope of returning to Brennans on his own, given the limitations imposed by the meager budget available to him at this juncture of life. However, lack of monetary advantage could not quell the desire to gaze on Bernadette O'Neil. To the contrary, it only served as an all-persuasive obsession to find another way to encounter her. Consequently, it wasn't overly difficult to achieve the conclusion that the pauper had no other resort than to wait outside the restaurant until such time as she might emerge. Then, he would present himself to her—and hope for the best. Finding out when Brennans closed was simple enough. He would ask Mr. Hogan to get off a little early, then lurk in an area from which the restaurant's entry could be scrutinized.

Mickey was a consummate schemer. Given that propensity, he evolved a plan whereby Billy Flynn, one of the fill-in barkeeps, might be utilized in his innocent conspiracy. If he could convince Flynn to post himself in the nearby alley and emerge to accost the young woman, then he, Michael Manion, could come to her rescue! How could she help but be impressed—and indebted to him? Billy seemed the perfect foil to participate in the plan. True, Billy was submsart, but he idolized Mickey because of his prowess as the best bouncer in Bogside. Furthermore, he was anxious to reciprocate for Manion's taking his side on many occasions. Nonetheless, he was sufficiently astute to obtain assurances that he wouldn't receive any injuries in the feigned rescue attempt. Flynn was fully assured after he grabbed the young woman's arm, the savior would quickly arrive on the scene and yell out, "Get your dirty hands off that lady!" Flynn could flee before Mickey had any need to land a blow. "There's no need to worry, Billy, nothing can go wrong!" No further convincing was needed.

On the first night of opportunity, the two conspirators were properly positioned. Since Flynn didn't know what the target looked like, the plan called for an obvious signal from the ringleader, so a conspicuous wave of Mickey's cap was settled on. Unfortunately, a heavy rain descended on them shortly before the expected appearance of Miss O'Neil, but the two plotters persisted undaunted. The lights at Brennans started going out, as customers departed one by one, followed by the owner and several of the staff. Finally, the door reopened, and Bernadette appeared.

Captivated, Mickey nearly forgot the signal. Coming to his senses, he clawed the wet cap from his head and waved it wildly. The motion spurred Flynn to an immediate response, and he groped for the young woman's arm, just as she was starting to open her umbrella. Simultaneously, Manion sprinted down the street. Only yards short of the rescue, he was shocked to see Billy suddenly crumble, emit a soulful groan, and grab for his crotch! The devastated would-be mugger was prostrate on the wet sidewalk when the would-be rescuer arrived. Instead of a grateful damsel in distress, Manion found himself face to face with an infuriated female in a defensive position holding the business end of her umbrella in a direct line to his own scrotum! "Are you next, you bastard?" she screamed.

Mickey caught himself and remained outside the range of the murderous umbrella. Bernadette cast on him the most malevolent look he could imagine, seemingly all the worse because of the beauty of the face from which it emanated. Mickey's return expression, which she perceived, was one of absolute bewilderment far exceeding the expression of simple shock. Complete silence descended for a few seconds. Then it was broken by Billy's groans and his devastating revelation, "Mickey, you said I wouldn't get hurt, and this hellion hit me in the balls with her fookin' umbrella!"

Now Miss O'Neil was the one with the bewildered expression, and her concentration was broken. Mickey took the occasion to wrest the umbrella from her hands. After stepping back a safe distance, he opened the umbrella and handed it to her. Bypassing Miss O'Neil, he bent and raised the stricken Flynn to his feet and slung him easily over his shoulder. As he walked away, with the moaning body of Billy swaying to and fro, he said dejectedly, "I'd like to explain, but you wouldn't understand!"

"Try me sometime," Mickey thought he heard her say.

Three different parties were left the work of analyzing the debacle that had occurred that night in front of Brennans restaurant. Billy Flynn was out of the loop. He knew only too well what had transpired, and he wished profoundly to forget. That possibility would be slow in coming, as the easy chair with Irish whiskey and strategically positioned ice bag had done little to assuage the horrific ache. Nonetheless, he was able to communicate between groans the sordid truth to Mr. Hogan.

Much to Billy's consternation, the senior man showed not the slightest hint of either sympathy or empathy. To the contrary, he found it uproariously comical. Raucous laughter, which Hogan generated, was sufficient to cause waves of motion in his glass of Bushmills. One crested the rim of his glass and sadly soiled a silk necktie of which he was particularly fond. Even this mishap did not quell his humor. Peals of laughter reverberated about the room until aching sides and shortness of breath induced Hogan to stop for a short respite. One more look at poor Billy, plus a conjured vision of the encounter, jump-started another round of most robust laughter When Hogan finally captured control and had the advantage of being free of the visage of Flynn, there was a return to his serious side.

While Hogan's cohorts, confreres, and customers were always captivated by his humor, it was the somber, calculating half of the Provo's Captain that had to this date ensured his success and survival As Con pondered the occurrence free of mirth, he concluded that Mickey was brash but resourceful in a very pedantic sort of way. He had all the needed martial skills! However, he was deficient in planning and the ability to divine all the things that could go wrong and make decisive contingency options a part of his schemes. "Well, boyo," he said to himself, in reference to Mickey, "we'll be taking you on your first mission tomorrow. We'll see how dedicated you are to the Cause and if you got the guts to stiff some Prod bugger when you have the chance!"

Two blocks away, Bernadette O'Neil was attending properly to her magnificent mane of burnished auburn hair. Gracefully downward, the hairbrush glided through the glistening strands from crown to tip. Her lithe limbs, of both upper and lower extremities, ached as usual. This was their way of protesting the indignities to which they were subjects, as a result of long hours of hustling on hardwood floors and bearing heavy trays laden with dinner dishes. As the brush dutifully stroked the final lock, Bernadette centered her head and looked at her own image. The face she perceived still appeared to have a certain aura of softness, belying the hardness that had invaded her inner spirit.

At times like this, Bernadette was prone to recall her childhood and her real surname, Donahue. "My pampered childhood," came as a self-reminder. Oh, yes, dear sweet little Bernadette, only child of doting parents who were Catholic to the core! They were among the few in Dublin to achieve social status in an environment where nearly all the papists were "worker bees" laboring out their lives in the hives of the Protestant upper class. Dear Daddy went off to America, got a position in a New York bank owned by an Irish émigré. He ended up very successful and was awarded the banker's daughter as the ultimate perquisite. Then followed a triumphant return to Dublin, where her father assumed the position of president of a major branch of his father-in-law's burgeoning banking empire.

Bernadette's thoughts became disdainful, as she recollected how her father had become a mere quisling, embracing the mannerisms and social aplomb of the Brit elite who dominated all the commerce in the Irish Free States. Yes, she had been a willing participant in this mockery, until her final year at the prestigious St. Cecelia's Academy—the only RC school in the Republic considered appropriate for the daughters of Catholic collaborators like her parents. Then, she met Bridgett O'Neil, a very free-spirited but brilliant urchin who was awarded a scholarship to St. Cecelia's.

Bridgett O'Neill's mother, or "Ma" as the scholarship recipient referred to her, took in washing and sewing. This being in response to the widowhood awarded when her husband was shot to death by the Brits in an IRA operation! Given her disdainful background, Bridgett was not one of the girls. Ostracism was her due, and no hand of friendship was ever extended, except for that of Bernadette. She was captivated by Bridgett O'Neil and engrossed by her tales of what real life in Ireland was all about—including entrancing stories of the struggle between Provos and Prods.

Bridgett was well schooled in IRA lore as an impressionable girl whose own

Da, Granda, and several uncles had suffered martyrdom during their short role in this present portion of the long war. As a result of this friendship, Bernadette was introduced to things other than insurrection. She developed more than a casual acquaintance with alcohol and marijuana. Discovered near graduation time, Bernadette was reprimanded by the Mother Superior. Her devastated parents saw to it that she received a full measure of religious counseling. In addition, a generous dose of psychotherapy was given in hopes of achieving the desired behavior modifications. However, Bridgett was dismissed, and her response to dismissal became apparent when her stiffened corpse was hauled from the river! The search had been generated by a grieving mother in response to a suicide note, which she found on returning to her dingy apartment with a large load of laundry to be done at a pitifully small wage.

After washing away the mud and weeds filling the hollows of Bridgett's face and hands and washing her hair, the coroner noted the stark contrast between the porcelain white skin and the purplish blue lips, fingertips, and toe tips of the suicide victim's rigid cadaver. He had previously cut away the sodden uniform and had noted the St. Cecelia's crest emblazoned on the pocket of her blue blazer. Consequently, he had informed the appropriate authorities of his findings. Thus, Bridgett was identified and her remains turned over to her mother.

Bernadette was denied attendance at the funeral; it was deemed fulsome to be present at the final rites for the hoyden who committed the most grievous of sins in taking her own life. Plus, there was the presumed immediate commitment of her soul to Hell for all eternity. However, God was gracious and inspired Father McHugh to decide that the poor, dear departed girl was overwrought and thus not fully responsible for her act. The Requiem Mass was very sparsely attended but provided solace to the devastated mother. Father McHugh urged the tiny congregation to pray for Bridgett's soul. He and Mrs. O'Neil took the words to heart and never missed a daily Ave for the rest of their days. The other attendees soon forgot.

Willful embers burning within the soul of Bernadette became fanned to a full conflagration, but she remained capable of confining them within herself. Bernadette's parents, confessor, and counseling psychotherapist agreed that she had accomplished an amazing metamorphosis and, exuberantly, proclaimed a complete cure. Plans were made for entry into Trinity College in the fall. Matriculation at the prestigious school was a rare achievement for an RC in those days; however, the banker and his wife had all the credentials to achieve that goal. The young lady who entered Trinity in fall 1947 seemed to have all the attributes one could only dream of—brains, beauty, and a bountiful supply of Punt notes of high denomination. None who encountered her were able to have their perception pierce the outward veneer, which cloaked the underlying rebellion.

High test scores and excellent grades were easy for Bernadette. While her parents were giving thought to locating the right young man from the right family to wed their delectable debutante, Bernadette was surrendering her virginity to a musician who performed at one of the student hangouts. Also, she had reacquired her taste for alcohol and marijuana—much to the delight of her current consort. Furthermore, Bernadette had abandoned her faith, apart from ceremonial attendance in her parent's presence. Bernadette the rebel prided herself that she had defrauded everyone. She was the beautiful, brilliant Miss Donahue, the model of decorum and possibly the most sought-after debutante in Dublin. She was amused to mull over how they would feel if they were aware of the slut that lay hidden beneath the veneer.

As time passed, Bernadette sensed there was an increasing chance that her sordid side would surface. Derek, the drummer and her lover, was chronically short of funds. Even the plentitude of punts she gave him failed to satiate his needs. Furthermore, he had graduated to hard drugs, necessitating a greater need for cash. Also noted with alarm, was the fact Derek was becoming abusive, verbally and physically. She could use accidental injuries to explain cuts and bruises to only a limited degree. Finally, he resorted to extortion!

"I need lots of money, Bernadette darlin'! I know you can get it—or certain photos will be posted on the bulletin board at Trinity!"

"I'll see what I can do," she said, and hurried out! "My God! You have been a fool," she said to herself. Then, a thought of killing him came to mind, but Bernadette had no confidence in the commission of the perfect crime. Also, given the fact that she would certainly be a suspect with adequate witnesses for any investigation, having been seen with him at the pubs or in his lodgings, quelled such speculation.

Bernadette had to think! For this purpose, there was a place she had sought out before. Pauper's Cemetery was easy enough to find, but the grave marker was not. Single stakes upheld a profusion of small, square tin markers. All had numbers, which attested to the final resting place of the nameless. Grave number 99061 finally came into view, and she placed a small bouquet reverently on the green grass that covered Bridgett. The Ave was left unsaid. Instead, she told her former friend that she was leaving. "Someday, I'll return and obtain a proper headstone for you, Bridgett," she said softly. A warm tear found temporary seclusion in her eye before being released to slowly traverse her cheek. She knew there would be little chance to keep the promise, given the new life on which she was embarking. Bernadette knew Derek would have no need to tell of her transgressions once she disappeared. She had lost nearly all her childhood love for her parents, but she still wished to protect them from certain revelations.

Bernadette's plans called for returning home one last time. She would clean out the remnants in her own bank account and take whatever cash might be in the house. A note would be written saying she was sorry, but she was going to America to find herself. Bernadette knew her heartbroken parents would exhaust themselves trying to locate her there; however, no one would ever look in Ulster! She would play her own role in fighting for Irish independence. That would be one gift she could provide for Bridgett! Also, Bridgett in turn would do her part, for she would be using her old friend's birth certificate to obtain new identification in the north. Fortunately, Bernadette had procured a copy several months earlier when trying to decide whether she would ever need a means of escape.

Chapter Eleven

❈ ❈ ❈

Upon arrival in Ulster's capitol, Bernadette purchased garb appropriate to her new status at a used clothing store, then proceeded to find reasonable housing in Bogside. Though not used to life on her own, she was clever enough to know that you didn't march down the street bearing a banner announcing, "I'm here to join the Provos." Bernadette took her time. Then, she found a job after convincing Brennan that she was a waitress, which was not an easy task for someone who had never hoisted a tray. The sage restaurateur, more impressed with her attraction for customers rather than her serving prowess, had finally agreed to a tryout. She was certainly a magnet for male diners, and Bernadette in time became very proficient as a waitress. Although she had used Bridgett O'Neil's identification, once in Ulster she found her forged papers easily amenable to alteration. This made it possible to append her own first name to the documents and permitted her the comfort of being called Bernadette Bridget O'Neil.

With her new identity and job, Bernadette felt that if she kept expressing sympathy for the IRA and Sinn Fein in an unobtrusive manner, then sooner or later someone would decide she might make a good recruit. She did just that and before long, she was approached. Since touts or informers were uncommon among women, her way was made easier. Finally, she came to the attention of Con Hogan. He had no amorous motives. Murderer, he might be, but adulterous never! He had a wife and eight fine children, which left no more needs in that direction to satisfy.

Bernadette was given little jobs and errands for a start. She might pass a note along with a dinner check or cross town on her motor bike to deliver guns, ammunition, or explosives. On several occasions, she had participated with other Volunteers in administering a savage beating to young Catholic women who had been found out to be dating either Protestants or British soldiers. Bernadette didn't relish this. However, she set about doing it with a vengeance as a perceived duty. Yes, she had aided the Cause, and she took pleasure in anticipating many more years of service in increasing responsibility. Bernadette didn't miss the money or her fine home in Dublin and certainly not the students at Trinity. She had considered them vacuous as well as contemptible. They had no sense of response to the Cause, which transcended all the nonsense in their sheltered lives.

Now, alone in her boarding house room, Bernadette had braided her hair and sat on the edge of her bed. She had no certainty as to what the young Irishman was up to at the occurrence in front of Brennans. However, she was extremely intuitive and decided it was some sort of ruse meant to ingratiate her to whoever he was.

The mystery man was in the company of Con Hogan the first time she had seen him. That meant he was new in the Cause and, like her, a dedicated Volunteer! Therefore, Bernadette decided that while possessive of obvious brawn and good looks, he might be somewhat of a bumpkin. However, this didn't disturb her in the least. Despite Bernadette's obvious fatigue, she resisted sleep, preferring instead to squander fifteen minutes more rest in favor of speculation as to what new means of attack the young man would take. She had no doubt that he was very strongly attracted to her. However, she was now realizing there was a very definite mutual attraction.

Meanwhile, thoroughly embarrassed by his ineptitude in the foiled rescue attempt of the past night, Mickey found himself unable to forgive or forget how he had bloody well botched up any chance to recoup his presumed loss. Mounting one vain attempt after the other to drive the image of such a glorious woman from his mind, he foundered in futility. Like a sailor enchanted by the Siren's song, he was helpless to avoid the shoals that lay ahead. What Mickey thought he grasped from her final words—imperfectly heard when he had swiftly departed bearing the writhing body of Billy Flynn—kept leaping to the surface of his sensorium. *Did she say, "Try me sometime," or "I'll get you next time"?*

Given the turmoil to which Mickey was subjecting himself, his performance as barman was slipping from near perfect to perfunctory. The overfilled glasses were a delight to the customers, but the amount of Guinness that overflowed only to disappear down the drain would have generated an outburst of volcanic proportions from Con Hogan. However, Hogan was at the moment attending to the final preparations for stiffing a Prod. Unbeknownst to Manion was the fact he would participate, and the operation would drive all other vexations from his mind.

Tuesday night was payday for much of Ulster's working stiffs, who included Sam Caarson—a foundry foreman by day and UDL Sergeant, arsonist, and gunman whenever the opportunity arose. Hogan had information from unimpeachable sources that it was Caarson who had torched a Catholic restaurant in the neighborhood. In the quid-pro-quo war of attrition between the Provos and Prods, such an action would easily earn retaliation in kind or a more lasting lesson of having your kneecaps explode, leaving you a stiff-legged cripple for the rest of your life! That would be reassuring if the capper wasn't a poor shot who managed to shred your popliteal arteries, leaving you dead from shock or bleeding to death. Fortified with a second whiskey and Guinness chaser, Con's informant went on to relate, "Fat Sam must have had the fever for fire that night and for no reason tossed his next Molotov Cocktail through the window of Danny Sullivan's little shanty. Danny had made it out. His burns were painful and disfiguring, but the physical suffering was of no consequence compared to the emotional torment arising from the incineration of his twin two-year-old boys and his near-term pregnant wife, Mary!" After receiving this information, Con Hogan decided that it was an egregious crime and could only be satisfied by the death of the perpetrator. This very night, Fat Sam Caarson would pay the piper in full measure!

"You'll be behind the wheel, Jerry lad, and Manion will be sharing the front seat. I'm bringing Danny here along, so he can see for himself that some measure of justice has been meted out to the SOB that murdered his family. We know that Caarson never misses staying for closing time at the Lambeg Drum every payday night. Being that his house is five blocks away, he should be staggering by just past twelve. I've reconnoitered it well. There's a nice, quiet, comfortably dark section of street near halfway between the pub and Fat Sam's house. Mick should be able to bound out of the car, and put old Sammy out with a solid blow to the jaw. That should crumple him up, so he'll be easy to stuff in the boot. Sure 'an we can have the hearing on the way to The Oaks. The verdict is a forgone conclusion! We can impose the sentence and be off in no time at all. Be out front with the car at 11:30 Jerry! We won't want to be postponing justice, would we?"

Mickey was summoned from his station behind the bar to make a timely entry into the waiting sedan. A full briefing was given regarding his important role in the abduction. No discussion was given of the events to follow. Mickey was unconcerned. His role struck him as trivial and easily accomplished. They waited a good fifteen minutes at the site of their planned ambush. Conditions seemed perfect. Only a rare window gave evidence of a light within heralding an awakened occupant. Talk was subdued, and Danny, who had come to realize how far out of his element that his grief had brought him, displayed no nervousness apart from occasional twitches.

At near the expected moment, a large man approached bearing in the right direction. A perceptible stagger was noted. In addition, a sonorous and dislocated, rambling conversation was being carried on with himself. Suddenly, Mickey catapulted from the car as the lurching man drew abreast. Surprised, Caarson—still possessing of a primitive alarm reflex—muttered an obscenity-punctuated question having to do with what was transpiring? However, the query was terminated short of completion, as the result of a hammering blow to his solar plexus, followed by an immediate slam to the left side of his head from a rock-hard elbow! Then, despite the man's weight, Manion supported him until Jerry Clancy opened the lid of the boot. Next, the two dumped the pole-axed victim inside. No one approached; no shades were raised. They were undetected and clear of the area within seconds!

Twenty minutes later, they were nearing The Oaks. Mickey was assuming that they had brought their man here to deliver a merciless beating, a lesson he would probably be chosen to teach. *No problem,* he thought as he patted his jacket to ascertain if his heavy leather gloves were in place. *No need to cut up me knuckles,* he thought. Shortly, the sedan came to a stop near a giant oak, one of many gracing the park-like setting and providing the name.

Caarson had recovered consciousness and was wildly kicking the metal sides of his temporary miniscule prison. Manion stood at the ready, as Clancy opened the lid. He had not noticed Con Hogan pulling out a small stepladder, hidden in some shrubbery, nor did he detect its placement beneath a massive, horizontally oriented limb The befuddled victim was sobering fast, and in the light of the full moon his terror-stricken face could not be overlooked. Hogan had returned and stood aside the opened boot with a leveled .455 Webley trained on the victim's face.

"Mr. Caarson seems to be in need of some assistance, Mickey. Give him a hand out like a good lad and see if you can get him to stand up straight like a proper UDL soldier." The condemned man was barely out and erect when his arms were pinned behind him by Clancy, who also bound his wrists tightly together. Hogan dug his gun's muzzle deeply into the side of Caarson's head just behind his left ear. "It's just a short parade, Sammy darlin', over to the little ladder there just three steps up, and you'll be able to look down on us poor Paddys.

You'll be closer to heaven, but just one step from hell! Give him a hand, Mick! I think Sam's feeling a bit weak in the knees!"

Manion knew moments before that this was no ritual beating. This was an execution, but he didn't waiver. The condemned man uttered every supplication his frenzied mind could conceive, but his executioners never paused or paid the slightest heed. When the pitiful, quavering figure had at last surmounted the final step, he stood precariously balanced as the noose was placed about his neck. The first of the eight coils were pressed hard against his skin below the left ear. This placement was actually irrelevant, as he wouldn't drop far enough to break his neck. He would strangle instead.

"Oh! God you can't do this to me," the doomed man shrieked.

"Shut your fookin' mouth, Caarson, and I'll tell you what I'll do! Never let it be said Con Hogan wouldn't give half a man a chance."

Then, Hogan paused and chuckled, wondering if the victim or his fellow executioners had picked up on his juxtaposing of the word *half* in the old canard. "I'm going to pop you in the knee." Then, he continued "and if you can maintain your position for five minutes—you're a free man!" Instantly, Hogan placed the muzzle of the heavy revolver against Caarson's knee—and fired. A horrific expression immediately emerged on the victim's face. Despite the shock and extreme agony, Caarson fought with all his reserve to maintain his position. Seconds later, the shattered leg went numb. Caarson listed to the affected side before lurching off the tottering ladder. The tightening rope halted his death screams. However, his corpulent body twitched convulsively in a grotesque dance.

The moon did not offer sufficient illumination to reveal the agonized distortion in Caarson's face.

Bleeding from the bullet wound subsided, as the driving pressure coming from the previously contracting heart ceased forever. Freed from the control of the nervous system, sphincters relaxed, thus releasing bowel and bladder contents. "Oh!—Sammy, you soiled your pants. What will your dear mother say!" snickered the ringleader.

Then, returning to the car, Hogan asked Mick, "Well, boyo, how do you feel about the struggle now?"

Mickey's face was ashen, but he stood straight, jaw set, legs planted firmly. "It's war, like you said, Mr. Hogan! You do what you need to do—and get on with it."

"That's the way to view it—Mick. Remember that if we don't win the war, it will be you or I—or one of our families—catching the slug or standing on the ladder!"

Hogan didn't inquire of Sullivan, who was retching uncontrollably near the side of the car. Nor did he seek the response of Clancy, who was back behind the wheel, pleasantly puffing on a cigarette. Hogan's large, powerful hand strongly clasped Mickey's shoulder as he neared the open door of the sedan. His firm but softly modulated voice said, "You did well, boyo! The first one is always the hardest!"

On return from The Oaks, the avengers dispersed. Danny Sullivan disappeared quietly down the lane, seeking sanctuary in a temporary bed provided by a sympathetic relative. Sleep would come, though only after a time, and not before the liquid contents of a bottle of Poteen held in shaking hands was replaced by air. Danny would soon immigrate to America; however, all the horrid memories of the past few weeks would remain until he plunged into the depths of despair. His descent was hurried by the alcoholic anchor to which he clung. Danny's Irish legacy, which he bore to the New World, consisted of the barest number of happy times. None of these were ever able to rise to the surface through the viscous, black pool of nightmarish memories created by the loss of his Mary and the children, in addition to his participation in murder—justified or not!

Hogan and Clancy suffered not in the least from stricken consciences. After a couple of self-congratulatory toasts to a fine night's work, they adjourned and went to their respective homes and families. They were free of any backward thought, apart from a satisfactory review of their planning and success.

Mickey retired to solitude in the confines of his room. Closing the door softly, he flicked on the light switch, activating the single bare bulb dangling from the ceiling. The incandescence was sufficient to illuminate his hallowed plaque. Once more, the stark words struck him hard. "Life springs from death, and from the graves of the patriot dead spring living nations." The words sank in, though in the present format they spawned a strong degree of incongruity. In a hushed and vehement voice, Manion spat out: "God Almighty—there will be a hell of a lot better chance for a living nation to spring out a live patriot, than a fookin' dead one! If you're a Prod—then that simpering sod Caarson is probably a patriot! However, nothing's going to spring out of him but maggots!"

Mickey tossed his cap and jacket on the bed, leaving space for him to recline alongside. He noticed a couple of leather fingers peeking from his coat pocket. "Didn't need these gloves tonight," he said to himself, adding, "I guess the rope was the way it had to be!" Stretched out and reasonably relaxed, Mickey ruminated over the activities of the night and his own feelings about what had transpired. Was he really cut out for this? If not, was it too late to back away?

From childhood, Michael Manion had always arrived at decisions by making up a structured list of pros and cons. In the ensuing minutes, his inventory of affirmatives became lengthy, while the negatives remained limited. He could be tortured, killed, or returned to prison, but hell, a man had to take his chances! Thought of his demise was sublimated by virtue of youth's inclination toward immortality. Deep inside, Mickey was that visage of natural law that he had never nurtured. Even after those long four years at the Maze, he had never truly rid himself of the concept that killing another human was intrinsically evil. Nonetheless, rationalism based on patriotism or revenge could certainly render it a moot point. All pangs of conscience or fear of death quelled, Manion gladly focused his thoughts on his pursuit of Bernadette O'Neil. His mind sprang to the challenge readily and sleep came soon thereafter.

Chapter Twelve

On the night of the Caarson killing, Bernadette had finished her shift and exited the door of Brennans in a high state of expectation. However, the street was empty. She thought perhaps her erstwhile hero would be waiting along the way, though each block added to her discouragement. By the time she inserted her key in the rooming house door lock, she was despondent. Shortly after arrival, Bernadette undressed for bed, leaving her hair unattended. "What the hell should I care?" she repeated to herself. "It's a fool's dream!"

On the next day at work, she was disconsolate. Brennan, who took measure of such things, noted she was uncharacteristically brusque with his patrons, but he paid little heed. He never considered a reprimand. Given the fact that most of his customers were men—and that statistically a goodly number of them found petulant women of greater allure—he had no fear of customer revolt.

For Bernadette, closing time came again at the demise of a dismal day. As she exited on to the sidewalk, she admonished herself not to partake in a repeat role of playing the lovesick maiden. Her downcast eyes sought a pathway among the uneven paving stones but fell instead on a pair of heavy, well-worn shoes. They projected below some reasonably pressed trousers. When followed upward, there was an outstretched hand of generous proportion holding a small bouquet. At the top of the vision was a strong, handsome Irish face, well accentuated by a pair of penetrating blue eyes, which harmonized with the broad smile forming just above a firm, well-set jaw. No words were uttered, but the bouquet was offered and accepted, thus obviating any immediate need for conversation.

Somehow, her empty hand found one of his, and, so adjoined, they proceeded up the street.

Only a block or so further on, he gently guided her into a coffeehouse and found a table and they both sat down. For a few seconds, Bernadette and Mickey just sat and gazed at each other, then both broke into simultaneous conversation, which in turn evoked mutual laughter. After finishing a second cup of coffee, the bogus rescue attempt and her response had been explained. Formal introductions were exchanged, though in her case the alias of Bernadette O'Neil was allowed to suffice. When it was time to leave, she led Mickey hand in hand to the place in which she lived. At the door, he ventured a kiss, and it was returned freely and fully. Seemingly, both had struck the other's lure and were now firmly hooked! Only time would tell in what direction they would be pulled by the attached lines and when if ever they would be brought to net.

At the first rendezvous between Bernadette and Mickey, the cornerstone for their lives had been set in place. However, time would pass before the mortar hardened and theirs was to be far removed from a whirlwind romance. Given their financial plights and work schedules demanded by their jobs, plus the extracurricular activities imposed by their status as Provo Volunteers, there was never a surfeit of time at their disposal. Additionally, it was a paranoid and dangerous world in which they lived. Other Volunteers were constantly incarcerated, despite precautions taken. When was one ever sure that the next zealot wasn't a tout planning to turn you over to the Brits for a sweaty palm full of pound notes or to bargain your freedom for theirs?

Nonetheless, both were possessive of a degree of equanimity far exceeding what one might expect facing the existing hazards. Eventually, a memorable Sunday occurred when Bernadette and Mickey were both free of duty, thus allowing an outing in the countryside on a fine summer day. Pooling a few extra pence, they took off on Bernadette's motor scooter, which was still running well despite meager maintenance. Funds for its purchase were the last vestige of those taken from Bernadette's parents. Shortly thereafter, she had assumed the personage of Bridgett O'Neil after shedding her true identity, leaving her disappearance as a daunting mystery that would haunt her parents to the end of their days.

Bernadette and Mickey partook of the largesse of Brennans Restaurant pantry. Thus, ample amounts of cold roast beef and other delectables were enjoyed that the restaurant had declared surplus and Brennan made available to his favorite waitress.

Bernadette was mildly surprised when Mickey declined one of the two ales she had brought along. "It's my Da," he said. "I have no desire to ever try it." He stopped there, leaving a conclusion to her intuition.

She was pensive for a time, then blurted out, "Mickey, I'm not Bernadette O'Neil! It's Donahue, not O'Neil." She was about to give a full explanation when he put his finger on her lips, thwarting further speech.

"Sure and I don't care what you're calling yourself. I've fallen in love with you the person and not your name!"

She leaned forward to kiss his finger, which had been removed from her lips though still remained close by.

Other secrets and thoughts were exchanged. Their personal portraits were broadened by each stroke of a verbal brush. That night, once again alone, Bernadette reflected fondly on the kisses and embraces, of which there were plenty. She had desired it not to stop there, but that wish was unrequited. "You're a strange man, Mickey Manion," she said to her pillow. "You must be the only Puritan in the IRA." Recalling her past licentiousness, she decided it might really be exciting to have a pure and proper courtship. "Sure'n, a girl should have at least one!" Bernadette smiled at the thin beams of light from a street lamp, which intruded through a crack in the shade, and then she surrendered to sleep.

Calendar pages flipped rapidly over from one month to the next, as if left to the will of a capricious wind, and Mickey grew in stature and reputation within the ranks of his chosen clandestine organization. Then, near closing time at the Blarney Stone on a blistery fall night inhospitable to the coming of customers, he was summoned to Con Hogan's inner sanctum. His boss was there, as was to be expected, but the surprise was the presence of Big Frank McGann, who had been absent from his life since that first day of freedom from the Maze. Given their respective and relative ranks, neither older man arose or extended a hand. McGann nodded and smiled, and the words were left to Hogan.

"Mickey, boyo, you'll be taking a seat now and listening to some propositions that should set your rebellious young heart all a flutter!"

Manion did as directed and slid into the remaining unoccupied chair. Noting the seated posture, McGann sought the rim of his whiskey glass, drained the residual, and beckoned for a recharge of the empty Waterford.

"Well, Manion, I'll get right to the point! There being no need for empty-headed Irish loquacity, though God knows I've mastered the art." McGann paused in favor of a generous draw on his cigar, followed by a satisfying, extended sip of the replenished whiskey. "You've handled yourself well since we took you in, Mickey. This little army has to grow to continue the fight, and it has done just that, I'm proud to say. When you get more soldiers, you need more officers, so we're giving you a fine promotion. Therefore, you're now a Cell Leader! You'll answer to me and me only. Con has brought you along better than anyone else could have. Now, he bows out of your life, except in some rare circumstances, which might call for a combined operation! Our survival demands that the average Volunteer knows little else than his mates in the same cell. You can't turn in whom you don't know, simple as that!"

McGann continued to explain that a new cover for Mickey had been created. He was to become the manager of a car repair shop located several miles away and sporting a large sign that proclaimed: "Sweeney's Garage—Limp In—Leap Out." The elderly owner would retain actual control of the business but would have no knowledge of any extracurricular activities. Two of the current employees were bona fide skilled mechanics; a third of equal competence would be requisitioned from another cell. The remaining three men of the cell would be employed or located elsewhere.

"Are there any questions?" Big Frank asked at the close of his briefing.

Mickey responded, "No, Mr. McGann, I've got me assignment, and I'm grateful for the honor. I won't let you or the movement down, sir!"

Though he didn't stand, nevertheless, McGann extended his hand. Manion took it with his own. To lesser men, the strength imparted in the grasp would have been bone crushing. However, to them, it was an expected display of respect earned by one and granted by the other. Also, Hogan came forward, extending his own hand in a similar vice-like display of acceptance and congratulation while saying, "We got a great cover story to explain your departure from the Blarney Stone, Mick! I'm going to tell everyone Johnny Hanratty beat the shit out of you, and you're scared to come back."

"Give me a break, Mr. Hogan, and make it Billy Conn!" They all laughed. It was an inside joke.

Hanratty was a recently retired professional pugilist in the heavyweight division, who had ascended quite high in the ranks of Irish contenders. Mickey had floored him with a single right in the midst of a bar altercation. Billy Conn, the Irish American, was challenging Joe Lewis, the heavyweight Champion of the World.

After the laughter subsided, the new Cell Leader standing near the door turned and said, "Thanks again, Mr. McGann and Mr. Hogan, I won't let you down!"

"I know, boyo. I'll miss you—and it is Con, when next we meet."

McGann smiled, waved one ham-like hand and called out, "Sure and now it's Frank you can call me."

Mickey headed straight for his room. Since it was well past the time Bernadette would have quit her shift, even the most brazen of louts wouldn't go a beatin' on a Rooming House door after midnight. Besides, sticking your foot on the next highest rung of the ladder—due to his promotion within the Provo ranks—was a milestone he could enjoy most fully in solitude.

Although Manion had begun to share some of his thoughts with

Bernadette, he had not as yet come full circle. Thus, he remained reluctant to include her in the most personal of his contemplation. The new Cell Leader remained alert, well beyond the usual self-imposed limits! Supine on the well-made bed, divested of all but his shorts and hands clasped behind his head, Manion stared at the errant moonbeams playing on his feet and reminding him of the anthem of the Irish insurrection, "By The Rising of the Moon." Adjusting his frame to the lumps in his mattress, resulting from numerous unrestrained springs, Manion exhaled deeply, though leaving sufficient breath to say in semi-silence, "You're on the way, Mickey!" Yes, he would enjoy the Command Position, and there was no doubt he would handle it with great competency! Young enough to think his fantasies could be fulfilled, Manion pictured himself on a plane with Sean Moylan and Dan Green, and those Irish heroes of mystic proportions heralded in his favorite song, "The Galtee Mountain Boy."

However, Manion was never purely altruistic. His pragmatic side called forth visions of increasing monetary reward. A car—and hell, he could even have Bernadette's scooter tuned up on the side. These thoughts Manion could share with her tomorrow, and that would be done, unless orders from Big Frank intervened.

Seven-thirty the following morning found Manion moving rapidly across the rain-slick paving stones to his new headquarters. Cap at a jaunty angle, jacket unzipped, and head held high, his appearance was a considerable departure from the frowning and stooped umbrella-wielding pilgrims, who shared the sidewalk as they all sought their personal destinations. Mickey's face appeared to welcome each raindrop, while the expressions of the others projected as formidable landing places. Turning the final corner, the Sweeney sign sprang into view. "Given my skill as a mechanic, maybe I should change the sign from 'Limp In—Leap Out' to 'Limp In—Towed Out,' if you're lucky!" Mickey had always got a laugh from his own humor. Few of his friends even knew that he had any. In the past, it had become easy to entertain himself. How did one act the comedian to a drunken sot of a father, or a mother who had no wind for a laugh, only enough to generate the next cough!

As Manion looked up, an elderly man—dapper in dress and fighting to preserve that appearance by means of a rippling umbrella held high aloft—came into view. Despite his best intentions and maneuvers to match, the man was less than successful in fending off the raindrops, as evidenced by the tiny rivulets springing from the bushy white eyebrows. These joined with others to form a sizable stream upon reaching the gorges between cheeks and lips, manifestations of the age he had achieved. Seeing the young man approaching and divining his mission, he said, "Are you Manion?"

"I am, sir, and I assume that I have the honor of addressing Mr. Sweeney."

"You do, as a matter of fact," was the elder's reply. Forthwith, he produced a ring of keys, which were delivered without further ceremony into Manion's anticipating hand. "It's all yours, Manion! I'll drop bye from time to time, but I won't be in your way."

Sweeney gave a half-smile, topped off with a nod, which released a small stream of rain water heretofore held in check by the rim of his derby. A similar gesture was returned by the new manager.

Soon, Sweeney was inside an old but pristine Austin, and there was instant response to the ignition key. Engine purring, the car was under way. Manion gazed after the auto until it rounded the nearest corner. After tossing and catching the keys a couple of times, he decided it was opportune to show the world he had enough sense to go in out of the rain. Finding the proper key after the third try, Mickey entered his new domain.

Formal survey of the premises had hardly begun when two figures entered. Studying the new Cell Leader, the first had little doubt that life wouldn't go his way should he choose to cross him! "Tom Brophy," he said.

Mickey quickly appraised the offered hand. Several fingers were angled in a way nature had not intended. No doubt a casualty of a slipped wrench. Black grease had found a permanent home beneath the nails, most of which were broken. Additionally, further dirt and lubricants highlighted the ridges of the heavy calluses on his palms and fingers. Manion was no Conan Doyle, but he appreciated the fact that If your cover was a mechanic, you sure as hell should fit the picture!

Dismissing study of the hand, Manion grasped it and focused on the face. Black hair and almost black eyes, with more than a hint of malevolence. Thin, spidery vessels coursed through the one-day stubble of bristly, black whiskers and the tip of an aquiline nose, giving it and the man's cheeks a reddish glow. *I wonder if it's exposure to the weather or the bottle,* thought Mickey on the way to evaluating the thin, cruel-appearing lips, which were paler by comparison. Craggy contours of the man's jaw and cheekbones blended well with a very prominent Adam's apple.

Manion's appraisal proceeded no farther, as the second man intruded. His hand was beefier and better kempt. However, there was no doubt he also was a mechanic. Unquestionably, his wedding ring played a role in the relative cleanliness. Kevin Walsh was a shorter man, in the process of extending his forehead at the expense of thinning red hair, dappled with threads of blond and gray. A pinkish complexion went well with his porcine features. At first glance, Mickey could imagine Walsh to be a bit on the slow side but dependable, while Brophy was considered an enigma in need of evaluation.

Brendon Moriarity was the last to arrive. *No doubt a rough participant in Irish football,* thought Mickey, who relied on the missing front teeth, misshapen nose, assorted facial scars, a mangled ear, and a very muscular, athletic physique to reach his conclusion. His other three cell members would come to be known as they filtered in later in the week. They were not a part of his immediate coterie, as McGann had explained.

Given the fact the garage was an actual viable business, there was work to be done. Brophy, Walsh, and Moriarity donned coveralls and proceeded to tend to the repair of various automobiles awaiting service. A fairly active banter was carried on, such as work and proximity would allow. For the time being, the Boss was odd man out! Such a game was constantly played by the soldiers of the Irish Republican Army. Mickey felt his way along. He was aware cell members were always fearful of the unproven and the possibility of a tout! Consequently, the full facts of one's curriculum vitae were passed out slowly. However, they would be known in good time.

Mickey was never the wastrel, though there was a surfeit of spare time for the new manager of Sweeney's Garage. He quickly picked up the art of car repair, and by the end of the second week Brophy, Walsh, and Moriarity were pleased to find that Manion was an asset. In three weeks, he was occasionally suggesting other ways to skin a mechanical cat. To their surprise, the advice Manion offered was frequently helpful, and once or twice was a much better than what they had contrived from their own experience. Furthermore, the boss had insidiously asserted his own personality; therefore, his position of Team Leader was readily accepted.

Three outside members of Manion's cell had finally made themselves known. At first meeting, all seemed dedicated and capable. Jimmy Plunkett stood out because he really didn't. His facial features, hair, eyes, and body habitus were such that he would in all probability be described as nondescript. This pleased Mickey, for he saw definite advantage in employing someone who looked like everyone—especially in all activities calling for a daylight operation when witnesses might be encountered. In addition, he was an expert welder and could do just as well with a cutting torch, while bomb making was Plunkett's strong suit.

Barry McConville was Jimmy Plunkett's antithesis, as it was unlikely any witness would soon forget him. Manion regarded the man as an Abraham Lincoln caricature. Close to six feet, five inches tall, he was slender with sinewy arms that hung too far down. Despite the length of his spindly legs, his fingertips achieved the crease in his knees when the arms were limp. After Manion's first impression, he noted McConville's left hand dangled even nearer the earth—by virtue of the fact that Barry's left leg was two inches shorter—an undesirable gift from polio. In motion, the man was pure gyration, which readily accounted for his nickname, Jingle Joints. His face was Lincolnesque in feature with its age appearing ten years beyond the chronological one. However, a large purplish-red birthmark on his right cheek diminished comparison to the real Abe.

Charlie Maher filled the last space; in fact, he filled it too generously. "Friar Tuck," said Mickey to himself well before grasping the corpulent hand. As Manion's appraisal would suggest, Maher was beyond the limits of simple obesity. An aggressive form of male pattern baldness had provided him with nature's tonsure. Charlie had little in the way of a neck to provide a pedestal for an overly large head, leaving the caput seemingly to be as one with the shoulders. Sufficient adipose tissue had found a home in his eyelids, so there was little to see but the pupils. His pug nose would do a bulldog proud, while the lips and rosy cheeks were in perfect accord. However, Charlie seemed cerebral. Therefore, he might be a major help in planning. He possessed insight, was far from brash, and was a stickler for detail,

Alone in his office, Manion sipped his tea, noting with disdain his fingers were developing the mechanic's manicure. *Irish Republican Army, what a fookin' misnomer that is,* thought Mickey. *A good part of my squad, while young, wouldn't get by the Recruiting Office door much less survive basic training*! Somewhere, from the recesses of his mind, Mickey recalled an old saying about playing the hand that was dealt you. *Well, I can do that,* he thought. *But with a hand like this, I better keep a poker face and be ready to bluff.*

During the shakedown cruise at Sweeney's, Mickey had not neglected Bernadette. Her motor scooter had been serviced with the care usually reserved for a Bentley, and she was elated. Given his current freedom in the evenings, Mickey was at Brennans door each night at closing time. Consequently, for Bernadette, the last hours of every shift passed with agonizing slowness. However, she felt amply rewarded when she beheld him standing there with his awkward smile accompanied by the omnipresent two-penny bouquet.

Sundays, she would have him for the whole day, and that would be the zenith of her week. However, at day's end, Bernadette always found herself alone with her thoughts. Then, she would mull over his increasing ardor but remained curious as to his reluctance to bed her. Their relationship was unlike any of the affairs in which she had partaken. Perhaps, this was due to some vestige of Mickey's religious training that he had been unable to shake despite his severance from the Catholic Church, which was a break she had also made. However, with further thought, Bernadette was reconciled by the fact she was happier than she could ever recall being in the past. *All things come to she who waits,* she thought. Then, she recoiled at the apprehension that some night he might be captured or killed, and her wait could be eternal. "Oh, Mickey, hurry up, my sweetheart! Only God knows how long we'll have together! Why did I say God?" was her next question. "Didn't I give Him up years ago?"

Meanwhile, during these first three weeks at the garage, there had been no requests passed down from Frank McGann, though he had stopped by and conversed with Mickey while getting his car serviced. Manion was quick to notice that although the sedan looked outwardly like a well-kept draft horse, the engine was pure thoroughbred. McGann's parting words were, "It won't be long, and I'll be in need of you, boyo!"

The summons came quickly, but Mickey was not unready or unnerved. In his meeting with Hogan and McGann in the back of the Blarney Stone, he was fully briefed on the latest depredations wrought by the Ulster Defense Association. Three Provos—all good lads—had been gunned down in a short, bloody ten-day period.

"We're through pissin' around," thundered McGann, coincident with the concussion of a massive fist thundering hard against the top of Hogan's desk. "Bad enough they stiffed two of us on the way to a day's slavery at one of their fookin' factories. But gunning down Billy Byrne standing in his own doorway, holding his new baby and just back from Baptism, is the limit! The bastards are two up on us since we stiffed Caarson, and you can see the sinking morale in the faces of our men. No more one on one at a time. Shit, we're going to take out a fookin' bundle of them. There's to be a UDF meeting and drill at their Lodge Hall on Friday night, and afterward many will be heading to the Lambeg Drum to fortify their resolve with whiskey. It's your party, Mickey! You know the location and the get-away routes. You have four days to put it all together. Can we rely on you, boyo?"

"That you can do, Frank," was Manion's response.

Given the task, Mickey became consumed with it. Bernadette would face an empty street as she emerged each night from Brennans. Well, she was part of the Cause, wasn't she, and the Cause demanded sacrifice, didn't it? All was part of basic training for a good Provo woman and a prelude to widowhood for many! Having completed that consideration, Manion was capable of extirpating Bernadette from his mind.

Chapter Thirteen

In a windowless, basement room of Sweeney's, the six cell members and their leader were locked in deliberation, which could have gotten out of hand if anyone had the temerity to question Manion's leadership. Discussion was well tolerated, suggestions were entertained, dissension was not to be considered. Two absolutely reliable automobiles would be necessary, and stolen ones would be untraceable. That order of business would be taken care of later that night, thus allowing their future transport to be brought to the garage for evaluation and necessary repair. This would leave a second night to secure an additional vehicle, should one of the initial requisitions come up a cropper. Very unlikely possibilities, since the foragers were skilled mechanics.

Charlie Maher had been quiet up to this point. Then, he raised his hand as pupil to teacher. "How about a small lorry for us heaving the bombs, Mick? We drive up in a car and you'll have to get out to throw them or lean out the window. It strikes me as better to have a couple of us with good strong arms in the back of a lorry!"

In little time, Mickey agreed. The others nodded silently. Instinctively, Mickey knew you led by example, and he indicated he would be one of the bomb throwers. Moriarity was the other obvious choice, and there was no hesitation in his rising to the occasion. Elated and encouraged by the success of his suggestion, Charlie Maher added his next thought.

"In case of pursuit, it would be a hell of a lot easier to fire at a following car from the open rear of a lorry instead of leaning out the car's windows or attempting to shoot through the back window. Yeah! I just happened to think none of us are lefties, and if you have to lean out and shoot with your left hand, you aren't going to hit much!"

Facial expressions around the table expressed acquiescence to Charlie's presentation. Then, in the time remaining, the cell members were left to ponder the matter of the bombs, and they were on their way to fusing a team. "Too bad that we don't have any of those potato mashers the Germans use to use," said Plunkett, wanting to make at least a token contribution.

"What we got is six sticks of dynamite and some black powder fuse," was Mickey's reply. Hearing his grenade suggestion squelched, Plunkett saw his second in the limelight being extinguished. Then, it came to him! Just two weeks ago, he had used his craft to weld a flowerpot stand for his mother.

"I got it!" he exclaimed. The idea seemed plausible.

"Make two and we'll try them out tomorrow," was Manion's recommendation.

Break-up of the meeting did not follow parliamentary rules of procedure, nor had Robert's Rules of Order ever been employed. Manion sent each on his way, along with a demand for secrecy and admonition to keep thinking out every detail of the plan. Also, he added that they should be back promptly at the appointed hour on the following night.

Plunkett arrived early, anxious to show off his creation. Each had a basket on one end made of metal staves welded together. Thus, the receptacle formed was about eight inches long and six inches in diameter. Protruding from the base was an eight-inch-long metal pipe of sufficient circumference to be easily held by a large hand. Three sticks of nitro fit easily into the basket, leaving considerable space to be packed with nails. Then the whole thing could be wrapped in tape to hold it all in place.

"Damn! I like it," exclaimed Manion. Not long after, it was determined they could—with sufficient force and good accuracy—easily shatter the pub windows. Next, they worked on the fuses. Four seconds was the detonation of choice. With considerable experimentation, the men concluded they had achieved their goal, or had at least came as close as possible, given the vagaries of burning rate in the impregnated black powder fuse. Was there a dependable way to ignite the fuses in the back of a moving lorry? Two sheltered carbide lanterns with a third as backup—were chosen for that purpose, as they were far more reliable than matches or a lighter.

On Friday night, at the appointed hour, the men converged on Sweeney's. Cars, bombs, and carbide lamps had been checked and rechecked. Plans called for the lorry to be driven to the Lambeg Drum—slowing considerably as it traversed the front of the pub. Brophy would be at the wheel with McConville at his side. From the direction they would approach, the latter man would have the entrance facing his side of the lorry and could fire his gun if necessary. From their meager arsenal, handguns were provided for all. Several had old .455 Webleys. The rest were issued American Colts or Smith and Wessons. In addition, Mickey could rely on an old 1898 8mm Mauser Rifle—beaten up but serviceable.

As soon as the bombs were delivered, the plan was to be off to rendezvous a dozen blocks away. Then, they would pile into the purloined sedan driven by Walsh. Another mile further on was rendezvous 2, where Plunkett would be awaiting with a sedan from Sweeney's garage, freshly serviced and out on a nocturnal test-drive. Given the fact that movement from one vehicle to the next must occur with split-second timing, and adding the consideration of six men crammed in one not very capacious sedan, Charlie Maher was selected to remain at Sweeney's to open the garage door on their return.

Manion and Moriarity were slouched in the open back of the track, covered by a light tarpaulin and thus rendered inconspicuous. Each clutched a handle of their oversized grenades. Burning carbide lamps were constantly checked. Their flames remained bright though not obvious due to the shielding. Two taps by McConville on the back window was the signal for one block to go! Mickey's three taps, as expected, answered those of McConville. Seventy-five yards from the pub entrance the lorry slowed, and there was a rapid succession of taps emanating from the lorry's cab. After hurling the tarp away, the two bombers stood upright. Timing their movements to those of the vehicle, Manion and Moriarity positioned themselves for the fuse ignition. Their plan had gone down with near perfection. Lit fuses sputtering, two strong, determined, and accurate arms catapulted the twin bombs upward and outward. On either side, the deadly canisters shattered the front windows.

For those in the front of the Lambeg Drum, there remained but a second to curse or scream. Those more fortunate in the back fell into deadly silence with a single thought, which was an intense fear of impending disaster. The lorry had not gone far but was far enough to escape from the main force of the shock wave and flying debris. However, no escape was possible inside, as the exploding dynamite unleashed hell's fury with a deafening roar and blinding flash. Those not killed outright by the concussion and fireball were scythed down. They were mutilated and shredded by the pounds of homemade shrapnel, which was a very lethal additive to each of the gargantuan grenades.

When the police and firemen arrived, they were revolted and sickened by the carnage they saw. Few of the patrons were physically unscathed. Those who survived would be forever branded mentally and emotionally. Meanwhile, at rendezvous 1, Mickey somberly intoned "Well, lads, I think we got their attention!"

Quiet prevailed between rendezvous 1 and 2 and from there to Sweeney's, apart from hastily whispered commands to move it!

As the men dispersed, there was a degree of subdued jocularity. However, it wasn't elation. Leaving that many dead or maimed behind in your wake, even if you didn't have to see them, wasn't quite like winning the European Cup. Mickey really didn't feel good, nor did he particularly feel bad. *It's just getting the other sod before he gets you*, he thought. *When it's Ireland—and you're Irish—what else can you do?*

Manion took off his heavy shoes, but his clothes remained in place. Exhaustion overwhelmed conscience, and sleep came quickly.

Early the next morning on the way to Sweeney's Garage, Mickey passed a newsstand that was the scene of frantic purchases of local papers. Shuffling off a few steps out of the crush of attentive readers, he sought eagerly for the details to be found beneath the blazing headlines, which accounted for the upper half of the front page. "TERRORIST BLAST KILLS AND MAIMS SCORES AT PUB—IRA SUSPECTED." Manion moved through the cluster to the vendor, careful not to topple an elderly lady, who stood mouth agape and seemingly mesmerized by the lurid details of the ghastly carnage. Coins were traded for the paper. As Manion had no intention of gawking while on the spot, he stowed it snugly under his arm in a folded state. Reversing his direction, Mickey dodged his way to the perimeter of the crowd and resumed his way to the garage.

Finding his desk, the principal perpetrator of the crime quickly digested the details. Seven were dead at the scene, including two women. Thirty-one had been taken to hospital, and several of those were indicated to be critical. Some were left sightless, and more than a few had parted with limbs that would never be flexed, extended, waved, or used to embrace again. *Protestant widows—Ulster's widow's pool had been enhanced once more. Protestant widows and fatherless children, no doubt anguished and cried just as hard as those on the Catholic side,* Manion thought. Then, he mused that of course; the IRA did not consist of Roman Catholics per se. He was Catholic by birth, but as a group they ran the gamut from pure patriot through fiscal pragmatist, idealist and even extended to Communist.

Ensuing paragraphs took a toll on Mickey, who had masterminded the slaughter, as though he was stuffing himself with spoiled food. Every verbal bite added to his feeling of unease.

Sensing the fact that he was becoming physically ill, Mickey realized an entombed conscience was stirring and trying to arise from the sarcophagus. Grasping his head in strong but tremulous hands, Mickey was suddenly aware of prayer, which was what the good sisters had always advised in the face of calamity. However, the anguished man reshuffled the thought, realizing he had long since freed himself from the bondage of religion. If there was a God, he really didn't care anyway. As a substitute, Manion started to recite the IRA Credo, but he got no farther than "Life springs from death." Bolting upright, Mickey spat out, "Shit on that! Am I any worse than those RAF and Yankee flyboys who dropped a 2000-pounder down some frau's chimney, then flew back to the Officer's Club for a round or two? I'm a bloody fookin' hero, that's what I am!"

Composure had returned to Manion by the time his trio of mechanics arrived. However, Brophy, Walsh, and Moriarity were sullen. All joviality was replaced by somber, softly spoken words. Expressions of fear formed on faces at the sight of an opening door or the sound of a horn seeking admission. Mickey didn't intrude on their private thoughts for a time, as he hoped for spontaneous resolution. Unfortunately, it never seemed to come.

Privately, the moods of the trio shared a single consuming horror, They had participated in a horrible murder—one that would surely impel the Crown to find the perpetrators and bring them to justice. Like shoppers on a massive spending spree, they might at some time have to confront the cashier. If it came your time to pay the tab, you didn't reach for your wallet. You extended your hands and accepted the cuffs. There was much to generate extreme anxiety when being hunted by the minions of Her Majesty! Fearful beatings were to be expected, as death by hanging or the firing squad was a thing of the past. However, back then only two seconds were needed for the hangman's knot to dislodge the second cervical vertebrae and sever the spinal cord. Thirty years of facing the boots and truncheons of the Guards was a far worse fate. If worries over officialdom were not enough, the men could always dwell on the possibility of the UDA seeking them out, finding them, and leaving them in hopeful anticipation of a bullet in the brain to end their agony.

Irresolution in the face of final judgment of a sinful life by a wrathful God was easy for the men to slough off, for it seemed remote. However, the chance of judgment by the Queen's Bench was certainly a more proximate possibility—and a more powerful progenitor of great anxiety. Also, at least one of the men arrived at the inescapable conclusion that if arrest, conviction, sentencing, and punishment might occur before too long, then pleading his case in a heavenly court might follow soon thereafter! This was a powerful stimulus for qualms of conscience.

Shortly before the lunch break, Manion took the men to task. He herded them into his office and closed the door. "You look and act like a fookin' bunch of schoolgirls who lost their virginity, are now pregnant, and facin' their Da holding a razor strap! We did what we needed to do, and we're soldiers fighting a war—not some bloody Jack the Ripper cutting up whores! We pulled it off—and none's the wiser. We got each other, and we got the army, and by God, we'll stick together and win our war! If we're going to let our fears pull us down, then go swallow your pistol barrel!"

Manion gave a strong pep talk and like a team down by what seemed to be an insurmountable score at half time they appeared to be stimulated. By quitting time, banter and productivity were near normal, as best Manion could tell. When the last had departed for the day, Mickey was once again alone with his thoughts. Were they only good lads in the face of adversity, or had he only witnessed bravado covering a core of cowardice—like so much paint and gilt?

Shortly, thereafter, the ringing phone, when answered, conveyed the voice of McGann. "Are you free to talk, Mick?"

"I can do that, Frank."

"Good. It was a great show! We'll discuss what the critics had to say ten o'clock at the Stone."

Mickey was responsive to the call. He was beginning to feel equality and was rather looking forward to receiving well-deserved praise. However, Bernadette would greet an empty street once again and proceed alone back to her flat, anxiety increasing with each step.

On this Blarney Stone meeting occasion, Manion's arrival at Hogan's was by automobile—a cherished perquisite of his new position. Entry to the pub was accomplished via a private portal in the rear. Caution was necessary, for there was no point in starting tongues wagging, especially just a day after the blast. Informers and spies were not prone to wearing a badge proclaiming their nefarious profession, nor did they display the mark of Cain, though it would make life a hell of a lot easier. You couldn't tell a tout from any of the neighborhood imbibers—so you did what you could and best rely on stealth.

The door resonated the agreed-on secret knock, which was the same as the Morse code for IRA. The signal was acknowledged, as evidenced by the protrusion of Hogan's face, the right side illuminated by a light from within, while the more sinister left side remained in shadow. "Mick, come in boyo! You're punctual as usual, right on time like one of those bloody Swiss watches no Paddy can afford."

Manion once again surveyed the familiar sight. Nothing new was expected. Square bottles of Bushmill's had a fluid level at half-mast, having surrendered the rest to the two omnipresent Waterford whiskey glasses, whose contents were drawn down well-nigh to the bottom.

Big Frank was up on his feet in a flash. His physiology existed in harmony with an alcohol blood level that would fell the average man. However, he was quite free of falter, and his speech had no hint of slur—though presumably it was energized by ethanol. "Mickey—darlin'—t'was a masterful fine job you and your lads did! You rattled windows all the way to the Brits' fine Parliament, twisted the Lion's tail, and have all the fookin' Orangemen lookin' over their shoulders!" The boisterous pronouncement was followed by a playful but still powerful punch in the ribs. Then followed the classic Irish handshake, wherein a goodly volume of spittle was expectorated on the palm of the hand before the two hands were clasped in a somewhat slimy grip, meant to display a firm bond despite its lack of appeal to aestheticism.

On the way to the proffered chair, a thought entered Mickey's mind. His own lads seemed so jumpy and depressed. He wondered what course of action they might take? On the contrary, his immediate superiors celebrated every victory and dampened every defeat with booze. How really competent and reliable were any of them? Well, better to remain insouciant, at least for the time, and bask in the praise he anticipated!

Manion received some, but it trailed off abruptly. Hogan was leaning back, a pensive expression on his face. McGann had built a pyramid with his sapling-sized fingers and was carefully sighting his one open eye, sporting a wrinkled, bushy brow, over the apex of the geometric figure that he had constructed. Then, Frank leaned against the back of his chair and appeared to aim the apex of the pyramid at an outstretched foot. Like a shot expected when he pulled an imaginary trigger, the words shot out, "Shit, Mick! We did a good and glorious thing for the Cause, but we can't sit on our asses waiting for the parade to go by."

The *we* in the front of the sentence was not lost on Manion Nor did he think the *our* in the end was inclusive of anyone. Nonetheless, he held himself in check and awaited the utterance of McGann's developing proposition.

Big Frank continued. "What we really need, boyo, is more good guns, explosives, and a few coins to spread around between our good lads, who are having a tough time of it. Even a patriot needs a little oatmeal, potatoes, and brisket in a larder. Old Napoleon said it all when he came out with that bit about an army marching on its stomach!" McGann continued. "There's a limit to what you can beg, and it would be damned tough to clean out one of the Brit's arsenals. However, a truckload of cash would be a great help to all of us. Wouldn't you agree, Mick?"

On hearing the predictable "Sure, Frank," McGann continued. "A couple of our good lads out in the country have a little farm that survived the potato famine and the clutches of the robber barons. They are located outside a tiny place called Bally Kelly, which is on the road between Londonderry and Limevady. It seems our lads just happened to notice that an armored car leaves Limevady at eleven A.M. every Tuesday, proceeds to Derry, before returning to Belfast. We assume it stops at Ballymoney and Ballymena on the way to Limevady. So, after they clear Derry and head for home, they should be loaded with cash. The best part is they'll be beatin' it back through very lonely countryside. It's a natural, boyo! Get your lads working on it—and plan for two weeks from this Tuesday at the latest."

After McGann's final words on the subject, he disassembled his pyramid and arose to replenish his glass. Hogan passed Mickey a map of the route the armored car would follow, and a detailed description of the brother's farm near Bally Kelly. McGann clasped Mickey's hand and wished good luck, which was reinforced with a broad smile. Within seconds, Big Frank had downed a quick shot of Bushmills, reloaded, and stood facing the departing Manion with upraised glass in a form of salutation. "If you have any special needs for the job, let Con know, Mick!"

Manion nodded in what seemed to be happy accord. However, inside, he was seething. This could be a hell of a devilish undertaking, which would be tough enough. But the wolves in his cell seemed to have changed to rabbits, which would surely not intimidate the British lion.

Manion was aware there were no medals minted by the IRA! He thought, *If you survived one job then you were a sixty-minute hero before the next one. If you didn't survive, you could wait in some special part of Hell until someone wrote a ballad about you.* Mickey doubted he would hear it from there. "I'll pull it off," he said to himself. "I'll rise to the top like I said I would! When I get there, I'll run this fookin' outfit right, not like some fortune teller reading the future from the bottom of a whiskey glass instead of the fookin' tea leaves!"

At last, there was time for Bernadette—not much, but some. Mickey was on-station when Brennans closed, and his beat-up pair of brogans caught the attention of both the green eye and the blue. A sweet smile evolved, tentative at first, then blossoming like an opening rose. Bernadette closed the short distance separating them in an instant. She flung her arms around his neck and proceeded to purge all her pent-up emotions in a passionate kiss. Mickey was quick to respond, though only after securing the safety of his two-penny bouquet. Finally, freeing themselves from their embrace, they echoed sentiments as to the degree each had missed the other. Hand in hand, they strolled up the lane until their little sanctuary, Garrity's Coffee Shop, was entered.

Mickey and Bernadette had an hour to spend before the lights would be extinguished and the owner would be ushering them out. Especially in the day's last hour, the little shop was nearly as free from eavesdroppers as a deserted slip of rock jutting out of the windswept Irish Sea. Garrity's suited their purposes and was used to good advantage to probe each other's inner thoughts. Bernadette had seen or heard all the news stories about the bombing besides picking up a good deal of tabletop discussion at the restaurant. Instinctively, she knew Mickey, this man she now loved, was involved. She wondered to what depth this extended.

Garrity had completed his last refill run. Soon, the apron would come off and the day's meager receipts totaled up. Bernadette cradled Mickey's right fist in her two hands, once soft and tender, though now toughened by the trays that she carried. "Mick you were in on the bombing weren't you?"

His fist hardened at the words, but a slight yet perceptible relaxing of the contracted muscles occurred as Mickey replied softly, "Aye! I was and that's all you need to know!" The meeting of their eyes brought out one of Manion's tight-lipped smiles and sufficed to eradicate any further curiosity on Bernadette's behalf.

Shortly, in front of Bernadette's flat, the two completed the last of a series of good-night kisses. Mickey was about to turn when his love reached out and said, "Mickey I would like to give you much more if you wish."

"I do so more than you could imagine," was the soft reply. Then, he continued, "Now is not the time, Bernie, but it will come, and we'll make up for all we missed!" Then, he was gone, though his parting words made up for his absence.

On the first Tuesday after the meeting with Hogan and McGann, Mickey departed Belfast while the city remained shrouded in black and no moon intruded. He was nearing Derry when the sun, having traversed the Russian steppes and wended its way across Western Europe to sparkle on the North Sea, finally agreed to present its pinkish-gold aurora on the rear window of Manion's westward-moving car.

During his solitary hours on the road, there was considerable time for thought and introspection. Was he on a fool's errand and one with a high probability of lethal consequence? Well, polemics wasn't his game, so accepting assignment was what he was going to do or die trying! For someone whose larcenous background consisted of no greater crime than hoisting some penny candy from a preoccupied merchant, this seemed like heady stuff. *I'm like the kid in the silly Irish story,* he thought. Then, Mickey reflected on the lines, "Daddy, I'm tired," said the boy.

"Keep on swimming," replied the father.

"Daddy. I'm really tired!," exclaimed the exhausted child!

"Keep on swimming," replied the father.

The boy, near sinking, replied one last time, "But Daddy I don't want to go to America!"

Chuckling to himself, Mickey was temporarily relieved of concentration on the real job, and his unleashed mind hastened to exhume another story.

The Maze prison library had given Manion access to more information than he ever had at his disposal in the short school tenure of his preceding youth. Mickey's mind had always been a scampering squirrel adding nuts and kernels to his horde. Sisyphus was one of the kernels that he had come across. Useless information, practically speaking, but personally gratifying. Mickey wondered would he be like the mythical king of Corinth, always pushing a monstrous rock up a hill only to have it roll down again, thus, forcing him to start over? Manion slammed his open palm hard on the steering wheel, then said aloud, "Michael Manion is different, damn it! If McGann wants me to swim to America, I can do it. This Sisyphus is going to get all his boulders to the top of the hill and keep them there!"

At least Hogan had provided a Derry map of reasonable accuracy, and the various branches of the Royal Bank of England were indicated by readily discernible circles. Reviewing the map, it seemed to make good sense to proceed to the branch located in the Southeast section closest to the highway to Ballymena, for the armored car would surely take this route on its return to Belfast.

Finally, locating his target, the strategist had time for a spot of tea and a trio of tasty biscuits slathered with good Irish jam. A churning stomach welcomed the relief, and Mickey found himself reasonably composed. However, that state proved short-lived when he considered the fact that this was only a scouting mission, not even a dress rehearsal! Sure as hell it was nothing that would get him killed or wounded! As Manion left the tea shop, there was a chance to scoop up a discarded newspaper, so he availed himself of the opportunity.

Looking around, Manion noticed that a small grassy square was present close by the bank. Several of the benches held men reading, as Mickey intended to do. "Well, I won't look any more conspicuous than those sods," he said to himself before coming to the amusing conclusion that the other men already present might also be planning a heist and had managed to get there before him!

Bells of a nearby church had no sooner pealed to announce the noon Angelus than the armored car arrived. When Mickey glanced over the extended newspaper, a driver and another man were visible in the cab. The latter quickly got out went to the vehicle's rear door and opened it with a key. From the back of the lorry, two more guards emerged; both were armed with holstered pistols. They proceeded into the bank pushing a small trolley, while the guard from the cab stood alongside the opened rear door hand at the ready and resting ominously on the protruding butt of a Webley.

Diverting his attention, Mickey had time to glance over most of the newspaper's write-ups describing the frustration of the RUC in not developing a quick lead to finding the perpetrators of the bombing at the Lambeg Drum. The officer in charge of the investigation was quoted as saying that a break in the case was expected momentarily, arrests would be made, and he expected justice to be swift in coming as well as harsh in degree! Manion had just finished saying, "I wouldn't bet my proud Prod ass on that my friend!" when the bank doors opened, disgorging the two guards.

The previous empty trolley was piled high with what appeared to be currency-filled sacks. While the guards seemed alert and ready for action, Mickey decided that if their movements were subject to intense scrutiny, they were actually more akin to actors playing out a role for the benefit of supervisors or spectators! He had never been a guard, and this was his inaugural attempt at holding one up. Nonetheless, the robber-to-be was gifted with great insight. "The fox is not a hare—never was, never will be! However, every fox has to figure out how to catch his first hare!" Mickey was in the process of doing just that.

Shortly thereafter, Manion returned to his car, then pulled away from the curb, keeping a respectful distance behind the lumbering armored car. This cautious interval was maintained all the way to Ballymena. Though not vain in the true sense, Mickey was aware he had a facile mind. Consequently, he fed it countless bits of information during the entire time he tailed his quarry. Nonetheless, penciled notes were made when and where the road permitted. Among his notes were the make-up of the armored car crew; the presence of thickened glass in the windscreen and side windows of the cab, as well as the tiny windows of the van. Also noted were what appeared to be two firing portholes on either side of the rear compartment! These would permit the guards to fire at outside targets. However, their ability to aim would be poor and field of fire quite limited. Mickey thought, *Yes the car is armored, but the steel skin is thin and would provide no protection against large-caliber rifle bullets!* These often had steel jackets and were possessive of sufficient weight and velocity to allow easy penetration of the thin armor of the lorry. *Simply a matter of physics*, he decided.

Physics held an attraction for Mickey, and once he was able to assimilate the vocabulary the principles and theories seemed almost self-evident. *One more gift from the Crown,* he thought. As to where the actual assault on the armored car would occur, he was not absolutely certain at this time. However, notice had been taken of a very narrow stretch along the highway, which would be easy to block. Fortunately, it was long and straight, thus providing good visibility for a relatively long distance. Block this, and the bank vault on wheels would simply pull into a lay-by and wait or turn around!

Just beyond the village of Ardmoire, a satisfying number of curves opened in the road. As Manion was coming out of one, he figured there would only be a short distance to stop if an obstruction was seen. Another advantage was the presence of deep ditches on either side of the road, so swerving off onto the shoulder would be disastrous! Finally, a short distance beyond was a gently sloping shoulder leading to clusters of trees. Mickey thought, *One could leave the road at this point, drive the armored car into the obscuring trees, and loot it at a reasonable pace!* Then, coming into Mickey's mind was the consideration that there would be a greater amount of booty to be had if one captured the treasure lorry after it stopped in Ballymena. "No!" he said to himself. "If the weasel is clever enough to get into the hen house, he should take the eggs that are there and not wait about until the hens lay more. An angry farmer could always come along!"

Full of fervor revolving around his plan, the plotter's night was spent in solitude. Attacking his notes for the third time, Mickey was pleased to ascertain he had carefully plotted the speed of his adversary along with appropriate though approximate times of passage through areas of note, especially that of the planned spot of the robbery. Still lacking was a well-thought-out escape route. That could be done on any day, as there was no need to follow the armored car for this purpose.

Also, whom should he select for his accomplices out of those available? After all, three of his men held jobs outside the garage, and one couldn't simply tip your hat to the foreman and say, "Sorry, sir, I won't be in tomorrow. I've got a lorry to hijack." Additionally, there was the question of whom to discuss plans with and at what appropriate time. Manion thought that the best-kept secrets are always the ones newly spun, leaving no time for dissemination! Finally, his pitiable arsenal was not up to the task, and augmentation was a priority. Hogan must be consulted and soon!

Chapter Fourteen

At day's end, Bernadette had regained a place in Mickey's thoughts. *Too late to see her now,* he reflected. *I think she wants to marry me, or at least have me act the part.* Mickey had a mental image of Bernie walking behind a poor wood coffin shouldered by Hogan, McGann, and some of his own crew. She was dressed all in black, her magnificent red locks hidden from view. He could imagine seeing her eyes through the veil she was wearing, and it was evident that one was green and the other blue. Tears that came from either eye shared the same crystal clarity. *Should one even consider a mate when you're doing my line of dirty work?* he thought. *She's far too nice just to use, and I love her too much to wish her a widow. I'll think on it,* Mickey told himself. *There is this job, and one or two I need to do for myself. Then, maybe old Sisyphus can stop rolling rocks for a while!*

Just forty-eight hours later, Manion was on the road once more, though this time he had the benefit of Charlie Maher as company, councilor, and co-conspirator. Given his girth, there was no pretense the man could ever be a fireball when it came to rapid deployment. That department should be left to the physically endowed, or at least to those with a half-measure. One fine brain was worth at least as much as two brawny bulls. This was a thought not unique to Mickey, but it served him well in the utilization of his tiny unit, and that's what counted. Additionally, Maher had the good fortune to clerk in a bookstore under the supervision of a lenient owner, and an occasional day off was not that hard to achieve.

For the purpose of today's reconnoitering, the opposite direction was followed, which was Belfast to Ballymena. Then, on to Derry, with the return route via Limevady and a planned stop at the Harrington Brothers farm just outside Bally Kelly. These were the men who had taken note of the armored car in the first place and, certainly, they might provide further intelligence or even formal assistance in pulling off the caper.

Ardemore was finally achieved, and Mickey was pushing through the town when Maher announced that his stomach was much aggrieved and couldn't they stop for a snack. A snack to Charlie was nearly commensurate to sustenance for six. Shortly thereafter, Mickey appraised Charlie as the last forkful of pie was lifted aloft from the now pristine plate. *No need to wash that dish,* Mickey thought. *Oh well! If you must be a glutton, then it's nice to be a fastidious one.*

When the curvy section of highway was coming into view, Manion pulled over at the first wide spot to check his notes and to explain his preliminary plans to Maher, who expressed initial unanimity. Once more, the car was pulled over at the site Manion had selected as being most appropriate for the actual hijack. "Let's walk it out," said Charlie, a pronouncement generated by the turning wheels within his mind. Mickey steered the car carefully down the gradual slope that he had chosen on the initial run. Then he backed it to a stop in the security of a small arbor of oaks.

Manion was first to exit, a maneuver gracefully and quickly performed. Maher was much slower in his self-extraction, which resulted only after a series of to-and-fro motions, punctuated by jerks and terminated by a grateful sigh when fully free and erect. Outside the confines of the car, Mickey was pleased to note his G-2 man was surefooted, surprisingly agile, and totally free of huffing and puffing when it came to surmounting a grade.

Shortly later, done with the examination of the area and explanation of what was expected to transpire, the two halted on a small knoll to silently mull over all that had passed between them. "I like it Mick, but—" There was a pause, and no words followed for a brief span until Charlie completed his sentence. "How do you actually plan to stop the armored car?"

"Well, you have to put an obstacle in front of it and if at all possible another behind," was the Cell Leader's reply.

"Yeah! What kind of obstacle do you have in mind?" was Charlie's response.

Maher's query put Mickey's own wheels in motion, but he was slow to reply. Carefully taking in all the natural and topographic features of the area, he went through a quick mental checklist. He thought that if for any reason you wanted to attract crows, you didn't put up a scarecrow. It was far better to use something natural that might provoke their interest, but not scare them away. That rules out digging a ditch, even if they had the time. The same would hold true for felling a tree and dragging it into place. Cars crossways in the road with a group of armed men lurking about would surely provoke a gunfight. That was something he wished to avoid, not only from the standpoint of his own safety but also that of his men. Additionally, he had no reason to think the driver and guards were politically motivated. They were probably just poor sods trying to make their way in life. Why kill them if you don't have to? was Mickey's conclusion.

Rationalization, which Manion had used in the hanging of Caarson and bombing of the Lambeg Drum, came up short in its application to the target's crew. "We'll make it something pastoral," were the words resulting from the summation of his thoughts.

"Like what?" responded Maher.

Again, Manion responded to imagery, which generated various possibilities. A wagon loaded with hay came into his mind, teetering on the edge of consciousness, then fell from sight. That was natural enough, but how in hell did one steal such a wagon much less one loaded with hay and sporting a team of horses? Ready to dismiss that notion as absurd, Mickey was somewhat surprised to have the image reemerge, altered in a sensible way.

We could steal an old lorry. That would be reasonably natural. The Harrington Brothers would probably have the hay or could get it without suspicion. Furthermore, the distance between here and Bally Kelly is not prohibitive.

Manion passed the concept to Maher, who once again responded, "I like it!" The ruminations of the two plotters proceeded in silence.

After his initial breakthrough, Mickey found his own train of thought impeded by obstacles. Frustration became edged with fury. He had just issued an oath when Maher broke in, "The old lorry with the load of hay is fine, Mick, but we need two cars in addition. We station the lorry here, though we can't block the road for a long time. Otherwise, we could end up with a queue of cars all stopped in front of the armored car. The way I see it, we'll need a car to pass the armored one at such a place that it will pull by here five to six minutes before the armored car. The men inside will run up here and hide in the ditch. Our second car will follow right behind our prize and block it from escape once we get it stopped. We should have at least four or five of our lads on the spot to do the job. Also, it will provide us with two cars for escape should we need more than one!"

This time, it was Mickey's turn to add, "I like it!" Then, he said, "We'll take all the lug nuts off one rear wheel, except for one that we leave on loose. It should be no trouble to get the old lorry on the highway lose the wheel entirely and spill the hay!" When plans seemed to reach fruition, it was easier to replace a frown with a smile. However, all the i's hadn't been dotted, nor the t's crossed. They had to find a lorry and enough hay to spill.

Later, it proved to be easier to plan a heist than to find the Harrington

Brothers' poor little farm. After a wasted forty minutes, Mickey reached the conclusion the map Hogan had supplied would bring dishonor to the Boy Scouts. Furthermore, it was not possible to stop in at any farm and ask directions. Also, both were hindered, as they possessed that inexplicable passion peculiar to many men to avoid ever asking another human to help find their way. In addition, a practical reason existed, for country folk were especially wary of strangers. Should it ever occur that a connection between them and the Harrington Brothers came to light, then no doubt someone would be quick to remember the incident. A face would come to mind, with a good chance of a fairly apt description to follow.

Manion got a laugh out of Maher when he jokingly suggested sending him up to a door with a kerchief covering his face from the eyes down. However, a declining volume of petrol in the tank soon rankled Manion even more, causing him to stop abruptly and snatch the map from the hands of his navigator. For some reason, only the amateur cartographer might explain, the points of the compass had never been included. Nor had any city or town been designated, apart from the printed note, which stated "just beyond Bally Kelly."

"Shit!" exclaimed Mickey. "'Just beyond Bally Kelly' my ass! And going from what direction?" Concluded simultaneously by both pilot and navigator was the fact they had assumed the map was drawn in such a way as to coincide with the armored car's route.

"We'll try it the other way around, Charlie! Hopefully, lost is no worse on the left than on the right side of the road." Mickey was not unaware that the inept production of a map was easily compounded by their assumption, which was another form of stupidity. Added together, they could lead to a disastrous conclusion! Fortunately, this was not applicable to the search for the farm. But, if such mistakes were to occur in the operation—the tingle up his spine gave a better answer than any words.

At last, a small sign came into view. Though extremely weathered, a sufficient number of the crude letters clung to the split wood decipherable as Harrington. Leading to a small mud-walled cabin was a deeply rutted driveway. Only a steel-rimmed wheel left such groves. No pneumatic tire could have passed this way for a long time if ever, Mickey concluded. The poor little place was wretched and run down. He imagined it remained locked in winter's harsh embrace, and that spring always managed to elude it.

Of all the things visible, not one seemed incongruous. The few chickens scattering before them were content to move the minimum distance necessary to secure safety, as though they couldn't spare the energy for more exuberant run. Beneath the bedraggled feathers was little to suggest anything except the sparest flesh. Charlie, ever mindful of food, was quick to conclude one would be lucky to cook up a thin broth if the entire little flock were added to the pot. A thick and savory chicken stew lay well beyond expectation!

In a single stall were stabled a team of sway-backed horses. They seemed to lean against one another in an attempt to stave off collapse. Neither Mickey nor Charlie had any desire to analyze the goat, two sheep, or the cow. They couldn't avoid the dog, as he laid in a submissive attitude immediately in front of the door. The canine responded to having his underside scratched by agreeably offering a paw to shake. Answering a knock on the door, the Harringtons responded as a duo. Toil-worn men, they had smiles of greeting that indicated dental care had never been affordable. Nonetheless, they were as hospitable as circumstances would permit. Therefore, after partaking in their meager offerings, Mickey was pleased to hear Charlie politely turn down a second piece of soda bread under the pretense they had recently eaten just up the road.

Tim and Terry Harrington were eager to do what they could to help. They had no way of stealing a lorry, as they had never learned to drive. However, they could store one out of sight behind the manger. They could come up with hay. It would be a sacrifice, but they "would do their part!" Their words proved too much for Mickey, who sought his wallet and produced a fifty-punt note. This was the first one Mickey had ever latched onto just for himself. With bravado, he announced, "Fortunately, the army has funds to aid good men such as yourselves so, please take this to cover expenses." Given the expressions of gratitude, the newly created big spender from the city wondered if it might be the first fifty-punt note that either of them ever had in hand.

Details worked out, it was time for departure. At the door, Mickey again feigned prosperity and tried to quell the brothers need to express gratitude. He was happy to be free of the wagon ruts and back on the road to Belfast. Maher was dozing off. Hopefully, he would remain asleep, and there would be no need to stop for food.

Left alone with his thoughts, Mickey's mind went back to Tim and Terry. They were sharing one tiny farm, barely enough to sustain them. Once they were young, he knew, and like most young men would have had a desire to wed. But the place would never support two families, so one of them would have to leave. Mickey assumed it was somehow easier to pass up the conjugal life than put your own kin on the road with no place to go and no money to get there! *Why do such men join the Cause?* he wondered. Obviously, neither one would have any real interest in becoming the sniper or throwing the bomb, but they still wanted to do some little thing for Ireland, meager as it might be. *Perhaps,* he concluded, *if you think you are holding up the badge of the IRA even though it might be invisible it will somehow act as an amulet that wards off evil! Maybe it will even keep the poison black potatoes from returning.* Surely, Tim and Terry were well versed in that infamous part of history. The legend was given to them by parents and grandparents who somehow survived probably on the same pitiful acres. "I guess it's like wearing garlic around your neck to scare off vampires," Mickey concluded.

Mickey couldn't help but wonder if things would change for the Tims and Terrys of Ireland when they won their struggle? Interrupting his thought process, Manion glanced over, and Maher was still sound asleep. His snoring was rendered inoffensive by the hum of the engine.

Belfast was now attainable, as sufficient petrol had been procured from Bally Kelly's single pump.

Manion had the foresight to take the old though still serviceable camera from the garage prior to his scouting trip with Charlie. Mr. Sweeney had kept the venerable Kodak on hand for the purpose of providing a parcel of before and after photographs highlighting the quality of his smash repairs. These made up a prominent display, which could hardly be overlooked by any prospective customers. So the following day after their return to Belfast, Manion picked up from the film developers an envelope containing eight good-quality black and whites. These showed the ambush area to fine advantage, and they became the objects of scrutiny by his little squad. In a previous decision, they had already agreed that only five men would participate.

As Squad Leader, Manion felt Charlie was a handicap in some ways. However, Maher had shown he could move with alacrity when extra exertion was necessary. Inasmuch as they would be fleeing the scene in two cars, both of which had ample room, lack of space would be no problem. A proper lorry had yet to be stolen, but two suitable cars would be available from the garage. Each of these was to be fitted with stolen plates, as would be the lorry when it was procured.

Mickey made the assignments. Volunteerism was expected not requested. Brendon Moriarity and Manion would be in the lorry. Mickey could now find the farm, and Moriarity was extra muscle to load the hay and subsequently dump it when the need arose. Furthermore, being one of the mechanics, Moriarity would provide additional insurance in the event of that kind of problem. Also, he could remove or loosen the lug nuts faster than anyone else.

Charlie Maher would drive the lead car, which would be the one to overtake the armored car. Thus, he would arrive on station approximately six minutes in advance of it. Charlie knew the route, and arriving early would give him extra time to position himself according to plan. Brophy and McConville would occupy the trailing car. This would make it easy for them, as their only role was to pull in immediately behind the stopped armored car, thus blocking any attempt at escape.

Manion drilled them all in regard to shooting. He left no doubt the plan should go down without bloodshed if at all possible. "None the less, if one or more of the guards decided to be heroes and try to save the Queen's Purse, then we'll stiff them right then and there. These boys aren't UDA as far as we know, so we will give them one chance to see mother and the kids again. If they blow it, then it's their own bloody fault," was Manion's conclusion.

The three men who had not participated in the scouting trip were presented with photos to be studied at home. Briefing over, a dress rehearsal was on tap for Saturday. Barry McConville would have to think up a good excuse for absence from work next Tuesday. There would be no problem for Maher. Jimmy Plunkett would be out of the loop for this one, as would be Kevin Walsh, who would remain at Sweeney's as the sole mechanic on duty. Mr. Sweeney would manage the garage office without bothering to inquire as to why he was needed.

Time started to fade rapidly. Manion thought, *Time has a way of doing that when there is an absolute need to have everything in place.*

Stealing the right kind of ancient lorry wasn't quite as easy as it had seemed. At two A.M. on Friday morning Brophy and Walsh made it back to Sweeney's with a derelict of a vehicle. Although it was the right size, overall it was a real loser. Several of the tires had long since shed their tread. In spots, even the underlying rubber was worn away by the abrasion from the road, thus exposing the cords like muscle fibers in a flayed leg. Also, the ignition was dubious, and the clatter emanating from the engine left Mickey conjuring up images of the camshaft erupting from the engine block at any precarious second.

"Is this the best you could do?" shouted Mickey. "I'm supposed to drive this fookin' thing. It's a bloody refuge from the wrecking yard. Well you can bloody well fix it, assuming you're capable of such miraculous things, or you can go steal another."

The prospect of working nonstop to restore the wreck along with facing Manion's continued fury seemed less threatening than returning to the darkened streets to purloin something better. Tired minds, aching bodies, bruised knuckles, and the wrath of a now-tyrannical boss, coupled with a berating seemed far better than encountering a police patrol. "The more times you return to the well, the better the chance to lose the bucket," was Brophy and Walsh's reflection on the old canard.

They proceeded to work harder. Then, Mickey opened the garage door, started one of the cars at his disposal and roared outward. The two mechanics already hard at work jumped at the sound of screeching tires. One second later, the brakes squealed in outrage, then the sedan roared backward. A furious Manion bellowed out the car window, "Get a hold of Moriarity and have him get his ass over here so he can help you bolt this bucket of shit back together!" Tires spun on the concrete, leaving behind a miasma of burning rubber. However, their antagonist was gone and attempted resuscitation of the lorry, which was in extremis, now could proceed.

Mickey parked quietly in the rear of the Blarney Stone. His temper was partially assuaged. A single bar-laced window emitted a wan, yellow light. This proclaimed to the alley and all entering its domain that Hogan remained inside. White knuckles drummed out the signal.

Shortly after, as Manion negotiated the opened door, he was confronted by the graceful narrow barrel of a broom-handled Mauser pistol. Lowering the muzzle, Hogan proclaimed, "Where the hell have you been, Mick? I've been waiting for hours!"

Mickey's temper reignited with uncharacteristic occurrence in the company of his superior. "I've been working and worrying my ass off over this heist," came the stinging reply.

"Listen, boyo! I was handlin' jobs bigger than this when your diaper was full of kak. Can't you handle the heat, Manion?"

"Yeah! I can handle it, and I damn well expect you to come up with something to help."

"Over there wrapped up in the blanket. Help yourself." Hogan said no more as he busied himself with the pistol. With the muzzle pointed safely at the ceiling, he curled his right thumb about the knurled surface of the gun's round hammer, securing its position, thus preventing its uncontrolled fall as the trigger was pulled. Slowly relaxing his thumb, the hammer was eased forward until it contacted the rectangular head of the pistol's bolt and its centrally located firing pin. Thus, safety ensured, the Mauser was laid aside next to a glass of Bush.

Mickey, his back to Hogan, carefully examined one of the two guns he had taken out of the blanket. Mounting the weapon to his shoulder, he brought it down, quickly remembering he hadn't stopped to verify whether or not it was loaded. Manion had never seen a 30-caliber M-1 Garand before, much less held one. However, firearms of any sort intrigued him, and he had a strong affinity for them. He observed a gently curved steel flange projecting from the side of the bolt. Manion rightly assumed it was the key to pulling the bolt back. Completing the maneuver, visual access to the gun's chamber was accorded. No round was present. The gun was safe to handle. Next was the dilemma of how to close the bolt, but that did not long pose a problem to Mickey's ingenuity.

"Con, it's a fine weapon, or I should say it looks quite fine at first glance. Does it function?"

"Why the hell wouldn't it?" snarled Hogan.

"Well, the firing pin could be broken or half a dozen other things," replied Manion. "Is there proper ammunition for it?" he continued.

"On the desk," was Hogan's curt reply.

After a quick visual sweep, Mickey noted two black steel magazines, each of which held eight rounds. The visible portions of the brass shell cases were relatively bright, as were the sharply pointed bullets, which were copper in color but primarily steel in composure and tipped in black. "These are what I wanted, Con, but where are the rest of them?"

"That's all we could turn up, boyo!" Hogan replied.

"Just right for a one-minute war," was the sarcastic response.

"Shit, Mick, you're holding up an armored car, not fighting bloody Monty and the fookin' Eighth Army. You would bitch and moan if they offered to hang you with a new rope. You're starting to worry me, Mick!"

"Well, Con, maybe you can put out your fears with another tote of Bush," was the harsh response.

"Oh! Fook you!" retorted Hogan. Their eyes met and tough a man as he was. the look Con received was sufficient to stifle any further outbursts on his behalf. Inherent in the complex nature of any possible altercation was the intimidating fear that Con could be taken, and the young man he was staring at surely possessed that potential. "Look. boyo. we are both a bit agitated. It comes with the job. I'll see if I can scare up some more cartridges, but they may not be armor-piercing like these. In the meantime, unwrap the other gun. It should make an artillery lover like you wet your pants."

Mickey stood the Garand in a corner and slowly undid the cloth covering of the second weapon. It was a Thompson .45-caliber submachine gun. The wood of the stock and forearm were scarred by dents and dings, however, they remained intact, as did the pistol grip. Much of the bluing was gone, and a light patina of rust had found a home in the denuded areas.

As with the Garand, Mickey cocked the bolt back, assured himself the gun was unloaded, then snapped one of the two drum magazines into place. It clicked reassuringly into position. Held at either waist level or against his shoulder, the weapon seemed to transfer a sense of omnipotence to Manion.

"There's 100 rounds for that one, Mick, and more on the way," said Hogan, voice firm but free of rancor.

Manion, looking up, said, "I'll be off now, Con." He didn't speak again, but busied himself in rewrapping his new arsenal. After stowing the cartridge-filled magazines in a canvas bag, he slung its strap over his right shoulder then cradled the weapons in his left arm. At the door, Mickey paused and said, "I'll deliver the loot here, Con. It will be around midnight on Tuesday." Again, hooded, nearly black eyes sought out Hogan's blue ones. Like a wireless communication, the silent message sent was *I'm not some bloody kid! I'm moving up. You can help me and in that way remain slightly ahead. In the future, don't toy around with me, or I'll run over you!* While there was no frank acknowledgment, Hogan's face registered acquiescence.

By Friday night, the derelict lorry was established as roadworthy, and all precautions were taken to ensure the replaced tires and other parts could not be traced. Mickey spent several hours coaching his small squad, as though he were a battle-tested veteran preparing them for their own little D-Day.

Very early on Saturday morning the entire group sallied forth, well in advance of the rising sun, which found limited success in trying to brighten the green velvet that carpeted the hills and dales of Ireland. That day, thick grayish clouds seemed to congregate and coalesce from all the compass points, and once bonded together, the brilliant rays of the sun were rebuffed. A one-day rehearsal was about to begin, and Mickey was determined it would be flawless. Otherwise, he would lack confidence that the real heist would be perfect in every way.

When the turn-off to the Harrington Brothers was reached, the lorry was the sole vehicle to depart from the stretched-out, inconspicuous mini-caravan. One of the cars remained at the side of the highway, with the occupants feigning motor trouble. The second sedan proceeded to Derry and a predetermined place of rendezvous. Manion and Moriarity were to load the lorry and help the brothers store it. Forty minutes had been allotted before the "stalled" car would come to pick them up. Since Maher was the driver, there was no need to be concerned about him taking the proper route.

Mickey found the poor little farm easily on this occasion, and its drab, dismal appearance was further warped and blemished by the somber sky. Not commenting, he duly noted Moriarity's sarcastic assessment, "The poor sods would be lucky to raise a handful of puny carrots on this God-forsaken place!"

"Yes, it's a pretty pitiful existence, Brendan, but all the largesse that our Brit overlords and protectors will allow. Maybe someday when we cleanse Ireland from their pestilent presence, men like these and thousands of others will have a go at prosperity. Givin' them a chance makes it all worthwhile." Mickey hoped it was a prediction that might see fruition. However, exuberance was restrained by virtue of four centuries of failure to achieve such a victory.

The Harringtons were enthusiastic welcomers and workers. Soon the lorry was loaded with an adequate number of bales. Then the vehicle was stored out of sight. Both brothers were beaming as Mickey and Brendan departed on foot. Turning at the gate, Mickey looked back and returned their waves. *Just like two workers in a tank factory,* he thought. *They don't go off to war but are ever so proud they have built a proper tank so someone else can go blast the bastards for them!*

A quarter of a mile up the road, Maher pulled up. Mickey and Moriarity climbed aboard, and they headed for the rendezvous in Derry. Manion thought that it did not seem anyone was aware of their visit. Stealth and anonymity were always the closest friends of those who dealt in clandestine matters. Shortly thereafter the link up with the second sedan went smoothly. Soon, both cars were at the hijack site, though well obscured by the grove of trees.

All discussion took place out of sight of the main roadway. There was no point in having some observant by-passer recall that five men were pacing up and down the roadside like a troop of surveyors, only lacking the tools of the trade. Later, return to Belfast was by way of secondary roads, which had been chosen as the best possible escape route. Quiet prevailed most of the way back, as everyone seemed engrossed in his own thoughts. No one suggested a stop for food, not even Maher. The five who were to do the job would be at the garage at four A.M. Tuesday morning. "Don't forget your gloves, a scarf for your face, and your fookin' gun," were Mickey's last instructions.

Not much was left of Saturday after the return to Belfast. Sunday was free for Mickey to see Bernadette if only he could divest his mind of all thoughts of the operation. Manion knew he could easily refrain from dwelling on things he had done; however, there was no such composure in regard to things yet to come. "I long to see her, but can't stand the thought of sitting there dwelling on this operation and listening to a dozen repeated requests of tell me 'what's bothering you. Mickey?' Even old Dante hasn't come up with a torture worse than that!"

As for Bernadette, she had begun to wonder if she was matriculating in some sort of course that was a prerequisite for widowhood. Apart from the noise of an occasional passing car, the click of her leather-heeled shoes contacting the cobblestones was all she heard. Bernadette thought the click was like some somber metronome beating out the measure for an aria of anguish. She paused, thus stopping the sound, but it brought no relief for the sadness. Her vision tunneled ahead, seeking out the stairs she would climb alone. No good-night kisses to leave her enraptured until next she saw him. Mr. Garrity, owner of the coffee shop, smiled and waved as she passed by, but Bernadette remained oblivious to him or the light in his window. They were incapable of penetrating the darkness of her mood.

Meanwhile, some members of the cell wished Tuesday would never come, while others wished it had come and gone. However, Mickey was quite acceptable of the fact that this Tuesday, like all those past and yet to be, would follow Monday. He remained outwardly unperturbed.

Tuesday finally arrived, and they departed Sweeney's at the appointed time. Tim and Terry were on station at the farm. The lorry was ready and soon under way. As the brothers bid them a solemn farewell, Mickey recalled an old newsreel showing Japanese crew members waving to their aviator comrades as they took off for the raid on Pearl Harbor. *I hope we enjoy the same degree of success,* he thought. Then, Mickey wondered if his own emotions were akin to those of the Japanese pilots.

Near the Bank of England branch, the two sedans were left on station. This would be their target's last stop before they intercepted it. Maher was alone in one sedan, Brophy and McConville in the other. They were in visual contact, and the bank was easily seen. Meanwhile, on arrival just proximal to the high-jack site, Manion maneuvered the old lorry onto the shoulder of the road. The spot was just free of the area where deep ditches began to parallel the highway. Moriarity opened the bonnet, and then proceeded to work on the lug nuts. All was in readiness as best they could determine. When an approaching car was seen or heard, they feigned repair. Otherwise, Brendon paced nervously, while Mickey leaned against a fender, reasonably relaxed.

At last, Charlie Maher was seen coming along at a good clip. He signaled as he passed, then pulled off into the waiting sanctuary of the trees. Mickey slammed down the bonnet of the old lorry and flung himself into the driver's seat. The lorry engine was turning over, but no ignition occurred! Although Mickey had been relaxed minutes ago, composure was disappearing rapidly with each soul-wrenching turn of the crankshaft. "Dirty, fookin', son-of-a-bitch," he cursed. But, then, the engine caught. An initial stuttering cough gave way to a roar. Releasing the clutch too fast, the old engine began to falter. Once again, near desperation Manion depressed the clutch, gunned the accelerator, and finally lurched on to the highway. The last lug bolt fractured at the opportune spot! Rim and wheel. free of final tether, took leave. As expected, the unbalanced lorry listed severely, spilling out several bales of hay. Soon, Moriarity and Manion were tossing out many of those remaining. Within seconds, there was a sufficient mass to block the road. Then, the two men began to act as though they were in the midst of a furious attempt to unblock the highway.

Their pantomime was short-lived before the armored car came rapidly around the curve. As soon as the driver saw what he presumed to be a genuine breakdown and a road-blocking mound of hay bales, he immediately applied the brakes. This action caused the heavy vehicle to swerve and shift before finally coming to a standstill just a few yards short of collision.

A mantra of shouts and curses from the driver and guard in the front seat ended abruptly, as Mickey grabbed the Garand from behind a hay bale and leveled its muzzle menacingly in their direction. "Out! with your hands up," he commanded.

The armored car driver and guard were startled yet keenly aware that the bullets lurking in the rifle confronting them could easily pass through the windscreen. "Bulletproof" it was said to be, but all bullets were not created equal, and they had no desire to flunk this test. As they began to emerge, the second sedan, containing Brophy and McConville, pulled up sharply behind the stopped armored car. As it turned out, there was no need to block the escape. Nonetheless, Mickey felt it was good to have some further gunmen on the scene. Manion ordered the guard to open the rear doors and commanded the men on the inside to exit! As practiced, Brophy and McConville covered the guard and driver on the outside, so it was unnecessary for Manion or Moriarity to walk past the firing ports in the side of the armored car.

With shaking hands, the guards from the cab produced a key and fumbled with the lock before full insertion was accomplished and the door opened. Given the easy surrender of the men up front, Manion assumed there would be no resistance. However, knowing assumptions sometimes pave the way to cemeteries, Mickey kept his rifle at the ready. A Webley muzzle was the first thing to emerge through the open door. The 200-grain lead projectile was second! The latter caught McConville near the inner edge of his left eyebrow. A livid hole appeared instantaneously, and the explosion of the doomed man's occipital bone followed in a millisecond. Immediately, Manion sprung toward the rear door and emptied the Garand's eight rounds!

Armor-piercing bullets had no respect for the flimsy plate intended to secure the safety of the vehicle and guards. Without significant impedance, they passed through both walls and both men's bodies. Life lay flickering in the one bandit and two guards. Soon, it was extinguished. Quickly, Manion ordered the living guards to place the three bodies in the rear compartment and get in behind them. With some difficulty, the grisly job was completed. Certainly, the reloaded Garand was a strong incentive.

Shortly after, enough of the bales had been removed to allow passage of the armored car. Driven by Maher, it soon found safety in the trees, along with the trailing back-up sedan. Mickey hid the Garand; however, he still had a .38 Colt in his waistband. Cars approached from each direction. Cap visor pulled down to obscure his face, Manion played the role of the penitent peon dutifully directing them past the remaining bales and broken-down lorry. Then, he had time to police the area picking up the spent 30-caliber shell cases and the clip, which was designed to be ejected when empty, before more traffic direction by Manion was needed.

Within minutes, Maher signaled all the usable loot had been transferred to the two sedans. Since coins were too heavy, only currency was taken. Tightly bound, the two live guards were left in the company of the deceased.

"What do we do with poor Barry?"

"We take him," said Manion. Dumping out a sack of coins, he used the bag to encase McConville's devastated head before carrying his limp body to one of the sedans and placing it on the floor of the rear seat. When all appeared secure, they left the scene. Soon, Maher, Brophy, Manion, and Moriarity were off on secondary roads, two to each sedan for return to Belfast. However, Mickey was quick to note that Brophy was coming unglued. He was a man in need of watching!

Cautiously, they made their way back to Belfast without incident and disbanded shortly thereafter. Manion gave Brophy the "war is war" speech with little impact, but decided to allow him a little more time. The shattered man was let go in Moriarity's charge. Manion told Maher that he would take care of McConville's body. He would see it was buried not dumped! However, it was his intention that it never be found. Barry would just be one of the unknown soldiers for the time being. Sometimes, relatives would be located and notified on the sly. But there was no need for a Brit coroner and Police Inspector to have a corpse to ponder.

Reviewing the operation, Mickey thought, *Charlie was rock solid*. He had balls there besides brains and blubber. Brophy had turned to jelly, and a sobbing, quivering man is hard to trust. If he couldn't straighten up, he would be of no use. Far better to stiff him, rather than listen to him sing at your trial. Moriarity was okay. He would measure up. As far as Manion was concerned, he was glad to have the job done. "Things could have gone worse!"

Late that night, moments before the witching hour, the cash was delivered to Hogan. Since a bill of lading did not accompany the loot, Mickey wasn't worried about extracting a mere 2000 pounds for expenses. All the remainder went to the IRA Victory Fund unless Hogan and McGann took a measure for themselves. Con seemed pleased at the size of the treasure. However, he wasn't particularly congratulatory, and the death of McConville was greeted only with a nod. "Yes, I could take care of the burial, but it would mean sending someone back out to Harringtons' Farm." Hogan seemed amused by Manion's surprise that the brothers' place also served as a clandestine cemetery. "One of the Corporal Works of Mercy, in case you forgot, Mick."

Chapter Fifteen

Once again, the little kiosk on the way to Sweeney's was a hubbub of activity. Mickey negotiated the impeding upright bodies holding their newspapers unfurled and outstretched to various degrees. They reminded Manion of main masts with partially hoisted sails in a small flotilla preparing to hoist anchor. Neither wind nor rain was playing havoc with the papers or their readers. Manion began to conjecture whether any of those engrossed in the story of the daring daylight armored car robbery ever thought they might be rubbing shoulders with one of the perpetrators. Likely as not they didn't. After purchasing a paper, Manion continued on his way.

In the privacy of his office, Mickey pored over the details, checking closely to see if the reporter's account of the Police Report was in harmony with his own recollection. He was pleased to note that serial numbers on the currency were not recorded. "Of course, that could be a ruse on the part of the RUC," he mused. Better yet, the value of the stolen currency was listed as "uncertain." Hogan and McGann would have a hard time coming up with a shortage in what they received by subtracting 2000 pounds from "uncertain!" Nonetheless, a disclosure of the actual amount might still be rendered in the future. Taking a cut might have been a mistake, if not for the fact that the unnerved Brophy had dropped a moderate amount of loose notes in the transfer. The act was witnessed by the others, and they would simply testify to this if questioned by Hogan or McGann. Mickey smugly concluded, "No need to think I dug my grave in pinching a little for myself!"

As he read the article, Mickey noted it was heavily weighted with commendation for Officer John Ormsby, "a true hero" who gave his life in a vain attempt to foil the hold-up. Also, the reporter presumed that Ormsby's sacrifice had resulted in the death of one of the gunmen, but nobody had as yet been found. Scant attention was paid to Jerome Porter, the other officer who was killed. Names of the two surviving officers went unmentioned. "I guess it's their due for not rising to the occasion and failing to shoot it out," mused Mickey. "I suppose old Ormsby will get the front side of a pound note chiseled on his tombstone, along with a tidy inscription proclaiming he died for this!"

Other good news pertained to a complete lack of clues or evidence. Otherwise, the report contained the obligatory statements about a massive manhunt, arrest thought imminent, and the IRA was suspect! "A whole page and out of that the names of the two stiffs were all they got right," boasted Mickey to himself. He didn't trouble to take in the names of next-of-kin or funeral arrangements. These details could be left to the sorrowing. Mickey did not count himself among their number.

Mickey's three mechanics showed up for duty the next morning. Walsh seemed all right. However, he hadn't actually participated in the operation. Furthermore, Manion hadn't expected a problem from Moriarity. So, he wasn't disappointed. On the other hand, Brophy was more furtive and weasely than before. He said little to the other three and was very evasive in regard to any eye contact. Mickey frequently observed him and took note of the fact that Brophy's eyes were always focused on someone's waist level or below. After repeatedly studying the man's behavior, a singular thought came to mind: *If you want to stay on this side of the sod, you better get it all together, Brophy! I'll give you five more days.*

After reviewing the garage's appointment schedule, Manion noted that Mr. Sweeney had booked a number of repair jobs during the day that Manion, Brophy, and Moriarity had been absent. All had been dutifully detailed in his exact penmanship, complete with flourishes that would do credit to the calligraphy of a century past. Walsh reported the old man hadn't posed a single question to him.

Late in the morning, Mickey received a terse call from McGann extolling some praise. But, more important, he indicated Mickey's cell could stand-down for awhile. Some of the others could start carrying their share of the load. "Yes, there was a funeral service for a dear friend." The euphemism obviously pertained to Barry McConville. This was good news for Mickey. Now, he would have time for Bernadette. Also, there was the matter of long postponed retribution, which was four years overdue! While Manion had sublimated that matter since his release from the Maze, it was still a molten ingot in his mind that would never cool.

Months had passed since Sam Caarson was found murdered by hanging, and the bombing at the Lambeg Drum was still unsolved. Now, two weeks had elapsed since the armored car robbery. For these two weeks, Chief Inspector Merlin Spencer hadn't had a second of respite. These were a small fraction of the crimes committed during that time, but they were the most high profile. Since there was nothing to link them, Spencer assumed there were different perpetrators, although not with certainty. "Why in hell couldn't I have been assigned a couple of good cases with a dozen witnesses?" the veteran cop anguished. "I feel like I'm straddling a razor with both feet off the ground."

Seemingly, there were constant, demanding, even sometimes threatening calls from every official who had access to a phone. Probably, the target of similar calls, his supervisor had hounded him all day, every day, and frequently into the night. He had heard from the Lord Mayor, the Governor, members of Parliament, and even the Prime Minister. Spencer was sure the Queen would have called, but for the fact he was far beneath her station. He thought it had to be the bloody, revolting IRA! However, despite his best efforts and those of his crew of fine detectives, the flimsy evidence collected was but a single step elevated from nonexistent. Frustrated, Chief Inspector Spencer verbally flogged his underlings at least three times a day; however, it brought no further results.

Spencer recalled the Caarson case. There were no known witnesses to the ceremonial hanging at the Oaks. A fragmented lead bullet had been recovered. However, ballistics doubted any match could be made, even if they had a gun, and they sure as hell didn't. Reaching the dead-end, which the Chief Inspector always encountered with the case, Spencer's mind homed in on the bombing of the Lambeg Drum. Again, there were no witnesses, no observed cars, and no threats—just bloody nothing! His investigators found only a few twisted steel fragments of what appeared to be flowerpot holders. These had no trademarks or fingerprints. That left him with what? Some 5000 anonymous suspects who knew how to use a welding torch! *Best chance of solving that one is a deathbed confession,* he concluded. Then, Spencer thought, *presuming the Queen's Ministers don't sack me long before some bastard decides to come clean as the death rattle starts.*

Now, one new problem blocked his path in the labyrinth, which confronted him the armored car robbery. *Perhaps, that will lead me out of this bloody Byzantine puzzle,* he thought before pulling the mental switch, which would send him down that track.

There were descriptions from the two surviving guards and a few passing motorists. A fat man, two brawny ones, a smaller rodent-like fellow, and a droop-sided, gangly-gawky one had been described. They all spoke with typical Fenian accents, just like thousands of others of their ilk. All had been masked, except for the dead one. However, he was no doubt well insulated under six feet of peat by now. "I suppose they'll dig him up sometime in 25,000 A.D. The archeologists will go wild and name him Londonderry man!"

They knew the tough guy had an American Garand, and the armor-piercing bullets that he fired passed through metal and flesh, then proceeded on their merry way. These were now as easy to find as one tuppence out in the brine somewhere between here and Nova Scotia. They say there is no perfect crime! Maybe that means an imperfect Chief Inspector investigated all the unsolved ones. "I could use a little bit of luck!"

Spencer's thoughts were interrupted by the mind-searing clamor of the telephone. *Another bloody fookin' complaining dignitary,* he thought with a grimace, as he reached for the phone. Relief registered over taut facial muscles, as the Chief Inspector realized it was only his wife calling. She complained that he hadn't been home for dinner in the past week. "Luck would have to wait." He was hungry and needed a few hours of respite, even in the company of an overly concerned spouse. Spencer knew she would be telling him her nagging was totally the result of concern for him! Though only partially true, Chief Inspector Spencer looked forward to seeing her as he headed out the door.

Late in the night, cobblestones resounded to the impact of two sets of leather heels. Thuds were measured, and the clicks gave rise to the impression of happy, fanciful feet. The sounds halted in front of Garrity's, then resumed again as the two entry steps were climbed in harmony. Their favorite table was found and occupied, and the coffee was quick in coming. On occasion, though busying himself with counting out the day's meager take, the old proprietor snatched a glance at the couple. With pleasure, he noted they were as enraptured as ever. As usual, Bernadette and Mickey's verbal exchanges were very personal but devoid of any reference to what official duties had kept them apart. Later, at the front of Bernie's residence, fervent kisses were exchanged. As he started to take leave, Mickey sensed the magnetism of her arms and eyes, which seemed to be pulling him toward her door. "Not yet Bernie, but someday not too far off!" That reply seemed enough to satisfy both for the moment.

Meanwhile, in Belfast, His Honor Sir Charles Collins had achieved eminence as one of the foremost justices of the Queen's Bench, a distinction afforded to few of the Roman faith. Along with the judicial trappings, he could afford a fine Victorian mansion on Malone Road staffed by proficient servants, plus a chauffeur-driven Jaguar sedan. Membership in all the right clubs had come his way and were used to proper advantage. Clarissa Collins was the quintessential jurist's wife and had few peers in how the role was played. None of their four children had followed in Sir Charles's legal footsteps. However, all had married well and achieved lucrative careers.

The sixty-five-year-old jurist was a model of achievement, as well as decorum. Some of his Protestant colleagues frequently wondered how Collins seemed to have no compassion whatsoever in handing down the hardest of sentences for Catholic malefactors over whose cases he presided. Obviously, no preference was shown to those of his own faith. In fact, the opposite was true. From time to time, His Honor had been the subject of vile threats issued by condemned criminals or vindictive relatives. But none had ever come to fruition. Since the last threat, considerable time had passed, and things seemed to be calm. Bodyguards, whom Sir Charles held in disdain, had been withdrawn some time ago.

Two members of the Collins household were creatures of habit. Sir Charles was first and foremost. Then, came Pandora, his full-sized white French poodle. At eight o'clock on a fine warm evening, the fair canine had laid her muzzle on his arm. This was a sure sign that her nightly perambulation at the heel alongside her master should begin. Strident barking followed to indicate Judge Collins should set aside his books and conform his schedule to hers.

"All right, you bloody beast! I'll get your lead, and you can start your promenade." Lady Collins looked up and smiled. Her Charles always went out of his way to please ladies of all species. Certainly, Clarissa had been indulged, and she harbored no jealously against her canine rival.

Once on the street, master and pet started on their familiar route. Shortly after, they encountered a very unfamiliar experience. Explosively, the door of a parked car opened, and a large figure clad in black erupted from the sedan. Judge Collins only had time to utter, "What the—" for the remainder of the sentence never left his lips.

Mickey knew the unsaid words would be "—hell is going on here?!" However, the words were irrelevant to Manion, as he knew precisely what was going on and why. Despite the fact Judge Collins was physically fit from many rounds of golf, sets of tennis, and weekend equestrian events, one hammer-like blow was sufficient to blacken the jurist's sensorium.

Pandora was no attack dog. Although she seemed upset by the intrusion into her routine, she displayed no belligerence, even when her unconscious master was dumped in the car. Then the door was swiftly closed. She stood for a while, looking after the disappearing car. Soon, it was gone. Like a jilted lover, she slowly trotted home, though not in such a hurry as to prevent investigation of intriguing scents along the way.

When Pandora finally arrived at the front door, she produced a series of harsh, unladylike barks that would alert all inside of her displeasure. Upon investigation of Pandora's barking, the maid quickly informed her mistress of the occurrence. Then, Clarissa Collins dispatched the butler, who returned thirty minutes later with no clue of the judge's whereabouts. Lady Collins's initial perturbation had changed to anguish.

Proper officials at the RUC were notified. The usual reassurances were offered. Search would commence immediately! Surely, His Honor would be found or show up soon, no worse for wear. Clarissa was devastated. Call were placed to her children, which produced nothing except further reassurances she did not need. *Time to turn to prayer,* she thought. *I'm out of the habit, but at least it's something I can do for Charlie.* On the way to find her rosary, she stopped to pet Pandora, who in her own canine conclusion had come to accept that something was indeed very wrong.

Mickey returned to Sweeney's and parked the car in the garage. Checking the judge, Manion determined he had a good, strong pulse and seemed to be breathing in a normal fashion. After securing his prisoner's wrists, Mickey hoisted the inert body over his shoulder and carried it to the empty storage room in the basement. Once inside, Manion lowered Collins to the floor before stepping back to assess the man's condition. "You'll have a mighty headache and a very sore jaw, Your Honor, but these will be the least of your problems."

When the man's hands had been untied, he seemed to stir a bit. This induced his captor to speed up the process with the aid of a bucket of water. Collins came awake; however, he remained in a dazed and befuddled state for a few more minutes. Finally, he was conscious enough to visualize his assailant and make a swift evaluation of the situation.

Glaring defiantly at Manion, the older man said, "Are you aware that you have accosted a Judge of the High Court and forcefully abducted him? If you have any wish not to rot behind bars for the rest of your life, then I suggest you release me immediately! That's the only way you will ever receive any possible clemency."

"You have it all wrong, Your Honor! You were never abducted. It's called taken into custody. Also, it's a shame you missed your trial. I held it while you were indisposed. However, awake or asleep, the verdict was a sure thing. I might add there was absolute legal precedence! You see I followed the exact same rules you did when you shipped me off to The Maze some eight-plus years ago."

Judge Collins eyed Manion defiantly. Weighing his options in regard to rushing him, Collins decided to play along with the charade in hopes of a better opportunity. However, the decision was instantly made for him when the Colt revolver appeared!

While the barrel and frame obscured two of the gun's chambers, four large-diameter bullets could be easily seen in the visible portions of the gun's cylinder. They seemed to stare back at Collins like small warheads peering out of silos. "So, what do you plan to do?" Collins said sternly, defiance still obvious in his tone.

With the muzzle of the gun concentrated on his prisoner, Mickey replied, "Stand up, Your Honor." When Collins was upright, Manion said, "Now peel off your fine, fancy duds, but leave your shorts on!"

"Go to hell," was the jurist's reply.

"All right, prisoner Collins, we'll play tough guy for a while." Manion's hand reached behind the chair he was sitting on and grasped a long length of radiator hose. Then he arose and moved toward the judge. Collins tried to ward off the blow but had no success in the effort. Mickey's blow with the heavy hose struck his back with great force. Screaming out in agony, the pain was sufficient to buckle his knees. "Last chance before the party really gets going, Your Honor!"

Defiance had evaporated from Collins. Now accepting the reality of submission, the frightened man divested himself of all but his undershorts. Mickey stood back and spoke. "Who said you can't teach an old dog new tricks? Now, get on your knees, prisoner." When his victim was positioned, Mickey intoned, "Charles Collins, for high crimes against the people of Ireland you are hereby sentenced to an indeterminate period of hard labor. In addition, the Court has determined that you have been a traitor to people of your own faith. Based on what some of them have suffered due to your perfidy special punishment will be meted out. Then, you can better appreciate the sorry circumstances of your victims. Are you surprised that a poor Paddy like me uses words like perfidy Your Honor? Well I learned that word and others when you had me paying tuition in one of your inhospitable palatial prisons. Michael Manion, age seventeen, sent up for four long years! Is it coming back to you? My dear mother scrubbed floors for nearly all of her adult life. Down on her knees, day after day, trying to help our little family eke out an existence. You pompous Brits and Brit sympathizers like yourself having decided that was the only work fitting for her."

Mickey stopped talking and tossed a piece of chalk to the kneeling judge. "Now, Prisoner Collins, take the chalk and draw a line on the concrete parallel to the walls. Go all the way around the room! Then, you move in one foot and start over again. If you are any good at all, you should end up in the center with a one-foot square."

Listening to the malevolent instructions and agonizingly aware of the leveled pistol, Mickey's prisoner did as he was told. However, by the time he reached the center of the floor, signs of discomfort were manifest. But he had no time for rest, as a full scrub bucket and brush were presented to him. "I'll be back in a few hours, Your Honor and I want all the chalk lines nicely scrubbed away! Incidentally, as soon as you complete your task, you'll be drawing new lines and starting all over. You'll keep it up until eight A.M. Then, I'll reward you with some fine rations. You can rest all the day until six P.M. tomorrow when you start the scrubbing once again."

Manion had arranged for a cot in his office. Though he found it an inconvenience to check his prisoner periodically, he was determined to mete out the sentence exactly as planned. Later, on one of his visits to the locked room, Collins was found sitting in a corner rubbing his reddened and abraded knees. However, at sight of the rubber truncheon, he was quickly back on all fours.

"Last warning, Your Honor, if I see you off your knees again during the work period, I'm going to really wail on you!" Collins's eyes were now pleading, though he said nothing. Manion locked the door and left. Upon return to his cot, he said to himself, "Six hours and he's a sniveling, broken man. I don't suppose he ever wondered what it was like at the Maze for four years. Well I had my go at it. I survived despite all the beatings and cruelty!" Then, exhausted, Manion fell asleep.

On his visit at six A.M., Mickey noted the jurist was doing his best to keep scrubbing; however, his efforts were severely diminished by pain and exhaustion. "You've done a decent job, Collins. But, you obviously don't have my Ma's stamina. She could go twelve hours straight without a whimper, at least until the consumption got her! She got sacked for being lazy. No one ever noted the bloody sputum she tried to hide in the rag she had for a handkerchief. Too bad that I don't have a few of her tubercle bacilli to blow your way judge! Well enough talk," said Mickey. Then, he placed a bowl in front of his kneeling prisoner.

Judge Charles Collins was revolted by the contents in the bowl—a large, blackened, and very moldy Irish potato. Collins averted his eyes. Manion spat out, "Not fine enough for the likes of you? Well that's your sustenance until you decide to eat it. However, I must warn you that it's in much better condition than it will be tomorrow or any days to follow. I'll let you off on your tatter for now, but I insist you have something to drink." As he passed the pint bottle of Poteen to his cowering prisoner, Mickey cocked his pistol, pressing it firmly against the judge's eye. "Drink it, Your Honor, it will chase the demons away and help you sleep. My Da found it to be a great comfort as he tried to get by under Britannia's loving rule."

Retching and gagging, Collins finally emptied the bottle's contents. Soon, he was too drunk to remain awake and gradually slumped to the floor. "Sleep well, Your Honor, you'll need your rest. You start scrubbing again in ten hours." Then, Mickey relocked the door. He was confident his prisoner would cause no commotion, especially one that could be heard in the noisy garage.

As predicted, there had been no sound arising from the temporary dungeon to raise suspicion that an inmate was held therein. When the day's work was complete and his crew departed, Mickey noted with some relief that Walsh and Moriarity seem jovial once more. Also, Brophy gave the appearance of pulling out of the emotional tailspin that had begun at the time of the heist. *Probably a good time to pick up a paper,* he thought. *I'll catch up on the news before I attend to his magnificence.* When Mickey arrived, the kiosk was deserted apart from the vendor, who was already in the act of closing up. Only a few papers remained. Though the information would have already turned stale for the majority of Belfast's citizens, it was still fresh to Manion. Headlines blared out: "HIGH COURT JUSTICE MISSING."

After purchasing a newspaper, Manion returned to his office. He noted that below the headlines there were printed some details and considerable speculation the reporters had been able to gather. Included were, "Wife and family mystified. Hospitals and morgue checked. Police mount massive search. No ransom note or calls received. Suicide thought unlikely. RUC say kidnapping must be considered!" Mickey dismissed all that had to do with the eminent Charles Collins's biography as well as statements by colleagues, friends, associates, and pastor. However, a picture of the local bishop along with a request asking everyone to pray for Collins did catch his attention! Manion said aloud, "A lot of good that will do." Also, he noted that the armored car robbery was allotted only back pages and listless description.

Though he was not a man given to gloating, Mickey was pleased but aware things could sour. Possibly, tomorrow's headlines could be reporting his capture. *Well at least there will be no photo of His Excellency, Bishop McCartney praying for me,* he thought.

Putting down the newspaper, Mickey decided it was time to check on his prisoner. Cautiously, he unlocked the door murmuring, "The bastard may be tougher than I thought, and he could try and jump me." However, it was a needless worry. Groans indicated that life remained a factor, although not readily evident from the body, face down on the concrete. Pistol at the ready, Manion nudged the inert form with his foot. This produced a few more groans but no additional sign of viability. Fortunately, Sweeney had seen fit to put a water spigot in the basement, so a couple of buckets of water were easily filled. Cascading cold water produced unequivocal moments of return to a semblance of cognitive function in Collins.

"All right, Your Honor, up on your knees like a good scrubwoman. It's time to lay down the chalk lines and then make them go away! You managed four rounds last night, but we'll be pushing for six tonight. Ma could easily have done twelve."

Looking up, the judge whispered, "I'm sorry, I just can't."

Mickey didn't reply. Instead, he pushed the judge's face below the surface of the water in the second bucket. Then, he held it there until he counted forty-five. On release, Collins gasped for air. He struggled to replace the carbon dioxide, which his body had accumulated, with the oxygen so desperately needed.

The process had barely begun when Mickey said, "Time to go bobbing again."

Terrified, Collins gasped out, "No! No! Please, I'll try!"

"See, all you needed, Charlie old sod, was a little incentive. Here's a new piece of chalk for you, and we have an endless supply of water. All that's needed is more enthusiasm on your part." Then, Mickey, adding exclamation to his order, employed a heavy kick to Collins's flank. Prisoner Collins's ordeal began again.

"Don't forget, Your Honor, we are going for the big six tonight. Don't let the team down!" At this moment, Mickey thought the sight of the Judge would be pitiful to most but not to him, as he had endured as much and more! Retribution in kind was neither cruel nor unusual, was his conclusion.

Chapter Sixteen

⌘ ⌘ ⌘

By the start of his second week of captivity, many changes were evident in prisoner Collins. Driven by hunger, he had gnawed on some of the blackened, rotten potatoes. As Mickey could judge from Collins's emesis, they weren't retained for long and were mixed with purplish clots. Manion realized these attested to the caustic affect of the Poteen on the stomach lining. Also, he noted that hours of scrubbing the floor on hands and knees had left Collins with torn nails and bleeding fingers. Septic sores covered both knees. Any scabs that formed were quickly abraded away. The anesthetic effect of the Poteen was diminishing. Therefore, the prisoner's desire for more was increasing steadily. Collins reached greedily for each new bottle and rapidly consumed the contents.

When day twelve arrived, Mickey sat on a chair and watched the judge purge another Poteen bottle of its contents. "You are a sociophysiologic wonder, Charlie! I'm afraid you've gone a bit past social drinking. What do you think they would say if I drove you over to the Country Club? You're catching up on my Da—almost to the same level he was when he died. However, you're lucky you don't even have to buy it. Poor old Da had to steal the money from my Ma to get his bottle. Look at yourself, man! That's the worst case of housemaid's knees I ever saw. Charlie, you should take a bath now and then. Much as I like to visit you, the stench is getting to me. If we stuck you back on the bench, you would clear the courtroom fast. I'm beginning to feel sorry for you, Your Honor. In fact, I've brought you a gift." Mickey tossed a crumpled suit of clothes on the floor in front of Collins's face. "It's my old freedom suit, Your Honor! I got it when I graduated from the Maze. Now put it on and we'll see if you don't look and feel much better."

Judge Collins's only response was to take another long pull on the bottle. Snatching it away, Mickey commanded, "Put it on, damn it, or your face will be kissing the mop bucket!"

Slowly, Collins donned the disheveled suit, which was several sizes too large. "Much too big, Judge, so we'll shrink it up a bit." Mickey grabbed a bucket of water and flung it full force into the Judge's face. "There, now give it a few days and your suit will look like it was tailored just for you." Not responding, Collins just knelt there staring at the Poteen bottle, which Mickey held in his hand. Then, he started licking his lips and finally extended a tremulous hand toward the bottle. Manion pulled it away, saying, "Not yet, Charlie, there's an old game I saw my Da play several times. I remember him being on a big binge, and he dropped his bottle. Next thing I knew, he was down on his hands and knees, just like you, licking the Poteen off the floor." Manion dropped the bottle, and he was not surprised to see the Judge trying to lick up the spilled contents. He shouted back, "Don't cut your tongue on the glass, Your Honor!" Then, he went out and locked the door.

When the evening of day fourteen arrived, Manion returned once more to the basement. Unlocking and opening the door, he observed His Honor High Court Justice Charles Collins curled up on the floor in a fetal position, flanked by two empty whiskey bottles. Prisoner Collins had been totally incontinent, and the old suit was befouled by urine, feces, and vomit. Fighting back a rising tide of nausea, Mickey looped a rope under Collins's shoulders. Then, he dragged the judge up the stairs and dumped his unconscious body atop a tarp in the boot of a sedan. Jolting action was enough to partially revive the prisoner, who started murmuring, "I need a drink, please I beg you, give me a drink!"

"No need Charlie, I'm setting you free. You can celebrate later on." Manion's words seemed to penetrate the alcoholic fog. Seemingly, there appeared to be a minute residual of his sensorium still capable of grasping the implication. For the first time since Collins's abduction and two weeks of utter debasement, a spark of hope emerged. Manion heard the word "free" repeated several times before he closed the boot lid.

Mickey parked the car in the place he had previously scouted and selected. A moderate degree of rain was falling, so the black slicker he put on was appropriate to the conditions. Next, a black knit cap followed and rubberized gloves. Then he was ready. When Manion opened the boot, Judge Collins was more alert than he had been for many days. Befuddled, he kept murmuring "free" with an occasional "thank God!" The thought alone was enough to stimulate him to try and help get out of the boot. With Mickey's assistance, he managed to become semi-erect and capable of slow, faltering steps for a short distance. Going agonizingly slow, at last they reached the abutment of an overpass. Mickey halted, and Collins murmured, "Free, free, why stop?"

"They'll pick you up any minute, Your Honor," softly retorted Manion. Two minutes passed, and Collins was becoming agitated. But, in his present condition, his movements were ineffectual.

"Here they come, Charlie! Can you hear them?" Despite his obtunded condition, Judge Collins was able to discern a sound, which rapidly increased in volume.

Some primordial center within Collins's brain was able to decipher the sound as an approaching tram. "Why put me on a bus?" he slurred.

"You're not going on the bus, Charlie. You're going in front of it," whispered Manion.

Immediately, every vestige of alcoholic fog evaporated from Collins's brain. "No! No! For the love of God, I've got a wife," begged the judge.

"I don't believe in God, Your Honor! So, what I do or not do isn't for the love of Him. It's for little Sean, me brother who some rich Brit bastard drove over in his fookin' Bentley. The RUC didn't even bother to look for the fooker. They just came to pick up the body."

Judge Collins screamed out, "Think of the law!"

"I did," replied Mickey. "Hammurabi's Law—an eye for an eye and a tooth for a tooth!" Now, the bus was just yards away.

Initially, the driver of the heavy tram saw nothing, but he would never be free of the sickening sound of the impact. To the police, he could only describe it as "like a huge pumpkin dropped from a great height, then exploding on the concrete!" As the body flew forward in reaction to the violent force of the great mass of the bus, he saw the victim's face illuminated in the headlights! Truly an image from Hell, it was burned into the surface of his mind's eye.

Shaken by the experience, the driver continued that "if you look directly into the sun, it sears your retina, and you are forever blind!" Having looked at an image far worse than the sun, he would never have the comfort of being blinded from the sound and sight. He would never escape from either. When the tram jolted, after colliding with the man, he was aware a wheel had passed over the body. If there was any cause for relief in the driver's plight, it was the fact he never had to look under the bus.

Judge Charles Collins's devastated body had made its way to the Coroner's Office, where Dr. Clifford Lewis, the Duty Autopsy Surgeon, confronted it. Leaning against a stark, white tile wall, Diener Jack Ross was awaiting the physician's response. Dr. Lewis was a well-trained forensic pathologist. Thus, he was subject to encountering human bodies or pieces thereof in all manner of condition and state of decay. However, he had never managed the degree of complacency found in most of his confreres. Today was no exception, and Ross took unrestrained delight seeing the physician grimace as he pulled back the sheet exposing the judge's remains.

"Good God!" exclaimed Dr. Lewis. "Buzzards wouldn't bother with this one. At least, you could have hosed him off, Jack," continued Dr. Lewis.

"Come on, Doc, you know there aren't any buzzards in Ireland. The great St. Patrick chased them all away along with the snakes. Besides, if I had cleaned him all up, you would have chewed me out for washing away vital evidence. I felt all queasy just taking off his clothes, and I needed time to recover well didn't I?"

"Sure, Jack, your ratio of recovery to work runs about four to one. Did you find anything in his clothes?"

"Sure, rolls of 100 pound notes and a will leaving it all to me."

"Damn it, Jack, grow up will you? I would like an answer!"

"Well I haven't yet but I will," complained Ross.

"Then get at it and do a careful search," replied Dr. Lewis.

Ross shuffled off, and then turned saying "Maybe he was a KGB spook. Shall I call MI-6 if I find out his name is Dimitri?"

"Just get the hell out of here and do what I asked," hissed Dr. Lewis. Then he added, "Find Abbot and send him in here to give me a hand. I've had enough of you for the day."

"Touchy touchy," replied the retreating assistant.

Also a Diener, Carey Abbot was one with a professional demeanor. "Good morning Dr. Lewis," were his first words. Immediately, Dr. Lewis felt more relaxed, replying, "Good morning, Carey. Do you know anything about this man?"

"Yes, sir he was hit and then run over by a tram on its last run of the night. He must have died instantly. Also, I suspect he was a heavy drinker. His blood alcohol was above 0.3 and certainly his look and aroma would point to the fact he was a derelict."

Dr. Lewis started dictating his observations into a suspended microphone. "White male approximate age of sixty, height seventy-one inches, weight 165 pounds. Body appears better nourished than I would expect in a chronic alcoholic of long standing. There are no spider telangliectasis to suggest cirrhosis. Nor is there any indication of jaundice, which might stem from hepatic disease." Dr. Lewis continued on to describe in full detail all the external injuries and deformities, which had surely occurred due to the initial impact from the tram, then saying "the subsequent trauma was incident to the secondary impact of the body with the street." Finally, "the massive changes were wrought by the tram's heavy wheels passing over the man's chest."

"This is interesting," said Dr. Lewis softly.

"What is that sir?" replied Diener Abbot.

"Well there is little skin left on either knee, and it surely appears there are chronic abrasions and infected ulcerations. Coupled with that both the finger and toe tips are all abraded and the nails cracked and worn down! For some reason, I don't understand, this man spent a lot of time on his hands and knees. He couldn't have been wearing shoes, or his toes wouldn't look like this. Find Ross and see if the knees in the man's pants are worn away then get back here."

With his assistant temporarily gone, Dr. Lewis gingerly pulled back the lips of his subject. Though a number of teeth had been avulsed by the multiple impacts the body had suffered, many were left intact. Dr. Lewis was astonished at the remarkable state of repair, despite the fulsome condition of the oral cavity in general. "You are not the usual derelict," he murmured to the corpse.

Abbot had not yet returned, so Dr. Lewis decided to use the saw and remove the calvarium from the cadaver. Soon, a problem arose due to the extensive fragmentation of the skull. However, he finally succeeded, and the brain was exposed. As Dr. Lewis expected, much of the brain was reduced to pulp. Furthermore, there were no signs of cerebral atrophy inconsistent with the man's estimated age and certainly no indications of alcoholic encephelopathy in portions left intact. He found no surprises in the thoracic cavity. Ribs, heart, great vessels, and lungs had responded to the weight of the tram, which had been transferred through one heavy wheel to the body pinned underneath. His abdomen was of more interest. Surely, signs of trauma were ubiquitous, but there was no gross indication of cirrhosis. On the other hand, the pancreas was edematous and inflamed. There were definite signs of acute pancreatitis, and these were surely commensurate with the changes of acute, hemorrhagic gastritis starkly evident when the stomach was opened. No doubt, Dr. Lewis surmised, the microscopic evidence gathered from tissue samples that he removed would provide additional information. But, for now, Dr. Lewis was sure he was standing on the edge of a mystery hoping to be able to peer inside and provide answers.

As he pondered the riddles, the forensic pathologist's contemplation was interrupted by Abbot's boisterous return. "Sorry for the delay, Dr. Lewis. It was that wretched Ross. He wasn't where he should have been, so I went looking for him. Finally, I tracked him down to the furnace room! The wretch had already burned the clothes, but I caught him red-handed going through this!" Abbot's extended hand held a fine Moroccan leather wallet in pristine condition. "That bastard Jack said he was planning on giving it to you, but frankly, I doubt he was!

I presumed you would want him turned over to security, Doctor, so that is where the son of a bitch is now."

"Thank you, Carey! I'm not really surprised about Ross. Hopefully, we can now sack him and get his sorry ass out of here." As he finished his statement, Dr. Lewis opened the wallet. The name on the driver's license matched the embossed initials CPC, which stood for Charles Perceval Collins.

Nearby, Chief Inspector Merlin Spencer carefully replaced the telephone on its cradle. All his best efforts at composure were necessary to accomplish the task in such a fashion given his present temperament. Much more satisfying would be to smash the receiver on the desktop, then stomp the cradle into oblivion. Phone calls from all levels of the pecking order above that of Chief Inspector had relentlessly continued to harass and abuse him. In his twenty-plus years as a policeman, he could think of no parallel. The desultory voice of Ulster's top cop had just informed Spencer that London had decided to intervene unless real results were forthcoming. Forty-eight hours was the mandate! The high-bred voice, gilt-edged with an Eton inflection, had even asked if he had considered retirement. "No, sir," was his reply. The response received was "Perhaps you should!"

"I can't even work on the damn case," was Spencer's bitter assessment, directed solely to himself. Loosening his tie, he let his body sink back in the chair. Spencer decided that he couldn't and wouldn't let the bastards grind him down. "Illigitimi non carborundurn est," as the Romans would have said.

Shortly, thereafter, a figure appeared in the Chief Inspector's doorway. It was one he knew well, for they had started out together as foot patrolmen or bobbies. They were comrades and had all the characteristics of good policemen should possess. One had more knowledge in some areas, while the other was more proficient in others. When summed up, both Chief Inspector Merlin Spencer and Chief Inspector Paul Foster were outstanding in their chosen fields. Seeing Foster entering his office uplifted the spirits of his friend.

"I've joined your selective little club, Merlin! As you know, I was assigned Judge Collins's case and produced no results and made no arrests. Now, His Honor's body has turned up in the morgue. Kidnapping, torture, and murder is the verdict from atop the totem pole. To make things worse, the last phone call I got insinuated the judge would have been rescued alive if I had done my job. So, the two of us, hopelessly cursed with all the inabilities known to man, appear to be solely responsible for all the unsolved crimes in Ulster. Maybe I should hand in my badge fully addressed with the place I would like them to insert it!"

Spencer smiled at his friend saying, "Yes! Paul, you've joined my club, which seems to be a two-man Legion of the Damned. Well, my friend, I say we both hang in there and hang together. Every one of their damned leprechauns can't be lucky forever. These Paddies made a mistake somewhere, and we're the ones who will find it sooner than some haughty bastards from London!"

At least on the surface, this seemed to give them both a bounce. They shook hands and exchanged a couple of playful punches. Then they went back to try and glean even a hint of a clue from the pitiful evidence gathered to date.

Later, on his way out well past usual hours, Chief Inspector Spencer was surprised to encounter a very red-faced Sergeant. He was wiping tears from his cheeks, as he sought in vain to quell his tumultuous laughter. Another patrolman, who had been laughing just as hard, caught sight of the Inspector. Shock short-circuited whatever impulses had given rise to the unfettered manifestations of humor. He abruptly came to attention! The Sergeant followed soon after, as embarrassment replaced glee.

"What's so damn funny Hicks?" Chief Inspector Spencer asked sternly.

"I'm sorry, sir, but Richards here told me he ran into the greengrocer. You know, sir, the one whose lorry the Paddies stole for the bombing. At any rate, the man said it had never run so fine in all the years he had it. Then, the poor fellow said it would be wonderful if they would steal it on an annual basis. I guess it struck us as funny, Chief Inspector." Hicks was about to start laughing again; however, the hard gaze of his superior quickly aborted that.

"Hicks! Get that damn lorry back in here, and get the one from the armored car robbery as well!" Spencer realized they had meticulously combed the inside and outside of both vehicles looking for prints, though no one ever thought to look really hard beneath the bonnet. An old vehicle that runs better than it ever had must have been professionally serviced. You could wear gloves, so as not to leave prints on the dash or steering wheels. But how many mechanics wore them while working on the motors? Would there be a similar anecdote from the owner of the second lorry? Time would tell. Maybe the leprechauns' luck was running out after all.

Soon, in the RUC garage, the greengrocer's old lorry occupied center stage. Quickly, it was surrounded by a large cast of sweating, silently swearing mechanics, fingerprint specialists, and other various forensic types. Each individual was doing his utmost to appear totally engrossed, while doing all possible to avoid collision with his colleagues. They all hoped to take on the mantle of Sherlock Holmes and be able to say, "Look at this, dear Watson," or in this case "Spencer." Meticulous in their work, they all hoped to find the clue that others had missed. In reality, they were convinced nearly to a man that it was a wild goose chase with the chaos of a Chinese fire drill. The first few hours had been wild enough. But it became much worse after the key man had approached the Chief Inspector with negative results and a chorus of "Sorry, sir, didn't find anything, don't think there is much more we can do, sir!" As for Spencer, who sat backward astride a chair with his arms resting on the back, these were excuses and not statements of fact.

Realizing he was only forty hours short of the end of his career and possibly on the brink of forced retirement, Inspector Spencer had but one response, which was stated in the harshest of terms and voice strident emphasis. "Then, take the damn thing apart piece by bloody piece!" The men felt like they were dealing with a creature possessed, and they were on the inside of the gates of Hell. All knew there would be no escape until the lorry was reduced to an amorphous pile of parts. Their dismal judgment had been rendered by the Chief Inspector!

Three hours later, Nugent gave vent to an epithet when he envisioned a couple of telltale smudges on the undersurface of the rotor cap. Crimmons, a fingerprint analyst, added several expletives of his own as he carefully examined the finds. Then, he opined, "Yes, they were made by fingers. But, the details are so poor that it was a million to one they could ever be matched with any reliability."

Nonetheless, Crimmons would take all the component parts to the lab and study them with every means at his disposal. However, he had no reason to believe this would achieve anything. Rather, it was a good ploy to extricate him from the scalding cauldron in which they were all emerged. On the way out, Crimmons imagined how wonderful it would be if he could volunteer to take them to MI-5 Headquarters in London. Better yet, deliver them to the FBI in America to see if they could come up with something. "Oh well," he decided. "Much better 100 yards away in another building than continue to stand helpless in front of Spencer's glaring eyes!"

For reasons they didn't fully understand, even in retrospect, the mechanics had started on top of the engine rather than on the bottom. Close on to midnight, some of the crew who had vacuumed the inside of the lorry cab for the sixth time or gone over the bed an equal number of times, reported once again to Spencer. "We got a few hairs. a couple of fibers. and a few fragments of dried vegetation. We can catalog it all and maybe something will turn up we can tie it into! But that's about all we can do, sir, as God is our judge."

Truly depleted, the air of the crew's resignation was palpable. Also, Spencer was encountering the ebb of his own tide of enthusiasm. He had expected the receding waters to expose all the rocks and reefs of uncertainty, which had torn into the soft underbelly of his already weakened self-confidence. Then, suddenly, there were more expletives! Nugent emerged from underneath the lorry on a mechanic's creeper. What appeared to be bona fide fingerprints in the relatively weak light of his mechanic's torch seemed to stand out vividly under the brighter incandescence of the workshop's overhead fixtures. Nugent didn't bother to get up but chose to propel himself recumbent to the Chief Inspector's feet.

"I think that I truly found something, sir. Have a look at these!" There on the edge of the oil pan in a spot free of heavy oil accumulations and dirt were what surely seemed to be distinct whorls and lines. To the naked eye, they really appeared to be distinguishable prints!

With all the care that might be accorded a hot bottle of nitroglycerin on a rock-strewn road the evidence was carried to the lab. "Prints confirmed, damn good ones at that! Who the hell they belong to, we don't know but I'll break my arse trying to find out," was the enthusiastic response of Crimmons. "I'll start right now, Inspector," he added. "If nothing turns up by dawn, there will be a fresh crew in, and they can work them until I get back." Fervor in Crimmons became a communicable fever! Everyone seemed to have regained his enthusiasm. As quickly as Spencer's own tide had ebbed, it now surged again, covering all the rocks and reefs exposed such a short time ago.

On the next morning, just as Chief Inspector Spencer was drawing his crew into a huddle preparatory to a "good work lads" speech, a patrolman entered the room. "Beggin' your pardon, sir, but some fellow named Crimp is here to inquire if he can get his lorry?"

Spencer looked pensive, then smiled, "Tell the good man he can have it now if he wants to haul it away in a wheelbarrow! Otherwise, it will be sometime bloody next week." Those words were the tonic that his men needed far better than a pep talk. Happy faces appeared all around. Grins were broader when he dismissed them for the day with orders to "sleep in a couple of extra hours." Then they could better face the reassembly of the dismantled lorry. Now was not a propitious time to tell them about the second lorry from the bank car robbery, which might arrive any time.

Chapter Seventeen

Mickey's interest in the wares of the kiosk completely subsided after purchasing a newspaper, which detailed the funeral of High Court Judge Charles P. Collins on the front page. In reading the edition, Manion purposely bypassed the captioned photo of the grieving widow in mourning attire. The cardinal was consoling her, up from Dublin for the service. Mrs. Collins was pictured surrounded by adult sons and daughters accompanied by in-laws and a considerable number of grandchildren. All faces bore strained lines of grief. On several, a handkerchief could be seen dabbing at the lachrymal manifestation of profound sorrow. Mickey thought, *I've had my sorrows, too, and they have all been borne without any eminence providing a shoulder to cry on. A Paddy's tears were simply salt water running down the gutters of his checks!*

On page two of the newspaper, there was a long list of the dignitaries in attendance at Judge's Collins's funeral service. These were classically listed in order of rank and importance. Mickey reflected, "How different from my little brother, Sean, and my baby sister, Maureen. Da and me carried the little pine boxes with Ma walking behind, sobbing her heart out. Not a soul outside the family attended, but Father McGuire with all his pious intonations and rubbish about God's will. Some God! That would let a Bentley-driving Prod fooker smash a beautiful little boy's body. When Ma died, Father McGuire managed to get six parish volunteers to pack her to the graveyard. However, by the time Ma got away, the consumption had her so emaciated they hardly needed six pallbearers. I could have probably carried the coffin by myself. I would have preferred that to six strangers who came on like a half-dozen Simons of Cyrene!"

Mickey recalled bitterly that instead of helping to bear his mother's coffin, he had to half-carry his blind-drunk Da. Then, he remembered the ignominious halting of the pitiful procession, so Da could vomit up his ration of Poteen and half his stomach lining. However, when it finally came his father's turn to die, he had his fellow IRA Volunteers hoist the box along with himself. They got the job done, without Father McGuire! There was no further need of the reverend's soliloquies concerning the will of God. Then, Mickey had two more irreverent though not disparate thoughts as he tossed the newspaper in a trash bin.

First of Mickey's irreverence's concerned Father McGuire. *It's too bad old Father McGuire didn't byline all the crime stories for the newspapers and wire services. Then, instead of proclaiming 'IRA Terrorists Suspect,' they would all simply read 'Police Place All Blame on God's Will.'* Mickey's second reflection was, *If the SOB in the Bentley was an instrument of the Divine, then why the hell can't I be one?* These two thoughts provided fodder for his inner humor, little jokes he could enjoy all by himself. Shortly after, as he turned the key in Sweeney's door lock, Mickey's mind was presented with a mental image of a massive blast leveling the cathedral and burying all the dignitaries in the rubble. *Now that would be a fine example of all God's will occurring in just the right place and time.*

Hearing him laugh, a passerby could only wonder what was so funny about opening a door. Quickly, Mickey entered the garage. After tossing his cap on his desk, Manion allowed himself one last reflection. "If the so-called Almighty is going 'to will' something, I wish he would make it easier for His helpers like me to accomplish our part!" Then, he envisioned the difficulty in blowing up the cathedral, especially in view of the extreme security. "Easier to tow a Howitzer into Buckingham Palace and through the door to Lizzie's bedchamber," he concluded. These produced another laugh heard only by him, thus free of interpretation by any interloper.

Daily work at Sweeney's had been going well. On one of his rare visits to the garage, the kind old owner congratulated Mickey on his managerial skills. As usual, he asked no questions pertinent to extracurricular business. Seemingly, a record number of repairs had been done the preceding month. Records indicated there would be even more vehicles "limping in and leaping out."

Despite a limited and deficient education, Manion had taken on the bookkeeping with a high degree of proficiency. So far, Brophy had remained an enigma, while Moriarity and Walsh were steadfast and natural acting as always. However, something about Tom left Manion uneasy. Brophy seemed much like a painting on a wall that appeared slightly canted. Manion felt left with the feeling that you should view it from different angles. If the picture truly proved to be askew, and you were possessed of even the slightest degree of obsession and compulsion, then you had to straighten it. Pictures were easy. Volunteers in the

IRA were tough. If someone were truly off-kilter, you didn't change picture hangers or the center of gravity on the wire. No, you killed them! That's all there was to it.

In the following weeks, Manion met twice with Hogan and Frank McGann. Word had come down from on high to cool it for a while. The hornet's nest had been deeply disturbed by the hanging of Caarson, the bombing of the Lambeg Drum, and the armored car robbery and murders. Now, they were even more angered by the presumed kidnapping and assassination of High Court Judge Charles Collins! In some respects, the IRA leadership was as mystified by the Collins case as was the RUC.

McGann was and remained closer to Manion than any other higher-echelon men in the pro-Ireland organization. He alone suspected that Manion was responsible for whatever had occurred to the magistrate. This intuition McGann kept to himself. He feared that the council, if made suspicious of Mickey's involvement, might decide that he was a loose cannon in need of restraint. Under such circumstances, restraint meant extermination!

Meanwhile, Hogan's personal animus toward his lieutenant persisted unabated since their heated exchange some weeks back. However, the pragmatic side of the pub-owner realized Manion was a valuable asset not to be wasted. Also, there were smaller jobs of the kind that didn't generate headlines, especially if they occurred to a Fenian. In these, Mickey was called on to play the enforcer on many occasions. However, his activities did not exceed a couple of knee cappings to those whose militancy in the Cause was under question.

After a light supper, Mickey returned to the garage. He could pace around in it without need of concern that his feet impacting on the thin floor of his room would enrage the tenant underneath, provoking him into pounding on the ceiling. For some inexplicable reason, Manion had decided long ago that meaningful thought relied on motion. Perhaps coming down on his feet juggled the thought loose. This was another example of Mickey's humor.

After taking a few steps, Bernadette came to mind. How many times had he seen her? Thirty or thirty-five, max! Mickey knew that he wanted more than a kiss at the door. But was he really ready to get married or enter some kind of relationship that would produce the desired level of intimacy? Three tours of the garage floor later, Mickey conceded he was terribly naive in worldly things. It wasn't about sexual matters. "I didn't grow up in a one-bedroom flat and remain ignorant of those events." He recalled feigning sleep and watching his parents, or at least watching them before the TB bug and the Poteen bottle stifled any desire.

Pragmatic considerations were these: "Could we ever move in together without producing some sort of certificate to the snoop who collected the rent?" Mickey had never even known of anyone who had not married in the Catholic Church. Did the Prods even give licenses or perform the rituals for Paddies? He had no desire to have a priest tie the knot and assumed the same held true for Bernadette.

After a couple tours more, suddenly, another thought emerged. *Did the beautiful Bernadette even want to live with him? Maybe she just wanted a fling!* Looking at the clock, Mickey realized it was time to pick her up at the restaurant. He would approach the subject when they stopped for coffee. Mickey's pacing stopped when he reached his office and grabbed his cap. "Damn it, if I can successfully hold up an armored car, I should be able to convince Bernie to live with me one way or another!"

That night, when Bernie made her egress from Brennan's Restaurant, Mickey was there holding a bouquet. Twice as large as usual, and she wondered what it might portend. Momentary distraction did not keep Bernie from noticing that Mickey was wearing new clothes and shoes. Thus, she gave an appropriate compliment but continued the speculation already unleashed. Mickey presented her with the flowers and took her arm. Then they made straight way for Garrity's coffee shop, which remained their destination of choice.

Mickey's new shoes squeaked, though he seemed oblivious, and Bernadette made no comment. Once ensconced at their little table near the rear, they remained silent for a time, apart from thanking the proprietor for the coffee. Manion reached for her hands, found them, then looked into her eyes. "I've been thinking Bernie," he said.

"I hope so," she replied.

"What does that mean?" Mickey shot back.

"Well if you didn't think, Michael Manion, you would be a vegetable, and I couldn't imagine you in that capacity."

Instantaneously, the comment struck Mickey as an insult, and his ire started to rise. First, he blurted out, "You mean like some bloody carrot ready to be tossed into the stew!" Then, he noticed the sparkle in the blue eye, and the mischief in the green one. Any hostility on his behalf evaporated.

Bernie smiled saying, "Thinking of what?"

"Well us," came the response.

"Well us what?" Bernie questioned.

Mickey hesitated, then said, "Well us joining together like man and wife."

Bernie's hands retracted swiftly, and the motion startled Mickey. When their eyes again found each other, Bernie portrayed a quizzical expression. "Is this a proposal or a proposition Mickey?" she said soulfully.

"It's a proposal damn it," came the response.

"I'm glad for that," were Bernadette's next words. She followed with,

"However, there are things I feel that you should know. Deep in my heart, Mickey, I have the feeling that you are very deep into serious matters with the IRA ,and I think I have the right to know."

Mickey took her hands back into his, saying, "You have the right to know that I love you. The rest shouldn't matter! You do things for the Cause, and I'm not asking you about that."

"Oh! Mickey, for God's sake! I deliver a few messages here and there, drop off an occasional gun but that's petty stuff."

Manion's face steeled, and the next words had a degree of sharpness. "Bernie, what I have done and will do, you are better off not to know. Can't you just cherish and be happy with the things we can share and leave the rest alone?" Mickey could sense that she was coming to terms with a degree of surrender regarding the implications of his words.

However, her capitulation was not complete, for she said, "I must have at least one question answered. That is, could a bullet or prison bars someday come between us?"

He felt compelled to answer, "Yes, Bernie, they could."

This was a reply that caused dismay. Bernie's shoulders sagged slightly. A tear formed in each eye. She fought to maintain its precarious position on the parapet of each soft lower lid before it was displaced by others competing for the same limited space. *Life is a roulette wheel,* she thought. *Spin it enough times, and the ball will ultimately end on double zero. Well I don't know how many days or years I'll get to play, but I'll leave all my bets on the table. I may lose sooner or later! However, at least I can live out the rest of my days in the knowledge I enjoyed the richest of days at one time.*

Immediately the little cascade of falling tears halted, and a smile was kindled. "Yes! I'll marry you, Mickey Manion, and I do mean *marry!* I plan to have your babies some day, and I'll not be birthing any bastards."

A smile lit Mickey's face, and he exclaimed, "Great! How do we do it?"

Bernadette was astonished. "How do we do what?" she cried out in a voice loud enough to cause Garrity to loose count of the day's proceeds.

Mickey was taken aback, then, finally stammered, "Well, given my lack of love for the Church, we can't go there. So, how do we get it done?"

"Michael Manion, you are a lovable but sometimes childish man! Did it ever occur to you that despite a Protestant form of apartheid that a couple of ex-RC could get married in a legal ceremony? In fact, you may do the same thing in the south." Bernie continued on asking, "When is this to take place?"

Having Bernadette acquiesce so suddenly left Mickey unnerved. He would have liked to respond, "In a year or so," however, he knew that would put her in a state of extreme pique. Therefore, Mickey decided on a month, thinking it could no doubt be stretched a bit. Currently, there were no assignments from McGann of which he was aware. However, there was one more personal project, which he needed desperately to complete. It could be done in thirty days, he was sure. Mickey's reply finally came, "We should be able to go ahead within a month."

Bernadette was ecstatic, exclaiming, "I'm not sure how long we'll journey through life together, Mickey, but it's a trip I want to start as soon as we can." She leaned across the small table and kissed him fervently. Glancing over at the couple, Mr. Garrity felt fulfilled, though he had not done particularly well at the till that day. Watching their joyous departure, then, noticing the fabulous one-pound-note tip didn't hurt a bit either.

When it came to falling asleep, Mickey's proposal and its ramifications produced no insomnia in the male half of the Manion and Donahue duo. Conversely, he awoke earlier than usual. Much like a heavy imbiber with a hangover, Mickey's morning arousal was in a state of confusion, as he tried to recall exactly to what he had committed himself. By the time Manion passed the kiosk and had taken note of the complacency present, things seemed well sorted out. Yes there had been a promise of a month, but months were made of days, and forty-five of those weren't much more than thirty, at least from his perspective. As for Bernadette, he couldn't imagine someone who would marry you in one month but back out in one and a half months or even two months. Something could always crop up with the IRA. That was for sure.

More important to Manion at this time was his unrequited desire for further personal revenge. To a degree, the business with the judge had assuaged his vindictiveness. However, it would never be completely expunged until the score was settled with the three guards at the Maze that he loathed the most. Manion felt this trio had gone far past the line in brutality and needed to perform some suitable expiation. Considerable thought had been given as to how, when, and where. Certainly, it couldn't be like the penance enacted on the judge. What he had decided on would be worse, in all likelihood. At least worse if it were done in the way Manion planned. He hoped the whole scheme would provide a high probability that the three guards would suffer greatly for a long period of time—perhaps for the rest of their lives.

Manion had considered many options, including tracking the scum down and smashing into them with a car or trying to put a bullet in their spines. However, such attempts carried a high risk of apprehension for the perpetrator. Hitting a target with a rifle at long range could result in instant death rather than the prolonged suffering that he desired. Since firearms captivated Mickey, he had done extensive reading on the subject and had discovered the shotgun.

Due to his interest in the shotgun, Mickey became very familiar with all the nuances regarding gauges, chokes, size of shot, and the ballistic characteristics inherent in the diameter of the pellets. From his studies, Manion had reached the conclusion that a standard twelve-gauge's load of one and one-fourth ounce of number 2 shot would have a tight pattern of about thirty inches in diameter at forty yards. This would pretty much cover an adult's abdominal and pelvic region. Therefore, delivery of the pellets could be affected at a relative long distance. Extreme accuracy was not a problem, as number 2 shot could be expected to penetrate deeply enough to produce perforation in the intestines and bladder, as well as savage the sexual organs. Also, it was possible that major arteries could be severed within the abdomen, pelvis, or groin and exsanguinations ensue. However, Manion would just have to gamble on that. He figured chances were that some Brit surgeon could stem the bleeding before they expired. Maybe, they could live and get gangrene in their legs.

Leaving that imagery, the question for Manion now was could he set up three successful shootings before their marriage would occur, and Bernadette might have more accessibility to the secrets of his life? More than once, Mickey had produced mental images of the guards, Carter, Grimes, and Stillton, lying in hospital beds. He pictured three men with a hydra of rubber tubes emerging from the abdomen and groin attempting to cast off the poisons generated inside by their leaking guts. Mickey knew that patients often slowly ebbed away in pain and solitude when visitors stopped coming, rather than facing the noxious odors of pus and fecal drainage. Therefore, once again, Manion answered his own question with a "yes."

No full-dress parades, pipe bands, and lavish burials for you bastards, he thought. *That's for those heroes who die suddenly in the line of duty, not for some sod who rotted away from something that happened six months or a year before!* Mickey knew where they lived and quite a bit about their routines. *I'll try for number one within ten days,* he thought. *If it goes down right, I should still have time for the other two in my prenuptial grace period.*

Shortly after Mickey opened up, Kevin Walsh arrived at Sweeney's Garage, and it was evident that he was mildly agitated. "There is something I think you should know, Mick," were his opening words.

"What's that?" Manion asked.

"My wife, Laura, had me stop by the greengrocer's yesterday. When I went in, he was talking with another customer all excited like. He told her that the police had come and taken his lorry back to their garage and tore it completely apart. After they got it all stuck back together again, they returned it. That's when one of them told him it was all worthwhile because they found something very interesting. He didn't say what it was, but all this worries me, Mick! What do you think we should do?"

"There isn't much we can do, Kevin," Manion replied. "They either found something or they didn't. You know as well as I do that we cleaned it up good before it left here, and everyone who rode in it wore gloves. We sure as hell didn't leave a box of return address stickers inside. I doubt we got anything to worry about, but I'll check around and keep you posted."

Mickey intended to gloss over the revelation. However, it was like thinking you had a worm under your skin. You wished it would go away. But you hated the thought that it would break onto the surface, and you would have to confront the loathsome thing. This was news Mickey felt that he should share with someone higher up the feeding chain. Hogan was out since their confrontation. That left only Frank McGann.

Mickey placed a call to McGann. "I need to talk to you about Mr. Blue," he said to the leader. McGann knew "Mr. Blue" meant the police.

"Well it will just have to wait until Woody gets back from the south at five P.M.," replied McGann. In turn, Manion understood this to mean a meeting at the south entrance to Woodville Park, which was in West Belfast, and the time would be five o'clock.

McGann was punctual; however, Mickey had arrived a little early. He stood near the gate, acting as though he were making a concentrated study of the sign listing Park Regulations and Rules. McGann took shape in Mickey's peripheral vision at the time the older and larger man stopped in front of a vendor. He purchased a large bag of nuts. Then, McGann ambled by and Mickey caught up with him shortly thereafter. Sensing the Cell Leader at his side, Big Frank said, "It's a nice day for a walk, boyo. An opportunity to work out the kinks in the muscles and perhaps some that got into our plans as well. I'm sure the Queen's lackeys won't mind us strolling through this fookin' park as long as we don't poison the pigeons or plant our Paddy arses on their polished benches. Now, tell me what is up, boyo."

Mickey reiterated Kevin's story with all the details of which he was aware. Then, he added some thoughts and speculations of his own. Big Frank remained silent throughout the recounting. Whenever Mickey would drive home a point, his Chief's only response was to cast another very large handful of peanuts to a swiftly growing armada of pigeons following in their wake. Finally, McGann paused, screwing up his eyes, as they caught the glare of the late afternoon sun. Then, he said, "Nice thing about pigeons, they're completely non-sectarian. A peanut is a peanut whether a Paddy or a Prod tosses it out." McGann resumed walking with Manion at his side.

A few minutes later, Big Frank stopped once again saying, "Look boyo!

There is a 99 percent chance the RUC doesn't have a fookin' real clue, and so you needn't worry. If you want to play the short odds, then you can probably expect them to come and get you. In that case, you can turn yourself in and worry about us coming to get you. Or, you can hang yourself and save them the trouble. Third option is to shoot it out and take some of the bastards with you! The last solution is to hide in a cave and live like a hermit or go to the south. Better yet, you go to America and buy a bar in Boston."

"You know, Frank, I'd kill myself before the Brits will ever get me back. But I'd rather shoot it out first if that be the case. However, if the time comes and I can escape, then I would need your help," said Mickey.

"I'm way ahead of you, boyo," Big Frank replied. "There's a camera shop over on Broom Street just west of here. The sign reads "Smythe the Shutter Bug." In addition to the name, there's a picture of a big bug sitting on top of a camera. You can't miss it! Smythe will take your photo and make up a proper set of identification papers for you. But he will give them to me. I'll be the one to decide if and when you need to run."

McGann tossed the half-empty bag of nuts to Mickey, saying, "Take care of me pigeon pals, boyo!" A few feet away, he turned and called back "When did you plan to tell me about you and Miss Donahue alias O'Neil?" Mickey looked surprised, but did not answer immediately.

McGann continued, "Old Brennan is a pretty shrewd judge of the moods of one fair colleen, boyo! He doesn't miss much, nor do I." Big Frank set out again, then turned once more after only a half step. He smiled revealing several gold posts in the gateway of his mouth. "Incidentally, boyo! You might be interested to know that I already own a bar in Boston." This time, McGann continued on his way. Mickey distributed the rest of the nuts to his newly found avian friends. Then, Manion left to find Smythe the Shutter Bug.

Coincident with Michael Manion's visit to Smythe's camera shop, Chief Inspector Merlin Spencer was bending over the back of Crimmons in the Fingerprint Section. The fingerprint expert felt totally spent and was nearly convinced that the comparison of the prints lifted from the lorry to another set from the files would probably reduce him to the end stages of catatonia. In addition, the Inspector was breathing on his neck. The hot breath was odious enough. But it was somehow supercharged with a combination of aromas. Crimmons imagined these were being generated by the guv's morning kippers, a garlic-laced pasta at lunch with a serving of limburger cheese, and a cheap cigar, quite recently smoked and probably chewed on as well. He wondered if Spencer's stomach had revolted and refused to pass the refuse downstream.

❈ ❈ ❈

Small volumes of miasma conveyed to his nose by each of Spencer's exhalations was bad enough. However, Crimmons was convinced he would probably become ill if the Chief Inspector allowed a full-fledged eructation. Crimmons could bear no more.

"Excuse me, Inspector, but I find it dreadfully hot in here! I'm going for a glass of water and to open a window if you don't mind." Spencer voiced no objection. However, his facial expression was that of a man who needed to defuse a very powerful bomb within thirty seconds. Meanwhile, his assistant had just left him holding the wires from the detonator after saying he would be back in a few minutes.

Crimmons did return composed and started a search of the last file. Inspector Spencer resumed his position. Fortunately, fresh air had invaded the gap between his mouth and Crimmons's nose, thus allowing the technician to continue in more wholesome surroundings. Just one-half hour later, Crimmons blurted out, "Bloody sorry, Chief Inspector, but I haven't been able to come up with a match. Perhaps MI-5 would have something. Shall I send the prints to them?"

A booming voice, coming from just behind his head, emitted a single word, "Juveniles!" The word came through loud and clear.

"Juveniles, sir? I thought we were looking for adults."

"Damn it, Crimmons, you weren't born a man. You have to become one. If you are a terrorist, then maybe you had some practice as a felon sometime earlier in your life. Now get the bloody kiddie criminal files and have a go at it!"

Chief Inspector Spencer seemed calmer after the outburst. Then he announced that he was hungry and would return after grabbing a bite. Crimmons wished the same opportunity was afforded to him, but it was not. At least, he could continue his work in solitude, hoping Spencer would find something bland to eat. Unfortunately, Crimmons's hopes were dashed when the Chief Inspector called back, "I'll be at the Mohti Mahal! For some reason a good curry appeals to me."

Upon his return, Chief Inspector Spencer stared incredulously at his technician. Instead of leaning intensely on his desk with magnifying glass in hand, Crimmons was sitting relaxed in his chair. His tie was straight and freshly knotted. His hair was slicked back, and a smile of happy contentment was displayed on an upturned face. Seeing Spencer coming his way, Crimmons reversed the direction of his teacup, and the freshly steeped cup of Darjeeling tea was brought to rest on its saucer. "Hit it lucky, gov, only a half-hour after you left. Thomas Francis Brophy is your man! He made it into the records as a thirteen-year-old purse pincher. Then he graduated to pilfering from cars. Apparently, Brophy wasn't satisfied with just the contents, so he started stealing the whole damned vehicle. Here's a mug shot. Weasely-looking character, has criminal written all over his face."

Crimmons continued, "Also, there is some frosting on the cake, sir! The old lorry used in the armored car robbery was sent over from Londonderry, but it was stolen here in Belfast. The owner didn't turn in a stolen vehicle report to us but did file one with the insurance company. Apparently, he gave them a highly inflated estimate of its worth, hoping they would pay him handsomely. I guess he thought they were dumb, which they are not. Anyway, a fine set of Thomas Francis Brophy's prints also showed up on the side of a wheel rim, which held a newly installed tire. A second set of prints was present on the undercarriage; however, we have no make on those yet. I've initiated instructions for records to turn up an address for this weasel. They should be on it first thing in the morning. Now, if there's nothing else, Chief Inspector, I'm off to down a pint or two."

His superior responded, "Good show, Crimmons—bloody good show!"

Left alone, Spencer pulled out a cigar. He bit off one end, lit the other and took a passionate pull before exhaling in near ecstasy. "I got my break," he said jubilantly. "I should be able to start collaring this group tomorrow." Then, Spencer remembered his forty-eight-hour deadline had passed. "Hell, what's a few hours? They wouldn't hold that against me, would they?"

Early the next morning, Spencer was in looking for someone to hound. However, his urgency wasn't theirs. Frantically, he paced the hallway in front of the ID. and Location Section. Belching clouds of smoke arose from his lit cigar clamped hard between uneven teeth. He evoked a simile of a frigate maneuvering through a land-locked sea at flank speed while in the process of laying down a smoke screen. At last, an early bird arrived, and he was quickly loaded down with instructions. These would cover all his near-term activities and those of all his mates as soon as they arrived on station. Searching for the whereabouts of Thomas Francis Brophy was of the highest priority. No rest, no lunch, no tea breaks, no trips to the loo until Brophy was found.

After giving his specific instructions to the men and women of the ID and Location Section, Spencer decided the next step was to bring the news of their success to High Commissioner Malcom R. Marriott.

Half of the alphabet was festooned behind the High Commissioner's name to inform the world of all the orders and honors he had received. Sir Marriott wished all to know the level of his distinction. Also, he was the same gentleman who had solicited Spencer's early retirement just two days ago. Spencer surmised that Sir, Marriott would surely not be in before ten A.M. or "tenish," as he was prone to say. There was no point in skulking about his resplendent office awaiting his Lordship's arrival. *No, I'll return to the catacombs of the humble working class and badger them. Besides, if Malcom the Magnificent does arrive, the roar of his motorcycle escort will document his entry on the premises. Certainly, that will be audible from the trenches.*

At the time that "tenish" was beginning to give way to "elevenish," the cacophony of the motorcycles became noticeable. At the same moment, Frobisher announced a street address of a rooming house, which was the nighttime habitat for Brophy, the prey they so earnestly sought. Spencer made for the stairs with the paper on which Brophy's address was written clutched in his hand. *Protocol be damned,* he thought. *I can afford to be assertive once in my life!* Spencer brushed by the aghast secretary and entered Sir Malcolm's capacious suite unannounced.

After entering the office, Spencer was about to say, "We tracked down one of the bastards, sir!" However, the words seemed to be pushed retrograde down his larynx by the most malevolent sneer to which he had ever been subjected.

"How dare you have the insolence to break into my office in this fashion Spencer?" came the stinging rebuke from Marriott's snarling lips The High Commissioner venomously continued. "Your churlish behavior goes far beyond a lack of civility. It is boorish. Do you hear? Boorish and totally intolerable!"

"But—but, Sir Malcom," Spencer stuttered. "We've located a suspect who is linked to the bombing and the robbery. I was very anxious to give you the details. No offense was intended. I do apologize for the intrusion. I guess that I was overly enthusiastic, sir, and I am most sorry for what you have aptly described as my boorish behavior." Chief Inspector Spencer's assertiveness had crumbled, and he tried to take refuge behind a wall of self-effacement. However, the reply was, "Too little too late, I'm afraid Spencer!" The Commissioner turned to face a third person in the room, thus making his contrite underling aware of the other man's presence for the first time.

"This is Edward R. Terwilliger, Deputy Director of MI-5 and in charge of domestic terrorism. Mr. Terwilliger is here from London and will be taking over this investigation!"

Spencer looked hesitantly at his announced replacement. His jaw dropped, and his arms hung lifeless. He felt as though he were trapped in a vacuum. His lungs were striving to find even a molecule of oxygen.

Terwilliger advanced toward Spencer like a Saracen prince, anxious to strike off the head of a captured Christian Crusader. The tone of his voice coupled with a malevolent sneer disguised as a denigrating smile cut Spencer as surely as a razor-sharp scimitar. "Teddy Terwilliger," he said, hand outstretched. "I'm afraid I didn't catch your name?"

"Chief Inspector Merlin Spencer," replied the devastated man. Now his title seemed almost nauseating to utter; an introduction of Chief Inspector Boor seemed more appropriate.

Spencer grasped the extended hand, which contracted very firmly on his own. Terwilliger's handshake sent the message "Health club and I can bench press twenty-five stones." The appendage was an extension of a model physique, resplendent in an impeccably tailored Savile Row suit. While his hand muscles were like bands of steel, the skin was quite soft. However, tan like his face, the hand reflected hours spent in tennis, golf, or yachting—gentlemen's pursuits rather than murder scenes, or back alleys, and dimly lit cramped offices.

Teddy's exquisitely trimmed mustache proclaimed a degree of masculine superiority, while his eyes were cruel and calculating. They seemed to say, "I'm shaking your hand, old boy. But I consider you much as I would a fish that expired much too long ago and without ever receiving the benefits of refrigeration." Finally, Terwilliger withdrew his hand, turned, and headed for a chair. He reminded Spencer of a superior boxer, who had never even broken into a sweat and was now returning to a stool in his corner of the ring so he can enjoy the sight of his fallen, bloodied opponent, struggling to regain his feet long into the count of ten.

Again, Sir Malcolm's voice boomed out. "Good God, Spencer. You are dismissed! I assume that is an order to which even one of your intellectual capacity can respond."

In reply, Spencer stuttered, "Sir Malcom," as he unfurled his left hand to reveal a crumpled and sweat-dampened paper, which he had carried triumphantly just minutes ago. "But sir I have the address of a suspect," Spencer gasped, as he extended his hand holding the disheveled paper.

"Indeed, sir. Agent Bodine of Mr. Terwilliger's staff will contact you shortly, and you can brief him on your meager accomplishments. In the meantime, please absent yourself and absolutely take no independent action. If you should be needed for any further activities, the Deputy Director will notify you through members of his staff. Now, we have very important matters to discuss. Close the door on the way out!"

Completely devastated, Spencer lurched to the entry. As he was closing the door, he was certain he heard Sir Malcom say, "Teddy you must try the sweetbreads at the Oak Room. I think they are the finest I've had, and I'm anxious to get your opinion. Shall we be off?"

"It sounds jolly good, Sir Malcolm," were the last words the Chief Inspector heard before the solid door clicked shut.

Chapter Eighteen

At 3:15 in the afternoon, Agent Bodine finally came to find Chief Inspector Merlin Spencer. The Chief Inspector had spent the preceding four hours explaining to his group that from then on London was running the show. This was hard for them to accept, especially since they had ascertained Tom Brophy was employed as a mechanic at Sweeney's Garage. Knowing where it was located, they had every reason to believe that he was there at this very moment.

Disappointed, Spencer was slumped in his chair, head tilted right. His right thumb supported the parietal bone of his skull, leaving four fingers to rhythmically rub his forehead from time to time. The sliding digits frequently trapped an errant lock of his thinning brown hair. Moistened by perspiration beaded on his brow, it hung down, limp and damp. Periodically, Spencer would mumble to his gathered squad, "They got the hot shots over from London. Don't need the bloody locals anymore. We're as welcome as whores at the Vicar's Sunday afternoon tea!"

At least upon his arrival, Sergeant Bodine turned out to be a real-life policeman. Despite his association with Deputy Director Terwilliger, there was no way Bodine would ever lord it over them. He treated Spencer with deference addressing him as "Chief Inspector" or the more familiar "Gov" for Governor. Similarly, those on the Chief Inspector's retinue were treated as equals.

"I see you and your men have located this Brophy's workplace, Chief Inspector. Reading all the reports, it's apparent that you have all worked your asses off and done a fine job of police work! You've made it easy for us to come along and snatch the glory. I'll be first to admit we don't deserve it. But then we all know how most of the big boys play. At least I can say, Chief Inspector, that Deputy Director Terwilliger would like you to personally show us the place. Not much of a reward, sir. But when you are only the messenger like me, you don't have any choice in the matter."

Shortly later, Spencer selected a large sedan from the police motor pool. The car could easily accommodate six men, which would include himself, Terwilliger, Bodine, and three others from MI-5. Before entering the vehicle, Terwilliger withdrew a well-cared-for 9mm Browning Hi-Power from a shoulder holster and chambered a round. Then, he released the magazine and added one more cartridge before reinserting it. The gun was now loaded to a maximum capacity of fifteen rounds. Spencer was surprised to see the weapon, as he had never suspected the man to be armed. *Just shows how much you can hide in a well-tailored suit,* he thought. Other MI-5 agents had Colt revolvers in the newly fashionable (for England) .357 magnum caliber guns. Spencer was armed with his venerable Webley .455, which he was allowed to carry on special occasions. Certainly, this was one of those even though he was under strict orders to remain with the car.

To Spencer, the rank and file of MI-5 seemed intense and rather keyed up; whereas the unflappable Terwilliger treated the whole matter as an inconvenient but mildly adventuresome lark. *We will see,* thought Spencer. *These aren't a bunch of London thugs to be easily suppressed by a squad of truncheon-wielding bobbies. These bastards are killers with little to lose. Most of them shoot back, and some are damn good shots.*

Before driving away, Spencer whispered to Sergeant Masley, "Dan you know that you are to have no direct involvement in this operation. But you might round up a few of the lads and stand by at a discrete distance. I have a feeling that the party may get rougher than these modern-day Sheriffs of Nottingham anticipate."

Dan nodded. "We'll be there, gov. Tally ho, like the foxhunters and Spitfire pilots say."

Soon, the agents were under way. In a short time, the car pulled up in front of Sweeney's Garage. Silently, Chief Inspector Merlin Spencer said, "They'll be leaping in, but I wonder how many will limp out or get carried out." He didn't have long to wait for the answer, as Spencer's passengers had already emerged and were walking silently toward the garage door. Bodine was in the lead, Terwilliger right behind him, with the other agents grouped closely to the rear.

Just as the assault team reached the door, Brophy looked up. Instantaneously, he recognized what they were and the mission they were on even before he saw the drawn pistols. A shrieking curse was his first response, while the second was an overwhelming desire to flee. Deprived of anywhere to escape, he was driven to try and hide himself. So he dived beneath the car he was servicing. This action saved his life for the moment. However, given the circumstances that prevailed after his capture, Brophy had considerable time and reason to ponder whether it was the best choice?

Moriarity and Walsh responded to Brophy's screamed alarm. Immediately, they sought out their Webley pistols, which were secreted but readily available at their work stations. Both men were partially hidden behind cars. Thus, they had an advantage over the MI-5 group, clustered in a relatively open space.

Moriarity sensed an opportunity. He popped partially upright and fired three rounds at Sergeant Bodine. Two of his three shots were errant. However, the third was lethal, as the bullet made its way through the policeman's neck, severing the right carotid and left vertebral arteries in its oblique passage. In addition, it transected his spinal cord, which was interposed. Initially, Moriarity's reaction had made it possible for him to vanquish his first foe, but at the same instant it made him vulnerable to the others.

Terwilliger responded first and double-tapped his Browning Hi-Power in the classical way to deliver two shots in very quick succession. Unerringly, a pair of 115-grain jacketed bullets sped to the center of Moriarity's massive chest, where the energy that each conveyed were fully absorbed. However, the mass of muscle plus thickness of his sternum and ribs prevented entry into the thoracic cavity. Thus, his heart and lungs were spared violation. A look of surprise on Moriarity's face was commensurate with the two hammer blows just received. Nonetheless, he was still conscious, defiant, and determined. Moriarity's slackened arm holding the Webley began to straighten, elevating his revolver to a position of aim.

Firing his Browning again, Terwilliger's third bullet met very little resistance. It passed virtually unimpeded from the entry point just two inches above the bridge of Moriarity's nose and on through his brain. Now, looking even more surprised, his body went totally limp. Moriarity slowly sank to the floor like a great glob of molten wax.

So far, Walsh remained unscathed. However, he was no true gunman. Muzzle blasts and reverberations of the shots fired so far had left him dazed and somewhat disoriented. Walsh knew he didn't want to die. "Oh God! I want to hug Molly and the kids," he murmured, visualizing their apparitions as he raised his revolver. That was his last conscious and earthly act. All three remaining policemen concentrated their fire on Walsh. Most of the bullets struck home. For a moment, his body seemed suspended, jerking convulsively to the tune of the discharging revolvers like a macabre puppet's dance. No strings were necessary, as all his movements were in response to the energy delivered by each of the slugs that struck home. Kevin's reunion with Molly and the three little moppets would have to await the hereafter. His earthly opportunities had all expired!

Manion had been preoccupied with bookkeeping when Terwilliger and his men arrived. However, the first gunshot report made for a quick trip to reality. His Thompson submachine gun was quickly procured and the safety moved to fire position. One round was already chambered, waiting for the strike of the firing pin to ignite its primer, thus propelling the bullet on a lethal journey. Forty-nine more rounds held in a tight circle within the drum magazine awaited their turn. Several feet higher than the workshop, the office floor gave Manion an advantage of elevation and line of fire.

Below, staring abstractly at the fallen body of Walsh, were the rank-and-file policemen. As yet, they had not attempted to explore the condition of Sergeant Bodine. Deputy Director Terwilliger was standing unruffled, observing the crumpled remains of Moriarity. Manion observed this man and the appearance on his face of a smug smile like that of a hunter, trying to decide on which wall he would like to display the trophy head he had just brought to bag.

Mickey's Thompson roared, and the detectives were up-ended, like ten pins, unable to resist the inertia of a giant bowling ball. Terwilliger responded immediately! His Browning swiftly leaving the set arms position to bear on the source of the gunfire. In this initial second, he was unable to shoot because his men were between him and his assailant. However, there was never to be a real opportunity again, for a small squadron of 230-grain 45-caliber bullets soon entered his chest. Rudely, they terminated the function of a heart that had served him well for thirty-seven years, and had there been any fellow alumni present, they would have not recognized the cherished school tie. Forever altered was the pattern by the addition of three large holes and an enlarging crimson deposit. This was spreading out widely, obliterating the prior sharp demarcation of the resplendent diagonal stripes. These had told all in the world, elite enough to know, that this had been a Cambridge man!

Meanwhile, at the first sound of gunfire, Chief Inspector Spencer did not erupt from the waiting car. He hoped the MI-5 men were far too professional to be getting wiped out by IRA gunmen. If he was to arrive on scene when the battle was over, it would surely appear melodramatic. "No, I was told to wait! I'll be a proper puppy, and do as I've been told." However, as he was thinking of congratulatory words for Bodine, thunder and lightning struck. Spencer had spent several years of his young manhood trying to stay alive in a trench in France. Immediately, he recalled the staccato of the Maxim and Vickers machine guns, which had conversed with one another across the expanse of no-man's land in the Fields of Flanders. The thudding, jackhammer sound he heard was not that of the of the Vickers or Maxim species. However, it was surely of the same genus. It was a machine gun!

Spencer threw himself from the sedan. He ran to the garage at a speed that he thought middle age had forever deprived him. His Webley was in hand when he reached the door. Everything was quiet! But the pungent aroma of burned smokeless powder pervaded the air. Spencer gambled a quick glance inward and noted a powerfully built young man clenching a Thompson. There could be no mistake! This was an IRA gunman that he had to take down. As his revolver discharged, the Webley bucked violently in the Chief Inspector's hand. The Paddy winced but didn't fall.

Once again, Spencer's finger tightened on the trigger, and he could see and sense the rise of the hammer. However, suddenly, a 230-grain bullet delivered its devastation to his right shoulder even before he heard the report. An odd sensation emerged! Spencer felt no pain, but his arm was becoming a flail. His hand was unable to retain possession of his gun, which was slowly slithering from his weakening grasp. As shock started to embrace his body, Spencer felt his knees begin to buckle.

Soon the gunman was moving closer, and the Chief Inspector was staring unbelievingly into the black eyes of the angel of death! The Thompson's muzzle was scant inches in front of his face, and the bore stared at him remorseless like the sunken eye of a cyclops. As the man's trigger finger tightened, Spencer wondered if he would see the bullet coming or even the flash that would announce its flight. The next sound Spencer heard was the loudest of his life. No explosion, only the dull click of metal striking metal!

"Fookin' firing pin is broke," screamed Mickey. Then he brought the barrel down hard on Spencer's head. The Inspector was enveloped in oblivion as he slumped to the floor. Just as Mickey was reaching for the Webley, he spied Terwilliger's Browning lying near his body. Since it was the better prize, Manion's intention was to use it to finish off this last of his attackers. With the gun in hand, he was about to deliver the coup de grace when the sound of sirens filled the air!

Converging swiftly was the Reserve Force, which Spencer had arranged for with Sergeant Masley. "I'll kill you later," Manion hissed at the unconscious Spencer. Then he dashed outside and piled into the abandoned police car. It started immediately, responding well to the accelerator. Glancing back, Mickey observed that no pursuit car was following. However, he realized there would be numerous witnesses ready to describe a car hurtling down narrow streets. Consequently, Mickey forced himself to maintain a conservative speed. Then he noticed the sticky, red and warm flow of blood dripping from his right hand on to the steering wheel. His shoulder had been hit and was starting to burn.

However, Mickey could move it well despite the pain. *It can't be too serious,* he thought. *But, it sure as hell complicates escape, running around with a crimson sleeve and leaving a bloody trail like a wounded deer!*

Manion was now a good mile from the garage. However, he seemed to feel as though he were center stage in the middle of a massive orchestra whose only instruments were police sirens. "If I don't abandon the car soon, it might quickly become my hearse," he mumbled. Only one-half block ahead, an RUC car burst through the intersection with its claxon proclaiming the urgency of the mission! "Fook this!" muttered Mickey. Then, pulling to the curb, he exited the vehicle.

Near the corner, Mickey noticed a Catholic Church. *It would be saint this or that in all probability*, crossed his mind. However, the name was of no importance. Realizing he had no good way to hide the blood-stained sleeve, Mickey noted thankfully that some coagulation must have occurred. No longer was there any active bleeding, only a gentle ooze. "Walk quickly but refuse to run," he warned himself. Faces he passed seemed to say, "We know who you are, Mickey Manion, and we know what you have done." He glowered at them, wanting to grab them around the neck and scream, *I did it for you! Don't you understand? Are you going to be a Judas and sell me out for England's silver?*

At last, the church door was within reach, and Mickey entered rapidly. *Good thing about Catholic Churches,* he thought. *There are lots of doors, and they are open most of the time,* not stopping to consider that he was seeking sanctuary inside a church of the faith that he had rejected. From his youthful experience, Mickey knew the holy place would most likely be deserted. Maybe a few old biddies inside lamenting all the sadness, which had come their way. But they would pay him scant attention. Few men would take the time to pass a moment with the Lord. At this hour, they would most likely be finding a pub!

Mickey sought out the Sacristy, not bothering to genuflect or cross himself in the Sanctuary through which he had to pass. As expected, it was unlocked, so he entered rapidly. Seeing a sink, he quickly washed the blood from his hand. Mickey wished to remove his shirt to examine and dress the wound, but decided that this would be too time-consuming. In addition, he was fearful that he might dislodge the fragile clot and renew the bleeding.

Having scant hope any street clothes would be present, Mickey checked the closet, and he was right in that regard. "I sure as hell can't flee the scene in a purple chasuble or other vestment," he uttered. However he noticed a white linen alb that might be useful. Rapidly, Manion tore it into strips, which he utilized for a makeshift pressure dressing, then applied it to his wounded shoulder. Another closet contained a row of neatly hung cassocks for the acolytes. Figuring most would be for boys, at last he found one suitable in size for a mature man. Savagely, he tore away the garment's skirt and high-necked Roman collar. Finding it was large enough, he tucked the torn bottom inside his pants and left his own shirt collar to hang outside the neckline. Then, looking in a small mirror, Mickey decided it did not look as weird as he had feared.

While tucking in the torn lower end of his newly crafted garment, Mickey was gratified to feel his money belt containing the 2000 pounds which he had taken at the time of the armored car robbery. Next, Manion wrapped the Browning Hi-Power in the remnant of the cassock and made for a rear church entry. "Good old Catholic churches," he said once again. "Lots of doors and almost always open!" Then, another reflection came into his mind. *Necessity might be the mother of invention, but urgency was surely the mother of innovation.*

Out in the alley, the fugitive was once more aware of sirens. They seemed to be converging on the spot where he had abandoned the police car. Now there were a number of police whistles interspersed. To Mickey, these sounded for all the world like a flock of small birds, trying to compete with the boisterous calls of far bigger ones. He could foresee that everyone on the other side would like to be the one who got him! *Well, when it's daylight, and I'm on foot, there really isn't anywhere to hide, so why not stick with a winner?* he decided.

Remembering Our Mother of Perpetual Help Church was probably only about ten blocks away, Mickey headed in that direction. More relaxed now, he even managed a smile for several passersby and managed to say, "Pretty exciting day," to one couple just after two police cars tore by. On reaching the church, he found the sacred decor at Our Mother of Perpetual Help was considerably different than that of the church he had recently departed. However, the open door policy was much the same, and the worshipers were just as few.

Before entering, Mickey had noted the sign in front proclaimed that Confessions were heard before each Mass at 6, 8, and 9:15 A.M. and noon as well as Tuesday evenings after Devotions. All the Masses have been said hours ago, and it wasn't Tuesday, Mickey realized as he entered a Confessional, purposefully selecting the priest's compartment because it had a chair. Mickey was damned sure that he wasn't going to spend the next hours on a kneeler, which was all there was to be found on the penitent's side.

Sitting in the chair, Manion managed to doze off several times. Each time that he awakened, the comforting feel of the Browning clutched in his right hand was his initial awareness and his guardian angel. *One with a barrel and bullets,* he thought. *No need for those fellows with the wings that they feature in the catechism.*

Near midnight, Mickey left the church. This time, the doors were locked but only on the outside. Soon, he was in the street. Now, Manion figured it was a half-hour walk to McGann's at full pace, or forty-five minutes doing it surreptitiously.

Finally, Mickey reached Big Frank's. Inside, a few lights were on, indicating that all had not accepted Morpheus's nocturnal invitation. Manion's knock on the door was that of the established code, and the response was a rapid opening. Then, a massive hand on the end of a ponderous arm emerged to propel Mickey inward.

"Good God, boyo!" McGann exclaimed "What the hell happened?"

Mickey started to explain. However, the IRA Leader, appreciating Mickey's exhaustion, pushed him into a chair before allowing him to continue.

"Well, Frank, you said that it was one chance in a hundred that the RUC would ever find us. But somehow they came up with the winning sweepstakes ticket." Then Mickey went on to explain in great detail all that had occurred. At the end, he said, "There was one of the bastards down when I started shooting. I got four of them, maybe five! Incidentally, tell Hogan that the next time he passes out those Mafia violins to have some new parts added!"

All during the narrative, Big Frank had been decanting the Bushmill's bottle at an Olympian rate. While far from intoxicated, he was getting loquacious and found humor in Mickey's last remarks as well as his explanation for his somewhat bizarre attire. Then around 2:30 A.M., McGann's chauffeur Seamus arrived. He helped his boss clean and bandage Manion's wound. Also, some fresh clothes reasonably well fitted were produced, and Mickey dressed in his new attire.

After Mickey had changed his clothes, McGann handed Manion an envelope, which he had procured from a desk drawer and commented, "Smythe was smooth and fast! Here are two sets of ID, one for the south, and the other for the States. You can be a Yank now, boyo! But from now on you're Michael Moynihan. Same first name, the second one phonetically close enough. Mickey Manion is now history! Incidentally, boyo, there are 500 punts in the envelope. That's all I could scare up with the short notice you managed to provide. It should get you by until we settle you in somewhere."

Mickey expressed his gratitude. He was truly in the other man's debt. At the same time, he was pleased to have it confirmed that McGann was unaware of the 2000 pounds he had taken from the armored car job. Otherwise, the hand, which was passing the notes might be trying to choke him instead.

Appearing to be genuinely sniffling just the slightest, McGann admitted, "I hate good-byes, boyo! But, there's a fishing boat in the harbor that's waiting to take you to Skerries, or Na Sceri if you favor the Gaelic, a nice little port down south. No doubt they're anxious to put some Irish Sea under their keel. You've got to go by boat, as the border crossings are closed up tighter than a miser's purse."

Suddenly, Mickey exclaimed, "I can't go Frank! I've got a woman that I love and I have to see if she'll go with me."

McGann smiled slightly, then replied, "If you are referring to Bernadette Donahue-O'Neil, and I know you are, then I'm sure she'll be leaving to join you. However, the fair Colleen is either asleep or pacing the floor, frantically awaiting word of you! Since she's inside a Rooming House filled with other folks, neither you nor I nor Seamus here is about to go play some fookin' mandolin under her window. Nor are we going to sing some mournful tunes in hopes of luring her outside. I promise she'll join you in Skerries if I have to kidnap her."

Placing his hand on Mickey's shoulder in a fatherly gesture, Big Frank continued. "Now be off, boyo! Before the Bushmills blubbers get me all weepy. The fishermen will get you a place in Skerries and a quiet doctor to fix you up." McGann embraced Mickey hard, hurting the wound considerably, but Manion bore it well. Shortly, with the trusted Seamus at the wheel, the car made it safely to the proper wharf in Belfast Harbor. Manion and the driver shook hands. Welcomed warmly by the crew, Manion and the *Angel of Erin* were soon well out in the inky Irish Sea. No running lights were visible. Only the diesel hum and the phosphorescent St. Elmo's Fire marked the fishing boat's passage.

Chapter Nineteen

❈ ❈ ❈

The sun was well up in the sky by the time waves could be seen, dashing against the guardian rocks protecting St. Patrick's Isle. *Surely an uneven contest, the stones showed the wear over eons of time,* Mickey thought. Breakers of today, like those of 1000 years before, were being reduced to spray and foam, as they receded slowly back into the maelstrom from whence they came only to await the wind, which would restore their lives. Water, soft as it was, would always break when confronting stone. Despite this, it was a silken abrasive, which would reform the rock molecule by molecule over the millennia! He observed the gulls and terns whirling overhead. Their raucous calls erased the softer sounds of the wind and water. Mickey noted that the *Angel of Erin* responded well to the sudden command to turn starboard in search of Skerries's snug harbor.

Reflecting back, Mickey realized he had slept nearly all the way. Exhaustion had molded his body to the sparse space of his bunk. His nervous system, and those tiny gyroscopes housed in his middle ears known by anatomists as the semi-circular canals had remained oblivious to the boat's response to troughs and crests. Thus, he had not experienced the slightest symptom of seasickness. Now, Michael Manion alias Michael Moynihan was fully alert and on deck when the *Angel of Erin* hove to and the hawsers were tossed and tied.

Moynihan observed the number of houses visible, and then tried to enumerate the men on the quay. He was unaware that in Skerries, all events no matter how mundane were accorded the same degree of importance as another passage of Halley's Comet! Then, he became disquieted after noticing that one of the men was in uniform. Reflexively, Mickey felt for the reassuring butt of his Browning, hidden beneath his coat. However, his hand had not even become acquainted with that of Inspector Bogue when it was obvious that the man posed no threat. He was Officer Congeniality, and the only question asked was, "Did he enjoy the trip?" No documents were requested. Apparently, word had traveled ahead that the *Angel of Erin* was transporting one of those Yankees—an American on a quest to experience the greatness of old Eire.

After shaking hands with most of the men, Mickey nodded to the remainder. Finally, he was placed in the auspices of Kevin O'Toole, who did a masterful job in dislodging him from the ring of the courteous and curious. Mickey's new host led the way toward the center of town.

Meanwhile, the well-wishers and welcomers remained knotted on the quay, vying to give impressions of the visitor. Bogue commented, "It is funny to have a Yank who speaks with a Northern accent," however, Duffy quelled him. He stated bluntly that "the great Irish American actor Pat O'Brien had no accent at all. So, you can never be sure of what to expect from Americans, even those with roots in the Old Sod!"

Each person stated his or her observations, negative or positive. These always evoked a response quite the opposite until at last they dispersed. Many departed in the same direction, which was toward Finnegan's, a pub where matters of such importance could be discussed in proper perspective. Consequently, Inspector Bogue was left alone, for he was the only one who had any duties, though his were precious few! Probably, there would not be any more new arrivals for a month.

Inspector Bogue was not entirely devoid of curiosity. Indeed, he had wondered about Mickey's accent and was not mollified by Pat O'Brien's explanation. Also, this Yank didn't seem to have what might be construed as American clothes. Furthermore, he noted that there was no sign of luggage, which Bogue thought a world traveler should possess.

Nonetheless, Bogue did have some of the keen perception and extreme suspicion of *Les Miserables'* Inspector Javert. Thus, he was even giving thought to Mickey as a possible Jean Valjean. Cognizant of the gun battle that had occurred in Belfast on the preceding day, it was all beginning to add up. Additionally, the "tourist" was favoring his shoulder, and Kevin O'Toole could be seen leading him to the surgery of Dr. Cobain, an unusual first stop for a visitor. Throw in the bulge, just discernible under the man's windbreaker, and the irrefutable conclusion was that Moynihan (if that was really his name) was an IRA gunman on the run!

"Could be me," reflected Bogue, whose father was killed by the Brits at the Dublin Post Office in 1916. However, a life of poverty and deprivation, which was all a widowed mother could provide for five children, had served to subdue any fervor for an active role in the rebellion. Instead, he grew up to be a conservative man, complacent in the role of civil servant, but proud of the fact there was a decent roof over his family's head and good food on the table.

Pleased by his personal percipience, Bogue smiled softly. Let all the others think that they had a new John Wayne, *The Quiet Man* among them, and glory in their good fortune. He knew better! Still somewhere in Bogue's gene pool resided a bit of unwavering patriotism. *God bless this man for doing what I am reluctant to do*, he thought. *I would be worse than Judas to turn him in!* Bogue glanced at his watch. Duty was done for another day. Perhaps, he, too, should visit Finnegan's pub. A pint toasted to Ireland wasn't a bad idea!

Meanwhile, departing toward the center of town, O'Toole guided Mickey straight to see a Dr. Dennis Cobain. Briefed in advance, the kindly physician was fully aware of the etiology of his new patient's trauma. After deftly removing the dressing, he examined the entrance and exit wounds.

"I have to probe," said Dr. Cobain after completing irrigation of the bullet tract. "It may hurt quite a bit! I can give you a shot of morphine if you wish."

"That's okay, Doctor! Do what needs to be done. I'll grit my teeth," replied Mickey.

Small as the tip of the forceps was, Mickey felt that it hurt like hell. He was feeling a little faint and quite aware of the cold beads on his forehead, not unlike the condensation on a frosted glass exposed to the sun. Moynihan was having second thoughts regarding the proffered opiate when the searing pain subsided, and the forceps withdrew.

"Well, well, what's this?" proclaimed Collins, exhibiting a small piece of fabric held tightly in the instrument's jaws. "It would have been producing a pint of pus in a few days, lad! Good we got it out now." The doctor continued, "The bullet picked this up on the way in, but left it behind before exiting."

Thorough irrigation of the bullet tract was performed. Then, penicillin was administered by injection, and more was sent along for continued oral therapy. Dr. Cobain requested Mickey to return in two days. Patting him on the good left shoulder, he said, "We're thankful for what you on the front lines do for all of us."

After leaving Dr. Cobain's office, O'Toole guided Mickey to the widow Mrs. Finucane's Boarding House. She had a small but clean and well-appointed space available. Mrs. Finucane informed Mickey that dinner was several hours away. "Please make yourself comfortable Mr. Moynihan." Then, just at the time Mickey's foot touched the first step, his landlady called out, "Oh! Mr. Moynihan, Mr. O'Toole said to tell you a young lady—he didn't give her name—will be coming to town tomorrow. I understand that she will be staying with Mrs. Conroy on the other side of town." Mrs. Finucane's message provided a great relief for Mickey for although he felt a hell of a lot better off than twenty-four hours ago, he was tormented by the absence of Bernadette.

Early the next morning, Mr. O'Toole phoned with word that Bernadette would arrive on the two P.M. stage from Belfast. However, unfortunately dissemination of the news was not limited to Mickey alone. Anxious to see Bernie, Moynihan arrived fifteen minutes early at the bus depot.

He was dressed in a newly purchased suit, which had been altered quickly but satisfactorily. Freshly shaved, Mickey had added a bit of pomade to his unruly hair. Having obtained a small bouquet in route to the depot, he was the essence of the classic beau.

Bernadette was the fifth passenger off the bus. Exuberantly, Mickey embraced her. Then, in spite of his painful shoulder, he lifted Bernie off her feet and held her high like a grand prize! No sooner did he set her down and commence to bestow a passionate kiss when he became aware that they were encircled. Mrs. Finucane had just arrived, and five other women were already present. Along with the women was a quartet of girls ranging from prepubescent to upper teens. Taken aback by a chorus of throat clearing, the couple were embarrassed, resulting in a downpour on their reunion. Ten wet blankets clustered so closely dampened their ardor! Thus, the couple separated as introductions progressed, though Mickey was still in possession of one of Bernadette's hands, allowing for a telegraphy of sorts.

Introductions were no sooner concluded than welcoming banter began. All of it was quite inane but seemingly beyond omission as far as the ladies were concerned. Then, Mrs. Conroy took charge of Bernadette with the solemn announcement that "Miss Donahue must be far beyond exhaustion as the result of her lengthy bus ride. Surely, a nice bath and nap were quite in order. Mr. Moynihan may call on her after dinner!" Although greatly disappointed but totally unprepared to confront the ladies, Mickey acquiesced.

Dutifully following Mrs. Conroy, Bernadette was relieved that she had let Mickey use her real last name, Donahue, instead of the alias O'Neil. She felt using the name borrowed from her deceased friend would be needed no more. For as soon as she and Mickey married, Donahue would be gone as well. Bernadette Moynihan alone would persist. Meanwhile, as his love was marched off lock step surrounded by her sanctity squad, with younger ladies carrying her solitary suitcase, Mickey stood chagrined. He was left with a mental picture of Joan of Arc headed for the stake. Moynihan did take some small comfort when Bernadette turned, smiled, and waved her bouquet.

At the appointed hour, Mickey arrived at Mrs. Conroy's Boarding House and was ushered solemnly into the parlor. "Your young lady will be down soon, Mr. Moynihan. Please make yourself comfortable." Bernie came downstairs quickly. She was radiant—even more beautiful than he could recall either in real life or memory. They embraced in a puritanical fashion, both assuming that more desirous displays of affection could wait until they were finally alone. Such was not to occur. For Mrs. Conroy returned in a flash with tea, and seconds later with cookies!

Just when it seemed a cherished moment of privacy was possible, their hostess proudly announced that her niece, Sinead, had volunteered to play the piano. She was a very talented pianist and a great vocalist as well. Had they been the entire audience, this situation would have been distressing enough, but soon the sitting room was filled to capacity by other relatives and friends. Then everyone had to sing, as was often the circumstances on such occasions. Bernadette was happy that she had been afforded singing lessons at St. Cecelia's Academy. Also, she was surprised that Mickey had a naturally beautiful baritone, which came across well despite his complete discomfiture at having been ambushed by Mrs. Conroy.

From the standpoint of the two lovers, the evening had been a complete disaster. However, both understood that it was an era not given to assertiveness, especially in dealing with dear-hearted people that really meant well. Moynihan was able to give Bernie a kiss on the cheek, as their hostess was ushering him out. Additionally, he managed to whisper in his love's ear, "My God! We're surrounded by sin fighters. I'd have an easier time trying to court a postulant in a cloistered convent than getting you alone in this place. We have to make a break for it and soon!" Then, Moynihan was ushered out.

First thing the next morning, Mickey was up and about. His initial stop was at the seat of city government. After inquiry, he was told that a magistrate could perform a civil marriage service. But the clerk appeared perturbed. She acted as though the man standing in front of her had asked if it were permissible to commit suicide in front of her desk. Moynihan ignored all the disdain and left with the details. Some time would be needed, but it was infinitely shorter than publishing Bands of Marriage in the Catholic Church if that were their desire. Certainly, this was not the case. Fortunately, Mickey was able to pass the plan on to Bernadette on one of the short periods of privacy they were allowed. She beamed with happiness!

Now, it was time to let Mrs. Finucane and Mrs. Conroy in on their plans. After hearing their story, both blessed themselves and looked totally aghast! Mickey surmised that they probably would have been less mortified if he had unrolled a prayer rag in their parlor, knelt toward Mecca, and started Moslem prayers. In seconds, Mickey had become a vile American, and in the minds of the town's gossips he was a depraved Yankee! He must have come under the satanic influence of Hollywood. "Poor dear girl, enraptured by such a

Svengali!" None would attend the service, considering it second only to a Black Mass as a matter of sacrilege. However, some of the ladies came to the conclusion that a small reception in deference to the lovely young woman would not be sinful. After much discussion, they decided this gesture would not suggest material cooperation in a non-Catholic marriage. Once the decision was made, that is what they planned.

Nervous and somewhat anxious, Bernadette and Mickey felt relieved that the marriage ceremony was mercifully short. Afterward, the lovely reception turned out to be fun. Unknown to Moynihan, some of the ladies thought a little rat poison in the slice of wedding cake going to the groom would be "just-desserts." However, they resisted the temptation. Actually, these dear folks could not remain disdainful for long. Soon, the reception was over. Finally, they were on the bus and snuggled close together!

Just prior to leaving Skerries, word had come from O'Toole that Big Frank had made arrangements for them to leave for America from Galway. They must be there by the 16th and check into the Dublin House Hotel. Mr. Bailey, the proprietor, would give them all the information they needed to know, and an Irish passport would be there for the new Mrs. Moynihan! "In the meantime, have a fine honeymoon." A 100-punt note had been passed along with the message.

The newlyweds' bus would take them to Drogheda, where they planned to spend the first night indulging in all that they had denied themselves heretofore. While en route, Mickey pulled out a little map, unfolded it, and passed it to his wife. "Where to after Drogheda, Bernie?" She studied it carefully. Then, she thoughtfully began circling a spot in the south of Killarney. Mickey was puzzled, "Why there, my dear? I thought you would like to see Dublin?"

"No Mickey! I saw it in another life. It's an old dreary city, and I have no desire to return."

"You didn't ever tell me that," he replied. "When were you ever in Dublin?"

With a smile on her face, she replied "I have my black secret, too, my love. You keep yours, and I'll keep mine!"

Mickey had no argument. "All right that's where we'll go. But, the place looks like it's on the edge of nowhere! I can't see why you would want to travel to such a place."

"Well I've never been there," she said with a smile.

"You've never been to the South Pole either for that matter," Mickey shot back with a laugh. "But if that's where you want to go, that's where we'll go. However, Mrs. Moynihan, in the future, I'll make all the decisions."

"Sure you will," said Bernadette liltingly.

At last, the newlyweds arrived in Drogheda and secured lodgings for the night. They had planned to leave the following day. But when ardor became too arduous, some additional time was needed for rest, so they remained for a second day. Then their journey began again, and they maintained a southwesterly direction as best they could given all the geographical considerations and bus routes with which they had to cope.

Bernie and Mickey spent their third night in Tralee, then passed through Shannon and Limerick. "This is where those silly poems started isn't it?" said Mickey.

"What silly poems?" asked his bride.

"You know, those five liners where all the sentences end in a word that rhymes," was his response.

"You've lost me, Mickey," was Bernie's rejoinder.

The groom stared out the window for a few moments then turned and said:

> *There was a lovely bride named Bernadette,*
> *Who hasn't grown tired of her husband yet.*
> *That gallant fellow is willing to bet,*
> *As the years go bye she'll have no regret!*
> *And my little poem will cause her no upset!*

"There you are, Bernie, a true limerick composed by the Bard of Belfast for the fairest of all Colleens, Bernadette Moynihan! Well how did you like it? If it made you upset, I'll have to change the last line."

"I thought it was absolutely charming and a work of pure genius," she responded in a very sweet voice with a hint of mawkish overtone. "However, Mickey, dear I doubt Mr. Shakespeare would feel he should be reincarnated to compete with you in the here and now."

Poet Laureate Moynihan took her response as a put down! A half-frown developed on his face, only to disappear when Bernadette gave him a little punch in the ribs followed with a kiss "I'll have to remember never to say anything critical to you in the next fifty years, Mickey. But after that you are fair game." As Bernadette spoke those words, she laid her head on his shoulder sighed and began to doze.

When Bernie awoke, Mickey announced they had only twelve more miles to go. His bride quickly noticed that the bus had nearly emptied during her nap. Apart from themselves and the driver, only a solitary elderly lady remained on board. "She must have got on during the last stop. I surely would have noticed the crate with the four hens inside if she had been here before I fell asleep. I imagine this will be one of the things I will always remember, Mickey, sharing our honeymoon trip with a bunch of chickens!"

"I'm surprised all that clucking didn't wake you sooner," he replied.

"No, they didn't bother me a bit. How about you?" was her response.

"The clucking wasn't so bad. It's the odor that got to me," was his rejoinder.

"Oh! You mean the droppings," said Bernadette.

"Well, left to my own devices I probably would have selected a more earthly term," Mickey responded. Then, he injected, "The aroma is pretty pungent." He laughed before adding, "The stink is bad enough but it also burns my eyes." This evoked a hearty laugh from Bernie, and merited her seatmate another poke in the ribs.

At last, the bus lurched to a halt like a tired old horse, an analogy so perfect that they would not be surprised to hear it snort and whinny. "Ballyskellig Hotel," the driver intoned. Quickly, the couple was out of their seats. Mickey hoisted down their grips, and they started down the aisle. In the lead, Bernadette paused as she drew abreast of the elderly woman sharing the seat with her cargo of pullets. Intuitively, Bernie sensed a word of greeting accompanied by a kind remark would be much favored. "Those are fine-looking chickens," she said sweetly. In response, the keeper of the birds straightened up as best she might. Spread across her shoulders, the worn old shawl was of little help in masking the kyphotic spine beneath. Slowly, a smile developed on the wrinkled, weather-beaten face. Although marred by the stained dentition that still remained, none of its warmth was lost.

Unfortunately, the elderly woman's clouded left pupil failed to generate a sparkle. However, that of the right eye made up for both. Perched atop her head was a black straw bonnet crowning her iron-gray hair pulled tightly in a bun. A few stray wisps of hair sought escape through the many holes left by straws long since departed from the once charming chapeau. Protruding upward from the shredded black ribbon was a single black feather. The long shaft was bent, creating a rakish angle! Though appearing ludicrous, it was lovely in a peculiar sort of way.

"These are lucky chickens," the old woman said with a lilting tone. "Look! they already laid me an egg!" After unwrapping her handkerchief, she proudly held up her prize for Bernadette to see.

"Lucky indeed," replied Bernie. Though no practiced conjurer, Bernadette had adroitly slipped a one-punt coin beneath the egg as she passed it back.

"God bless you my dear," came back in response to her charity.

"God bless you as well," said Bernadette softly.

Later, Bernadette would reflect on the event, wondering about the significance of intoning a blessing. Certainly, this was not the usual demeanor of a newly avowed atheist. However for now Mickey was pushing against her with one of the suitcases. She knew he was impatient to disembark, so she said no more. Her spouse thought about chiding her humorously when they were off the bus. But he decided it was indeed a tender act and Bernie would be hurt if he were to make light of it!

Arriving at the hotel, the innkeeper was as hospitable as he could be at the end of an unprofitable week. Sensing he might be dealing with newlyweds, he excitedly pronounced that they were fortunate to find space. For there were only two rooms remaining. He would show them both, and they could take their choice! Reasonably furnished, room number one was very cramped and had a single, small window with a view of the road. By comparison, the second room seemed to be palatial. They could easily walk around. Also, there was a table with several chairs and a double bed. When the curtain was drawn, the large window became a portrait. The setting sun was a dusty, golden-red and of a magnificence that no artist could paint. Shimmering, a pathway of similar striking beauty stretched from the burning orb all the way across the now tranquil blue Atlantic. Close by, it appeared like some magical road leading off to a kingdom of indescribable beauty. About the sun, small clouds of the most vivid pink and softest violet looked for all the world like gossamer angels.

The contest between the rooms was decided with the first draw of the curtain. "Oh, Mickey! It's so beautiful," exclaimed Bernie.

Mickey was unable to resist in the face of such expressed sentiment. So, he rose to the occasion, and somberly said, "We'll take it."

During their registration, the sign proclaiming the established room tariffs was in an inconspicuous place, and Moynihan was too unsophisticated to inquire about the charge. Therefore, the shrewd innkeeper added somewhat to the prevailing price, but not enough to dissuade his sole customers of the day.

Bernadette was up early the next morning. Her awakening wasn't rude, nor did it occur in response to the stertorous sound rhythmically emitted from the mouth of her sleeping spouse. She was beckoned forth by the call of some special Siren whose song was inaudible to all but her. Seemingly, it sang, "Come and see! Come and see!" Arising, Bernie braided her magnificent auburn tresses, donned suitable attire, and hastened outside in answer to the call.

Having reversed its position from dusk the day before, now the sun sent forth its fiery splendor from the east, where it dominated the heavens! Possessive of all the glory of its progenitor, a splendid shaft of light slashed its way through the scudding clouds to explode on an island off in the distance. The sight was such that Bernie could imagine Hyperion hurling a solar-tipped spear through the heavens then seeing its impact on the mammoth rock, which jutted upward out of Poseidon's domain. From the visible side of the great black stone flashed opalescent hues of orange and pink that dazzled the eye of the beholder!

Bernadette was moved to exclaim, "It's so beautiful! I wonder what it's called?"

To her astonishment, a voice from an unperceived source replied, "They call it Skellig Michael, miss. Centuries ago, a fine monastery was there, but no one abides on Skellig now. Out beyond is Little Skellig and closer in is Lemon Rock. Also, it's a splendid sight when the weather is grand as it is today."

Turning toward the sound of the voice, Bernadette saw an elderly gardener. Lowering his pruning shears, he tipped his cap. "Good morning, miss. I'm pleased that you enjoy our scenery! I never tire of it myself. It's quite glorious to look upon when we're not fighting the fog. Makes a believer out of you, doesn't it? I've been to Dublin twice. I never saw any of those piles of brick and stone that could hold a candle to it."

Bernadette avoided the reference to a Creator, but once again exclaimed, "It's so beautiful and entrancing in a strange sort of way. Is there any way one can visit it?"

"Sure and begora you would have to be a great swimmer," he answered with a laugh. "But for those less athletically inclined you can sometimes get one of the fishermen to drop you off on the way out. Then he will pick you up coming home. Of course, if they run into a storm, you might be in for a longer stay than you planned. However, if you are game, then check with Mr. or Mrs. Cooke, the owners. Not infrequently sea-farin' folk come into their pub and they can probably line you up for a boat ride."

"I will I will do just that," Bernadette replied. Then, she added, "Thank you so much Mr.—"

"It's O'Malley, miss, with Denny in the front, and you are most welcome! Also, welcome to the hotel. It's pretty slow this time of year. You and your man are our only guests."

Bernadette thanked O'Malley again. She didn't comment on Mr. Cooke's subterfuge regarding only two available rooms. She was ecstatic over the room, especially with the grand vista it offered. Additionally, what Mickey would do and say if informed that he was fleeced left nothing to conjecture.

While outside the hotel, Bernie found there were a hundred variable views, each competing to be the best. She decided Skellig Michael was nature's Taj Mahal, an edifice she would probably never see. However, just like the man-made wonder, Skellig's colors changed with the positioning of the sun, and the angle from which you viewed it. No matter who had come and gone from the time man first set foot on it, Bernadette claimed the island as her own! The deed was filed safely in her heart.

Seeking her husband to share her discovery, Bernadette rushed back to their room. However, Mickey was still fast asleep and far beyond sharing or caring. Soaking a towel in cold spring water, she applied it to his bare chest, and it did wonders to recall her husband from the Land of Nod. Not quite sure what Mickey's response would be, Bernie was still willing to experiment. He did awake with a start! However, he wasn't wrathful, but laughing. Thus, for the newlyweds, it turned into a wonderful day together.

At supper that night, Bernadette inquired of Mrs. Cooke, who doubled as maître d' as to whether or not they could hire a boat to drop them off on Skellig Michael. "I'll let you know in a moment dear. There are fishermen in the bar, and I'll ask around," was her reply.

Mrs. Cooke did not return. Instead, a tall man approached their table. Aromas of the sea had taken root in his clothing and were easily distinguished as he drew near. At first, they noted his ice-blue eyes. But distraction came with the perception of his eyebrows. These were black as ebony, very long, and furled like feathers on the tip of an eagle's wing. His exposed skin proclaimed, "I've fought the sea for forty years, and it hasn't beat me yet!"

"Evening, ma'am, evening, sir," he said. Husky and resonant, the voice was obviously used to battling the wind and never taking second place.

Mickey stood and extended his hand. "Michael Moynihan, glad to meet you. This is my wife, Bernadette." Mickey observed the man's handshake was very firm. Sensing a little more pressure in the fisherman's grasp, Mickey tightened his own. A reciprocal response followed, leading to a series of increments. Finally, both men came to the point where they knew their masculinity had been sufficiently manifest and a tie was acceptable.

"I'm Patrick Garrity, and I understand you want a ride out to Skellig Michael and back."

"Oh, yes! We surely do," Bernadette exclaimed. "Can we go tomorrow Mr. Garrity?"

"Patrick will do fine," he said. "However, tomorrow is out, as there is a major storm brewing. I doubt anyone would dare to venture forth. Certainly, not the likes of me with five mouths to feed. besides myself and the missus."

"How about the next day?" asked Bernadette.

"I rather doubt it," he said. "Once the old pot gets boiling out there, it may take a few days to simmer down. I'll keep the old weather eye peeled and let you know as soon as it's safe!"

Garrity departed with a smile. However, it didn't buoy Bernadette's depressed spirits. *We'll have to leave in a few days,* she thought. *Will I never see my island?* This was a question she couldn't answer. Turning into a nagging fear, it was one Bernadette was unable to dispel.

As predicted, a great storm came during the night. Upon awakening, Bernadette ran to her window. The beautiful portrait seen before had been ripped from the frame! In its place were massive clouds propelled across the sky like giant ships full-rigged with sails of black and gray.

Spawned by the glaciers of Iceland, the wind had increased and grown with each passing mile. What waves Bernadette could see through the mist and horizontal sheets of rain were ponderous. Soon, the waves formed great white caps, which were torn from their base and hurled ahead as a cloud of spray. No match for the Atlantic, the Irish Sea surrendered its own surface, and meekly joined in the tumult. For Bernadette, it was like looking into an open black coffin. She could not envisage anything to lift her sagging spirits. "Oh! Mickey," she proclaimed. "I'm so discouraged. I did so want to see my island!"

Mickey was sitting next to the pot-bellied stove, savoring its warmth. He was reading a book borrowed from the surprisingly well-stocked hotel library. "Look on the bright side, Bernie! It's a good time for planting seeds and starting things to grow."

She passed him a desultory look and replied, "Just when did you develop such an interest in farming, Mickey? I can't imagine anyone out trying to plant in this weather."

He put down the book and held out his hand. "I have no interest in farming, Bernie! That wasn't the kind of seed I was looking to plant."

Though thoroughly pleased by Mickey's diversions, Bernadette remained dispirited on the second day of the storm. Early on the third day, it seemed to be abating. However, there was no sign of boats venturing out or any messages from Captain Garrity. At least, being around her husband, life was never devoid of mirth.

At dinner, Mickey suddenly looked around furtively. Then, he bent over and whispered in her ear, "You know, Bernie, I've come to the conclusion that we are the only guests here. Do you think I should warn the Cookes that their rooms aren't full? Or, do you think the surprise would do them in?" Neither could contain their laughter.

Upon return to their room, Bernadette glanced at the drawn shade, which she had pulled down to shut out the sight of the somber sky. Then she noted that the windowsill was a pinkish hue! After dashing to the window, she pulled the cord, leaving the shade to the mercies of the contracted spring. "Mickey, look!" she cried. Only the upper half of a gloriously, orange-red orb remained and not a single cloud had the audacity to intervene.

The rest of the sky's color was an azure blue slowly giving way to purple before surrendering to the black of night. Bernie stood enraptured by the sight and unaware of the knock on the door, which Mickey answered. She did hear the fisherman say, "We'll be off at dawn tomorrow. Will you be coming along?" Skellig Michael was no longer a specter enshrouded in fog. Once again, her island had appeared for Bernie to see. Tomorrow she would visit, and the answer to the fisherman's query was "yes!"

Before retiring, Bernadette obtained an alarm clock from Mrs. Cooke. She handed it over with a straight-faced smile and proclaimed, "No extra charge for our distinguished guests." Bernadette smiled back, adding a gracious "thanks." But she withstood the temptation to add, "Don't you mean your *only* guests?" She felt Mrs. Cooke was a dear and not given to her husband's penury. Then, Mrs. Cooke added, "I'll have a fine lunch in a basket ready for you in the morning. Now sleep well and may the angels watch over you!"

On the next morning, Bernadette was fully awake well before the sun could send the golden messengers from its corona telling the sleeping world to await the dawn! She pummeled Mickey into a state of semi-awareness. By the time the alarm clock sent forth its strident call, they were both fully dressed. Then, as they arrived at the quay, they noticed there were a number of trawlers ready to get under way. In the softly diffused light, Bernie was able to make out the name of the last boat lined up at the pier. "Look Mickey! There it is *Patrick's Pride*."

Her spouse stood half-asleep, mumbling, "If that old scow is *Patrick's Pride*, his last boat must have been really something."

"Oh Mickey! It's a beautiful boat!"

"Bernie, my love, when it comes to getting to your island, you would probably say the same thing about the German battleship *Bismarck* just before it sank."

After hustling his passengers aboard, the fishing boat skipper and two-man crew cast off and brought the mooring lines aboard. Garrity introduced the crew to Mickey and Bernadette. One was his eldest son, Jerome, and the second was a nephew named Danny. After introductions, the skipper invited Bernadette and Mickey to come inside the wheelhouse. "It will be snugger besides saving you from a soaking if we whip up a bit of spray. I'm sure we are bound to do that. Besides, it gets a bit slippery out on the deck, and we may not be up to speed on a lady or man overboard drill."

With his passengers seated, the Skipper placed the gears in a forward position. However, *Patrick's Pride* made no progress. Instead, there was a terrible chatter of protest from the propeller shaft! In response to the fearsome sound of metal fighting metal with no sign of an emerging winner, Bernadette's index of concern rose steadily.

Mickey wondered if the brave Captain intended on going down with his ship. Then, he concluded it was a gallant fate in which they might also participate given the appearance of the poor little dory stored snugly on deck.

Presumably, it was intended as a wishful thinker's substitute for a lifeboat. For the moment, he took solace in the fact that the gap between the deck and dock was still leap able at least for him, trousered as he was. Unfortunately, it wouldn't go as well for Bernie, who would be badly hobbled in a long and form-fitting skirt. Of course, she could pull the damn thing up and jump! But modesty would be far better served if his spouse would simply slip into the water. Then, he could throw her a line.

Captain Garrity and crew remained entirely nonplussed, though Jeremy was observed departing his post and proceeding to the engine room. Mickey thought this was a bit of a misnomer given its Lilliputian dimensions. Then, Jerome bestowed two hearty blows on the gear housing with an oversize Stilson wrench. This resulted in a restoration of serenity for all but Mickey! He noted the Stilson had the same effect on *Patrick's Pride* as a jockey's whip to a thoroughbred coming down the home stretch.

Suddenly, the old trawler leapt from the quay, taking on each coming wave as though it was the finish line. Piercing the air with their shrill calls, the excited gulls cavorted and cartwheeled above. All of this provoked Patrick to comment, "When God gave brains to birds then he surely overlooked the gull! You would think, after centuries of watching fishing boats come and go, they would have figured out they'll get no goodies until you're returning and cleaning the catch of the day."

Not wanting to be deprived of a chance to participate in such a philosophical discussion, Mickey chimed in, "They're like the poor sods who vote for politicians! They cheer when their man gets elected instead of waiting to see if he accomplishes anything in office." This brought a hearty laugh from Garrity before he stopped to stoke his pipe.

In a relatively short time, Skellig Michael loomed before them in all its grandeur! Soon, Bernadette could define all the individual clefts, crevices, and cornices that dotted the massive cliffs as they were approaching. Thousands of seabirds clung tenaciously to the perches that made up their tiny fiefdoms. To Bernie, they appeared to mimic little winged soldiers. Each one standing proudly in separate little guardhouses seeking to protect the bounty of their nests from any predators, wheeling in the sky above. As the boat drew closer, the waves, which had appeared as tiny tongues tipped in white and breaking against the monolith's base, now were seen as great, bluish-green geysers! After colliding with unyielding stone, the energy remaining in their wrath was expended by hurling the fractured droplets skyward.

Bernadette's reverie was broken by Patrick's husky voice. "Well! There she is in all her glory! She's a grand sight. Some say she is the very edge of Europe with nothing left to the west of her. The monks have been gone now for quite some time. I can see why! An inhospitable place if there ever was one. I doubt you could grow anything there but more rocks, and there's too many of those already. You can almost imagine old Brendan the Navigator sailing by in his leaky hide boat wondering how far it was to the next sight of land!"

"Are there any buildings on Skellig?" asked Mickey. "There are still recognizable remnants mostly up on the top," replied Garrity. "When you get up there you can see Little Skellig quite clearly. It's quite a sight all on its own. Fortunately, there are a couple of serviceable quays still doing the job. I'll land you on this side, which is the lee side, and somewhat protected from the wind. We should be back about five o'clock, so try and be ready to jump on board. I see Mrs. Cooke fixed you a picnic basket. You should probably take out enough for lunch, and leave the rest at the bottom. You'll thank me when you're putting your foot down on what you'll think is the millionth step. Skellig is quite safe enough, unless you're the type that gets a thrill out of hanging over a cliff. Of course, you must stick with the well-marked steps. Some of the others are crumbling or are in areas where rock slides occur."

Patrick's Pride wallowed abreast the dock, and the two young crewmen competed to assist the beautiful lady to safety. Mickey was left to his own devices. Shortly thereafter, the trawler was on its way. Skellig Michael was theirs and theirs alone!

After visually confronting the seeming endless staircase of chiseled granite steps, Mickey stuffed one-half of the generous supply of food in a knapsack and prepared for the arduous climb. Then, turning toward Bernadette, he found she was nowhere in sight! After his third call, a response finally came. "I'm over here!"

Mickey called out, "Over here is where?"

"Behind the rock," she said.

"Why are you behind a rock?"

"Because I'm changing my clothes and I need to urinate, that's why."

Mickey sat down to wait. Finally, Bernadette emerged. This time, she was wearing slacks and sturdy shoes. "Where did you get all that stuff?" he asked.

"Mrs. Cooke loaned it to me, and I was carrying it in this bag," Bernie replied. "You didn't think that I was going rock climbing in what I had on did you?"

"Then why didn't you put this stuff on before we left?" he asked with some exasperation!

"Because I wanted to look nice," was her response.

"Seagulls are not nearly the mystery that women are!" was all Mickey could think to say.

Bernie and Mickey started their climb, which was punctuated with many stops. Some were for catching their breath but most for query. "I wonder what man came here first? What was he like? What did he think? Whose hands held the hammer and chisels to carve these steps? For those who attained the top, what sights did they see? Were there Spanish galleons, English Corsairs, or even Brendan, himself, sailing to the New World in a hide-covered boat? What drove them to forsake the world? Then banish themselves here to pray to some God who either didn't exist or was too busy to care for His creatures. What is it like here when the thunder boomed and the lightning hurled from the sky?" They conversed with endless speculations. Sure answers eluded them. Bernie could not help but wonder why she was there? Was it fate, kismet, joss, or God's will? She decided to stick with fate! Mickey didn't wonder why he was there. That was easy because it was what Bernie wanted to do!

When the couple weren't questioning or stopping for a kiss, they were fascinated by the marvelous sights that surrounded them. Seabirds were everywhere to be seen. Many were timid and remained aloof, but some were curious and allowed a close approach. All seemed intent that their calls be the most clarion of all and their aerial acrobatics the most daring.

"Oh, Mickey," Bernie exclaimed "I wish I knew them all by name."

"How on earth could you name them all, Bernie? You can't even tell which one is a girl and which a boy. You wouldn't want to call a female Bill, and some male Molly, now would you?"

Bernie's elbow found Mickey's ribs with sufficient force to elicit a grunt. "You know what I mean. I wish that I could tell what kind of bird they are."

" You want to know the genus and species" he quipped.

"No, not the latter just the common name."

Why didn't you say so to start with?" Mickey asked with a laugh before producing a tattered monograph from his backpack entitled *Birds and Flowers of Skellig Michael Island*. "I checked this out of the hotel library, but I'm not going to give it back to that crook, so it's yours to keep."

Bernie flung her arms about her husband's neck, kissed him with great ardor, and then exclaimed, "This is why I love you!"

"I thought it was because of my passion and good looks," Mickey retorted.

"That, too!" Bernie replied sweetly.

Soon, Bernadette and Mickey had identified gannets, razorbills, guillemots, fulmars, kittiwakes, herring gulls, shearwaters, storm petrels, and many greater and lesser blackbacks. There were even more species of flowers than seabirds. However, of all the blooms, Bernie was most enthralled by the armeria, or sea pinks, as they are commonly known. Also, some time was spent exploring the ancient monastic ruins accompanied by their speculation regarding the builders and occupants. Soon, all their time had elapsed, and now they must return to meet their boat.

By virtue of the long climb, the invigorating sea air, plus the glorious vistas from the top of Skellig, Bernie and Mickey were exhilarated! However, they were still famished after the food they had brought with them was gone. Fortunately, they could still look forward to devouring the remainder of their larder on return to the quay. Both seemed to share a wonderful almost giddy feeling.

"Oh Mickey! I wish I could stay here forever. I love it so!"

"Yes! You could sit here enraptured staring out to the sea, while I climb up and down the cliff to get the food," he replied with a chuckle. "I don't think that I would be very comfortable, sleeping on a pile of rocks for that matter," he added.

"What makes you think I'd leave you any time for sleep?" Bernie said in a somewhat seductive manner.

"Well if you are thinking about what I assume, then, all I can say is there would be more comfortable places to do that, too."

Upon return to the quay, the remainder of their food was devoured ravenously. But their appetites were still not sated. "If we lived here and kept eating like this, they would have to send out a large barge loaded with food every week," was Mickey's summation. Then, he quickly added, "*Patrick's Folly,* or whatever it's called is coming. I can hear it! Do you need to find your big rock to hide behind again, Bernie?" She needed to and did.

On the way back from Skellig, the old trawler seemed to hitch a ride on all the swells passing along with it. Slowly, Bernadette's Shangri-la began to fade from sight. But while the Island diminished in her vision, it grew larger in both memory and fancy. Somehow, she knew it was irrevocably attached to their future. Consequently, that night before sleep came, Bernie asked softly, "Mickey, we will get back to Skellig Michael one day won't we?"

"Yes Bernie, someday. Someday we'll get back!"

Late the next day, Bernie and Mickey boarded the bus to take leave of Ballyskelly. They were ticketed to Galway. Now, it was time to pass on to the future, whatever that might be. Mr. Cooke was sorry to see them go, mostly for monetary reasons. True, a couple of new pilgrims had come to stay. But none had opted for a suite despite his careful presentation and the usually unfailing ruse. Mrs. Cooke was genuinely sad, as was manifest by the hugs and tears, plus the expressed hope of them coming once again.

While Mickey was stowing the bags in the overhead bin, Bernadette waved from the window to Mrs. Cooke. Then she wiped her own fresh tears away. The bus pulled out, and the Inn at Ballyskelly was fading fast. Bernie looked down at her going-away gift. Although it was only a postcard, Mrs. Cooke had mounted it in a fine silver frame. It was a photo of Skellig Michael, which Bernie would keep until the end of her days.

Victimized by the erratic bus schedules, Bernadette and Mickey finally arrived in Galway the next afternoon. While on the journey, Bernadette had been reflective, as was her nature. She found it difficult knowing that Dublin, her parents, and the home in which she had been raised were just over there to the east! Bernie hadn't thought of her parents very much while she was in Ulster, as it had been easier to wall them off. *Something like the Great Wall of China,* she reflected somberly. This led her to wonder which side of the wall she was on. Bernie finally concluded that it was she who was on the outside! She represented the Mongols, while her parents were the staid citizens of Cathay. Well she was the free spirit, for Mongols could roam as they chose, independent of society's constraints. Would she ever see them again? Were they still alive and well? Chances are they were. For they were relatively young and in good health the day she took her leave.

Starting to tiptoe into Bernadette's conscience was a little remorse. Then, other nagging doubts arose. Maybe she was no Mongol after all. Perhaps, she possessed a siege mentality, holding herself within an emotional castle with the moat deeply filled, and the drawbridge up, while the portcullis was down. Then, Bernie glanced over at her napping spouse. She reached over and touched his hand lightly. "Well, Mongol or whatever, I'm with the man that I love, and we're doing what we think is right."

Suddenly, the words of their wedding ceremony leapt into her mind. "Until death do us part," she said silently. Then, she realized that for them the expression might not convey longevity, which most couples assumed. There was a simple solution for that. *Make every day count as ten. If we beat the odds, think of the wonderful bonus we'll have at the end.* These thoughts brought solace to her heart and generated a kiss of sufficient passion to awaken Mickey instantly.

CHAPTER TWENTY

After studying the register bearing Mickey's signature, the desk clerk at the Dublin House Hotel raised his eyes to observe the signer. Then he said, "Mr. Moynihan our manager, Mr. Bailey, has some news from a mutual friend that he would like to convey to you. Would it be convenient to see him now?"

"That would be fine," Mickey replied.

"Right this way, please," said the man behind the desk. Mickey nodded to Bernadette. This was a sign she was to remain in the lobby, causing no umbrage on her behalf

The clerk quickly came to a door marked "Private," knocked twice, opened it a crack, and addressed the person inside. "Mr. Moynihan has arrived, sir! Shall I show him in?"

"Of course," came a gruff response.

Mickey passed through the now fully opened door just as Bailey arose. He was a tall man, although a bit gaunt and typically black Irish when it came to complexion, eyes, and hair. Most striking about him was the empty sleeve smartly pinned up where the right arm used to be. Bailey extended his left hand, and Mickey quickly compensated to accept it. "Have a seat, please, Mr. Manion, or more properly now Mr. Moynihan, he said.

"Mickey will do just fine," was the reply given as he slid into a chair.

"I used to be in the same work as you, Mickey. One day, the RUC caught up with me and carted me off to one of their cherished correctional institutions. I tired of the hospitality after a few years. So, I went over the wall one night and caught a .303 in the upper arm as a going-away present. They didn't catch me or kill me, though it was close in the latter regard! After spending a week on the run, half of it coiled up in the dirt, the poor arm was so badly infected that it had to come off. Well at least I was happy that I made it all the way to the south. The right arm is buried here, so the rest of me can join up with it once again when the time comes."

Bailey changed the topic, saying, "I had a long talk with our mutual friend, McGann, last night. The news from Belfast isn't good, I'm afraid. One of your cell—Brophy is the name—apparently dove under a car when the RUC arrived. The bastard never put up a fight at all! Worse than that, he did more singing than Bing Crosby! As a result, the Brits have taken Maher and Plunkett into custody along with Mr. Sweeney. Also, two old bachelor brothers named Harrington, as I recall. Fortunately, you're safe, as is your new bride. None of those arrested can come up with McGann or Hogan's names.

"They put up one hell of a manhunt looking for you. But the fact you're sitting here is a pretty good argument they had no success. Big Frank has a high opinion of you, and you can be sure he'll follow up when you get to Boston and beyond. I can vouch for that, as he did well for me and I'm happy to reciprocate when I can. As I understand, you both have valid-appearing passports and a marriage license. Here are a couple tickets to get you aboard the *Star of Galway*. She's a freighter, but she carries twelve passengers. It's not first cabin or the *Queen Mary*, but it beats the hell out of steerage!

"The desk clerk will see to getting you up in time, and a car will take you to the dock. The room here is on the house, and so is the food. Best of luck to you and the bride, Mickey, and thanks for what you have done for the Cause!"

"Not nearly as much as you!" replied Mickey, noting the empty right sleeve again as he extended his left hand.

"One more thing, Mick: wanted posters can have wings, and sometimes the Yankees can be very straight-laced. We wouldn't want them sending you home to mother. The *Star of Galway* is on the slow side and a great opportunity to grow a beard. Also, here's a pair of old glasses that somebody left in the lobby. They'll probably screw up your depth perception. But, you'll look like Clark Kent when he's not in the blue and red outfit!" This was good for a chuckle.

On the tide, the *Star of Galway* raised anchor and passed gracefully from Galway Bay to the Atlantic. Boston was eleven days away. Neither Bernie nor Mickey knew what awaited them there, apart from the need to report in at the pub that Big Frank owned as a very absentee landlord. Meanwhile, the *Star's* cruise to America was well to the west of Skellig. Consequently, Bernadette would not glimpse her magical isle. Her little silver-framed photo would have to suffice.

The Old World was fast disappearing in the wake of their ship. A New World awaited, and they had some foreboding. However, both knew the earth was a globe, and they wouldn't sail off the end! That was an advantage over those who sailed west a long time ago.

Just as there are no road signs deployed on any sea, sure knowledge of location is bestowed only on the masters of the sextant. Also, they know the position of the telltale stars on which they rely. Consequently, in Ulster, at the exact second that the brazen bow of the *Star of Galway* transected the line of fifteen degrees west longitude, a large knot of the curious were clustered about the kiosk where Mickey used to stop. None of these took note of his absence. Nor did anyone seem to discern the photo on the front page of the newspaper was of a man who had frequently stood in their midst. Fully unfurled, the banner headlines proclaimed "MYSTERY OF JUDGE COLLINS SOLVED."

Details of the Collins story were ensconced in much finer print. They heaped great praise on Chief Inspector Merlin Spencer, while tossing only a few kudos the way of his friend and colleague, Chief Inspector Paul Foster. Articles went on to reiterate the heroic actions of Spencer in what had become known as the "Showdown at Sweeney's." As he was the only survivor from the law enforcement side, the glory of that day passed quite naturally to him. In addition, he had suffered a grievous wound in the performance of his duty. Furthermore, Spencer was believed to have wounded the IRA gunman and terrorist Michael Manion, who was still at large. Mickey's photo occupied a correspondingly large space, inasmuch as his evasion of capture continued to be quite newsworthy.

Foster had done the investigative legwork. However, Spencer, from his hospital bed, had urged him to make an extremely detailed search of Sweeney's Garage. Initially, Crimmons thought it was a colossal waste of time to perform his art in the basement. He felt there was little in that place to hint of any relationship to crime. "I must be going daft, checking this old bucket for prints," he murmured. However, prints were present, and one very clear set did not belong to the garage owner, Manion, or any of his men! Something about the pattern caught Crimmons's eye, for it appeared quite similar to a set he had taken at the morgue several weeks back.

Returning to his office, Crimmons's hunch led him to the second file, and he pulled out a sheet for comparison. He had no doubt that Justice Collins had touched that bucket, and the only reason would have been that he was held a prisoner there.

Thus, Mickey, out in the Atlantic, had another crime for which the Crown would charge him! Also, the connection with Judge Collins would lie heavily on the heads of the surviving members of his cell. Brophy, Maher, Plunkett, and poor old Sweeney had no knowledge of the judge's incarceration, and they would plead their innocence. However, that would lead to nothing but shaking heads, glowering eyes, and looks of utter contempt. From a practical standpoint, it was just one more murder added to at least six others. Therefore, one more life sentence, without possibility of parole, was not really a meaningful addition.

Newspaper accounts of the crimes did not mention the fact that when Foster and his squad of police broke into Mickey's room, they found no hint of where he might have gone. No address book, travel brochures, matchbooks, or indented note pads provided a clue. A single item did catch their attention—an old metal plaque that proclaimed "Life springs from death and from the graves of the patriot dead spring living nations." Foster grew livid as the words took root. He ripped the plaque from the wall and subjected the old metal to all the torque his hands could apply! Finally, the plaque surrendered its wholeness. But it gained a little revenge when a jagged piece cut deeply into the Chief Inspector's thumb. Foster hurled the fragments away, reached for a handkerchief to stem the flow of blood, and cursed all the "fookin' Fenians," especially Michael Manion.

Other factors not meant for the news were High Commissioner Marriott's scathing rebukes from London. Also, his absolute disgust that he was unable to wreak any vengeance on Foster or Spencer, as they were now held in the highest esteem by all Protestant Ulster. Instead of forced retirement, they were on their way to promotion and higher pay. Furthermore, the private pronouncements of Deputy Director Edward Terwilliger's superiors did not in any way resemble the public acclaim accorded him. Therefore, he did have a fine funeral service complete with Honor Guard, splendid eulogies, and posthumous commendations. His men slain in the same gun battle received only token recognition. Consequently, rank would seem to have its privilege on both sides of eternity.

Spencer and Foster would retire some years later. But their future exploits would never achieve the notoriety surrounding the "Showdown at Sweeney's." However, it was reassuring that they would serve out their time and end up with full pension until their final days. In particular, Spencer would always have some remorse that he had been unable to collar Manion. However, he achieved some comfort on convincing himself that the terrorist had probably died from the wound he had suffered and was buried in an unmarked grave. Also, shortly after the showdown, High Commissioner Marriott died from a coronary artery occlusion with associated massive heart attack. He had just finished a second course of sweetbreads at his favorite club.

Meanwhile, having wallowed her way across the North Atlantic, the *Star of Galway* was eleven days from the city whose name she bore. In a very small cabin, sandwiched between others of similar size, Michael Manion, now

Moynihan, was starting to stir. Then he bolted upright, striking his head a resounding blow on the berth above and, at the same time, bringing to life his deeply slumbering wife. Bernadette shook her head, rubbed her eyes, and slowly shook the cobwebs away. First, she murmured somewhat incoherently, "What happened, Mickey?" Then, very soon, Bernie's imagination leaped out of her clouded sensorium to bestow a stark image of the ship's side laid wide open by the jagged teeth of some monstrous, meandering iceberg.

Bernadette suddenly screamed, "Are we going down, Mick?"

"We're down about as far as we can go unless you wish to visit the engine room," he replied while still rubbing his head.

"I'm serious Mickey! Are we sinking?" Bernie cried out.

"If we are, the water hasn't reached our version of steerage," he responded. Mickey placed his feet on the bare deck, then said, "The floor's still hot from the boilers, and the engine is still rambling. It looks as though we may still have time to make it to the lifeboats or at least you can. They'll probably want to leave me behind and send women and children first. I hope this tub has a band. I don't want to be out on the deck singing 'Nearer My God to Thee' a cappella while the ice-cold Atlantic is creeping up my legs!"

"Mickey, for God's sake, be serious," retorted Bernadette.

"I thought we decided He was the product of smoke and mirrors," her husband responded in a jocular fashion. "Besides, if He really is up there somewhere, I'm sure He would want me to die smiling!"

"Mickey!" Bernadette said her voice icy with consternation. "I asked you a simple question because I'm scared, and all you give me is this song and dance routine."

"You're wrong, Bernie, I haven't put anything to music, and this cabin is far too small in which to dance. I have, in what I consider to be a humorous fashion, tried to inform you that we are not going under. This poor man's *Titanic* is still afloat and in no danger at all. The shock you felt was my head smashing into your bunk! You're in far more danger of losing your spouse from a concussion than you are to be a permanent guest of Davy Jones But, this bloody cabin reminds me of my prison cell. The only difference is that there are no bars on the door."

Bernie had regained her sense of humor and said rather coyly, "I can think of a bigger difference."

"What's that?" he shot back.

"You have me," was Bernie's response given in a sensuous overtone.

"You're right there, Bernie," Mickey responded with obvious pleasure. He caught her as she exited the upper bunk, hugged her tight and started to contemplate a return to the bottom bunk. However, the ship began to slow. A loud blast bellowed out from the *Star of Galway's* horn! Lesser horns sang out from various compass points. Then, Mickey realized that no doubt the tugboats were scampering like children about their mother's skirts, and vying with one another to lead the *Star of Galway* to her berth. Quickly, Mickey moved to the tiny porthole and peered out. Then, he exclaimed, "Throw on something quick, Bernie, and we'll go up on deck. We'll soon be going by the big, tall lady with the torch!"

Rushing topside, they confirmed that they were passing the Statue of Liberty, and a new life was waiting in America. Skellig and Ireland lay far behind at the very end of the ship's wake, which had long since been erased by the waves.

Clearance at Immigration was a breeze, thanks to the splendid forgeries that Big Frank McGann had provided. Noting the Immigration Officer studying first his passport photo, then his face, Mickey smiled broadly. "I know, Officer, the beard is new. My wife likes it." This brought a smile from the official in concert with affixation of the Official Stamp and a gracious acknowledgment that all was in order.

Once outside, Mickey did a quick study of those who were hailing cabs, and he soon procured one. Shortly, the new émigrés were on their way to Grand Central Station to board a train that would take them to Boston. However, the cab ride through Manhattan was like something from a different world. Dissatisfied with their inability to see the tops of the skyscrapers, Bernadette and Mickey leaned far out of the cab's windows so as not to miss a single thing! After a couple of blocks, the gruff voice of the cabbie boomed out in Brooklyn's classic accent, "Look, buddy! If you and the lady are hell bent on losin' your heads when we go by a bus, then leave five bucks on the seat so I can get my fare, okay!"

Without ever retracting his head, Mickey shouted back, "I'll be happy to do that if you'll promise not to take more than a nickel tip and then put the change back in me pocket." What the cab driver replied was not heard due to a blaring horn, but Mickey felt it was just as well.

Their train ride to Boston did not seem long or tedious, for there were thousands of unfamiliar sights. After arriving in Boston, another cab was hailed using Mickey's newly acquired skill. This cabbie was strictly "old sod," five years out of County Mayo with the name of Corkery. "Sure and I know McGann's Bar. I've even met Big Frank a time or two." Soon, they were left at the curbside in front of the bar. Shortly, the cab driver pulled away, better off than expected because he also received the tip that the New York cabbie forfeited by his rudeness. Once inside, Bernie guarded their valises, while Mickey made inquiry. He was back in moments, shepherded by one of the bartenders, who showed them to the office of Billy McHugh.

On meeting McHugh, Mickey observed that the proprietor of this part of Big Frank's American empire was far beyond portly. Nonetheless, his obesity was reasonably well obscured by an expensive tailored suit. A large shock of pure white hair was well coifed and contrasted sharply with a beefy, red complexion. This would be described as "very rare" if speaking of a porterhouse steak. An unduly large and bulbous nose was the focal point on his face. Pores in the skin surrounding the engorged proboscis were deeply prominent, giving the appearance of orange skin. A mosaic of spidery blue veins surrounded his nose, then spread out like a web to reach the far perimeters of the face. Mickey observed that they were so obvious that one's imagination might prod the observer to look for the spider.

As Mickey approached, a very beefy hand was extended, but the body to which it was connected did not rise. A gravelly voice proclaimed his name, then said, "It's my pleasure to welcome the Manions to Boston." McHugh's porcine eyes squinted at Mickey, and he could sense the exhilaration of enjoyment lurking therein.

"It's Moynihan, I'm afraid," replied Mickey, as he grasped the outstretched hand. A bone-crushing grip he meant to deliver was far reduced in magnitude by all the adipose tissue resident in McHugh's hand. Mickey sensed it was like squeezing a large ball of dough and expecting it to wince!

Full-disclosure discussion between Mickey and McHugh followed. As usual, Moynihan turned down the proffered drink, and Bernie quickly accepted, feeling well in need of one. First, McHugh gave them the good news, beaming all the way through the presentation. Big Frank had made all the arrangements for them to take over and manage a bar in South Boston named Barney's. They could keep 60 percent of the profits for themselves, and 40 percent went to McGann by way of a Swiss bank account. Details would be furnished later. Also, McHugh explained that living quarters were above the bar, which were rent-free.

McHugh's broad smile displaced his chin sufficiently to add several layers to an already double one. Mickey smiled back, saying, "How's the business been there?"

"It hasn't," said McHugh, with his smile undiminished.

"You mean it's new and hasn't opened yet?" responded Moynihan, trying to maintain some level of enthusiasm.

"Oh! Its been open for at least eighty years, but closed for about two months ever since the riot."

"The riot!" gasped Bernadette before aspirating a small quantity of the drink that she was sipping, thus setting off a coughing spasm.

"That's right," replied McHugh. "It was after an Irish football game! South Bay Bombers lost, and they were all there drinking. Benny Brogan, your predecessor, said the wrong thing and touched it all off."

"Where is he now?" queried Mickey.

"Hopefully in heaven," said McHugh, his already prodigious smile enlarging even more. "Someone hit him hard on the head with a garboon!"

"I presume the place is a mess," said Mickey. A black Irish scowl was forming hard on his face and drove the smile from McHugh's.

"Well it's definitely what we would call a fixer-upper. I can have someone run you over there tonight if you like," was the portly man's response.

"Just give me the address, and I'll see it in the morning," Mickey stood up and took the slip of paper from McHugh and spit out, "Good day to you, sir." He grabbed Bernie's hand, and they departed.

She looked and felt crestfallen. "What will we do now, Mick?" she said sadly.

"Find a fine hotel and celebrate our first night in America," replied Mickey.

"But, you don't drink," she said.

"I know that," he replied. "But there are other ways to celebrate!" and he gave her a fine pinch, along with a certain knowing look.

Chapter Twenty-One

❈ ❈ ❈

Mickey and Bernadette spent a romantic if not restful night at the Ritz-Carlton, further enhanced by the removal of his beard, which she detested. Fortunately, the money belt containing the purloined cash he had kept following the armored car robbery was still well stuffed, but unobtrusive around a slender rock-hard waist. When Bernadette awoke, she was surprised to find her husband sitting up in bed, studying the Boston phone book.

"Mickey," she murmured. "What on earth are you doing?"

"Celebrating!" he replied. "For the first time since we left Ireland, I can sit up in bed without crackin' me noggin on the bottom of your bunk. Second, I'm studying what they call the Yellow Pages here in the States. I've made a list of all the folks we got to see to resurrect this benighted pub that we fell heir to. Here's the list! It reads like the roster of the Irish National Football Team. See there's Murphy's Wholesale Wine, Beer and Spirits, Dumphy's Bar, Restaurant and Furniture, etc. As soon as we have a bite of breakfast, we'll go have a look at this tomb that we're supposed to operate. Then, we'll turn in to a couple of credit convincers."

"I wish that I had your optimism," replied Bernie demurely.

"Don't worry Bernie. It's highly contagious, and you'll probably contract it before we find a cab."

Shortly later, when the taxi driver picked up the two passengers in front of the prestigious hotel, he appeared somewhat astonished and unnerved when his fare presented the address to which they wished to be taken. His expression suggested that he had just been requested to proceed to a location somewhere on the other side of the River Styx. Had he not needed to have both hands on the steering wheel, he might have made the sign of the cross.

When he pulled up in front of the skeletal remains of the ill-fated Barney's, the cabbie haltingly said, "I won't be able to wait!"

"No need," shot back Mickey, as he paid the fare and proffered what was by his standards a generous tip. This was Moynihan's response to the driver's beseeching eyes, which seemed to indicate that he was deserving of a munificent one.

As Bernadette was being helped from the taxi, she reflected quickly and said, "Mick, we didn't get a key."

"Who needs one?" he replied. "There isn't any front door, and even if there was we could still go through where the front window used to be."

Bernie had barely cleared the taxi door before the car was in motion. Apparently, the driver felt that acceleration was necessary as he sped away.

Entry into the shambles once known as Barney's was precarious! However, Mickey and Bernie picked their way through broken glass and other debris. "I suppose it could be worse," sighed Bernadette. "At least, the walls are still standing."

"See! You have already contracted the enthusiastic spirit," laughed Mickey just before kicking a broken chair from his path. "You've got to hand it to those Irish Yankees. This place looks worse than the Lambeg Drum did after we bombed it!"

"That Mr. McHugh said there were living quarters upstairs," Bernadette said hesitatingly. "Do you see a stairway?"

"I think that it's behind what's left of the piano," Mickey responded. Then he put his shoulder into the instrument's sorry remains and gave a powerful shove. The old upright toppled, and as it hit the floor, a couple of surviving keys found remaining wires, producing a pair of discordant notes. "Out of tune," was Mickey's response. Then, he went on adding, "Mind your step, Bernie, the banister is gone!" Upon arrival in the living quarters, the new Mr. Moynihan sighed disconsolately and said, "This is terrible! It looks and smells like a pigsty."

"You're wrong love. No respectable sow would occupy this place. Well! We've seen all we need to see. Let's start seeing folks about resuscitating this corpse."

By mid-afternoon, all that was necessary had been accomplished. The results were the same wherever they went whether it was Boylan's Sign Company, O'Mally's Trash Cleanup and Hauling, or Murphy's Wholesale Wine and Beer. At first, the owners seemed incredulous on hearing the new customer's request. However, it didn't seem to take long to get better acquainted! Just before the time for rude dismissal, all the owners had the occasion to be the target of

Mickey's nearly black hooded eyes looming out of a scowling face with a ship's prow of a firm, set jaw. If it were necessary to look further, they were confronted with a pair of huge, hard hands sporting scarred rock-like knuckles fully supported by wrists larger than most ankles. Soon, all the suppliers came to decide that it might be pragmatic and healthy to acquiesce. Then they could spend the rest of the encounter risking a rewarding glance at the lady who had come along and sat smiling and non-confrontational. Surely, it was a pleasure to catch a peek at her face, a glory to see the locks of gleaming red hair, and pure intrigue to ponder what was so beguiling about her eyes!

Within two weeks, Barney's was no more. A new establishment had taken its place. Like a phoenix arising from the ashes, the Shillelagh arose! The name was proudly bannered in raised, gold letters against a field of black enamel, which was also bordered in gold and tastefully stippled with small shamrocks of vivid emerald green. Furthermore, early on, Mickey had decided that Bernie was not to live above a bar. Consequently, a very nice apartment had been leased in a much better part of Boston. Although the money belt was shrinking in girth, sufficient funds remained to carry them through until the Shillelagh was a success, of which Mickey had no doubt. Meanwhile, on the wall of their new apartment's bedroom, Bernie had hung her cherished photo of Skellig Michael. *Someday*, reflected Mickey, *I'll replace my little plaque that I left behind in Belfast. But for the time being I have other things to do!*

Bernie had not been allowed to see the Shillelagh until the renovation was complete. On inspection, she was awestruck at its appearance, though deeply concerned about the cost. The only response she received from her husband was, "Don't worry, Bernie, I've got it all planned out!" Indeed he did, for Mickey was becoming a fixture in South Boston. This allowed him to become privy to all that transpired there. Moynihan's personal safety was ensured because if there was anything a South Boston tough could recognize, it was someone tougher!

Planning the opening of his bar, Mickey thought, *I'll need some music. But, I must start out small, beginning with just a fiddler.* Several inquiries produced the same name. Frankie Finnegan, along with the caveat "If you can ever sober him up!" Moynihan located Finnegan and gathered him up just before two of Boston's finest were about to do the same. Safely away, Mickey stood the intoxicated musician up against a wall. Then, he malevolently asked Mr. Finnegan, "Would you rather fiddle, be dead drunk, or simply dead?" Quickly, the words blew away Frankie's alcoholic fog, and he soon came to the conclusion that he was facing either a benefactor or a destroyer. By week's end, the delirium tremens had ceased, and Finnegan no longer had hallucinations of mice and spiders emerging from the wall.

Within seven days, Finnegan had accepted being abstemious, and by opening night Mickey declared him "fit as a fiddle!" Moynihan did warn his one-man orchestra not to play any tunes that were morose. "Bad for business Frankie! Play something sad and all the customers start crying in their beer instead of drinking it." Bartenders and bouncers were recruited from among Boston College's largest and most intimidating athletes. Moynihan decided that valet parking would come along when business required. Parking attendants would come from the track team, while security resulted from the presence of two immense tackles from the football squad.

In Moynihan's mind, the Shillelagh was never meant to be a neighborhood bar. He meant it to be a mecca for all the Irish American zealots, who craved a bit of slumming with the Shanty Irish. He would provide a safe harbor for such frivolity. Soon, Frankie Finnegan was scouring the city to put together the finest ceilidh band outside Ireland. The Shillelagh would become a lodestone for all the would-be Fenians in the area. Also, the Shillelagh would become a conduit for the funds, which would be contributed by the wannabes to the real revolutionaries in Ulster and Old Erin!

Inside of six months, the Shillelagh's front door was never free of a waiting line, apart from nights of torrential downpour. A much larger marquee helped solve that problem. Given the Irish ambience, large numbers of partygoers felt it was worth waiting until the next inebriated customer was assisted to the door so they could secure a seat. However, in the event you were the right person, or recommended by one of them, entry through the side door was easily accomplished. Furthermore, the old living quarters had become Moynihan's resplendent private office and a good place for IRA business. Now made of carved ebony, the banister had been replaced and went very nicely with the green carpet.

The Shillelagh proved to be a bigger success than Mickey could have imagined! Before too long, all the debts were paid in full, which was something his suppliers had never envisioned. Moynihan always made the last payment in person. Totally free of intimidation, Mickey replaced his original glaring face and bare-knuckle diplomacy with a smile. Also, McGann's Swiss bank accounts were burgeoning. Consequently, Big Frank sat smiling in his Belfast office, wondering if he should spread some of his treasures around and open an account in the Grand Cayman Islands. McGann thought the name had a nice ring to it. Furthermore, if it were ever necessary for him to go to ground, it would have much greater appeal than Zurich.

To McGann, the image of a beach-front villa seemed to appear through the smoke of his cigar. He had no problem visualizing himself ensconced in a chaise lounge under a palm tree's umbrella, a glass of Bushmills in his hand. "That's a place I could enjoy," he mused. "Yeah! I'd be free of some stogy Swiss banker treating me as some subject of suspicion when I'm not half as suspicious as they are. Yes, the next deposit goes to the Alligator," he decided on after reflection on the symbol displayed on the Cayman Islands flag.

Turning to a codified set of books, McGann studied them. These indicated deposits in various banks in the names of clandestine companies. One account was IRA money, and good old Mickey was the primary source of that as well. His protégé was the way McGann thought of Mickey and he had the Yankees digging in their pocket bottoms! After a couple of stiff drinks and a few protest songs by Mickey's star performers, they were lining up to shell out a month's pay. Big Frank mused that if they added Maureen Sullivan singing "Danny Boy," while plucking at her Irish harp, they might even mortgage the family home. "Mickey, boyo, It was a fair day that I ran into the likes of you."

Bernadette was for the time being retired from her previous occupations. She had nearly forgotten the time spent waiting on tables at Brennans. However, the memory of meeting Mickey there and wondering if he would be waiting outside at closing was far beyond erasure. On occasion, while on shopping trips in her fine new Buick, she would call to mind her IRA message assignments. *I wonder who got the old motor bike?* Bernie would ponder. *Well, I hope it was someone who needed it. I have my fine new car now. Besides, I'd look a sight bouncing along on a motor scooter in the eighth month of my pregnancy.* Bernie knew that her husband had been elated at the news. But he had become somber when asked what they should name the baby.

However, after reflection, Mickey had responded almost piously, "If it's a boy, the name will be Sean." His little brother's memory would haunt him always, for he regarded Sean's death as murder. Apart from that reflection, Mickey remained his usual happy self, frequently kidding Bernadette about the fine dumpling she had in her pot.

Bernadette basked in her role as a developing matron. She had a fine new home to preside over and furnish, plus Beth, the new maid, to supervise. In regard to the Shillelagh, Mickey shared all the significant decisions with her. Otherwise, Bernie remained outside that part of her husband's business world that was private. On occasion, a little suspicion and jealousy crept into her mind, as she knew that many of the female patrons and certainly most of the entertainers were very attractive! Bernie had every reason to think that they would find her husband most appealing. In addition to his rugged handsomeness and sense of humor, he was becoming quite affluent. Last, she was aware that an aura of danger seemed to surround him. These were qualities that many women would surely find terribly provocative. In truth, such seductresses were not in short supply at the Shillelagh, and most were not the least bit reticent to play the temptress. However, this was something Bernadette and Mickey had never discussed, nor would they ever in the future.

In reality, Bernadette had nothing to fear. Mickey planned to be faithful come whatever. If propositions occurred, or he was subject to a surfeit of flirtation, all the women attempting to beguile him received the same admonition. Mickey's little speech was firm, to the point, and very sincere. Always delivered with a smile, it went like this: "Sorry lass, but there are two things I don't need rolling around my desk. First is loose cannons, and the second is loose Colleens. They have a lot in common!" Very few tried a second time, and if they did, his response was far less allegorical.

Meanwhile, Bernadette's pregnancy had been free from complications. Baby Sean was born healthy, weighing a bit less than ten pounds. Despite hours of studying him, Bernadette decided the baby was pure Mickey. She was unable to perceive a single feature of her own or those of her family. Nonetheless, she was absolutely pleased. Bernie decided that if there was anything finer than having one Mickey around, it was having two! Both parents would have liked the birth certificate to read "Sean Rory Manion," but the assumed surname of Moynihan was used by necessity. Bernadette thought about a Christening, but dismissed the possibility, knowing full well how her husband would feel about such a thing. In addition, she had grown to feel comfortable as an agnostic. *Why not just let things be?* she decided.

Sean was just over two years old when Liam was born. Bernadette was finally able to recognize a few Donahue features in their new baby. However, they were subtle, and there was no question that Manion was the predominant gene present.

Bernadette took great pride in her role as mother. Rarely did she feel a need to be free of her children for any length of time, so baby-sitters were used infrequently. Also, happiness resided within Bernie for two other reasons. Fortunately, there was never a sign that Mickey had come to be bored with his sons, as some other Irishmen she had encountered seemed to be. Furthermore, despite doubts that had arisen years back, Mickey never seemed to be bored with her. "He's a fine man for an atheist," Bernie would sometimes say to herself.

Though the following four years proved to be fallow, Bernadette's gynecologist had pronounced her as fit as she had ever been. Occasionally, due to this turn of events, Bernadette would feel a little dejected, for surely there was no lack of trying. Once or twice, she started to tell herself that it was God's will. However, she quickly corrected that concept and substituted bad luck or fate in its place. Happily, despite the dearth in offspring, life with Mickey was nonpareil when it came to good times and excitement.

Fortunately, the Shillelagh was busier and more popular than ever. Soon, it would have a running mate named Skellig Michael, and the new restaurant would be opening in a week. Bernadette had no doubt that most non-Gaelic speakers would mispronounce the name. But they would soon come to learn that it was pronounced "Skelly" ending in a y rather than a g. Mickey had given Bernie rein to decorate and staff it. Bernadette had enthusiastically received the challenge. Therefore, Skellig Michael had an exterior and interior fascias of Irish granite just like that of the island. Resplendent carpets of emerald green were enhanced by the finest of polished brass. Also, exquisite dark hardwoods and a quartet of Waterford chandeliers were deployed in obeisance about the magnificent central chandelier, a full twelve feet in length and suspended from a thirty-foot vaulted ceiling.

Direct from Ireland, professional bartenders and waiters were some of the finest. French was the nationality chosen for the chefs, and that was Bernadette's sole exclusion protecting her from being totally ethnocentric. No protest songs were to be sung or heard at Skellig Michael. Customers were to hear only the music of the most talented Irish harpists, pianists, and violinists that could be found. In addition, the tenors and divas chosen to perform would surely melt your heart away.

Bernadette spent one night a week away from the family to supervise and act as Skellig Michael's hostess. She had chosen her managerial staff with extreme professionalism and was proud to note that Skellig Michael was a great success with or without her presence. In addition, extreme happiness was manifested when Mickey met her by the door at closing time. His old worn brogans and shabby suit were replaced by Italian finery. Also, there was now a little gray sneaking a peek around his hairline. Mickey always held a small bouquet, as he was never ostentatious when it came to flowers. *Nevertheless, there are no sweeter ones anywhere to be found,* thought Bernadette.

One of the great delights for the Moynihan family was travel. Sean and Liam took to it naturally like baby seals swimming beside their parents. Money was no problem at this juncture in their lives, so in all of their journeys they traveled first class. Sean and Liam were quite pampered little boys. However, at ages seven and nine, there was no discernible indication that they were then, or would be later, overly spoiled. While traveling, two family rules were strictly observed. No cathedrals, chapels, or monasteries were ever part of their itinerary, nor did they ever visit Ireland or any part of the British Isles." Both Bernie and Mickey had up to this point been unable to shake the feeling that some face in the crowd might notice them. Consequently, the mind of the curious might grope for the placement of a name to go with the face.

Trips to the Orient, Australia, South America, and much of Europe were mainly for entertainment and intellectual enrichment. However, for Mickey, travel to some specific areas of the world was heavily spiced with intrigue, which created great excitement. Bernadette was not oblivious to this. She was well aware of private meetings between her husband and others in certain cities, as well as clandestine side trips, taken by Mickey alone. He had been up front in telling her that it was IRA business. However, he stopped short of providing specifics, and this fueled her speculation. Nevertheless, she was able to tame her curiosity to the point that explanations were never demanded, nor did she ever try to look at his personal notes or papers. This was just as well, for Mickey kept all coded in such a manner as to have been a formidable task for even a world-class intelligence unit to decipher.

Given his inborn Irish proclivities, Moynihan took a certain delight in providing an occasional clue to Bernadette. Almost always, these were in the form of some elegant gift. Mickey was well aware that his wife had an analytical intellect that would be prized by the KGB, CIA, Mossad, or even bloody MI-6. Thus, a certain gemstone in a particular setting, an exquisite piece of crystal, lace, or leather item could have only come from a particular place. Bernie would study the gift, decipher it, and come up with the proper conclusion. For instance, when Mickey brought her pearls, after studying them she decided they had come from the Arabian Sea. But she knew they hadn't been to Arabia, nor could Mickey have made it there and back in the time that he was gone on his side trip. "Just where could he go from Athens, conduct his business and return within twenty-four hours? Lebanon seemed a good bet." She knew at that point in time all the treasures of the Middle East were readily available in Beirut, and so was access to the Palestine Liberation leaders.

Bernie mused, *What could the PLO provide the IRA?* Then, she thought, *Guns, maybe, and training facilities in the Becca Valley probably!*

Earlier, Mickey had brought Bernie some exquisite crystal. She had decided that it had to be Czech. Besides crystal, she remembered that they exported Semtex. When Bernie had received the exquisite necklace and tiara, she had noted they were damascene in pattern. But the threads of green and white gold had been inlaid in yellow gold, rather than steel, as was the case with classic damascene. Bernadette decided the probable country of origin was Libya. Especially, she surmised, considering the short length of time that Mickey was absent from the villa they had rented in Toramelinos on the Costa de Sol of Spain, this country fit the scenario. "What else was in Libya? Moammar al-Gaddafi, of course, and another source of arms and munitions."

As it turned out, Bernie was rarely (if ever) wrong in her analysis. Mickey had readily embraced the concept that "my enemy's enemy is my friend!"

Indeed, Moynihan had visited all of these places and found areas of common interest, sources of supply, plus friends and supporters in high places. Also, he had secured training facilities for IRA commandos. Furthermore, Moynihan had procured arms shipments to Ireland, and these arrangements had never become known to MI-6 or their collaborators. They had seized the mother ships Escuna and Claudia chartered by others, along with the shipment of arms they contained, and this had become a cause célèbre for MI-6. The Libyans did not appreciate the loss or the publicity. Therefore, in the future, they decided to deal solely with Mr. Moynihan. For they fathomed the fact that behind the smiling Irish face lay the guile of an Arab trader. He could be trusted and depended on.

During some of his side trips, Moynihan met a number of times with Big Frank McGann. Several encounters took place in Switzerland, a couple in the Cayman Islands, and one in Cuba. In the latter, Mickey was distraught because he couldn't find a single intriguing gift for Bernie in that place. *If ever there was anything worth getting excited about, Old Fidel must have buried it*, Mickey thought. Then, he added, *I doubt she would be enthralled by a box of cigars!*

At previous meetings with Big Frank, Mickey was readily cognizant of insidious changes in the physique of his mentor. But arriving for their final meeting in Cuba, it proved to be a shocking revelation. When he greeted McGann, Moynihan observed the ravishing of his body, which was occurring with morbid acceleration. Gone were the sculptured, rock-like masses of bulging muscles encapsulated by taught, firm flesh. Now, severely atrophied, they barely stood out in contrast to the ligaments and tendons to which they were attached. Sallow skin hung like clammy bunting from his arms and face. Gone was the color of vitality. For Mickey, the remaining hue could be construed as the harbinger of death!

McGann's once proud, massive jaw line was now lost above a grotesque waddle of turgorless flesh. Jaundiced sclera served to extinguish the light in formerly flashing blue eyes. What color did remain in Big Frank's face apart from icterus was attributable to the rosacic cyanotic hue. This was part of the ugly rhinophyma that effaced a formerly handsome patrician nose, which had miraculously remained unscathed in numerous brawls. Only the massive bones predicated by some primordial gene attested to the man McMann once was. Mickey's mind was filled with allegories. Did Big Frank remind him most of a slab of ice cream, left too long in a warm dish? Or, perhaps a pitiful old lion long starving and trying to move about in a shabby hide ten sizes too large? Perhaps, a once proud man o'war left lying broken on a reef with its ribs and spine exposed, its sodden sails swirling about in the sea's ebbing tide was most fitting of all. Before conversation commenced, Mickey made one last observation. Many arterials were present on Big Frank's face. Poorly oxygenated blood coursed through them. Thus, they stood out in a cyanotic blue, like tiny roads drawn on a yellowed map. *All roads led to Rome in Caesar's time. But in the impending end of McGann's era, they all led to Bushmill's distillery!* decided Mickey.

Sometimes, Moynihan had asked his mentor if it was time for him to return to Ireland and take up the Cause. However, he always got he same answer, "No, Mickey, boyo! You are doing a fine job, a splendid job. We don't have anyone else who could come through for us like you have. We need you just where you are!" Though the answer remained the same, the delivery was deteriorating. Sentences became phrases between phrases. Deep inside, Mickey knew that he could be going back to take over, invited or not! He was no stranger to recognizing manifest destiny, nor was he in any way timid about seizing on it.

Mickey engendered one other stimulus, on seeing the sadly dissipating McGann, and that was checking his own physical status. When that time came, Moynihan was not concerned about his own physical well-being, for he was a fitness fanatic, either on the road or back home. In Boston, his neighbors often encountered him out doing roadwork well in advance of those years when it became an American passion. Thus he was considered a bit of an eccentric, which didn't bother him in the least. If the same inquisitive neighbors in the environs of the Moynihan Mansion were aware that he was also a student of martial arts, their curiosity might have turned into concern. Mickey had immediately favored Tae Kwan Do as a means of accomplishing his goal, which was the devastation of any opponent in a rapid and less tiring manner. However, he did inculcate a few of the finer points of the other martial arts forms into his repertoire.

Moynihan's interests included sports, and a modicum of publicity had come his way by virtue of his prowess at regional trap and skeet shooting competitions. However, his finally honed skills, in reference to big-bore rifle shooting and pistol marksmanship, was kept under wraps. No trophies or medals were given for expertise with timers, detonators, Semtex, or other explosives. But if there were, Mickey would have qualified for a trophy case full of them!

Physical fitness and sports were important to all the Moynihan family, and the sons, Sean and Liam, found soccer to their liking. They were quite good at the game, especially due to the encouragement and coaching of their Da. Mickey disliked the American name for the sport. He preferred to refer to it as "football," like most of the rest of the world. This caused confusion and consternation on behalf of other parents whose sons played with Sean and Liam's teams. They thought of football as the game of the National Football League. "Why call that football?" Mickey would demand. "You never use your foot at all unless you punt, place kick the bloody thing, or you're trying to kick your opponent in the groin! You should call it something like 'smash and tackle.' As for "Soccer," it sounds more like a sport for wife beaters."

Sailing was the family sport in which all participated. They had worked their way up, through the smaller boats, to a sleek thirty-six-footer. Mickey looked forward to something even larger, but decided that would have to await the time when Sean and Liam were bigger and stronger. Thus, they would be capable and competent in the handling of such a craft. Meanwhile, they all loved the water and the wind plus the challenges that arose.

In particular, Bernadette loved the boat and every moment spent on it. She especially enjoyed the times when they ventured beyond Massachusetts Bay. Often, they would head either south around Cape Cod to seek New Bedford, or coursing north, they would search for Cranberry Island, which would point the way to Bar Harbor in Maine. Always Mickey felt that Bernie was an extraordinary delight when she had the helm. Nimble afoot and possessing the balance of a ballerina, she became as one with the skiff and the sea, and Mickey took extreme joy just in gazing on her. Given greater life by the wind, her magnificent burnished red locks seemed flecked with gold! As he took in this visage, Mickey thought of her hair as a glorious pendant, enlivened by the breeze and undulating from the slender staff, which was Bernie's body. Surely, no proud and broad pendant ever flew from any admiral's mizzenmast that could match Bernie's.

At times, Bernadette would study the compass, then let the wind tease the sails to the point they would cajole the craft eastward. As it took this station, the prow would be pointed to the mystic isle whose name was beautifully emblazoned on the stern, the *Isle of Skellig Michael*. It called to her as surely as did Sinbad's sirens. She always felt unfulfilled, as she returned to course. But someday her time would come, Bernie knew.

Chapter Twenty-Two

After a few years, Michael Moynihan was as respected as any Irishman in a city, which was a mecca for a great many of them. In many ways, his newfound prominence ran contrary to his nature. While the bouncers he employed for the Shillelagh were probably as tough if not tougher than any to be found in Boston, with only one exception, Moynihan had never laid a hand on anyone. He was always amused at how the members of his security staff could smilingly assist the drunk and disorderly out of the Shillelagh. While "assisting them," they appeared like tuxedo-clad Boy Scouts helping a gravely ill man through rush-hour traffic.

For Moynihan, the single exception came on a Tuesday very near three P.M., a few hours before his "No-Neck Squad" would don their tuxedos and take up unobtrusive positions in the bar. Mickey was at his desk making out checks when he became aware of a brief commotion outside his office. This was what he referred to as "half a fight." A few harsh words were exchanged, which were undecipherable through the thick mahogany door. Barely audible, the sound of something big, bony, and hard striking a much less resistant object and followed by a soft thud was evident to his attuned ears. This had all the earmarks of some gorilla laying someone out for the count, presumably his day manager!

Suddenly, his door flew open. Two very troublesome apparitions swiftly entered Moynihan's office. In a guttural voice, the first entrant called back to an unseen underling, "Watch the door, Frankie!"

"Yeah, boss," was the response.

Moynihan didn't draw the easily reachable Browning Hi-Power from its accessible resting place. Instead, he leaned back in his chair and smiled. After a very quick appraisal of his uninvited guests, Mickey said in a surprisingly soft voice, "Well, gentlemen. To what do I owe this honor? We aren't making any Mafia movies here at this time. So, I'm not sure why central casting sent over a pair of gorillas like you."

Moynihan observed that the first man—dark, slender, with aquiline nose and black, hawkish eyes—had all the appearance of a small, savage raptor. His partner was immense with ape-sized extremities although lacking the hair. This man's nose was that of a pugilist, as were his ears. A surfeit of gold teeth occupied voids left from the departure of the natural ones. Mickey's eyes were drawn to the man's knuckles, which looked like bosses between the horns of a Cape Buffalo. Yet this curious inspection produced no intimidation in Moynihan. Instead, he thought, *Ursus must have been the easy winner in the half a fight which he had heard outside his door.*

Suddenly, the man proclaimed, "Look you Paddy asshole! You need some insurance, so to speak, and we're here to collect the first weekly installment!"

Speaking firmly, Mickey replied, "Well there's more to me than the anatomical landmark you described." Then, feigning a look of concern, he asked timidly, "How much would that be?"

"About three G's a week to start," snarled the hawkish one.

"That's pretty expensive! I'm not sure I can afford it," replied Moynihan.

"You can afford it better than you can afford loosing your balls!" he hissed. Moynihan's adversary was now brandishing a switchblade.

"I see what you mean," Mickey said in a stammering fashion. "I'll get the money from the safe. But please don't hurt me. I've got a wife and kids!"

"Stop begging and open the friggin' safe," was the enforcer's response.

Glaring malevolently at Moynihan, the big man remained silent. However, he kept pounding one huge fist into a cupped hand of equal dimension. Mickey paused as though he was too terrified to proceed. Then, holding the switchblade, the smaller Sicilian extended his arm toward Moynihan. He was dumbfounded when Mickey's manacle-like hand encircled his wrist, propelling him forward in perfect rhythm, with his wrecking ball knee smashing into his lower rib cage. Cracking ribs produced a sickening sound, which was followed by great gasping. As the man fought for a measure of air to pacify his lungs, he fell writhing to the floor.

"Well that's taken care of Guido, or whatever the hell your name is. Now it's your turn, Rocco!"

Reacting, the huge Sicilian curled his monstrous fist and swung a roundhouse right. Moynihan ducked, just in time to avoid the extremity, which whistled above his head like the trunk of any angry elephant. Off-balance due to the failure to land his blow, the hood gave Mickey his opportunity. In a classic Tae Kwan Do maneuver, Mickey whirled bringing his right leg around in a high arc, thus permitting the heel of a well-polished Gucci to land solidly on Rocco's chin, with telling effect. Crumbling, the giant fell to the floor with a resounding thud despite the richly piled carpet.

Outside, the third mobster was holding off a number of the Shillelagh's staff with a drawn pistol. Well aware of the sounds of battery emanating from behind the door, he wrongly assumed that his compatriots were teaching the owner a lesson. A tap on the shoulder corrected that conclusion. Turning slightly but sufficiently, he presented a broad target for the fleshed-out sledgehammer fist, which preceded the sleeve of a well-tailored Italian silk suit. Carefully, Moynihan straightened his jacket and massaged his knuckles. Then he smiled at the relieved, distraught staff saying, "Haul these goons down to the meat cooler. We need to talk to them more!"

Little trouble was encountered conveying the two lightweight hoods to the very commodious meat locker of the Shillelagh. However, the huge one was a much greater logistics problem. Consequently, his removal was deferred until the brute was sufficiently conscious to stagger on his own. Once all were assembled inside the refrigerated room, the door was secured. Then, the three erstwhile goons were doused with cold water. As a result, they became a shivering, soggy though alert trio! Mickey wasted little time in initiating the interrogation, commencing with "Who in hell sent you three freaks?"

Still holding his ribs, the hawkish hood glowered at the other two, and it was obvious the *code of muerta* was to be upheld. However, since his respiratory tract was now sufficiently functioning at this point, he spat out a few words directed at Moynihan. "Go f--- yourself, Paddy!"

Mickey smiled broadly and replied, "That may be some type of Sicilian sport, but it's anatomically impossible for we Irish! Well I know it wasn't the pope who sent you here, so we may have to participate in some fun and games to get your answer. Jocko, get a hand lorry and bring us three empty beer kegs, and a bunch of towels like a good lad. We're about to see who can sing like a canary!"

Jocko departed enthusiastically, drafted a couple of helpers, and returned with the requested articles. "Good man," Mickey said. "Now, line the kegs up in a row end to end and put some towels in front and back, so they won't roll." Jocko did as directed. Moynihan stood back smiled at the kegs then, at the three mobsters. "Fortunately, gentlemen, you get some practice runs, before we get to the finals! All right! I want you to go over, pick out a keg, and stand on top of it."

The man, who had guarded the door, now addressed as "Luigi" by Moynihan, started to move. But a snarling command in Italian from the raptor-like hood dubbed "Guido" stopped him in mid-movement. "I see we have a language problem," were Moynihan's next words, strongly embellished with an Irish brogue. Brandishing the mobster's seized switchblade, Moynihan approached the ringleader. When the razor-sharp blade was just inches from the mobster's face, Mickey asked softly, "Which eye first, Guido?"

Defiance drained from the man's eyes and was quickly replaced with abject fear. Arising he moved slowly to the first keg, mounted it, and teetered in position. Quickly, the other two men followed. Luigi did poorly as a result of his tremulous legs, while Rocco seemed fairly adept. "See," said Mickey, "nothing to it. Let's go on to event number two. Tape their hands behind them fellows. Then remove the towels from the kegs." Thereupon, Luigi lasted only three seconds before his barrel rolled, and he fell hard against the concrete floor. Guido was next at five seconds and Rocco surprised all with a full ten-second stand.

"Time to move to the finals, gentlemen," were Moynihan's next words. Then he followed with, "I know you will all do better this time because you'll have a lot more incentive!" Moynihan ordered the towels replaced to stabilize the kegs. Then, the terrified trio was assisted to stand on their tops. Mickey walked slowly to the far wall of the room, followed by the eyes of all present. Reaching up, he grasped three meathooks, slid them across the rail, and adjusted the chains that held them. Next, he placed the sharpened tip of a hook under each man's chin. "It's time to take out the towels. So gentlemen on your marks, and may the best man win!" Terror was experienced by the trio, and was manifest in their pallor, diaphoresis, and tremulousness.

"Stop!" screamed Guido. "Don Carlo sent us."

"Sounds like a brand of olive oil to me," laughed Moynihan. "Does he have a last name, and where do I find him?"

"It's Don Carlo Carboni," they shrieked in unison. "He has an office in the back of the Trattoria San Tomosa on 7th Street South."

"You did well, gentlemen, and I must say that you're good sports. I'm going to declare it a draw, so you will all get a prize!" The thought of this offer, after what they had narrowly escaped, brought renewed terror to all of them. However, their retainers removed the meathooks and helped them down. Then, they allowed them to collapse on the floor, still shivering with fright as well as from the frigid temperature in the meat locker. Mickey whispered some detailed instructions in Jocko's ear, which brought forth a raucous laugh from the younger man. This did little to alleviate the fear in the three contestants.

Returning to his office, Moynihan put on a bulletproof vest beneath his shirt. Also, he added a shoulder holster, complete with a loaded Browning Hi-Power. Then, he changed to a more generous fitting suit, which he obtained from a closet. This suit was specially tailored to conceal his accoutrements.

Satisfied by his reflection in the office mirror, he went to his car and headed for 7th Street South.

Upon arrival at his destination, Moynihan slid the Cadillac into a nearby parking spot, just as patrons were entering the Trattoria de Tomaso. As soon as he went through the door, it was apparent to the maitre d'hôtel that this was not the usual pasta aficionado. His eyes swept from Moynihan to a pair of pin-striped bruisers stationed like the pillars of Hercules abreast a door in the rear. A scowl emerged on the man's face, as he inquired of Mickey's needs, though his voice was flavored with contempt. "Mickey Moynihan to see Don Carlo. I don't have an appointment, nor do I intend to wait for one!"

Just as many others had learned, a person didn't look into this man's face and think it prudent to remain offensive. Consequently, the maitre d' picked up a phone, pushed a button, and carried on a rapid conversation in Italian. When the communication was ended, the man replaced the phone on the receiver. Suddenly, his demeanor became obsequious. "This way, Mr. Moynihan," he said. Turning, he led the way to a door in the back. The pin-striped pillars were still stationed at the entry. An obvious tumor was present in the left armpits of their suits, these being less discretely tailored than that of the man's closing in on them. As they approached the door, no doubt due to the body language of the headwaiter or some eye signal that Mickey could not perceive, the guards stood aside. They remained alert, but lacked any sign of aggressiveness.

As Moynihan entered, Don Carlo looked up, but didn't rise or offer his hand. He was not what Mickey expected. Instead of being some pseudo-don, he might have been a count. Moynihan took measure of the man. Neither spoke for some seconds. Moynihan observed Don Carlo's manicured hands, perfectly coifed hair, and impeccably tailored suit, which were attention getters even leaving aside the massive gold ring featuring a nabob-sized diamond. Furthermore, his watch and cuff links showed that there were no soft spots in this man's sartorial standards.

What really caught Moynihan's eye was the man's face. Unquestionably, it had been the recipient of numerous facials, which were probably given by some exotic masseuse, who no doubt offered other services as well. Then, as their eyes met, Moynihan thought of a magnificent dagger, which he had seen when the family visited Topkapi in Istanbul. The sheath was magnificent, every ornamental detail done to what seemed to be beyond perfection. He remembered that inside the sheath was a blade of finest Damascus steel. Moynihan decided that regardless of how super-suave this man looked on the outside, there was real steel on the inside. No doubt he had been a Mafia soldier, bomb and acid thrower, torturer, and merciless killer. Also, those manicured hands had probably twisted many a garrote. Carlo had fought his way to *capo* and now he was *capo con tutti capi*.

Don Carlo was no less observant. *This Moynihan is powerfully built, but there is much more than brawn. He moves like a tiger, and those eyes! They are like looking into the nozzles of a pair of lighted welding torches. They are not like eyes that would accept "no" until the fires were extinguished, and that would be a dangerous undertaking!* Instinctively, the Italian knew that they would both best profit from rapprochement rather than war. Did the Irishman feel the same?

Speaking first, the Don said, "Mr. Moynihan," and Mickey replied, "Don Carlo." Then he continued. "I was paid a courtesy call by three of your salesmen today. After listening attentively to their offer, I decided that I wasn't interested."

"Is that so?" replied Carboni.

Mickey continued, "I have a fair idea how your insurance contracts work. I'm convinced that I would do best to remain self-insured! Now, I fully realize that you have an army of highly proficient, premium collectors. However, I have several platoons of very dedicated Paddys. Also, a fine stockpile of that Bohemian putty called Semtex and a squad of snipers who would do the Marine Corps proud. Now, I don't give a tinker's damn what other ethnic groups that you choose to 'insure,' but let's agree to leave the Irish off the policy! Italians and Irish have the same colors in their flags, although the stripes are not oriented the same. I think we should base a truce on that, agreed?"

Don Carlo sat back and smiled. "Wops and Paddies united against the world! Yes, I agree." He reached out his hand. Then, one steel vice closed on another.

"Well, Don Carlo, if I can be of lawful assistance at any time, don't hesitate to call me," replied Mickey, as he turned to leave. Just as he reached the door, Moynihan looked back and smiled broadly, saying, "Enjoy the parade, Don Carlo!" Then he was gone.

Sitting back in his chair, the Godfather was pleased with how the encounter went. *Who needs this part of the protection racket anyway?* he thought. *I've a hundred more lucrative irons in the fire, and the bombing business is a much bigger public relations problem than it was in the 1930s.* Then, Don Carlo thought of Moynihan's closing remark and was curious. However, at that moment, he became aware of blaring music that rattled the wineglasses on his bar. Jumping up, Don Carlo made swiftly for the door, opened it, and proceeded to the street outside. Immediately, the two pin-striped pillars fell in alongside him, right hands probing their shoulder holsters.

Don Carlo was astonished by the sight and sound that confronted him. He observed a very large sound truck with all six horns turned up to maximum volume. A rope ran from the back bumper and was looped about the necks of his three henchmen, pulling them along single file. They were almost nude, but that wasn't what caught his eye. Rather, it was the fact that they were all painted a very vivid kelly green! Music that blasted forth was very appropriate. The tune was called the "Wearing of the Green!"

One of Don Carlo's bodyguards shouted, trying to make himself heard above the din. "Shall we get some men together and retaliate, Don Carlo?" While looking at his boss, the bodyguard was shocked to see him laugh uproariously.

"No, Paolo. Go save those poor bastards and give them a bath!" Simultaneously, Don Carlo removed the perfectly folded handkerchief from his breast pocket to wipe away the tears of laughter. *Surely*, he thought, *it is a sight that one could never recall having seen before and one unlikely to see again*. Then, the Don looked at the moistened cloth before returning it to his pocket. He noted that the handkerchief was Irish linen of the finest quality!

On the evening after his encounter with Don Carlos, Mickey arrived at the Skellig Michael just as they were closing. A big smile on his Irish mug was cloaked by a beautiful small bouquet, which he handed to Bernadette. As soon as she had accepted it, Mickey's arms encased her in an bear hug. Although a few hapless blossoms were crushed in the process, most were spared by Bernie's quick evasion action. "I've got great news my dear! You'll have to hear what happened today."

"I've got great news as well," replied Bernie.

Each was convinced that their news should wait for the other to start. Silence prevailed, until Mickey finally said, "I spied a new little coffee shop just down the street. It doesn't close until one A.M. We'll go there, grab a cup, flip a coin, and determine who goes first—deal?"

"A deal!" replied Bernadette.

A true hole in the wall, the coffee shop looked clean and the sign proclaimed "Little Joe's Java." "It reminds me of Garrity's coffee shop in Belfast," said Bernie.

"I thought you might like it, as a kind of reminder of the bad old days," Mickey replied as they entered. The owner was surprised at the well-heeled appearance of his two late-night customers. He had thought of closing a little early, but here was a chance to ring up a pair of twenty-five-cent coffees. Also, if they had been out partying, a couple of stale donuts might be sold as well. However, all they requested was coffee, so the donuts were out. As he filled the cups, the owner surmised that they must be a couple engaged in an extramarital affair. He felt there could be no other explanation for their choice of Little Joe's Java. No one they could possibly know would see them here. Also, they looked entirely too much in love to be married to each other.

"Well what's your good news, Bernie?"

"Not so fast, sir! As I recall, we were to settle that question by a coin toss."

"Sorry, I have no coins," beamed Mickey. "I can toss $100 bill up in the air and see if Benjamin comes floating down face up! It's the best I can do."

Bernie didn't reply. Rather, she opened her hand to reveal a one-pound coin. "We can use this," she said with a smile. "Also, if you have a $100 dollar bill, why is it that you are always asking me if I have any money when we go shopping?"

"You never give a man half a chance," replied Mickey smiling.

Predictably, Bernie won the toss. Her husband would go first. Mickey took great pains to describe every detail in regard to his run-in with Don Carlo. Try as he might to enhance it, the truth was so outlandish as to defy embellishment. Bernie laughed at every pause and often in between. When the conclusion was finally reached, Mickey looked at his watch and declared, "Thirty seconds until closing. The runner-up can now proceed!"

Bernie took his wrist, turned it, and watched the second hand. With barely two seconds left, she sweetly smiled and said, "I'm going to have a baby."

"A baby!" exclaimed Mickey. "You beat me again!" Then, leaning across the table with clasped hands, the two kissed. However, never wishing to lose without a laugh, Mickey proclaimed, "If it's a boy, we'll call him Don Carlo Moynihan."

After they had left the restaurant, the owner proceeded to their table. He had seen the lady withdraw two shiny quarters from her purse and leave them by her cup. To himself, the man muttered, "What can you expect from a couple of paramours, who are happy as hell when she gets knocked up!" He thought of his own wife, nodded his head, and said aloud, "Wait until Alice hears this one!" Then, as he cleared the table, the neatly folded $5 bill beneath the gentleman's saucer came as a surprise. "I'll be damned," were his final words.

Chapter Twenty-Three

Nature's clock had been properly set, and Bernie's gestation time was correct to the day predicted. They had another son, and one at odds with his predecessors. Red hair was the big difference, chromatically indistinguishable from that of his mother. At last, a few of Bernie's chromosomes had eluded Mickey's dominant ones and now proclaimed themselves to the world. Michael Moynihan Jr. had Mickey's name, but he would never be the spitting image of his father, as were Sean and Liam. As to personality, only time would tell, but for the time being he was a quintessential baby who demanded food and change when his parents wished to sleep, while he slept only at inappropriate times for them.

Three weeks after the birth of Michael, Mickey was off to the Cayman Islands to see Big Frank McGann. On their meeting, he received well-deserved thanks for the continuing supply of money and arms. The IRA chieftain was just past fifty-five years old, but no one would have been astonished to see age seventy-five on his passport. However, Moynihan was surprised to note the older man's deterioration had seemed to stabilize. *He could go another four or five years,* Mickey thought. *I suppose he's a good argument for embalming with Bushmill's.* Fortunately, their meeting went well. Then, for the first time, his mentor raised the question of Mickey succeeding him. Moynihan voiced ready acceptance, but deep within his inner self he withheld full consent.

After their meeting was over, and he was on the plane back to Boston, Moynihan wondered if he was terminally stricken by the American virus? Did he really wish once again to fight actively for the Cause? Well he needn't decide that now! Moynihan thought this could be isolated on the far edge of his compass for things to be considered. Then the stewardess offered him a cocktail and was politely turned down. When she proffered a magazine, he accepted. As Moynihan started to read the first article, the print seemed to fade out. In its place arose the ghastly image of a small metal plaque. He didn't need to read the words, as they were well known to him. Nonetheless, they were repeated silently: "Life springs from death, and from the graves of the patriot dead spring living nations!"

In the following months after the meeting in Cayman Islands, McGann was somehow able to divert disaster until early January 1970. However, when the time came, it was manifested by a physical maelstrom as a result of his malignant hypertension. McGann's heart, which had served him so well in the past, could no longer compensate. Additionally, a small artery in the left parietal lobe of his brain was unable to cope with the head of pressure to which it was subjected. A rupture of the fragile artery occurred, leading to an intracerebral hemorrhage. Consequently, his entire right side was paralyzed. While reasonable thought persisted, it was no longer possible for McGann to verbalize his thoughts. Big Frank's ability to communicate was limited to mere shakes of the head, or a crude scrawl, formulated by his intact left hand.

To make matters even worse, the hypertension had wrecked havoc with McGann's kidneys, while the Bushmill's-induced cirrhosis had finally conquered his liver. Consequently, it was pretty much a matter of total system failure. Therefore, upon review of his overall condition, the physician in charge of his case shrugged his shoulders. Then, he whispered to the intern, "If Mr. McGann had a control panel like that of a submarine, then all the lights would be red! I'm afraid it won't be long until he submerges for the final time."

As the physician spoke these words, three thousand miles to the west, a related event was occurring. At about eight P.M., a tapping on Moynihan's office door was light and obviously generated by female knuckles. Mickey was seated at his desk in the Shillelagh and just about to embark on one of his hourly gladhand tours through the bar. These were good for business, and especially good for contributions to the IRA. Just the chance to squeeze Mickey's hand, get a clap on the shoulder, absorb his smile, and hear the fifteen-second sound bite was enough to induce the donor to increase his pledge. Sometimes, this was in multiples to which he would have cringed a few minutes earlier.

"Come on in," Moynihan exclaimed. Megan Cassidy entered. She was one of the Shillelagh's best cocktail waitresses. Although dressed modestly for her role, obvious parts of her anatomy were fighting the constraints of the uniform, which Moynihan had mandated when waitresses had been introduced to the bar several years back. The owner had decided that more bees would come if there were a honey around. Bernie had agreed. In fact, she had hired a number of the cocktail waitresses for both the Shillelagh and Isle of Skellig.

Since the majority of the girls had come from well-ordered, moral upbringing, solicitation of customers had rarely been a problem. On rare occasions when it did arise, the bartenders or no-neck ushers, as Mickey referred to his bouncers, swiftly advised the owners. Termination was instantaneous.

After approaching Moynihan's desk, Megan spoke immediately. "There is a man here to see you, Mr. Moynihan. All he would say is to tell you that Big Frank sent him. What shall I tell him?"

"Send him in, Megan. I'll want to talk with him."

"Yes Mr. Moynihan, right away, sir."

Then, Mickey added, "Oh! Megan! You might check the uniform supplies and see if there's a little bigger one on a hanger." The girl blushed and replied that she would certainly do so, then she left.

A few seconds later, Seamus O'Neil entered. Years had passed since Mickey last saw him. But he was still readily recognizable though a bit more cadaveric, though still a man of ice like any good wheelman should be. "It's been a long time Seamus. What's behind the surprise?"

O'Neil replied instantly, "Big Frank is dying, Mick. Hell, he could be dead by now! I've been in and out of these fookin' airplanes and airports for almost twenty-four hours now."

"You could have called," replied Moynihan.

"It's the way Mr. McGann wanted it," replied the driver morosely. "He wants you to come back with me and take over. The troubles are much worse, Mickey! The movement is splintering. Everything is going to hell."

"When are you going back?" asked Moynihan. "First flight out tomorrow with or without you," responded the messenger.

After intently studying Mickey's face, Seamus quietly intoned, "Let me know what you decide." After placing a card inscribed with his phone number on the desk, O'Neil departed.

Mickey felt as though his body was being consumed by a great blowtorch inside him, and it grew hotter by the second. He murmured, "Things were different in the old days. You just got your assignment, and it might get you killed. But, otherwise, you had nothing to lose. Now, there is everything to lose—Bernadette, the boys, the business, and the good life. What am I going to do?"

Suddenly, he thought, *If I were on the shore, and a drowning man called for help, would I holler back 'Wait until I take off my fine suit and fold it'? Oh yes! I have to give someone my Rolex so I won't lose it! One more thing, I should call my agent and make sure I will be covered by my insurance.* Ireland was apparently drowning, and McGann was sinking even faster. Then, Moynihan picked up the phone and dialed Seamus. When he answered, Mickey asked "Which airline?"

"Aer Lingus," was the reply.

"The time, Seamus?"

"8:30 in the morning."

"That's too soon for me," was his somber reply.

Mickey was at Skellig Restaurant when Bernadette was ready to leave. She noted the usual bouquet wasn't evident. Instead her husband wore a grimace that mimicked Risus Sardonicus.

"What's wrong Mickey?" Bernadette gasped. "You look like you would have to get better to die!"

"I'm dying in a way, Bernie," was his only response. Shortly, they sat quietly in the moving car until a few blocks from their home. Then suddenly, Mickey blurted out, "We're moving back to Ireland."

"No Mickey! For God's sake! Say it isn't true! I love our life here. How can you just up and tear us all away?"

"Big Frank McGann is near death, Bernie. Also, the Troubles are worse by far. Seamus flew over to tell me that I'm needed. I or we have gotta go."

"I'd rather go to hell," Bernie screamed. They both recoiled at the vehemence of her invectiveness, as it came across like an epithet to their marriage.

For the first time in their union, they slept in separate beds. In the morning, Mickey left the house early, as he wanted to see Seamus off from Logan Airport. From there, he planned to go obtain visas to the Irish Republic, as well as Ulster. Mickey supposed that he should change his mind, but it was made up. Had his wife forgotten Ireland? Were the Troubles nothing to her now? Had the States sucked away the fervor that she once had like some huge red, white, and blue leech?

Objectivity was absent from his self-examination. Anger prevailed and prohibited any rational or prudent thought. At this point, he wasn't repelled at the possibility of separation or even divorce. "Sean and Liam will come," he surmised. Suddenly, Mickey was buoyed up by the thought of his two progeny taking up the Cause under his tutelage. *The red-haired brat—he's her favorite—can stay here with Mrs. Nouveau Riche Moynihan! If we all go down in the war, I have no doubt she can find a fine black mourning outfit at one of Boston's fashionable shops. Go to the funerals? Hell, no, just have the ashes shipped to Boston. They'll look fine on the mantel in a copper urn!*

An analyst would have told Mickey that his anger and tirade were a means of eluding the path that a prudent and loving man would take. These were qualities that he usually possessed in full measure, but now they were discarded. In reality, Mickey would never be able to part from Bernie unless he could irrationally convince himself that she had become a traitor to him and to Ireland.

After seeing Seamus off, proper visas and first-class airline tickets were procured by late afternoon. Then came the mandatory stop at the Shillelagh to announce his departure. No explanation was given! Proper questions arising from concern by the senior staff were fended off or responded to with either an evasive or desultory reply.

"When will you be back Mickey?"

"How the hell should I know?" was the response.

"Where can we reach you if there's a problem?"

"Call my wife!"

Therefore, upon his departure, speculation was rife. Were there legal problems, a pending divorce or an IRS audit? When the news reached the lower echelons, Megan Cassidy, now in a more modest size twelve, was quick to recall the vulturous visitor of the previous night. This recollection fueled speculation but ignited no fires. When Mickey returned home, there was no Bernadette to confront. Kathleen Garvey, the cook, housekeeper, and nanny reported that she had gone to Skellig Michael. "She seemed awfully upset, Mr. Moynihan, but didn't say why!"

Mickey's only response was "humph" issued through curled lips. However a little later much more like himself with Sean and Liam, he spent quite some time explaining his departure. His two older boys seemed excited by their father's upcoming adventure to a degree that prevented them from any sadness over what might be a prolonged separation. "I'll be sending for you as soon as I can," said their father. "You'll love Ireland, and you'll be proud to do your part in freeing her from British tyranny!"

Sean and Liam were infused with altruism, admiration, and a spirit of adventure as Mickey hugged them and spoke of his pride and love. Michael received little more than a frown and a passing pat on his red-capped head. No attempt was made to help him blow his nose or dab at the tears that coursed down his chubby, rosy cheeks. *Just like your mother,* Mickey thought. Shortly thereafter, he departed in a cab, for the night would be spent in a hotel, safe from the "two forlorn weepers," which he would have to confront if he remained at home. *Tomorrow it will be Boston to Shannon and hopefully a late flight to Belfast.* No longer did Mickey have concern about being recognized, for he felt that as far as the Brits were concerned he had ceased to exist. After all, he wasn't Jack the Ripper, and there wasn't anyone around making an effort to perpetuate the story of Mickey Manion.

Upon his arrival at the Belfast airport, Seamus O'Neil picked Moynihan up, as previously planned. "You got here just in time, Mickey! Big Frank is only a few steps ahead of the maggots. His doctors give him a week or less."

However, when Mickey saw his dying mentor, the prediction seemed almost optimistic. McGann extended a quavering left hand, while his right lay as a limp, fleshy rag. Although the IRA chieftain tried to speak, no words issued forth from his sagging lips. The left side of his face reflected a meager degree of animation, while the right side was flaccid. Meanwhile, the sister-in-attendance repeatedly wiped away the drool issuing from the crevice between his paralyzed lips. Mickey noticed that Big Frank's sclera and skin were deeply jaundiced, and if Mickey had the benefit of Sir William Osler's clinical acumen, he would have recognized the fetor hepaticus, which indelibly marked the aroma of the breath in a person whose liver function was teetering on shutdown.

McGann's left hand fumbled across the starched, white sheets and found a pencil. Sister Kelley recognized that the man's eyes were pleading for paper. She produced a small tablet and placed it in proximity to the quivering pencil point. McGann's letters were nearly illegible, and the line of words highly irregular. However, Moynihan was able to decipher: "Take everything. It's all yours."

"I will, Frank. I'll run it right for you and for Ireland!"

Meanwhile, the nurse made no attempt to decipher the cryptic note or verbal response. Concerned with her patient's welfare, she declared that Mr. McGann was exhausted, and it was time to leave. As he was departing, Mickey caught sight of a Roman collar on a man entering a side door. *I didn't think old Frank would go crying to his God at the end, but he was always the type to cover all the bets,* Mickey thought. *He is going to have a hell of a time writing out all of his sins on that tablet.*

On the next occasion that Mickey saw Big Frank, he was at the wake. While gazing on his deceased mentor, Moynihan thought it was sad to say, but McGann looked better dead.

Having arrived at McGann's wake early, Mickey noticed that it was a quintessential Irish function. Supposedly, it was held for the purpose of bringing family and friends together to mourn the deceased as the one who got away, expressed colloquially. Not infrequently, Mickey knew the mourners got overly enthusiastic in the manner they assuaged their grief. Also, if the supply of alcohol was adequate, anything from an orgy to a riot might ensue. Consequently, Moynihan was relieved to find that no professional mourners were present. They seemed to have fallen from favor, which was just as well. However, he noticed a bevy of old crones, screaming and carrying on like a pack of banshees. Consequently, he thought, *They could drive even the abstemious to drink*. Then, Seamus O'Neil caught Mickey's eye and beckoned him to a small sitting room. This would offer a degree of privacy and, in addition, shelter him from having to stare at the embalmer's art now in the stiff form of the departed McGann.

Upon Moynihan's entering the room, Seamus began. "I've talked with most of the cell leaders and chiefs, Mick. You have never met any of them apart from Con Hogan. Of course, this was the result of our desire and need for secrecy. I've tried to explain to them that Big Frank chose you as his heir apparent. A few said 'fine,' but a lot said 'What the fook do we care?' That group included Hogan. Now, McGann knew there was bad blood between you. But in some ways McGann was naive. He frequently saw loyalty where none existed. You may have inherited a rebellion instead of a kingdom!"

"I'm not interested in squabbles or internal warfare," Mickey replied. "Tell me how many faithful soldiers would be on my team?"

"Probably twenty-six," Seamus replied.

"Now tell me about the Provisional Wing, which I hear has sprung into being."

"News travels fast," replied O'Neil. "They're a splinter group. Primarily a bunch with a more incendiary nature. It's said that they want to move out of the penny ante stuff and launch into the big time. They consider the original IRA to be lacking in guts, too scared to pull off any action that will kick the British Lion in the ass, not just tweak his tail."

"Do you know anyone near the top?" asked Mickey.

"Terry Kelleher," was the reply. "He's a sadistic SOB, but he knows his stuff. You want to meet him, Mick?"

"I do," responded Moynihan.

Shortly later, Moynihan paid his respects to the widow McGann, who was in the company of a few close relatives. Then, he decided to leave the wake. On the way out, Mickey ran into Con Hogan. As soon as their eyes met, the feud begun years ago was reignited! Hogan had come to the wake half-inebriated. No doubt, he would be completely so before the evening was over. Already, the alcohol had produced enough false fire in him that he was not shy on inhibitions but filled with bravado. "Well sure and if it isn't the former Irish, now fookin' Yankee big shot. Or, maybe I should have said big shit! If you're looking to take over the operation, you'll end up takin' over McGann's resting place in the box! I advise that you stick your tail between your legs or up your ass, Manion! Get yourself back to Boston with your red-headed whore." Then,

Hogan turned slightly to make certain his words were appreciated by the massive disciple who followed him.

Since Mickey's arduous training in martial arts had left him with hands like slabs of steel, his right hand moved only twelve inches, aimed directly at Hogan's solar plexus! His extended fingers were like four parallel pieces of rebar propelled by a massive spring. Their tips thrust deeply into his antagonist's flabby rectus muscles. Then, they coursed upward to his diaphragm, seeking to contuse the ventricles of his heart. These resided in intimate contact to that muscular structure, which partitioned Hogan's chest and abdomen. Mickey's maneuver was capable of killing if the thrust were not interrupted. However, he held back sufficiently. Hogan remained alive but felled like a toppled tree.

Hogan's bodyguard caught his collapsing boss and called out, "What the fook did you do to him?"

"Nothing," said Mickey calmly, as he started out the door.

"You'll pay for this," screamed the bodyguard, who was out of action as he continued to support the unconscious Hogan.

"I suppose I will," snapped Mickey. "Here's a down payment!" Then, the heel of Moynihan's shoe came down with great force on the instep of the threatener. As a result, several of the bodyguard's tarsal bones were dislodged from the anatomically correct position. Although this could be rectified, a skilled orthopedic surgeon would take quite a while to make it right, and extreme pain was the result for the recipient. Having made his point, Moynihan continued out the door.

After returning to his hotel, Mickey thought about calling home. However, because he was remaining spiteful, the call was postponed. Instead, he lay back on the bed with only a single lamp aglow. *I should go back to Boston,* he thought. *I don't seem welcome, and from what O'Neill says the Cause has turned into a clown's game. Between all the opposing ambitions, the rivalry and the touts, it's more like a Mafia gang war than a patriots' rebellion!* Mickey was about to call the concierge and inquire about flights to Boston. Then he thought, *Maybe that's why I am here.* Replacing the phone on its cradle, Mickey murmured, "I'll see Kelleher tomorrow and make up my mind!" This was his last conscious thought after a catastrophic day.

On the following day, Seamus picked up Mickey at his hotel. Outwardly, Manion alias Moynihan seemed his usual buoyant self. However, the old wheelman could sense a current of deep unrest below the placid surface. O'Neil spoke, "They finally got Hogan's heart beating regularly after putting the jumper cables on him a couple of times. What the hell did you do to him, Mickey?"

"He must have a poor constitution," replied Mickey. "I just tapped him with my index finger to emphasize a point."

"Were you emphasizing a point on Corkery's foot as well?" laughed O'Neill.

"No, the oaf must have slipped on one of Big Frank's fine carpets and twisted it. That kind of fellow tends to be accident prone!"

Mickey wasn't about to disclose any more information and switched to a new topic. "Isn't that where Garrity's Coffee Shop used to be?"

"Yeah! That's the place," remarked Seamus. "The old man and his wife died a few years after you left."

"Well I can see the neighborhood is improving," stated Mickey. "Now, instead of a good cup of coffee, you can get a flying dragon tattooed on your ass!"

"That's progress," replied Seamus. "I guess some of the newer residents prefer cannabis to caffeine."

"My God! What happened to Brennans restaurant?"

"Just another example of Irish mortality," replied O'Neill. "Only for Brennan it wasn't father time, it was a UDL time bomb, as best we could tell."

"It's a shame to see old Brennan's fine place turned into a fookin' pizza parlor," said Mickey in a half-hushed tone, which became increasingly sotto voce, as he thought of Bernie and all the nights he had waited outside.

"Are you wondering about the old garage, Mick?"

"I do sometimes," he said. "But, I don't want to face that ghost now."

A few moments later, the car pulled up to the door of a warehouse. Peering eyes could be discerned through the single small window in the center of the portal. Then the door opened and O'Neil drove in and turned off the ignition. An acne-scarred youth trying to portray an "I'm tough" look approached fondling an Armalite, as the Irish chose to call the M-16 .223-caliber rifle. "You Moynihan?" he sneered.

"No, I'm the Archbishop of Canterbury," snarled Mickey. "Stop wavin' the fookin' gun around, or I may decide the barrel is a thermometer, and I'd take your temperature the awkward way!"

Keeping his surly countenance, the punk did change the position of his gun in deference to the big man's remark and his appearance, which seemed to enhance the gravity of his threat.

Leading the way, the pimply one stopped at a door that was obviously the entrance to an office in the rear of the building. After tapping on the door with the butt of his rifle, he said "They're here, Terry." Mickey heard footsteps approaching the other side of the door, but the cadence was unusual. After he opened the door, Mickey observed that the man standing in the entrance was a caricature of an Irish leprechaun. He had unruly red hair and a beard but was minus the green suit and hat. Standing about six feet and no more than 165 pounds in weight, obviously he was not given to strenuous workouts. Once Mickey had navigated the face and torso, he then noted the carved, mahogany peg leg. Terry Kelleher was aware of the curiosity it produced and was given to wearing it for effect. Obviously, it was the cause of the bizarre clunk-tap sound that Mickey had heard.

Moynihan was not impressed with the strength of Kelleher's grip, but along with Seamus he accepted the proffered chair. Their seated host was first to speak. "Do you prefer Moynihan or Manion?"

"Try Mickey," was the response.

"Well to what do I owe the pleasure of meeting an ex-patriot, now returned patriot, Mickey?"

"I'll cut to the chase," said Mickey. "I came back because it was McGann's deathbed wish. From what I've seen, and O'Neil here has told me, the old IRA seems to be disassembling. The Troubles are worse. UDL and the rest of the Prods appear to be getting the upper hand, and the Brits are sending Tommys over to shore things up. I was in the middle of things twelve years ago. Now, I want back as a major player in the Provisional outfit."

"I've been hearing about you—nothing like starting at the top," was Kelleher's response.

"I spent my time in the trenches before I had to flee a half-dozen murder raps. I've raised hundreds of thousands of pounds for the IRA, most wasted, I presume! Also, I'm in good speaking terms with the bad-ass leaders of most of the terrorist organizations in the world, as well as a number of Communist elite, who are careful about whom they supply. If O'Neil here is correct, I've got a couple dozen good men who will have me as their leader. Take it or leave it in twenty-four hours, Mr. Kelleher! In forty-eight hours, I'll be back in Boston."

Mickey arose, motioned to O'Neil, and went out the door. His quick exit alarmed the punk, who raised the muzzle of his Armalite in Moynihan's direction. With blinding speed, Mickey twisted the gun from the young man's grasp. Then he removed the magazine before pulling back the bolt and thus ejecting the chambered round. In less than forty-five seconds, the weapon was field stripped, with the parts strewn over the floor. "If you can't get it back together, then try calling "Dial a Prayer!" Now open the fookin' door!"

Kelleher's call came within twenty-four hours. On the other end of the line, the voice came through crisply. "Mickey, the Board of Directors has agreed to your proposal. You come in as a full partner. However, we wish to make it clear that should your efforts not be in good faith, it might place your position in jeopardy, if you know what I mean!"

"I know exactly what you mean, as I feel quite the same in regard to the current directors," replied Mickey. Steel was in his voice, and the edges were sharply honed. Kelleher's voice paused, signifying a short deliberation of Moynihan's response.

Finally, Mickey heard, "Well I guess we've all entered into an agreement that we can live or die with. Please have O'Neil take you to Corporate Headquarters tomorrow night at eight P.M." Then, there was a click and a dial tone. The die was cast!

As Mickey was about to replace the receiver, impulse altered his motion. Instead, he secured the services of an overseas operator and put a call in to Boston. His plan was to talk to Sean or Liam, or so he had convinced himself. By the third ring, he remembered the time difference. The older boys would be at school, and he couldn't talk to them now. *I'd best hang up,* he thought. As the receiver was departing his ear, Bernadette's soft "hello" became audible. *I can't talk with her,* he thought. When her voice said "hello" again, his resolve vanished. "It's Mickey, Bernie." He expected her to hang up, or scream, "I don't want to talk to you!" Neither occurred.

Although Mickey heard no sniffling, their were tears in Bernie's voice. While these crystal droplets are generally manifest by sight or touch, hers seemed audible. "I tried to hate you, Mick, but the love wouldn't let go. I'll come to Ireland and bring the boys, if that is what you want." There was no reply. "Are you there, Mick?" she asked plaintively.

Finally, she heard, "Yes, I'm here, and that's what I want."

"What about the business, the house, the cars and boat, Mick?"

"We'll need to keep the bar and restaurant. We'll have to get a small townhouse, but the rest have to go. I'll get us a fine place here, Bernie. You and the boys will come to love it, I'm sure. We'll both have to fly back to Boston to check on things once in a while. That's why we'll need a small place to stay in on occasion. In no time at all, we'll be as happy as we were in Boston, maybe more so, Bernie."

Although Mickey tried to put conviction in his voice, there was no sign that it was contagious. "I hope so, Mick," said Bernadette softly. Then, she added, "But over here, I was never troubled by the wondering."

"Wondering what, Bernie?"

"Wondering if you'll come home alive!"

"If you're here, I'm sure that I will," he said in a vain effort to instill a little humor. "I'll call you again in two days," Mickey said. "We'll compare notes and give a progress report. I love you, Bernie," was his closing remark.

Her reply, "I wish it was more than you love Ireland, Mickey."

"If you need me, I'm at the Connaught Hotel, Room 424. Give my love to the boys!" The call was over.

For the first time in her marriage, Bernadette was faced with trying to divine her husband's raison d'être. Was his desire to return to Ireland a matter of true noblesse oblige or simply solipsism?

On the next day, Bernadette called a friend in the real estate business. Although she tried her best to make joie de vivre sprout through the hard clay of her heartbreak, Bernie remained uncertain as to her success. "Eileen," she said in mock enthusiasm. "How would you like to sell our house?"

"You're kidding," replied the realtor. "Sell the place that you've spent all our last luncheon together raving about?"

"Well, uh, Mickey has a smashing business opportunity in Ireland. It's a once-in-a-lifetime deal, and you know we are Irish after all. It would be wonderful to go back to our roots, and the boys will absolutely love it."

"Are you really certain?" asked Eileen quizzically.

"Sure," replied Bernadette.

"Well it's a beautiful place, and I'm positive that it will sell fast if the price is right."

"What do you think it's worth?" was Bernadette's response.

"I'd say $400,000," was Eileen's estimation.

"Fine," replied Bernie, with no conviction in her voice.

"Want to sign a contract tomorrow?" asked her friend.

"Sure," was the reply.

"I'll see you for lunch, and I'll buy." Eileen closed off the call more excited about her probable commission than perplexed by her friend's very unexpected decision.

After hanging up the receiver, Bernadette stared dejectedly at the phone. "I'm such a fraud! Am I a fool as well?"

Meanwhile, on the other side of the Atlantic, Mickey was also dealing in real estate. Located in Grey Abbey was a fine granite manor house. Splendidly situated on the West Bank of Strangford Laugh, there was moorage for a boat plus acreage for horses and nearby schools of quality. Distance to Belfast wasn't too great, and the road was good. Also, Mickey felt that the relative isolation should dampen suspicion. Seemingly, it was the ideal location for a newly rich Irish American atheist who dealt in the clandestine.

While Mickey was looking for a new home, Bernadette had found a very attractive townhouse. However, it would forever be simply a Boston base and never a home. Also, she found no problem in readily disposing of the cars and boat. Automobiles she could bear, but the boat tore her heart asunder. *If I ever have another, I'll name it* Skellig Despair, she thought glumly. Their home sold last, though she was unable to participate in the glee of the new owners and Eileen. After the papers were signed, Bernie backed slowly down the driveway for the last time. *Oh, my God!* she thought. *It's like being hoisted off an operating table and placed on a gurney. As they wheel you away, you look back and see your legs lying there, amputated from your body! You want to scream 'My legs I need them.' However, they just keep wheeling you away.*

Sean and Liam were excited about moving to Ireland. They asked whether they had to wait until tomorrow to get on the plane? However, little Michael's tears were being absorbed by the cheek of Buster, his well-worn teddy bear pressed tightly against his face. From the back seat came the little boy's solemn words, which further wrenched Bernadette's soul, "When I'm big, Buster, I'll make lots of money, and I'll buy our home back. We'll live there forever and ever, just you and me!"

Chapter Twenty-Four

❈ ❈ ❈

Although the manor house outside Grey Abbey was quite striking by local standards, to Bernadette, it was mindful of a mausoleum. Gray granite seemed incapable of retaining or enkindling any warmth, either from the standpoint of the thermometer or the temperature of the soul. At times, Bernie felt that if she looked hard enough, she would find a crypt within to entomb her spirit, which seemed to be dying. Outwardly, a reasonable degree of bravado was manifest, and Mickey, Sean, and Liam didn't seem to notice any desolation. In town, Bernie found that the people were curious, though reasonably friendly. A few overtures to join local ladies groups were accepted by Bernie, with a feigned enthusiasm. Perhaps, she might find a friend or two sometime, but no priority was given that assignment.

Mickey purchased Irish thoroughbreds of good quality for Bernie, himself, and the two older boys. A pony was secured for Michael. "As soon as we can get glued to the saddle, we'll join the local hunt club," Mickey had said excitedly. *Thrill of competition and potential danger would be another stimulant for him*, Bernie thought. *As for me, I feel much more closely aligned with old reynard.* Bernadette's horse was named Guinevere. She was basically a gentle chestnut mare, though given to schizophrenia at the sound of the hunt master's horn. This seemed to generate a metamorphosis, thus turning her into a female Pegasus. As a novice equestrian, Bernie was much more comfortable with the meeker side of her mount's split personality.

On many an occasion when she could slip off by herself, Bernie would give Guinevere her head, knowing the mare would instinctively trot to a nearby brook, where the water was cold and clear and the grass long and sweet. Here, the still-young woman could cry the tears of concern that she felt as a wife and mother. Bernie would frequently lean far forward in the saddle, wrap her arms about the horse's neck, and let the tears flow. Sometimes, when the breeze freshened her long, loosened locks of burnished red, she would meld with the mare's chestnut mane, producing a surreal image.

Recently refitted, the new sailboat was quick in coming and was fifty-five feet of speedy elegance. Mickey and the two older boys sailed it to their private quay to fetch Bernadette for her inspection. Again, with feigned excitement, she hurriedly followed along to see the new boat. However, Bernie stopped to grab Michael's arm so he could join in the festivity. This was a compulsion that seemed unshared by the others. When the inspection was complete, Mickey took her to the stern. "See, Bernie, it has no name. We're leaving that up to you. In town, there is a sign painter who does boats as well. I'll give you his name, then you can bestow whatever appellation that you choose!"

Several days later, Mickey was chagrined to see large letters, resplendent in gold, proclaiming the name of the family's pride to be *Sargasso,* instead of the *Isle of Skellig Michael II.* Shortly later, on entering the kitchen, he found his wife conversing with their new cook and housekeeper, Mrs. Hennessey. Their conversation was interrupted by Mickey exclaiming, "Why did you name our new boat *Sargasso?* Didn't you know that is a sea off the West Coast of Africa, which is choked with weeds? All the sailing ships that entered were forever stuck! The crews died, and the hulks became ghost ships."

"I'm sorry, Mick, I knew that it had something to do with the sea, and I thought it sounded kind of exotic. I'll have it changed."

"Wait a minute, I have changed my mind!," exclaimed Mickey. "The *Sargasso* is perfect from the standpoint of being facetious! Instead of being stuck and going nowhere, it will sail right by anything else on Strongford Lough and possibly the Irish Sea as well. It's the perfect play on words! You're a clever Colleen, my love."

Mickey picked up his wife, twirled her around, and bestowed a fervent kiss. Poor Mrs. Hennessey had never observed such behavior at her previous places of employment, nor did she partake in the merriment. She had cut her thumb instead of the cucumber and was busy at the sink cleansing the wound. Bernadette never let on that she was well aware of the legend of the Sargasso Sea and how she felt it pertained to her.

Sean and Liam were instant outsiders at the nearby St. Andrews Academy. Given their American accents, the other students felt sufficiently emboldened to serenade them with a rendition of "Yankee Doodle Dandy." However, the concert was short-lived when one of the singers suffered a cut lip and broken incisor from a solid right delivered by Sean, while Liam accorded a second singer a black eye! As it turned out, the fight was much shorter than the time Bernadette spent in the Headmaster's Office trying to explain and apologize. Nevertheless, in the ensuing months, the two brawlers continued to win their father's adulation while remaining one step ahead of expulsion.

Readily apparent to Bernadette was the fact that although Sean was very intelligent, he was equally intemperate and intransigent. Liam was not as intellectually endowed but well gifted with guile. Consequently, by year's end, Bernadette was growing concerned that they would never be successful in any profession, apart from one of intrigue and violence. To make matters worse, Bernadette felt they had both inherited Mickey's physique and cunning but none of the gentleness he so frequently displayed. "Oh! My dear little Michael," she would sometimes whisper, "You are your mother's last hope!"

In spite of her fears, Bernadette was grateful that when Mickey was at home, which was most of the time, he was the hub of all the family's activities. What transpired in Belfast, its environs, and elsewhere, was shrouded in secrecy. *Just as well,* reflected Bernadette. *I don't really want to know, and it's far better the boys never find out what takes place when their father is away.*

Nonetheless, she maintained her own intelligence service correlating Mickey's days of absence with occurrences of a particular variety reported in the news. She noted just last week he had received a phone call, then quickly announced that there was business to attend to in Belfast. Soon, he had departed in the vintage Aston Martin he had acquired. Another one of his passions, the car was one that he delighted in working on. Mechanical acumen acquired at Sweeney's garage had never deserted him.

Mick had returned late, as he said he would. Despite her husband's admonitions, Bernie had stayed up to wait for him. "Who knows?" she said. "Sometime, he won't be coming home. Perhaps tonight is that fatal time!"

Finally, there was the bright beams of auto lamps sweeping down the driveway followed by the whine of the Aston Martin's precisely tuned engine. Soon, Mickey entered with a smile and bestowed a warm embrace and a kiss.

"How did things go?" Bernie asked plaintively.

"Smooth as silk," he replied jauntily.

She thought, *If I didn't know better, I could believe he was just returning home after selling a huge insurance policy and acting like a normal man returning to a normal wife.* Then, Bernie added to her innermost self, *It may have been a policy of sorts, but not the type that Lloyd's issues.*

On the next morning, as Bernie was helping Mrs. Hennessey set the table, the news report coming over the radio drew her attention. Excitement was evident in the reporter's voice, as was common when calamitous news was reported. "Royal Ulster Constabulary officials seem to remain perplexed by yesterday's shooting death of Neville Porter. Mr. Porter, who managed the Bennington Cricket Team, collapsed suddenly near the end of yesterday's match. Medics who came to the scene found what appeared to be entry and exit wounds from a bullet. Police investigators interviewing witnesses were unable to find anyone who could recall hearing a shot fired. At this juncture, the police are uncertain as to whether or not this was an accidental death from a stray bullet or a homicide. This reporter has ascertained that Mr. Porter is known to have strong ties with the Ulster Defense Force, which might fuel speculation that it was indeed an assassination. If so, no person or group has taken credit, nor is anyone certain as to how the victim could have been gunned down without anyone being aware of it."

Bernie had no interest in the rest of the news report on the weather. She fumbled with the dial, and finally found what she would have considered pleasing, soft music under ordinary circumstances. Then she pondered. *I left all of Mick's guns in the townhouse in Boston. He never even suggested that I try and ship them here. He doesn't have any guns, and even if he did, how could he shoot someone in a crowd and not have a single soul hear or see anything? No! It couldn't have been Mickey!*

If Bernadette had known what Mickey and Alexis Zellanova knew, she wouldn't have been so certain. Colonel Zellanova was KGB, although he was posted in Belfast's Russian consulate under the shopworn euphemistic designation of Cultural Exchange Officer. He had arranged for a Draganov 762X54 sniper rifle, which had come via diplomatic pouch. Then, he secretly delivered it to Moynihan. A fine weapon, the Draganov was superbly suited to its role, as a long-distance death delivery system in the hands of the right person. The ten-power telescopic sight with which it was equipped was optically perfect. On several occasions, Mickey had sighted the gun in over on the West Coast of the republic. Many memories were brought back by the place selected, as it was the same site to which he had been taken years ago when McGann had recruited him.

Most of the rest of the planned assassination was the result of good footwork on behalf of Seamus and Mick. Since the target managed a cricket team, they believed undoubtedly he would be at all of their games. Time and place was no problem at all. However, the next hurdle was higher. Moynihan knew that at a great distance, say, near a mile, hitting a man-size target could be more good fortune than skill. Wind, humidity, and all the ballistics such as bullet weight, velocity, and trajectory, if not estimated with near absolute certainty could make all the difference in the world as to who goes to the hereafter! Foul it up and you end up with a wounded man, who will be forever cautious in the future. Worse yet, you could stiff some granny, who came to cheer for her grandson.

Mickey, like nearly all snipers, preferred his shot to be at 1000 yards or less. He wondered if there was such a place. O'Neil found one on the fringe of the fifteenth fairway of a nearby golf course that was almost exactly 1000 yards from the spot where their victim would be standing at the scheduled games. Wooded, it provided reasonable cover, plus a significant muffling of sound. Additionally, the number of golfers usually using the course on a weekday morning were minimal. He had every reason to think that this would be a winner.

On the given day, Mickey drove to the golf course in a rental car. His garb was that of a golfer, complete with jaunty cap. Now alert he skirted the fairways and made his way through the bordering woods to the place, which he had selected from the information that O'Neil had supplied. Along the way, Moynihan was careful to mimic the appearance of some hacker earnestly seeking a lost ball in the dense rough. In his golf bag was the Draganov surrounded by an arrangement of golf clubs. Shaped like the head of a driver, a wooden attachment had been placed over the rifle's muzzle, then covered with a knitted mitten like the other woods.

Finally, Moynihan was in place. From a pocket of his golf bag, a camouflage netting was secured. This he used to cover himself, as he lay in a prone position. Also, similar material had been used to enshroud the heavy barrel of his sniper rifle. Moynihan had used dull earth-tone paints on the scope, as wrapping it would have denied him acquisition to the wind velocity and elevation knobs. Current weather prediction had been for occasional light breezes; however, the few blades of dried grass Mickey dropped showed no sign of wind agitation. Therefore, he had every reason to assume the weather prediction was correct.

After waiting patiently, at last Porter was seen in the scope. A center post with cross-hairs was Moynihan's favorite reticule. The tip of the post was exactly on Porter's mid-sternum. No one was behind him, which was good, for he knew that a bullet expected to pass all the way through the victim could claim someone else as well. Two birds with one stone was not always advantageous. Consequently, the best thing that could happen was for the projectile to exit Porter's body and forever be lost somewhere in the field. In the event that the projectile had to traverse an additional body, it might not exit and be easy to recover.

Carefully, Mickey controlled his breathing, for it was an important factor. To a degree, some snipers could control their cardiac contractions as well. This prevented the minute pulsatile movement that occurs in the body as a whole. Some thought this motion could potentially alter your point of aim by a fraction of a degree. As far as Moynihan was concerned, this was fine for paper targets of the Olympics. However, he doubted it would bear significantly on who lived or died!

A very slight contraction of the pad on his right index finger was all that was needed to activate the set trigger of the Draganov. This would release the firing pin, allowing its pointed end to indent the primer. Shortly, Vulcan's fury was unleashed by the exploding powder, and the bullet was on its way. Traveling at over 3000 feet per second, the 1000 yards was transited in less time than it would take to say "good-bye Porter." Visualizing the point of impact on the man's shirt front, Moynihan knew that he was dead before he hit the ground.

Quickly surveying the surrounding area, Mickey observed no sign of other people or sounds of alarm. In seconds, the Draganov was put back in his golf bag, neatly camouflaged as before. Then, on the way back to his car, Mickey encountered a foursome of golfers near the club house. One of them asked, "Did you hear anything that sounded like a shot?"

Manion smiled broadly and said, "Well, sir, all my last shots went into the water hazard on fifteen. If they made any sound at all, it was a kerplunk. I'm heading back to the car for more balls. I'll get one across that pond sooner or later."

A different member of the foursome yelled, "Good luck! That hole can ruin anyone's day. See, Frank, we told you that you were imagining hearing a gunshot."

In the following investigation of Porter's death, the Constabulary remained clueless. An assailant was never found.

Over the ensuing months, Mickey, working in concert with Seamus O'Neil, managed a number of successful unsolved assassinations. As personal exploits these were satisfying. But in the overall picture, he realized that his efforts were little more than trying to empty the Irish Sea with a bucket. Also, as Mickey kept count, there were more Catholics than Protestants being killed. Of the twenty-six men that he had inherited from Big Frank, three were now dead. Unfortunately, the other twenty-three were near worthless for anything more than a knee-capping, and that needed strict oversight.

Initially, Moynihan had high hopes that the Provos were a new breed, kind of an IRA elite, like the Rangers in the U.S. Army. However, in reality, they turned out to be lacking in skill or motivation. As a group, they fit the hackneyed phrase "All talk and little action" to a tee. Kelleher and the other three leaders were great for clandestine meetings, secret passwords, and grandiose plans. Altogether, they hadn't eliminated half as many English soldiers, RUC officers, or elite members of the UDL as he and O'Neil had done by themselves.

Early on, Moynihan had bankrolled them, providing high-quality arms and explosives, all to little avail. Through his contacts with the Cubans, Libyans, and

Palestine Liberation Organization, Mickey knew that willing Volunteers who were sufficiently motivated were welcome for training. He felt that it was entirely possible that over a few years a real crack commando force could be formed. However, the usual response that he got for suggesting this was, "Fook that! I'm not going to go fry out in the desert with some rag head," or "Me and my boys swelter on some forsaken island with a bunch of greasers? Piss on that!"

Demonstrations of proper techniques and a well-run guerrilla-type operation were ineffective as well. One day, Moynihan and O'Neil took Kelleher, Danny Feeley, and one of the other chieftains to a place of ambush, which they had planned out well ahead. This spot was very near the border with the Republic, and the dirt road skirting the boundary was patrolled by a British armored car. When the steel-plated vehicle was broadside and well within range, Mickey touched off the rocket-propelled grenade. The projectile impacted on the armored car and detonated. Inside, searing flames lashed out at the occupants, and those who didn't die from shrapnel wounds wished they had. Then, the Provo quartet easily escaped on two motor bikes Mickey had provided. The rocket launcher had come through the good grace of Alexis Zellanova and was surely not a fair cultural exchange for the five British soldiers who were killed.

Once back at a safe house on the Republic side, the bikes were stowed. Then Moynihan thought a critique of the operation would be in order. He was hopeful that Kelleher and Feeley would be impressed. "Well, gentlemen what did you think?"

Kelleher replied, "Well, it was okay as a hit-and-run operation, but they'll probably hush it up, and all the folks we're trying to win over will not hear about it."

"As far as me," piped in Feeley, "I'm not much for crawlin' about out here in the peat. What if they had sent a chopper out and gunned us down when we were on the bikes? Did you ever think of that Mr. Tactician?"

Mickey needed all his control to keep from wrenching the man's neck enough to break it. Glaring at the two men, he spat out, "Hell yes! If you kill them all instantly, as I've shown that you can do, then, who is going to radio for a helicopter?"

Moynihan continued. "In the event they did have time, then a shoulder-fired surface-to-air missile would take care of the problem! Don't you see that if you plan it right, you can disable the armored personnel carrier? Let them go ahead and send for a helicopter, and you can shoot it down. If you have good men well trained, you could ambush other APCs or even tanks coming to the rescue."

Feeley piped in again. "I like it better getting them in the streets. There you know your way around and where to hide!"

"Just how the hell many have you ever got, Feeley?" screamed Moynihan.

"I got my share," he replied limply.

"Let's get back to Belfast. I need a drink," injected Kelleher. "I'm sure the instructor here doesn't have any around, being the teetotaler that he is."

Shortly thereafter, Mickey was happy to come to the spot in the countryside where Kelleher and Feeley had left their car. He would be well rid of them. Then O'Neil drove him to a second location, where Mickey was to pick up the Aston-Martin. As Moynihan was getting out of the car, O'Neil said, "Those two are a couple of assholes!"

"You're right, Seamus," replied Mickey. "We know that part of the anatomy isn't capable of rational thought. Pushing out shit is its only purpose in life!"

On his way back to his home, Mickey's mind was filled with thoughts, and they all seemed to be of a disturbing nature. The syllogism that he kept repeating was, "*Something is wrong with Irishmen!* Well, there isn't anything wrong with me so it can't be universal. Logically, I should say that there is something wrong with some Irishmen or most Irishmen. What the hell is it? As a people, we have many fine qualities, but one of them isn't winning wars." Who could he compare them with? There were the Scots who were Celts, just like his own people. They had fought the Brits for centuries with some semblance of success at least up until Culloden in 1745. How about the Slavs? Chetniks under Mihelovich and partisans following Tito, who had taken on the German Wermacht and SS for almost all of World War II. They had made the Nazis pay a grim price. Next, the Israelis came to mind. They also fought the Brits, but were a hell of a lot more successful. What he wouldn't give to have a bunch like the old Israeli Stern Gang. Now there was an organization of dedicated freedom fighters.

Also of note was the fact that a number of the original group ended up running their future government. They had the advantage of taking on Britannia soon after a horrendous war and at a time when world sentiment was against colonialism. In addition, the Brits didn't have the advantage of a number of million Orangemen with their own constabulary plus a host of paramilitary types back then. Last, the Stern Gang wasn't considered a bunch of fanatics ostracized by other Jews. Conversely, the IRA and Provos are by and large rejected by the government of the Republic and a considerable segment of the populace. Moynihan continued his appraisal of the cause. *I'm sure that there are even a fair number of Irish in Northern Ireland who want to accept the status quo. We don't suffer from a shortage of quislings,* he thought.

Mickey was beginning to sense he was drifting toward disillusionment. Swiftly, he pulled the Aston-Martin to the side of the road, placed the gears in neutral, and applied the handbrake. Once out of the car, he leaned against it and studied the sky. He thought, *You couldn't miss the luminance of the full moon if you tried.* As he stared up at the vacuous expression in the face of the man on the moon, an old patriotic song came to mind. "By the Rising of the Moon" had always been special to Mickey. Starting to hum the tune, he didn't vocalize the lyrics. They were left to pass in quiet through his mind.

"I'll fight my own war," he decided. "Who needs rock-throwing, slogan-painting teenagers, or melodramatic funeral processions for dead Provos, who were too dumb to successfully plan an operation? That's it! I'll have my own force de frappe. We'll kill British soldiers and government officials, as well as the top dogs of the Ulster paramilitary. Provos can continue their penny ante stuff with the indiscriminate bombing that blows up more baby carriages than armored personnel carriers. Sooner or later, any Irishmen with sense will realize that there is someone out here, who is doing it the right way. They will rally about me, and we will win!"

Once back in the car and heading home again, Mickey reflected on his scheme. Was it mad cap, grandiose, and so overly stuffed with bravado as to create unattainable goals? *Possibly so,* he thought. *But it's worth a go!* Suddenly, a thought crossed his mind, and it made him laugh. An inside joke he had thought up, and only told it to himself. The mental image that induced his mirth was a banner headline in a Belfast paper proclaiming "THE GREEN PUMPERNICKLE STRIKES AGAIN!" "No! I'm not going to intrude on that Scarlet fellow's turf, and I won't be changing clothes in the phone booth, but I'm going to make sure they know I'm around!"

Mickey did meet with the Provo chieftains one last time. When they were all present, his eyes swept those of the others. This action was slow enough that they were easily able to discern how much fire lay behind his pupils. "I'm going to disassociate myself from you gentlemen," he said. Then, Mickey continued, "I'm much aware we have some philosophical differences, and I see no way to resolve them. I'm going my own way, and you can continue on yours. No hard feelings; just pretend that I never existed."

Slowly, Moynihan rose from his chair, ever watchful for any aggressive movement by the others. Feeley and a man named Coffey started reaching for weapons. However, Kelleher was mindful of how quickly Mickey has disarmed the punk with the Armelite, and he had every reason to think Mickey was armed. Guided by prudence, he raised his hand to quell the actions of Feeley and the other man. Quick as the movement was, it had hardly been instituted when they were all aware that Mickey's Browning Hi-Power was out and leveled in their direction.

Slowly, and with reasonable calm, Kelleher said, "No problem, Moynihan if you want out, then you're out!"

"I love a happy farewell," replied Mickey. Then, he was gone.

"We'll have to stiff that fooker," cried Feeley after Moynihan had departed. Then, he added, "We'll stiff O'Neil as well!"

"Don't be in a rush," replied Kelleher. "You kill O'Neil, and Moynihan will know who did it. I don't doubt he would have much trouble doin' us all in! Someday there will be an opportunity."

In time, after his disassociation with the others and with the assistance of Seamus O'Neil, Moynihan assembled his cadre of followers. All these men exhibited qualities much like his own, though O'Neil was getting to be at an age where he was not quite up to the arduous tasks. However, he was a splendid planner, recruiter, and intelligence gatherer.

All in their twenties, the other eight were as near a match for England's Special Air Service personnel as Moynihan could contrive to train them. Also, they were as well armed as the SAS, possibly even better. By necessity, their training was given by elite instructors within the Communist bloc. However, the majority of planned operations they conducted needed only a few of his squad. Preoperational briefings were never conducted in the same place, and they were generally handled by O'Neil. Moynihan's participation was primarily limited to what they considered major strikes and the introduction of new weapons and tactics. Three safe houses were set up in the six counties of Ulster and were located in rural or suburban areas. In the Republic, two houses were just south of the border. All had been chosen with meticulous attention to detail, leaving scant chance they would be the subject of curiosity or accidental discovery.

At one major meeting, which he did attend, Moynihan addressed his men in solemn tones. "It is my concept to ration successes. We'll have more than our share of them, but we'll never set a pattern, nor will we ever become too greedy at this stage of the game. Maybe we'll launch a couple of quick strikes in different locations the same day, then drop out of sight for a couple of weeks, or a month.

"Although nameless, we do exist, and nameless we'll remain until it suits our purpose to go public. An enemy is more prone to remain confused chasing a phantom. Give them a name to chase, and it increases their determination. Newspapers won't hound them to eradicate an organization that doesn't exist. But they sure as hell will ride their asses to eradicate some mythical Jolly Green Rangers if we start calling them up claiming such a group was responsible for their most recent disaster. Also, I want to make it clear that none of you are to have any friends or contacts with any of our brother competitors. That would place us all at risk! You could get swept up in a dragnet, or as we all know, touts or supergases are not in short supply. So, all your friends and girlfriends must be those of a neutral bent, or even opposed to the IRA and Provos!

"One last thing! We're good, but we're not perfect or invincible. One of us could be captured, and they have clever ways to make you talk. I don't mean to be melodramatic, but I have a supply of cyanide capsules in case you think that you'll ever have to rely on one. I don't ever intend to put any of you on the spot, so I'll give each of you a capsule. In the case you think that you can tough out any interrogation or you intend to shoot it out to the end, then throw the capsule away in private. That way, no one will ever know who might want one, and who doesn't."

Moynihan's talk seemed to satisfy the men, and all felt more closely united and more impressed with their leader. On the following week, the British forces lost one Saracen APC and a helicopter, then a second Saracen three weeks later. There were no clues found, and no braggadocio claims of success.

Over the next five years, Moynihan's little commando squad kept up their depredations against what they deemed the enemy establishments. They managed to down another helicopter and one light observation plane, both with highly portable air-to-ground missiles. Three more Saracens were claimed by rocket-propelled grenades or tow missiles. In addition, there were a number of bridges, railroad tracks, electrical substations, and high-tension power lines destroyed. On occasion, the British Army could hush up the destruction of armored cars or even the aircraft. However, it was difficult to explain to any angry populace and inquisitive reporters why a bridge on a well-traveled lane suddenly ceased to exist. This was especially so when debris, obviously part of the original structure, lay scattered about the countryside. When the people became frightened and greatly inconvenienced, then the politicians were provoked, and those in charge of maintaining order harassed. Thus, the Army, MI-5, and the RUC were feeling the heat. The elevated temperature spread to Britain. Parents, wives, and siblings of slain British troops demanded to know what precisely happened to their loved ones and what was being done about it.

Fortunately for Mickey and his little band, there were nearly always one or more groups quite happy to compete in claiming credit for what his group had done. This had two different effects. Intelligence officers, who found themselves at war with Mickey's marauders, were becoming more proficient at tracing the calls of those making spurious victory claims. As a result, more arrests took place. Although this took some bona fide members of the IRA or Provos off the street, no decrease was observed in what was deemed terrorist activities. In fact, there was an increase because Moynihan continued his operations. Also, a number of other groups tried to mimic them. Copycats were by and large far less successful. Nonetheless, they increased the need for more police, more soldiers, and a greater number of patrols.

Another effect was confusion and bewilderment on behalf of the Parliament of Ulster, the British Parliament, and all their minions. Endless hours of surveillance followed by arrests and interrogations did provide a few convictions for unrelated offenses. However, after all the mind-numbing work, they always ended up knowing this group couldn't have blown up the bridge or other facilities because they simply were not sophisticated enough. In the end, many an irascible interrogator was ready to bang the prisoner's head or his own against the wall. When they finally got the prisoner to admit he blew up the armored car, then asked, "What with?" The classic, fraudulent response was "dynamite." Obviously, this fellow didn't know that it was a tow missile. He probably didn't have the foggiest notion of what one was! Consequently, the usual decision was, "Well, best get him to confess to something else and salt him away." In the meantime, the ones they really wanted remain as invisible, as they were years ago, and the political fires kept raging.

In addition to the frustration of the intelligence-gathering community, increased demands were made on Army personnel and equipment. In some areas, tanks were employed rather than APCs. Alternate plans included shadowing Saracens with troop-laden lorries or helicopters. Questions arose regarding what to do about bridges and power stations. Should they be guarded around-the-clock or by sporadic patrols? So far, Moynihan and his group had certainly not brought the Lion to his knees, but they were a very meddlesome thorn in his paw.

Dilemmas were not always one-sided. Certainly, Mickey and his group had their share of frustrations. However, overall, they were proud of their successes, but success tended to breed a desire for more. Moynihan thought, *How do you balance daring against prudence?* For years, Mickey had fought this problem out within his own mind. He would have liked to take out an APC along with one or more troop-laden lorries all at the same time. Was that too ambitious? Maybe yes and maybe no! Sun Tzu was full of good ideas on how to overcome your enemy. However, they didn't have radios or helicopters in his day. Response time for a rescue effort was a hell of a lot slower when the cavalry was coming on Mongolian ponies. Besides, old Sun Tzu was used to dealing in big numbers. Far different when you limit yourself to nine and you know them all like brothers. That makes it a hell of a lot harder trying to decide who you are willing to sacrifice.

Mickey laughed, as he thought about the fact that he wasn't quite at the point where he wanted to sacrifice himself. "Should they get me on a good-odds mission that's one thing, but I don't have the right-shaped eyes for a kamikaze. Well, the squad is anxious for action, so I'll be innovative. I'll cook up something, and see if Seamus can punch any holes in it. I'm light years away from launching a blitzkrieg," he mused to himself. "I wonder what old Montgomery, Patton, or Rommel would have done with ten guys including themselves? The way I figure it, I'm about 9,990 men short of a Panzer Division, and I don't have any tanks at all!"

Once again, Mickey buoyed his spirit up with a little self-denigrating humor within the privacy of his own thoughts. *I guess I'm a bit more like Robin Hood with a Draganov instead of a bow and arrow. I wonder how it will all end? Well someday, I'll find out! But in the meantime, daydreaming is not known for producing results. Let me go on to bigger and better things. How do you wipe out a Saracen and a lorry filled with troops without getting whacked yourself?*

During the years that Mickey savored the successes that came his way, Bernadette had realized at least a modicum of complacency. She had noted there was far less business for Mickey to conduct in Belfast. However, he was obviously doing something on those days and nights when he was away from home. Whatever it was required no bookkeeping. Sure, it was business of a sort, but it wasn't commercial. Both he and she took frequent trips to Boston, though grand fun was experienced mainly during school holidays, when the whole family made the trip. However, when it was Bernadette and Mickey alone, then it was sublime, for that was when her husband was solely hers, and she had no fear of a dreaded call announcing his death or arrest.

As for the businesses in Boston, they were doing well, and the income was good. The people left in charge were honest and diligent. Nonetheless, they couldn't be expected to pour their personalities into achieving the same degree of success that the owners had managed on a full-time basis. *Oh how I wish we could abandon Ireland with all its troubles and woes*, thought Bernadette. *Would Mickey ever decide when he had done enough, or for that matter, would he live sufficiently long to confront reality?*

In addition to spousal concerns, Bernadette had more than her share of those of a maternal nature. Despite the fact their peers in the town and school were nearly all Protestants, both Sean and Liam manifested symptoms of having contracted the fever of Irish rebellion. Some of it came from Mickey, as he seldom missed the opportunity to strongly editorialize against any pro-Ulster pronouncements emitting from the radio or TV. During this time, TV was becoming an important factor and influence in everyone's life. Also, due to her finely tuned intuition, Bernadette was led to believe that the two older boys must be aware their father had a sinister side despite the fact it was never discussed.

As far as school was concerned, Sean did very well, although he was capable of doing better. Sports were of greatest importance, though an interest in girls was emerging; however, Bernadette noted not nearly as rapidly as the girls' interest in him. Sean was extremely competitive and aggressive in sports. Now nearly as big as his father and surely to be larger at maturity, he was a force with which to be reckoned. After the first school year, his fellow students realized that taunting Sean Moynihan was an open invitation to a thrashing. Consequently, such behavior stopped.

Regarding Liam, Bernadette was very concerned, for he constantly provoked dismay and frequently anger. Although Liam was probably as bright as his brother, however, he seemed to delight in courting dismissal via truancy or academic failure, rather than striving for any semblance of scholarly achievement. Like Sean, he was very gifted athletically and even better coordinated than his brother, though smaller in size. In rugby or football, Liam was truly a whiz! Unfortunately, any joy sensed when he scored a goal was usually quickly erased. Liam had amassed more yellow cards, red cards, and evictions from the game than any other player in school history.

Moynihan's second son was a dirty player and enamored with trash talk, not only to the other team's players but also to his own teammates, Sean excluded. Often heard was the comment "Liam takes more delight in trying to discreetly punch or kick an opponent in the balls than score a goal!" While Sean protected his brother on and off the field, Mickey freely chastised him. Often, his father's powerful hand held Liam by his shirtfront, feet well off the floor, with his voice bellowing, "Liam what the hell is wrong with you!" On a number of occasions, Mickey took the strap to him.

However, for Liam, behavior modification was temporary at best. Sometimes Bernadette thought, *If it weren't for the fact that Liam could be so much fun and wonderfully accommodating on family outings, his father might have beat him severely.* Frequently, she struggled with her husband's dichotomy. *My dear Mickey,* she would think. *You can go around killing people for the Cause, but you'll brook no compromise when it comes to sportsmanship. You have a mystifying honor code!* Then, she thought, *Am I so much different? I never killed anyone and I doubt I ever will. Nonetheless, I delivered guns that permitted others to do so and now I seem to be suffering a conversion. Who is right and who is wrong?*

Trying to protect family relations, Bernie never did show Mickey the girlie magazines she found in Liam's room. She felt her husband was probably the most chaste killer in the world. "No telling what he might do if he found out!" she murmured. Instead, Bernie threw the torn pages of pornography in Liam's face and shrilled, "Anyone who would look at that stuff would drink water from a dirty toilet. Now go burn it or I'll tell your father!" Bernie never found any more magazines. However, not given to self-deceit and appreciating Liam's guile, she didn't think he would desist.

As for little Michael, he always seemed free of fault. Actually, Michael wasn't little anymore. When the squeakiness wasn't there, a baritone voice was emerging, and a copper-red whisker or two could be found emerging alongside a freckle. On more than one occasion, Bernie imagined Michael Jr. in a black soutane with a Roman collar. "What is it that brings that up?" she would muse. "I thought I purged myself of the popery years ago." Then, she would conclude with, "Probably some type of Freudian mental quirk because he happens to excel in Latin. Well I might not believe in God, but angels are a rather nice vestige to preserve and my little Michael is surely one of them." As far as Mickey was concerned, Bernadette found him a fine, loving father to his third son. Despite that, she seemed to sense that her husband sometimes regarded his youngest progeny as an Irish setter might on finding a Labrador in the litter he had sired.

Sometimes there was yet another part of Bernadette's life that she revisited. She knew her mother and father were still alive, for on occasion she felt compelled to place a phone call. Though deeply moved at the sound of their voices, she never spoke. If she held the receiver to her ear long enough, she could hear, "Hello hello! Is there anyone there?" That wasn't much, but it was a contact, which seemed to preclude finality. *You just can't forget your parents!* she would think. *No more than I can forget the real Isle of Skellig Michael.* Then that memory would induce her to seek out the little framed photo from long ago given to Bernie on her honeymoon. Bernie had no photo of her parents, only a fragile recollection. *I could go back to Skellig Michael, I suppose. Also, see my mother and father, but for some reason I feel compelled to wait until all this uncertainty in my life is over.* As Bernie replaced the Skellig Michael photo in her jewelry box, her eyes misted, and the same old question would arise: "Will it ever be over?"

Chapter Twenty-Five

❈ ❈ ❈

After several weeks of soul searching and a good deal of surveillance, Mickey decided it was time to strike again. He noted a fine dirt road headed east from Newry curving toward the border between the twenty-six counties of the Republic and the six counties of Ulster. This was a road known for smuggling guns and explosives into Ulster. Best yet, it ran past the base of Camlaugh Mountain, which provided an excellent vantage point for Moynihan's plan. By himself, for three Wednesdays in a row, Mickey made the drive on a speedy motor bike, wonderfully adaptive for cross-country use. His arrival at Camlaugh Mountain was always timed for dawn. Fortunately, there were no roadblocks along his route. Of course, Moynihan knew that he could possibly run in to a roving patrol car. However, as usual, he was prepared. Close to the mountain ran a splendid little stream, with ample trout, plus salmon in season.

Cautious as always, Moynihan carried precisely the right equipment for angling, plus a bona fide license. When the mountain base was achieved, enough daylight enabled him to proceed across country to his vantage point. *They should be along in an hour or so,* he reflected. *I might as well have a little hot chocolate and make myself comfortable. I might even try to catch a fish,* was his next bemused thought.

Then, at 0745 hours, a small column of motorized vehicles came into view. Sporting a light machine gun, a Jeep led the little parade. Approximately 100 yards back was a Saracen armored car, and in the rear a lorry with eight armed soldiers in the back, plus two in front. Using a range finder, Mickey could quite accurately estimate their distance from him and the space between them. On the following two Wednesdays, the same patrol with identical make-up materialized at almost exactly the same time.

At their favorite drop site, four days after his last recon mission, Mickey met with Alexis Zellanova. Ever watchful, the Russian pulled up nearby Moynihan's Aston-Martin. Immediately, he went to the rear of his Zil and feigned inspection of his left rear tire. The act that followed was first class. After swearing indignantly in his native tongue, Alexis savagely kicked the hapless tire and proceeded to open the boot. Then came an exasperated waving of his arms and more invective in Russian.

Mickey got out of his car much in the fashion of a perplexed good Samaritan hoping to help his fellow man. Observing the pantomime that followed would have convinced anyone that the poor fellow in the Zil had a flat tire. Just now, he had discovered he had no jack. Soon, Moynihan produced what appeared to be a tool bag, opened it, and proudly held up the needed tool. Then, the Russian produced what appeared to be an old blanket. Someone watching would probably assume this would be used to protect the clothing of the tire changer. Soon, working together, victim and Good Samaritan had the tire changed. Next came a demonstration of effusive gratitude for help given.

All the tools went back in place, along with another tool bag, which had appeared out of nowhere. However, the tools in this satchel were meant for destruction, rather than repair. They included three land mines and four claymore mines. No actual thanks was given by the distraught motorist, instead the dialogue was frank. "Do you think I'm running a supermarket for explosives Mickey?"

"No, Alexis, it's more of a boutique!"

"Good luck," spoke the Russian.

Mickey nodded and replied, "Dosvedanya!"

All of the mines were devised to be detonated electronically, rather than by applied pressure. Otherwise, the lead vehicle would explode the first one and the others would stop. Also, the possibility of accidental detonation by a wayward cow or farm lorry laden for market could be avoided.

On the fourth successive Wednesday, Mickey was on the road earlier than usual. Previously, Moynihan had arranged for his squad to be in designated places as lookouts or possible rear guards if needed. Rotated among the five, Mickey was always grateful for their presence. Assisted by cell members, the explosives had been left at designated sites by O'Neil on the day before. Although Seamus's vehicle had suffered mechanical problems, there had been more than adequate time to hide the mines in between occasional passage of other vehicles. Aided by Jennings and Carey, Mickey found them easily.

Carefully, the men placed the explosives in desired positions under cover of darkness. Mickey quipped, "Nothing so grand as hands-on experience. Do it wrong and it's a hands-off experience!" Then, he withdrew to his vantage spot on Camlaugh Mountain and waited. Land mines buried beneath the road's surface could be fired independently by electrical impulses of variable frequency. Conversely, Mickey knew, the claymore mines were tuned to the same frequency. As a whole, the operation was far from exact. However, it was planned out as well as possible. He realized there were many variables. Vehicles might be closer together or further apart than he had foreseen. That could foul things up. But then, Mickey felt, you had to play the hand you were dealt. The first mine was placed directly in front of a willow tree. Number two was exactly aligned with a large rock, and third mine was at the corner of a fence line.

"Here they come," Mickey hissed under his breath. When the Jeep was in position, the first button was pressed. Violently, the road erupted, tossing the Jeep in the air. Obviously, there would be no survivors. Carnage was even more evident to the drivers of the other vehicles, as they fought to brake them to a halt. Both the lorry and Saracen were close enough to the designated spots that damage or destruction could be predicted. Next, the Saracen was knocked on its side, though not rendered asunder. Damage to the front of the lorry was extensive, and injuries to the two men in the cab was extreme or fatal! Those in the rear were obviously stunned but mobile.

Screaming orders, a Sergeant ordered his men to dismount. Simultaneously, the crew of the armored car were exiting through an open hatch. Then Mickey pressed hard on the last button, releasing the fury of the claymore mines. However, the mines planted near the devastated Jeep were overkill, for the crew was already dead. But the steel spheres released from the last four had a telling effect on the numbed survivors of the other two vehicles. Deadly pellets scythed across the open spaces, killing or maiming a number of soldiers.

Far from perfect, thought Mickey, as he sped away on the motor bike. *Now I'd best get the hell out of here!* Fortunately, the frozen trout that he had brought along had thawed. If stopped, he could surely say, "Yes, Officer, I was fishing. Did pretty well, as you can see." No one ever stopped him, but the bombings did make the news. Bernadette was greatly relieved when the motor bike came down the drive. She tried to put it all together while she was helping Mrs. Hennessey prepare trout for dinner.

At last, Sean graduated from secondary school, much to the relief of his mother. He opted to enroll in Coleraine University. Sports remained foremost in his activities, but maturation enhanced the young man's desire to learn, as evidenced by the appearance of his name on the Dean's List. Bernadette was euphoric, but Mickey was ambivalent. However, it did please him to see his son achieving status in areas where he had been deprived.

Conversely, Mickey fretted about whether or not more openness and authoritarianism on his own behalf would have kindled more of a patriotic spirit in his son. When such thoughts crossed his mind, Mickey would say to himself, "How many martyrs need the family supply?" Just as he was on the verge on saying "no more," another inner voice would whisper, *We need all the good men we can get!* Pondering these self-exhortations, Moynihan decided that it's time to inculcate him slowly, though he never seemed to get around to commencing the indoctrination. However, that really didn't matter, as Sean had already started the process.

Finally, it was time for Liam to graduate. He did receive a diploma; however, the Headmaster and faculty felt that it was more a warrant for release rather than a reward for achievement. Parents and siblings dressed for and attended the ceremony, but Liam was in absentia. Bernadette was crushed and Mickey furious! When the absentee finally came home, Bernie pleaded with her husband for equanimity. Mickey did his best to comply, but try as he might, any pathways to compromise with his errant son ended in cul-de-sacs.

"Why not try a year or two at the university?" Mickey asked. "You could pick up a little business acumen and give us a hand with our business in Boston."

"That doesn't appeal to me," snapped Liam in a surly voice.

"Then what the hell do you want to do?" shot back his father in response.

"I need to find myself," replied Liam.

"That's a good one," replied Mickey. "Why do you need to find yourself? I can tell you where you are. You're right in your parent's parlor. It would make more sense to say 'I want to find my way.' Then, once you admit that, perhaps your parents could give you some direction!"

Discourse went on for sometime and grew more heated. Even Bernadette's patience wore thin. Realizing she was on the brink of losing her composure, Bernie was certain Mickey was about to explode. Finally, she said, "Let's all take a breather. I can see we are all getting overwrought. Perhaps, we can reconcile our differences tomorrow."

Suddenly Liam stomped from the room, bolted up the stairs, and slammed his bedroom door. Mickey sought the outside in hopes his ignited anger would cool. For Sean and Michael, it was the telly.

Nothing on TV was of interest, but it did lend a distraction of sorts. Bernadette was left alone in the kitchen, too distressed and depleted to seek a tissue to wipe away the tears. A damp dishcloth was used instead. A sudden memory erupted in her mind. She recalled her parents, kneeling in prayer to invoke Jesus and the help of Jesus's mother, Mary, or some surrogate saint to come to the family's rescue. "All nonsense," she sighed. Nonetheless, she wished that she could convince herself otherwise. However, she was filled with spiritual inertia, and no prayers issued from her lips.

Later, when Mickey came back inside, Bernie was more composed and said softly "It looks like we have a prodigal son."

"That's more mumbo jumbo from Rome. Reminds me of Jonah, Noah, and all the other fairy tales. I'll stick with Grimm if I want to dwell on the make believe!" Then, seeing how distraught Bernie was, Mickey gave her a kiss and said, "He will come around in the morning. Let's get some sleep!"

However, their second son did not come around in the morning, for he had left during the night, along with nearly 200 pounds in cash from a pried-open desk down in the study. Liam found his way into the seamy side of Belfast, like a young shark beginning predatory life in the sea. Only a small portion of the purloined pounds was needed to rent a dismal flat on George Street, just off Queen's Street, in the Catholic Dockside section of the city. He wasn't entirely sure why he selected a Catholic neighborhood, as no known heritage existed in his mind. There was no shortage of sin or sinners in the Protestant area; however, they were nearly all employed and thus not as laissez faire as the Paddy. Perhaps, it was because life seemed looser with more trees bearing forbidden fruit to pick. Alcohol, never present in his home, was abundant, and he freely imbibed. Tartlets abounded, leading Liam to purchase the favors of a few before finding there was a ready supply of amateurs available. Cast out a good line, and he could catch one nearly every time.

Marijuana was next on the menu. Finding he liked it, Liam ordered more. Fortunately, being innately snobbish, on seeing the derelict junkies strung out on smack, avoidance of the hard stuff seemed prudent. Within a couple of weeks, friends were found, and they were fonts of information on how to obtain easy money, either from criminal activity or welfare schemes. "Sell some pot, earn enough to supply yourself, and have a pocketful of punts left over in your pocket. Be sure to avoid the Constabulary, as well as those elements of the IRA and UDF, who found drug peddlers mortally if not morally offensive." Liam seemed to excel. Why wouldn't he? Ever since he was thirteen years old, he had managed to dabble in vice under the very noses of his observant and strict parents.

Sooner or later in the Queen Street bars and coffee houses Liam realized that you would encounter the IRA. Over in the corner of a neighborhood pub with six shots of Bushmill's beneath your belt and a protest song wailing lament in your ears and a sultry little slut pressed tight against you, the Republican fever could become infectious. Suddenly, Liam was aware that carpe diem, "Live, drink, and be merry," wasn't quite fulfilling enough. Perhaps, he needed some adventure. He thought, *Even a liberal could find a little altruism within himself.* So when the music ended, he inquired of Katie Brannigan, his female companion for the night, "Do you know anything about the IRA?"

"My brother died for it. Do you need to know more?" she asked.

"Yes I do," was Liam's answer.

Katie accompanied Liam back to his rooming house after the bistro closed. Snugly ensconced in the confines of the squalid garret, she gave freely of her favors and narrative. "It's the Provos you should be joining here," she said. "They're the new wave and the real hope for Ireland! My brother Billy saw it right off. Sure he was killed by the SAS, but he went down fighting hard. Everybody in the Catholic section of Dockside was at the funeral. I cried a lot, but I was proud of Billy. Seein' the turnout helps you make it through, as well as keepin' the hate going for the fookin' Brits and their Orange stooges. I've done some gettin' even myself. A gang of us set upon a couple of Prod bitches and beat the crap out of them. Then, we ripped off their fine clothes and tarred and feathered the whores. If I had a knife, I would have carved them up a bit. I would have liked that!"

"You keep mentioning Catholics," Liam queried. "I assume all the people with the Provos and IRA are Catholic. Do you go to church?"

"If I did, I wouldn't be cuddled up naked on the bed, love," was Katie's response.

"Then, why do all of you keep saying you're Catholics?" was Liam's next question.

"Because we have it in common—and it's the reason we get such a shitty deal. However, when you're piss poor, can't get a job, and they want to toss you on the dung heap, you look for something new. Kind of a new religion, where you pull the trigger on a gun, instead of piously fingering some rosary beads hopin' for the Second Comin'. The Catholic Church is the soil in which we seeds were all planted. It's just that some of us come up onions, and the rest are heads of lettuce."

Liam Moynihan acquired two things from his tryst with Katie. One was his first introduction to the devastating symptoms of gonorrhea, the other a fervor to take up the Cause. In time, thanks to the efficacy of antibiotics supplied for free by a neighborhood clinic, the urethral discharge and urinary discomfort disappeared. However, the fervor remained with him, especially since he never sought a cure. Liam was hooked for life when the mousy little mate in his tryst turned up dead. Someone had witnessed Katie's participation in the beating and degradation of the Protestant girls. Word got back to one of their fathers. Highly positioned in the UDF, he was easily able to see that revenge was accorded to Katie and her friends. They were abducted, tried, and sentenced to forty lashes each.

No one could have known Katie had congenital heart disease, for she didn't even know herself, never having seen a physician. Her compatriots survived, but were scarred for life. Katie's heart wasn't up to the test, and it stopped somewhere near the twenty-fifth lash. Her torturers felt no remorse, for the chief instigator was heard to say, "The bitch died on us. Well, we can still make use of her," and so they did. Sometime after midnight, the torn, nude, and emaciated body was hung from a light pole on Queen Street, with a sign hung around her neck, simple but to the point, reading, "Justice for a Paddy whore." Liam attended the funeral. As it had been for her brother, there was a fine turnout. Most of the mourners left the service shaking their heads. However, Liam was among the few who went to seek a recruiter. He was about to become a Volunteer!

No great difficulty was encountered in finding someone to sign Liam up in the Provos. Terms of enlistment in that organization were extreme and could cause eyebrows to rise or the jaw to slacken. However, Liam was unperturbed. Joining the Provos, like signing up for any regular Army, usually meant for the duration of hostilities. That was generally a finite time. However, the struggle of the Irish against the English was already four times longer than the 100 Year War. Still, there was a degree of optimism that victory would come within the lifetime of the present participants, presuming their longevity wasn't curtailed by a bomb or bullet.

Liam gladly accepted all the admonitions about the consequences of early retirement or betrayal. Knee capping and assassination of those who, tired of revolution or decided to talk with the other side, were certainly not classified secrets. As a matter of fact, Liam thoroughly agreed with such deterrents. In a cell led by Kenny C. Casey, Liam started out as a simple soldier. For reasons of his first two initials being K.C., the leader was nicknamed Echo. Liam's cell leader was tough and mean. However, Moynihan was not intimidated but rather stimulated to be tougher and meaner.

With flying colors, the new cell member passed all the initial tests. In the event the Provos felt there was someone in need of a good thrashing, others would kick the hard parts; however, Liam took particular delight in a well-placed kick to the scrotum. He found this much more rewarding than the old soccer games, where you had to hold back and only got in a single blow. Out on the street, Liam could really put his heart and boot into it! Before long, he had achieved some acclaim due to the fact that his victims frequently ended up needing to have one or more of their testicles removed.

Knee capping also became a favorite indulgence. Frankly, most of Liam's peers were reluctant or squeamish about performing knee injuries, especially the first time. Such was not the case with Liam. At his first opportunity, he took the old Webley 455 without hesitation. Then the person to be punished was forced on his side with both knees tightly opposed. Liam pressed the muzzle hard against the outer surface of the upper knee, saying softly, "Why waste a bullet? I can wipe out both the fooker's knees with one shot." After cocking the exposed hammer ceremoniously, he paused and exclaimed vehemently, "Welcome to Cripple Land!"

Liam's perverse bravado didn't go unnoticed. Within a few months, Echo gladly promoted him to be his Lieutenant. For the first time in his life, Liam had found ambition, and he fully intended to ride the wave all the way. Indeed, he had some of his father's traits. However, the difference lie in the fact that Mickey followed Hammurabi's Code because he truly thought it was just. He never really enjoyed its application like his second son.

Though Liam found enforcement and maiming to his liking, there were some aspects of his new profession that he felt were banality itself. The Provos had found him a menial job in a warehouse, which he detested. Liam's work ethic was no better than his study habits. On the first day, he would have been sacked before lunch if the foreman was not afraid of provoking a Provo reprisal. Additionally, the recently created gunman was chronically short of cash. He had given consideration to peddling some drugs on the side. But he abandoned that plan after participating in the torture of an active pusher.

Apart from drugs, the IRA and its Provisional Wing were partial to virtually all felonious activity. Just as long as you "protected" Catholic merchants, the protection racket was acceptable. Those were the merchants who were trying to eke out a living, attend Mass, and receive the sacraments, apart from Last Rites. These poor souls were considered noncombatants and noncontributors, who only wished to remain neutral when it came to political causes.

Echo and Liam staked their claim to a ten-square-block area. Low-key examples were made of those initially reluctant to pay their premiums. Soon, collections were good. However, they would never be grand enough to sate the avaricious appetites of Echo and Liam, but higher-ups had somewhat of a heart, plus a degree of pragmatism. Far better to desist when you have extracted enough to impoverish the policy holders and still bank on a steady level of revenue. Alternatively, the Provos could keep raising the bar, put them all out of business, and end up with an empty purse.

Echo's cell was allowed to deduct expenses before submitting the rest of the money to headquarters. As a result, they had a fair fling at their concept of the good life. This was especially so since sex and booze were essentially free. Liam moved to what was considered an upscale apartment for the area. Among its features was a feather bed shared frequently with his latest liaison. Consequently, the foreman was overjoyed when his lazy lout of an employee became too affluent to appear for work. Extra Aves were said at evening family prayers in thanksgiving!

As a perk for reaching rank of lieutenant in Casey's cell, Liam was issued an Armalite in .223 caliber. He delighted in the feel and look of the weapon; the magazine capacity of thirty rounds, and its selective fire capabilities. However, with one pull of the trigger, only one shot fired was not for him. Full auto was the way to go. A day didn't pass that Liam didn't ask Echo when he could finally use the gun. On a special Tuesday, instead of an answer, "How the fook do I know?" Liam heard, "Tomorrow!" This was followed by "You'll like this job, I promise."

Word had got around that it was Derek Atwell who was responsible for flogging the Catholic young women and the death of Katie Brannigan, plus the repulsive exposition of her body. Consequently, Liam was ecstatic at the opportunity to stiff the man. His only regret was that Atwell's death would be sudden. Accordingly to their plan, a suitable car was stolen for the raid. Jimmy Brady would drive and share the front seat with Brian Mulcahey. Both were armed with hand-me-down Colt 38 specials; however, one of these (unknown to its carrier) had a weakened hammer spring. In the rear seat would be Liam and Casey, who were outfitted with Armalites. A tip had come in from a Paddy handyman at the Rover car dealership that Atwell was slated to pick up a new car at two P.M. Therefore, the would-be assassins positioned themselves, where they were relatively inconspicuous, as they were still uncertain that the delivery would take place. They didn't have a photo of their intended victim, but his description seemed straightforward enough. Plus, they knew it was a sure thing that the car was new, four door, and dark blue in color.

At half past two, such a car emerged through the gate. "Hit it, Brady," screamed Liam and Casey in unison! As the tires squealed, their stolen car careened forward. Soon it was nearly abreast of the slowly moving blue sedan. Liam called out, "That fooker won't get much of a test drive!"

"Your shot, Liam," hollared Casey. Moynihan's window was down, and the muzzle of the Armalite quickly came into play.

Suddenly, Mulcahey screamed out, "Oh shit! He has his wife and brat with him. We can't do anything now." His last sentence was never heard as its stature in sound was obliterated by the staccato explosions of the Armalite's cargo.

Just in front of the driver's door, the first round hit. Then the rest stitched an irregular path upward and rearward. Holes in the metal looked neat and precise, but the glass erupted in terrible disarray. Atwell's brain tissue was just erupting through the hole in his left parietal bone when a second and third bullet struck five-year-old Sarah! The doll she held was no impediment to the passage of the high-velocity projectiles. They passed right through Raggedy Ann and then little Sarah before rending the heart of Nancy Atwell. Then the weight of the lifeless driver slumping against the steering wheel compelled the shiny new sedan to impact on a store front.

As the Provos sped away, an intersection was just ahead of the racing escape car. Brody was pushing the speed and fighting the wheel. Suddenly, he screamed, "It's a fookin' patrol." Concomitantly, four British soldiers in a Jeep were crossing the intersection about seventy-five yards ahead. They heard the deadly rattle of an Armalite spread down the street in a deafening crescendo. One second later, they saw a dark blue Rover careen wildly before hitting the store front. Then they spied a black car racing directly toward them at high speed. Quickly, their minds extrapolated the facts. As a result, their Jeep was left to block the intersection, and the occupants piled out, unlimbering their weapons at the same time.

First to reach a point offering some security was a sergeant. Immediately, he fired a quick burst at the windscreen of the black sedan hurtling toward them. Some of the steel-jacketed bullets were errant, but three impacted on Brady's most vulnerable parts, and death ensued instantly. Responding, Mulcahey ripped the dead driver's hands from the steering wheel. Thus he was able to avert collision with the Jeep. Reaching across, Mulcahey raised Brady's lifeless foot from the accelerator and tried to gain control. Amazingly, this proved advantageous to the three surviving gunmen, as it allowed the get-away car to come to a halt without devastating impact. Knowing it would take too long to extricate Brady's body from the driver's seat, the three survivors threw their doors open and scrambled away from the stalled car.

With his rifle pointed and ready to fire, one of the British soldiers was closing fast on Mulcahey. As the soldier was about to pull the trigger, the toe of his boot caught the edge of a paving stone. He fell headlong before impacting on the street's hard surface. Somewhat dazed, the trooper raised himself to a kneeling position and scrabbled for his gun. Mulcahey was a scarce ten feet from the soldier. Looking into the man's face, he raised his Colt pistol aiming directly between his enemy's eyes. Finger pressure on the trigger was exerted, and the hammer raised until the sear released and allowed it to fall. Instead of the explosion, which both men expected, only a sharp metallic click was audible.

Fate had decreed that Mulcahey had drawn the defective revolver. The good one remained tucked in the waistband of the bloody trousers shrouding Brady's corpse. Had Brian tried squeezing the trigger again, he might have had success. Even though Mulcahey knew that weakened hammer springs are like that, for sometimes they impel the hammer of the gun hard enough to detonate the primer and sometimes not. Yet he was dumbstruck! His outstretched hand was as if frozen. However, trained as he was, the soldier suffered no such paralysis. Instantaneously, the rifle was raised and fired.

Liam and Casey had been running down the street, but they turned at the sound of the firing just in time to witness a most macabre sight. At least ten rounds form the soldier's weapon tore through Mulcahey. His body seemed to twitch convulsively with each impact. Exiting his back, the velocity of the bullets was still high enough that they were not perceptible. This was not true for the fragments of flesh, spouting blood, and the tiny shreds of his shabby shirt that flew from the man's back. His body began to sink toward the street in harmony with the crimson stain descending toward the belt line, bidding adieu to life!

Stopping momentarily, Liam fired at the still-kneeling soldier. But his aim was faulty. Instead of killing the man, bullets ricocheted off the paving stones. Some few fragments of the splintering rock struck the man's face and kept him from firing again but did no significant damage.

"Run for it," shouted Casey, and the two of them took off fast.

Years of sports training proved to be Moynihan's salvation. He was well ahead of Echo and had just reached the entrance to an alleyway when another burst of automatic weapon fire sounded up the street. Stopping, Liam looked back. Casey was down, screaming in pain and trying to stanch the blood spurting from the inner aspect of his right thigh. Two soldiers were quickly on him. One kicked the Armalite aside. Then, they grabbed him by the arms and pulled him upright.

Liam's decision was instantaneous. Echo was alive, he could talk. Echo could name him! The last twenty rounds in the Armalite erupted from its muzzle and streamed down the street. One caught a soldier very near the bridge of his nose, with lethal effect. Two others tore into the second soldier's flak vest, stunning and wounding him, though not seriously. However, the bulk of the burst tore into Echo's heart, lungs, and spine. No longer suspended by his two captors, his body crumpled to the street, then slowly unfolded, totally inert.

Liam was satisfied. He was three blocks away when the Brit reinforcements arrived. Swiftly, he hid the Armalite behind some trash cans. Hopefully, it would be there when he came back that night. "Too bad about Brady and Mulcahey." However, Liam felt no real misgivings over Echo. He could have ended up a cripple. Surely, he would have had to endure years or even life in prison, and he could have talked!

Liam's bubble of elation burst as soon as he found the security of his room. Calm defiance and a sense of immortality he had experienced in the street gave way to cold shivers, then paranoia! Quickly, he pulled down the torn shades on the one small window and rechecked the door to make sure he had bolted it. "Damn it," he hissed. "I had to ditch the Armalite. If they come for me now, I'm defenseless." Trembling hands reached for a streaked glass in which he quickly poured a goodly measure of Bushmill's. Liam's first attempt to drink was sloppy, resulting in overflow from his mouth and a small degree of aspiration. When the coughing ceased, a second gulp was attempted with greater success. By the time the glass was emptied, a calming effect on his physiology was starting to occur. However, it did little to quell the fear in his mind. "Think it out," he said. *Was I recognized? The soldier wouldn't know who I was. Anybody else? Shit! How would I know? When you're running for your life, you don't study every face you rush by and think 'do I know that guy?' Could that have been the woman from the pharmacy? Would they tell even if they did recognize me? Fingerprints—could I have left any somewhere? What difference would it make? I don't have any on file. There would be nothing with which to compare them.*

Liam's complacency faded immediately. *Yeah, but if I'm ever picked up in the future, they would have a file. Steady, think it out! Start from the beginning. The car? No, I was wearing gloves right up to the time I fired on Atwell. I stuck them in my pocket.* Immediately, Liam jammed his hand in the left pocket of his trousers. Nothing. His heart was racing as he tried the second pocket. Tactile information fed to his brain told him of the presence of leather. *Was there one or two?* "Two," he said aloud with a long sigh of relief. "Yeah, but I wasn't wearing them when I opened the door after the crash. Oh shit! how about the empty magazine I took out of the gun and all those empty shell casings that I loaded? They could all have prints! What if they find the gun?"

About to pour more whiskey into his glass, Liam desisted and began to feel nausea as panic descended on him. *Best to get out of town,* was his next wild thought. *And go where?* was the second. *What about my oath to the Provos? Would they understand, or will they end up hunting for me?* Suddenly, sounds of a heavy shoe kicking the bottom of his door doubled his heart rate and sent his pulses throbbing through the four corners of his body. Then, a stern voice said, "The big man wants to see you Moynihan!"

It couldn't be the police, Liam thought. *They would have announced themselves, then broke the door down. It must be the Provos.*

Tentatively, Liam's hand went for the door bolt and threw it back. When the door opened, two very large, hard-looking men were standing there. Then the one furthest forward said, "You look like hell kid! The boss wants to see you and discuss today's action."

The second man snorted and added, "Maybe, he needs to clean up, Curly. He looks like he pissed his pants!"

Feeling some relief, Liam assumed a little defiance. "I just lost my best friend," he snapped, then added, "How the fook am I supposed to look?" However, by the time they got to the car, all Liam's bravado had returned. He even felt cocky enough to have them stop long enough to retrieve the hidden Armalite. About fifteen minutes later, the car pulled over to a curb. Soon, he would be meeting someone far further up than Echo in the Provos leadership. *Put on your best face for the interview,* Liam thought.

Darby McKevitt was not what Liam expected. No bruiser was this man. Instead, he gave the appearance of a hard-riding, tough as nails, slightly superannuated jockey, who could have won a thousand big races. No better application of the old canard "Looks don't deceive," than this man. Indeed, McKevitt was a legendary jockey. If any doubts persisted, they were removed by the impact of his handshake. Darby's hands were oversized, and when they clasped yours, you could readily appreciate why thoroughbreds responded to the reins when he rode.

Once seated, Liam looked into the ice-blue eyes of McKevitt. No twinkle was there. His eyes were sapphire, hard, and cold as ice.

Darby spoke. "Who finished off Echo, Moynihan?"

Liam was about to give a somewhat flippant answer "the Brits," but stopped short. Finally, he replied "I did."

"Why?" was the one-word question bolting next from Darby's lips.

Liam responded slowly, "I had but a second to decide. Casey was hit badly, but he may have survived. Suddenly, I thought they might induce him to talk. Even if they didn't, he had several murder raps hanging over his head, and they could salt him away for years. On the other hand, if he buckled under torture, he could have given them names of others in his cell, and no doubt some of his superiors!"

"You mean like me," the ex-jockey snapped. To Liam, the obvious answer under the circumstance would have been "yes." However, he paused under the scrutiny of McKevitt's freezing stare.

While in school, Liam's test scores were always poor. A dismal performance resulted not from stupidity but personal delight in answering just enough questions to pass. For this reason, his instructors were always perplexed that when they gave him a trick question, it was always answered correctly. McKevitt's last question was a trick question. Finally, Moynihan responded, "I didn't kill him because I was trying to save you, sir, because I didn't know who you were."

"Your answer isn't entirely satisfactory, Liam. But, it is honest and saved your life!" Extra meaning was added to the chief's words when his left hand gently pulled a Walther PPK from under the desk, then laid it on the surface.

"I'm putting you in charge of your cell, Moynihan. Also, here are some strong words of advice. You better get to know all your men very well, including the three new ones I'm sending over to you. In the event you ever stiff someone else in your group, you had best be able to document your decision with something better than guesses! Also, be sure one of your boys doesn't pull the trigger on you to save you from the possibility of a long prison term or ratting out on us. I'll send for you from time to time. Should you need to get in touch with me, go to Eddy's Bakery, and be sure you insist on talking to Eddy himself. I'll inform him who you are. Fritz and Curly will drive you home. They'll probably be surprised or disappointed they don't have to bury you."

Liam shook McKevitt's hand again and turned for the door. His spine felt a chill as he opened it, still feeling the ice-blue eyes that followed him. He had nearly flunked the exam. *Screw up another,* Liam thought, *and there will be no tears in Mr. Darby McKevitt's eyes when he lets the hammer drop!*

The following months went well for Liam. His group was performing solidly, and their operations went off without a hitch. Meanwhile, Sean was doing fine work in his studies and sports pursuits. Sometimes, to his mother, Sean would express concern for Liam, who remained incommunicado. However, in truth he didn't feel any. As far as Sean was concerned, he envisioned his younger brother as enjoying independence as much as he was. "Liam will turn up when he gets bored," was the way he handled it.

Concurrently, Mickey Moynihan and his gang of ten pursued their own war. Nothing as spectacular as the ambush of the small convoy, but the punches they threw were landing solidly. Moynihan's opponents in the RUC and British Army, including the elite SAS, were feeling the hurt. However, they weren't staggering yet, and he was a long way from a knock-out punch. "I've got a lot more rounds left in me," he would tell himself "I'll just keep jabbing with the left and someday I'll be able to smash them with a right upper cut!"

As for Bernadette, she was like a mother bird who lost a fledgling from her nest. Oh how Bernie wished she could fly about until she found it. However, there was little Michael to tend to, and he surely needed her. In the meantime, Bernie only hoped that Liam would learn to fly before a fox got him. Frequently crossing her mind was the thought that it would be nice to fortify her hopes with prayer. But she never seemed able to surmount that hurdle. As for her husband, Bernie sometimes sensed Mickey would always respond with, "Don't worry Bernie! Like the lost sheep, he'll turn up someday, wagging his tail behind him."

Chapter Twenty-Six

❈ ❈ ❈

Two years passed, and Liam never returned home. No bodies turned up, so everyone maintained the hope that he was alive and presumably well. Sean was near graduating, and there was no doubt that it would be with honors. Mickey was still the quintessential thorn in the lion's paw, for in addition to smaller encounters, another convoy had been hit. A bridge was blown in front of the leading Jeep, then rocket fire was poured in while the other vehicles tried to turn on the narrow road. *Yes,* Mickey thought. *The lion limped when he stepped on his sore paw, but he kept moving nonetheless! I'll have to come up with something like a good dose of rheumatism,* was Mickey's conclusion. *A barracks would be nice, but I don't have the men or resources. I'm surely fighting a glacial revolution. Sometimes, it seems as though I'm sitting watching sea battles on a great rocky cliff and waiting for the stone to change shape. If only all the factions could unite and be in solidarity with the populace, we could take out a barracks. Hell, we could take on a couple divisions. Well such an occurrence is only a pipe dream. I'll just have to keep banging away with my little hammer and chisel.*

Despite her concerns for husband and son, Bernadette remained radiantly beautiful. She continued to seek out happiness wherever it could be found. One day, she happened upon a solitary silver strand among her ravishing locks of red. Also, a couple of tiny wrinkles were just discernible at the corners of her eyes. Bernie sighed and tweezed out the single errant strand. Then, she applied a little extra moisturizing cream along the outer edges of her eyes. "If it were not for Sean and Mike, I'd be all silver," she murmured. Then, a little half-smile into the mirror beckoned a couple of dimples and the blue eye and green eye beamed appreciatively.

Little Michael had become "Mike" in the household. Now the diminutive appellation seemed inappropriate to a lad who had crested six feet and seemed destined to stretch a bit more. As Bernadette was putting down her hairbrush, she thought, *Thank God I'm doing well with two out of three.* Then, her reflection in the mirror registered dismay. "There you go again," she said. "Here I am thanking a God that I can't pray to. Is He just a figure of speech, or does He really exist? *I'll think about it again when I spot a couple more silver threads. It's time to pick up Mike,* was her replacement thought. *Where did I leave the car keys? At least I can still find them without glasses. How about that!* Suddenly, Bernie remembered that just next week she, Mickey, and Mike would be off to Boston. So on the way over to pick up her youngest son, Bernie was already planning where to shop and what to buy. She didn't realize that when they returned to Ireland, an unexpected event would await them.

Meanwhile, within the Provos, Liam was gaining recognition. Since their initial encounter, Darby McKevitt had no reason to find fault with him. Young Moynihan had done well in his assignments and had increased cash flows by comparison to the long since buried Casey. However, unfortunately for Liam, kudos from one war quarter can create jealousy in another. Liam Moynihan along with four of his cell had held up a small bank branch with no casualties and very good results. Liam thought it was a cause for celebrating. Not having had the pleasure of seeing Rosie Carey for several nights, Liam looked forward to her company for a night of partying and additional favors after the pubs closed their doors.

Rosie was an outlandish dresser under ordinary circumstances, but she had outdone herself for this occasion. Consequently, Liam took special note when he picked her up. Pretty much devoid of inhibition, Rosie had left nothing to anyone's imagination. Instead of being even slightly embarrassed by his date's dress or lack thereof, Liam, already partially inebriated, was enthralled. He started leading her toward the "Cove, where they usually partied, but Rosie insisted on the Embassy, the club in which she felt all the action would be taking place. "The music is far better, love, and they have a fine dance floor. You want to show me off don't you? Or, do you want to hide me in a corner of that stupid Cove."

"The Embassy it is, Rosie! I'll keep you out dancing, at least as long as you can stand up."

"You've had a head start love. I'll be out there doing a jig when you're under the table," was her raucous reply. This was accentuated by a swinging sequined purse that hit lightly on the side of Liam's head.

Making good on his promise, the couple missed only a few dances during the initial two hours at the Embassy. Only because of the desire to imbibe more Bushmill's and a single visit to the loo to relieve themselves had kept Liam and Rosie off the dance floor. However, off in a corner, a party of five men were also doing some serious drinking. Liam's father would have readily recognized two of them as Terry Kelleher and Denny Feeley, whom he had known during his short association with the Provos. Mickey had thoroughly disliked these two in particular and made it known every time he had come in contact with them.

Filled with animosity, Kelleher's slurred speech was punctuated with expletives and invective as he threw down another shot of whiskey. Then, he reached for the next glass in a short row destined for consumption. "McKevitt should have given us that bank job! All we get is the fookin' tough stuff. Who the fook did he give it to?"

One of his more sober associates replied, "I thought you knew."

"If I knew, he would have the shit beat out of him, Darby or no Darby!"

"Well, you don't have to go out of your way to do that," replied the more sober man. "That's him out there! He's doing the jitterbug with the whore who has the big knockers and the glow-in-the-dark red dress that's doing a poor job holding them in."

Kelleher fought the alcoholic haze and drink-induced diplopia, trying to bring Liam into focus. Partially successful, he suddenly exclaimed, "I know that fooker from someplace!"

"You're drunk, and you're mixing him up with his fookin' Da," mumbled Feeley. "You know the big shot American who joined up with us briefly, then told us to kiss his ass because we didn't like his fookin' soldier games."

Kelleher seemed to sober perceptively, and his eyes hardened. The pupils stood out from the heavily bloodshot sclera. "Go get Jumbo and Turk," he said to one of his underlings. "I'll be looking forward to them working this fooker over!"

Jumbo and Turk, Kelleher's most imposing enforcers, were on station in the alley when Liam and Rosie departed the Embassy. Liam was definitely in his cups, and Rosie was not lagging far behind. Their pathway led them past the alley entrance, and they were negotiating the passage with obvious difficulty. Following behind the couple, Kelleher indicated to the two heavyweights that Liam and Rosie were the targets. Jumbo sized up the situation and stepped out of the alley to confront the tipsy couple. In a raspy voice, he called out, "Hey slut! Let me take care of that fairy. Then you and me can go home and have a good time. You'll love being with a real man!"

Jumbo's slurs ripped through Liam's alcoholic fog to create a livid anger. "Shut your mouth you big fooker!" was his shouted response. Thereupon,

Jumbo closed in rapidly, while Turk slipped around to the side. Liam threw a hard right, but it landed well off the mark of his antagonist's jaw. Brass knuckles on Jumbo's huge fist easily found their target, as Liam's jaw fractured in two places, and he was propelled backward into the encompassing arms of Turk.

Now Rosie joined the action, swinging her purse as hard as she could at the leading assailant's head! Her blow landed but resulted in no damage, apart from the fact Jumbo had to explain to a suspicious wife why he had two red sequins embedded in his bushy left eyebrow. Backhanding Rosie, Jumbo split her lip, bruising her left cheek and periorbital area. Also, the blow upset her balance. As a result, the stiletto heel on one of her red patent leather shoes was broken. Her downward spiral ended when her head struck a garbage can, rendering her unconscious. Liam, nearly obtunded by the first savage blow, was held upright and solidly pinned by Turk. Egged on by Kelleher and his mates, the mugger proceeded to deliver a savage beating to the victim. Liam could offer no retaliation or even mount a defense.

His nose was next! It offered no resistance to the brass-encased knuckles. Blows that followed were mostly to his abdomen. He could only manage an extended, rasping gasp in an attempt to quell the searing pain in his lungs and trachea as he fought to secure even a few molecules of oxygen for his starving lungs. Finally, Turk let him drop to the pavement. Liam's body lay inert, apart from a few convulsive movements, when Kelleher closed in to deliver a savage kick to his ribs and groin.

Shortly, after Kelleher and his cohorts departed, Rosie slowly returned to consciousness, though her face and head hurt painfully. Her lacerated lower lip was still trickling blood, and the left eye was swollen shut. As her sensorium began to clear, she looked about for Liam. Finally, she saw the outline of his body in the subdued light, which reached the ingress of the alley from an adjacent street light. At first, she was sure that he must be dead! However, swiftly and with trepidation, Rosie forced herself to seek out a pulse. Some hope arose when she found his skin was still warm. Then, a feeble pulse brought reassurance. "I've got to get help," she screamed.

Immediately obvious to Rosie was the fact that her ruined shoe defied ambulation. Kicking them both off, she ran in her stocking feet on to the deserted street. Finally, Rosie's screams for help found the ear of one good soul who was concerned enough and brave enough to get involved. Hearing the claxon of an oncoming police car, she knew that help of some sort was on the way. Then, Rosie's mind began to clear faster when she realized questions would be asked and answers required. She had a reasonable idea of who the attackers were. Kelleher had been two years ahead of her in parochial school before he dropped out. Rosie had spotted him when she had turned to see who might be behind them. Then, Jumbo had launched his attack.

Rosie thought what if she told the police, *Yes, officer, that's right, officer. It was just a friendly scuffle between a couple of Provos. Oh yes, it was Kelleher that started it.* She realized that any semblance of that story would get her killed for sure! Rosie had just time enough to spill out the contents of her battered purse grab her wallet and Liam's then slide them under a garbage can. She hoped a later retrieval would be possible.

Rosie's contrived story, which the police received, was that they were attacked by a gang of club-wielding youths. They must have been Protestants, officer, because she heard them yelling "the Paddies don't have enough money, let's work them over!" At last the ambulance came, and Rosie was able to ride along to hospital. However, she wasn't reassured when one of the attendants looked at Liam's limp form and shook his head.

When Liam arrived at the trauma center, it took precious little time to ascertain there was a high probability that his spleen had been ruptured. Fluid was present within the dependent portion of the left hemothorax, and the left flank was bulging and firm, while laboratory studies indicated considerable internal blood loss. Deemed an emergency, Liam was rushed to the operating theater.

Rosie provided them with Liam's name and address but was unable to tell hospital personnel of any next of kin. Rosie's lip was sutured and application of an ice bag recommended for her swollen left eye. Next, they suggested that she depart for home and that she could check on her friend in the morning. Fortunately, a nurse was kind enough to loan her cab fare, as the distraught young woman was without funds, having left her billfold beneath the trash can. No one commented on her ensemble—at least, no one within earshot.

Upon returning to her rooming house, Rosie quickly donned more suitable attire. Within minutes, she was back at the alleyway and very grateful to find the wallets and cash safely in place. After returning to her room, Rosie decided that she should check Liam's wallet to see if it might indicate the existence of any relatives. He never talked about any, but then he never said anything concerning being an orphan. *Well, he has plenty of money,* she noted.

As Rosie searched Liam's wallet, she noticed there were no photos. However, the contents included scraps of paper with telephone numbers, a couple of business cards, an expired credit card, and a driver's license. Behind the transparent window was a blank card. Rosie removed the card and turned it over. She noted that it was one of those "In case of emergency" cards. Names and a phone number were listed. Unlike other numbers on the card, it was obvious that one was outside Belfast and could be his parents.

Do I want to stick my nose in? she thought. *Of course I do,* was her decision. *If I might be dying, I would certainly want my folks to know!* Quickly, Rosie grasped a handful of coins and proceeded to the nearest phone booth. *Terrible thing to be calling at 4:30 in the morning,* she thought. *But it's just like on the telly. All the gruesome things happen in the night!*

After the phone rang only once, the voice that answered was strongly baritone and fully alert. She hadn't awakened anyone. This person had already been up. In a hesitant voice, Rosie asked "Is this the Moynihans?"

"Who wants to know?" was the response.

"My name is Rose Carey. I'm a friend of Liam Moynihan. If you are his father, then I need to tell you that he was badly beaten and might not live. They took him to the hospital and are operating on him right now."

"Which hospital?" asked the man in a grave tone.

"It's St. Luke's, here in Belfast. I'll be going over there soon to see how he is doing. Do you want me to call back when I find out more?"

"No, I'm on my way. Thanks for the call." Then the line went dead.

It was lucky that Rosie called when she did. Mickey Moynihan was about to leave on a scouting mission. Instead, he would be speeding to Belfast to see if his son would survive. Mickey decided not to awaken Bernie, for it would take too long to explain. Also, she would have to dress. *Best be there as soon as possible. Explanation can come later!*

Mickey's Aston-Martin, given free rein and as full a throttle as the talented driver could sustain, managed arrival at St. Luke's Hospital in the shortest possible time. The drive seemed shorter and less nerve wracking than the interminable delays encountered trying to pass from one layer of medical officialdom to the next. At last, a knowledgeable person with a desire to render assistance was found.

"Your son Liam is still in surgery," said the solicitous sister. Mickey accepted the kind hand that touched his, but it wasn't solace he desired. Knowledge that Liam would survive was foremost in his mind. But revenge was nipping at its heels. "You can wait in the lounge, Mr. Moynihan. Dr. Massey is a fine surgeon. I'm sure that he'll do the best for Liam. I'll tell him that you are here. I know that he will come and discuss everything with you as soon as he is finished." Having completed her oft-repeated narrative intended to allay apprehension, the sister removed her hand and waited for a reply.

"Thank you, sister. You have been most helpful," were Mickey's parting words, as he sought out a chair.

Some two hours later, Dr. Massey arrived, as predicted. He looked tired but managed a wan smile. His thin lips were turned upward, elevating a well-groomed mustache. Mickey took this as indicating things went reasonably well.

He felt that down-turned lips were usually associated with, "We did everything possible to save him. It just didn't come out the way we would have liked." Then, Dr. Massey's words confirmed the father's conjecture, and details followed.

"His spleen was ruptured and had to come out. Broken ribs are painful, but they heal in time. Fortunately, there was no indication of a punctured lung. If all goes well in the next twenty-four hours, then Dr. Caine, one of our best reconstructive surgeons, will work on the fractured nose and jaw. We have every reason to think there will be an excellent cosmetic result. Jaws, of course, are a problem because you have to wire the teeth together to immobilize the fragments. That leaves the patient taking sustenance through a straw. Onerous, but bearable," he concluded. Then, Dr. Massey inserted a little chuckle in an attempt to buff up his bedside manner.

"When can I see him?" asked Mickey solemnly.

"Oh, best wait until evening," was Dr. Massey's response and adding the hackneyed suggestion that Mickey looked exhausted and could well benefit from rest himself. A pat on the shoulder concluded the discussion. Dr. Massey was back on the other side of the swinging doors guarding the surgical sanctuary before Mickey could respond. *Come back this evening?* he thought. *That leaves time for retribution, but retribution on whom?* Then, Mickey thought of calling Bernie, but that would complicate matters. She would insist on coming immediately. He wouldn't be able to leave her at the hospital with, "Wait here honey. I'm going out for a little revenge." No, he must find out who was responsible, and take care of it now if possible!

I'll call Seamus O'Neil, he decided. *Maybe there's some news out on the street. Nothing like this happens that someone doesn't know about it besides the bastards that did it! Why in hell didn't I call three hours ago, instead of sitting here like a clam in the sand? Stupid ass,* he said silently, in self-rebuke. Mickey's mind was clouded, and he just avoided collision with a young woman in the hallway. "Pardon me, miss, I'm not looking where I'm going, I guess." About to brush by her, Mickey had a fleeting glance at her face, and it was a wreck.

Moynihan's mind quickly sprinted to a possible conclusion. This young woman had already been treated, as evidenced by the bandage on her lip. However, the covering did not completely hide the tails of sutures used to close a wound. *If someone was already taken care of, then why would they be coming to the waiting room, except to check on another person? Could be one possibly injured at the same time.* Mickey was about to turn and ask, "Are you Rose Carey?" when a hand touched his arm. A hesitant voice inquired, "Are you Liam's Da?"

Rosie had the advantage in recognizing a man, who surely appeared to be an older version of Liam. "I am," Mickey replied, "and you must be Rose."

"Yes, sir," she responded. He noted that the left side of her face was swollen, and deeply violaceous edema had completely closed the left eye. Mickey could sense fear in the right one. He thought that if one could brush away the signs of trauma, she would appear quite pretty. Fortunately, Rosie's clothes of the day were far more modest than the strumpet ensemble of the prior evening, and her behavior followed suit.

"I need to talk to you, Rose. Let's go somewhere away from here. Would you like a sandwich or something?"

A weak smile emerged; however, it put traction on the sutures on Rose's lip causing her to wince. "I would try a bowl of broth, but my mouth wound makes it too sore to even think of trying to chew."

Soon, they were seated in a small café. Mickey waited until her spoon was projecting above the level of the remaining broth before asking his first salient question. "Who did this to you and Liam?"

Rose looked terrified. "You won't tell the police will you? If it ever got back that I was a snitch, I might get killed!"

"They are the last ones that I'll be talking to," he replied. "This is a personal matter that I'll be handling in a personal way."

"The two goons who beat us are known as Jumbo and Turk. They work for a man named Kelleher. Once I heard someone say that he might be a Provo. Where they live, I can't tell you." The look she saw on Liam's father's face, told her that a confrontation of some type would soon occur. "Oh God, Mr. Moynihan, you can't let anyone know you talked with me. These bumps and cuts would be nothing to what would happen to me!"

"Your secret's safe, Rose."

Mickey smiled at the distraught young woman, then produced a clean linen handkerchief. Tears were streaming from her right eye and at least one was trying to escape the swollen confines of the left eye. Rose blotted away the tears from the good side, but a single soft dab was all she could manage contralaterally due to the extreme tenderness. Then Mickey pressed a 100-pound note in her hand. "You'll need some car fare," he said softly. "Also, if you're like most ladies, something new to wear will help erase the bad things. Go back to the hospital as soon as you can, and please check on Liam. There is a matter I must attend to, but I don't think it will take too much time. I'll see you over at St. Luke's."

After leaving Rose, Mickey thought, *Will I find Kelleher and Feeley at the garage where I met them in years past, or have they moved? It wouldn't take long to determine if they were there.* Immediately, Mickey went to his car and drove to the old location. He glided the Aston-Martin into a parking place nearly a block from the garage. While the throaty exhaust system was a pleasure to him, it could be a warning to others.

After walking to the side door of the garage, he found the latch was secured and unresponsive to his attempt to open it. Producing a lock pick, Mickey inserted it, and the tumblers yielded readily. Returning the instrument to his pocket, Mickey reflected on the fact that it was one more skill acquired thanks to his Communist benefactors. Fortunately, the door hinges were not given to squeaking, and his entry was silent. Quickly and quietly, he approached the pimple-faced punk that he had encountered years back. He had aged but obviously not in any way beneficial. Deeply absorbed in the centerfold of a well-thumbed girlie magazine, his alertness level was minus one. A knock-out blow quelled the voyeur's concentration on the lascivious layout of the lustful lady displayed. Then, Mickey eased the limp body to the floor, and estimated the erstwhile guard would be out for at least fifteen minutes.

As he moved stealthily toward the inner office, raucous voices were audible. One was definitely Kelleher. The other could be Feeley, but it was hard to be sure. Slurred speech and overkill in the use of fulsome expletives were reasonable signs they had continued their imbibing from the previous night. His hypothesis was confirmed by the clink of a bottle neck on the edge of a glass. Mickey slid the Browning Hi-Power out smoothly as a safeguard. His desire was not to kill them, but he had no intention of being surprised in case anyone inside had ready access to a weapon. Throwing the door open, Moynihan entered, gun in hand.

Kelleher and Feeley were the sole occupants of the office. They couldn't have been more surprised had Mephistopheles suddenly appeared in a great ball of fire and brimstone! One look at Moynihan's face left them wishing it was the demon instead of the man they faced. Feeley was in easy reach, and the barrel housing of the Browning struck hard against his left temple, sending him sagging to the floor! "Now, it's just you and me Kelleher," Mickey said scathingly.

Greatly frightened, Kelleher was desperate. His right hand flashed out, grabbing the neck of the nearly empty whiskey bottle. His attempt to smash it against Mickey's head was futile. Five vise-like fingers encircled his wrist.

Moynihan's other forearm took the place of a fulcrum. Kelleher's arm was the lever as his elbow joint was rended asunder and the splintering bones created a sickening sound. But it was nothing in comparison to the terrific pain that Liam's persecutor experienced. Soon this was measured in the decibels of his scream. Indeed, Kelleher would have been fortunate if the pain had induced unconsciousness, but it didn't, nor did the following karate chops that fractured his nose and then unhinged and exploded his jaw! Kelleher was barely conscious when Mickey's stiffened, rod-like thumb probed deeply into his left eye socket, rupturing the precious orb that lay within. The last words the Provo chief heard before passing out were, "Come against me and mine again, you bastard, and this will be just a taste of what you'll get next time. I promise you'll beg for death!"

From photos, Mickey had known of the existence of Turk and Jumbo. Also, he had seen them once or twice, and he recalled they apportioned part of their nonhostile hours to a pub down by the wharves. The avenger's next stop would be Salty's Pub. Upon entering the Pub, from recollection, Moynihan noticed the two thugs seated at the bar were just whom he wanted to see. Not remembering "which enforcer was which" made scant difference to Mickey in regard to the initial encounter.

Intentionally invading their space, he asked sharply, "Which one of you is Jumbo?"

Turning, the larger of the two started to snarl out "Who the—" when a hammer-like blow to his jaw curtailed the rest of his sentence, for the initial response had provided all the verification Mickey needed.

Jumbo was stunned, though far from out! After spitting out fragments from several teeth and shaking his head in an effort to clear it, the thug started groping in a pocket for his brass knuckles. Meanwhile, Turk was taken aback, and before he could respond, Mickey slammed his forehead into the bar with a force sufficient to render him senseless.

Then violently angered, Jumbo was up and ready to kill. The enforcer's massive fist armored in the brass knuckles whistled through the air inches above Moynihan's ducking head. However, Jumbo had no chance to recover either offensive or defensive posture before Mickey's shoe heel caught his right patella with full force. Grunting wildly, he reached down to his fractured kneecap. Next, Mickey's rock-hard elbow came across mightily to smash into his opponent's jaw! Jumbo was stunned, and felt as though he would pitch forward onto his face. Gamely, trying to ward off collapse, the mauler raised his head slightly. At that point, Mickey thrust his knee with terrific force into the chin of the teetering man. Jumbo hit the floor like a fallen oak and lay just as still.

By this time, Salty's other patrons had scurried out or moved as far away from the action as the pub's confines would permit. The heavily muscled, weather worn, and tattoo-embellished owner, Salty, was considering intervention on behalf of his two regulars, but prudence interceded. Compliance was immediate when Mickey glared at him sternly and asked for the bung starter. Though normally used to drive the firmly seated stoppers or bungs from the opening in barrels of ale, it was not Moynihan's intention to employ it for that purpose.

Jumbo was first. Mickey put both of his flaccid hands on the brass bar rail and smashed them repeatedly with the large hammer-like instrument. In seconds, both of Jumbo's hands were reduced to a grossly swollen mass of purple pulp. Still in place, the brass knuckles were firmly cemented by the magnitude of the encompassing edema. Moynihan felt a little compassion for the surgeon who would have to try and remove them, but none for Jumbo.

Next to succumb to Mickey's wrath were Turk's defenseless hands. When his work was completed, Moynihan returned the bloody hammer to Salty. Gagging at the sight of the starter, well covered with blood, bits of flesh, and tiny shreds of bone, Salty dropped the instrument in revulsion. Salty had seen a lot of revolting scenes in thirty years at sea, but none were more ghastly than the visage of four utterly destroyed hands that he faced on the other side of the bar! Then, looking up, he realized that Moynihan was gone. Mickey wanted to check on Liam. Afterward, he would confront the problem of breaking the news to Bernie.

Upon returning to hospital, Mickey was given a specific room and directions on how to get there. Thus, he was relieved from the frustration undergone on his initial visit. Upon entering, he found that it was a six-bed ward and obviously not conducive to communications of a private sort. A curtain shielded Liam's bed from vision but not from sound transmission. Pulling the corners of the drapes apart, Mickey peered inside. Liam looked devastated. Nevertheless, he was obviously able to clutch Rose's hand and sustain the pressure of her head on his shoulder. When Liam noticed his father's presence, only defiance registered on his face. Soon, Mickey's facial features changed in response. Gone was the look of relief that attended his entry, and a scowl replaced it.

Finally, words came. "I'm glad to see you made it through the ordeal, son." Then, Mickey reflected, *Strange. Son almost seems like a foreign, inappropriate term. How soon a wedge can develop.* Then, he continued. "I'll be going to get your mother. We'll be back first thing tomorrow."

Liam's response was short and, as best Mickey could discern, his son had said, "Don't hurry." Rosie said nothing. Instead, she shifted her position slightly, as though she was attempting to place a barrier between them. Then, thinking it might be shock or that post-traumatic stress syndrome, Mickey turned, feeling deflated, and left.

On his way out, Mickey encountered Dr. Massey. "Oh! Mr. Moynihan Your son seems to have turned the corner." Following was the usual mantra, "Fortunately, he's young and in good physical condition and, of course, the surgery went very well." Instead of ending in the self-congratulatory note, the surgeon added the usual caveat, "I will be monitoring him closely for infection that could change my prognosis. As I mentioned to you before, reconstructive surgery will be coming up soon. I imagine Dr. Carter will be attending to that." Mickey tossed off a cursory "Thank you, Doctor," and left.

On the way back to Grey Abbey, Moynihan's driving was at a much slower pace than the hurried journey to Belfast. That was eighteen hours ago, but it seemed like an eon. When he arrived, Bernadette was waiting up. However, Mike had gone to bed hours before.

"Where have you been, Mickey, for God's sake, where have you been?" Bernie's face reflected relief and anger simultaneously. However, the first emotion dissipated rapidly. leaving the second to ripen unchecked. "I can't stand this uncertainty any longer!" she screamed. Mickey remained silent but reached out and pulled her into his arms. At first, she tried to push him away. But then relief returned, and she clung to him desperately.

Bernie's emotions were all peaks and valleys, as Mickey related what had happened to Liam. One second, she anguished over her middle son. The next, she abhorred her husband. In the end, she accepted the fact that she would always love Mickey even though his devotion to Ireland and all it entailed was beyond her comprehension. At last, she quietly said, "We best get a bit of rest. Mrs. Hennessey can watch over Mike for a few days. We had better go to Belfast together, and see if we can bring Liam back into our lives."

When Mickey returned to the hospital with Bernie, they found Liam in a sullen state. Fortunately, Rose was absent. They felt that if there was hope of some type of reunion, it would come easier if only family were present. Additionally, Mickey felt that Bernadette would find Rose's dress and demeanor not to her liking. Liam did manage a wan smile for his mother and accepted her hand in his. However, there was nothing but a nod for his father, and it didn't erase the defiance mirrored in his sullen, slit-like eyes. At the end of a half-hour, the visit was becoming an ordeal, and his parents took their leave.

Once outside, Bernie anguished over the pain Liam was suffering. Denying rejection, she went on to say, "We really can't expect him to converse, Mickey. It's the fractured jaw. He can't talk without great pain."

But Mickey remained disconsolate and abruptly replied, "I would have expected a warmer welcome from a rock!" However, Bernie and Mickey stayed in Belfast for the following ten days, and went to see their son at least once in every twenty-four hour period.

During these ten days, the swelling in Liam's face was slowly, greatly alleviated. Also, the widespread bruising had progressed from purple through magenta and on to a subdued saffron. Liam's appearance indicated there was strong evidence that the reconstructive surgeon Dr. Carter had applied his skills successfully with an excellent cosmetic result. However, Liam remained very noncommunicative, and the few words he did say were difficult to distinguish. To immobilize the fractured jaw, it had been necessary to wire his teeth together. Thus, it was like listening to someone speaking through tightly clenched teeth.

Another impediment to Liam's proper enunciation was the fact that the doctors had removed several of his front teeth so a soda straw could be inserted, permitting him to take in liquid sustenance. As a result, a strong lisp further distorted his mumbled words.

Both Sean and Mike had come to Belfast for several visits. However, their presence did little to assuage Liam's antipathy. Then, on post-operative day ten, both the treating physicians were seen by Mickey and Bernie. Their beaming smile bespoke "Didn't we do a fine job?" Bernie thanked them profusely, but Mickey could manage not more than nodding in accord. Even that meager motion was performed without enthusiasm. Before parting, Dr. Carter informed the parents, "Liam is sufficiently well recovered for discharge. How would you like to take him home tomorrow?" Bernie put on a happy face, but ambivalence hid just below the surface. Obviously, a response was required, so she responded in feigned merriment, "How wonderful. We'll look forward to that."

Once outside, Mickey squeezed Bernie's arm and said softly, "I hope good comes from taking Liam home. It was tough enough visiting a belligerent rock in the hospital. I don't really know if I'm up to having one seated at the kitchen table!" Bernadette was trying hard to come up with ameliorating words. However, her attempt was short-circuited when a very small man approached and blocked their way.

"A moment alone, Mr. Moynihan, if you please," requested the diminutive though extremely wiry male of middle age.

"Wait here, Bernie. I'll be but a moment," were Mickey's words to her.

As soon as they were positioned face to face, the other man said, "Let me introduce myself I'm—"

Completion of his sentence was halted by Mickey's cutting words, "I know who you are Darby McKevitt, as I've wagered a few punt either on you or against you! What the hell do you want of me?"

The ex-jockey's assertiveness was not diminished by the harshness of Mickey's words. "I'm a patriot, Mr. Moynihan, and I have reason to believe you have been one or still may be. You should know that I'm on the top in this area. Liam is one of my officers. Over all, he's a good one, and I take care of my own. Kelleher is one of my officers, as well, and he has served me faithfully. I would have punished him myself, though I suspect not to the same degree that you did. In short, I don't appreciate you jumping into Provo business like the hammer of God! However, I can see that you are obviously a man of action. There might be a place for you on my council if you are interested."

"I have no desire to be a horse in your stable or respond to your bridle, Mr.

McKevitt. If your management were as good as your mouth, Liam wouldn't be in hospital. Keep Kelleher on a short leash, McKevitt. Otherwise, you may be short an officer, and there could even be a vacancy at the top! I believe that's where you said you were." Turning away, Mickey started his return to Bernie's side. Although the Provo chief had more to say, he was not about to try and block Mickey's departure.

Mickey and Bernadette decided to return home to take care of some business, planning to return the next day for Liam's release from the hospital. On the way back to Grey Abbey, there was commentary. Then, after a fitful night, Bernadette packed a few of Liam's things so he would have a decent outfit to wear on discharge from the hospital. However, upon return to the institution, both were shocked to hear a litany of guttural gibberish coming from what had been Liam's bed. Their son was gone! Now, a disoriented derelict had taken his place.

On inquiry, the Charge Nurse smiled and said, "Liam Moynihan left with his wife. Well, I think she was his wife. It was quite early this morning."

Bernadette was crushed. In a pleading voice, she said, "He must be in Belfast, Mickey! Shall we look for him?"

"If he wanted to come home, he would be here. Bernie. I don't recall the father of the prodigal son undertaking a manhunt for his misbegotten progeny, and I'm not about to break with tradition!"

Over the ensuing few years, Mickey steadfastly kept his word and made no effort to contact Liam. Mike was flourishing in secondary school. Sean, now graduated from the university, seemed to delight in the role he was given in managing the Boston businesses. Bernadette had striven to resume a quasi-normal life outwardly, but she achieved only limited success inwardly. Often, it seemed to her that Mickey, Sean, and Mike pretty much regarded Liam as deceased. Never able to accept this concept, Bernie sometimes contemplated looking for Liam, but she never undertook the search.

Meanwhile, the battle for full Irish independence continued on, gaining slowly in fury. The Cause was fueled by incidents, such as Bloody Sunday in Derry on January 30, 1972, when British paratroopers fired on an unarmed civil rights procession. During this time, Mickey maintained his squad at ten men in number. His little group was known for its elan and camaraderie. Also noteworthy was that a member could retire if the exigencies of life so dictated. Mickey found there was no shortage of very able replacements. Successes against enemies continued, and his squad's identity remained secret.

During this period, Darby McKevitt was gaining in stature, for his command increased in numbers, as well as degree of violence committed. Also, a tenuous truce had been maintained between Liam Moynihan and Terry Kelleher by keeping them well separated.

In the case of McKevitt, a threat of execution was an added impetus to deterring any sign of disobedience on behalf of his now senior lieutenants. Jumbo and Turk, the once feared enforcers, were long forgotten. Deprived of any meaningful existence, Jumbo drank himself to death, as he downed innumerable bottles of Poteen clasped as best he could between the pitiful claws that had once been hands. Turk had also endeavored to drown his misery. However, instead of killing himself secondary to cirrhosis of the liver, he pickled his brain. Institutionalized with a diagnosis of alcoholic dementia, he eked out his final days restrained, one among many in a ward of similar sufferers.

During these years, there was a modicum of happiness in the curtailed Moynihan family. Sailing, riding, travel, and social events helped fill in the void. Mickey as always was sufficiently circumspect and careful to avoid suspicion by the authorities. As best he could tell, Sean and Mike were unaware of the clandestine activities in which he indulged. On occasion, they did wonder about his solitary fishing trips, but their curiosity was allayed by the fact he always welcomed them to come along on those of a genuine nature. Bernie did notice that Mickey talked in his sleep much more frequently than in the past. She couldn't help wondering if the effects of all the stress was becoming accumulative!

Chapter Twenty-Seven

※ ※ ※

A fine spring day had come to the area of Strangford Laugh, and the sun was welcomed back after several weeks' absence, its warm rays teasing the wildflowers to life. That element when added to the rain-bestowed moisture absorbed in the previous fourteen days, caused the flowers to erupt in a kaleidoscope of vibrant color. From every tree, green leaves were springing, and the carpet of grass was as emerald as anyone had ever seen. Meanwhile, the Laugh, itself, appeared like an irregularly cut sapphire disrupted only by the occasional white feather capped waves, which were provoked by the capricious breezes. Mickey was out riding Warlord, a magnificent Connemara stallion. Moynihan and horse were totally simpatico and absolutely synchronous. To a viewer, they presented a magnificent mount with a human appendage growing from the horse's back. Much to the joy of man and beast, their ride had been furious. Only a single mile separated them from the stable, as Mickey prudently slowed Warlord to a walk for the purpose of a gradual cool down.

Meanwhile, Mike was departing school at the end of a scholar's day. Recently, he had become accustomed to walking home with Lorrie McMenamin, who lived a scant distance from his own house. Both were always noted to maintain a measured pace. Obviously, they enjoyed each other's company and were quite disposed to prolonging it. "Like two copper pennies," mused a lady as they passed, noting the sun-kissed red locks they bore.

At home, Bernadette was enjoying the day greatly. For the first time in several months, she sensed a resurrection of her spirits. Someone watching would have thought it curious that she was smiling and talking to a down comforter, which she was flapping vigorously while presenting it to the sunshine and heavenly fragrant spring air. "I'm just like you," she said. "I've gone through a dreary winter, and I'm surely in need of a good flapping to rid me of all that's stale and dusty." Folding the renewed comforter carefully, Bernie went back inside the house greatly bolstered.

As Bernadette passed through the kitchen, Mrs. Hennessey called out, "I'll be going to town for some shopping Mrs. Moynihan. Won't be long! I thought I'd fix you all a fine Irish stew, and I need a few things to add. My Granny's recipe, you know. She would toss and turn in her grave if I left anything out."

"Take your time, Mrs. Hennessey. I see you already have this evening's supper well under way."

"Oh Mrs. Moynihan," the housekeeper called out. "A package just came. Do you want me to open it?"

"That's okay," Bernadette called back. "I'll see to it after I put the comforter away."

As she neared the door, the older woman called back one last time. "You should have let me do that Mrs. Moynihan."

"Don't be silly," replied Bernadette. "You have plenty to do, and I enjoy a little housekeeping now and then."

Bernadette returned to the kitchen and noted the package on the counter. Picking it up idly, the label came to her attention. "Express delivery" was prominently displayed. The label indicated it was a gift package from Ocean Treasures Fish Market in Belfast, and a separate sticker stipulated "Refrigerate at once." However, there was no indication of who might have ordered it. Her first inclination was to place it unopened in the refrigerator. Bernie decided if it were fish, she had better inspect it to make sure that it was fresh or frozen. In the event it was the latter, then it should go into the freezer.

Despite the name of Warlord, Mickey's superb stallion had never heard cannon fire, or a bomb explode, nor had he ever been ridden toward the sound of a gun! As he and his rider passed by the kitchen, the windows shattered, and the vision was followed a microsecond later by a deafening explosion! Every muscle in the splendidly sculpted horse seemed to contract as one when he reared on his hind legs. Thrashing the air with his front legs, Warlord's eyes went wild, and an equine scream bellowed from flaring nostrils. If it were not for his strength and agility, Mickey would have been thrown off. Worse yet, the rearing stallion could have lost his balance and fallen backward on his rider. After no more explosions were heard, Warlord became subdued, allowing Mickey to dismount and bolt for the kitchen.

A gas explosion? Was Mrs. Hennessey seriously hurt or even dead? Within feet of the door, the horror present in this thought overwhelmed him. *Could Bernadette have been in the kitchen?* A primordial scream erupted from his lips, and it conveyed but a single word, a single hope and a single fear. "*Bernie!*"

As Mickey burst through the door, there remained a considerable amount of dust and smoke in the kitchen. An initial whiff informed his nostrils that it was the peculiar aroma of Semtex. His blood pressure arose to nearly lethal levels, while his pounding heart contracted wildly. Nothing in life could have prepared Moynihan for the soul-annihilating vision that now confronted him.

Bernadette was on the floor; her back slumped against the refrigerator. Her once beautiful face was scorched obscenely, and much of her ravishing red hair was singed away from a terribly burned scalp. Iron nails and fragment of nails protruded from the baked flesh of her chest and face. Once again, Mickey screamed, "Bernie!" with a fury bordering on madness! Feebly, Bernadette raised her arm, and called out "Help me, Mickey for God's sake, help me!" Her upheld hands were nearly fingerless, for the slender digits had been blown away by the force of the contents in the package she had opened.

Moynihan swept his wife into his arms and raced for the garage. Just coming down the driveway, Mike was horrified beyond description by what he beheld. Speech would not come. Seeing his son, Mickey screamed out, "Call the hospital! Tell them to get doctors and see about a Med Evac helicopter. Let them know I'm on the way!"

In her fading consciousness, Bernadette grasped the meaning of the words, and they brought a little surge of strength. In as loud a voice, as possible, she said, "I don't need a doctor, Mickey, I need a priest!"

Tenderly as possible, Mickey placed Bernie in the back seat of the Bentley. In his mind, he tried to block out the sight of seared flesh, the hideous protruding nails, and the remnants of burned blouse still adhering to the blistered skin of her chest. Tiny fragments of brittle, singed hair broke away and fell to the seat, forming a little halo around her head. In seconds, the car was racing for town

As soon as the car screeched to a halt, Mickey lifted Bernie's limp body and placed her on the gurney brought by several alerted nurses. Two doctors were already there, and they swiftly started examining their severely burned and wounded patient. Orders were issued for starting IVs administering morphine, type and cross-matching of blood, chest radiograph, and monitoring of vital signs.

After checking the X-ray, the doctors conferred with each other in whispers. Then, one turned to Mickey, and said, "It looks very bad, Mr. Moynihan. Some of the nails penetrated your wife's lungs. They are collapsing, and her chest is filling with blood. We're not thoracic surgeons, and our facilities are limited. We don't know what further we can do here. She needs to be in Belfast."

"Did you call for a helicopter?" Mickey yelled loudly.

"We did, sir! But, there was a bomb blast in Derry just a short while ago and available helicopters are all in use. We have asked them to try all other sources, and they're working on it. Hopefully, they'll come in time."

"Then get an ambulance!" Mickey shouted.

Soulfully, the other doctor responded, "They wouldn't make it in time, Mr. Moynihan. Our best hope is finding another helicopter. We will start some plasma, and we can aspirate some of the blood and air from your wife's chest. God willing, we can keep her going."

At that second, the Emergency Room door opened and an elderly priest entered, with Mike following closely behind. He had heard his mother's words. So, after calling the hospital, Mike had mounted Warlord and raced the great horse in an effort to find the priest his mother had requested. After they entered, the clergyman put on his stole. From his pocket, he removed a small flask containing the holy oil used in the sacrament of Extreme Unction. "I'm Father Mulligan," he said in a soft voice. "I think we can work around each other. So, you doctors do what you can, and I'll do the same."

Upon seeing the priest, Mickey was furious. But for some strange reason beyond his comprehension, he couldn't bring himself to intervene. Thereupon, the priest made the sign of the cross with his tinctured thumb on Bernadette's forehead and whispered the prayers for the dying in her ear. Somewhat miraculously, she stirred into consciousness and became aware of what was happening. Into Father Mulligan's ear, she whispered her confession. Then he whispered the words of absolution into hers. When it was over, those present could sense a smile on Bernie's face. Very weakly, she called out, "Mickey are you there?"

"I'm here Bernie," he said softly, "and so is Mike." Raising her shattered hand, she sought out her husband's face and finally found it. "I'm blind, Mickey. I'll never see you, and Sean, Liam, or Mike again. Hopefully, I'll be seeing God soon. I love you!"

Then, at that very second, Bernadette Moynihan released her soul in search of heaven and her Creator.

For the first time since his little brother Sean had died, tears found their way to the eyes of Michael Moynihan. Father Mulligan approached, intending to offer words of solace. "You must accept it as God's will, Mr. Moynihan. Bernadette died in His Grace, and we have every reason to believe she is with Him now."

Suddenly, Mickey was consumed with wrath! Had his reflexes not been slowed by emotions, the blow from his cocked fist would have smashed into the cleric's face. Just as the punch was to be released, Mickey became aware of a pale face crowned with red interposed between him and the priest. His hand was stilled, but his voice was not. "Curse you and your damn God," he shouted before storming out.

Realizing decisions had to be made regarding Bernadette's funeral, Mickey faced them with grim determination. Despite the fact that his wife had received the Last Rites of the Roman church, he was adamant that the papists play no role in her burial. Sean, now well versed in atheism, agreed wholeheartedly, but young Mike pleaded affirmatively but to no avail. In the event that Liam was even aware of his mother's murder, he remained odd man out! Therefore, he was neither sought nor heard from in regard to funeral preparations.

During a period of solitary, anguished remembrance, Mickey came across Bernadette's old photo of Skellig Michael. *My dear Bernie, you never got over it, did you? Why did I never see how much it meant to you? The sailboat in Boston, the restaurant, and your faded little photo; yet you never asked to go back! I suppose you were waiting for me to take you there, but I never did. Always too busy with what seemed to be more important things. They don't seem so important now.*

Mickey was wracked with guilt. However, at least there was a solution regarding the funeral. Bernadette would be cremated and her ashes deposited on her mystic rock. Perhaps there her spirit would find some rest. Mickey was in hopes this choice might grant him some relief. However, unfortunately, it never did. Gray ashes, softly descending from the sky to dust a rain-slicked rock, hewn by capricious winds over many eons, would never replace the opportunity to share it as one. For ashes don't smile or laugh, hold your hand, or accept your embrace. They are only molecular residuals of what was once but could never be again!

Following the cremation, Mickey and Sean took the ashes-filled urn south. From a chartered helicopter, the tiny cinders were given over to the charge of the wind. Mickey knew that he would never be free from remorse; however, as in the past, vengeance would be his ally.

Mike didn't go along. Instead, he stopped by St. Brendan's Church because he thought it would be a good place to talk to God, and that was something he desired. Mike wasn't bothered by having no knowledge of formal prayers, apart from the fact that his friend Lorrie from school had once kidded him about not knowing the Our Father. She had said wistfully, "How are you ever going to get to heaven, if you do not know how to pray?"

"Why would I want to go there?" Mike replied with a hint of adolescent chauvinism in his voice.

"Well don't you want to be in a place where you will be happy forever and ever?" Lorrie shot back.

"Why would I be any happier there than here?" Mike responded.

"Because you'll be with God, silly." Then Lorrie laughed, poked Mike in the ribs, and ran off down the road. Although she was soon caught up with, there was no further talk of theology or eternity. Warm hands joined together seemed much more important at that moment.

At this saddest time in his life, Michael decided he had no need for the Our Father, for he doubted it said the words that he wanted to say to God. Shortly, when his conversation ended, the grieving young man immediately recognized that God didn't talk back. Nonetheless, he was more at peace than he had been before, and that left him with something to think about. Then, on the way past the cemetery next to the church, Mike paused and studied the head stones. Tears flowed from his eyes when he thought how much better it would have been if his mother was buried here. *I could come and tell her that I miss her, and how much I love her. You can't talk to ashes, even if you could find them,* he decided. *If mother is in heaven, maybe God can give her a message.* A little solace sprang from the thought.

Following Bernadette's funeral, such as it was, an inquest was held. Fortunately for Mickey, it was conducted by local authorities, more given to sympathy than suspicion. Naturally, many questions were asked regarding known enemies—who might resort to such a dastardly deed? All of Ireland, especially the six Northern counties, was unfortunately overly familiar with bombings due to the fact they were so common. Fervently, Mickey denied any knowledge of a single IRA or Provo member much less one who was a sworn enemy.

As a defensive maneuver, the grieving husband did recall past problems with the Boston Mafia and their protection racket. However, these were dismissed as such a long shot that contacting American authorities was not fully justified. One of the local inspectors independently advanced the possibility that Mrs. Hennessey could have been the target. After all, there was a notation in the files that her brother had once been detained on suspicion of planting a bomb for the IRA. However, the charge had been dismissed. But the inspector refused to abandon his intuition until his superiors informed him that they thought both the theory and theoretician were a bit loony. Also, questioning of Mrs. Hennessey produced not a single scintilla of evidence. All she could recall was that there had been a knock on the door. Needing time to dry her hands, straighten her apron, and rearrange several errant wisps of hair, it could have taken a minute or more to open the door. The package was there, but she saw no messenger.

Police interviewed the owners of all known businesses who made deliveries in Grey Abbey, especially concentrating on those that might originate in Belfast. However, it was all to no avail. Poor Mrs. Hennessey, though a meticulous housekeeper and marvelous cook, did not possess the attributes of a steel-trap mind or encyclopedic memory. After many hours of questioning, her recall flickered slightly, allowing the good woman to advance the notion that the package might have had something to do with food. Fifteen more minutes of intense interrogation prompted her to opine that it was fruit. "Yes, it was definitely fruit. I'm sure of it!" Canvassing of all fruit vendors, who provided delivery, failed to show a single one either in Grey Abbey, Belfast, or anywhere in between who could provide any help!

Analysis of explosive residue did confirm that it was Semtex. Naturally, no such dealers were listed in the phone book. Authorities knew it was produced in Czechoslovakia; however, the middle man could be anywhere from Dublin to Djibouti. Also, nails are among the world's most common and generic articles. Trying to trail that lead would result in producing more insane inspectors than clues. Now it seemed to boil down to whatever information might be garnered from an extremely thorough study of package remnants that had contained the explosive device. However, the wrapping was nowhere to be found!

Without hesitation, Inspector Dixon recalled that he had placed every recovered scrap in a plastic bag. "Yes, I'm sure I gave it to Officer Clyde and instructed him to take it to the evidence room forthwith." Inspector Dixon knew that this particular officer was likable but subsmart.

Reluctantly, Clyde recalled that he had put it in the back seat of his police car, and unfortunately, his trip to headquarters was detoured when he received a radio call to intervene in a domestic dispute. Arriving at that scene, he had found a distraught young woman with two howling infants. Her husband had battered her, then left! He caved in to the woman's pleas to be safely delivered along with the newborn and two-year-old to her own mother's home. Finding no drunk wife-beater to arrest, Officer Clyde decided to play knight errant and do as requested. He explained that the trip was relatively long, and the diapers of both infants were changed en route.

Frustrated, an extremely angry Chief Inspector gathered more demoralizing information as the inquisition continued. Officer Clyde reported that the soiled diapers had been placed in plastic bags. However, the stench was formidable! Therefore, it seemed the only rational thing to do was to get rid of everything before it permeated the car. "Yes, sir," he said with his head now drooping. "I must have thrown out the evidence bag along with the rest. Sorry Chief Inspector!" Contrite Officer Clyde was more sorry still after spending a week at the local garbage dump in a hopeless attempt to find the evidence.

At the formal inquisition into the bombing, Mickey gave a perfect performance of a grieving husband whose wife had been brutally murdered by some terrorist act. In testimony, he indicated that the bombing seemed mindless, possibly even an error. Police had no suspects, no clues, and no hope that any would be forthcoming. Instead of arrests and convictions, Moynihan left the inquiry with vacuous words of reassurance echoing behind him. "This case will remain open until we bring the murderer to justice Mr. Moynihan. We'll never rest, sir, until justice is served. It's our number one priority!"

Mickey nodded in agreement, then picked up his pace to distance himself from police and reporters. "Justice will be served," he said under his breath. "But it will be mine, not yours!"

Later, home alone, Mickey discarded the role of actor. He had been good at it. In this particular setting, he felt that Lawrence Olivier couldn't have done better. No one had seemed to see through it, or to think he was other than what he portrayed. He was the grieving husband entirely shocked and bewildered by such a horrible tragedy, which had no motive!

Meanwhile, after his mother's death, Sean had left his father pretty much alone. Like a good big brother, he seemed to be devoting his time to his younger sibling. Remaining distant, Mickey ate little, conversed rarely, and appeared to confide only in his horse, Warlord, with whom he shared nearly all the daylight hours. One of the guest rooms served as his haven for the night. So great was the pain that he could not reenter the bedroom they had shared. Handling and seeing Bernie's personal things was beyond bearing. If he looked at the bed or a dress, he could see Bernie in it, and her own sweet, personal scent still pervaded all.

At times, Mickey Moynihan pondered about the degree of depression he needed to suffer to be pushed over the edge so that he might tumble in to the pit of despondency or even suicide. One day, as Mickey was returning home, Warlord was spurred into a full gallop. His master decided that he needed no tranquilizers or psychiatric counseling. Revenge was the only nostrum desired! Sometime and somewhere, he would find out who was solely responsible for Bernie's death. In the meantime, everyone was fair game. Odds were, it had to be a Prod or a Brit. Thoughts of "putting a thorn in the paw of the Lion" were behind him. Now, cutting off the head of the snake who killed Bernie consumed all of Moynihan's being!

Sean and Mike were pleased to behold the resurgence of their father's good spirits. In public, as well as in their presence, he was gradually returning to the personage they were familiar with and loved. Privately, Mickey had improved, but he conceded to himself that life would never be the same. There could still be light in his life, but it was destined to remain forever as twilight. Gone was the brilliant sunshine that he could bask in and be rejuvenated, for Bernadette had been his sun goddess! She was gone, and there could be no other to replace her. He could love Ireland, fight for her, and possibly die for her. But the Emerald Isle was not a subject of worship, in his opinion.

One night, after young Mike had gone off to bed, Sean approached his father. "What do you plan to do about Mom?" he said solemnly. The question, and its abruptness in presentation, took Mickey by surprise. After pausing for contemplation, Mickey decided to parry the question with an oblique reply in an effort to draw Sean out regarding his exact meaning. Finally, he replied slowly, "I placed her ashes on her island, as you know. Beyond that, I'll just go on missing her terribly for the rest of my days!"

"We'll all be doing that," said Sean. Then the timbre of his voice hardened perceptively. He continued on, "I'll get to the point! Someone murdered Mother! The police have been totally feckless. Someone has to avenge her death, and I assume that will be us!"

Mickey looked intently into his oldest son's eyes. *Strange,* he thought. *It's like looking into a mirror!* At last, he said, "I didn't know you were an avenger Sean."

"Yes and you don't seem to know that I've had a good idea of what you have been doing for many years," was Sean's response.

"What does that mean exactly?" Mickey shot back.

"It means that I'm pretty sure you have been conducting your own war of independence on behalf of Ireland! Logically, I would assume Mother's murder was somehow related. That being so, you'll be obliged to do something about it! What I'm trying to tell you is that whatever you are planning, I need to be a part of it!" Again, two sets of eyes sought each other and locked on firmly.

"You are either very intuitive, a snoop, or both," replied Mickey. "However, if what you say is true, why should I risk your life in such a vendetta?"

"You'll do it because if you don't, I'll seek satisfaction on my own, and you are aware that I'll probably screw things up. Conversely, if you train me, I'll be in a position to help you, and you can watch out for me."

Mickey offered no denial or confirmation, but continued with, "Boston is where I need you, Sean."

His son replied, "The business is doing well with the managers that we have. I can continue to monitor them part-time, but the major concern in my life is to do something for Mom and for Ireland! That's what Liam is doing, isn't it?"

Mickey replied sternly, "He may be doing something for Ireland. He sure as hell isn't doing anything for his Mother! I appreciate your desire and candor, Sean, really I do! I'll think about it, and we'll discuss it further."

Sean arose, straightened to his full six feet, three inches, and replied, "Don't think too long, for I intend to start out soon either by myself or at your side!"

Mickey lay awake long hours that night. "I wish I could ask you, Bernie," he said quietly. "You would be against Sean signing up with me. Maybe for once I would listen, and you could convince me that it was far better for him to lead a normal life. You and I never had one really. But I loved every moment of the one that we did have. No doubt, I got you killed because of my ways. Stupid of me never to have spent any time thinking about that possibility. Maybe if I had I would have changed, but that option is gone forever."

Thoughtfully, Mickey continued. *I see a lot of me in Sean, and I suppose some in Liam, maybe young Mike will be all that's left in the end. Hopefully, he'll remain more like you. That would probably be for the best. Forgive me, as you always did, dearest Bernie, but I feel that I should accede to Sean's desires. Ireland can use one more devoted son, and I can use his help in avenging you. If you could speak to me, you would probably say 'Oh Mickey I don't want revenge.' But you have to understand so much has been taken from me in this life that revenge has become my soul!* Unconsciously, Mickey's arm reached out, seeking the warmth and softness of his wife's sleeping form. Finding nothing but rumpled bedding, it was akin to total emptiness. Finally, sleep came at last, troubled though it was.

One night later, after young Mike had retired, Mickey and Sean followed up on their discussion. "I've thought over what you said, Sean, and I'm willing to let you play a role in avenging your mother. In addition, I've thought long and hard on who might have been responsible. As best I can determine, it is highly unlikely to have been the SAS. In my experience, that's really not the way they operate. So, that leaves one of the U groups as primary suspects. We have never discussed them, and I'm not sure how knowledgeable you are regarding them. UDA is an acronym for Ulster Defense Association, and UFF stands for Ulster Freedom Fighters, and UVF is the Ulster Volunteer Force. Also, you can add in the UFF, which is a splinter group of the UDA. Last, there is the UDR, or Ulster Defense Regiment. They are a nasty bunch of bastards, even though the British Army is supposed to be monitoring them, since they are a quasi-government force."

"Why would any of them have any knowledge of you?" asked Sean with a quizzical expression.

"I don't really have a clue," responded his father. "As far as I know, I've covered my tracks very carefully. However, it could possibly go back to the old days. Before I met your mother, I had spent four years in the Maze prison, after being caught in an IRA bombing that went bad. Following that, I joined the IRA and was head of a cell. We pulled off some jobs, which I won't describe, and they got a lot of notoriety at the time. A couple of my old group were captured. Maybe, they gave evidence that led someone in my direction though I can't figure out how."

"That's all we have to go on?" asked Sean, in a frustrated tone.

"Not exactly," responded Mickey. "I have some enemies on the Paddy side as well. There is a fellow named Kelleher who was responsible for all of Liam's injuries. I paid him back with interest, but he may have more guts than I gave him credit for having. Possibly, he decided to raise the ante!"

"Well we could end up taking revenge on the wrong people," Sean interjected.

"No, I—or I guess it's we now—will keep on assailing the Brits and Prods. They are the ones that we are at war with, and we will keep eradicating them because that's part of our war. Should we happen to stiff one of them who was in any way tied to your mother's death, then that will be a bonus. In the meantime, we'll keep on shuffling the deck until we encounter the ace of spades! When that card comes up, it won't be a simple matter like a bullet in the chest for them. They will be asked to pay a very special price!"

"When do we get started?" asked Sean, now exhibiting some eagerness.

"I start tomorrow," replied Mickey resolutely. "You will start in about nine months if you last—and if you are ready!"

Now Sean responded with unrestrained resentment in his voice. "What the hell does that mean?"

"What it means is that you are not applying for a position as a plumber's apprentice and if you screw up the worst that can happen is a flooded kitchen! Screw us up, Sean, and it's forever in a prison that you can't even imagine! Or, if we're lucky, we'll both get stitched with a long burst from a Brit machine gun and die in the street. Nine months in the Becca Valley, with Mustafa and his merry little band of assassins and then you'll be of use to me! Hard words, I know, but it's a take-it-or-leave-it proposition."

Suddenly, the billowing sails of Sean's ambition went slack. He had never conceived there would be any conditions imposed at all, much less any as onerous as these. Was he only a pretentious bravado after all, or could he back up his lofty suggestions with fortitude? *Even if I'm not strong enough in my convictions to play a role in avenging Mother, it is not possible for me to be viewed as a coward in my father's estimation!* Sean decided. So he arose abruptly and said "Make all the arrangements." Then, Sean turned to leave.

"Are you certain?" said Mickey sternly.

"Certain," said his son, as he left the room.

Now, alone in the room, Mickey had misgivings about the proposition and his presentation to Sean. After a few quiet moments, he murmured, "Do what you think is right and then leave it be!" Next, Mickey's thoughts turned to Alexis. KGB Colonel Zellanova was still playing the ludicrous role of Cultural Exchange Officer in Belfast. Again, he would be his intermediary. *I could go ahead and try to make all the arrangements myself,* he thought. However, Mustafa and his superiors will be much more likely to dance in tune with a puppeteer like Alexis than they would for Mickey! "Besides, I want Sean to have some special training that he sure as hell can't get out in the desert." Having made his decision,

Mickey left the house and drove to a public phone to make an untraceable call to his Soviet friend.

After Moynihan's phone call to Alexis, Sean was in the air only two days later. His itinerary was as much a Byzantine labyrinth as ever was devised. Mickey couldn't be sure who might be watching, especially after Bernie's death! Should anyone be keeping track, they would be led into a rabbit's warren that should defy even their best efforts to follow. On his departure, Sean was grim, and Mickey wondered if this was a sample of how his eldest son would be on return or *if* he would return? Mickey knew the training could be very dangerous, and some trainees of the Hezbollah didn't always graduate alive. For some, commencement took place in a body bag!

After Sean's departure, the ensuing months passed quickly for Mickey. More time was spent with young Mike. Over time, the rapport between father and son expanded incrementally. Mike quickly became an avid angler, reasonably accomplished equestrian, and better than average chess player. Also, he surprised Mickey by showing an affinity for shooting sports, such as trap and skeet, and coming close to besting his father in their *mano a mano* competitions.

Shotguns were one thing in Ireland, but rifles were another. Despite the fact Mickey recognized Mike had the makings of a superb rifle marksman, he assiduously avoided that particular sport. He knew that you couldn't be sure that a fingerprint might not be needed to purchase a rifle legally, and that would surely be tempting fate. Also, Mickey had no desire for anyone in Ulster to have any concept of just how expert he was with a rifle. Additionally, Mickey saw to it that the shotguns they employed were always kept in the vault at the shooting range, appreciating the fact that the best alibi was always the iron-clad one.

To his father, young Mike seemed to be innocence itself. Mickey resolved to do his best to keep him in as close to a prelapsarian state as was possible. This decision was in deference to Bernie's memory. Some might think that Sean and Liam were already on the road to perdition, though Mickey didn't agree. Nevertheless, he resolved to do what he could to keep Mike unsullied. Of course, this was unless the exigencies of life brought about some future event as yet undetermined necessitating otherwise. Meanwhile, Mike asked no questions regarding his father's frequent unexplained absences from home. Mickey wondered if this was a manifestation of the fact he was naive and undefiled? Perhaps Mike was very perceptive but inclined to keep his own council. Time would tell, for time was never reluctant to speak out when it so decreed.

In regard to rapport between Mickey and Sean, there was no increase. In fact, it was quite the reverse during the first few weeks in the Becca Valley. Sean hadn't been in the camp for more than an hour before developing an absolute loathing for the place and its occupants. He felt that personnel from the

Commander on down were uniformly swarthy, sinister, sadistic, and strongly malodorous. Geographically and weather wise, the camp seemed like the last outpost of the nether world. Propelled by the always present winds, the sands were constantly in motion. It abraded your skin and invaded your clothes, and it seemed incapable of scattering the clouds of flies and other noxious insects that filled the air and from which you could not escape.

While it was chilling to the bone at night, the desert was a solar furnace during the day. Sean felt as though his skin was burned deeply into the dermis with his body as a whole totally desiccated. However, he noted that officers and other trainees seemed to enjoy the deterioration of this Farenji that Allah had bestowed on them. Sean had thought he was in top physical shape, as his days of varsity sports were not far behind him. Also, he had maintained a strenuous conditioning program since graduation. Soon, young Moynihan realized this was not the case when he would collapse after a long run or march and no medics came. He was left to limp or crawl back when he revived. Anyone bereft of the strength or willpower to crawl perished! Your body would be stripped before decomposition was too far under way, then it was left to rot. Camp policy demanded that no one else suffer the hardship of burying a weakling, especially an infidel.

Despite the fact that Commander Mustafa was supposedly Sean's father's friend, there was never any favoritism shown. Instead, it seemed to be disdain. Haji, the Head Drill Instructor, went far beyond disdain. Brutality seemed to be his game, and it stopped just short of annihilation. Matched with the Drill Instructor in martial arts and hand-to-hand combat training, Sean often thought that the man was going to kill him. Application of a choke hold would draw one's attention. But maintaining it to the point of unconsciousness terrorized all except the most resolute. Fortunately, Sean possessed that quality in abundance.

In time, it became clear that the spirit of the Gael was deeply embedded within him. Sean hardened greatly as the weeks passed. Somewhere near the last trimester of his training, Haji came to the realization that he had more than met his match. Sean was bigger, stronger, and now faster. In the last hand-to-hand match, it was obvious to all that he had the advantage. When Sean's steely forearm was locked in place about the instructor's neck, he briefly considered killing the man; however, *I could possibly need him in the future,* he thought. Releasing the strangle hold, he pulled the gasping Haji to his feet and embraced him. Allah had smiled on the infidel, and Sean was welcomed as a brother. Then, before his departure, Mustafa put on a splendid feast to fete the graduate, now nearly as dark as they and just as sinister.

Sean was funneled back toward home via Istanbul. Enough true sons of the

Prophet were encountered in route that knowing glances supplanted the customary stamps on his passport.

Sean's Turkish visa was still valid. Also, not by chance, a certificate authorizing a course of study at a Turkish University found its way into his possession. Furthermore, all the records of travel to and from the Becca Valley vanished just like those footprints in the sands of time.

Sean's arrival in Paris was punctual. No longer needing oblation of his travel records, he had chosen British Airlines for the final leg home and welcomed the opportunity to hear proper English spoken, plus the chance to read a magazine in the same tongue. Engrossed in his reading, and savoring a sip of Bushmill's between pages, he was oblivious of the passenger who slid gracefully into the first-class seat beside him.

Suddenly, Sean was aware of a familiar fragrance gently tickling the sensory endings of his olfactory system—Chanel's Russian Leather, no doubt about it. Quickly, he recalled that his mother had once bought a bottle of the cologne. She wasn't wild about the scent and was going to discard it. However, his father, given to penury on rare occasions, applied a little as aftershave lotion and declared his fondness for it. The Russian Leather scent had been removed from the Chanel line years ago. But Mickey had somehow managed to secure what might be considered a lifetime supply.

Unobtrusively, Sean turned slightly to determine who might share his father's paradoxical whim. First, a pristinely pressed leg of finest quality suiting material came into view. Before he could correct from peripheral to central vision, a voice unquestionably his father's said, "Are you enjoying your Bushmill's, son?"

Sean was so nonplussed that he didn't respond in a resounding filial salutation. He could only say, "Sorry, Dad, I wasn't expecting you."

"Errant sons never do," was his father's response. Then, Mickey gave Sean a hard elbow in the ribs and was pleased his son didn't flinch. "I don't mind if you have a libation now and then, Sean. You didn't have a father who drank himself to death, as I did. I sell it in Boston, and I would have gone broke if no one ever drank it. Just keep in mind that the Irish are particularly susceptible to the alcoholic flu bug."

"I will, believe me!" replied Sean, while wishing airplanes had windows you could dump things out of quickly.

Since the public area of an airplane cabin was not conducive to discussing what was foremost in their minds, conversation was limited to small talk, mostly happy and entirely nonsuspicious. Sean did wonder how his father had come to be seated next to him. Smiling, Mickey said, "Oh! There are gnomes, trolls, and leprechauns behind every tree and under every bridge. They see all, know all, and will tell all to those they hold in esteem. There are even some in airports wearing leather coats and peeping out from behind newspapers." Both father and son were in good humor as the announcement was made to prepare for landing.

After landing in Belfast, and in the privacy of the Aston-Martin left parked at the airport, Mickey embraced his son. Then, he sang out joyously, "It's great to see you, Sean. You're dark as toast, and harder than month-old soda bread. Tell me one thing: how long were you with Mustafa and his mugs until you stopped hating me for sending you there?"

"I haven't ceased yet," replied Sean with a laugh, adding, "Maybe next year!"

In a firm voice, Sean asked, "How is the battle going?"

"Oh! We keep banging away," replied Mickey. "Sure and it's no blitzkrieg, as we've seen no white flags fluttering from atop Ulster's Protestant bastion Stormont, or the English House of Parliament, nor has anyone approached with a signed treaty of unconditional surrender. Incidentally, I understand via one of our cooperating commissars in the East that you got to splash around a bit in a Bolshevik pond and they found you to be quite an accomplished aquanaut."

Always amused by his father's descriptive phraseology, Sean laughed and said in mock humor, "I assume you are referring to the frogman training. As a matter of fact, I did excel. Who wouldn't want to swim, after spending months in a hell that Dante Alighieri didn't have the imagination to describe! Incidentally, what was that all about?"

"You will know in good time," replied Mickey solemnly. "For now, let's just say that it might get us closer to the head of the lion. In the meantime, let's plan on a week or so of rest and relaxation. Mike is dying to see you, and Mrs. Hennessey is all flustered with plans to drown you in vats of her Granny's infamous Irish stew. Sometimes, I think she is demented and fancies herself the feminine equivalent of Escoffier and Grandmaster Chef of the Cordon Vert School."

"I thought it was the Cordon Bleu," responded Sean quizzically.

"Not if you're Irish," responded his father. "It has to be green instead of blue!"

Soon, they were in the driveway, and Mike ran out to greet them. He was amazed how much his oldest brother appeared to match his concept of a commando. But he never asked why or how. Mrs. Hennessey observed only that Sean looked overcooked by the sun and, surely in need of gaining some weight. However, there was no talk of Liam until the good lady and Mike had retired. When questioned, Mickey said only that Liam remained submerged, but like the Loch Ness monster, he'd surface sometime!

During the following two weeks together, all were filled with experiencing and expressing the fun-filled joie de vivre they felt. Nevertheless, whenever they rode on horseback, they seemed to sense the presence of a phantom filly with an empty saddle. Out at sea, in their yacht *Sargasso,* they sometimes thought of the burnished red hair that had always been their proud pennant. Like shipwrecked sailors adrift on the sea seeking the sight of gulls to indicate nearness of land and safety, they looked vainly for the resplendent red tresses. Finally, each came to the admission that Bernadette would never again be at the helm of either the *Sargasso* or their lives.

Now in possession of martial arts skills he never would have imagined a year ago, Sean was eager for action, and it was all Mickey could do to hold him in check. Nonetheless, the son acknowledged his father as the leader. Thus, Mickey remained the governor, which monitored the speed of Sean's racing engine.

However, as Sean reached a peak of physical fitness, Seamus O'Neil had finally reached the point of becoming superannuated. He knew it, as did Mickey. At a private meeting, Moynihan came to the point with his faithful consigliere. "Seamus, for years you have served me well, and no one has been a more devoted Son of Ireland. I think it is time for you to rest on your laurels, spend more time with the missus and your grandchildren, as there must be more than fifty by now." Mickey's broad smile confirmed that his statement was a spoof. Nonetheless, the elderly volunteer felt constrained to partake in the repartee.

"Lord save us, Mickey. I'm not some heathen sultan with a harem. Jessie and I can only lay claim to thirty-one, at least up to yesterday. I haven't checked today to see if there might be a change." They shared the laugh that Seamus's statement generated, then they grew more serious.

Continuing their conversation, Moynihan said, "If you are agreeable, I would like you to take Sean under your wing for a month or so and teach him all your craft. How to reconnoiter without tipping your hand, setting up a site, planning escape routes, and all that. He's a great lad, but impulsive. So don't feel bad about reining him in and pulling on the bit if need be. Once you tell me that you're satisfied, Sean will be taking over for you. Incidentally, there's a fine pension that goes with honorable discharge. You won't ever be in need."

"Thank you, Mickey. You know I'll do my best for you, Sean, our squad, and of course for Ireland. However, there's one duty I'll not set aside, as long as I live. I still have good connections along with a nose for smelling out rats. A murderous bastard is out there someplace—the killer of dear Bernie. I'll search for that scum for as long as I live and shamrocks grow."

Like high-voltage current passing through terminals, all the feelings of two men, who totally relied on each other over years of constant danger, were transmitted through their joined hands. Then, Mickey called in Sean, and the three of them discussed his job in the next operation. Action at last, though not the combat that Sean desired, but it was a beginning. Shortly thereafter, teacher and student departed.

Left alone, Mickey's thoughts quickly swung in the direction of a fine, big bridge on a busy highway, which provided commuters going to and from work a means of passage over a deep river. As a result of some of Mickey's work on prior depredations, the bridge was guarded on both sides where the highway crossed. "I doubt the Brits have any guards bobbing in the water all night. I always wanted to have a Navy." Smiling, he drew from a simple but highly secretive file code on index cards, which produced the names of two in his group that were tops with explosives, plus how and where to rig them. As a bonus, they could swim like porpoises. "I need this excitement," he concluded. "It will help dispel the haunting. Besides that, I wouldn't want Sean to think I'm becoming an emeritus."

According to plan, three weeks before the job was scheduled, Mickey playing the role of the consummate Izaak Walton spent an afternoon of angling near the bridge. In case a soldier guarding the structure was curious enough to try and discern the face below the fisherman's floppy-brimmed hat, he would see a very bushy Prince Albert beard and mustache. Also, Moynihan wore a pair of heavy horn-rimmed spectacles without prescription but bearing lenses as thick as bullet-proof glass. While fishing, the erstwhile nimrod determined the center support of the bridge was the critical part of the structure, and it was so constructed that explosives could easily be deployed for devastating effect. Best of all, there was a partially submerged tree just twenty-five feet upstream.

Returning home, initially Mickey planned to use a small rubber raft, but after further thought that idea was abandoned. Three men, dressed entirely in black, and riding in a raft of the same color would be difficult to see on a moonless night. However, they might show up as silhouettes. Additionally, a small raft could become easily overbalanced and flip. Such an incident could produce sounds, which would surely raise an alarm. A new plan much more to Mickey's liking was devised. Consequently, three weeks later, Billy Cox, one of Mickey's ten operatives, stole just the right pair of cars. Wearing thick rubber gloves, as his leader had demanded, the cars were near new requiring no repairs. "Once burned, twice shy," was Mickey's credo, drawing from bitter lessons of the past. Then, one car was well hidden in a wooded spot 200 yards downstream from the bridge, while the other car would convey Mickey and two preselected members of his group.

Moynihan and two of his men were driven to the upstream embarkation point by a fourth newly chosen member. Once they were out of the car, it was driven away and quickly abandoned. Then, the three men who were left put on black wetsuits with matching life vests. Loosely roped together, the current carried them silently down the slow-moving river. They had sufficient buoyancy to easily carry adequate explosives, detonators, and timing devices.

As they drifted slowly and soundlessly toward the bridge, it was easy to detect the large protruding limb of the sunken tree snag. They attached to it the far end of the rope, which bound them together. This would suffice to hold them in place against the center strut despite the pull of the river's current. Once the explosives had been placed, and the timer set, they cut the anchoring rope and drifted away, as silently as they had come. Soon, they would escape the area via the car left down downstream, and Moynihan exalted in the fact that his plan had worked perfectly!

At seven A.M. on the next day, the intense, bearded angler whipping the water with his line and attached wet salmon fly was one-half mile downstream from the bridge and seemed acutely unnerved by the sound and shockwave of a terrific explosion. Immediately, he left the river and stowed his gear in a nearby car. Surely, that debris drifting slowly down the river would ruin his fishing for the day.

Of course, the angler's consternation was false, and totally unlike that of a genuine nature shared by the Army and police detachments, who had hurried to the site where the bridge once stood. Attempts to investigate the cause of the explosion were greatly hampered by the task of explaining to hundreds of stranded motorists that the bridge they had used for years had ceased to exist. Furthermore, it was complicated by the need to try and explain to an angry and frightened populace that it took place despite all attempts at prevention.

Soon after the bridge destruction, Sean was finished with his indoctrination under the guileful tutelage of Seamus O'Neil. Shortly thereafter, both went to the Moynihan manor house for one last conference before the man Mickey regarded as a devoted seneschal retired from action. Each in his own way, found it to be a very touching adieu. Seamus spoke first.

"Sean is much more than I could have hoped for, Mick. He's first class in every department. Tough, resourceful, analytical plus loaded with tactical savvy. I think he can shoot as well as you; runs a hell of a lot faster on twenty-year-younger legs, and swims like a dolphin."

Mickey laughed, saying, "You could have phrased it so I didn't come up sounding quite so over the hill."

Before parting, O'Neil looked Mickey Moynihan hard in the eyes; however, the hardness didn't cloak the perception of a tear poised on the brink of his eyelid. Had it not been that his life had been filled with every anguish that readily begot tears, even in the most stoic Seamus probably would have generated another tear. This would have dislodged the first, which would have coursed slowly down his cheek. However, composure aborted the second tear, allowing the first to sink from view. "You know where to find me if you need me, Mick," the older man said solemnly.

"I do!" Moynihan replied somberly. "Now go, live to be 110, and be a proper Granda for all those red-headed ragamuffins you are responsible for Seamus."

Before leaving, O'Neil took Sean's hand hard in his, and their eyes locked before a mutual manly embrace was exchanged. Now, it was Mickey's turn. Although the routine was the same, time expended and strength of the exchange was commensurate to the greater bond they shared. Seamus turned quickly, as the second tear had reemerged and others were forming behind it. Also, he was loathe to show any sign suggestive of weakness. In turning, Seamus missed the sight of hard-fought tears forming in Mickey's eyes. Lifting his left arm, he swiped at his nose with an available sleeve, no doubt a resurrected vestige of a youth long past. "Thanks for everything, Mick," he called back.

"There is no thanks required for paying just debts," Moynihan responded. Then followed a couple of audible sniffles and "Fookin' allergy," and O'Neil was gone.

"Those are big boots to fill," sighed Sean.

"They are indeed," replied his father. Mickey continued, "Men like Seamus should receive their nation's highest honor, but Ireland isn't like any other place. You don't get the Order of the Shamrock here like the Blue Max or the Pour Le Merite that the Krauts used to give out. Let's just hope the old boy stays retired in peace, never turned in by a snitch, tout, or one of those damned Supergases as they are now called!"

After Sean's filling of Seamus's position, Mickey and Sean pulled off several successful assassinations. These were the result of long-range sniper fire, and each was scouted out by Sean. Coming from far away, a single bullet took the lives of two prominent members of the Ulster Defense Force. With Sean observing, the first shot was fired by Mickey, while the roles were reversed for the second. Mickey noted that his son was cool and concentrated as he squeezed the trigger of the Draganov. Fine optics of the powerful telescope revealed the crimson blush emerging from behind the victim's necktie, just as the eyes fixed, and the body sagged.

Sean showed no emotion, neither remorse nor perverse elation. His father felt that is the way it should be, and there was no need for concern. Sean had accepted the role of a soldier, as Mickey had done. Pity, anguish, or self-recrimination were not to be a part of this war. Each fallen foe was but one more step in a long march to victory. This is the way it had to be!

Upon return to Grey Abbey, Mickey spent several days working on their yacht. Within the ranks of his squad was a talented sign painter and when the boat cast off from the quay, late one night, it was no longer visibly bearing the name Bernadette had bestowed. Instead, a painted canvas bearing the name *Seraphim* had been cleverly attached to the stem, as a *ruse de guerre*. Beneath the angelic appellation was painted *Rothesay Bay*, which was meant to indicate its home port was on the outer fringes of the Firth of Clyde.

Vividly, the first rays of an awakening sun illuminated a Union Jack snapping resolutely from the masthead at the beckoning of a fifteen-knot wind. Coming in from north of the Orkney Islands before scraping the crags of Ben Nevis, the wind then descended on the Irish Sea. While Sean and two others tended the sails and other shipboard duties, Mickey was at the helm. At this point in time, only the captain knew their mission. Others assumed it to be most portentous, but were content to patiently await the disclosure.

Tacking skillfully into a quartering wind, Mickey took full advantage of the *Seraphim's* nautical attributes. When Runabay Head came into view, they were comfortably ahead of schedule. With graceful vigor, the boat responded to a helm thrown hard to port, while the sails blossomed fully at the behest of a now following wind. Before long, the lee side of Rathlin Island was presented to their eyes, and Rathlin Sound was entered.

Beyond the protective embrace of the island, the wind proved less amicable, and foul weather gear was mandated. Fortunately, Mickey, Sean, and their sparse though adequate crew were immune to the malevolence of mal-de-mer, so they pushed on undaunted. As the hours passed, it became apparent that Boreas, the god of wind from the north, would pay no umbrage to the fact that it was August. While the *Seraphim* shook off Neptune's wrath and seemed to enjoy the duel, it was obvious to Moynihan that he and his crew teetered on exhaustion. Sanctuary was sought, then realized, as they crossed the bar into the Laugh of Foyle.

Riding at anchor in the lee of Magilligan Point, the gentle undulations of the *Seraphim's* hull were a welcome relief from the more convulsive motions encountered on the open sea. Soon, the captain became cook, and a fine and hearty dinner was set before them. Though abstaining, as always, Mickey allowed Sean and the others alcoholic libations of sufficient volume to induce relaxation and mild euphoria, while running no risk of incurring any vengeful side effects imposed by Bacchus.

Dawn found only ripples on the surface of the briny sea nearly landlocked within the Laugh. Within minutes, the anchor was weighed and unfurled sails were allowed to present their soft bellies to a strong, pleasant breeze. Then, out on the Atlantic, while still skirting the shore, the sailors were pleased to find Boreas had withdrawn from the sea, leaving it open to Eurus, the god of wind from the East. He proved to be a benign deity, yet steady in exhortation, seeming almost a coconspirator to Mickey's plans.

Arriving a full day ahead of schedule, the *Seraphim* presented its proud port side to Rossan Point before cleaving the center of the channel between the Island of Rathlin O'Birne and Malin Beg. Fair sailing and swift passage across the wide mouth of Donegal Bay was accomplished with ease. Before long, the *Seraphim* presented its alias painted stern to the southern extreme of Rosskeragh Point, and the proud bow cleft smartly into the pacified waters of Sligo Bay. Pulses quickened, for Mickey had fully briefed Sean and the other two men during the night they spent in the Laugh of Foyle.

Mickey's words had unleashed an adrenaline rush, though it paled in comparison to what they now experienced. As soon as Sean had taken the helm, his father scrutinized a detailed map with great deliberation. Exact location of the small village of Mullaghmare was ascertained and deliberate directions given. Then, one at a time Mickey and his crew disappeared into the capacious cabin to emerge a short time later in disguises of their own choosing.

Heavily bearded, Mickey now appeared as a weather-beaten captain. Sean was jaunty in white pants, a blue blazer topped off with an ascot, dark glasses, and a pristine cap. O'Malley, sign painter and now sailor, had added adequate stuffing to considerably oversized clothes. Now, he appeared to be an obese, lubberly person incompetent of meaningful shipboard activity and simply along for the ride. Fitzgibbons was last arriving on deck, presenting himself as an apparition of a Teddy Boy going to sea and crowned with a Beatle-style wig that would have done Ringo Starr proud. While Mickey knew some may consider this theatrical, he realized that witnesses best remembered the outlandish. If all went well, there would be possible pursuit, so better let the hounds chase the fox described emphatically as the one with the purple tail!

O'Malley sprawled in a deck chair, while the Teddy Boy and Yachtsman Dandy furled the sails, as the Ancient Mariner stood steadfastly at the wheel. Like an aquatic arrow, the *Seraphim* sped along in response to the propulsive effort of a finely tuned and powerful diesel engine. Ahead was the village of Mullaghmare. As predicted, a fine dowager of a yacht outfitted with resplendence as might be expected lay quietly at anchor. Mickey noted an occasional glow of sunlight, which reflected off binoculars trained on the *Seraphim* by the curious aboard other craft, either at anchor or in passage. "Take a good look, and lock it in your memories," he said quietly. At last, a vacant spot on Sligo Bay far enough from the nearest boat. Mickey wanted to prevent shouted banter being delivered by megaphone from loquacious types, who were always anxious to feign friendship or assuage curiosity. Best of all, they were within 200 yards of what he had called the "Dowager Yacht!" A very accurate range finder had confirmed for Mickey his initial visual estimate.

Twilight lingered on Sligo Bay, while azure sky once predominant in the western half of the heavens was losing its sheen. Nonetheless, beauty (though fading) was for the moment glorious! Pinks, lavenders, and reddish-gold; all came into play as the setting sun threw a goodnight kiss to the Emerald Isle. When day had finally surrendered to the foraging sable night, the inky blackness came alive from the diamond-bright brilliance of myriad stars and galaxies, which burst from space, mocking the lessened luminescence of a scimitar moon.

Raucous voices and music broadcasted from some of the anchored yachts, where bottle-bearing boarding parties had been previously evident. Apart from the anchor light, the *Seraphim* was entirely blackened out. Facing into the silky, soft swells, the boat pulled lightly on its anchor chain like a tethered puppy tired at the end of a day at play. Off in the distance, Mickey observed the Dowager Yacht was just visible in the blade of soft, yellow light derived from the moon's single illuminated quarter. Slowly, the yacht's anchor light rose, then sank, in harmony with passing swells.

Active and purposeful movements were occurring aboard the *Seraphim*, not discernible to any except the participants. Sean sat astride the gunwale fully outfitted in black scuba gear. After a squeeze on his shoulder by his father's powerful hand, Sean slid softly into the ink-like sea. Soon, Sean's head and hands broke to the surface, and a streamlined canister was passed to him from the deck above. Shortly, there was a second and last submersion, which produced no sound alien to that of waters lapping the hull.

For Mickey, anxiety increased with the passage of time. When on his own missions, minutes seemed to race. However, it was not the same when his son was out there! Representing every moment in a mission clock, the cogs seemed to grind against the timing wheel with fear intruding during every excursion of the pendulum. *Sean was due to be back in an hour, but that was twenty minutes ago!* Mickey wondered if there had been a deadly mishap. *Could Sean be lost or disoriented out there somewhere? Could the oxygen tanks be near depletion?* However, the curse formed from concern never left Mickey's lips; for suddenly, like a glass-faced sea lion Sean broke through the water just feet from the *Seraphim's* stern quarter.

Greatly relieved, Mickey helped bring his son on board. Then, in record time, the *Seraphim* was under way, pushed to full throttle! Clear of Sligo Bay, their disguises and scuba gear were placed inside a crab pot and consigned to the depths. Parchment-hued sails, Union Jack, and canvas stern cover emboldened with the name *Seraphim* were weighted and followed soon after, disappearing in the depths of the ocean.

When the sun's corona had flared sufficiently, the North Atlantic stirred to life. Hungry, though seemingly happy, gulls cavorted above the pristine, white sails of a yacht bearing north. *Sargasso Grey Abbey* was emblazoned on its stern, and the Stars and Stripes snapped in the wind from atop the mainmast! On board, the crew looked athletic, energetic, and tan. For all the world, they appeared as though they had come straight from San Diego, California.

Meanwhile, attached to the hull of the Dowager Yacht, the limpet mine had heeded the command of the timing device housed within the portion of its cavity not filled with explosives. Suddenly, a horrendous eruption wrought complete devastation to the yacht and occupants. Immediately, a massive search was ordered, as there was little doubt that it was a terrorist act! No clues or possible bombers were found on the shore or anywhere nearby. Consequently, the sea was suspect as a means of escape. Air and surface patrols were instituted. While searching, a sea plane noted the *Sargasso* and studied it carefully. "About the right size," said the copilot.

"Wrong-colored sails," called one of the observers into his throat mike.

"Wrong name, too," called out another, who then added, "besides that he's a bloody Yank."

"Who else would wear shorts and sport a Hollywood suntan!" chortled the first.

"Well I'm calling it in," exclaimed the pilot. "It's the only thing we've seen even vaguely fitting the description."

"Yeah! The description of a bunch of hungover yacht freaks."

"Based on the recollection of those blokes, I'm surprised we're not out looking for the *Graf Spee* or the *Scharnhorst*," chimed in the first observer.

An hour later, the *Sargasso* was boarded by an officer and five crewmen from a patrol boat. Far from reluctant, the yacht's captain was hospitality itself. Mickey and Sean had absorbed enough of Boston to sound as though they just stepped out of the Commons. O'Malley and Fitzgibbons were readily passed off as a couple of Ulsterites serving as crew on the boat. A case of Guinness was offered as a gesture of goodwill, but declined by the awkward young officer to the dismay of his crewmen. Before boarding his gig, the lieutenant politely requested Mickey to call his Captain should they happen to encounter a mystery boat named *Seraphim*.

"As long as it is not under command of John Paul Jones, you can count on us," replied Mickey with a smile. "Keep on looking for the fox with the purple tail!" he said under his breath. After the gig cast off, they were not bothered again.

Though the world was shocked by the savagery of the bombing, the epicenter of anger was in London. One of the victims was a lady who happened to be a baroness. Also, two young men were killed; one was a local lad, who was acting as a pilot, the other was related to the most distinguished victim. He was a royal and a hero of World War II. Suspects and theories abounded! Foremost in everyone's mind was the Northern Command of the IRA since there was more than ample evidence that they were planning just such a dastardly act. Meanwhile, with feet braced on a heaving deck and spokes of the wheel locked hard in his hands, Mickey murmured, "They can all take credit for his Lordship, but we're the ones who have the satisfaction of having done it!"

Upon Mickey and Sean's return home, young Mike was overjoyed and wanted to hear all the tales of adventure. "The worst part was outrunning those Viking longboats," said his father with a laugh. "Next time, I'll take you! Sean isn't much good with a sword and even worse with a spear. However, you have to promise to wear one of those steel helmets, with the horns coming out the sides!" Then, Mickey decided to discuss Mike's future. He knew that his youngest son wanted to engage in business. Already, Mickey had decided to send Mike to school in Boston and, after discussion, found him receptive. Mike was very bright and extremely affable, a natural in all sports, and Harvard had accepted him. Soon after Mickey's decision, Mike was on his way to Boston.

Mickey's decision had a deeper reason, for he was fully cognizant of the fact that one of his sons and presumably a second son were fully engaged in fighting the Brits. Their futures could evaporate at any moment in a violent way. Michael was different. Despite his masculinity, he was the embodiment of dear Bernie. "If it is to be that only one of us survives, then best it be him," was Mickey's rationale. He and Sean could continue their war and perhaps Liam was out there somewhere doing the same. "That was three eggs in one basket. Better the last egg be in Boston!"

Chapter Twenty-Eight

Indeed, Liam Moynihan was continuing the war for the Cause. Darby McKevitt, jockey par excellence and now patriot, had managed to keep him separated from Kelleher. Consequently, no murder or mayhem had occurred between them, though plenty had been perpetuated on the Protestants of Ulster, as well as their British protectors. However, one day they were both in the same part of Belfast, though on different missions. Liam along with a single associate was in the process of fleeing the site where they had just gunned down a UDL man walking his daughter home from school.

Just eight blocks from the scene, their speeding car suddenly came to an intersection blocked by a British Saracen armored car and several police vehicles. Liam turned the wheel and applied the handbrake in such a way as to cause a purposeful skid, which should induce the car to do a 180-degree turn or loop a Brodie, as it was described in street parlance. After Liam's maneuver was performed successfully, he was about to accelerate back down the street when the sound of metal impacting on metal tore at them in a deafening crescendo. Immediately, it was followed by bursts of automatic weapons fire. No rounds impacted on their sedan or ricocheted off the cobblestones of the lane or brick houses on either side. Obviously, the police and Army intrusion was not meant for them but for someone else.

Desperately, Liam glanced in the rearview mirror, which revealed a man running toward them as best he could with one wooden leg. After another burst of machine gun fire, the man staggered and dropped the Armalite he was carrying out of his dead and useless hand. Crimson stains appeared on the shoulder of his shirt, then spread down the sleeve as the blood was wicked by the cloth and accelerated by gravity. "He's one of ours," screamed Liam's associate. Then, the middle Moynihan son recognized the staggering figure approaching them was none other than Kelleher. Another burst of fire cut the fleeing man's normal leg, along with the mahogany one from beneath him. More crimson dappled the cloth of his trousers before he lurched and fell.

Some phantom force seemed to paralyze Liam's foot, preventing it from jamming down on the accelerator, and he would never be able to logically explain his next reaction. Some unfathomable reflex forced him to vault from the car, as he screamed to his associate, "Take the wheel!" Then, Liam sprinted toward the wounded man. Fortunately, he had extricated his own AR 15 at the time of leaving the sedan. Noting a British soldier was running toward Kelleher with his rifle at the ready, Liam got off a short burst, disabling the would-be captor.

Although Kelleher was conscious, he could provide little in the way of enabling. Finally, Moynihan had his former nemesis slung over his shoulder. Still, he was able to maintain a grip on his weapon. Suddenly, only a few yards from the sedan, Liam experienced a searing pain in his left thigh. Velocity-wise, the bullet that passed through it was such that the projectile had arrived in advance of the sound, heralding its release. Nonetheless, Liam was able to turn drunkenly and fire back at his assailant. Encumbered and wounded, the return fire was hopelessly inaccurate, but sufficient to propel the soldier into a sheltering doorway.

When Liam reached the car, the back door was open, and Kelleher was dumped unceremoniously within. Then his rescuer threw himself on top of him, and the driver didn't wait for Liam to scream, "Get the fook out of here," as he was already accelerating wildly, while Moynihan struggled to close the door. Meanwhile, the soldier had recaptured his bravado. From the doorway, he emptied his magazine at the fleeing car. Bullets punctured the body of the sedan, but none registered on targets of significance. Then neighboring teenage toughs, sizing up the situation, were able to tip over several parked cars, thus blocking the street and delaying pursuit.

Ten minutes later, the riddled sedan was safely ensconced in a garage. Immediately, the driver contacted McKevitt and pleaded for medical assistance as soon as possible!

Just minutes before McKevitt came, a trusted doctor arrived at the garage. However, the triage didn't last long, as the doctor spent only a few minutes with Kelleher, then moved on to Liam. His assessment was complete by the time the Provo chief entered the scene. Kelleher lay stretched on a cot, and even a layman could ascertain he was in extremis. A sheen of cold sweat covered his nearly alabaster skin and hairline, except where it was beaded on his upper lip. Violaceous color of both lips, fingertips, and ears bespoke of cyanosis.

McKevitt looked at the physician, and he asked the mandatory question, "How does it look, doctor?"

Despite his clandestine role, the practitioner retained compassion for his charges and was restrained from shouting, "Can't you see he is nearly dead?" Instead, he took the chief aside and whispered, "This one would be an uphill battle in a major trauma center with loads of blood and a fine surgical team. Lying on a cot in a poorly lit, dirty garage with you and the mechanic as surgical assistants, it will be about ten more minutes before we pull down his eyelids so we don't have a dead man staring at us. However, the other one got a clean shot through the thigh. He's stable enough to sneak into my surgery. There we can give him a little anesthesia and irrigate the wound. Plus, we can grab an x-ray to make sure the bone was missed. Loaded with antibiotics, he should do well. I'll get him on the way. It will be your job to take care of the corpse in whatever way you see fit."

Darby was a tough man, but his hand recoiled slightly when he touched Kelleher's face. "Terry, can you hear me lad?"

"Yes," emitted between shallow gasps was just audible.

"You're hurt bad, Terry! I'm afraid you won't make it."

"I uh ... I fig ... figured that ... out ... myself," came out in a fading response.

"I don't know if you want a priest, Terry, but even if you did, I doubt there is time."

Seizing on the last remnants of strength, Kelleher did his best to communicate the few sentences he deemed most important at the termination of his mortal existence. Some of it was hard to decipher. Due to his premortem dyspnea, the feeble words emerged like Morse code letters transmitted with great delay. Darby tried hard to slowly piece it together to determine what had been said, as the last nerve impulse that Kelleher's heart received didn't get past the atria. That vital organ never beat again.

Since McKevitt was a confirmed atheist, he made little of Kelleher's mumbled contrition to a God that didn't exist. Also, Terry's pleas for a proper burial would go unheeded, as would the request for his mother to pray for him. "Sorry, Terry, we'll have to find an isolated peat bog for your resting place," McKevitt said softly. Now, the other information Kelleher had confided was the only thing of importance!

On the day following Kelleher's death, Mickey had been out exercising Warlord. He was still mounted as the horse was walked slowly toward the paddock door. Suddenly, McKevitt emerged from behind a tree. Still in the midst of congratulating himself for having caught the great Mickey Moynihan unprepared, he stopped when it became apparent the rider was holding a Browning Hi-Power leveled at his head. Quickly recovering his aplomb, McKevitt called out, "That's a fine stallion, and you sit him well, Mr. Moynihan. You don't mind a surprise visit do you?"

Mickey was replacing the gun in the holster beneath his jacket, but he responded, "If you like surprising people, Mr. McKevitt, hide in the shade! Even small men, behind trees, cast shadows when the sun seeks them out." Dismounting, Mickey added, "I assume you didn't come just to compliment my horse. What is it that I can do for you?"

As the former jockey nuzzled the stallion's broad nose with a practiced hand, he replied, "I'm more conversational over a fine cup of tea, and I assume you might be willing to offer me one?"

Soon, Moynihan and McKevitt were seated in the study. Mrs. Hennessey served tea, then left them in privacy. "Your son Liam was wounded in action yesterday! Soft tissue of the thigh only, according to the doctor. A complete recovery is expected, and no one is looking for him. You might be interested to know that he performed a gallant action. As a matter of fact, he risked his life to save none other than Terry Kelleher. Unfortunately, it was all in vain. Kelleher died a short time later."

"Is all this meant to provoke concern for my son or bereavement over Kelleher?" responded Mickey sharply.

"The former is up to you. The latter I assume is not to be expected. However, Terry made a deathbed confession of sorts. It was he who delivered the bomb that killed your wife!"

Mickey's knuckles grew white, as he clutched the arms of his chair. With jaw set, he glared at the jockey. "Kelleher killed her! Is that what you are saying?"

"He was the messenger, but he didn't build the bomb."

Mickey vaulted from the chair and screamed, "Then, who in the hell did?!"

McKevitt felt unnerved but fought to keep it from notice. Slowly, and with great deliberation, he said, "It was Con Hogan. He's hated you for years. The bomb was meant for you, but he was no less happy when he learned it killed your wife. I assume it is a matter you want to take care of yourself, Mr. Moynihan?"

Mickey's face revealed a malevolence greater than McKevitt had ever seen. No response was necessary, but the confirmatory words were issued at last. "That I do!" was all Moynihan said.

The little man rose to depart. "I'll let you know how Liam is coming along. I plan to make him my lieutenant. Do you object?"

"That's up to you and him," Mickey replied. Immediately after that, the door was closed behind McKevitt. He was gone. Mickey found Sean, and they left together for Belfast, full partners in fury and committed to revenge!

Meanwhile, no doubt Con Hogan's defensive demeanor was dulled over the months that had passed since his dastardly act caused Bernadette's death. Complacency ended when Mickey and Sean apprehended him as he was about to enter his car. Despite the fact that Hogan had been excessively liberal in the amount of Bushmill's consumed that night, the abduction had a sobering effect on him. Quickly bound, blindfolded, and gagged, Hogan was slammed into the back of the old Bentley Bernadette had once driven. While on the way to Grey Abbey, Hogan thrashed about a bit, and there were occasional indecipherable mutterings through the duct tape across his mouth.

On arrival, he was pulled roughly from the car and stood upright. Then, Mickey ripped off the tape covering his mouth and eyes. Hogan tried to get his bearings. He looked into Mickey's face and realized that it was the Angel of Death that stood before him. Nevertheless, he still had sufficient bottled bravado coursing through him that he shouted, "What the fook is this all about?"

Mickey's response was as cold as a corpse. "It's about the murder of my wife!"

"What if I did kill the red-haired whore?" Hogan shouted. "You can't touch me. I'm too big in the IRA!"

Mickey hit the cell chief across the mouth with an open hand. The force was sufficient to stagger Hogan and deeply split his lip. "You dirty fooker," Hogan screamed. "You could at least give me a chance!"

"You will have a chance, Hogan, a far better one than you gave Bernie." The condemned man seemed to rally slightly at the thought of a chance, and after the ropes were removed from his legs, Hogan walked willingly down to the quay and boarded the *Sargasso*.

Sean fastened Hogan's hands to the mainmast. As the *Sargasso* cast off under diesel power, he sat quivering and speechless. Mickey and Sean were silent as well until Mickey consulted his sonar and said, "We're here!"

Freed from his tether, Hogan stood upright. Marked by a few lights that were still on, he could see that the shore was about a half-mile away. As a youth, he had been a strong swimmer. Perhaps land was attainable despite the chilling temperature of the water.

"You wanted a chance," said Mickey. "Well we're giving you one! Take off your clothes and put on this wetsuit. You'll do far better with that on, the water being the temperature that it is."

Hogan's spirits were immediately buoyed. The fool was actually making escape possible. Desperate as he was, the murderer let thoughts of revenge begin to fill his mind.

Once the wetsuit was on, Hogan thought of running for the railing. Mickey was ready for that and said sardonically, "Don't consider breaking for it now, Con! I won't shoot you; I'll eviscerate you instead." Sean still held a pistol, but Mickey was brandishing a large and deadly knife, and he stood between Hogan and the rail. "Besides, you need all the advantage you can get. That's why we have the diving tanks for you. With a little instruction, even a drunk like you can get the hang of it."

Hogan was filled with relief thinking it would be a hard swim, but with the suit and tanks he could make it. What at first had seemed like sure death was ending up like some sort of initiation ritual.

With mask, mouthpiece, and tanks all in position, Hogan was led to the railing. Life-giving oxygen was flowing into the mask, allaying a new fear that Moynihan might be giving him a poisonous gas. Sitting on the gunwale, back to the sea, Hogan was startled when Sean affixed chains about his ankles. "You dirty fooker," he screamed. "You said I would get a chance!"

"I'm keeping my word," Mickey hissed. "You have an hour's supply of oxygen, and down there, alone in the dark and cold, you have a chance to wish you had never killed my wife. On the way down, your eardrums will rupture. But you won't go deep enough to die from the bends. However, if you decide you want to come up, you can use this." Mickey pressed a diver's knife into Con's trembling hand. "Should you wish to free yourself, then cut through both of your knees. There's a joint space where there's only flesh! You needn't try and saw through the bones."

Next, the chain locked to Hogan's ankles was connected to an anchor. The last thing he saw on the surface was the great metal weight arcing through the air as Mickey and Sean heaved it out together.

For Con Hogan, the searing pain from his exploding eardrums was nothing compared to the sheer terror that consumed him. At last, the anchor touched bottom. Buoyed by the wetsuit and his own oxygen-filled lungs, he was suspended like some mortal sea mine in the inky blackness. Before madness took complete control of his mind, horrific images of Bernadette flooded his sensorium. At last, it was too much, and he dropped the knife, choosing to reach up and rip off the mask. Then, Con Hogan welcomed the sea water into his lungs.

For several days after Hogan's execution, Mickey was terribly unsettled. Although it had nothing to do with remorse or pangs of conscience, nevertheless he began to audit the ledger of his life. Bernie and the boys had been his greatest assets. However, his wife was dead, and Liam had seemingly fallen into the deficit column. Business in Boston had been exciting and made him rich. Although the businesses were not booming, as they had been under his direct supervision, the revenues were still grand. They were far more than adequate for his needs. In a few short years from now, Mike could take over in person, and Mickey had no doubt that all the excitement and grandeur would return.

Moynihan's thoughts turned to his private war. From memory, a long string of what appeared to be successes were easily retrieved. However, once they were analyzed, doubt crept into his mind. "Was Ulster any closer to independence and union with the Republic? There were no less British soldiers, Protestant militants or police. Like toadstools, three more seemed to crop up for everyone you pulled out. Ranks of the IRA, Provos, and splinter groups expanded slowly, but never outpaced the opposition. Worse yet, there seemed to be continuous internecine war within the Republican ranks! Mickey had only to look at his own experience, for he had drank a full measure from that cup of bitter brew.

Next, Mickey came to dwell on his sons, which led to an effort to find a convincing argument that he had been fair to them and to Bernie. *Mike at least is insulated from all of this! Sean on the other hand seems as dedicated as he was. There is no reason to suspect that he would abandon the Cause, even if urged to do so. Liam is, and I presume always will be, the Lone Ranger and a reckless one at that. I fear more for his life, but I'm not part of his decision-making process, and I doubt I ever will be.*

Beginning to feel disconsolate, Mickey called on the aid of his private humor. Frequently, humor had been his salvation as well as the key to "unscrewing the inscrutable," as he liked to put it. Moynihan always took pleasure in considering himself a bona fide soldier. So it wasn't difficult to conjure up a proper military analogy. "In the event I was an officer of the rank that I deserve in a real army, I could add a hash mark to my sleeve signifying four years of service. Well I'll serve with all possible diligence for four more years, then restudy it!" This decision released a wave of resurgence in his spirit compelling Mickey to find the notes he kept secreted. Then, he could begin to plan his next campaign.

During the time of doubt, the image that had propelled its way into Moynihan's consciousness was dispelled and had vanished without a trace. However, at the time, it was disturbing to have that image break its way out from some lock box within his brain. At the time, Mickey was seriously considering giving it all up when an image from an old holy card that Sister Mary Stephanie had given him popped into his mind. It was a picture of Christ in the Garden of Gethsemane and the caption read, as best Mickey could recall, "Father, if it be Thy Will, then let this cup pass from me."

For some reason he didn't comprehend, Mickey felt guilty and profane in coming up with any comparison between himself and Christ. "Why do I get uptight over some silly thought from the past? Surely, it isn't any more of a sacrilege if there is such a thing than suddenly conjuring up a picture of Buck Rogers from a comic book?" Shortly the matter was laid to rest when Mickey recalled that the good sister was better known for how hard she could box your ears. That card was the only one that he had ever received, while the number of times he had been the target of her yardstick were many.

Continuing their private war, during their next tour of duty, Mickey and Sean along with their squad of ten had many successes by their own standards. Of course, others viewed them as vile acts of terrorism, murder, and mayhem. Meanwhile, Liam was established as McKevitt's trusted adjutant. Rumors abounded that the two of them were responsible for the bombing at Brighton, which came close to killing Margaret Thatcher. Having come to the conclusion that they botched it, Mickey started working on his own plan to show them all how it should be done. *I'll concentrate on the Iron Lady,* he thought. *If that goes well, there are many more of the royals to go after.*

Further rumors linked his son and the ex-jockey to the bombing in London's Hyde Park, which killed four members of the Household Calvary and eight members of the Royal Greenjackets Band. Mickey was incensed, not by the death of the soldiers, which he considered a patriotic act, but the scurrilous part was the killing and maiming of a number of fine horses. He cursed McKevitt roundly for being a traitor to all things equine, especially since they had made him rich and famous! Immediately, a check for £1,000 was sent to the Royal Dublin Society to help replace the dead horses and treat the wounded ones. Others could contribute to the fund for widows and orphans.

When his four-year hitch was drawing to a close, Mickey knew he would be good for at least one more if a British bullet didn't intervene. Sean was even more enthusiastic than his father. However, he was close to marriage, and Mickey thought strongly of insisting that Sean retire. However, nothing had changed with Liam, and he was still the enigmatic phantom, prodigal son, while young Mike, now sporting the title of Michael Brendon Moynihan, was garnishing all sorts of accolades at the hallowed Harvard Business School. In addition, even Mike's part-time efforts were breathing new life into the Boston enterprises. Michael Jr. wrote his father, proudly announcing a record second quarter of revenue. However, Michael didn't mention his fiancée, as that would be left for a surprise on his father's next visit. Immediately, Mickey wrote back that "it was great news, but as an MBA seeker, you should take inflation into consideration before proclaiming supremacy!"

Chapter Twenty-Nine

※ ※ ※

Early Monday morning, Iain Cameron was at his desk in Wellington Barracks. He felt a little let down, as the great day on which he received the Victoria Cross was consigned to history. Now, Claire and his parents were back from whence they came. While available by phone, a receiver tethered by a cord could only convey speech, and though intonation could add warmth to words, it would never be the same as seeing the face from which words came. Many well wishers stopped by his desk or caught Iain in the hallways to bestow their congratulations. While he appreciated these appendages to yesterday, they didn't quite elevate him from the emotional trough in which he had fallen.

Finally, Iain decided that the realization of the great event, now ended, should best be replaced by anticipation, but anticipation of what? Since it was July, he could think of no momentous occurrences that might take place in the seventh month. Cameron's mind went blank, and so was the sheet of paper on which he had intended to make notes for the Malay Manual. *Well, I can be resourceful in regard to these pristine sheets of note pad,* he thought. This gave rise to a series of doodles including a caricature of a Scottish red grouse standing proudly on a stump. He was about to add some feather details when the importance of August burst into his mind. "Bloody hell," he exclaimed, loud enough to startle a corporal about to close a file door and causing him to forget to move his thumb to a place of safety before the heavy door closed on it. However, the poor man's verbal response to the predicament never registered on the captain, whose mind was now locked on the Glorious 12th!

Opening day of grouse season was of extreme importance for all those gentlemen and ladies for whom shooting the wild flying game bird was an avocation, which few other adventures could match. In addition to the shooting, the Glorious 12th also marked the opening of Highland social season. shooting parties frequently moved from one estate to another, where hosts vied to provide the greatest number of birds under the most variable of circumstances.

Competition extended to cuisine as well, consequently the nightly dinner parties were truly gala events. Excitement generated by the Glorious 12th was not limited to the gentry alone. Gamekeepers and their assistants were often quite celebrated, for it was their knowledge and management (or lack thereof) that made the difference between splendid, mediocre, or, that category most feared, "ghastly" hunt. Dog handlers were next in line, and proud were those whose canine charges never lost a downed bird. Less heralded were the ghillies. Those stalwart men were the ones who minded the horses, filled or emptied their pannikins, and made sure all that was needed was brought, and all left was carried away. Last on the list were the beaters, who marched dauntlessly through the heather and bracken waving and snapping their flags. Their purpose was to cause the birds to flush and fly toward the line of shooting butts or stations, wherein waited the hunters or guns, as they were called colloquially

Iain exploded from his trough of disquietude and now danced with delight. Of course it was perfect, and Claire would be enchanted, he was sure. "Fortunately, there would be scads of time just for them to walk and, more importantly, to talk." Cameron's newfound enthusiasm spread like a virus. His doodle sheet was discarded, and new paper began to fill with cogent thoughts for the Manual.

Earlier, Major Wilson had passed behind Iain and noted only doodles for the day's work, so on his last pass, he was most pleasantly surprised at the number of pages produced. How well he knew what it was like to bask in glory and adulation, only to see gold turn to lead soon thereafter. Wilson thought, *It's a contest that each one faces in a different way. Fortunately, there are those who look deep inside themselves, find what they need, and continue on their way. Unfortunately, there were some who would never again find themselves. They simply faded away.* Then, the major smiled inwardly, as he thought, *Captain Cameron will never fade away.*

Although Iain was going to call Claire on Saturday night, his new plan was too exciting to postpone, as it was like a condor chick, anxious to crack the shell and escape the egg. As soon as he could break away from his mess mates, Iain placed the call. After the third ring, the voice that answered his call to the Sister's Quarters had that "So, I get to talk to Sir Galahad" tone when she indicated that Claire was there. "Please hold, and I'll try and find her."

At last, the voice he loved said "Miss Campbell here."

"Just who I wanted," Iain said, and then went on. "Claire, I have the most wonderful idea. How would you like to come to my parent's place up by Dunkeld for the Glorious 12th?"

Very few people, male or female, in Scotland have no concept of that particular date. Claire knew it had to do with hunting, but she had no real knowledge of all the nuances involved. "Isn't that where you shoot at birds?" she replied somewhat hesitatingly.

"Yes that's the most important part," Iain said.

"I don't know anything about guns Iain, and I wouldn't really want to try and shoot something if I did."

Iain laughed, then said, "Claire, dear, for most of the ladies, it's a splendid social event; sort of like going to the derby for the horse races. Everyone has a great time, and no one but the jockeys ever ride a horse. I'm going to try and get away on Wednesday, the 11th. I could pick you up on the way, and bring you back on Sunday? You would love it, I'm sure, but not as much as I would love having you come. Please try and get away Claire. I want to see you so badly!"

"I'll try," Claire blurted out before she could contain it.

"Great," came the response. "I'll call you back on Saturday. I really miss you."

"I miss you, too, Iain," came softly in reply.

Even before she replaced the receiver, Claire began to feel disturbed. *Why can't he just come and see me?* she thought, *What's so important about some dumb bird shoot?* Given the vagaries of logic, Claire abruptly departed those questions without an attempt to answer and, immediately, moved on to "What on earth do you wear to such a thing?" As an old dictum from Thomas Aquinas stipulates "from nothing, nothing comes." As a young nurse, Claire knew instantaneously that if you know nothing about what to wear, you could spend the rest of your life thinking and, in the end, the result would be the same.

Claire's mind turned to the foreboding about difference in their religions, which had come to her notice in London and now returned to haunt her. She was swift to recall the little lines, which appeared in Aunt Jane's face when the question of her going to the Anglican services was raised. Yes little lines of dismay that had much to say and, thus, leave words unneeded. This would surely end in disaster. Iain would never convert, nor would she. His parents, nice as they were, would be absolutely opposed; hers, too, for that matter. *Damn Henry VIII,* she thought. *If the old libertine hadn't been so lustful and left well enough alone, this problem wouldn't exist.*

Claire gave vent to some anger, which flushed her cheeks and much enhanced her beauty, even though Iain wasn't there to admire it. "Claire Campbell, or the dreamer and fool," were the words of remonstration she next applied. "You don't really need this. Give it up. Let it go!" she continued. However, the self-abasement provided no relief, but did spawn a decision. "I don't need this. I need Iain Cameron," was her conclusion. "I love him, and I need him. Maybe it will never work out, but if I'm to slip and fall, then so be it! I'll keep on trying to make it work. If I'm to fall off a precipice climbing my own Matterhorn, what difference does it make if I come tumbling down from halfway up or from the top? The fall will get me either way!"

Now, since the agony of her major decision was set aside, at least temporarily, Claire faced once again the dilemma of a wardrobe. She realized there would be no possibility of remaking or altering an existent garment. She might as well consult her closet in hopes of finding a costume suitable for a mermaid.

Iain had no such problems when it came to clothes, for a well-tailored Harris-tweed shooting coat with matching breeches and cap along with a drawer full of Tattersall shirts could be readily retrieved from his armoire at home. These would be de rigueur for the shoot, but far down the line of importance when compared to the gun you used. Cameron conjured up a vision, and a matched pair of Holland and Holland Royals came into view like some marvelous mirage without the heat waves. There was no need for heat waves, for few things can warm the cockles of a grouse hunter's heart as sure as a matched pair. They are assembled with consummate skill, as they are made up of two shotguns exactly the same in all dimensions and without perceptible variance in weight.

Pair production is an achievement most difficult since the density of wood coming from the same Circassian walnut tree will vary from one piece to another. Thus, while all the stock and forearm dimensions of the guns are exactly the same, the weight could vary by several ounces. This would be unacceptable to the most discriminating marksman. Essential to the shooter is the necessity that the two guns feel, balance, and mount absolutely the same. From his grandfather, Iain had inherited his pair of Holland and Holland London Best guns. In addition, the old gentleman had passed to his grandson nearly the exact body size and build, so the guns fit him perfectly. Indeed, they were a precise fit, in that they were like an extension of his arm.

As his exhilaration grew, Iain was moved to jump to his feet and mount a make-believe gun to his right shoulder. His left arm was extended with the hand embracing a fanciful forearm. Suddenly, it struck him that the phantom fowling piece seemed a bit off to the right. Cameron's euphoria froze like a fine mist of water at absolute zero! "You stupid ass!" he said with disdain. "How could you forget that you are now blind in your right eye?" Immediately, Iain realized that he had been so distracted by his surgery, the medal, and Claire, that his blindness had not remained in the forefront. Additionally, apart from minor problems with depth perception, he hadn't really been that much aware of the handicap.

He found no problem with driving, reading, or any of the usual things one did; however, it was not the same with shooting.

Iain knew that a shotgun would fill a thirty-inch diameter circle with hundreds of pellets from forty yards away, and a neophyte would think it easy to hit a target. They would be unaware that mounting such a gun to the right shoulder, and using the left eye to sight, could result in having all the pellets pass as much as three feet to the right of the target. That was intolerable! He could think of no alternative but to shoot left-handed. Would it be possible to do this, and attain even very mediocre success in the three short weeks that his grand scheme allowed? Well he could play the underdog, roll on his back, expose his throat and soft underbelly, and allow his legs to point limply upward, or he could stand, erect curl his tail, and growl. Iain decided to growl, as it was his nature. Tomorrow, he would call Holland and Holland and make arrangements to see their staff and also try the facilities of the shooting school they maintained in London's outskirts.

Fortunately, progress on the Malay Manual was proceeding at a phenomenal rate, so on Tuesday Major Wilson was greatly pleased and happily added an extra hour off to his charge's request for two. "Certainly, Captain, come in early, pile it on, and be off at 1400 hours for the next three weeks," was his response to Iain's request. So, with Cameron at the wheel, the Austin Healey negotiated London traffic like a fine polo pony dashing for the goal. At last on Audley Street, Iain quickly found No. 20. Large gold letters on a background of black proudly proclaimed Holland and Holland Ltd. Cameron found a parking place between the firm's showroom and the nearby American embassy.

Once inside the door, Cameron was greeted by William Burton, manager of sales. Iain started to introduce himself but was stopped by the elderly man's recognition. "Yes, Captain Cameron, I was told of your phone call earlier on today, but I also remember your many visits over the years with your father, the General. How may I be of service?"

Iain quickly related his predicament, and the older man listened intently. "Always a way when you have the will, Captain. You told me that you have been shooting your grandfather's pair of Hollands." Turning, he withdrew a leather-bound book from a nearby shelf. "Here we are! Colonel Alexander Justin Cameron. One matched pair of Royal Ejector in twelve-gauge, two and one-half inch chambers, barrels twenty-nine inches, etc. You might be interested to know someone penned in a note indicating your grandfather spent two days selecting the wood for the stocks. This was considered a record at the time, and I suspect that it may still stand!"

With a complimentary smile, Burton continued. "Well, let's see what else we have here. The stock length should still be quite appropriate for you, and according to the entry in our log, it is fifteen inches. Drop at heel and comb will probably suffice, but the cast-off will be a problem. As I'm sure you know, cast-off is an indication that the stock was carved so that its comb or top is located slightly to the right of a line, which would come straight back from the rib between the barrels. Many right-hand shooters have a cast-off of one-eighth to one-half inch. This will be a problem for a left-handed shooter. Basically, there are two solutions. We could carve a stock curved way over to the right. The degree of curvature would be approximately the distance between your pupils. Such a stock would allow the shooter to mount the gun right-handed, but sight with the left eye. Drawbacks are several, as it would take a number of months, as there would be two to produce. Also, there is the matter of cast, possibility of fracture, due to the relatively acute angle in the thinnest part of the stock, and, lastly aesthetics!"

Burton continued with his opinion regarding aesthetics. "Personally, I think such a stock is bloody ugly, but that's based on my own bias. Especially at your age, the transition from right to left should be relatively easy. Most of the shooters who switch are our geriatric customers and are of an age where blindness in one eye is more prone to occur. I'm happy to say, many of them become as good a marksman from the sinister side, as they were from the dexterous or vice versa. Now, if you wish to give it a go as a left-hander, we will need to bend the current stock into a neutral or slightly cast-on orientation. Presuming the left side of your face is relatively the same as the right side, then I would guess we would need an eighth of an inch cast, which would mean we would bend them first to neutral, then slightly to the left."

"Did you say *bend?*" asked Iain quizzically, as he had always thought of gun stocks like table legs, and could not imagine you could bend one, though he was aware that wood could naturally warp.

"Yes, Captain, *bend* is quite correct. You can't bend a thick piece of walnut very much, but by applying hot oil and the correct pressure, you can bend it at least a half inch without injury to the wood or damage to the finish. I'm going to call Boyd Walker, who I'm sure you know is our top instructor at the shooting school. Boyd has had a wealth of experience and fantastic success in teaching the unused half of your body to perform as well as the part that you are leaving behind. Is it possible to make it out to the school by four P.M. for a number of days?"

"I'll certainly do so, Mr. Burton, and I'm most appreciative of your assistance and encouragement," Iain replied. They shook hands, and Captain Cameron turned toward the door feeling far more buoyant than he had on entry.

Just as Iain reached the door, Burton commented, "One last thing, Captain. Don't get too good too fast! We wouldn't want you out shooting your father right off. There is no one more competitive than the General and, if you were to best him, he might decide to cancel the order he placed for a full set of Royals."

Iain paused. "My father placed an order for a new pair?"

"Not a pair, sir, but rather a set. You know, one gun in every gauge from .410 through .28, .20, .16, .12, and all the way up to .10. We're quite thrilled about it, as the set is the first one we've been commissioned to build since the war."

"Yes, I'm sure you would be," said Iain with a smile.

Out on the street, Cameron whistled softly and shook his head. "That will be a magnificent collection," he murmured, "but damn expensive!" Then, he thought, *I wonder how father plans to finesse mother on this one?* Since boyhood, he knew his dear parents had a little game all their own. It was a quid pro quo, for which only they knew the rules by which they played. However, it usually became evident that if one of mother's relatives came to stay for a lengthy period, a fine new Labrador or Springer puppy would suddenly find its way into the kennel. Conversely, his mother had donned a beautiful pair of emerald earrings within a week of the time father took delivery of an exquisite matched pair of Purdey Best guns. Given Iain's estimate of the cost of the General's order now in production, he wondered what his mother would claim in return.

Iain chuckled as he groped for the car keys and thought, *It's all so funny! In many ways, they are sort of penurious, and it usually a relatively long time between acquisitions. However, when the fever strikes, then scheming begins.* Fortunately, all the toys that his father so loved took a long time to make. Mother seemed to have no trouble finding an item of equal or greater worth that she desired within seventy-two hours. Consequently, it was and probably always would be "tit for tat" in the Cameron home.

Although it had been several years since Iain had visited the fabled shooting school of Holland and Holland, he recalled the route. Despite the early build-up of traffic, he arrived early.

His mentor to be shook hands firmly and said, "Please call me Boyd, or BW, and I'll call you Iain. I was a gunnery instructor for the RAF all during the war, and I came to abhor military titles, so please bear with me." Cameron found the concept consoling and readily agreed. "Let's start with some basics, Iain. I understand from Bill Burton down at the shop that you were a very fine right-handed shooter, but, thanks to the Chinese souvenir, you wish to go to left-handed shooting."

Boyd continued. "In the past, you were obviously able to develop a sight picture. That is to say, when the barrels were properly aligned and sufficiently in front of the target, you knew automatically it was time to pull the trigger. I am, of course, referring to incoming birds or targets. The sight picture and need for lead, or being out in front of what you are shooting at, would be different for going away or crossing targets. That is all programmed into your brain, and that organ doesn't give a damn if the signals it receives comes from both eyes or only one! Therefore, you already have 60 percent of the routine mastered. The remaining 40 percent will be tougher because your brain became used to telling the left hand to swing the gun, and your right hand to pull the trigger. Your right shoulder and the right side of your face learned to know when the stock was in position and felt right. So the sight picture is exactly the same. All that is necessary to do is convince your two sides that they can switch roles and be just as happy."

BW suggested, "Let's go over to the standard trap range and get started. Holding a gun and pulling a trigger far outweighs words."

For this part of the training, Iain stood on a portion of a crescent-shaped walkway, which was exactly sixteen yards behind a concrete bunker. Five positions, equidistant apart, were designated on the walkway. Shooters generally fired five rounds at clay targets, one person at a time from each position. Always, the targets flew out and away from the shooter. Some came out as straight-aways, and others angled to the right or left.

A mechanical device with an arm and strong spring threw the targets at speeds up to sixty miles per hour, and they were released when the shooter called, "Pull!"

Walker slipped a double-barrel twelve-gauge shotgun out from a soft leather case and handed it to Iain. "Have you ever shot a TRY gun, Iain?"

"No, Boyd, I haven't," Iain replied, as he noted that the gun's barrels and receiver were all H & H and superb, but the stock was a monstrosity. It was made up of many sections of well-finished but straight-grained dark walnut. All were held together by a number of screws, which could be adjusted to change the dimensions in a multitude of ways.

Like his grandfather and father, Iain had a special love for the exquisite walnuts from the arbors of England and Bastogne in France, the mountainous regions of Turkey, and, of course, Circassia. How grand it was to gaze on this ligneous matter so splendidly shaped and finished, and also see the exquisite polymorphic veins of blacks, browns, golden tans, and variegated antique ivories, which only nature had the artistry and time to blend in such beauty and perfection.

Opening the action of the gun, Walker checked the dual chambers to be sure they were unloaded. Then the gun was passed to Iain along with the remark, "It's empty. I assume you noted and agree?"

"I do," he responded.

"Very well," said the instructor. "Close it, mount it to your left shoulder, and point it at exactly the bridge of my nose. I know that's against the old rule that you don't point a gun, even an empty one, at anything you don't intend to shoot. However, it's the only way we have ever devised to start tuning the gun to the man."

Iain complied with directions, and some adjustments were made. Then the exercise was repeated three times more.

Having completed his routine, Walker exclaimed, "Let's shoot! Start on position 3 in the center and blast away."

Iain's fist shot was a miss, while the second target was chipped, however, the third shot was a more solid hit. More adjustments were made and more shots fired. His final score was seventeen out of twenty-five. "That was pathetic," said a downtrodden Iain.

"It wasn't fantastic, but it sure as hell wasn't pathetic," snapped BW. "It was a pretty damn good first step on a trek of unknown length at this point. If you had broken all twenty-five, you wouldn't need my help, and I might as well give you a loaded gun to point at my nose."

The next round of twenty-five produced a score of twenty-one. Student and instructor were both pleased. "We'll stop for now Iain," BW said. "Your left shoulder was never introduced to recoil before, while the right side was used to the pounding. We'll go at it again tomorrow. When we get to twenty-three out of twenty-five, we'll switch to incoming targets from the high tower. I think you'll get your share of grouse on the Glorious 12th!" Both looked forward to the following day, as they had a pleasant departure.

While Iain was engaged in perfecting his shooting, Sister Campbell embarked on her own quest. Claire finished her shift at three P.M. but chose to relinquish an extra one-half hour to detail the condition of her patients to the group taking over. This was all part of the nurse's report, which was both a cherished and necessary routine to ensure proper patient care. Then Claire changed rapidly from her uniform into her very best day dress and made straight off to Marie's Ladies Fashions and Accessories on Princess Street. She browsed about, though she saw not a single item that in anyone's wildest imagination might be construed as something in which to shoot, unless you were planning the murder of an unfaithful lover.

With the usual salutary greeting, a smiling clerk approached her. "May I assist you?"

Claire decided that if she were about to appear as a country bumpkin, then why not ask the obvious question? "Do you have anything appropriate for attending a grouse-shooting event?" were the words which emerged from her sweetly smiling face.

Then from the clerk came the response: "For day or evening?"

Claire was puzzled. She reflected on "day or evening." How could you shoot anything in the dark? However, she was not bewildered long, for an intellectual sun quickly arose and cast the clerk's question in light. Of course, Iain had mentioned dinner parties, and that was obviously to what the clerk was alluding. "Oh! I'm very well set for evening," lied Claire, with mannerisms that added credence to her deviation from the truth. "I just can't seem to find a thing for the day, and I'm not sure what to do." A sigh and slightly downcast look were added for emphasis, stimulating the clerk to call on every compassionate instinct at her disposal.

"Well, we have nothing here that would suffice for a day on the moors, my dear. However, I did hear several of our customers speak of going to Dicksons." The last word spoken seemed to transform the clerk's face. Suddenly, she appeared like a person who, having just found a purse filled with gold, came and offered to share it with you.

"Dicksons," repeated Claire.

"Yes. It's at 21 Fredrick Street, just a few blocks from here." Then the saleslady raised her arm and pointed poignantly to the southeast, as Queen Isabella may have done when she sent Columbus off to find the route to India.

"Thank you so very much," said Claire. "You have been such a help to me."

"My pleasure," was the reply.

Still thirty minutes were left before the shops were slated to close, so Claire proceeded quickly and soon found her way to the desired destination. Upon entry, she felt very ill at ease, amid all the guns and sporting paraphernalia She imagined herself to be in a circumstance tantamount to a man in a lingerie shop trying to buy foundation garments. At last, she spied a mannequin dressed in what surely must be ladies' shooting attire. Claire approached the display with alacrity, much like a shipwreck victim swimming to a piece of floating wreckage. Actually, she found the ensemble more attractive than she had imagined. Made of a splendid tweed, it was of loden color, which would compliment her. True, it seemed a bit Victorian, but then these events were supposed to be reminiscent of that era. There was no doubt that it was tailored to best display the feminine form.

Moving her eyes from side to side, Claire tried to detect the presence of a clerk, or other customer, in the extremes of her peripheral vision. No one was detected, so she reached unobtrusively toward the price tag dangling from a sleeve. Her hand was only inches away when a deep baritone voice spoke out, "May I be of help, miss? You must be getting ready for the Glorious 12th."

"Oh! Ah, yes I am," she said softly.

"Well I daresay that would be most attractive, miss. If you should like to try one on, I can certainly get Mrs. Bell, our seamstress, to assist you!"

After glancing at her watch, Claire replied. "I just love it, but I am running late. Perhaps tomorrow."

"Splendid, miss," said the clerk affably

As Claire was leaving Dicksons, a feminine voice, polished in tone, modulated by self-assurance, and quite upper class in diction rang out. "Oh! Mr. Scoresley, I'm in desperate need of something new for this season! I couldn't be seen dead in last year's things. In fact, I just gave them all away to the Salvation Army Thrift Shop. Now, I can look Robert straight in the eye, and say that I just had to get new things, Robert dear. I simply didn't have a thing to wear." A stilted and somewhat throaty laugh followed, which Scoresley naturally felt inclined to acknowledge with a beaming smile.

"I'm sure we can please you as always, Mrs. Claredge. We will lay out a selection of our finest things, then call on Mrs. Bell to assist you." Pleased that the salesman was now casting his lure at a bigger fish, Claire used this opportunity to exit gracefully. Oh yes, she was able to quickly snatch the sales tag, and make out the price of £60, sixteen shillings. "Never on my salary," she concluded.

Claire's foray into Dicksons had not dampened the spirit of her shopping spree. Instead, she exited the shop excited and somewhat effervescent. "I will go to the thrift shop," she murmured. "Mrs. What's-her-name married to Robert Who-so-ever may be a snob, but she's a size eight snob, I'll bet! I can't imagine there will be a long queue of thrift shop habitués all waiting to buy a shooting outfit, size eight. I might just be lucky!" Then Claire glanced at her watch and decided it was too late to find the Salvation Army Thrift Store. Besides, she hadn't the foggiest notion where it was located, apart from the fact that it wouldn't be on Princess Street or any street nearby. Claire decided she would find the address tomorrow and seek her treasure that afternoon.

On the next day, Claire arrived at the Thrift Store near four o'clock, wearing what she had decided best fit the image for the occasion. As she stepped inside, an elderly lady, obviously an employee or volunteer worker, approached her. "Good afternoon, young lady. Is there anything special you wish to find, or are you just looking about?"

Now Claire was fully aware of the fact that she was really a bit vain. Consequently, given her pride and the nature of the store, she had conceived that a certain degree of silly subterfuge was desirable. "Yes, I hope you can help! You see I'm in a play, and I need a costume like you might wear to go hunting," she said with a disarming smile. "Naturally, I don't wish to pay a lot for something I'll never use again."

"I'm afraid I can't help you, dearie," the older woman replied with a little dismay. "However, I'll ask Margaret. She is more aware of some of the donations that might have just arrived."

Claire's effervescent bubbles began to burst, a few scattered ones at first, then they came in a flurry! Just as she thought the final one would pop, the inventory expert arrived, and Margaret's face became greatly animated, as though she thought she was about to unload the largest white elephant in the land. Claire was whisked to the corner of the store, and there under a sign labeled "To be sorted and priced," was just what she had hoped she would find.

Certainly, the garment was pristine. Surely, Robert's wife could never have worn it through the bracken. Indeed, it looked as though she had never sat down in it. "It will be nine shillings if you would like it, miss," stipulated Margaret, who had suddenly taken on the demeanor of an Arab rug merchant.

"Well, that's a lot," replied her pleased customer, "but I really need it for act one." Then, Claire spied a rack of what appeared to be quite beautiful evening ensembles. She decided to enlarge her charade, and suddenly blurted out, "I nearly forgot the third act! Do you have anything one might wear to a dinner party?"

Shortly after, a very euphoric young woman left the smiling clerks at the counter. She was loaded down with enough dresses and accessories for a ten-act play, plus her greatest trophy the shooting ensemble! As she was leaving, Claire felt a pang of conscience because her pride had led her to a series of white lies, but they were still lies. *I am sort of an actress,* she thought, *and this may be a role that I'll play just once. I hope God will understand.*

Chapter Thirty

❈ ❈ ❈

When Iain arrived every afternoon for the next seven working days, Boyd Walker was waiting. His pupil was constantly breaking twenty-three or more out of each round of twenty-five targets when he was shooting over a standard trap-shooting layout. Now, Walker decided it was time to advance to firing at high-flying incoming targets. These were launched from a high, unmanned steel tower approximately forty-five yards in front of the shooter. The clay pigeons, as they were sometimes called, sailed approximately twenty-five to thirty yards above the marksman's head, and their angles of approach were variable. Direction and velocity of the wind, if any, could also produce some degree of modification in the target's behavior. This often added substantially to the difficulty of breaking them.

After Iain's very poor showing on the initial two rounds of twenty-five, BW had made a few more adjustments in the TRY gun. "I am pretty well convinced that I can't improve further on perfection," he said after tightening the last screw. "The only thing left is to work on the nut at the butt end of the stock."

Iain tumbled to the innuendo immediately, and said, "I think the nut is so rusted it's beyond turning."

Walker smiled, then replied, "I love a perceptive pupil, Iain, and I have a specially formulated penetrating oil in my bag of tricks, just for you nuts that are tough to turn. Let's try another round," the instructor said, while handing his pupil a fresh box of twelve-gauge cartridges.

After Iain missed two targets in a row, forceful words came forth from Walker. "Damn it, Iain, you have to get over being afraid to miss, because that is precisely what you are causing yourself to do. Look, you're bringing your gun up with the target way too far out. Then, you follow it and follow it. By the time you pull the trigger, you have already stopped your swing and started raising your head. Watch this!" BW picked up his own shotgun, fed a cartridge in each chamber, and closed the action. When a target emerged from the tower, he called out, "Here it comes; watch it!" Instead of mounting the gun, which Iain had done, Walker held it at the ready, as the clay bird sped toward him. At the last second, he mounted the weapon and swung the barrels out in front of the flying disk, all in one fluid motion, then he fired. The target disintegrated, apart from one small piece about the size of an orange segment. Then, he fired again, and it also dissolved. He called for a second target and repeated the same masterful maneuver. This time, the target was reduced to a puff of smoke.

"All right, your turn," Walker said to Iain, and Cameron called, "Pull!" This time he waited longer than previously, but not long enough. "That's better, Iain, but you're still following the target too long. Just hang on like you're trying desperately not to pee in your pants, but you can't find a loo." Being a friendly, relaxing form of advice, this brought out good results in the pupil.

When the session ended, Cameron was consistently in the twenties. Before parting, BW gave him a pat on the shoulder and said, "Tomorrow, we go head-to-head, or mano-a-mano, if you're into the bullfight business. I think it's important that we introduce some competition into it. That's frequently a real edge honer."

After leaving his instructor and on the way back to the BOQ, Iain was musing about the prospect of trying to compete against Boyd Walker, for the man was legendary. Many were aware of how it all began. When he was a boy, BW had lived on a tiny farm situated quite close to the boundary of the shooting school. Resonant sounds of the erupting shotguns had always intrigued him. At age twelve, his curiosity rose to a fever pitch, leading him to sneak beneath the fence and hide in a wooded grove. From his vantage point, Boyd was able to meld the sight of breaking targets to the sounds he cherished. Fortunately, it happened that he came under the scrutinizing eye of a temporarily unoccupied instructor, who was a kindly man. Despite the disparity in age between him and the trespassing urchin, the young lad was recognized as a kindred soul. Young Walker was offered a position as a trap boy, which he gladly accepted.

Although Boyd was not really sure what being a trap boy would entail, he quickly discovered it meant huddling within the confines of a concrete bunker and trying gingerly to place clay targets on the blade of a fearsome metal arm, which was enslaved to a gigantic coil spring. Though he was intimidated at first, it gradually became great fun, and he never lost any of his fingers, which at first he had feared might happen. In a couple of years, he was big and strong enough to cock the machine by means of a long lever. This was connected to the trap or catapult by means of a lengthy rod that ran from the bunker to a position behind the shooters. At last, out in the open, he came to the attention of many of the marksmen. One very kind, elderly gentleman bestowed on young Boyd the greatest gift of his life: a London Best gun made by Charles Lang.

The stock of this gun had been shortened to fit the gentleman's grandson, to whom it was given as a gift. However, the young man was quite disdainful of shooting and returned it, to the grandfather's sorrow. His grandson was a dashing type and did develop a fondness for fast cars and finally flying planes. As a result, he qualified for the RAF. On his first sortie, he missed a Messerschmidt 109; however, the Luftwaffe pilot was more proficient. His rounds strafed the Spitfire's petrol tank, and the grandson was incinerated in his cockpit. The grandfather forever ruefully wondered if the London Best gun would have made a difference. Certainly, the Lang did make a difference in BW's life. When he joined the service, he soon became the most celebrated instructor for the RAF School of Aerial Gunnery.

Boyd Walker dazzled students by his ability to break hundreds of targets in a row, shooting from the hip. After World War II, he won all of the coveted awards in trap, skeet, International or Olympian trap, plus having the reputation as the man to beat at all the live pigeon shoots on the Continent.

Yes it would be something to compete against BW. Again, Iain recalled his underdog analogy, Obviously, there was no way that he could beat the fabled instructor at this stage in his life. "But, bloody hell, I can stand on all fours at least and growl at him once in a while."

Competition between Iain and BW was a one-sided though spirited event. The two decided they would shoot 200 targets each. BW smashed 98 out of 100, as compared to Iain's 86 targets. Instructor Walker had a superlative 99 out of the second 100, and Cameron posted a very credible 91. BW shook hands with his protégé and said, "You did very well Iain. The nut on the end of the stock is not a problem any longer."

"Thank you so much for all you've shown me, BW. I'm truly in your debt."

"As a matter of fact, in a couple of weeks you may truly be in my debt," said Walker with a wink of his dominant shooting eye. "Your father has invited me to participate in your shoot. We'll let the loaders and dog handlers keep track, and I'll spot you ten birds. Winner gets a fine fifth of MacCallum single-malt from the looser."

"It's a bet!" said Iain with a smile. Then, he added, "I don't suppose the loser will be offered a drink or two?"

"Well a generous man like myself might be willing to sacrifice a dram or so, to let the loser assuage his grief," replied BW. Their exchange brought a chuckle from both, then BW added, "Incidentally, Iain, have your father send us your pair of Hollands. I've got all your new dimensions now. We need to bend the stocks, and there's precious little time left before the 12th." They both departed on that note.

Days seemed to race by, and Iain thought, *Time is strange. While each hour is comprised of an unchanging number of seconds, urgency seems to invariably speed their passage.* At first, preparations for the Glorious 12th were leisurely, but by the 10th of August, they were at a sprint pace. Holland and Holland had refurbished their twin beauties, bent the stocks perfectly, and delivered them to Captain Cameron. The Malay Manual was complete and considered excellent in quality of content. Major Wilson was very pleased, so he was a pushover when Cameron's request for leave was made. Iain was truly ready, apart from topping off the Austin Healey's petrol tank. However, his telephone calls to Claire far exceeded the number he had originally rationed, and a persistent eavesdropper would have noted the telephonic exchanges were much more freely punctuated with terms of endearment, as well as stipulations regarding the type of desideratum from which they suffered. Finally, there was only forty-eight hours to go.

Meanwhile, due to a common human frailty to put the worst thing off until last, Claire fell victim to it once again. All of her secondhand finery had been folded and carefully placed in valises of good quality, mostly borrowed. Also, she had endured the chiding of her compatriots with good humor. None of them had ever gone anywhere necessitating more than a single suitcase, so it came quite naturally for them to dream up little quips like, "Bombay is quite far off, Claire. Do you really think you are taking enough things?" She always had a pert response. However, had that not been the case, she would still be far better off to ignore the jests than mash her dinner dresses in a single carrier.

Surely, the worst thing Claire had put off was absolutely the most important, for she had put in no request for time off! What would happen if permission was unattainable? Given the fact that she had been granted humanitarian leave during her mother's illness, and also had time off to attend the awards ceremony for Iain, she was really pushing the limit. Various supervisors at ever higher levels of the echelon would do no more than suggest that Sister Campbell try one rung higher up. At last, she reached the pinnacle, Miss Phoebe Farqharson, Supervisor of Nursing Personnel. She was best known as Farkie by all she intimidated, which for all intents and purposes was everyone, doctors included. Claire's intention was to fight danger from a distance, so a carefully penned request was submitted. Her vain hope was that when a tiger blocked the path that she must take, it would somehow be satisfied with being tossed a small morsel of meat, rather than relying on the traveler's remains for sustenance!

Claire realized that this tiger was by no means sated, for she received a summons to appear in person when her shift ended. Consequently, at day's end, she approached the tiger's lair with a degree of tribulation. She felt it must exceed that of Mary, Queen of Scots, on confronting Elizabeth's black-hooded executioner, standing ax in hand beside a blood-stained block.

At Claire's approach, Miss Farqharson set her pen aside, and glowered above the upper ring of her spectacles. "Well, Sister Campbell, I see you have the audacity to request additional leave time." Then, given her penchant for the pernicious, the supervisor continued. "I should like to call your attention to the fact that you are employed at a hospital, rather than being some free spirit at a holiday resort." Smugly, the supervisor smiled, as she anticipated the imminent capitulation of the petitioner. Instead, she found herself cast in the role of the Dauphin as he looked into the eyes of Joan of Arc about to outline her plan to lift the siege of Orléans.

Claire's countenance must have sparked some ray of unrequited love, deeply hidden in the older woman's past. Suddenly, Farkie turned from flint to frosting, and she blurted out, "You are a fine sister, Miss Campbell, and it would be heartless not to make an exception for a special occasion."

Astonished, Claire replied, "I'm so deeply appreciative, Miss Farqharson," in unison with the warmest smile.

"Have a nice time, my dear," came the reply.

Claire left, wondering why everyone so feared Miss Farqharson, while Farkie was left to ponder her own change in demeanor. "Maybe, it was remembering Charlie," her only fiancée, whose Lancaster bomber never made it back from Bremerhaven.

On the appointed big day, Captain Cameron pulled into the parking lot close by the Sister's Residence. Fortunately, his baggage consisted of only a heavy luggage case, wherein resided the Hollands and his toilet articles. All else was already at his parents' home. At first, he ignored the many faces peering out from nearby windows. However, his jubilant mood finally led him to wave and smile. Intervening glass hid the blushes of the recipients and fully muffled the girlish giggles. Then, with judicious arrangement, utilizing all available space in the tiny rear seat, boot, and luggage rack, the containers filled with Claire's wardrobe were safely and snugly packed. They roared off with a wave and a toot of the horn. Iain thought, *It's like beginning a honeymoon,* then arose four more words: *I wish it were!*

Just north of the Firth of Forth Bridge, Claire's cheek found Iain's shoulder. Though neither commented, both felt how perfectly it fit there, and how wonderful it felt. After many tribulations, all their plans had finally worked out, and they were on their way to the Glorious 12th. Fortunately, the old Austin Healey purported itself well, and before long, it was idling pleasantly at Capercaille's gatehouse. Immediately, a joyous reunion took place between Captain Cameron and his former Sergeant Major Sandy MacPhee, now retired from the Scots Guards but no less stalwart in monitoring the entry gate. Claire was introduced to Sandy and his wife, Molly. Then, when the young couple took their leave, the older pair stood in the roadway waving. However, Molly's free elbow found its way to her spouse's ribs, and he noted her head was moving in an affirmative nod. Thirty years of decoding his wife's facial expressions made him aware of what she was signifying. "I like her, and I believe she's the one for him!"

When the entryway of the manor house was achieved, the household staff came quickly in response. Iain was beloved, and their admiration had always been reciprocated. Obviously, that facility reserved for the young laird was passing freely to his lady. Mother, father, Annie, and of course Aunt Jane were soon in attendance. All the emotions and embraces that make up loving reunions were much in evidence. Soon, Claire was whisked away under the feminine pretense that after such an arduous and possibly harrowing journey, freshening up and a nice warm bath were of absolute necessity. On the masculine side, hearty handshakes and a wee bitty dram or two of single malt were all that was required.

Later, at dinner time, all were thoroughly refreshed in one way or another, and they eagerly sought their places at the magnificently appointed dining room table. A quick survey of the fare indicated they would not be famished for long, and gluttony would not be easily avoided. All the ladies appeared radiant in their dinner dresses, especially Claire, who was wearing a beautiful blue frock. In their own way, the gentlemen were no less resplendent. Many were vested in formal Highland dress; the remainder in tuxedos or formal military attire. Guests included Boyd Walker along with his wife, plus Geordie MacCallum's parents, General and Mrs. MacCallum. In addition, other invited guests were a French general, a noted American sportsman, and two other high-ranking British Officers all with their spouses. Furthermore, places at table were also found for friends of yesteryear, as Mary Cameron would never neglect those widows who had always cherished this gala event when their husbands, now deceased, had come to shoot.

Dinner was magnificent, as all had come to expect, though easily equaled by the conversation, toasts, and boasts plus friendly jibes and jokes. The hours fled too swiftly, and despite reluctance on the part of all, time for sleep arrived. Breakfast would be early and eaten eagerly, for shooting would commence exactly at eight A.M. However, Claire and Iain did manage to extend their curfew sufficiently for goodnight kisses, warm embraces, and words of love.

At seven the next morning, a small motor pool had assembled in the driveway ready to accept the guns and their gear, plus those of the ladies who chose to watch. In order to avoid confusion, Iain had earlier explained to Claire that the term "gun" had a dual meaning, applying to either a participating shooter or his firearm. In her tweed attire, Claire was quite smashing! Though she wouldn't be shooting, the ladies usually dressed as though they might be shooters. Iain hurried over to her and quickly handed her some type of strange device. "Grab this, Claire, you'll need it!" About thirty inches long, it appeared to consist of a rounded length of hardwood with a ferrule and pointed projection on one end. On the opposing end, there was what seemed to be a pair of stirrups, which were hinged and attached to the wood. Unattached portions of the stirrups were joined by a broad leather band. *Why would I need this?* Claire thought. She tried vainly to get an answer from Iain, but he was totally engrossed in getting everyone seated in a Rover.

On his next pass by, she called out, "Iain," and his attention was caught, so he came to her. "What is this thing?"

He grinned and replied "It's a shooting stick," and was off again.

Claire became alarmed, and she held the device very gingerly, thinking it might have some sort of a hidden trigger and should she touch it inadvertently, it could go off. On his next pass, she stepped in front of him and said with some exasperation "Is this shooting stick loaded?"

This time, he winked and said, "It will be when you sit on it." Then, again, he was gone.

Claire thought perhaps she should lay it down and step away. However, she feared that someone could kick it while passing by, and it might discharge with fatal results. Keeping what she thought might be the barrel pointing skyward, Claire stood for some time.

At last, Iain approached her and took her arm, saying, "Ride in front with me, Claire. We're ready to go at last!" He was surprised when she stiffened, looked at him defiantly, and said, "I am not going anywhere until you take this gun and put it someplace safe."

For a few seconds, he looked at her incredulously before her dilemma dawned on him. A broad smile blossomed on his face, and Iain said repentantly, "I'm sorry, Claire dear. I did say shooting stick, didn't I? And you assumed it could be a gun."

"You also said it would be loaded when I sat on it," she replied somewhat spitefully.

"This is what I meant," were his next words. While trying to look contrite, Iain was doing his best to hold in the laughter building inside himself. "You see, you plant this pointed end in the ground at an angle. Then, you open up the other end, and it forms a little seat. It really is a big help when you tire of standing."

"Now, I can appreciate what you meant when you said it would be loaded when I sat on it." Her words were emitted from a frowning face.

"I'm truly sorry, Claire," This time his words carried much more conviction.

"I'm sure you are," she said with a huff. Then, at last, she got in the Rover.

On the way to the area where the first drive would occur, all the animated conversation was between Iain and the passengers, as Claire was silent. Then, when he turned into the area where the dogs and handlers were assembled, he happened to note the telltale fasciculations arising from Claire's anterior abdominal wall, before being transferred, and becoming manifest in the front of her jacket. Such movements could be spawned by a person starting to cry or attempting to suppress a giggle. Slightly turning, Iain expected to see tears, but none were there. Instead, the giggle could be held in no longer, so out it came along with a follow-up smile directed only to him.

Soon the small convoy reached the area designated for the first drive. At this juncture, various elements partaking in the exercise began a rapid deployment. The beaters, under the careful supervision of assistant gamekeepers, were sent by a back road to the far end of a swale approximately three-fourths of a mile away. Once there, a line of advance would be formed with each beater about twenty yards apart. When signaled, they would slowly move forward toward the line of shooters. So doing, they would maintain a perfect alignment. This exact formation was ensured by having an assistant gamekeeper in the center, plus one on either flank. Also, of extreme importance from the safety standpoint was that their advance be halted before they came within range of the pellets fired by the shotguns.

Making up eight shooting positions or berths, the shooters were also spread out in a straight line. These in effect provided a reasonable degree of cover and camouflage for the gun and his loaders. On a good drive, literally thousands of grouse might be flushed and, as a result, shooting could be very fast and furious. For this reason, the matched pair of guns came into prominence since it was not possible to load a single gun as swiftly as desired. In addition, with constant firing, the gun would readily become too hot to handle. This explains the rationale behind having a loader.

When the shooter had discharged both cartridges in the double-barrel shotgun, he passed it quickly to the loader and exchanged it for the other gun, which the loader had just reloaded. The exchange was strictly a matter of synchrony and harmony between shooter and loader. When they worked very well as a team, it was possible to do more shooting. In addition, the treasured shotguns would escape dents, dings, and scratches. As far as the gun owners were concerned, the exchange was quite similar to the rapid handling off and receiving a pair of Ming vases. Collision was to be avoided at all costs; consequently, it was a formidable exercise in concentration and coordination. While it didn't result in death or disability, as might be the case with two participants in a high-wire trapeze act, it still could be distracting, devastating, and damned expensive, if one were to end up with a very deep dent in a £300 piece of 500-year-old walnut tree! To play the adult version of patty-cake in the best way possible, many shooter's brought their own loaders with them. Unfortunately, Iain was at a great disadvantage.

Sandy MacPhee had volunteered to load for him, but they had no opportunity to practice as a team. In addition, Iain was now left-handed, therefore, the gun exchange would be all the more awkward. Consequently, it seemed most pragmatic to improvise. Thus, it was decided Sandy would act as stuffer, rather than a loader. This would mean that after expending the two rounds in his gun, Iain would open the action, which would cause the empty cartridges to be ejected. As soon as this occurred, Sandy would stuff two fresh rounds in the now empty chambers. After the tenth round was fired, they would switch guns. This should make it possible to shoot nearly as fast as the others, with less risk of collision, plus avoidance of overheating.

To the rear of the shooting line stood the dog handlers with their excited charges. The retrieving corps was made up primarily of Labradors. They were beautiful dogs with glistening coats of black, chocolate, and yellow, although those of ebony hue predominated. A goodly number of dappled Brittany and Springer spaniels were also in evidence, as were the rare Golden or Chesapeake retrievers. Observing the dogs was of great importance to Iain, as he loved just to gaze at them. Especially, he was fascinated by their ability to mark a downed bird, locate it in the dense heather, and bring it back, holding it tenderly in their mouths. Some dogs were quite capable of marking and locating a wounded bird that had finally come down a half- mile away. No good sportsman ever wanted a wounded bird to suffer unduly or any dead bird to remain unfound and thereby wasted.

Several other things didn't escape Iain's scrutiny. Despite the fact these dogs were brought by many owners, it was very rare that a dogfight ever occurred. In fact, all the canines could be counted on to honor another dog's retrieval. *If people would act as well, it would be a far nicer world*, he often thought. Then, Iain's attention was drawn to a pair of newly arrived dogs who were the pride and joy of the French general his father had invited to participate. Iain was aware that dogs of this breed had at one time been known as proficient retrievers. However, seeing them now, surrounded by Labradors and spaniels, made them seem totally incongruous. At the same time, they came across as appearing haughty, if not openly arrogant.

Just then, Iain's father passed by and said softly to his son, "The white one, the bitch, is named Marie Antoinette, and the black one is a male named Robespierre. As you can tell, General LeClaire has a sense of history and humor. I hope he can control them, or our usually well-behaved retrievers may revert to their primitive state, and we'll have the canine equivalent of the Battle of Crecy. Well, so far so good!" Neither Marie Antoinette or Robespierre gave the appearance of wishing to dirty their paws mixing with the hoi polloi. They remained disdainful and aloof.

Meanwhile, Iain's mother took Claire in hand and steered her to a spot of relatively open ground behind the shooting stations and well as to the rear of dogs and handlers. Further back stood the ghillies with ponies bearing paniers, plus several horse-drawn wagons. "This spot will put you right behind Iain, Claire. He has drawn Number Six for the first drive."

"Number Six," replied Claire, with her face bearing a questioning expression.

"I should have explained." said Mrs. Cameron. "All the guns—that's what the shooters are called, draw a number from one to eight, if there are eight guns, as is the case today. On the first drive, you go to that position. Then, you move to a higher number on each subsequent drive. After you reach the highest one, you start over with number one. The idea is that in any given drive, there may be more birds fly over one location than another, so that person will get more shooting. Therefore, it's simply an attempt to even out the odds and try to provide the same opportunities for all."

"I see," said Claire. "I suppose they have been working this out for a long time, and it is nice to come up with a more fair system."

"I will be just over there with Mrs. Randold, Claire. Her husband passed away several years ago. The Colonel was a splendid shot. Effie loves to come and watch. I guess it brings back some of those happy times they shared. She had a mild stroke about six months ago, and I feel obligated to keep an eye on her."

"Well, that's very sweet of you Mrs. Cameron," said the younger woman.

"She's a splendid lady, and I'm pleased to do it." Mary Cameron replied. "At any rate," she continued, "Effie will stay through lunch. Then, I'll take her back to the house for a nap. If you need anything or have any questions, I'll be right over there, my dear."

This is a good spot, thought Claire. She could see Iain's head and back projecting above the wall of his shooting butt. Way off in the distance stood a line of people holding flags. Suddenly, there was a single blast of a hunting horn, which slightly startled her. Claire observed Mr. Finlay, Chief Game Keeper, was waving his walking stick high above his head. Simultaneously, the distant line started moving toward them, and all the white flags were waving and snapping in unison. Soon, little black specks could be seen in the sky above the beaters' heads. They appeared to fly on for a hundred yards or so, then land again.

Though Claire had never attended such an event before, nor had she ever owned a dog, it was easy for her to appreciate their excitement. Heads were raised with their eyes seeking all the degrees of angle from 0 to 180 degrees, and there wasn't a still tail to be seen. Even the bobbed, stubbed tails of the spaniels were twitching, while the other breeds were swinging with abandon. Then, Claire noticed the two large standard poodles that she had seen before. When they had previously come to her attention, she had wondered why anyone would bring a poodle to a bird shoot. Before, they had looked totally bored, but now they seemed electrified.

Before long, the black specks on the horizon began to grow in size and numbers, as birds took to flight in advance of the approaching line of beaters. With anticipation, the shooters stood poised and alert with their loaders crouched beside them. Suddenly, two shots rang out on the far left, and a single bird from the brace flying high above cartwheeled earthward. Then, followed a short pause before the barrage began. Dozens of grouse were coming hard and fast every moment, and the shooting was markedly increased in tempo. Claire saw Iain miss a single with both shots. Then he downed a pair in quick succession.

Quickly, she learned that as a spectator sport, this was far different than sitting in the grandstand watching at a distance from the soccer pitch. Birds, flying thirty to forty yards up and going forty miles an hour, are likely to come crashing down well behind the row of guns, even when hard hit. Thus, Claire found herself in the center of the drop zone and soon appreciated that a careful watch for falling birds was a necessary measure of self-defense. Surely, a one-to two-pound grouse coming down from forty yards up could surely ruin one's hairdo, or possibly their entire day!

Soon, another potential hazard was to become familiar and convince her to divide her attention between sky and land. Having just seen a grouse shot well above Iain's head, which surely appeared to be falling in her direction, she stepped aside to avoid the collision. However, her peripheral vision detected something of concern, and this sent an alarm directly to Claire's brain.

With a burnished coat, the exact same color as a chocolate bar, a very large dog had also seen the same bird falling, and he was running full tilt to retrieve it. The aerial onslaught was forgotten in a flash, as Claire jumped to avoid what surely appeared to be a charging behemoth. Unfortunately, she zigged rather than zagged, and a collision plus what seemed personal peril certainly seemed imminent. However, the alacrity of the large Labrador's reflex saved the day. He braked sharply with all four paws, slowing himself sufficiently to allow an evasive maneuver. Claire found herself standing rigid and wincing, but no impact came. As he flashed by, the dog looked at her with his soft yellow eyes and seemed to fashion a canine smile. She could almost imagine him tipping his hat, had he been wearing one! Soon, the dog returned, bearing a bird in his mouth, and he was obviously pleased with himself. This time, the Lab was trotting at a leisurely pace and, as he passed, turned his muzzle toward her, so Claire might appreciate his prize.

Now, the shooting was becoming more sporadic, and Claire felt she had won her spurs. When she looked about, it was obvious that many of the spectators had employed their shooting sticks to good advantage. "I might as well go whole hog," Claire decided. "If I can set up pulleys for patients in traction and handle surgical instruments, I can certainly use one of these."

Carefully, Claire set about trying to appear to be the polished veteran and was pulling it off quite well. The stirrups were extended laterally, thus stretching out the broad interposed leather strap, and fashioning it into a reasonable facsimile of a seat. "Simple enough," she said to herself. Then, a sideways glance showed her the pointed end of the stick should be stuck in the ground at a slight angle. Claire felt a bit smug, as she prepared to sit. Indeed, the pointed end had penetrated the sod, but it had come to rest on a large rock with a convex superior surface. Consequently, the rock remained steadfast; the shooting stick slipped, and an alarmed Claire headed earthward. The impact knocked some of the breath out of her, as well as a good measure of recently acquired self-assurance.

Iain's mother was first to the rescue. "Are you hurt, Claire? Poor dear, you must be, you're crying."

Claire raised her hand and pushed away the dislodged tweed hat that teetered on her brow, as well as an errant lock of hair, which clouded her vision. "I'm not really hurt, Mrs. Cameron. My tears are pure frustration. I'm a disaster and a laughing stock."

"You are none of these, Claire. You are a fine young lady and a good sport. Now, let me help you up and brush you off. No damage done, my dear, and that's good, as you look beautiful."

"Thank you Mrs. Cameron. That was very kind of you," replied the still distraught Claire.

"Please call me Mary," the older woman said softly. Then, she continued, saying, "First a little advice, then a story. When you plant the pointed end, be certain to push hard. Then, you can be sure that there's no nasty rock to cause the point to slip off.

"Now, the story. Many years ago, another young woman came to a shoot and was given a shooting stick on which to sit. Right in the middle of a crowd, she got it out. After looking it over, she decided the end with the strap must be placed against the ground. If she had asked or looked about, she would have known better, but she didn't. Obviously, she finally concluded that you couldn't sit on the pointed end. But you can imagine the raised eyebrows and smiles she generated before coming to the correct conclusion. That same young woman now grown older is telling you the story about herself of over twenty-eight years ago."

Claire laughed at the event described, and Iain's mother dabbed away the last tear on Claire's cheek, and said, "Pratfalls are kind of funny, too." Then they both laughed, just before hearing two sharp blasts of a hunting horn, which indicated the beaters were nearing a point where it was no longer safe to shoot. Now, the first drive was over, and there would be two more before lunch.

At last, lunch came, and it was a splendid repast in which the attendees participated with gusto. Along with two of the more stalwart ladies, Claire and Iain's mother were present. At least in a peripheral way, this was an opportunity to share in a man's domain, and the ladies enjoyed it immensely; also, the gentlemen were enthralled to have them present. After all, it was a chance for the men to show the fairer sex just how they purported themselves among their peers. In a sense, it was probably similar to the knights of old, gathered in a celebratory mood to discuss the outcome of all the jousts that had taken place in the day's lists. Now, however, the jocular banter revolved around those splendid shots observed, a string of misses even more accurately noted and recounted, and all the obvious awkward situations and foul-ups.

Most notable among the foul-ups occurred when one of the two shooters riding to the third drive happened to pick up the other's spectacles. These were housed in similar cases and lying on the car seat between them. Uproarious laughter occurred when General LeClaire described, with great humor and self-deprecation, how he became aware of the switch only after noting that he was seeing double. A single grouse appeared as two, and he kept shooting the wrong one! When the supply of humorous antidotes had been well covered, the conversation switched to the dogs.

Many outstanding feats of retrieval were described. However, the most noteworthy event was an "affaire de la coeur." General Cameron was shooting from the butt next to General LeClaire, and both were doing extremely well. As a result, the Frenchman's poodles as well as Cameron's Labradors were kept most busy. On one occasion, Ebony (one of the Labs) was far downfield on a long retrieve. On the way back, he encountered another grouse that Marie Antoinette had as yet not located. Since he was of extreme size for his breed, he had no difficulty in managing to carry the two dead birds in his capacious mouth. As Ebony passed by the searching poodle bitch, he suddenly stopped and dropped the second bird in front of her. Marie rendered, according all who could see, what seemed to be a very coquettish canine smile before picking up the bird. Then, Ebony approached, and they stood muzzle to bird-filled muzzle. The black Lab's long tail was swishing to and fro, with a happy cadence, while Marie's powder puff–tipped cauda seemed to be all a twitter.

Finally, the apparent flirtations came to the attention of Robespierre, who was starting out on another retrieve. Doing his best to mimic a fighting bull from Pamplona, the gallant poodle charged toward his Labrador rival in the most bellicose fashion imaginable in a dog of that breed. However, Robespierre slowed his charge considerably, as Ebony's towering 120-pound frame and four very large well-exposed canine teeth confronted him. Resentful of the intrusion, the Labrador was ready to wage war, having already dropped the grouse from his mouth. Robespierre did not fully succumb to intimidation, and so produced a less than frightening growl. However, there was no responding bark from Ebony, as he simply stared at the poodle with a "go ahead and try me if you feel lucky" look. Marie stood between the would-be combatants, though not in the line of fire. She looked from one to the other, quite like a zealous fan at a Wimbledon tennis match. Her last look was at Ebony. Then, she turned and went to Robespierre, wagging her curtailed pompom. Ebony looked forlorn, but he soon picked up his bird and delivered it to the keeper's hand.

Tradition remained intact, as there was to be no dog fight at a shoot on the Cameron estate. Naturally, the French version and conclusions were far different than those of the English. However, the presence of the ladies constrained any ribald comments in either language.

After gourmet fare, a glass of fine wine and dram of single-malt was enjoyed by all the participants before they embarked on the afternoon's three drives. As always, the shooters policed themselves in regard to drink. A single glass of fine wine and a single tot of whiskey gave vigor to the afternoon shooting. To deviate from the self-imposed moderation would be unthinkable. Intoxicated shooters were never tolerated.

After lunch, Iain's mother and several of the other ladies returned to the house. However, Claire was determined to see it through, treating it as a rite of passage and something that would please Iain. That was very much becoming something she wanted to do, so she remained until late afternoon when the final drive was complete. She noted the guns returning to the manor house a bit more reserved, and some quiet was observed. Fatigue was pervasive after a long and arduous day of shooting, though after a warm bath and change to evening attire, they would be rejuvenated. All would proclaim it as one of the most splendid days of shooting they had ever experienced. All looked forward to an exceptional dinner complete with toasts and boasts, tributes, expressed tribulations, and an unsurpassable demonstration of the funniest and friendliest repartee.

Soon, the Rovers were all back in the driveway, and their occupants were bound for the front door. The Camerons had never expected their guests to use another portal, even though they might be carrying a bit of residual mud on their Wellingtons. The Camerons' house was a happy home for guests, as well as family.

Iain held back and reached for Claire's hand. "We have loads of time before dinner, Claire. Do you feel up to a little walk?"

"Yes I do," she replied with a smile devoid of any sign of fatigue. He took her arm, and they headed off on a pathway.

At a discrete distance from the house, Iain pulled Claire toward him. They embraced, then followed with a long passionate kiss. When they parted, Iain held her hand and looked in Claire's eyes. "Well what do you think?" was his query.

"It was a wonderful kiss," she replied softly.

"I intended it to be, silly, but I was asking about the shoot."

"Don't ask a Campbell questions out of context, Captain Cameron. You could get surprising answers," came as her humorous retort.

"I'll remember that," he replied. "Come along with me. I want to introduce you to a very dear friend. Then we can discuss the shooting in proper context, I might add."

Still fifty yards from the kennel, though downwind from it, they became quickly aware of unrelenting boisterous barking. Iain knew this could only be interpreted as a song of joy by a very happy large dog too long separated from his beloved master but now sensing imminent reunion. Claire stood back during the full five minutes it took for Iain and Simba to express all their affection. Once he was fully reassured, Simba was content to proceed on a walk. He remained at heel, ever so close to his master's left leg, appearing like a tawny appendage.

Along their path was a small grotto with an ancient stone bench, and the vista provided was equal to any in Scotland. "Let's stop here," exclaimed Claire. "It's so beautiful!"

"Women have said that here for 200 years," replied Iain.

"I hope they weren't all going on walks with you," said Claire from behind a pixie grin.

"I'll never tell," replied Iain.

Then Claire proceeded to sit close to her escort. Suddenly, she was surprised by a tawny wedge energetically pushing them apart. Simba had his muzzle nestled on Iain's thigh, but was still able to aim one soulful eye directly at Claire. "Ah! He's a nice dog," she said, somewhat awkwardly.

"Well he generally is, but he isn't right now," said Iain. "Dogs are jealous creatures by nature, and they surely seem to have some innate sense when there are competing forces about. As a result, he instinctively realizes only two choices.

He can bite you, or he can push you away. As befits a canine gentleman, Simba has elected the latter."

Claire smiled and said sweetly, "Will he ever get over it? I kind of miss the closer proximity to you Captain Cameron."

"He will when he falls in love with you also," replied Iain tenderly.

Fortunately, as nearly all dogs are prone to do, Simba finally decided personal comfort was more important than intrusion. Therefore, he gradually let his body subside until he reached a fully recumbent position with his chin lying softly on his outstretched, comfortably crossed forepaws. Thus disposed, Simba was able to keep both large brown eyes fully focused on the interloper, who had the audacity to compete for his master's attention.

Claire was fully aware of the fact those large brown orbs bore no sign of remission. But, nonetheless, she pressed her recently acquired advantage and deftly moved to occupy the crevice between them. After Simba's initial intrusion, she wasted no time in embracing Iain and soliciting a kiss, which was followed by several more. Simba raised his head and wrinkled his nose, as only a distraught dog can do. Then, he was compelled to whine, but it was to no avail. Thus, he sought solace in somnolence.

Claire began to sense that early passion was beginning to teeter on the brink of impropriety. Therefore, she pulled slightly away, cleared her throat, and said softly, "Perhaps, we should discuss Simba, shooting, or something."

Iain smiled and replied, "Yes, that might be a good idea. Let's start with Simba."

Having heard his name, the dog cocked one eye open and flicked the ipsolateral ear. he did not rise, but rather lay quietly, suggesting that he might be content to enjoy the recounting of his adventures in Malay. Claire sat engrossed by Iain's narrative. Completely free of embellishment, the tale was transfixing. When the story was complete, Claire leaned forward and planted a kiss atop Simba's head.

"I've fallen in love with him already," she said. "Is there any hope of reciprocity do you think?"

"If a dog isn't barking, then he usually talks with his tail. Please note how he's tapping the ground, and that's a pretty good sign you're winning him over, I'd say!" The smile on Iain's face was a mirror of that on Claire's.

"Let's talk about the shooting. Did you enjoy it, Claire, or just barely endure it? Be honest now. I can readily decipher deceit," Cameron said jokingly.

"Well, sir, I adhere to the Sisters' creed. If you have cancer of the lung, I'll never tell you it's just a bad cold, so you'll be relieved. In all honesty, I am—well, I guess rather ambivalent. I do like the excitement, and I guess for want of a better word, the pageantry as well as the revelry. However, I do feel sorry for the birds, as it seems rather sad to see then shot from the sky. I guess it's the nurse in me. I would like to patch them all up and send them flying away once again, though I know that I can't. Maybe that is silly, or at least sounds that way. I hope you understand."

"I do, Claire. In fact I would have been disappointed if you had answered otherwise because it would have run counter to my image of you. As a matter of fact, I felt the same way as a boy. Back when I was nine or ten, my father took me along to observe. When he had finished shooting, not seeing me, he sought me out. I was sitting by a pile of dead birds, softly stroking their feathers with tears on my cheeks. From my father, there was no admonition to grow up and be a man. No he sat down beside me, wiped away the tears, and talked to me. He said 'I know why you are sad, Iain, but you must remember that we are all like birds flying through the sky, and sooner or later, we all plummet to earth. I suppose you might think to shoot a grouse is a harsh thing. However, Laddie, you don't see the chicks shiver and die in the wet, cold heather when the spring rains or the late snows come to the Highlands. Pellets from my gun provide a far more merciful death than that which comes from the raven, the hawk, fox, or ticks. Also, you must bear in mind that shooting provides jobs for many who would otherwise have none. Know also, my son, that the birds provide revenue for the estate, not only from some of the shooting parties that pay a fee, but also from the sale of the grouse and hares to the fine restaurants of London and other major cities.'"

Iain's father had gone on. "The land is not really good for anything but raising heather, grouse, and sheep, so they are our main crops, so to speak. Lastly, Iain, the good Lord did provide us some of His creatures for our recreation and enjoyment. Given all the stresses of life, one needs a bit of that. I'm thankful to God I'm able to do it, as I love it so, and I hope you will one day as well."

"So, Claire, here I am doing what my father loves and enjoying it fully as much as he. I hope you understand that it's a combination of pleasure, with a bit of reality thrown in, and pragmatism. I suppose that in a profession where you may have to kill other men, that hunting in as humane a way as possible doesn't seem so grievous!"

"Thank you, Iain. The story you were told by your father was a big help to someone who is still a little girl in some ways."

"Stay that way," he whispered, before they kissed again. Then, it was back to the manor house to prepare for dinner, and all the gaiety that would accompany it.

Later that evening, the dinner was as gala as anyone could imagine. Not a single soul was reluctant to participate fully in the joyous banter of toasts, boasts, and roasts, which went on unabated well into the last of the day's declining hours. General LeClaire held his audience enraptured with a very well-embellished account of the dalliance between Marie Antoinette and Ebony, culminating in the intrusion of the dauntless Robespierre. The narrative was of a quality only a Frenchman thoroughly imbued with all the art and subtitles of *joie de vivre* and *joie d'amour* could contrive. He employed ample double entendres, which the more worldly found uproariously humorous. Yet they were absolutely nonoffensive to the innocent, less worldly, or sophisticated.

Not to be outdone by his French counterpart, General Cameron gave a hilarious account of a safari with Simba. Seemingly, General Cameron became enchanted by Iain's description of the dog's uncanny ability to detect the scent of Chinese insurgents from a great distance. Thus, one day he procured a grouse wing and presented it to Simba's nose for evaluation. Immediately, his interest was aroused, and Simba ran to the door while barking to be released. On attaining his goal, the dog turned and beckoned Iain's father to follow him. Once outside, the dog proceeded to the nearest moor, making sure to maintain a pace the General could easily follow.

As soon as he reached the heather, Simba went on point, turned, and looked at the General as if to say, "I know they are here. I just didn't know you were interested in them." Of course, General Cameron didn't know what the dog's nose knew, so he approached closer out of curiosity. Ten yards from the dog, the old warrior was startled by the sudden eruption of a large covey of grouse, which took to flight. "I knew right then that I was looking at the most natural hunter the good Lord was kind enough to create. Then, the dog looked at me askance, as though he wished to say, 'What is the point in all of this? I found them, as I thought you wished me to do, but then, you did nothing.' It was, as if he expected me to shoot! Strangely, Simba didn't seem to miss the fact they weren't shooting at us. Needless to say, I ran back to the house and procured a fine Holland. Then, I raced back to the moor with as much exuberance as an old campaigner's legs would tolerate.

My companion seemed to recognize a gun for what it was, and his enthusiasm increased exponentially. After proceeding a farther distance out in the heather, again, Simba went on point. This time, I was ready and well content to poach one of my own birds well out of season. Again, Simba held steady as a stone. I reached the ten-yard mark, as before and yet another covey exploded skyward. I fired both barrels and brought a brace to bag. They were splendid shots, I might add, and certainly instant kills. Simba gave me what I interpreted to be a 'now we're getting someplace' look! Then, he ran to the sites where the birds had fallen, and I couldn't believe my eyes. I had just witnessed two unbelievable points by an untrained dog and now he was appearing to be a splendid retriever."

Savoring a generous sip of single-malt, the General paused while teasing a bit of ash from the tip of his cigar. Meanwhile, his audience sat entranced, waiting for the preconceived culmination. Finally, the senior Cameron started the epilogue. "Indeed, Simba did pick up both birds in his mouth one after the other. I have never witnessed a more tender hold on birds. He headed straight for me; head held high with obvious pride. As he came close, I reached out to take the birds. This most natural of all hunting dogs stopped, eyed me warily, then he turned and ran as fast as he could to a bracken some 100 yards away. At fifty paces, I could see clouds of feathers filling the air above his head. Thirty yards closer, it was quite apparent he had field dressed both birds and devoured those parts considered delectable. Consequently, it was obvious to me that I had 50 percent of a fabulous pointer, while the second 50 percent was a selfish hound who claimed all the birds as his own. I wouldn't have scolded Simba so harshly had he at least shared or given me one bird. My hope was that Iain would have time to train him, but I can see that is what will take up my time in the off-season. In the meantime, Sergeant Simba has been relieved of duty and confined to quarters."

Accolades for the finest story of the evening were given General Cameron, and a few roasts followed—all in good humor, for those who had a series of bad shots and misses. True marksmen were not left unscathed, as they received their measure of jibes and jests. Then, as he noted approach of the witching hour, the General finished the last draw on his cigar, and placed it in the ashtray to extinguish itself, as all fine cigars do. After reconnoitering his whiskey glass, he ascertained there was sufficient volume to mete out one last toast. This would suffice for a potable taps and bring this fine day to a closure. General Cameron arose and stood proudly in the unmistakable posture of a real soldier. Immediately, the others followed and, when all were standing, the General proposed a toast: "To God, Queen, and country!"

After the glasses were lowered, General Cameron added rather wistfully, "A second toast to a young and beautiful lady who has graced our presence these past two days. All of these undertakings were new to her. However, she has participated vigorously, followed them intently, and found a place in our hearts. If Iain has no time to train Simba, I believe it is because he seeks fairer game. With all the love and pride a father can command, may I propose a toast that he be imminently successful in the hunt!" Following were many chimes that rang forth from the softly colliding rims of crystal glasses, as all looked on Claire and Iain. Each man recalled the joy of pursuit, while each woman reflected on the thrill of being pursued.

Although Claire was taken by surprise, she was not in any way embarrassed. Instead, she was mystified and happy. Her right hand was tenderly grasped by

General LeClaire and kissed most properly. "Bonne nuit, ma cherie," he said. Then, he turned and smiled at Iain saying in French, "The lips I leave for mon capitan."

Part of Claire's nature always responded positively to praise, and certainly it had been forthcoming in Iain's father's toast. In the event that a physician, supervisor, or patient complimented her performance, she would strive to do even better and thus endeavor to perpetuate their high opinion of her. So it was at the next day's shooting. Claire noted happily that it wasn't really necessary to work at it. Before long, she began to perceive what constituted a truly great shot. Furthermore, an appreciation of the dogs and their handlers was evolving, and all the mechanics and variations of the drives. Also, the teamwork between the shooters and their loaders was falling into place. Although she remained a bit uncomfortable with the killing of the birds, she found herself secretly speculating on whether or not she could hit one. Inwardly, Claire smiled as she began to muse about having Iain teach her how. Then, suddenly, a little black cloud insinuated itself and began to block out the sunbeams, which danced on the tiny parade of her dreams. Would that future ever come to fruition?

Now, Claire's little parade was rapidly becoming peopled by historical characters. Henry VIII was astride his charger. Queens Elizabeth I and Mary were borne along on somber palanquins. Soon, Archbishop Cranmer and Cromwell were falling in line, alongside Fisher, Moore, and Dunn Scotus. They glared fiercely at one another, but fell in step. The grimmest apparition was that of her parents and Iain's, displaying the same scornful grimaces as they joined separate columns.

Despite the near trance-like state that Claire had succumbed to, her functioning instincts alerted her to the fact that a well-shot bird was plummeting from the sky and hurtling toward her head. Nimbly, she dodged the stricken bird, allowing it to miss her by inches. Just as suddenly, she adroitly moved again, thus avoiding collision with Robespierre, charging to make his retrieve. Her two spontaneous arabesques did not go unnoticed. Cheers went up from the handlers and ghillies, as well as other spectators to the tune of "Well done, Miss Campbell," or "Well done, Claire!" Surely, it was not the dance step of the Royal Ballet but quite splendid under field conditions. The old self-remonstration returned to her: *If you want to reach the top of the peak, then keep climbing, Claire. Should you slip and fall then, so be it!* Immediately, the cloud was gone.

Meanwhile, happily for Iain, it had been the grandest of days though the shooting was over. In the number of birds bagged, Iain had closed rapidly compared to his father and BW. However, he fell a few short despite Claire's cheers and exhortations. A mock ceremony was conducted, and Boyd Walker was presented with a fifth of MacCallum single-malt, as the wager demanded. Then, it was back to the manor house for yet another sumptuous feast. Adieus would wait until the morrow.

Time remained for a walk before dressing for dinner, so Claire, Iain, and Simba sallied forth. Since Simba seemed uncertain as to whom to heel beside, he decided to lead. Soon they found the bench and vista, then Claire and Iain found each others arms and lips. Simba found contentment in the soft grass, head nestled on outstretched paws, master of all he surveyed.

"Did you enjoy the day?" Iain said softly.

"Oh! Iain I really did," she replied. "I was so very proud of how well you shot. Surely, it shows you can overcome a handicap if you have the will."

"I'm even more proud of you," was his response. "You have captured everyone's hearts these past two days. Of course, I surrendered mine some time ago."

Looking into his eyes, Claire asked, "Do you really mean that, Iain?:

"Of course I do, Claire, and I hope you'll receive my surrender and grant me very honorable conditions," he said smilingly.

"You mean that I will let you keep your sword," was Claire's lilting riposte. Then, both laughed and kissed. "I wish it never had to end," said Claire. "It's been my first real visit to faerieland."

"I feel the same," Iain added. Then, he added, "Faerieland today, Never-Never Land tomorrow, for it's back to work and grim reality for us. However, we know the way to the land of enchantment, so I'm sure we can find our way back!"

"Promise?" she said.

"Promise," he replied.

They returned to the house via the kennels. Rubbing Simba's ears affectionately, Iain said, "Be a good dog until next time, Sergeant Simba. I'd invite you to dinner, but knowing your barrack manners, you would probably end up standing in General LeClaire's plate, while gobbling Madame LeClaire's Yorkshire pudding." Simba accepted the closing of the kennel's door with an expression of absolute dejection, at which he excelled. However, it changed to a canine version of a smile when Claire impeded the closure and bestowed a kiss on top of his head.

Though it did not seem possible to surpass perfection, all were so fervent in this quest that this goal was achieved at the final night's dinner. Claire and Iain would not be present after the Sunday break, when no shooting was allowed; however, the others would continue on for a few more days at Capercaille, then move on to other estates. Suddenly, the mood changed in the final moments of that day. Older attendees were reminded that they would soon be losing the two brightest stars in their tiny galaxy.

Claire was surprised and much moved by how reflective, sentimental, and even tender the old soldiers could be. She guessed it might stem from all the final good-byes said to friends known for so short a time. To look on the young, especially those in love, perhaps softened the sorrows imposed by the past and the remembrance of many repetitions of Taps played for those who would no longer march at their side; also, all the slow march steps taken beside the caissons bearing their comrades. Undoubtedly, memories were awakened of the days of desperation punctuated only by the shortest of tenures in the company of their families. Such a life left an indelible stamp! All of this was very manifest in the final toasts, also rather overwhelming when all glasses were raised, and Bobby Burns's immortal "Auld Lang Syne" was brought to life in their voices.

On the next morning, the driveway and front steps of the house were overflowing with guests and staff, as well as Iain's parents. Once again, Iain had found room in the ageless Austin Healey to store all the luggage, which included all Claire's costumes. These had proved to be perfect. Kisses and hugs were exchanged between Iain and his parents and the ladies present. Strong handshakes were accorded the gentlemen and senior staff. Claire got hugs and kisses from all the ladies and gentlemen. Then, as the gears meshed, the car was in motion.

Claire looked back and noted that all the old soldiers were saluting. She wasn't quite sure what to do. Then, suddenly, she compulsively saluted back. A roaring cheer came up from the assembly.

"What was that all about?" asked Iain, who missed the event by virtue of negotiating a curve in the driveway.

"Oh, Iain, I'm so embarrassed. Your father and the other men started saluting as we drove off and, for some reason that I can't explain, I felt compelled to salute back. I feel like Shirley Temple in *Wee Willie Winkle,*" she said with a strong note of embarrassment in her voice.

"As I recall, Wee Willie Winkle came out rather well in that movie!" he replied.

As they approached Dunkeld, Claire suddenly became aware of church spires and the fact that it was Sunday. No doubt Iain was going to attend Mass at the Catholic Church. Much like her spontaneity in returning the salute, suddenly, she blurted out, "I'm not one, don't you know?"

Iain frequently given to the quick quip, which though given in jest, was often received otherwise replied, "You're not one what? A movie star, a mole in MI-6 or—a what?"

There was silence! Immediately, he perceived the jest was inappropriate. Then, as soon as Iain pulled the car over to the curb, his first sight was that of large and glistening tears teetering on the levees of Claire's lower lids. "Oh

Claire, I've been the fool again and said something to offend you. I meant to be funny, but obviously I wasn't. Please tell me what you meant."

Claire's index finger served to blot away some of the tears from the corners of her eyes. Then, the back of her hand was used to spread out those that had negotiated her nasolacrimal ducts and had not been recalled by her sniffles, sitting perched on her upper lip.

"I'm—I'm not a Catholic," she stammered. "I'm an Anglican." And her tears and sniffles began again with greater intensity.

"Bloody hell! I know that. I was going to drop you off at St. Mark's, and pick you up after I go to Mass at St. Andrew's."

"How did you know?" she sobbed.

"Aunt Jane told me weeks ago," he said somewhat sternly.

Now Claire was crying harder than ever, distracting Iain to halt the conversation long enough to produce an unsoiled handkerchief. "Dry your eyes, Claire, or you'll miss the service," he said in a mildly commanding manner.

Claire started to dry her eyes, then suddenly replied with some ferocity. "But you'll always be a Catholic, and I'm always going to be an Anglican."

Iain took the handkerchief from her, deciding he would be more adept at the clean-up than she. Becoming more calm, Claire was starting to look presentable again. But fearing a fresh flow of tears, Iain said firmly, "Are you aware that both churches accept mixed marriages if certain conditions are met?"

"Is that a proposal?" she blurted out.

"Aye, it is," was Iain's reply. Instantaneously, the response was joyful and affirmative. The faerie tale had taken on new dimensions. Her dreams were coming true. She would have a lifetime to ensure they remained that way.

Soon, Claire was deposited at St. Mark's with a few moments to spare, while Iain arrived at St. Andrew's just in the nick of time. However, each maintained the rush of euphoria surrounding the proposal and acceptance until midway through their respective services. Beyond that, little niggling doubts began to ripple the smooth surfaces of their equanimity. Being a common human foible, it began to seem as though they were catapulted into a momentous decision without sufficient reflection and possibly lacking full consent of the will. If both had written down all of their thoughts during that time and compared them, they would have been nearly carbon copies. What would parents and pastors say and think? They both came up with duplicate answers. "Are you sure? Rather sudden isn't it? How long have you known him/her?"

For Claire, the foundation of her faerieland, so firm forty-five minutes ago, was beginning to seem unsteady, and Iain was starting to feel as though he had just ordered his platoon to advance before he had sent scouts ahead. Then, just before the Anglican and Catholic services were drawing to a close, each found themselves searching for words that would indicate they might have been hasty, yet free of any insincerity or rebuff. However, neither found a single suitable sentence.

Shortly after the services were over, the Austin-Healey pulled to the curb in front of St. Mark's, and Iain sprang out to open the door. Although it was a cloudy day, nevertheless, a happy little beam of sunshine managed at that very moment to find a small aperture in just the right cloud to allow the sun to caress Claire's cheek. Both looked deeply in each other's eyes. The doubts were gone, and they would never return.

Travel time back to Edinburgh was spent making very positive plans for their wedding under the most propitious of circumstances. Iain and Claire had every reason to feel that his parents would bestow their blessing. However, Claire opined that her mother and father might be more resistant, as they had never even met him and the difference in religion might prove a higher hurdle. At her first opportunity, she would call them to lay the groundwork. "No," said Iain, "in my regiment, the officer leads the charge. We'll go to them together, and together we'll discuss it with your mother and father."

"I like your plan, Captain," his new fiancée said sweetly.

Later, for the habitués given to rushing to the rear windows of the Sisters Quarters overlooking the parking lot at the slightest perception of a turned-off engine or a closing door, a difference was noted. Claire and her Captain were embracing and, strangely, they appeared as one rather than a pair in intimate proximity. Very intuitive on occasion, the first of the three heads peeking out beside the blinds said, "Something is different," and the second murmured, "Yes, but what is it?" Excitedly, the third shouted, "I'll bet they're engaged!"

Perhaps hoping to secure confirmation of their speculation, Claire's baggage after being unloaded was whisked away by the curious trio. Though no substantiation came in a verbal fashion, the trio seemed to sense an aura indicating their intuitions to be correct. All were sure that it was true. He must have proposed and she accepted. They noted a long parting kiss.

On separation, Iain said, "I'll call you every day."

"No you won't," Claire shot back. "We must start saving for our honeymoon and the future. I am going to be allowed a say in the finances, aren't I?" asked Claire, somewhat resolutely.

"Aye, every good regiment needs a fine Quartermaster, and I think you will fill the bill," Iain said with a smile, continuing with, "So, I'll call you every other night unless I'm desperate. One last thing," he said. "I intend to set everything in motion. I'll talk to my parents first then discuss our engagement with the Catholic Chaplain. Ordinarily, marriage bans would have to be published, but I don't think that is a necessity in the military. We must be optimistic that it will all work out the way we wish. Let's keep our feet on firm ground and avoid any quagmire of indecision."

"Aye, that we shall do, Iain, my love." One last kiss, then they parted.

Iain couldn't get the leave to return to see his parents personally any time in the foreseeable future. Also, they wouldn't be coming to London soon, and consideration must be given to seeing Claire's parents first. Consequently, there was no alternative but to telephone his mother and father, though it would have been far better to have done it face to face.

Therefore, when Cameron had his parents on the phone, he proceeded factually and forthrightly to explain his engagement to Claire. No interrupting questions or comments were made, so Iain continued. "I have discussed the matter of a mixed marriage with the Catholic chaplain," he said. "As I expected, he indicated it was not ideal in his opinion but permissible nonetheless."

"Might Claire convert?" asked his father.

"Certainly not at this time," responded Iain. "I'm of no mind to force the matter. She's a very spiritual young woman and steadfast in her own faith."

"What about children? Would she agree to raise them Catholic?" was his mother's first question.

"Yes, most definitely," said Iain. "I know that I must sound very impetuous," said the son. "But she's a wonderful young woman, and we are deeply in love. I hope you will give your blessing to our marriage."

For ten seconds, there was silence, though the span seemed infinitely longer. Finally, his father said, "I wasn't always an old curmudgeon on the General Staff, Iain. Believe me, there was the time that I, too, was an impetuous gallant. However, the decisions I made, especially regarding your mother were the best of my life. So, you have the permission of your father, but the case rests with your mother."

"As a mother who knows her son, there will be no veto from me. I can't think of another woman with whom I would be happier to entrust you."

Then in a chorus, they said, "God bless you Iain! We'll say some prayers that Claire's parents are as easily convinced, as we."

After hanging up the phone, General and Mary Cameron sat silently for a few moments. Then she said, "You gave in more easily than I would have thought, General. If you would have held out, I might have had to play my trump card. We do have our little game of quid pro quo, and I could have asked for a favor in compensation for all those Holland and Hollands that I saw you sneaking into the gun room."

The General, in unaccustomed manner, stomped out his cigar and replied gruffly, "We play that game only over material things and not those of a spiritual nature. You should know that, Mary Cameron! Besides, I've been very impressed with Claire and decided several days ago that Iain would be a damn fool if he didn't ask her to marry him. As far as the guns are concerned, I was planning on taking you on a wonderful trip to Africa. All first cabin of course."

"First cabin, my foot!" she shot back. "Maybe on the ship, but then it would be some old tent, and I've never slept in a first-class tent! You would be having the time of your life blasting away at charging cape buffalo, while I would be sweltering and swatting tsetse flies. I'll accept a cruise to America with a train ride to California, then back through Canada."

The General noted Mary's chin was raised to the defiant level, and she had that fight-to-the-death look in her eye. "All right, we'll go to America," her spouse replied with an unconvincing scowl.

"Aunt Jane can come as well?" asked his antagonist.

"Yes, she may come, I suppose." A note of an edge was in his voice this time, but she knew it was a bluff.

"For an old curmudgeon on the General Staff, you're kind of cute," she said.

"You are a hell of a poker player, Mary," was the General's reply. He was already halfway to the bar, unwrapping a cigar en route.

Chapter Thirty-One

In the days following their respective returns to Edinburgh and London, Claire and Iain were performing their duty functions admirably well. Nevertheless, they managed to find adequate time for planning and plotting. To their joint dismay, there always seemed to be gaping holes in most of the plans they constructed. Always, it turned out that Plan A depended on Plan B, while B was forever contingent on Plan C, and so it went all the way to Z. On their fourth phone call, both admitted their inability to unscrew the inscrutable requests for leave and the proper notice for resignation from the Nursing Staff. In Claire's case, this must of necessity hinge on the disclosure of their engagement and securing her parent's approbation. Pure and simple, that was priority number one!

Postproposal dilemma number two was when could they see her parents? Discussion brought out the fact Iain would have the first weekend in September free. Any chance during the following four weeks looked dismal indeed. "No chance for me at all that weekend," Claire sighed. They were both totally disconsolate, and it was obvious in the tone of their voices.

"I'll keep working on it," said Claire in softly inflected words, which Iain could only imagine as the precursor of tears.

"I don't know about your outfit, but in mine St. Jude is the Patron Saint of the impossible," responded Iain. "Let's gang up on him and see what transpires."

"If I get off, it will be a miracle," was Claire's response. Then she added, "Will that make me a saint in your outfit?"

"Sorry, but you need three for canonization, so you'll have two more to go!"

"Well you have to start somewhere," Claire said. "I'll give it a go." After that bit of levity, they pledged their love and rang off.

Late the following afternoon, Claire received an unexpected summons to the office of Miss Farqharson. Since one was rarely if ever called to see Farkie unless they were in trouble, this seemed more like a command rather than a simple invitation. After a quick examination of her conscience, attendance, and duty performance, Claire had no inkling of malfeasance for which she might be guilty. But then, few were ever on the same wavelength as the supervisor.

Exactly at the appointed hour, Sister Campbell presented herself with her appearance impeccable. As always, she was posture perfect and prideful in bearing, which was obvious though not arrogant. Miss Farqharson consulted her watch, which hung from a gold chain fastened to the top of her gleaming white apron, starched to a degree of stiffness one might find in a Roman soldier's breast plate. Since chit-chat was never part of Farkie's lexicon, her first words were predictable.

"I'll get right to the point, Miss Campbell. Some of the outlying districts have been calling on us to furnish volunteers for the Children's Inoculation Vaccination Program. I have reworked the schedules so as to provide them with three qualified volunteers. You will be going to your home city of Oban on the first weekend of September. Of course, bus fare will be provided. Since your parents abide there, you will need neither food or lodging, and this lessens the drain on the medical funding, which is scarce enough. I presume you will be most happy to comply, Miss Campbell. It might be nice to visit your parents for a change, might it not?"

"Indeed it would Miss Farqharson, and I'm most grateful for your consideration." All of Claire's willpower was necessary to maintain her composure. She would have liked to throw her cap up in the air and shout, "Thank you St. Jude!" and give Farkie a hug, which would dent her steely apron. Instead, Claire restrained herself until well out of range of the supervisor's supernormal hearing. A few witnesses to her solitary celebration may have wondered if Claire had gone daft. However, she really didn't care.

Linking the lovers, the telephone line on the next night's call carried only elation as they made future plans. Claire would proceed by bus to Oban and prepare her parents for Iain's impending arrival. Jointly, they decided that she would not break the news of the proposal, lest it appear she was guilty of duplicity. Iain should arrive on Saturday afternoon, then he would proceed to the clinic. As soon as Claire completed her assignment, they would see her parents together. Iain did feel somewhat remiss, as he wished to have met Claire's father earlier and have an opportunity to discuss proposing to his daughter. However, fate had decreed otherwise, so they would present their case as honestly as possible.

Surely, Iain hoped for accord, but one way or the other, he was not about to lose Claire for any reason.

Iain arrived at the regional clinic barely fifteen minutes before Claire's duties were to conclude. When the receptionist asked if she could be of assistance, he politely told her that he was waiting for Miss Campbell. "She is just about finished up," the woman replied. "The children just love her. She has a way of making a jab in the arm seem like an adventure to them. Miss Campbell will make a fine mother one of these days."

The emphasis was obvious and brought a smile to Iain's face. His reply "I'm counting on that," produced a reciprocal smile from the receptionist.

Minutes later, Claire appeared. Regardless of what she wore, Iain considered his fiancée beautiful, but in the uniform she looked angelic. "Thank you for all the help, Mrs. Nevis. I don't know what I would have done without you."

"You did all the hard work, Claire. However, if I made it a little easier for you, then I'm elated. Twelve to three tomorrow, my dear, and that should finish us up. I suppose I may see you at church services in the morning with your parents."

"I'm sure you will Mrs. Nevis. Oh! How silly of me, I didn't introduce my fia—uh, friend, Captain Iain Cameron. He's with the Scots Guards and is visiting for the weekend."

"A pleasure to meet you," said Iain courteously smiling, then extending his hand to warmly clasp that of Mrs. Nevis.

"Have a wonderful visit, Captain, and please enjoy Oban."

"I'm sure I shall," he said.

Once outside, they locked hands, as a more public display of affection would not be appropriate. Nevertheless, all the feelings needed to be communicated were transmitted via their enmeshed fingers. Once the car was in motion, Iain asked, "How did it go?"

"Could have been worse," Claire answered rather tensely. "I didn't say we were engaged; just that we were very fond of each other, and I wanted them to meet you. Their faces seemed to ask how could you be very fond of someone you just met, but they didn't verbalize it. However, the rest of the evening and this morning, I seemed to be the object of profound parental politeness. It's not at all what I'm used to from mother and father. Hopefully, we can square everything up in the limited time we have, Iain, but I'm worried."

Claire was taken aback when Iain suddenly swerved to the side of the road. "What's wrong?" she exclaimed.

"It's nothing serious," he replied. "I just don't happen to know how to get to your parents' place."

"I thought you perhaps scouted it out," she said. "It's the white frame, three-story hotel just ahead. Rather hard to miss in what is basically a one-street town." That little bit of humor seemed to ease their tensions somewhat. Iain pulled into the tidy parking lot, and they took their first steps toward an uncertain ending.

Little time elapsed before Iain was face to face with Claire's parents. While their handshakes offered were firm, their countenances seemed inquisitorial, leaving young Cameron feeling like a Trojan horse. No particular words of welcome were spoken or was he invited to bring in his luggage.

Turning to his daughter, Mr. Campbell said, "Claire someone needs to run the desk, while your mother and I speak to Captain Cameron. I presume you haven't forgotten the routine, so please see to it. Please come into our sitting room, Captain." Claire was obviously dismissed, but obedient to her father's wishes. Iain paused to let Mrs. Campbell proceed, then fell in behind her.

Iain heard the door latch solidly behind him, signifying Angus Campbell's entry. Surely, it seemed as though court would soon be in session. "Please be seated, Captain." Iain moved to the proffered chair but remained standing until Rachael Campbell was seated. Obviously, the little gathering was to be confrontational, as Captain Cameron found himself directly facing his judges, who were seated side by side. Iain's mouth felt dry. A drink of something, preferably one with a high percentage of ethanol would have been desirable, but even a glass of water would be most welcome.

From what seemed to be the enemy's side, the first volley rang out immediately. This was fired by Claire's father and was of an acerbic nature. "Captain Cameron, there is an old saying that 10 percent of the populace fail to get the message. Mrs. Campbell and I seem to find ourselves relegated to that category. We were abruptly told last evening that you and Claire were quite fond of each other. Also, it turns out that our daughter has spent weekends with your family. We did know about her going to London for your award ceremony, but were led to believe she was doing it out of professional respect for a patient. We were unaware of the shooting safari until last night. Naturally, we are hurt that it was not discussed with us in advance. Suddenly, to now learn of this deep affection is a bit much for us, I'm afraid. What do you have to say for yourself?"

Though his adversaries' volley was accurate, Iain was not pinned down. "Mr. and Mrs. Campbell, Claire and I have known each other for approximately six months. On the two occasions we were in each other's company, our actions were entirely chaste and, for the most part, we were thoroughly chaperoned. Failure for us to discuss her visit to my parent's place—"

Claire's father cut in with, "Come now, Captain. You're being a bit modest. We are aware that General Cameron has a sizable estate."

"Very well," said Iain. "Failure for us to discuss her visit to my parent's estate was inexcusable, and I offer my profound apologies. It was a regrettable oversight, but not an action meant to deceive. I wish to be totally honest with you at this time.

"On the morning we left Capercaille Manor, I was in the process of driving Claire to the Anglican church service. She thought I was taking her to the Catholic Mass because somehow she assumed I believed her to be of my faith. Claire suddenly exclaimed 'I'm not a Catholic,' or words to that affect. I told her I knew that. Then, I explained that mixed marriages were acceptable to both of our faiths. Claire asked me if my words were indicative of a proposal, and I answered 'yes.' This may all sound incomprehensible, or be taken as indicating the highest order of sophistry; however, despite the spontaneity, I believe what transpired was absolutely meant to be."

Claire's mother looked bewildered. However, her father remained steely-eyed above a tense, firmly set jaw. Angus Campbell was about to speak, but Iain held up his hand. His voice boomed out, "Wait!" This was not a request but a command requirement. The order seemed to kindle obeisance in the older man. Perhaps, it was a resurgence of the conditioned reflex resulting from four years as an enlisted man in Montgomery's Eighth Army. The steel in Mr. Campbell's eyes softened, as his jaw slackened slightly. No sound emerged from his tightened lips.

Iain sensed at least one more opportunity to press his point, so he continued. "Mr. and Mrs. Campbell, I am a man of honor and means of my own. Certainly, any good man would recognize that Claire is beautiful in every way the term could be applied to a young lady. I have known her long enough to appreciate and respect all of those qualities. I revere her, and I'm sure there will never be anyone who would make a finer wife, companion, and God willing the mother of my children. I love her deeply, and I have every reason to think she feels the same about me." Emboldened, Iain began to say "I will marry her with or without your blessing." However, he caught himself in time to change "will to wish" and the final phrase to "hopefully with your blessing."

Recovering his aplomb to a certain degree, Claire's father finally spoke. "We do not share the same religion, Captain. I believe that to be of prime importance."

Replied Iain, "We do share the same God, sir. Our rituals and Sacraments may differ, but I daresay we strongly share the same moral values. Rubrics should take no precedence over ethics."

"I can't see my daughter as a papist," shot back Angus Campbell, with more flint present in his tone. Meanwhile, Rachael Campbell shook her head, part in accord and part in protest to even the thought of such a prospect.

"Your daughter isn't going to become a papist, if that's the term you wish to employ, nor am I ever to become an Anglican or a Roundhead," replied Iain. "The Reformation was nearly 500 years ago, and there hasn't been a Catholic or Protestant burned, beheaded, or hung for over 100 years as far as I know. The Scots fought the English or their predecessors for 600 or 700 years, but we live in seeming harmony now. I'm not aware of any Englishman being refused the hand of a Scot's daughter. Why do people, whose common bond is the same Ten Commandments, have to carry on so sadly? I've fought alongside Englishmen, and no doubt you did the same with Catholics, Mr. Campbell. My last friend, a fellow officer, was buried—at least what remained of him was buried—in an Anglican service. Do you think my heart was less devastated, or my tears less sincere, because he wasn't a papist?"

"Children," Rachael Campbell said quietly. "Is it true they must be raised Catholic?"

"That is non-negotiable, Mrs. Campbell. However, there is no bigotry taught, nor would I ever tolerate it. Any children of which we might be blessed will be raised with the understanding that I know of no better person than their mother."

Claire's parents looked at each other, and their faces perceptively softened. Their eyes carried messages in a code not readily deciphered by Iain. Then, suddenly, Rachael changed direction. "You are a soldier, Captain, and we assume you intend to stay one. That raises the question of becoming a premature widow. If Claire, or I mean any young woman, marries a soldier, there is always that possibility! Am I not correct?"

"You are, Mrs. Campbell. I could try and delude you and say 'oh well you can get hit with a bus while waiting at the stop.' However, when you've heard the bullets whistle by, as have your husband and I, then you know it's a lot more dicey than waiting for the tram. God willing, I'll always be spared. But, should He deem otherwise, I promise whatever years we might have together will be as happy as I can possibly make them. Also, Claire will be well endowed if ever I were to fall." With these words, Iain grew pensive, and the scar diagonally delineating the lids of his right eye seemed to become more apparent. Obviously, the cicatrix served as a testimonial to the possibility of such an occurrence.

Again, the eyes of Claire's parents locked on each others. Iain was aware that Mrs. Campbell had gained recognition of what was silently being conveyed in the face of her spouse. Soon, there was a barely perceptible nod of accord. Shortly thereafter, Angus Campbell arose, saying, "I understand there is a movement afoot called ecumenism. I don't fully comprehend all the facts and details, but I understand it to be very well intended. Obviously, if ecumenism is to be implemented, it has to start somewhere. Perhaps, we should be among the first to give it a try. Before we start, I think a couple of drams of Scotch whiskey would be in order. Rachael, please call Claire. I'm sure the desk can spare her for a few minutes. In fact, the night clerk has probably already arrived. I didn't realize it is so late."

Claire answered the sudden and unexplained call to come to the parlor. On the way, she was tremulous and utterly surprised when she opened the door. Those three people she loved most in the world were standing in a circle. Well-filled whiskey glasses were raised, and she heard her father say solemnly, "To ecumenism!" All was explained at a very happy and sumptuous dinner served in one of the hotel's private dining rooms. Again, Claire's parents were once more themselves, and first names had entirely replaced formality. Most important, Iain was still there.

Early the next morning, three Campbells and one Cameron strolled down the main street of Oban. They had started the day in solidarity, and so it would remain except for the transient separation when the Cameron split off in the Catholic direction and the Campbells headed Anglican. Angus Campbell hollered to his future son-in-law, "Don't fall asleep during the sermon, Iain. We'll compare notes when we rejoin and determine who received the best one!"

"If ours isn't any good, then I'll make up a better one and win the contest!" was Iain's smiling retort. Claire and her mother laughed, and the former was so very happy that her father's real personality was back in proper form. Now, it seemed that the two men in her life were starting to genuinely like each other, and Claire considered it a most wonderful omen.

Nurse Claire was off to clinic soon after they returned to the White Heron. Therefore, her parents took the opportunity to show Iain the highlights of their town. "Come along, Iain. Rachael and I will take you on the grand tour of our city."

"Village" corrected his wife.

"Let's compromise with town," came the rejoinder, along with an attached chuckle.

"I would sincerely like that," said Iain. "I'm all yours."

Obviously, Oban was primarily a one-street town with side streets sprouting here and there. Many of its young would come of age and leave for other places. Still, there would always be that comfortable cadre whose dreams and ambitions would be fulfilled right there.

At the edge of town, a vista was found from where they could see all the town and much of the surroundings. In the little harbor, a few trawlers were observed. Still more, under way, were obvious in the distance. In acknowledgment, they bowed and bobbed to the passing swells like partners in a dance. From this vantage point, the White Heron stood out. Like many of the charming little hotels and shops that neighbored it, their hotel was decked out in whitewash highlighted by contrasting trim.

"From the time of its origin," Angus Campbell explained, "Oban had always been intimate with the Irish Sea, as had its inhabitants, and the sea can be a jealous mistress. Over the centuries, it had claimed many souls from this little town, holding them in the bosom of her depths for eternity." From Iain's vantage point, the gray sea wall and backdrop granite cliffs looked much like an oyster shell with Oban nestled there like a pearl.

After returning from sight-seeing, shortly later, Claire was out of the clinic at three o'clock sharp, and it would have been wonderful if they had the luxury of languishing over a delightful dinner. However, reality had to be recognized, as it was a relatively long trip back to Edinburgh and much longer to reach London. Thus, by necessity, they were hurried off by concerned parents. A well-packed and most savory lunch along with thermos of coffee was stowed in the Healey's small rear seat. Parting waves were exchanged and kisses thrown.

Iain was about to release the clutch when Claire's father called out, "Iain, I forgot to mention that our sermon wasn't too good. You win the wager."

"Our sermon wasn't too good either, so we're even until next time," replied Iain.

Shortly after leaving, Claire's head found a comfortable cradle on Iain's shoulder, and soon she was asleep. Though it had been a vexatious weekend, the ending was all bliss. Claire had felt wonderfully happy and very serene, and when serenity prevailed, sleep was often forthcoming. Iain would have enjoyed the stimulus of hot coffee to keep him roadworthy; however, he wouldn't trade a dozen cups of coffee for the presence of the sweet head nestled on his shoulder.

On the following day after his return to London, Iain was putting the finishing touches on the manual dealing with the warfare in Malay. He was through with the glossary and half-finished with the index. Some communiqués from the Commanding Officer, Scots Guards Malay, were lying immediately adjacent to his work, and Iain dourly noted that it had become the "Malay Emergency." Along with Geordie, he had gone off to war. His friend, Alpha Platoon, and a lot of good men had died or been maimed there. A war was a series of actions, where two sides fought, and some men perished for one reason or another. What the hell was an *emergency?*

Soon, a mental image came to Cameron's mind.

A group of politicians were sitting in a closed room having a heated discussion. One man said in a whining voice, "I say, we just can't call this a war. That word is quite alarming to constituents."

"We can't use campaign," said another. "That sounds too much like a long bitter struggle, which could be part of a war!"

"Campaign might also be construed to be part of a political party's drive to be elected, reelected, or whatever," opined a third.

Soon, the face of yet another man blossomed into a smile "I've got it," he exclaimed.

"You've got what old fellow?" the others chimed.

"Let's call it an emergency! It's the perfect word, which catches a little attention, as we desire. Best of all, nearly everyone has a different definition of what it is. To one person, it's being in the middle of a concert, and suddenly wondering if you unplugged the iron. For another, it's being tardy at work because the car wouldn't start. For the fairer sex, it might mean being four days beyond when your period should have started. Usually, it is never understood as anything terribly serious. Conversely, should a civilian airliner crash with 175 aboard, or a giant meteorite smash into London, it would be a calamity. We would surely never call it an emergency."

"Splendid indeed," the others joined in. "The Malay War shall become the Malay Emergency."

As Iain studied the communiqué, he noted the killed in action and the missing. *Thank god the numbers were relatively small,* he thought. Statistically, they might be considered of minimal significance. After all, 10 men killed out of 5,000 in the field is only 0.005 percent. Hardly a number to get excited about. However, it's 100 percent for all their loved ones left behind. Some awards had been meted out, and it was nice to be recognized and honored, as he had been. How about those poor souls, who expired from a malaria-induced rupture of the spleen? Were there any medals awarded to those killed by plasmodium? Were there any parades for those who stepped on a fecal-contaminated punji stick? If there was, they probably wouldn't be marching in it. That's hard to do when you lost a leg due to gangrene. "Call it what you want, gentlemen," Cameron murmured. "What it comes down to whose bayonet reaches whose belly first for those men, it's war!"

Iain was about to return to the completion of the index when Major Wilson approached, saying, "Iain, a few moments in my office, if you would."

"Yes, sir, I'll be right there." Immediately, the young Captain fell in right behind his superior, so neither felt it necessary to observe a reporting protocol.

"Have a seat," said Wilson, pointing toward a chair. "Two things to discuss," he said. "The first is aggravating, but we can live with it. Those at the top, it would seem, have decided that the Manual on Jungle Warfare written by General Sir Walter Walker is to be the bible for everyone. He is, of course, the hero of the War in Burma, and General Sir Walter is said to know all there is to know about fighting in the bush. As a result, our labor is lost without any love from the High Command. Needless to say, I considered your efforts in our project to be superior in all respects. Our manual will be consigned to the Regimental Archives. Perhaps someday it will be dusted off, and a future historian will compare it to that of the General's and decide who might have shown the greater insight. In the meantime, your Service Record will reflect my highest praise for your efforts.

"In comparison to what I have to say next, I'm afraid this disappointment and frustration rather pales. Oh hell, there is no way to put this nicely. I guess soldiers shouldn't expect that, so Iain, I have become privy to information indicating you are being issued orders to return to Malay on 1 November."

For Iain, the sound of the words just heard were as devastating an experience as if his head and neck were bared on the block, and he heard the rushing, rasping sound of the descending guillotine blade. He recoiled slightly but otherwise displayed no emotion. Wilson's and Cameron's eyes met and locked solidly. Major Wilson's registered profound regret, while Iain's reflected resignation backed with resolve.

"I can't say how sorry I am, especially in light of your wedding plans. If I had a chance, and it were possible, I would take your place. However, Her Majesty apparently has no need of one-lung soldiers outside the confines and comforts of Regimental Headquarters. It would seem that as a result of rotation policies and debilitating illnesses, Captains are in short supply. Coupled with that is the fact that you have the reputation and experience. Again, I'm truly sorry, Iain. However, as we are all aware, in the Army, *sorry* is nestled in the dictionary somewhere between *shit* and *syphilis* and probably less meaningful. I have contrived to find a special ten-day assignment for you, which I'm sure no one will even question, or fully understand for that matter. This will allow you time to see your fiancée, as well as your parents.

"Just between you and me, Captain, I was engaged when I learned that I would be hitting the beach on D-Day. Of course, I couldn't discuss any details with Angela, but she knew the invasion was impending and fervently wished us to marry. I decided it wasn't best, as I might die. I survived, but she was killed by a V-2 rocket; one of those cute little toys of Werner Von Braun. I did marry after the war to a fine woman that I love and share two children with, nonetheless, I've always regretted not having Angela as my wife for even such a short time. I'm not telling you this in anticipation of anything horrible happening. Rather, it's a well-meaning suggestion that you might consider seeking your full measure of human happiness as soon as opportunity permits. I guess that's it, Iain."

Major Wilson stood, and Captain Cameron jumped to attention, with his hand starting in a salutary motion. Then he curtailed the reflex and extended his hand to grasp the one that his superior offered him. "God bless and watch over you, Iain," said Major Wilson, whose face was locked in that particular expression strong men employ when trying to alleviate tears.

"Thank you, Major. I'm most appreciative, and consider you a friend, as well as a superior officer," said Iain solemnly.

As Cameron was leaving, Wilson called out, "The special ten day assignment officially commences at 0600 tomorrow, Captain, but you are unofficially free the moment you leave this office."

"Thank you again, Major!" This time Iain did salute before leaving.

Quickly, Iain decided that he had to see Claire in person since such news as he had to convey would be devastating enough face to face, and it seemed too terrible for transmission by telephone. After necessities were rapidly packed, the Healey headed north. When Iain reached his destination, it was still dark. However, an all-night petrol station in the outskirts of Edinburgh provided him an opportunity to make himself presentable. Unfortunately, though, it did little to erase the tension lines evident beyond the fringes of lather on the face reflecting back at him in the restroom mirror. He could not help but think, *How frail are little laugh and smile ripples. They can be so quickly ablated by anxiety and replaced by much deeper etchings of concern.*

As the Healey glided into the hospital parking lot and the ignition was turned off, it sounded like a semblance of the neighing of a tired old horse. A greatly fatigued body requested sleep, only to be rebuffed by the alert mind that dominated it. The thought of a nap struck Iain as being inane, like a condemned man selecting his final meal. "Who in hell would be hungry before their execution?" he mused, as he noted long rays of sunshine were now assaulting the eastern battlements of Edinburgh Castle, which loomed above him on the awakening horizon. However, the black muzzles of the great cannon protruding through the crenels on the ramparts remained silent. Iain felt like the sun was a friendly invader, and its rays of light allowed by the translucent clouds to fall on the castle had come back each day for years numbering in the hundreds. Surely, no one would try and repulse the sun, even if it were possible. Now, he noticed the British colors were rapidly ascending the flagpole, which stood silent and alone above all else. Soon, he would carry that flag back into battle. *God grant I need not die beneath it,* he thought.

Before long, Iain noted the little knot of sisters exiting their common quarters and making for the hospital. As always: prim, pressed, and dazzling white, they were a happy group. No Grenadier Guards could have been more presentable. In the center was Claire, a beautiful nucleus surrounded by her compatriots, who jostled about like so many excited electrons in outer rings of an atom. Her face was absolutely radiant, at least until she noticed Iain standing by the car. Claire's expression of happy surprise became one of alarm when she looked at him. He had come because of something terrible! Immediately, the aura infected the other nurses, as Claire bolted and ran to him. The other sisters continued on their way silently, with only furtive looks behind vainly attempting to ascertain what might be happening. Already, her beautiful blue eyes were reflecting anguish, while the finely sculptured chin became tremulous.

Claire threw herself into Iain's outstretched arms, which quickly encircled her, then contracted, drawing her hard against his chest. His lips were well within range of her ear to convey even the softest spoken message. Claire heard the words, "I've been ordered to return to Malay on the first of November," yet, she couldn't fully perceive the message.

"It can't be true! I just can't believe it," she said, as the words echoed back to her. They were the exact same words that cancer patients used when informed they had a deadly disease. However, Claire would not and could not deceive herself. "Tell me all, Iain, I have to know." Iain repeated all that Major Wilson had told him, apart from the anecdote about Angela, the young lady he had left behind. "Is there nothing you can do to change it, Iain?"

"Possibly," he replied. "But it would fly in the face of my honor, my family's honor, the regiment's honor, and especially that of the medal I just received. Perhaps that sounds selfish and vainglorious, especially in the light of the love I have pledged to you, Claire, but it's the type of man I am. The same man who desires you above all else but who is unable to elevate desire above duty. I hope you understand."

"I do, my love," said Claire. "When I said that I would marry you, I knew it meant I would be a soldier's wife. Also, I have my honor, and though it's kind of premature, I accept my duty to be a good soldier's wife. I only ask one thing from you, my dearest."

"What is that?" asked Iain, while still holding her tightly.

"I wish us to be married before you go," she replied. "It's the only way I'll be able to bear this."

"Will your parents agree?" he questioned.

"I am certain that they will, as there shall be no need for defiance on my part," Claire whispered.

"Very well, Claire. I promise you will be Mrs. Cameron as soon as I can arrange it."

"I guess it's the old stiff upper lip for me," Claire said, as she wiped away a tear and did her best to mimic a solid fixation of her face. "However, I'm glad to be in surgery today. You get to wear a mask, and you can hide a lot behind one of those."

Gently, with his curled index finger, Iain elevated Claire's chin, then looked deeply into her eyes. "I love you more than anything, Claire Campbell."

"Soon, Claire Cameron, if you please, sir." They kissed, and then Iain was gone, for though it would be a quick and unexpected return to Oban, he felt it was his obligation to personally discuss the matter with Claire's parents. Knowing they were splendid people, he also thought they would understand and give their blessing. After Oban, Iain planned to be off to see his parents. He had no doubt they would agree. What else could they say when they had done the same thing several wars ago?

Again, the Austin Healey was on the road, and the direction was westward away from the Firth of Forth and on to the Firth of Clyde. As he drove along, to Iain's mind came thoughts of how intertwined Scotland's history of commerce and cities were with its Firths. Edinburgh was nestled near the tip of the Firth of Forth, and Glasgow occupied a similar position on the Firth of Clyde. Here was the spawning grounds of some of England's and also the world's greatest ships, whether they be ocean liners or man-o'-war. The Firth of Moray was home to Inverness. Perth and Dundee arose from the banks of the Firth of Tay. Meanwhile, Iain's current destination, Oban, was perched on the Firth of Lorn. *Perhaps, it would have been better named the Firth of Forelorn*, he thought momentarily. Then, he rebuked himself, for the title was not apt. Certainly, he was going there to inform Claire's parents of his orders to Malay. Though his initial meeting with them had started out with a confrontational manner, it had ended in happiness. "Don't worry, Firth of Lorn," he murmured. "Too much happiness has sprung from your banks for me to bestow such a dismal name on you. If I ever choose to change your name at all, it would be to the Firth of Claire!"

Iain checked the palms of his hands. Noting they were dry, he realized that this was a sign of advanced fatigue. Consequently, at a vantage point overlooking storied Loch Lomond, he pulled off the road and parked. Although his mind still did not wish for a period of somnolence, there was some center in his brain that was rebelling, and Iain knew it was capable of shutting down the entire power supply with little or no notice. Far better to get a few hours of sleep and survive, rather than chance a fatal crash. With the Healey's motor shut off and the brake set, Iain leaned back in his seat. Momentarily, he thought of the anonymous Scot prisoner of long ago, awaiting his execution in the Tower of London. He had penned the poem "Loch Lomond," now turned ballad, to his love. Starting to sing the words softly, the exhausted traveler was barely into the first stanza when he fell fast asleep.

At the sound of a closing car door, Cameron was brought back to his senses. Someone had stopped for photos of Loch Loman, and their arrival served as his alarm clock, which now said one P.M. Oban was two hours or less away, so Iain continued driving and on his arrival, Angus and Rachael Campbell were at the hotel's desk. Forewarned by their daughter, they knew what to expect.

Mr. Campbell spoke first. "Claire rang us up, Iain, so we are aware of your orders to Malay. We deeply appreciate the fact you have come to discuss the situation with us in person."

"Iain looks as though he needs a good lunch," Rachael interrupted. "Discussion can occur between bites." Suddenly, Iain realized that he was famished. Nothing had entered his stomach apart from three cups of coffee and a donut obtained at the petrol station hours ago.

Well into his second sandwich, Iain paused and addressed Claire's parents. "All of this comes as a great shock. As a soldier, I suppose it shouldn't, though after all it is a human being that buttons on the uniform."

"Aye, I remember it well," was Angus's summation.

"What about your wedding?" asked Claire's mother.

"As Claire may have told you, we would like the marriage to occur before I leave for Malay." With this reply, Iain surveyed their faces, and there did not appear to be signs of rejection. He continued. "Perhaps it seems melodramatic, or one could even state that it is temporary insanity, but it is the way we feel. Nonetheless, we have resolved not to be rash. You were kind enough to approve of our marriage just a short time ago. This turn of events was unknown then, but it does change matters greatly. You raised Claire to be the fine young woman that she is, and I respect all the love and sacrifices that went into it. If you feel the wedding is best postponed, then we are resolved to respect your wishes. Maybe you may wish to discuss it in private?"

"We have done that already, Iain," the older man replied. "A good hour was spent discussing and thrashing through the would be, could be, and a whole long list of what ifs. However, in the end we discarded them all in favor of what's best. What's best for two young though mature adults, who deeply love each other, is to be married and embark on as long a cruise together as the Almighty will permit." Angus reached for his wife's hand and squeezed it lovingly, signifying they were linked in body as well as mind. Rachael didn't speak, but her softly nodding head and eyes shining with understanding and approval more than sufficed for words.

"You'll stay the night, Captain. An old Sergeant can give orders as well. Certainly, a good dinner and fine Bordeau will do wonders before a few hours in a soft bed."

"Aye, Sergeant," said Iain with a smile. "Your order is accepted."

Chapter Thirty-Two

❈ ❈ ❈

While outside consulting with the gardener, Mary Cameron's highly tuned ear perceived a familiar sound, and it could only mean the return of Percy with Iain at the wheel. The General always named his cars and like Bobiecka, the Austin Healey's appellation was related to war. When people looked puzzled at the reference to Percy, her husband would always smile and say, "Named after Harry 'Hot Spur' Percy killed at the Battle of Shrewsbury in 1026."

Immediately, Mary excused herself and walked quickly toward the car. After one look at her son, she knew something unexpected and fearsome had occurred. Already, he was out of the car and standing when she arrived. "Iain, what is it?" she inquired.

"Orders back to Malay," he responded.

Then Mary embraced her son and held him close. *Why couldn't a mother's embrace protect her son like it used to before he became a man?* she thought. However, she knew the answer that it was that transition which made him a man.

Tenderly, Iain hugged his mother and followed with an affectionate kiss. "Is father about?" Iain inquired.

"No, as you might expect, he is out shooting just outside Aberfeldy. He did promise to be home for dinner, but then, you know your father."

At the appointed hour, the General did arrive for dinner. All the facts were well presented and discussed by dinner's end. However all three were aware of the one question that was most important to resolve, though as yet not raised. As might be expected, the General took command.

"As you know, Iain, because we have so often discussed it with friends in a humorous, anecdotal fashion, your mother and I faced a similar decision. Should you and Claire decide, as we did, it will surely be with our blessing."

"Indeed, it will," said his mother resolutely.

So now all the bridges were crossed, and approximately six weeks were left to plan a marriage and have a little honeymoon before confronting Malay. Suddenly, Iain's mother arose and left the room. Soon, she returned holding a tiny silk bag. After she opened it, the single content was passed into her son's hand. "This was your grandmother's ring, Iain. Your grandfather served in Africa on several occasions and brought the stone back with him. I have my own ring, and this one has been searching for a finger to encircle for many years now. I think you will find that Claire has just the right finger to make this ring feel at home once again."

For Iain, soon it was another morning and another departure time. As mother, father, and son stood beside Percy, there was gravity in their voices, but all were bearing up well. Embracing his son, the General said, "It's tough, lad, but think of it as one more set of skirmishes. Like all things in life, even war doesn't last forever. You've been through it once and in a sense it's easier the second time around. You've shown that you've matured in the skills to survive and in those to vanquish your enemy. I have every confidence you'll come home safely."

Men, especially soldiers, thought his mother, *are proud of their prowess, and sure that skill will be their salvation, while mothers and wives are left to anguish over the errant bullet that defies courage and guile. Please God, grant me some peace of mind and preserve my son,* was her silent prayer. Aloud, Mary invoked the angels and saints. Also, she told Iain of their pride in him, and the joy they felt over his coming marriage to Claire. Shortly thereafter, Percy responded to the spur of the accelerator and headed south to the Firth of Forth and Edinburgh.

After Iain's arrival at the hospital's parking lot, he awaited Claire at the end of her shift. When she emerged, the smile she gave was wan but her demeanor resolute. After they kissed, she laid her cheek on his chest, and through softly pursed lips she whispered, "All went well with mummy and daddy and your parents?"

"They are as fully supportive as they could be," Iain replied. "We have an appointment with the Chaplain at the Castle," he continued. "I told him I couldn't be sure of our exact arrival time, but he was kind enough to give us some leeway."

"Do I have time to change clothes?"

"Probably," said Iain, "but I won't permit it. You look so angelic in your uniform that he will think you are celestial, and he won't be able to refuse us any request." Iain's spark of humor enkindled a similar response in his wife to be.

"I thought all angels were boys," she said with a little smile.

"I'm not sure they have any gender," he replied. "But I've always had a preconceived notion of what they should look like, and you fit the bill."

On arrival at the castle, Major Loran Marsh, the Chaplain, was awaiting them, and introductions were exchanged. Quickly, they were ushered into his office and appointed chairs. Although a Major in the Army, he was often called Father by his constituents, and it was a term with which he and Iain felt most comfortable.

"How can I help you two?" said the Chaplain with a broad smile, above fingers arranged in a steeple-like fashion.

"We wish to consult with you about getting married," said Iain. "Also, there are various ramifications and, I suppose, complications that we will endeavor to explain."

Thereupon, the priest cocked his head, smiled broader still, and said, "I'm all yours and all ears."

In a very efficient manner, which amazed his fiancée, Iain recounted all to the Chaplain. As a woman, Claire felt she would have been prone to more explanation. However, when it came her turn to answer questions proffered by the Chaplain, she did her best to maintain the tempo set by Iain. Father Marsh studied the faces of the two petitioners intently, for after thousands of battlefield confessions and more administrations of the Last Rites than he wished to recall, he had become a shrewd judge of character. These two manifested a purity of soul that greatly impressed him. Slowly, beginning to tap the two halves of his finger-formed church spire, the Chaplain spoke.

"If one were to seek to find impediments, they would find two," he said. "One, you are of different faiths, and strongly anchored in your beliefs. That is both good and bad, but I believe the good far outweighs the latter. However, you must always remember that a difference in faith is a hurdle, and it can be one you cannot easily step over without fear of tripping. Conversely, you can make it so high that it would be impossible to fly over. Last, there is the question of marriage in haste. As I see it, in your own minds, you are firmly convinced that it is what you fervently wish to do, and have come to the conclusion it is what God wishes you to do. Furthermore, you have consulted your parents and have their approbation. In addition, you have come to me and pled your cases rather well, I might add. The hopelessly headstrong and impetuous would have dashed off for the nearest civil service and never given it a second thought."

After a pause, Chaplain Marsh continued. "Indeed, you have convinced me that God wishes you united at this time. I can bless your marriage and will be delighted to do so on the 20th of October. That will give you time for a short honeymoon if Iain's Regimental Commander concurs. Before you leave, I will give you a blessing. Claire, you may stand because you look so angelic in your uniform," the Chaplain said with a wink. "The Captain, of course, should kneel."

After the blessing, they shook hands, then Major Marsh added, "Keep me posted, Iain. We both know the vagaries of the Army. The certainty of their decisions has not attained that of the Almighty."

After a shared laugh, Iain said, "Aye, Father Marsh, you can depend on that!"

Then, it was back to the Sisters Quarters with more good-bye kisses and embraces, while their love and yearning for each other was increasing exponentially. Meanwhile, for the curious at the window curtains, as they were still unaware of what was transpiring, they decided whatever was happening, it seemed to be going well.

After leaving Claire for his return trip to London, Iain permitted himself the luxury of a hotel overnight stop in Leeds. Then, off on an early start, he was in front of Major Wilson's desk before noon. His senior officer was surprised. "I didn't expect you back so soon, Captain. You know I gave you the week, and it still stands."

"I have some bartering to do Major," Iain replied. "Claire and I are to be married with our families' blessing ten days before I depart. Leave for a wee honeymoon would be much more appreciated at that time than now. In addition, I'll have roughly five weeks until the wedding. If it is at all possible, I would like to spend several weeks at Church Crookham."

"The Gurkha training camp?" responded Major Wilson with puzzlement evident in his voice.

"Yes, sir, for two reasons." I found out I can use a shotgun on birds quite well shooting left-handed, but I need expertise with the rifle and other weapons as well. I understand they have proper range facilities there. Second, I want to try and considerably improve my ability to speak their language. In addition, it is my hope to convince someone there to assign me some Gurkha troops. My orders indicate that I will take command of a company out in the bush. I could surely use some Gurkhas!"

After Major Wilson smiled, he said, "Most probably a rumor, but there's an old story about a certain Lieutenant Cameron who purloined some Gurkhas last year about this time. Also, the story suggests a certain Sergeant in Personnel was reassigned after several Gurkhas came up missing. At his inquiry, he kept mumbling something about Operation Kukri, and telling his Commanding Officer that he was surprised his Senior Officers were unaware of the directive."

With an entirely too innocent appearance, Iain replied, "Of course, there isn't a grain of truth to the story. However, I would like to emulate this bold lieutenant and obtain some Gurkhas myself, but it would all be according to the book!"

"Of course," replied his superior, barely able to refrain from a deep laugh.

"I'll see what I can do, Captain," was the Major's next statement. "Check back at 0800, and should have something to tell you by then."

After this instruction, Iain saluted, then left to find a haven for his tired body on his BOQ bed. In moments, he found himself reflecting on a similar scene just a year ago, though it now seemed like eons had passed. Iain remembered being on an identical bed in the same building when the Happy Warriors received their orders. He could picture his clumsy attempts to pack, and perfectly recall inebriated Geordie's arrival to the room. Soon, the scene was replaced by one of carnage, where his friend along with his entire platoon was annihilated. Iain's eyes moistened. Always the passionate observer, he quickly noted that the socket that held the glass replacement eye was quite as proficient at proffering a tear as the intact one. Iain realized that soon he would be traveling east, accompanied by Geordie's ghost and all the love and concern Claire and his parents could send with him. The former would be most hard to endure without the latter.

At 0800 hours on the following day, Captain Cameron entered Major Wilson's office. Looking up, the Major smiled and said, "I presented your request to the Colonel, Captain. As expected and much like most senior officers, he glowered and said 'What the hell does he want to do that for?' As a subordinate, I have learned that it's best to just stare wistfully at a corner of the ceiling, rather than answer right away. Given a little time, they almost invariably answer their own question and, then, end up by saying 'Go ahead or tell the damn fool it's out of the question.' Fortunately, for you the answer was 'Go ahead and try.' Then, I reached the Adjutant at Church Crookham, who said he would broach the subject with the Commanding Officer there, and try and let me know by noon."

"Is there anything I can do here to help, Major?" asked Iain.

"Not really, but check back around 1300."

"Yes sir! Thank you, Major," was Cameron's reply.

Meanwhile, as a kindness to Major Wilson of the Scots Guards, Major Polk of Gurkha Training Command, Church Crookham, was bearing Iain's request to Colonel Upham, the Camp Commander. Upham surveyed the teletype for only a few seconds before exploding. "Some bloody Scots Guard Captain wants to come here to do a bit of shooting, learn Gurkhali, help himself to some Gurkhas, and then ride off into the sunset?! He certainly has no shortage of effrontery," fumed the Colonel.

"I say, Polk. Is this that same Cameron that stole three of our men in Malay and ended up with the Victoria Cross instead of a court-martial?"

"One and the same, Colonel," replied the Major, whose mustache always seemed to twitch in harmony with the senior man's rising ire.

"Well he can bloody well go piss up a rope." Major Polk answered.

"I'll send a message indicating your disapproval, Colonel." When the Major was nearly out of the office, a stern call to return was heard. "Yes, sir. Is there something else?"

"This Captain Cameron, is he possibly related to Brigadier General John Alexander Cameron?"

"I believe him to be the General's son, sir."

"Uh, Polk, change the reply to 'Special arrangements can be made.' Have Captain Cameron proceed to this command and report directly to me on or before 10 September."

"Very well, Colonel. I will see it's transmitted." Then, the Major turned slowly, purposefully delaying his exit. As he expected, the Colonel was motivated to explain his change of mind. "I owe this General a favor, Major, and it's my first opportunity to pay him back."

Subordinates never asked why. However, if one were clever in producing a conspiratorial look, then more often than not, you were told why. After sitting smugly for a moment, the Colonel cocked his head and produced a smile, which was of the type usually forthcoming when reflecting on some fond memory from the distant past. "General Cameron, then Major Cameron, was my Commanding Officer during those dark days when Jerry was pushing us out of France, and we were all trying to get to Dunkirk to bail out. At an abandoned château, we had set up a temporary headquarters. Hardly dry behind the ears, I was a very junior Lieutenant and convinced I would be killed at any moment. I became enamored with the concept of carpe diem. You know, seize the day, live, drink, and be merry, lest tomorrow we die."

Removing his glasses, the Colonel stared off rather blissfully at nothing in particular. Shortly later, he continued. "I discovered a cache of fine Margaux in the château's cellar. In my youth, I didn't appreciate the flavor and bouquet, but I had no trouble in appreciating the wine's effects. After finishing one bottle, I decided to go for a walk. By chance, I happened to encounter an extremely comely mademoiselle, whose morals turned out to be even looser than her bodice. Overcome, I decided to sneak her into the wine cellar for the last bit of amorous delight I was likely to have in this world. An inebriated young Lieutenant pulling a giggling young French woman behind him through a debris-strewn cellar is not particularly given to stealth. Therefore, my attempt at dalliance came to the attention of the Sergeant of the Guards just about the time when the young woman's knickers were nearing half-staff. Taking me in tow, the Sergeant presented me to Major Cameron.

"My captor was quickly dismissed, and I found myself standing at some semblance of attention before the towering man. Even now, I can recall my eyes looking into his, which were the darkest blue and meanest that I could recall. Periodically, I would stare downward at his immense, hairy hands with freckles all over them. Suddenly, he hissed in a voice that I could imagine the Almighty might employ on the day of final judgment. 'Lieutenant you are a disgrace!' Then his knuckles grew more white, and he continued. 'I'm giving you one more chance and if you are ever brought before me again, I'll close the door and claim you tried to assault me. Then, I shall proceed to beat the holy hell out of you, after which you will be placed under arrest and await court-martial! Is that clear Lieutenant?' 'Yes, sir,' I slurred. I've never heard anything clearer in my life.

"Then the Major recalled the Sergeant and told him to pour a gallon of coffee in me and not let me urinate until I had finished it all. Needles to say, from that day on, I was a model officer. General Cameron never brought it up again, and he always treated me with an even hand, as he did all junior officers. Yes, Major, I owe the General a favor. I want to see how this young pony compares to the old warhorse."

In just forty-eight hours, Colonel Upham met Captain Iain Cameron, and he observed that the young officer was the image of his father. However, he was no pony and certainly not an old warhorse. Instead, the man at attention across the desk was a strong young stallion. His eyes were just as blue and intense as his father's, and the knuckles were just as big. After much discussion, the two men found many interests in common. So, with the Colonel's aid, encouragement, and planning, Iain plunged into a four-week period of intense preparation.

His marksmanship became superb with a great variety of weapons, However, for distance shooting, he switched to a M-1 Garand in 30 06 caliber. All the Lee Enfields at his disposal had their bolts on the right-hand side, and he was never able to satisfy himself in attaining a very rapid working of the bolt when it was necessary to reach across with his left hand. Although Iain's fluency in Gurkhali was deemed quite adequate for the field, he continued to enhance his skill. A surprise awaited Captain Cameron, for Kulbar Ghale, nicknamed Cool Beer, one of the original Gurkha trio Iain had commandeered, was stationed at Church Crookham. Cool Beer had been wounded in Malay and sent to England for recovery. Now he was fit and anxious to return to action with the great, tall Scot. In addition, Cool Beer had been promoted. Therefore, he was ideal to watch over Iain's Gurkha detachment. They would fly out together.

During the time that Iain had spent at Church Crookham, he had felt very remiss in being away from Claire. However, they both took comfort in the fact that his absence now, which allowed for preparation for survival, might well be the key to his safety and return. With many wedding preparations under way, the time was going fast.

Claire came from her shift and saw Iain standing in the parking lot. They ran to each other with arms unfurled. Their collision was gentle and kisses warm and tender. From his pocket, Iain procured the little silk pouch and removed the ring, which he slid on Claire's finger. She was amazed and thrilled at the same time.

"Oh! Iain, it's so beautiful, and the diamond is so big!"

"It was my grandmother's," he replied. "I'll have it reset for you if we can find a good jeweler."

Claire looked at the setting, and it was antique to be sure. However, it seemed the perfect match for the stone, so she replied, "No, dear heart, they have been as one for all these years, and I never wish to see them apart. I like to think of them as bonded together for always, as we will be soon."

Shortly, after Iain had departed, the other sisters were all aflutter. Claire was cherished and respected by all her compatriots, and her impending departure generated a degree of sadness in each. As would be expected of her, Claire went to pay her respects to Farkie on her final day, as she had already given notice of leaving. Her supervisor was uncharacteristically quiet, though she did sincerely congratulate Claire and wish her well. However, if anyone had seen Miss Farqharson after Claire left, they would have noted a handkerchief held close to her eyes and considerably dampened by blotted tears. However, for Claire, after all the good-byes were said, much still had to be accomplished.

Meanwhile, Iain was thinking, *So much to do, and so little time to do it. Worse yet, when all is done, there will be only one week to savor the fruits of our efforts. Then, I would be whisked away back to the Green Hell they call Malay. Claire will be left to wait, wonder and worry. Certainly, it is all deplorable but hardly unique. They will suffer, but hopefully survive. Capture the happiness we can now, then return to reclaim our dreams.*

Finally, all was in readiness.

Though the wedding party was small, it was tightly bonded. They gathered in the same chapel where Mary Queen of Scots had fervently prayed so many years ago prior to her beheading. Iain's and Claire's parents stood close by, along with Geordie's mother and father. Also, Sandy MacPhee and Molly, plus a smattering of relatives and close friends were present. Iain's younger sister, Annie, made a beautiful bridesmaid, and Major Wilson was best man.

In its reverence and simplicity, the service was beautiful. With the exchange of traditional vows, there was no doubt in anyone's mind that only death would render them apart. Then, after an intimate and lovely reception party, the newlyweds took their leave, anxious to compress all the happiness they could into seven short days. Only fitting, Percy would be their honeymoon car.

Once the bride and groom were nestled inside, Percy sallied forth across the cobblestone ramp of Edinburgh Castle and purred his way north toward the Kyle of Lochalsh. Though Claire knew they were heading north, the final destination was meant to be a surprise for her. Then, she saw the sign indicating their entry into the village of Balmacara and that Lochalsh was only a few miles beyond. Suddenly, she exclaimed, "Oh! Iain, are we going to Skye?"

"Yes," he answered softly, "but we'll be using the bridge and not going 'Over the Sea to Skye,' as Bonny Prince Charlie did."

Slowly caressing his cheek, Claire demurred, "I just love hopelessly romantic people, and I'm glad I married one."

Smiling, Iain continued. "Actually, Mrs. Cameron, we are going to Portree, to be exact."

Claire held his arm tightly and began to sing "Over the Sea to Skye," in a beautiful soprano voice.

Before long, they arrived at a renowned inn perched on a cliff just to the North of Portree. However, Claire was dismayed that there seemed to be no sign of life, but posted on the door to the lobby was a small sign that read "Greetings Captain and Mrs. Cameron. We turn in early this time of year, but your room is ready—the Bridal Suite. There is a fine fire going in the hearth, plus a chilled bottle of champagne and some cold cuts on the table. Make yourselves at home and enjoy your stay. We'll see you sometime in the morning (or afternoon)." This had been signed by Mr. and Mrs. MacPherson, the owners. Also, in parentheses was the phrase "married fifty years."

In the days following, the bride and groom indulged in the fulfillment of their union, as it was a pleasure they had denied themselves during their courtship. In the honeymoon suite was a great bay window offering a glorious view of the charming inlet, which thrust its way like a crooked finger into the cliffs surrounding the Sound of Rassay. On days when the weak fall sun managed to make the scudding clouds scamper away, and the Highland mist dispel, they could see the Isle of Rassay off to the east. Boats of varying size, color, and description plied their way to and fro from the snug harbor and anchorage. Birds of the sea were profuse and much alive in their aerial acrobatics, and so clamorous with their calls. Autumn's chill nights had worked their wonders on the trees, leaving a palate full of color on every limb. Portree was their land of enchantment, and it was to be indulged to the fullest in the few days they were to have, then carefully folded away, hopefully to be unfurled and recalled time and time again.

On one of several walks into the village, Claire noted a small painting in an artist's shop. This scene seemed to capture all their thoughts and happy moments in Portree. They decided it had to be purchased and must be hung in every future house they were to have. Although expensive, given their budget, they felt, *How could we put a price on the picture of our dreams?* Forever, Claire and Iain would be happy they made this decision, for much too soon it was time to leave; however, they carried a part of their dream with them. The MacPhersons, who had left them the note, saw them off personally. In so doing, they remembered themselves, as they once were, over fifty years ago, and this helped rekindle every joy that they had known.

As planned, Iain and Claire returned to his parent's home so he could gather up his gear and say his good-byes. Fortunately, there was time for a walk before dinner, and Simba had to be included. As they came to the vista with its bench, Claire and Iain sat down, but Simba was obviously dismayed. Instinctively, he knew that something was to occur, and there would be no part for him. He sat on the ground with his chest pressed tightly to his master's leg, muzzle resting on Iain's thigh. Simba's eyes were deep wells filled with all he wished to express.

"Can you take Simba with you?" asked Claire.

"He's asking the same question," said Iain, "so I'll tell you both. Sergeant Simba, I would love to take you with me, but I'm, not sure the Army and the RAF would agree. In addition, I must tell you that dogs have far shorter lives than men. You really only have time for one war, old friend. You nearly died trying to save your first master, and you were instrumental in our victory over the Serpent. So, Simba, you have had your war, and you deserve to live out your days in contentment. Besides, I have a new duty for you. While I am gone, your new mistress will be visiting from time to time, and I must have someone dependable to walk with her and share this place." Then, all three sat silently for a time before they returned together to the manor house in complete accord. However, dinner was solemn that night despite the efforts of all to make it otherwise.

On the following morning, at another farewell in the driveway, all the participants were resolute, though the ladies did have an occasional dab at their eyes, and a sniffle was not to be avoided. Sister Annie was now a young woman and gave her brother a kiss commensurate with her status. She also kissed Claire and told her how happy she was to have her as a sister, then she started to cry.

For Iain and his parents, it was a re-enactment of the scene that took place hardly more than a year ago. Claire kissed and hugged them both, then as she started for the car, General Cameron said, "Claire we would like you to have the Healey while Iain is gone, for it would make it much easier for you to come and see us and your parents."

After thanking them, Claire said, "I'll take good care of Percy because he is named after Harry Percy, who died in the Battle of Shrewsbury in 1046." Then she put her arms around the General's neck, kissed him again, and began to sob. The elder Cameron suppressed his own tears by virtue of setting his teeth so hard that they were in danger of splintering.

"I'm sorry," said Claire. "I guess I'm not really much of a soldier's wife." However, she quickly regained control.

Iain's mother looked deeply into the young woman's eyes and replied "I've seen no finer, my dear Claire," as the couple departed.

The plans were that Iain would catch a flight to London from the RAF facility in Edinburgh. Together, they called Claire's parents, and Iain said his good-byes. At the end of the conversation, Angus said softly, "The sermon bet is still on, Iain, after you return."

Shortly afterward, at the RAF Station, Claire steeled herself, though she felt disembodied. Iain clutched her, held her ever so tight and kissed her. "I love you with all my heart Claire!"

"And I love you, Iain."

Just then, a Sergeant hurried by and hollered, "We're ready to button her up, Captain!" One last kiss and Iain was gone. Standing alone, Claire watched the Dakota until it turned from an airplane to a speck, then finally a phantom.

Chapter Thirty-Three

※ ※ ※

Upon Captain Cameron's arrival in London, there was little time for reflection. Since another plane was waiting, it was simply a matter of grab your kit and go. Reconciling himself to the vast feeling of emptiness that prevailed, he took some comfort in knowing his six Gurkhas were all on board. Additionally, several fresh young Second Lieutenants would be on the flight, plus some enlisted men and noncoms. He could look at the faces and tell who was going back and who had never been to Malay. Resignation reigned on the faces of the former, and anxious anticipation masking the faces of the latter. Their plane was a DC-4, being more commodious, faster, and of longer range than the Dakota. *I suppose this is better*, he thought. *At least if you are anxious to get to hell sooner in slightly more comfort.*

Two of the young lieutenants approached him. "We beg your pardon, Captain, but would it be possible to have a few words with you? We understand you will be taking over Delta Company, and we will be under your command."

How frightfully young and innocent they look, he thought. However, they couldn't be more than a few years younger than he was. But why dwell on that? *Just put it aside and help the lads, as best you're able.* So, replying to their inquiry, Cameron said, "Certainly, please seat yourselves anywhere you can, and I'll brief you to the best of my ability. I am Captain Iain Cameron, and you are?"

"Second Lieutenant Jeremy Chism—" However, the "sir" that was to follow was aborted at the first consonant, as the young officer, heedless of his location, smashed his head into the top of the fuselage.

"No need to come to attention in the confines of this aircraft, Lieutenant

Chism," Iain said with a little smile. Although the young man appeared dazed, he soon recovered his composure, while softly massaging a developing hematoma. Second Lieutenant Byron Ogilvie was more cautious and introduced himself in a crouched posture.

"What's it really like in Malay, sir?" asked Ogilvie.

"As you may have heard, most refer to it as the 'green hell,'" said Cameron. "Some have come up with more sordid descriptions, but I'll spare you the expletives." As Cameron continued the briefing, the young officers sat silent, as their Captain gave them a very comprehensive narrative on the geography, flora, fauna, climate, plus logistical conditions. Cameron made no attempt to spare their sensitivities, nor embellish the conditions they would face, as they were odious enough. Then, he added, "I'm sure, gentlemen, of the questions now forming in your minds but are loathe to ask: Can I make it; am I tough enough; will I survive? Only God knows the answer to the last one. As to the other two, I can only say have faith in yourself and in your training. Be always guided by duty, honor, and the greatest respect for your men. Never, never be too vain to ask counsel with your Sergeants; if done in the proper manner, you will gain their respect, not their disdain. Remember, my headquarters, wherever it turns out to be, will always have an open door or an open tent flap. I have every confidence that you will do your duty and do it well. Now, let's see if we can get some tea or coffee and a sandwich. I'm hungry as hell."

Soon, it was dark, and the first refueling stop was an hour or so in the future. Sliding somewhat back in his seat, Cameron realized that he was tired, and sleep would eventually come, but he had no desire to seek it yet. *Strange,* he thought, *how the mind becomes attuned to the harmonies of the reciprocating engines and the whirling of their props.* He seemed to be developing a single lyric for the droning sound, and it was as if the engines kept repeating, "Claire, Claire, Claire." Then they would change pitch when altering speed, and it would come across as "Geordie, Geordie, Geordie." When pushed to maximum, he could imagine the thundering engines screaming, "Malay, Malay, Malay!" With his heart near breaking, he thought, *My dearest Claire, you are now far behind, and Geordie now long dead, but Malay lies ahead somewhere beyond a dozen horizons yet to be crossed.*

Finally, the plane reached the Crown colony of Hong Kong, and it was one of the stops that Iain had made with Geordie. They would be on the ground for possibly as much as eight hours, for the crew had become aware of an engine problem. Though it wasn't serious at the moment, nevertheless, they felt it prudent to fix it now, rather than end up as drop-in guests in a small section of a very large Pacific Ocean.

After deplaning, gradually Cameron and some of his fellow passengers worked their way out of range of the pungent odor of lubricants, aviation fuel, and engine exhaust. At a distance, the air was fresh and strongly scented with the aroma of jasmine. When perceived by the olfactory sense, it had a tranquilizing effect on one hand, but also stimulated the mind to recall all the sweetest memories of life. Iain's thoughts started with Claire, tripped nimbly through his parents and sister, boyhood, and standing with Geordie in this exact same place. Then, Claire's image returned, and with it, Iain became even more aware that it was very warm in Hong Kong, and a very obvious change from the autumn, which was now far behind. *It's like going to hell in stages!* Iain thought.

Now, the final leg was just hours away. As Cameron turned to view the city off in the distance, it was easy to conjure up images of buccaneers, flint-hearted merchants, tai pans, concubines, tongs, governors, coolies, opium, and silk. Then, his vision centered on little knots of men, not too far separated, but standing aloof. *Fine Commanding Officer you are,* he thought. *You're so engaged in your personal reflections that you are oblivious to the welfare of your men. Of course, there is a limit on the amount of socialization allowed between ranks, but that should never preclude me getting to know the man covering my back or who will carry me to safety when I am wounded, and help bring me back when I'm dead. Also, I should know the men that I would place in harm's way with one of my orders, which they must obey.*

Quickly, Cameron strode to where Lieutenants Chism and Ogilvie were standing in sweat-streaked uniforms trying to look proper and official. Certainly, Captain Cameron knew the feeling as they stood at attention and saluted. He returned the salute followed immediately with, "At ease. Come with me, gentlemen." Then, he set off toward a small cluster of Scots Guards enlisted and noncoms. More salutes followed and another, "At ease," plus a repeat of "follow me." Soon, they were in front of the six Gurkhas, bringing smiles to their boyish faces. First, he singled out Cool Beer, who had been at his side in Malay before they were both wounded. Cool Beer was now a Havildar, or sergeant, and his English was reasonably good. "Sergeant Kulbar Ghale, I will speak to the officers and men in English. Please translate for me, so all present will know of my desires."

After surveying all of them, Cameron spoke slowly though forcefully. "We are Scots Guards and Gurkhas, different in race, religion, and skills, but we are to become united as members of Delta Company. We have a common task and a common enemy, so if we work together as brothers, I have every confidence we will share in a common victory. Look about you now and resolve that you will do your utmost to protect and befriend every man you see, and that you will carry over this feeling when we join the main unit."

Following Captain Cameron's talk, smaller brown hands were clasped by white. Various shades of eyes looked deeply into others. Resolve to do what the Captain had said was reflected from one to the other. Then, Cameron went off to see if he could find a single bottle of beer for each of the assembly. Shortly he returned in a Jeep piloted by a commissary Sergeant. Ample beer was on board. As Cameron drew close, he was happy to note Second Lieutenant Chism was in deep discussion with Sergeant MacFarlane, a returnee to Malay, and a damn fine soldier. Also, Second Lieutenant Ogilvie was busy examining the keen edge of a kukri, while the Gurkhas and other men looked on intently. Captain Cameron liked what he saw in this fraction of Delta Company. It was yet to be seen how they would fit with the main body; however, he was determined his men would be molded together like the parts of a sword, and he would persevere until the blade was razor sharp.

At last, they arrived at Kuala Lumpur. Although the Sergeant who collected them and the officers that briefed them were mostly new to Cameron, he noted that a few familiar faces remained. The oppressive heat and humidity were the same. As soon as arrangements were made, they were off in a small convoy of Jeeps and lorries to their final destination, which was Bandar Bahar, not far from the Muaa River.

Delta Company consisted of three platoons. Two were at full strength; however, Charlie Platoon had been cannibalized, consequently being at only 60 percent strength and primarily used as a reserve platoon. The captain Cameron was to replace had been flown out to the nearest medical facility after being wounded. Now, First Lieutenant Stewart was acting commanding officer. A gaunt man, taciturn by nature, he struck Cameron as being a good officer but debilitated by malaria and dysentery. Lieutenants McKendrick and Caldicot seemed to know what they were about. Unfortunately both Stewart and McKendrick were to be rotated out as soon as Ogilvie and Chism were ready to assume their roles. Thus, in a short time, there would be only one experienced officer and two neophytes under Cameron's command. *Thank God,* he thought, *for a number of excellent, experienced Sergeants and solid, dependable enlisted men.*

Because there were no patrols out at this time, on his arrival the new Commanding Officer of Delta Company addressed his entire command. Speaking directly to the hearts of all present, it was a solid speech. Changes would be made. All platoons would have essentially the same number of men. Consequently, in effect, they would be somewhat undermanned. However, they would be equal. Cameron didn't like the concept of a reserve platoon, as he felt it tended to make the members feel like misfits, and there were to be no misfits in Delta Company. Continuing, he exhorted the old hands to be patient, though firm with newcomers. For the latter, he urged them to learn fast and learn well. To all the men, their new Commanding Officer explained that "they were not just a squad, platoon, or company, but rather a dedicated team, or even better, a tough-as-nails fighting family. Physical training and martial arts training were both to be mandatory, and he included himself. However, for all units about to go on patrol or just back from one, there would be a day off. Everyone was to choose a buddy, and they were to be certain that their counterpart took their antimalarial medications and any other medicinal exactly as prescribed. Cameron's address was spirited, and their was no indication that their new Commanding Officer's words were not taken to heart. The men realized this man was no martinet, but a lean, tough follow-me type of soldier. If they were to survive and be successful in this dirty, damn "emergency" to which they had been committed, they couldn't imagine a better leader.

Three months had passed since Captain Cameron had assumed command of Delta Company. By Malay standards, they had been good months. As a result of action against the enemy or from illness, casualties were extremely low, and the success enjoyed by Delta was exemplary. Ching Peng was the recognized leader of the Communist terrorists, as they were now called. Having returned to Malay in 1946, he had raised an army in hopes of turning the country into a Communist state, and he had become a determined enemy of his former allies. The Medal of the British Empire awarded him along with the medal bestowed by King George V was no longer alluded to, nor did anyone much care to recall that he had marched in the great post World War II Victory Parade in London some two years prior. Despite the successes of many of the British Forces' Units, Ching Peng's army still numbered about 5,000 men. They were tough, resilient, and seemed able to survive for at least a week on a cup or so of rice and an occasional fish.

English forces for the most part needed far more sustenance; therefore, Cameron, like most commanders, limited his patrols to a week or less. Limiting of patrol time included Cameron's half dozen Gurkhas. Of course, he was aware that true Gurkha units sometimes were on patrol for as much as a month; however, that type of operation was never part of his plans for Delta. As far as armaments for his men were concerned, Cameron had chosen an admixture of Lee Enfield M5 jungle carbines, plus assorted automatic weapons ranging from American M2 .30-caliber carbines to Bren guns. Additionally, due to the martial arts training he had insisted on, all the units under his command were far above average in hand-to-hand combat.

Radio communications between units or with Headquarters were nearly as inadequate as they had been during Cameron's first tour. Few radios were available, and those that were transmitted poorly in the mountainous terrain. "Little better than two empty tin cans connected by a string," was Cameron's conclusion, as he bent over a crackling receiver proclaiming a garbled message, or a silent one with no message at all.

As Company Commander, one of Cameron's first directives was the deployment of two squads from both Alpha and Bravo Platoons on a "search-and-destroy mission." Iain felt the two Lieutenants who had accompanied him to Malay had matured sufficiently to be given a modest field command, especially since each had a very seasoned, savvy Sergeant to back them up. Recently the Communist terrorists had been active on both sides of the Muaa River. Therefore, two squads led by Second Lieutenant Ogilvie and Sergeant Hendry would patrol on the north side of the river and were given the code name "Tortoise." Second Lieutenant Chism and Sergeant Paisley, with their two squads, would patrol on the south side of the river and went afield with the code name "Hare." All of their intelligence reports had been correlated with what information could be gleaned from the local aboriginals. To the best of anyone's knowledge or analysis, they had determined that the Communist units were small in size, and it should be possible for either Tortoise or Hare to cope with any resistance they might encounter, with the resultant elimination of additional terrorists.

These patrols were expected to be in the field for approximately forty-eight hours. Punctually, Tortoise returned to Headquarters. They had encountered a small band of marauding, insurgent terrorists and were able to confirm the killing of four and capture of one. In turn, they had suffered no casualties, apart from a minor flesh wound to one of the enlisted men.

Meanwhile, dusk was descending like a foreboding curtain, but Hare had not returned. Captain Cameron stood confronting the map on his desk with a rod-like index finger tracing the route Hare should have taken. Certainly, there were no places to promenade in Malay. You fought for every foot you covered coming or going. *Bloody hell, they should be back by now.* Then Cameron decided, *If they're not back in the morning, I'll go find them myself.*

Moments later, there was a commotion outside his makeshift office. Iain headed for the door and caught sight of Sergeant Paisley. He looked exhausted, but there was more than fatigue that haunted his face—desperation was lurking there as well. Captain Cameron accepted and returned the subordinate's salute. One look at the man, and Cameron knew he had no more reserve to call on.

"Grab a chair, Sergeant. Do you want whiskey, water, or both?"

"God bless you, Captain, I can use both, but a Scot needs the whiskey first." Although Paisley was a small man, the bones of his forearms appeared to be shrouded by cables of steel. Wisps of pewter gray fringed the margins of his hair, which was otherwise pure obsidian, little different in hue from deep-set eyes that stared out from a face tanned to the color of teak.

Paisley quaffed half the whiskey, then set the glass aside. "I lost Second Lieutenant Chism and Private Barclay, Captain. Oh God! We spent all day yesterday searching, sir. I'm sorry Captain. I let you and Delta down." Then,

Sergeant Paisley kept shaking his head, as though the motion might somehow clear the sordid thoughts from his mind.

Captain Cameron replied, "I think it unlikely you are to blame for anything, Sergeant, but I need to know exactly what happened."

Paisley reached for the whiskey, then withdrew his hand and wiped his brow instead. "We got into a wee fire fight Captain. Nailed three of the terrorists for sure, and possibly wounded several others. I was checking the bodies out, looking for maps or other information. We were all down in a defensive mode when apparently Lieutenant Chism told one of the men that he was sure he heard moaning coming from a small distance away. He told Private Barclay to follow him. Corporal Farlayer called to them, 'Don't go,' but they didn't stop. Suddenly, all hell broke loose, and we were in another fire fight. Grenades were coming in, and we were throwing them back along with some grenades of our own. If we hadn't been in a proper defensive position, we could have been cut to pieces. As it turned out, some of us picked up some shrapnel from the grenades, but all turned out to be walking wounded, sir. All except the Lieutenant and Barclay."

Looking at the Sergeant, Cameron said one word, "Dead?"

While holding his head in his hands, Sergeant Paisley looked up replying, "Oh God! I don't know." Then, after looking at the whiskey glass, he again refrained, and his anguished eyes looked once more into those of his commander. "When the firing stopped, we carefully looked around, sir. Three more dead terrorists, but no Lieutenant Chism and no Private Barclay."

"Any sign of blood or their weapons, Sergeant?"

"No weapons, sir, and any blood that was apparent had obviously come from the dead terrorists. We searched for the rest of the day but found no trace. I decided that I had best bring the men home than to keep it up. Did I do right, sir?

"Yes, Sergeant, you did exactly what was right."

"What do you think happened, Captain?"

"I think they were captured and hurriedly led off," said Cameron. "I'm sure that if they were killed, the terrorists wouldn't have hauled them off for a Christian burial. In the event they were wounded, the bastards would have simply slit their throats. No, Sergeant, they were taken alive for reasons not apparent as yet. They obviously don't have information so valuable that they would want to torture them to obtain it. We are hardly holding any D-Day secrets to ourselves. No, I think there is a more obvious and probably despicable reason, but I'll find out one way or the other."

Cameron refilled his Sergeant's half-empty glass, saying, "Drink that, then go get some rest. However, on the way, find Lieutenant Caldicot and send him to see me."

When Lieutenant Harry Caldicot arrived, Iain was again poring over the map. He explained to his subordinate the plans he had made. "I'm taking a detachment out at first light and Harry, you are to be in charge of Delta until we return."

"Why not let me go Captain?" was the officer's reply.

"Thank you, Harry. But if this is a fool's errand, then it should be led by the fool that thought it up."

After Cameron had completed his plan and was seeking a few hours sleep, he became aware of a knock on his door. The Sergeant of the Guard was there, and beside him stood a disheveled man. In the poor light, it was apparent he was affecting a wan smile, which only served to enhance his suspicious appearance. "He just showed up at the gate, Captain. Says he knows what happened to our Lieutenant and Barclay and needed to talk to our Commanding Officer."

"Bring him in, Sergeant, and sit him in a chair, then stand by." Cameron turned on several of the lights before confronting whatever kind of messenger the man might turn out to be. Now, he had a devious expression accompanying his wan smile.

"Are you the Commanding Officer?" he said haltingly in broken English. Then, he continued: "I want to help our great British protectors and save the two men that Captain Wah Mei, the evil Chinese, has captured."

There probably aren't two aborigines in the whole province who speak English this well, thought Iain, *and this chap isn't one of them.* However, out loud, he said, "Please continue," and the man smiled more broadly.

"Thank you, Captain," he replied. The larger smile provided sufficient luminescence within the man's mouth to show at least one dental filling. Cameron thought, *Odds are one thousand to one this fellow is a plant.* But he let the story unfold.

"Your officer and man are at Wah Mei's camp along the river," he said. Then he asked, "May I see a map? I will show." Quickly, the man pointed to a small spot of land projecting into the south bank of the Muaa River.

"They are here, Captain. You must rescue them soon."

"Why?" responded Cameron. This question drew a surprised look, though no comment from the Sergeant of the Guard.

Answering, the man replied, "Because Wah Mei is going to bring my poor people in from all the surrounding area. He intends to feed your men to the rats, showing how cowardly they are and how you are powerless to save them. He feels it will teach them that the Chinese are the true masters of the world."

"Thank you so much for telling me," said Captain Cameron.

"May my humble self go now, perhaps with a small reward?"

"First tell me when this is to occur," said Iain.

"In the morning of the day to follow this one," was the answer he received.

"Yes, you can go. You can go straight to the stockade. Arrest him, Sergeant! I'll see more of him when I return." Then, Cameron decided that all of his plans must be changed. Consequently, he set about doing so and was satisfied with the results.

Birds of Malay were just beginning their raucous welcome to the rising tropical sun, which they seemed to enjoy but man could only endure. At this appointed time, though Captain Cameron had excused the exhausted members of the just returned Tortoise and Hare detachments, all others were assembled for briefing. In a deeply resonant voice, Cameron began his address: "Men of Delta Company, we know, for certain, that Lieutenant Chism and Private Barclay have been captured by a group led by a Captain Wah Mei. We are not certain they are still alive, but we must assume they are. An informer, who I believe to be a spy, has come to this camp to let us know that it is the intention of this Wah Mei to publicly torture our comrades in a most hideous way. This may or may not be true, but I believe it is. Also, I believe that it is all part of a carefully contrived trap. I have a plan to try and rescue Lieutenant Chism and Private Barclay. Obviously, my plan is filled with assumptions. If any assumptions prove to be false, then certainly failure might ensue. It is my intention to lead this effort, and I ask for sufficient volunteers to aid me. By my calculations, thirty-six would be the optimum number." Then, looking out at the men, Iain hoped at least that number would step forward. However, at that second, every man present advanced forward without a single laggard being observed.

Iain let out a small gasp. This was one of the most moving moments of his military career. "Men of Delta! You know your comrades, your country, and yourselves. In the history of war, no unit of any size could possibly stand more proud. I am enormously grateful and respectful of your courage and resolve. Much as I would like to take you all, that would be imprudent, for there is this camp and this flag to defend." With these words, every eye turned to the Union Jack wafting slightly from atop the staff to which it had been hoisted minutes before.

Continuing, he said: "Sergeant Ronald McAllister and Havildar Ghale please come to my office. However, before I dismiss you, men, may I salute you with all the affection and sincerity in my soul." Thereupon, Captain Cameron stood at full attention and rendered the most splendid symbol of military recognition, and it was returned by all with equal affection.

Minutes later, Ghale and McAllister stood with their Captain, intently focused on the map in front of them. "Havildar Ghale, you and the five other Gurkhas will come with me. This trail, which runs along the river and leads to what we assume to be their camp, is quite wide and easy of passage. I believe the site was purposefully selected in expectation that we would blunder up the trail as fast as we could. It is my best guess—and I emphasize *guess*—that there will be a well-prepared ambush set up along the trail, approximately 1,000 yards from their camp. Therefore, any forward unit we send rushing along the trail to the rescue would be allowed to pass. Then, the machine guns that I presume are deployed would open on the middle and rear units. As soon as they heard gunfire, the main group of terrorists would come charging out of the camp and attempt to annihilate us all. My plan is that, Ghale, you and your men and myself will start up the trail at nightfall. We will walk as stealthily as possible along the south side of the river until we reach a point approximately 1,500 yards from the camp. There we will split out on both sides of the trail, trying to stay about ten yards apart. From that point on, we'll be crawling bush by bush until we find out who's there and annihilate them."

Rising slightly, Sergeant McAllister cleared his throat, so Cameron sensed a question was coming and asked, "A comment, Sergeant?"

"Begging your pardon Captain but how will you know when you are that distance from the camp?"

"Left to myself, I probably wouldn't, Sergeant. However, remember that our Gurkha brothers come from Nepal. Once you get outside Kathmandu, there probably aren't three road signs in the whole country. From the time they could walk, these Gurkhas found their way from one place to another because they had the uncanny facility to damn near recognize any stream and every rock. Fortunately, they have gone along the trail many times. I trust, and I have to trust that they will know, just as surely as they know their way in the Himalayas."

"Aye, sir," replied McAllister, looking a bit incredulous.

"Now, Sergeant, let's discuss your role. As you well know, I've had you all out paddling dugout canoes on many occasions. I suspect some of you may have thought it all rather silly, but now we are going to try and use it to our advantage. I need you to select twenty-nine men who paddle the best and can do it most quietly. Hopefully, the same group will contain our best marksmen. I have timed our canoe training on several occasions. If you all put your backs into it, you should be within a half mile of their camp when we are beginning to clear out the ambush that we are expecting."

"Sir," said McAllister with more than a hint of exasperation. "How will I know when I reach that point? There won't be any of these rock readers with me?"

"All you need are your ears, Sergeant. There is a good-size waterfall on a tributary right where I want you to stop and wait. If you had never been outside the Glasgow city limits in your life, you would have no trouble recognizing it."

"Then what?" said McAllister.

Patiently, Captain Cameron said, "If you hear gunfire, attack the camp! Otherwise, I'll send one of the Gurkhas to tell you when to proceed further up river, and you can all start paddling like hell."

Continuing his instructions, Cameron stated solemnly, "Sergeant McAllister, if no Gurkha comes, or no shots are heard, you should return to camp at dawn and assume we failed." Then, he added, "If all goes well and you do attack, remember to warn your men to recognize their targets. We sure as hell wouldn't want to kill Lieutenant Chism and Private Barclay or mow down some hapless natives forced to attend this despicable event!"

Further discussions followed, along with additional questions, then all seemed to be understood and agreed on. Now, it was time for Ghale and McAllister to brief their men and attend to their weapons and the dugout canoes. Also, there were letters to write and entrusted to those left behind.

Iain penned a letter to Claire and one to his parents in his broad handwriting, knowing he was placing thirty-six men plus himself in grave danger in hopes of saving two soldiers. If he lost more than two men in the effort, how could he reconcile it? Cameron decided, "You can't always reconcile your honor. You have to respect it and react to it. Would Claire understand that I am gambling our future?" In his heart, he knew she would. As a nurse, would she refuse to tend a patient with a deadly, highly infectious disease out of fear that she might contract it? No, not Claire, for her sense of duty and honor were as deeply inscribed as his own.

Shortly afterward, as nightfall descended on them, the same jungle birds that serenaded the dawn were becoming silent in the dark. Aware of the hour, Cameron checked and found all of the men had been inspected. They and their equipment were in readiness. Scouts had been sent out to check their route, though there was no reason to suspect they would be under surveillance. Nonetheless, they had no doubt that Wah Mei knew that Delta would come to rescue their men. Cameron thought, *Thank God our approach will not be as expected!*

By 2000 hours, Sergeant McAllister and his men were putting their dugouts in the oily black waters of the Muaa River. "Look up, lads," he hissed. "We have a long pull ahead of us, and a rendezvous we dare not miss. Fortunately, there is enough moonlight for hand signals, and there is to be no noise or talk unless I indicate we have come within the range of a whisper. It's silence for now. You can shout your bloody heads off when it's all over!"

Meanwhile, Captain Cameron had reached the trailhead, where he gathered his small band of Gurkhas about him. Speaking to Ghale, he said, "No further opportunity will come our way. Every man must know exactly what we are doing. If my Gurkhali is not adequate, then please interrupt me and clarify for them. Also, impress on the men that it is absolutely necessary to ask any questions now."

Then, all the plans were thoroughly covered. Ghale further expounded on every detail that might be unclear, and all questions were answered to everyone's satisfaction. From that point on, absolute silence was essential, except for the "tiger." When Captain Cameron had discussed the fact that bird calls could obviously not be used in darkness, Ghale broke out in a manly Mona Lisa smile. Cameron knew something was coming, but had no idea of what it might be. "Captain," said the diminutive brown man, "Lance Naik Sherbadahur has on many occasions entertained us with his ability to mimic a prowling tiger's nocturnal sounds, and in all modesty I have learned to do nearly as well. Tigers are not common here, but there are a few in this region. Several times, we have seen them with our own eyes. However, more frequently we have come across their spoor. Once or twice, the great cat's recent kills have been encountered. May I make a suggestion, Captain?"

"One would be appreciated," replied Cameron.

"Thank you, sir," was the response before the Gurkha continued. "Let me go up the right side of the trail with two men, while Lance Naik Sherbadahur and two others should be with you on the left side. Then, as soon as we sense the presence of our enemy on either side, an appropriate sound for a hunting tiger would be given. Very surely, this will alert all of us and the terrorists as well. However, for them it will be most distracting. Any sounds that we make in our advance will be associated in their minds with the approach of the great predator. No doubt, thoughts of those massive teeth and claws ripping into you will be unnerving. Still you can't shoot at the sounds to kill the tiger or drive it away. To do so would betray the ambush and unleash a fury in their Commander, such as it would have been far better to have been eaten by the cat. Frightened men are easy to find, and when we do—" Ghale said no more, but drew his thumb across his neck in a gesture far more poignant than any words. Acceptance of the strategy was evident in Cameron's face, leaving the use of words redundant. Since they were clustered together, Cameron's erect thumb was the only sign necessary to initiate their action.

Now, it was time for Cameron and the Gurkhas to proceed. Since the trail was well worn and broad, they gambled and maintained as fast a pace as possible until Ghale thought they had almost reached the point approximately 1,500 yards from the camp. Besides the Gurkha's uncanny ability to know where they were located in a place they were familiar with, Iain took comfort in the fact that the waterfall where McAllister was to stop would probably be audible to them as well.

As it would be impossible to achieve any measure of stealth carrying rifles, Thompsons, or Winchester trench guns, Cameron and his Gurkha team were lightly armed. Each man had a well-secured pistol, and each Gurkha his kukri. As for Cameron, he wore his dirk, and though he was bereft of his Scottish broadsword, he had not entirely relinquished his heritage. In a special scabbard, between his shoulderblades, was a miniature replica of a Scot's battle ax. This was smaller but otherwise identical to the favorite weapon of Robert the Bruce. Iain was sure that he could use it as effectively as the wee brown men from Nepal used their dreaded knives. This was reassuring to him, for when the 1,500-yard point was attained, they would spread out.

They were ready. Finally, their objective was reached. Seconds remained before they must separate, and Cameron raised his right thumb and whispered the Gurkhali word for "tiger." Taking advantage of the sparse time, he studied his Gurkhas intently. The natural foundation of their teak-hued skin had been carefully layered with mud. However, a few soft moonbeams had dodged through the jungle's canopy, revealing six sets of gleaming white teeth signifying an equal number of enigmatic smiles. Obviously, it was as though they were off on an exciting adventure and could hardly wait to start.

Although the smile that their Captain returned was forced, they accepted it with enthusiasm. Six others thumbs were now raised, and the Gurkhali word for "tiger" came out in a near harmonious whisper.

When the approximate 1,500-yard point was attained, they spread out. Thus, Cameron was furthest to the left and closest to the river. Lance Naik Sherbadahur was located on Cameron's right and closest to the trail, and the remaining two Gurkhas were interspersed between them. Ghale had place himself on the right margin of the trail with the other two Gurkhas flanking him. Approximately ten yards separated each man on either side.

At that exact same moment, Captain Wah Mei set down his rice bowl and watched the approach of his subordinate, Wai Li. "Should we not deploy more of our men Comrade Captain?" said his subordinate.

"You are too easily agitated, Wai Li. Spend more time reading and learning from the writings of Sun Tzu and less time fidgeting like some nervous bride awaiting her lord and master."

"But surely the Scots should be here soon," replied the Lieutenant, not completely cowed by the rebuke.

"The Scots will come up the trail and plan to attack us at dawn," Captain Wah Mei sneered. "They are as predictable as lice on a beggar."

"Perhaps they will not want to take the risk," the other man said softly.

"After all, we have only two of their men, and such a small number could be judged insignificant."

"You are a fool," snarled Wah Mei. "A Scot's honor will require they act boldly to rescue their unfortunate comrades. Speaking of which, we must prepare them for their role in the festivities that we have planned. Now, take ample men and bring them to the site we have prepared."

On the dirt floor of a small bamboo cage in which they were imprisoned, Lieutenant Chism and Private Barclay were sprawled, looking at each other hauntingly. They had not spoken since they were warned by the Captain that their guard had orders to shoot them in the event they tried to communicate in any way. However, both stirred and looked apprehensively at the approaching squad of men. Then, their cage door was opened, and the man in charge motioned for them to come out, so they arose stiffly and hesitantly. "Remember name, rank, and serial number," Chism whispered to Private Barclay. Quickly, a rifle butt hammered his back, sending him sprawling and gasping for breath. Guards dragged him the rest of the way to a clearing in the center of the camp, where Captain Wah Mei awaited them.

"Well, well," he said. "Look at our Scots Guards. We are not so haughty now, are we, my friends? I'm sure you are wondering about my English. May I inform you that I am Captain Wah Mei of the Chinese People's Army. Also, I received a Master's Degree in Engineering from the University of Birmingham in 1937 well before I came to despise your capitalistic ways."

Wah Mei continued. "I am expecting your comrades to come to your rescue near dawn. I'm sure their efforts will be spurred on when they perceive your screams!" Then, after the Captain's nod, both prisoner's were grabbed and placed astraddle over horizontal, thick bamboo poles, supported by upright posts about four feet off the ground. Immediately, both men's arms and legs were tightly secured beneath the poles. In this painful position, a feeling of sheer terror filled both men, and their faces reflected it.

"This is actually a European invention," mocked Wah Mei. "Rather like riding a horse, but don't worry, you can't fall off. Since your weight rests entirely on your pelvic bones and breast bones, the pain will become agonizing in a short time. However, I have a diversion for you that will help take your mind off your distress." Quickly, their heads were encased in small bamboo cages, and Wah Mei said, "Please observe that there are little doors right in front of your faces oh! brave Scots." Then, the sadistic Captain nodded once again, and this time his men appeared with similar cages, but these were compartmentalized, and each contained two enormous rats.

After the rat receptacles were locked in place, Wah Mei strode forward, addressing Chism and Barclay. "These rats have been starved for days, my heroes of the British Empire. If they weren't separated, they would try to eat each other, but now they must continue fasting and await access to your faces. Do you think they will relish an eye first? Or perhaps a soft lip? Although the nose and ears are rather chewy, I understand. One more thing! As an engineer, I have contrived one other little device to add to your anticipation. Above each of you are two buckets, and the upper one has a hole on the bottom, which allows water to drip slowly into the bucket below. Then, the bottom bucket has a rope, which is attached to the gates. When the bottom bucket is heavy enough, it will pull the gate up, and your friends will come to visit you. If you don't scream, and you listen carefully, you will be able to hear the water drip. This is my version of the venerable Chinese water torture. Some have said that by itself, this is enough to drive men stark, raving mad. With the rats as an added feature, perhaps madness awaits you. Conversely, you may wish to try and make yourselves raving mad now. Who knows, in your fantasies, you may welcome the rats feasting on your faces." Then, Wah Mei laughed, and said, "Pleasant dreams!"

Chism cried out, "You sadistic monster!" Barclay was more to the point and bellowed "Fuck you, you commie SOB!"

"Shall I have them whipped Captain?" asked Wai Li.

"No," replied the Captain. "They are only belligerent schoolboys. Soon, they will be screaming their lungs out, begging for mercy. Their sound will be a great stimulus for the would-be rescuers to blunder into our trap," the leader said with a leering smile.

"But Captain what if the filling buckets raise the gates too soon?"

"That will never happen, Comrade fool. The gates are latched, and the buckets will not open them even if they are full of water. Of course, they do not know that, nor were you clever enough to observe it. I will open the gates myself when it is time."

Meanwhile, Cameron studied the luminous dial on his wrist watch. Progress up the center of the trail had been relatively swift. However, when they concluded that they had attained the point approximately 1,500 yards from the Communist camp, forward momentum had become glacial. Since the only possible way to advance was in a crouch, they slowly tried to separate the nearly invisible vines and foliage as fast as they could, all the while hoping it was a vine and not a deadly viper. As Iain's heels pressed into the softened jungle floor, he would sometimes ponder if it was the final step toward disaster and death. *God has known for all eternity what I may soon learn*, he thought, as he continued on slowly.

Now, it was nearing 0500 hours, and any ambush would have to be deadly near. Turbulent, rushing water cascading from the cataract on the Muaa River had been audible for some time. Suddenly, his hackles rose, while his heart responded in an irrepressible tachycardia, as the first sound of the tiger erupted from the area where Ghale must be located. Seconds later, a tiger response came from his immediate right, as Sherbadahur replied. Anyone having heard a real tiger intimately close by in the eerie darkness would surely think they were encountering another and it was hunting him. Worse yet, there were two! These tigers were approaching, as best the dug-in terrorists could discern, and they were caught in between.

Whereas Cameron's alarm had rapidly subsided since he knew the etiology of the cough-like breathing and interspersed roars, his enemy did not. Ensconced along the trail, all the terrorists experienced the fullest reaction to fear. Fighting the desire to flee, they froze in position. Gasping for breath, twitching movements, and, in the case of some, incontinence of bowel and bladder could not be constrained. Hammering pulses in their ears diminished auditory acuity, making it difficult if not impossible to determine if they could hear signs of the tiger's movements, but the calls were excruciatingly clear! Unable to overcome his fear, one man bolted for the camp. Enraged, his officer was about to shoot him, then realized that would alert his enemy, give away his position, and result in unimaginable consequences. Even so, he did manage to strike another soldier starting to bolt across the forehead with the butt of his pistol, rendering him unconscious. Unfortunately for the first fleeing comrade, he fell very near Sherbadahur. Apparition-wise, the last thing he saw when his head was still adjoined to his body was not the gapping maw of a tiger but the glistening blade of a kukri seeking his neck. Eternity was entered silently.

Though Cameron's senses were not as keen as those of the Gurkhas, he nevertheless was becoming fast attuned to the proximity of his foes. Sounds of movement were coming from many quarters. Were these being made by his men, and would they betray their presence? Answering his own question, Iain decided, *No, in all probability they will enforce the nightmare of tigers nearby. After all, these great striped carnivores can make noise with impunity, for what do they have to fear? Surely, there are no other animals in this locale that would provide intimidation.*

As predicted, the terrorists were incapable of escaping the tentacles of their dilemma. Although well armed with grenades, machine guns, and assault rifles, they could not fire and betray their position with no enemy in sight. Trigger fingers were not deployed, but voices could not be stifled. Whispers gave way to more audible voices, especially those arising from the leaders trying in vain to achieve silence. Though the Cantonese language was undecipherable to Captain Cameron and his men, the inflections and timbre associated with panic in any language were evident.

Two of Cameron's Gurkhas began crawling silently to the right, while Iain and the other one continued on to where they had heard an enemy's voice emanate. Suddenly, the loader of the first machine gun heard a dull thwack and felt the rain of warm fluid on his face and neck. Then, as he turned abruptly, the gunner's head was slithering off his shoulders. Pupils of his eyes were wide though not yet fixed. The loader did not hear the second thwack, nor if he could answer would he positively say that he had felt it. Simultaneously, two riflemen deployed nearby sensed impending doom. However, they took no offensive action, as they were so unnerved that they were incapable of doing so. By reflex, their hands started to raise in the sign of surrender, only to reverse in a futile gesture to catch the heads tumbling from their torsos. For the Gurkhas, the initial action had gone very well and very quickly. With cocked thumbs raised, the two Gurkhas smiled and whispered "tiger."

Meanwhile, on the left side of the trail along with the other Gurkhas, Captain Cameron was now within sight of the second machine gun deployment. Obviously, the group of four men were extremely agitated, as was determined by their jerky movements and whispers. Also, their attention would be directed toward the tiger one second, then to the position where their compatriots had called from just moments ago. Now that site was deadly silent. As they approached the enemy, Cameron had a tight grasp on the haft of his miniature battle ax, and a heavy leather thong attached to the handle was wrapped around his thick wrist. Now, he was close enough and it was time! Sharpened to a razor's edge, the crescent-shaped blade of the double-bitted weapon easily transected the enemy soldier's soft cap with little more resistance offered by the bony plates of the skull. After entering in the midline, the blade passed downward through the great fissure that lies between the hemispheres of the brain. His loader was as shocked and surprised as was the enemy soldier at the other emplacement.

Immediately, Iain's powerful wrist wrenched the ax from the first victim's head and swept it in a short arc, allowing the upper blade to cleave into the loader's neck at the angle of his jaw. This half-arrested its motion, but not before it had sheared the great vessels of his neck and transected his spinal cord. Quickly, Cameron whipped around to see who else might confront him; however, the two headless bodies posed no danger. His Gurkha had seen to that, and silently, he was kneeling, cleaning the blood from his kukri. Then, as best they could determine, there were no further enemies on their side.

To the right of the trail, similar success had been achieved at the first machine gun nest. Ghale and his men were now nearing the second. Whispered as it was, the talk of the terrorists was frantic, and more than four men's voices were audible. One of the voices seemed authoritarian, but the others did not. However, they all seemed turned in the direction of the last tiger roar, completely unaware of the infiltration. Ghale and his two men advanced like three confident cobras, ready to strike. Sounds of the two kukris severing flesh and bone came with the familiar sound. Then there was the eruption of geysers of blood from the surging flow through the separated carotid arteries. Lifeless heads tumbled with mouths still formed in the first syllables of words they were about to whisper. Ghale whirled and brought his blade diagonally across a third man's neck. From that position, he did not have the force to decapitate, but the result were just as lethal. Then the Gurkhas sprang to their feet. There were two more enemies to kill, and it must be instantaneously or the alarm would be given.

One man was no problem. He was kneeling with his arms hiding his face in a position of absolute submission and horror. As the knife sang in its descent, both wrists were severed along with his head. Ghale threw himself at the sixth man, with his deadly blade ready to strike. Obviously, he was an officer, and must be the one who seemed to speak with authority. Pistol raised, the officer had it pointed directly at his chest. However, now Ghale would not, could not stop! He must kill the man before he fired. Suddenly, there was a flash of light, a reflection only, but it appeared at the officer's wrist just before the blood erupted and the hand fell away. Still another reflection, and the head followed. On the face of the officer, was a look of bewilderment, which vanished as it made contact with the earth. Ghale had never felt as close to death as in this moment. He found it a strange sensation, one he would have to remember and analyze. Then, from behind the fallen officer, another Gurkha emerged. He smiled and whispered, "Other tigers also like to have fun!"

At the Insurgent's Camp, after having sent Wai Li out thirty minutes before to ascertain the readiness of his unit, Captain Wah Mei was awaiting the return of the Lieutenant and his report. However, the fool had not returned, and he was angry, though for Lieutenant Wai Li, he was beyond worrying about the wrath of his Commander. As time elapsed, Wah Mei sensed there was something radically wrong; otherwise, his underling would have come back. Could the Scots have somehow infiltrated his men and slain them without a sound? Wah Mei decided he must accept that as a possibility and prepare for an assault. He had approximately forty men left in his camp, plus one machine gun. He decided that if his forward positions had been overrun, then of necessity the assault would come by way of the trail. Therefore, preparations were made accordingly. When all seemed to be in order defensively, Wah Mei made his way rapidly to the place where his two captives were awaiting possible rescue or a more heinous torture and death than either could have ever imagined.

For Lieutenant Chism and Private Barclay, their positions on the bamboo poles was agonizing, though not so horrible as the mental anguish associated with the thought of rats ravishing their faces. They prayed silently and on occasion shouted encouragement to each other. "The Captain will come," repeatedly shouted Chism. "Aye, sir, I know he will," was always the reply. Several times Barclay shouted, "I'm keeping my eyes shut, Lieutenant, it seems to help." "Good man," responded Chism. Although the Lieutenant had conceived the same idea, the visions that came to his mind were almost worse than looking at the rats. At least if he looked, he could be sure the little gates were still in place. He could hear the water drip from one bucket to the other on the rare occasions when neither he or Private Barclay were not moaning. Maybe it would take days before there was enough water in the bucket! There could even be some evaporation. For a while, any thought that offered even an infinitely small hope was welcome. For now, he just wanted to die with some dignity. Lieutenant Chism had heard in the Korean War that some POWs had just laid down and died. Sometimes he even thought, *If I could just go mad, I would be free from this nightmare!*

After approaching his prisoners, Captain Wah Mei said, "I take pleasure in your groans gentlemen; however, I need screams." Pushing hard on each man's buttock, and forcing their pelvic bones against the bamboo, he did elicit a scream from each of them. Then their tormentor raised each gate that separated then from the rats about one-half an inch. Seizing on this opportunity, the rodents tried to push their heads through the slender openings. Thus, the rats' faces were less than an inch from the flesh of their victims. One of the rats substituted a front leg in place of his head and managed to graze Barclay's lip with his filthy claws. No one would ever know who screamed first, nor did it make any difference. Given the hideous fate awaiting them, they had already been absolute in their bravery. Suddenly, wild, frantic, and pleading screams were audible to Captain Cameron and his Gurkhas, but unheard by Sergeant McAllister out on the river due to the proximity of the waterfall.

Immediately, Cameron dispatched Sherbadahur to locate McAllister and his contingent, who were still on the river. "Tell them to paddle like hell and engage as soon as possible." The Gurkha disappeared into the brush with the urgency in his Captain's voice driving him through the dense vegetation. Fortunately, Cameron and his remaining five Gurkhas had the foresight to gather up some of the submachine guns and spare magazines from the slain enemies. These would prove to be of much greater advantage than their pistols or the edged weapons they had employed so devastatingly just minutes ago.

Shafts of sunlight were now starting to appear through the keyhole apertures in the jungle canopy which enclosed them. Birds were silent and scattered in flight, with the only prevailing sounds being the terrified screams of Chism and Barclay sounding like a primordial plea that seared one's soul. "Take cover as you advance, and be sure of your target," Cameron said to his Gurkhas. Then, in unison, they all started forward, with Cameron's trigger finger tightening, as each revolting scream came from the lips of their comrades.

Sherbadahur found McAllister. Stealth was no longer a need, as alacrity had taken precedence, each man in every canoe plunged his paddle into the murky waters of the Muaa River, and their coiled muscles pulled the paddles aft over and over again hurtling them toward the impending battle. "Take cover when you hit the beach! Mark your targets well and kill the bastards," McAllister shouted.

Meanwhile Naik Private Karbir Gurung had deployed himself far out on his Captain's flank. Portions of a deployed enemy machine gun and its crew were visible to him through the great fronds of the plant that separated them. Though he had no direct order from his Captain to open fire, he realized that if any of their group became suddenly visible, they would be immediately cut down. Slightly to his right, there was more space between the fronds. Distance and direction seemed perfect for the grenade that left his hand, and it landed near the gun carriage still sputtering. The crew had little time to react or reflect on their final second of life, for a large number of shrapnel fragments found ample flesh to cut through. Now the crew was dead, and the gun was inoperable.

Captain Wah Mei was on the way to see his prisoners. This time he had decided the gates would be fully opened and the rats would have their feast. Momentarily, the grenade's concussion stunned him, but he escaped the steel hornets that flew from its case. After Wah Mei's head cleared, he rushed back to his troops. "Kill them! Kill them!" he screamed. Then, he added, "I'll kill any man who leaves his post."

Now the element of surprise was no longer of concern to Cameron and his men, so they began to open fire, but their targets were limited, due to the fact the terrorists were dug in well. Also, Wah Mei's threats had the desired effect on his soldiers, and they were soon pouring withering fire toward Cameron and his men. A bullet impacted on Gurung's shoulder, fracturing the head of his humerus, then sped on its way. Though he felt the pain and winced, he continued his search for a target. Also hit was Naik Private Bala Ram Pun as a bullet creased his thigh, and it made him very angry.

Having expended one magazine from his captured PPS-41 submachine gun, Cameron had one more, then he would have only his pistol and ax. Also, he realized that he and his men were pinned down by the greater number and fire power of the terrorists. However, he was certain that he had killed several of them and had observed others hit by his men. Then, several bullets whistled by his head, and one transected the stem of a large frond, which fell in front of his face, further decreasing Cameron's very limited field of vision. "Bloody hell," he swore. "Where is McAllister?"

No sooner were the oath and question out of his mouth when the answer came to his ears. The very welcome *whump* of the 303s along with the sharper crack of the .30-caliber carbines were growing more and more evident, as were the shouts in English. Now, most of the terrorists were turning to face their new enemy coming from their right flank. Attack from this direction made their dug-in positions precarious. Conversely, advancement by Cameron and his Gurkhas was now made safer.

From a new position twenty yards forward, Cameron saw Chism and Barclay lashed to bamboo poles with their heads encaged. Despite the battle raging around them, they were both still screaming uncontrollably. Suddenly, it seemed there was a clear pathway to them. Cameron sprang up and raced toward them; however, two terrorists jumped up along his route. Immediately, they were cut down by the last rounds remaining in the magazine of his captured weapon. When Iain reached the captives, his ax was raised. The rats would die! Then, a sudden shout of "Captain!" stopped the ax in mid-air. The voice was Ghale's, and it was meant to alert him to the appearance of Captain Wah Mei. Whirling, Cameron saw the villainous countenance of the Chinese glaring at him with a hatred only found in hell.

His enemy's Tokarev pistol was pointed straight at Cameron's chest, and a finger was already depressing its trigger. Iain heard the series of blasts and expected the impact. However, out of nowhere, the form of Ghale had hurled toward the Chinese with the kukri in his extended arm, seeking the enemy's throat. All the bullets in the burst cut into Ghale's chest. As his body fell lifeless, the kukri still clutched in his hand cut through Wah Mei's ear and buried itself near the base of his neck. Though it was not the lethal blow the gallant Gurkha had intended, it did stun his mortal enemy. Instantly, Cameron hurled his ax with all the strength he possessed. By now, the sun was brilliant in the clearing and reflecting on the whirling blades producing a deadly kaleidoscopic effect. One ax bit found Wah Mei's sternum, cleaved through and rent his heart. The dying Chinese clutched at the protruding bit, lacerating his fingers to no avail. Immediately, Iain sprung toward the tortured prisoners. They were free at last!

Wah Mei's troops began to flee. Many enemy used the hapless aborigines, whom their evil leader had assembled to witness torture of the Scots, as human shields. McAllister and his men were reluctant to kill these innocents, so some of the enemy escaped. Nonetheless, it was a solid victory and a fortunate rescue. However, it would do little to enhance the body count that London desired in "the emergency," which they had declared. But it had been war for Delta and the exhausted members, who now began to let their adrenaline subside.

Tired as they were, they looked up to see Captain Cameron kneeling beside the lifeless form of Havildar Ghale. Gently, he covered the face with his jacket, and there were a few tears mixed in with the beads of sweat on his face. Then, all the men apart from the posted guards gathered around, saluted their fellow comrades and the little, brown man from Nepal who had given his life for the tall, white man from Scotia.

Shortly, the wounded along with Lieutenant Chism and Private Barclay were swiftly loaded aboard the dugout canoes, and Ghale's body was also solemnly placed on board. All captured weapons were destroyed, and the remains of their dead enemies were placed in a common shallow grave. For the men of Delta, it had been a victory that had tested their mettle against the most trying of conditions. Since it was no El Alamain, Monte Casino, or Crossing of the Rhine River, Whitechapel would regard it as an insignificant encounter, and just one of many that had occurred and would occur in "the emergency."

Chapter Thirty-Four

Bone-weary men walked down the trail with Captain Cameron as they returned to Headquarters. While they had little to fear from whatever remnants might remain of the terrorist unit, nonetheless, they were cautious since it was never prudent to get sloppy in Malay. Caution and adherence to military dictums were what tilted the odds in your favor. Once in the safety of camp, the soldiers could unwind a bit, and nearly everyone did. Upon their arrival, the wounded had been triaged, and those in need of further treatment were readied to be evacuated. In the cases of Chism and Barclay, there were question marks. Despite sedation, their nightmares were still in full control of their thoughts. Time alone would tell if they would ever be fit to return to full duty or some useful niche in society. *They could be criticized along the way,* thought Cameron. *But how many critics had ever faced what they did?!*

Time was now well past 0200 hours of the day following the rescue, and Delta's Commander was at his desk. He had written a lengthy, accurate report on the heroism of Havildar Ghale. Statements of other witnesses would be appended and sent along. "This man more than deserves a Victoria Cross," he said quietly. Then Captain Cameron's mind turned to thoughts of the young widow of Havildar Ghale, and the single child he had left behind in Nepal. Iain knew that Ghale had only one leave home during his service for the British Empire, and it was barely time enough to beget one child. Hopefully, Ghale's body would be returned to Nepal. In his mind, Iain could picture a babe who passed through boyhood to become a young man and a son of the Himalayas. When the Galla Wallahs came to recruit, Ghale had presented himself to them, and then gloried in his acceptance into the Gurkhas. Now, they were sending his body to some far-off funeral pyre. Relatives and friends would be there cloistered in a little knot to pay homage to this man. Iain hoped the sun would shine on that day, so the massive snow-capped peaks of Dhaulagiri and Annapurna would be resplendent in all their glory. Then, the mountains would bid farewell, as Ghale's ashes found the waters of the Kali River and were carried onward to the Gandak and finally to the Ganges River. Hopefully, they would ultimately wend their way to the Bay of Bengal and the Indian Ocean. This was what the Goddess Durga had decreed, thus, Iain wished it to be fulfilled. Cameron knew the British Empire was not generous to its adopted sons, and the little family left behind would be deprived if left solely to the largess of Her Majesty's Exchequer. "I shall see they do not want," Iain murmured.

At 0300 hours, Iain had completed new letters to Claire and his parents. Letters most recently written before the engagement were retrieved and locked away. *You write in a different way when it seems likely you may perish,* he thought. *Hopefully, I can reopen these when I'm seventy and reminisce.*

Later, before sleep came, again Iain thought of yesterday's action. Suddenly, it struck him as strange that if two rugby or soccer teams compete, it is called a game. Yet, if eleven men are trying to kill eleven other men, then you have to call it by some diminutive title. Certainly, it would surely seem that the politicians, the press, the General Staff, and yes even the people are caught up in the grandeur of war. But for those hapless souls fighting, it simply boils down to me or the other chap. What possible difference does it make to the ordinary soldier whether he is one of 100,000 men fighting another 100,000, or one of 40 soldiers up against another 40. Either way, you live, die, get wounded, or captured." Then he thought, *Also, the personal publicity that you receive will be exactly the same, which is an easily predictable zero! I wonder if many people ever thank God or whatever entity they are beholden to that they have someone like us to step out front and receive all the punches?* Then, he murmured "Not very likely," before falling into a coma-like sleep.

Slowly, the months in Malay ground away, and whatever force of nature that set the thermostat in the Green Hell left it on high enough to boil the body and bake the soul. Passing weeks brought new faces attached to feet, sometimes impaled by a punji stick, or bodies pierced with a bullet. However, morale remained high and casualties low, and enemy losses kept mounting. Delta was doing its job and doing it very well. Nonetheless, with the passage of time, Captain Cameron sometimes thought of himself as a block of ice mistakenly left out of the freezer, which day by day was slowly melting away. Would he return home before he completely evaporated?

Finally, the day came, and Captain MacIntosh was to take over command of

Delta Company. He was a fine fellow with a good record. However, despite the ecstasy of returning home, Cameron couldn't shake the sorrow of leaving what he had come to think of as his Delta, and the Change of Command ceremony left none untouched, for it was far more personal than most. As Cameron moved along the ranks from one man to another, he saluted each, met their eyes, and shook their hands. After saying good-bye to each, he did something they had never seen before. Their departing Commander took ten paces, turned, and saluted to nothing at all. Then, he took four side steps, stood at attention, and saluted four more times. Every man there came to the realization that it was his way of honoring the five men of his Command who were killed in action. Cameron stood longest at the fifth position, and there was no doubt that was the one he had assigned to Ghale.

Finally, Iain was on the way home. Somehow, he wished all the miles that separated him from Claire, his parents, and Scotland could be compressed or better yet eradicated. With a smile, he thought that unfortunately the RAF possessed no magic carpet, so he would be home when the wheels kissed the tarmac for the final time. As Cameron's plane ascended, then banked, it afforded Iain one last look at Kuala Lumpur. Staring out the window, which served as his camera lens, images were transmitted through Iain's one good eye to the retina, whereupon they were gathered by all the rods and cones like pollen on the legs of a bee. Only an instant was needed for transfer to the inner reaches of the cerebrum, where they would remain archived throughout his life. Then, they were impressed on his sensorium, which is the photographic film that man uses to capture and forever retain the images making up the hallmarks of their lives. Iain caught all that he would ever need to remember before a meandering cloud was imposed, and he felt it was like closing the cover on a book.

While Captain Cameron had methodically conjured up within his mind the images of those he loved, the droning engines seemed to harmoniously produce the names most dear to him. Malay was not among the names he heard, for Claire's name was by all means the most prominent, but "Geordie" would be discernible from time to time, and "Ghale" was added. Iain wondered if he should let them go, or was it even possible for him to do this now? Next, he thought, *Many officers can exorcise such thoughts and, perhaps, they deemed it appropriate. But no, I'll never attempt to purge them from my thoughts*, he decided. *I'll not let the tragedy of their deaths cloud my judgment. But, conversely, I'll not put other men in harm's way without revisiting the potential consequences. Perhaps I'm best suited for the small war,* he thought. Then, Iain corrected himself and used the euphemistic politically correct "emergency." *I know and remember them all. If memory ever fails me, they are inscribed in my diary. I suppose in a long war there would be too many names coming too fast. Well, I hope to God, if that ever be the case, I'll still recall them all or at least preserve the list. When you die for your country, the least you deserve is to be remembered!*

At long last, the final landing came, as the screech of the plane's tires boldly attempting to adhere to the tarmac resounded throughout the cabin. Iain heard the flaps manipulating the flowing air, while the reversed propellers clawed into it. Soon, they were taxiing, and in minutes he would disembark. No different than any returning soldier, Iain straightened up after coming through the door, and his only thought was to see who was there. However, the person that he sought did not stand out because of stature, for that person was small. Then, he saw her face, and the radiant aura surrounding it rendered all the others indistinct, for it was Claire!

Soon, they were pushing their way through the assemblage from opposite directions and at last they met. In their tight embrace, pounding heart thrust out against pounding heart. Encircled arms held them together and, at the same time, kept the rest of the world away. Tightly pressed lips prevented speech, though at the same time they said all that was needed to say. Claire's warm tears found little channels between their faces, and they were the warmest, sweetest tears that Iain had ever felt.

When all the documentation was complete, Claire and Iain piled into Percy. Always, it seemed, the Austin Healey possessed a personality transcending its inanimate state, and its engine purred to perfection all the way to the Savoy, where they would have some time alone. Their two sets of parents, who had also been young and much in love, decided to give Claire and Iain their reunion all to themselves. They knew the young couple would be visiting them in a few days, and their meeting could wait until then.

After arrival at the hotel, Claire and Iain were ushered into a beautiful suite at the storied Savoy. Having enjoyed only one week of conjugality in their married life, now they would be together again, and since Claire was a very bright young nurse, she knew it was a most auspicious time to be with her husband. When the hotel porter tipped his hat and opened the door, she happened to think of St. Jude, and wondered if she should ask him for a second favor. *Why not?* she thought, then silently added, *Ask and you shall receive.* Iain was somewhat puzzled by the little laugh lines in her face, as they entered. However, they were soon forgotten in the privacy of their room.

In the following week, there were idyllic visits to Oban and the White Heron to visit Claire's parents, then on to see Iain's at the Cameron Estate, and it was a splendid week for all. At the Cameron Estate, Claire, Iain and Simba once again found their bench and vista. Intently, Simba listened to his master's recounting of the skirmish on the Muaa River. At its conclusion, Simba raised his head and sniffed the air. His eyes stared off into space, and he seemed to recognize some vision there. Then, Simba came to his master, placed a paw on his knee and looked directly into his eyes. Gently, Claire touched Iain's arm and said, "Oh, Iain. It's like he understands everything you said."

Her husband took her hand in one of his, while stroking Simba's head with the other. "He does Claire," was his reply.

After visits with their parents, Claire and Iain returned to London, where they would remain for at least the next twelve months. He was reassigned to Regimental Headquarters Scots Guards and, during that time, worked tirelessly to see that Havildar Ghale was honored with the Victoria Cross posthumously. Also, Cameron made sure that the family of the brave man who saved his life would receive annual funds from a trust account set up in their name by an anonymous donor. Meanwhile, Claire set about becoming a model housewife and happy participant in Regimental social gatherings. Then, about six weeks after their arrival, some of her exuberance seemed to be diminished during the morning hours, and Iain seemed perplexed by strange, untimely requests for bizarre foods. Of course, Claire was fully aware of the etiology of her symptoms, but wanted to wait a few more weeks before sharing the secret with her husband. One morning, while drinking some weak tea and trying to hold down a couple of soda crackers, she suddenly laughed saying, "You know, St. Jude, I just asked for the pregnancy not the morning sickness. You pulled one over on me, but I forgive you."

After Iain had been dispatched at odd hours to procure a dozen ice lollies, peppers, pickles, and unusual flavors of ice cream, thoughts of possible conception occurred to him. Having deposited the latest acquisitions in the fridge, Iain gave his wife a demonstrative hug and said, "When is the baby due?"

Claire blushed and stammered, "What did you say?"

Iain stood back and repeated slowly, "I said, 'When is the baby due?'"

"How did you know?" she replied.

"Well Mrs. Nightingale, I an a soldier. That is true, and I suppose the Professor of Obstetrics at one of our leading maternity hospitals would have arrived at the diagnosis sooner. But, alas, even I can recognize *enceinte* after enough exposure to the symptoms. When all the morning belching and burping, along with a sudden distaste for your favorite cereal started, I must confess I was worried about ulcers. However, I discarded that theory when you started consuming hot peppers at bedtime."

"I was going to tell you this week, honest," said Claire, while looking a little sheepish.

"Good, it would have been awkward in nine months," said her husband, feigning indignation.

"Are you mad at me?" replied Claire, now looking a bit baleful.

"*Furious* is the word," replied Iain.

"I'm sorry," responded Claire.

"Sorry for what?" exclaimed Iain, then he continued. "Sorry for making the happiest man in the world even happier?! Well I intend to get even," he continued. "I'm going to wolf down half of your ice lollies and maybe even one of those red peppers. After all, the punishment should fit the crime." Then, grabbing Claire, he lifted her up, swinging her around and kissing and hugging her a dozen times.

Both husband and wife were equally thrilled to share the news. Upon her release, Claire proceeded to the fridge and returned with an iced lolly and a hot pepper. "I'm paying my fine," she said.

"You can save those for your next hunger crisis," replied Iain. "I've decided on a very large glass of single-malt and then we'll call our parents," which they did shortly after. Angus and Rachael Campbell, the General and Mary Cameron all fell into a third-place tie as happiest people in the world on hearing the disclosure.

When the Glorious Twelfth of 1951 came about, Claire was not an active participant. Her tweed ensemble of 1949 was much too small, and she was no longer sufficiently adroit to dodge falling birds. Nonetheless, she was the toast of the evening parties, as all the old friends were back. They rejoiced in the fact they were present at the time this wonderful young couple had fallen in love and happier still to know their union had borne fruit.

Iain Alexander Cameron Jr. was born in the morning of August 29, and at eight pounds, six ounces, he was a good-sized baby. Also, he possessed a lusty cry that was most evident during the witching hours. In the same chapel where his parents were wed, his baptism took place two weeks later. Long since, thoughts regarding who was right and who was wrong in the Reformation had been set aside. Only friendly competition remained, solely directed at who got to hold him. Since the tiny lad was nearly devoid of hair, and the color of his eyes seemed to be most likely blue, as was that of his parents and grandparents, no decision was reached, as to whom wee Iain most resembled.

After Claire's postpartum recovery was sufficiently far along, the original trio of Iain, Claire, and Simba, now enlarged to four with wee Iain, made their way to their beloved vista on the Cameron Estate. Never misplacing a paw, Simba was very respectful of the tiny newcomer. Nevertheless, when opportunity was presented, he would carefully nuzzle the baby with his soft nose. "Simba seems to adore wee Iain," Claire said, as she snuggled her head against her husband's shoulder.

"He has good sense," responded Iain. "He knows a winner when he sees one!"

"Do you think Simba was ever a father?" were Claire's next words.

"I wouldn't be surprised," said Iain. "But if he hasn't been, I suspect that he will be soon."

Claire was surprised, so she asked, "Is there something I don't know about?"

"Yes but I was going to tell you this next week," Iain said with a laugh.

Catching the rather sweet innuendo, Claire laughed along with him. Then, she nudged him in the ribs and exclaimed, "Tell me! What is the secret?"

"Well it seems that my father has a friend, an old campaigner, who now resides in Rhodesia. He is coming to visit and is bringing along what has been described to be a beautiful Rhodesian Ridgeback bitch named Rhoda, as a gift. If all goes well, we should be blessed with a litter of little Simbas and Rhodas in a few months."

"Do you think the pleased look on Simba's face indicates that he understands?" asked Claire laughingly.

"I wouldn't be at all surprised," was Iain's response.

Time passed quickly, and it wasn't long until Iain Alexander, or wee Iain as he was often called, abandoned hitching and crawling for his first attempts at ambulation. Frequently, Iain would return to their London flat to hear Claire voice the opinion that she should have concentrated on pediatric nursing, rather than surgery. "He always seems to be two steps ahead of me," she would say. "I have all the drawers and cupboards tied shut to keep him out. Then, I need something, so I have to open them. While I'm doing that, he finds something else to get into. I've never said 'No no,' so many times in my life." Iain would nod his head in agreement with Claire's pronouncements and complaints but was paying far more attention to wee Iain, who laughed with joy every time he raised him up above his head.

"Are you listening to me, Iain?" asked Claire with a bit of bite in her voice.

"Certainly, my dear," he replied, then said to the toddler, "Mommy wants to trade you in on a different model."

"How young do they take cadets at Sandhurst?" Claire said with frustration evident in her voice.

"Eighteen years, not eighteen months," replied her husband. "Besides that, they require a candidate to be potty-trained."

"I didn't know that was a prerequisite in the Army," Claire shot back. Then, she smugly noted that her final verbal barrage had got Iain's attention.

"Oh! The acerbic Campbell retort," he responded, along with a broad smile and canted head. Iain continued, "Mrs. Cameron you have just enough time to put on your new dress and get ready for dinner. I've made reservations at the Savoy Grill for two, and took the liberty of retaining Mrs. Brixton for a three-hour stint as a nanny. I can tell when a good soldier has spent too many hours in the trenches."

Claire beamed, then exclaimed, "Oh! How I love the two men in my life—the big boy and the little one."

Since separations have always been part of a soldier's life, Captain Cameron's was no exception. Temporary assignments came along with frustrating frequency. Sometimes, it was off to some remote spot like the Cambrian Mountains for training exercises, and once or twice to the United States or Canada. Foreign service was interspersed, and Cameron went to Egypt in 1952 with the First Battalion. Then, it was off to Sarawak and Sabah in 1956 to fight Indonesians. Of course, promotion did come, and on his return from Sabah, he was Major Iain Cameron. Then the Second Battalion was assigned to Redford Barracks in Edinburgh. This was the first time the Scots Guards had been stationed in Scotland for 250 years. Iain, Claire, and wee Iain were ecstatic to be so near to all those they loved. As for the newly arrived Justin Cameron, his happiness derived from a warm bottle and dry diaper, for now, they were a family of four.

Although many months of separation were a sad time for all, they seemed to strengthen the bond between them and enhance the love they shared. One of the little habits they developed was to hold hands on the eve of Iain's departure and recite a little ditty, "It's very sad when Daddy has to go away, but it makes it so wonderful when he comes back to stay." Now, their move to Edinburgh gave Claire the opportunity to have a real home. Consequently, she had obsessively looked at every suitable house in Edinburgh that fell into their price range. At last, she found the perfect one, and Iain loved it as much as she did. Now, they were first-time homeowners, and the initial thing to be placed in their little castle was the beautiful painting of Partree, for sweet were the memories of where their honeymoon had taken place. Apart from an occasional harsh word or a short sulk, there had never been any acrimony in their lives, and sometimes it seemed the honeymoon was going on forever.

With the Cameron family's relocation to Edinburgh, they were provided far more access to their parents. Wonderful weekends were spent, either at the White Heron in Oban or at the Cameron Estate with Iain's parents. Both sets of grandparents were slowing down a bit physically, though all remained very alert mentally. For certain, there was no abatement of the love they manifested for Claire, Iain, and the grandchildren.

When the next grouse season rolled around, the twelfth of August seemed as glorious as ever, and many converged on the Cameron Estate. Sadly, the makeup of those participating was changing. Now, General LeClaire was deceased and Colonel Edward Thornburn was an invalid after a stroke. Robespierre and Marie Antoinette had become very fond remembrances. However wonderful new people were found to fill the voids, but they were primarily Iain and Claire's friends. As the General was often heard to say, "You only have a small number of true friends in this life, and I've been blessed by having my share. I just wish they could have all stayed around as long as I have."

Another advantage to having a home came to be realized, as it was obvious to all that Simba was growing old. Up until now, he had always made a production of playing the puppy, but that time had passed. Kennel life was proving arduous. Long used and in past times abused, his joint cartilage was wearing thin. Arthritis had set in and was severe. Now, Simba's tawny fur was fringed with silver about his ever-nuzzling muzzle and between the worn pads of his paws. In the past, he used to gracefully descend into repose, but now he simply let himself collapse with a thud. Also, Simba had become gruff with the puppies he had sired, though he remained the submissive underdog to little Iain and Justin, who considered him their great, big teddy bear. For a time, the fenced-in yard of the new home was Simba's haven. When the clouds saw fit to let them pass, he loved to bask in the sun's caressing rays. At other times, he curled on his soft bed near the hearth eager to accept its warmth. Despite the pain associated with movement, Simba never relinquished an opportunity to be at his master's side. Also, the old fellow was still devoted to being privy to Iain and Claire's conversation and, as always, managed to convince them that he understood.

One day, Iain returned home to find Claire crying. "What's wrong?" he asked.

"Oh! Iain, Simba did a big puddle on the rug, but that's not what I am crying about. He doesn't seem able to get up, and his breathing isn't right." Immediately, they proceeded to Simba's side. He didn't raise his head, but fully raised his paw and wagged his tail, as best he could. Iain carried his dear friend to the car and proceeded to the veterinarian's office.

Upon arrival, Dr. Ward was quick to ascertain the special bond that existed between this man and this dog. After the examination, blood was drawn from Simba. "I'll run this right away, Major, and ring you up at home as soon as I have the results. I hate to say it, but things don't look good. I think his kidneys have given out, and he's in uremia."

Crushed by the news, Iain returned home, knowing he must share the news with Claire. That night, the four Camerons had little interest in dinner. Mid-evening, Dr. Ward called confirming the fact Simba's lab studies showed severe renal failure. Devastated, Iain called his parents, and he could tell they were taking the news no better than he.

Just two days later, a somber group of mourners stood sadly at the little pet cemetery on the Cameron Estate. Sergeant Major Sandy MacPhee had gathered together a piper, bugler, and a small Honor Guard from among retired Scots Guards. Also, he had made a fine coffin of Scottish pine lined with the Cameron tartan. A proper campaign ribbon, and a small replica of Iain's Victoria Cross were placed beside Simba's still body. Then, he decided it seemed fitting to cover the coffin with the flag of the country that Simba had served.

As they stood by the grave, the Pibrochs that the piper played finally gave way to Taps, then the volleys fired by the Honor Guard rang through the glen. Not a tearless eye was to be found, as Scotland's rocky soil and peat moss–infused earth closed the grave in finality. Simba's body would remain in its embrace, but the memories of him would persevere, as long as Simba's legend was retold.

After the sad burial, all wended their way back to the Manor House. Then, wee Iain asked his father, "Will we ever see Simba again?"

"Yes, son, he'll be waiting at the Rainbow Bridge."

"What is the Rainbow Bridge, Daddy?"

"I'll explain it all tonight son," was the reply, and so he did.

As the years passed, little boys turned to big boys and, as most parents do, Claire and Iain noted that time seemed to pass more quickly. Every time the young mother commented on the rapid passage of time, her husband was quick to say, "As I've oft said before, Claire, one's life is like a whirlpool. On the top, the circles are wide and relatively slow, but as you get nearer the apex, they become faster and smaller."

One day, as Claire returned from dropping off Iain and Justin at school, she felt uneasy. An earlier queasiness had become full-blown nausea. Immediately, her nursing training surfaced, and she remembered putting cream on her oatmeal that morning. Also, the rich sauce slathered on the venison served the night before came to mind. Along with the rich dishes came recollection of family members cursed with gallbladder disease. Claire thought, *After all, I am a female and now approaching forty*. However, she wasn't fat, which was one of the triad of signs generally ascribed to gallbladder disease.

Finding a chair, Claire sat, apprehensively awaiting the onset of an upper quadrant pain. However, none came; instead, she had an overwhelming urge for a hot pepper. Like a heavy smoker out of cigarettes and driven to rummaging through every drawer and pocket, she examined all the nooks and crannies in the pantry, then all the half-empty receptacles in the fridge. Not a single pepper was found. Pickles and olives were tried but proved to be no adequate substitute.

Then Claire thought of St. Jude, for after the series of agonizing miscarriages, she had neglected him. Could it be that he had found a sufficient number of unanswered prayers in her account that he had decided an interest payment was due? Claire hadn't had a recent menstrual period; however, their timing hadn't been as absolute as they once had been. Since there was no pain or jaundice, perhaps she was pregnant, and her gallbladder could remain sacrosanct.

Sitting back in the chair, Claire decided, "Time will tell. In the meantime, it would be no doubt propitious to add some prayers to her account with St. Jude. Also, there was that other saint named Gerard Magella, the patron of pregnant mothers and those who want to be!" Thoughts of Gerard were brought to mind as a fact of her husband's faith, which Claire always felt was quaint. Perhaps, better said was "rather odd." *Why on earth or in heaven have a* man *as a patron saint of the pregnant?* Then, she thought, *Well, I guess all the female saints were nuns or virgins, so probably he got stuck with the job! Anyway, once you're in heaven, you should be beyond embarrassment,* she decided. So, Claire devoted no more time on that dilemma.

After telling Iain's mother that she had to run an errand, she made straight for the nearest purveyor of hot peppers. Then, Claire murmured, *I'll get some ice lollies, lime and orange, too,* she thought, as she sped toward the village. Prayers were said coming and going!

As the gestation period for humans had decreed, Claire gave birth about nine months later. Another Cameron came into the world with a lusty cry. Though virtually bald when born, the few hairs the little fellow possessed were definitely red; soon "Geordie" would forever be the lad's name. The choice appealed not only to the parents and grandparents but especially to Sir George Edward and Lady MacCallum. They had lived to an old age, still grieving the loss of their only son, so many years ago in far off Malay. Both of them, still very spry, were cheered by knowing this little boy would be a living memorial to their own beloved son, who they were sure awaited them in heaven. Given their age, they believed the reunion would not be long postponed.

Time passed quickly, and only days after Geordie had taken his first faltering steps, Claire received shocking news that her own dear mother had suffered a massive stroke. Though still alive, she was obtunded, and no hope of recovery was offered. Immediately, Claire, Iain, and the children drove to Oban, where they were met by Claire's devastated father. His saddened eyes greeted them solemnly, as he said, "These are supposed to be the golden years. But it seems like we barely had a glimmer of the treasures that we thought awaited us. May our dear God see fit to reinstate them in heaven." Then he broke down completely.

Forever, Claire was denied any further words from her mother. A single sign of recognition in response to her whispered, "It's Claire, Mummy. I love you," was all she received. When Claire lifted her tear-streamed cheek from her mother's sallow one, tiny collateral tears were left behind as little legends of love. Slowly, Rachael Campbell's only functional eyelid opened, and the open eye emitted the fullest measure of reciprocal endearment. As the lid closed, her sternum depressed slightly, and her spirit departed.

The funeral was an ordeal, despite the vicar's consoling homily and the supernal music and hymns. Family septs of the Campbell and Cameron clans were fully in attendance, and their loving condolences helped ease the grief. However, as all knew, only time was the balm that could ease the closure of such a grievous wound. Angus Campbell lovingly declined the invitation to come and stay at the Cameron Manor for a time.

"You're so over kind, my dears," he said to Claire, Iain, and his grandsons. "However, the old White Heron Hotel was Rachael's and my own little empire. I best stay busy and keep it going, or she'll be hounding me in heaven." Angus kept his promise, and his wife could have nothing but praise when he joined her almost exactly one year later.

At the loss of her father, Claire's wounds of grief were all reopened. With time, they would heal, but the scars would be deeper. Also, Iain and Claire were reminded of their own mortality only a few weeks after the funeral. Suddenly, their second son, Justin, whose nickname was Jud, looked around and somberly asked, "Father, will you and mother and grandmother be going to heaven soon?" With this question, little Geordie understood enough to compel him to return his pudding-laden spoon to the plate. Geordie's eyes widened!

Then, young Iain, confident in his growing maturity, answered brusquely, "Of course, they will." As better judgment interjected, he added, "but not soon!" He concluded with "We'll all be going sooner or later."

Iain eyed Claire and his mother, and they both seemed mildly distraught. Quickly, he raised his wine glass and said, "Ladies and gentlemen here's to later!" Six full smiles were forthcoming as their goblets were elevated.

Then, Mary Cameron held out her glass and said with some sincerity. "I think I'll have another!"

After refilling his mother's glass, Iain thought, *Sometimes, it seems that the pass-*

ing years are like candles all arranged in a row. Initially, they are tall and broad and appeared to burn on and on! Now, they are becoming shorter and more slender. However, Iain's humor won out, "Don't be the melancholy Scot," he reprimanded himself, adding, "there's time to fret about that when you find there's only one wee candle left in the box!"

At last, Iain was promoted to the rank of Lieutenant Colonel. Promotions were becoming hard to come by, and the situation was bound to get worse. Cameron knew that politicians have the dangerous habit of finding signs of everlasting peace wherever they look, then, they usually proceed to declare themselves solely responsible for producing it. He thought it was true that Brittania was no longer a great colonial power. In fact, there was virtually nothing left, apart from an island or two. Where once the sun never set on the British Empire, it now seemed to sink into the sea just west of Penzance, where Gilbert and Sullivan's pirates used to frolic. Regiments with hundreds of years of tradition were now being riffed or amalgamated. One was left to believe that tradition for many politicians started with the last election and ended with the latest scandal.

Cameron felt you could sense the anger and anguish at the Officer's Mess and in the Regimental social gatherings. In the great wars, there were thousands of casualties, but new men came in to fill the voids in the line. Now, the holes in the line were not refilled, and the line simply got shorter. By Prime Ministerial, parliamentary, and bureaucratic fiat, a burgeoning number of vacancies occurred by forced retirement. Massive cuts in defense spending were popular ploys to divert the Exchequer's funds to politically correct largess. Soldiers could always stop bullets, but ballots were for welfare recipients.

At first, Iain noted that the cuts were commented on with ribald humor. After a couple of drams or pints, an officer might be heard to say, "I understand all the Highland Regiments are to be amalgamated into one, and our kilts will be made out of the parliamentary tartan." Invariably, one man holding the glass next to the speaker would ask, "What the hell is the parliamentary tartan?" Then, the answer would come "Why it's all white, didn't you know? You can take off your kilt run it up the flag pole, to signify your surrender and bare your ass at the same time!"

"You're wrong," another drinker would interject "They are going to take a small patch of each regimental tartan and sew them all together to make a kilt. Then, that Regiment will be known as Her Majesty's Highland Patchwork Kilties." That would draw a laugh and an order for a new round of drinks. Humor could bring temporary succor for their distress; however, it was an ineffective weapon against political whim.

Many years had seemed to pass quickly, and wee Iain was no longer an apt subject for that title. Puberty had come and brought a baritone voice and harbingers of a beard. Also, in their own good time, Justin and Geordie were keeping pace. Claire and Iain noted that their eldest son was drawn to the healing arts. Sam could attest to that, for he was Simba's son, the new family pet and he appeared to be a canine hypochondriac. Sam seemed to enjoy physical examinations, along with all sorts of bandages and even some nostrums that the young physician concocted. Young Iain's Grandfather Cameron said that, "It was about time after 200 years that some Cameron was going to patch people up instead of trying to put holes in them."

Justin and Geordie seemed to have inherited all the military chromosomes, though the former was more bound to battleships and the blue sea. On, excursions to Oban, his grandfather Campbell had taught him to sail, and the salt air and sea became firmly anchored in Justin's heart. Meanwhile, young Geordie seemed to be the family's embryonic Scots Guard. *I hope the tradition will last long enough for you to grasp it,* Iain often thought.

Soon another traditional Glorious Twelfth had come, and a full compliment of happy hunters had made their "Haj" to Scotland's Highlands and the mecca of great grouse shoots. Iain was able to spend considerable time with teenage young Iain to make him a relatively proficient shot. For the first time in the young man's life, he would be allowed to participate in the hunt, at least to the tune of a single drive each day. Knowing the young are quick to protest an adult's decision regarding something they wish to do, Cameron was not surprised that young Iain was especially offended by the fact that he was allowed to place only one cartridge in a double-barreled shotgun.

"It doesn't make sense," he said, following with a frown.

"It does make sense," replied his father, frowning even more profoundly.

"But why? How can I compete with everyone else when I can't have two shots?"

"You are not competing with everyone else," said Iain sternly. "You are competing with yourself at your first-ever shoot There will be other people close about, and it's simply much safer for a beginner to fire a single round out in front, rather than be whirling around with a still-loaded gun. Furthermore, it will force you to concentrate harder in order to bag a bird. Your grandfather learned that way, and so did I."

"As a matter of fact, so did I," said his mother, lowering her book and peering over recently acquired glasses, perched on the end of her nose.

Young Iain blushed, laughed, and agreed. Then he did quite well the following day, despite his handicap.

Time had come for the last drive of the final day. A brace of hard-flying Scottish red grouse were coming hard, fast, and forty yards up, just to the right of the General's butt or shooting station. Quickly, his favorite Holland and Holland came up, swinging swiftly. Then he fired, and a cloud of feathers exploded. From the lead bird, the wings folded, and it plummeted to the earth. His second shot was a reproduction of the first, and it was a beautiful exhibition. Those that saw it roared their acclaim. A broad smile broke out on General Cameron's face as he handed the gun to his loader. However, suddenly, the smile changed to a look of awe, and the old soldier's head went to his chest as he collapsed.

At this time, Claire wasn't shooting, as she, along with Grandmother Cameron, were tending the younger boys in addition to inculcating them in the art of dodging falling birds and charging dogs. Upon seeing what happened, she gasped and ran to her stricken father-in-law. Mary Cameron was following her, and Iain was running from a nearby shooting station. Immediately, the nurse in Claire was back in full force. As she hurriedly undid the collar of the General's Tattersall shirt, she could not help but note his pupils were beginning to fix. Her soft finger sought the site of his carotid artery, but no pulse was encountered by her palpating digit. When Iain and his mother arrived, Claire's streaming tears filled her eyes and ran like little rivers down her cheeks. Then, the subtle swing to and fro of her head shouted out the diagnosis without the need for words—Brigadier General John Alexander Cameron was dead.

Devastating for most men is the loss of their fathers, regardless of their age. However, when a man has the honor and privilege of having a father who is greatly loved and who loved you equally, it is especially hard. So it was for General Cameron's son. Devastated by his loss, Iain walked slowly across the great moor until he had reached the cairn on top of the glen. He sat for an hour with his mind calendaring many of the times he and his father had crossed the moor together. Simultaneously, mental photos began to appear, as though projected by some type of cognitive carousel. They started with himself as a very young lad who had just slipped and fallen in a bog. A great hand had reached down to grasp his small one, and a soft, though commanding voice said, "Come now, Iain, get out of that bog. I'm not about to lose you yet."

Then he recalled the first time he had bested his father at anything. As a teen, his first thought was not of the victory, but would his father be upset? Then, the answer had come quickly. His father had strode up to him, and there was no anger in his eyes, but instead a happy smile that spoke of pride. Then the same great hands had grasped his shoulders, and the piercing blue eyes anchored on his own. His father's voice that often had screamed "follow me, lads" when he had led a war charge in France, was soft but full. "Well done, Iain! I'm so proud of you, lad."

Iain thought, *Yes, a great father was your rod and staff. For as long as he lived, he would be your goalie in the game of life. You could be expected to play your heart out upfield, but if anything did get by you, then father would be there to back you up! God has decreed that I must now wear the mantle of protectiveness that Father wore so nobly for so many years,* Iain decided. *Well, I best show that I'm fit to don it. Here I am, sitting alone, shrouded in self-pity. Others need my comfort and guidance. I best be off and assume the roll that is my greatest legacy.* Iain arose and started for the manor house to fulfill his duties and prepare for his father's burial.

By the standards of London or Edinburgh, the funeral was not of magnificent scale. Nonetheless, there was a grandeur present that struck deeply into the spirits of all who attended. None were present who did not love or greatly respect the General, and in the case of most it was both. Due to Catholic tradition, a rosary was said in the village church on the evening before the following morning's Requiem High Mass. Next, the General's remains were brought to the Manor House by hearse, where the casket was placed on a caisson drawn by a team of great gray horses. As the pipes and drums of the Scots Guards and Cameron Highlanders were present, their drones filled the great glen with the traditional dirge. Then, the slow march began, and beside the flag-draped coffin was a magnificent black stallion. Empty boots were turned backward in the stirrups hanging limply from the empty saddle. The great horse's polished hooves pranced on the gravel in perfect cadence with the drums.

As the distance to the private family burial ground was close to half a mile, members of the family, dear friends, and fellow officers walked behind the caisson and fell in step with the drum's somber resonance. General Cameron's sister-in-law, dear Aunt Jane, was badly crippled with arthritis, and it was suggested she take a car to the grave site. "I'll hobble if I must, but by God, I'll go on foot like a good Scot kinswoman," she declared. No one argued with her.

After the grave was blessed by the bishop who had presided, and all the final prayers were said, Sandy MacPhee strategically placed a lone piper atop the distant cairn. Natures acoustics could not be outdone, as the plaintiff notes of "Going Home" softly descended on the grave site, as might one of the somber clouds clinging to the gray sky above. Then, it was the bugler's turn, and the solemn notes of Taps fled slowly from the bugle to seek out the granite rocks, which would give them new life in the echoes that were reborn. When infinity had captured the last reverberations, the salute was fired. Since the usual sharp reports seemed muted, Iain imagined they were not explosions at all, but speaking guns repeating, "Cameron, Cameron, Cameron!"

A folded flag pendant was presented to the widowed Mary Cameron, and she pressed it hard against her heart. Mary's tears ran by the shrouding veil she wore, but her body never quivered. Slowly, as Highland families do, each member added a bit of soil to cover the casket. The eldest grandson was stoic and reserved as was Jud, but little Geordie clung tenaciously to his handful of earth. "I don't want to bury Grandfather," he cried. "I want him to come back." All present wished that little Geordie's hope could be fulfilled, though they knew the man would rest here until the Resurrection, and someday, his remains would blend with that same soil on which he had so proudly tread. As the mourners left the cemetery, a gentle rain began to fall. For those in attendance, it seemed as though it was heaven's way to commiserate with those below. Surely, it appeared as though God's tears were joining theirs. They knew that only time would heal the sorrow, but the memory of General John Alexander Cameron would be preserved by generations to come.

Chapter Thirty-Five

✠ ✠ ✠

Since the funeral of the General, four years had passed, and on a blustery day at Military Headquarters, Lieutenant Colonel Iain Cameron's day was nearing completion. Before it was assigned to history, he decided there was time for contemplation. Having always been addicted to analogies, he was given to employing various animals to serve as subjects. On his desk, the calendar proclaimed that the year was 1968. All he had to do was turn over a couple of leaves, and his active duty to Queen and country would total twenty years. *I'm just an old sheep dog,* he thought. *Most of the sheep are gone, and the politicians are of the mind that all the hungry wolves have left as well! I suppose I could stick around in hopes my benevolent masters will provide me a warm place and toss me an occasional bone. But, then again, I might be kicked out in the cold, and left to try and subsist on hares that I am too old to catch. Should the Russians ever decide to become tourists in tanks and head west, I suppose they'll need me back. Of course, I will return, if needed! However, I feel the time has come to bow out gracefully,* he decided. Then, Iain continued his analogy. *This old dog shall find a new pasture, where only lambs scamper and play.* Actually, it was a concept he had mulled over ever since his father died.

Cameron knew well-to-do sportsmen were increasing in number in the United Kingdom, Western Europe, and, of course, America. He surmised that many of these would be anxious to have the chance to participate in the bird shoots of which he had the privilege to have partaken. Also, he was aware that taxes were becoming ever more onerous, and many landowners were hanging on by their fingertips. By leasing their land to shooting parties, any extra revenues generated would probably prove to be a godsend. That would certainly be true for the Cameron Estate. Yes, this was something he could really enjoy and be presumably profitable at the same time.

Iain's right hand found a pen, and a doodle appeared on the back of an expended Order of the Day. First, a semblance of a shop window began to appear and, then, it was neatly lettered CAMERON LTD. SHOOTING HOLIDAYS, FINE FIREARMS, AND ACCESSORIES. After looking at it, he decided that it really didn't strike his fancy. Something more catchy was needed. Before discarding it, Iain crushed the paper in his hand. However, the concept was left unwrinkled in his mind. His decision was to try it out on Claire and his sons tonight and his mother on the weekend. Then, Cameron arose, and when his tunic was buttoned and bonnet angled just right, he headed for home. As he left, the jaunty step, happy look, and smart salute of his Commanding Officer enlivened the Sergeant of the Desk, who turned to a glum Corporal passing by and said, "MacLeod, why can't you put on a smile like the Colonel? It would sure as hell brighten up this place."

After returning home, Cameron explained his plans to Claire, young Iain, Justin, and Geordie. They loved the idea of their father being much more available, and Claire was ecstatic. After listening to Iain's plan, Mary Cameron seemed the most animated that she had been since the death of her husband. Also, although she was and always had been a resourceful and talented woman, yet a quick review of the estate's books on the preceding day had left her with the feeling that the estate was exsanguinating and the ledger before her was turning crimson. Black was what she desired, and Iain's plan had the promise of being a fiscal alchemy, which would change red ink to black.

Over the next few weeks, Cameron went from soldier to salesman, as he met with dozens of landowners. He did encounter a few desultory dismissals, but most were interested and supportive. On occasion, splendid suggestions were offered, such as, "I've got two miles of property fronting the River Tay, Colonel. Have you thought of offering angling in addition to shooting?" Or, a landowner might add, "Will it be just for birds? I wouldn't mind providing some stag hunting for proper parties." Even one neighbor mentioned that he had shot Perdiz Roja in Spain, and he wouldn't be surprised if some of the *estancia* owners, who were also burdened under onerous taxes, wouldn't welcome an agent that could provide them with clients. Nearly everyone wanted to reserve some shooting for their personal guests, but they were anxious to experiment with the paying types—carefully screened, of course. Iain thought of his prior sheep dog analogy. *I guess I'm back at chasing the wolf away. This one bears a startling resemblance to the Chancellor of the Exchequer.*

Shortly thereafter, Cameron's request for retirement was accepted. Now, the final day had come. Cameron stood proudly on the Reviewing Stand. A review in honor of a military person was an age-old tradition in most of the world, and this particular one would honor Lieutenant Colonel Iain Alexander Cameron, V.C. He had never commanded a corps or a division of soldiers, having only risen to Regimental level. However, he would always be best known for leading a handful of heroes back in Malay. As Cameron stood at attention, the pipes and drums passed by first, followed by the companies assembled, and the guidon's pointed tips were positioned to pierce the sky until such time as they were lowered in respect to the imposing figure on the reviewing stand. Each descending foot and every bending knee were perfectly tuned to the music of the march. Among the marching men, some were present who had born the agonies of the Green Hell, Aden, and Suez. Due to their respect for this man, it produced an added bounce to their steps and induced them to hold the eyes right command and their salute just a little longer.

As Cameron stood, ramrod straight, precisely returning their salutes, he studied every man. Also, for Iain other visages appeared evident to only himself. Small brown faces, clothed with camouflage hats were there, led by Havildar Ghale. Sergeant Major Sandy MacPhee was next in line, and the limp was gone. At last, Geordie came by, with the bright sun burnishing his red hair beneath the Glengarry atop his head. In Iain's mind, it was as if Geordie was smiling at him and saying, "Well done, old friend!" Cameron's eye was misting, though one last vision remained, for there was Simba in his prime, tail erect and head held high.

Suddenly, the pipes were silent, and Iain was barely aware that the review was over. Immediately, there were clasps on his shoulders and hands reaching for his. When the well-wishing was over, Cameron proceeded to the small cluster of loved ones who awaited him, and it seemed as though he was crossing a river. He would never forget the marching boots, bugles, or battles since they would forever be a part of him.

Claire rushed to him, giving Iain the warmest kiss and tightest embrace of his life. Young Iain and Justin were next to embrace him, followed by his mother, Geordie, Aunt Jane, General Sir George and Lady MacCallum. Now, Iain had crossed the river, and it was nice to be on the other side.

Only a few weeks later, passersby noted the opening of a new business venture in Perth. Gold lettering indicated it was CAMERON AND COMPANY, LTD., AGENTS FOR ESTATE HUNTING AND ANGLING, also purveyors of the finest sporting arms. As proprietor, Iain was frequently there, and it was often said, "That fellow seems to know what it's all about." Since the venture was a success and continued to grow, it appeared they were right.

Though short of spectacular, the first shooting season for Cameron and Company was a solid success. For the first time in his adult life, Iain, always well steeped in the art of command, was forced to develop a strong diplomatic bent, especially in regard to the first American clients. Fortunately, none of them appeared in a Buffalo Bill ensemble. However, a few did not seem capable of rejecting camouflage clothing. Also, there was a great chasm in the choice of weapons. Given the fact that Iain had always shot with the genteel members of the United Kingdom sportsmen circles or Continental sophisticates, it had never crossed his mind to send a memo to Yankee clients that side-by-side double-barreled shotguns were considered de rigueur out in the glens. By good fortune, Cameron became aware that one of the Americans had come equipped with a Browning Auto 5, one of the world's foremost semi-automatic shotguns. However, these weapons were considered lacking in sportsmanship and thus were not used in the United Kingdom.

On their arrival, Cameron had met the party of eight Americans at the Edinburgh Airport. They had come from the Chicago area and appeared prosperous, affable, excited, and in general a fairly decent lot. After the greeting, Iain's assistants saw to their luggage, leaving Cameron time for small talk as well as pragmatic inquiries. Facing a ruddy-complexioned client, Iain asked his first question, "I'll start with you, Mr. Benson."

This was as far as he got, for the gentleman interrupted, smiled, and said, "Make it Burt, Captain."

Iain let his reduction in rank go by the boards. Then, he reinitiated his aborted question. "What gauge of cartridges will you be using? We'll be shooting in the morning, and I have to be sure that all your needs will be met."

As the reply registered, Iain nearly dropped his clipboard. "Twelve-gauge three-inch magnums, with number four shot if there's going to be high flyers!" Benson continued. "You don't use plugs over here, do you?" Cameron's gaping mouth and silence induced Benson, now somewhat incredulous, to further ask, "You know what plugs are don't you, Captain?"

"I'm afraid you have me at a disadvantage," replied Iain, with just a hint of testiness in his voice. Then, eager to educate a perceived neophyte, the Chicagoan boomed out, "It's a piece of wood you put in the magazine, so you can only shoot three times instead of five."

Obviously, Cameron was no stranger to magazine-type shotguns. After all, he had used a Winchester to lethal advantage in Malay. Yes it did hold five rounds, but it was used to kill other soldiers who were trying to kill you. However, even then, some of his peers considered it barbarous, and the use of such a gun to shoot grouse over Scottish moors was unthinkable!

"Well Mr. Benson, or Burt, we don't really need plugs, as you call them. We only use double-barrel guns, for they are considered eminently more sporting."

Thereupon, Burt Benson was no longer hail fellow well met, and a sneer was developing when he boomed out, "Hey fellows! Did you hear that the limeys only allow damn doubles? We gave up those old smoke poles in 1897!"

Mentally, Iain was totaling up the cost of refunds and airfare back to Chicago, when a more dapper gentleman previously introduced as Charles "call me "Chuck," spoke up, to Cameron's great relief. "I would have thought that you have an old double or two stuck in some closet, Burt. Now didn't you say that your family made their fortune in moonshine? All those old 'shiners had a double-barrel lying across their laps as they sat by the still. I've got an old L.C. Smith that I brought along for a spare. You can use that!" Mollified or not, Benson was subdued.

That evening, Cameron stopped at the hotel to check on his clients. First, he went to Burt Benson's room. After being admitted, he opened a case, which contained a pair of splendid Stephen Grant London Best guns from the used gun inventory of his shop. "I thought you might like to give these a try, Burt. They are yours to use during the shoot. In fact, I think they may give you a real advantage over your friends." Iain put one of the pair together and handed it to his quizzical client. "It's a beauty! Thanks, Captain," said the rotund American.

Fortunately, the Yanks enjoyed their shoot immensely and purported themselves well, and all rebooked for the following year. Furthermore, Burt Benson would be returning with a newly purchased pair of Best guns and be the envy of his associates. At their departure, good old Burt bestowed the heartiest handshake and, in addition, Iain was pleased to hear, "Thanks for everything, Colonel!" Restoration in rank was a bonus that pleased Iain.

Cameron's business prospered. However, unfortunately, all the French clients were not anywhere near on a par with the redoubtable General LeClaire, an august gentlemen whom Iain had always revered. Some were too wildly enthusiastic and not overly careful in what direction they were shooting. Italians could be even worse. Consequently, Iain always shrewdly employed countermeasures. Barriers, euphemistically named Franco Italian guardian angels, were placed along the sides of the shooting butts, thus making it nearly impossible for them to shoot one another. Cameron and his staff always used the acronym FIGAs, and were pleasantly surprised that no one ever asked what it stood for. In addition, insurance was purchased from Lloyds. Carefully, this cost was hidden in the shooting fee. As clients, the Germans were best of all, as they bore sufficient Prussian chromosomes to keep them all self-disciplined. Although the entrepreneur would never fully replace the soldier in him, Iain found it challenging, often enjoyable, and fortunately remunerative.

Claire was happy to entertain the wives who accompanied their husbands and found many of them very friendly, interesting, and educational. However, private shoots would always be her great joy, for they marked the gathering of the closest, dearest friends. Also, these gave her a chance to do a little shooting herself. After the season ended, she quickly reverted to full-time mother and matron of the manor house. This position was one that her dearest friend and confidant, Mary Cameron, mother-in law extraordinaire, had relinquished. Now Mary favored gardening, church, and charitable work as well as her most esteemed role, which was that of grandmother.

Happily, the fortunes of Cameron and Company, now Cameron and Sons, were burgeoning. Fortunately, most of the hard work was seasonal from the onset of the Glorious Twelfth to just beyond the New Year. However, the off-season was getting busier, for that's when all the brochures were sent out, the advertisements submitted, and the leases for shooting properties negotiated. Additionally, it came to Iain's attention that some of his clients, especially Americans, thought variety was the spice of life, and they had inquired if he could set them up with a shoot in Spain for Perdiz Roja, the red-tailed partridge, which abounded in the plains of Iberia. Others felt off-season golf tours to the meccas of the sport, like Troon, Carnoustie, and St. Andrews, were necessary to make life complete. Then there were the angler clients, who fervently desired to wet their lines in the rivers and lochs of Scotland or even in the pristine rivers of New Zealand or Patagonia.

After a desultory reading of yet another inquiry, Cameron frequently murmured, "Bloody hell what's next? Pheasant shoots in Ulan Bator in Outer Mongolia?" Frustration fanned his memory, and the name of Major Wilson, his old Commanding Officer at Scots Guards Headquarters, came to mind. He was elderly, but far from senile and an avid golfer and angler. Then, after more thought, Cameron decided that Wilson would make a proper business manager. Thereupon, Iain placed a call to Major Harry Wilson, Scots Guards, retired. After Cameron's explanation of his proposal, over the other line came Wilson's reply: "Splendid! I'd love to, and when do I start?" spoken enthusiastically.

Harry Wilson proved an able administrator and never added a single staff member until forced to do so by increasing volume. Certainly, Cameron's choice was wise and proved providential, as gross and net incomes continued to grow. Even if they hadn't, Iain would have only smiled and said, "What price should I be willing to pay for sanity?"

Iain kept lighting candles. As he had previously surmised, they just didn't burn as long as they had before; however, they were still bright years, though they were passing with increasing rapidity. Now, young Iain, their oldest son, along with Jud, were both enrolled in a fine boarding school in Edinburgh under the tutelage of the Christian brothers. Young Iain was still convinced that he wanted to be a physician.

In years gone by, dogs, no matter how much loved, were kennel housed.

However, Sam, who had followed Simba, lived to be ten, and Claire had convinced Iain that attainment of that age should provide parole from kennel life as they had done for Simba. When the ancient canine had passed away and gone to await his master at the Rainbow Bridge, Claire, always soft-hearted, said she missed a dog within the home. Iain thought one dog inside the house was enough. Nonetheless, Claire triumphed over his desires with feminine logic. She argued that since Duhb and Purdy were brothers, it would be unreasonable to favor one over the other. The two Labradors had differing personalities. Both were splendid retrievers and in addition were excellent hunters, able to find and hold birds as well as any setter or pointer. Similarity ended there, for whenever young Iain the fledgling physician showed up with his doctor's bag, Purdy would make for the nearest dog door—the first ever installed in the manor house. By contrast, Dhub, a natural hypochondriac would roll over on his back and proffer a paw for a bandage much like Sam used to do. After young Iain grew older and left to go to boarding school, Purdy seemed pleased, but Dhub was discontented. Consequently, Colonel Cameron, finding himself alone in the gun room with the two dogs, was often amused by their response when he took out a cloth to rub down a gun. Purdy had come to the conclusion that he was at last free of unwanted medical care and resumed his nap. On the other hand, Dhub would wave a paw and whine! Frustrating as it was, Iain never failed to bestow a bandage.

Claire and Iain noticed that second son, Justin or "Jud," exhibited a military calling, though it was nautical as he greatly loved the sea. Probably this was due to all the times that his Grandfather Campbell had lovingly taken the young man sailing. However, when the teenage years came along, air began to compete with water, and Jud wisely decided that he could serve both by becoming a naval aviator. Thereafter, his sights were firmly set on that target and never wavered.

As for nine-year-old Geordie, he desired to be everything that his big brothers aspired to be at least for a week. He was troubled that knights, especially those in armor, were no longer fashionable; and since becoming a king was highly unlikely, he settled on being "just like father."

"What does being 'just like father' mean?" Iain inquired after Geordie proclaimed his desire at dinner.

"I think it means being a sportsman," replied Geordie, innocently.

"What does a 'sportsman' do?" queried Grandmother Cameron, finding increasing amusement in the exchange.

"He does everything that's fun to do, and lets other people do what isn't fun," Geordie replied earnestly.

"Wise beyond his age," stated Mary Cameron before sipping her claret.

Registering consternation, Iain looked at his wife, seeking an ally from the feminine side. Claire shrugged while she cocked her head. Pursed lips with bulging cheeks and twinkling eyes were unmistakable signs indicating attempted suppression of a hearty string of laughs. At last, she was unsuccessful and gales of laughter erupted. Soon, Iain's mother succumbed to the contagion. Despite his dour expression, both his wife and mother seemed incapable of stopping. Finally, they were down to intermittent giggles interrupted by blotting at happy tears with their napkins. At last, the ladies were reconciled to getting their breath and easing the soreness in the muscles of mirth.

Geordie was perplexed saying, "I did not wish to be funny. I just want to say the truth."

Quickly, Claire replied, "The truth can be very funny, Geordie." Then, the laughter started all over again.

Consternation replaced perplexity in the nine year old, so he turned to his father and said, "Why are Mother and Grandmother laughing, Father?"

"It's one of those things that men never understand about women," Iain replied.

Upon this reply from his father, the next question came fast. "Why don't men understand women, Father?"

"One of the punishments of Original Sin, I'm afraid," was Iain's response. Then he also broke into laughter. Geordie didn't ask the follow-up question which arose in his mind, for it seemed just easier to join in the laughter. This little episode would remain as an inside joke from that time on in the Cameron family.

Since the birth of Geordie's namesake, George Edward Cameron, General Sir George and Lady MacCallum seemed very inventive when it came for reasons to visit the Cameron Manor. Subterfuge was unnecessary, for Iain and Claire knew that seeing Geordie was the closest thing to the reincarnation of their own son. On Geordie's tenth Christmas, a gift arrived and, when opened, it proved to be a miniature uniform of the Scots Guards. Quickly putting it on, Geordie was thrilled. Claire and Iain took their son to visit and thank the MacCallums. On their arrival, the elderly couple's eyes misted. Full-blown tears would await private moments. Succeeding Christmas presents brought a skean dubh, a dirk, and then a Scottish broadsword, all of adult size and finest steel that the Wilkinson Sword Company could produce. Given the adulation of his adoptive grandparents, and the legacy of his own father and paternal grandfather, George Edward Cameron was destined for but one career!

During these years, in keeping with his clients' requests, Iain traveled frequently to seek out shooting properties in foreign lands. With Grandmother Cameron still active and the MacCallums eager to lend a hand, it was possible for Claire to travel along, especially with young Iain and Jud in boarding school. They were pleased to rediscover each other.

For many reasons, these middle years were idyllic, though not entirely free of tragedy and sorrow. Aunt Jane, beset by a failing heart, had been pretty much confined to her London apartment for nearly a year. At last, that dear old heart was beyond response to digitalis and diuretics, and it totally failed in her sleep. She was laid to rest in their little private cemetery, attended by only a few. Time had decimated the ranks of her peers, and Mary Cameron was her only living sibling. After her sister's interment, on the way back to the manor house, Mary thought, *I seem to be the fulcrum between all the dear loved ones living and deceased. Soon, it will be time to let go. I should never want to outlive my children.* Lady MacCallum was the next to pass on, and the General waited only six weeks to follow. They went off to heaven to join their Geordie, leaving his namesake dedicated to a tradition they had helped germinate.

Passing years had not left Claire and Iain without sorrow. However, at the same time, the love they always shared was greatly enhanced and enriched by good times whenever they came. Fortunately, despite the fact that Iain's whimsical candles were shrinking in size, new ones always seemed to be in place when it came time to sing "Auld Lang Syne" and detonate a few bottles of champagne. During this period in their lives, Claire was becoming an inveterate traveler, and she loved every minute of it. Young Iain and Jud were ensconced in schools of their choice and free of need for parental supervision. Geordie still had Grandmother Cameron to watch over him while his parents were away. However, all three sons traveled with Claire and Iain whenever a hiatus in their school year permitted.

After a tour of some of the great estancias, Claire said wistfully, "I really loved Italy, but now I think Spain is my favorite." At this time, Colonel Cameron was courting Spanish property owners in an effort to provide greater variety for his shooting clients.

Iain was quick to reply, "Am I to understand, Claire Campbell Cameron, that you have forsaken Canada, Mexico, Columbia, Argentina, and the United States, which were deemed favorites just a short time ago? I can see that you have been unable to shake off the Campbell habit of fickleness. Hopefully, it doesn't extend to husbands."

"Well, sir, I must admit that Ernesto what's-his-name in Buenos Aires was most attractive. However, it's your good fortune that I have an aversion to polo players, especially those with mustaches. Since you have the Cameron need for continuous reassurance, please be informed that I love you with all my heart, and I always will."

While sipping the last drops of his Cardinal Mendoza brandy, Iain sighed, then set the empty snifter down. Reaching for Claire's hand, he spoke again. "You have given this Cameron all the reassurance he ever needed each and every day of our lives, Claire. But I must admit that I love hearing it again."

Smiling, Claire asked, "Would you like another brandy, Iain? It's excellent!"

"No," he replied softly. "I much prefer the company of the woman I esteem in a more intimate setting." They departed the restaurant hand in hand and made their way to a suite six floors above.

Before long, Jud was enrolled in the Royal Naval Academy. He was progressing rapidly toward the First Class year, then graduation and hopefully flight school. Meanwhile, young Iain had flourished in his premedical years and was now in his freshman year of medicine at Edinburgh University. Geordie seemed to be enjoying secondary school, but still regarded it as the springboard to Sandhurst and fulfilling his ambition to be an officer in the Scots Guards. Also, Iain's business was prospering far beyond expectation, and income proved to be excellent despite the onerous taxes levied by Parliament in the name of the Crown. Fortunately, Grandmother Cameron was frail but still sprightly and mentally very sharp. For the Camerons, everything seemed to be going well. Claire and Iain never failed to render prayers of thanksgiving, but they always added supplications that all would continue to be tranquil.

Busy years passed quickly and, for the Cameron family, more changes were in store, as two of their sons' graduations came at last, like all good things do for those who work and wait. Young Iain had been granted a residency in Cardiology at one of the world's renowned heart centers at Johns Hopkins in Baltimore. Though his parents were saddened to see him go so far away, pride dispelled loneliness as they said their good-byes. Then, Jud was soon in the sky and surely a source of concern. *Strange*, thought Iain. *I could be so cavalier when I was in danger, and here I am the reluctant, fretting parent when one of my sons chooses to embrace the hazardous professions of their forebears.* Then, he decided that prayer, pride, and patriotism would see him through. Meanwhile, Claire was content to shift some of her burden to St. Jude, though she was never able to escape carrying a corner of it within her heart.

In anyone's memory, the spring of 1972 had been the gentlest they could recall, and when the solstice came, it gave birth to a truly awesome summer. Any rains that fell were intermittent, warm, and fresh. Iain had not felt it hard to believe that some special angel was entrusted by the Creator to tend to the moors, glens, and braes to render them heavenly in sight and scent. Magnificent was the heather in profusion, and the bees seemed inexhaustible, as they scurried from one bud to the next. Iain was as busy as these gossamer-winged, black- and yellow-striped bodied nectar collectors with new hives to be planned and laid out; but for Cameron, there were shooting butts to be built or refurbished, plus endless details needing his expertise.

Along with the gamekeepers, assistants, and ghillies, the laird was out in the fields frequently, from the time that Sol erupted in the east, until gloaming captured the western sky. Cameron had little doubt that when the twelfth of August became the date on the calendar that it would prove to be the most Glorious Twelfth of all. Already, chicks had emerged from the myriad eggs carefully laid and incubated by thousands of Scottish red grouse hens. Fully nourished by the bumper crop of heather seeds, they had survived in great numbers and matured rapidly to become a vast flock of strong and high flyers. "Surely, the best-laid plans of grouse and men had all come to fruition," Iain murmured.

Meanwhile, as was her custom, Claire visited her closet to see what gowns were sufficiently chic and resplendent to reemerge for another season of gala parties. These would be the social highlights of what might be one of a nonpareil season. Before long, six dresses had failed to pass muster, and another three were on probation. Looking at the rejects and potentials, Claire's face formed a pretty little pout. "Am I overly vain and, surely, too extravagant?" she murmured. However, feminine logic soon commandeered her psyche, and vanity fell easy prey to pragmatism. "Surely, if Iain goes to all the trouble that he does to build his business, then, I shouldn't look dowdy." Consequently, her concern over extravagance was an easy victim. She decided her castaways would be donated, while the replacements would be carefully selected, so as to be beau monde for several years. Then, Claire was eminently satisfied that she had arrived at a decision in a Solomonistic though feminine mode. Therefore, she allowed herself a moment to consider another facet. "Men are so fortunate," she decided. "They can take the same shooting suits, kilts, and tuxedos, have them cleaned and pressed, then look quite resplendent. However, quite like menstruation and childbirth, a proper wardrobe selection was a fate shared only by the feminine."

Later, Claire stopped at the last bastion of a commodious closet, and she came on a closed up garment bag that she knew was there. Unzipped, it revealed her lady's hunting ensemble that she had purchased at the thrift store so many years ago. As Claire recalled the theatrical ruse employed when it was purchased, a soft chuckle was emitted. In the intervening years, a number of replacements had been bought and subsequently donated to the same shop. Some new damsel in distress might be out there somewhere, and a good deed would be repaid. However, this outfit had remained sacrosanct, for after Claire's marriage, a ritual was contrived. Each year, she tried on "old faithful." A dual purpose was intended. First of all was the joy of reminiscence! Second, it was of figure evaluation. Over all the years, except for the pregnancies, it still fit quite like the proverbial glove except for being a little tighter in the waist. Now, time for the test had arrived. Claire noted that the jacket was perfect in the shoulders and bust. But, oh dear it was more than snug at the waist, and the skirt was tighter still.

Disturbed, Claire profiled herself in the mirror. She saw, with mild alarm, that her abdomen was no longer scaphoid but mildly protuberant. Next, the scale was visited, and it was found in disharmony with her reflection. "My heavens," she said when the pointer stopped at 118. "I'm getting fatter, but I weigh two pounds less. No doubt it is middle-age spread and lack of muscle tone; both are reversible by a good exercise regimen." In that regard, Claire knew that she had been remiss, for it had been years since she had ran after scampering children or picked them up to carry them about.

On the next morning, Claire was up with Iain, and in answer to his jovial, "Good morning Lady Sunshine, you're up early," she laughed, and replied, "Lady Sunshine is getting in training for the Glorious Twelfth." Next, they shared a kiss, then Iain departed in answer to the gamekeeper's knock.

Soon, Mrs. McTavish, the Cameron family's beloved cook, placed a bowl of Claire's favorite oatmeal cereal before her, saying, "Piping hot, raisins buried in the bottom, cream and sugar on the side."

"I'll go dig for the raisins, Mrs. McTavish, but pass on the cream and sugar. I seem to be gaining a tummy," replied Claire.

"You're flatter than I was at fifteen, my dear, and don't forget that diets can be dangerous." Then, Mrs. McTavish, who liked to mother Claire, said she wouldn't resume her duties until Claire ate her cereal. Smiling, Claire said, "I'll be careful." Mrs. McTavish beamed and moved on to her work. Finally, the last raisin was disinterred from a mantle of oatmeal. "My appetite doesn't seem as good," Claire murmured, then added, "I've got myself psyched out," copying the parlance of her sons.

Rising from the table, Claire decided, "Well exercise and fresh air will restore me." Having dressed appropriately for a walk, she stopped in the hall to procure a tam. Labradors Dougal and Rory were lying there, looking forlorn. Iain had departed in such haste that he had forgotten them. Both were on the entryway rug, brows wrinkled and muzzles resting on crossed front paws. At Claire's approach, the eyelid on one side of Rory—the chocolate Labrador—opened slightly to unveil a yellow eye. Dougal did the same, although he was black, and his eye was brown. Both dogs looked like two old men, who had just seen their fortunes erased by a catastrophic market crash. These two dogs had replaced Dubh and Purdy, after they had passed on to take up station at the Rainbow Bridge. Rory and Dougal had been selected to be the new members of the "household guard," as Iain referred to them.

"Poor fellows," said Claire softly. "Your boss has gone and left you." Then, seeing a leash that ended in dual leads, Claire called out, "Would you like to come with me?" Though words were meaningless to the canine minds, the sight of the leash was not. Yellow and brown eyes became aglow, and black and chocolate tails swung in happy arcs. At least excellent training did restrain them from rearing up to lick Claire's face.

Once outside, Claire headed up her favorite trail, the one she had first shared with Iain and Simba. Nearly a month had gone by since she and Iain had walked it together. "Maybe, business is becoming too pressing," she concluded. Then, Claire remembered the old adage, "The hound knows the hand that holds the leash," and it was proving true. Although the two dogs would have been models of decorum under Iain's command, they felt free to test Claire. At first, it was just a little extra tug to pull away from the pathway to mark their territory on the bracken, which fringed the trail. At first, Claire was amazed and wondered if they would want to reverse sides on the way back, or would they be more interested in erasing the other's mark.

Keen to lower resistance on the leash, Rory and Dougal pulled just a little harder to reach another bush just beyond their tether. Barely a half mile from the manor house, Claire realized that she was tiring and decided to return. "Too much too soon," she said. Then added, "The dogs wore me out." Rather than admit she felt too weak to restrain them further, their leashes were unclasped. "I'll let them run free and have some fun," was her excuse.

During the next few days, Claire convinced herself that she was feeling a little better. Another half-mile walk was taken without the dogs and she really didn't drag nearly as much. *That's the nurse for you,* she decided. *You have a few natural aging changes and think you are just two steps removed from an autopsy.* Then, Claire's mother's discussion of menopause came to mind. Fatigue and decrease in appetite seemed to stand out in Claire's recollection. *Well, at least no hot flashes yet, but I'll be ready for them when they come.* This self-diagnosis did bring some mental relief. Her spirits were high when she embarked for Edinburgh the following day. All the fine dress shops on Princess Street beckoned to her, and yes she would drop off some things at the thrift shop.

In her buying spree, Claire had planned a variation, so a stop was made at a shop she had never patronized before. The premises had a sign that proclaimed its wares. As she parked and approached the door, Claire felt uneasy. She had chosen this shop, rather than one on fashionable Princess Street, because it granted her a degree of anonymity. When she entered, an obese woman approached calling out, "What can I do for you today dearie?"

Softly, Claire replied, "I would like to purchase a foundation garment."

"Spreading out a little, dearie?" the woman answered, as she broke into a smile with her overpainted lips separating to reveal stained and crooked teeth. Then, she continued, "We all do sooner or later, dearie."

After accepting the first garment proffered, Claire left it on when she redressed even though she felt it was restrictive and hated it. However, her abdomen was more flat. She decided the restraint seemed far better than facing a clerk on the fashion floor proclaiming, "You are a size eight in the bust and shoulders Mrs. Cameron, but I'm afraid at least a ten in the midriff."

"Oh! Well, that's what seamstresses and alterations are all about," she could reply.

On the first weeks of the hunting season, Claire felt quite well, and she stood up to the frenzied activity as well as ever, greatly enjoying the social events. However, by late October, exhaustion seemed to be setting in, and it was a struggle to appear effervescent. Claire knew that something had to be terribly wrong, and in early November, the charade was nearly unendurable. At times, she caught Iain looking at her apprehensively. When he would ask "Are you feeling alright, Claire?" she would brighten up and reply, "Of course, I feel wonderful, just a little tired I guess."

"Quite sure? Iain would say.

Then, her smile would broaden, and the reply was always, "As sure as a good nurse can be."

A few weeks later, Iain's questions implied increasing anxiety, and lines of concern indented his face. Finally, he said, "Claire I think you should see a doctor."

She leaned over and whispered in his ear, "It's menopause, but it only lasts for twenty years." Her feigned gaiety brought a half-smile to his face, but there was no humor underlying it.

On the next morning, Iain kissed Claire sweetly before he left. "I'm just putting in an appearance at Barclay's to reassure my clients. Then, best we take a week off and get some rest."

With her husband gone, Claire pushed back the covers and raised her nightgown. She noted that her abdomen was no longer in a state of slight protrusion, for it was beginning to bulge. In addition, it felt tense. Alarmed, she placed the edge of her left hand against the midline and pressed downward. Straightened fingers of her other hand were used to ballot her right flank The fluid wave, which was transmitted to the other side, came as a shock. *I've got ascites,* was her inner scream. "Oh! Why, why?" she kept repeating. She had no heart trouble, swollen ankles, or shortness of breath. She had never had hepatitis and, surely, the small amounts of alcohol consumed could never have caused cirrhosis. Was it possible that her ovaries had betrayed her and caused the fluid? If that was the case, it could still be benign. "I must face the truth," Claire murmured.

Then, she placed a call to her gynecologist and made an appointment to be seen at one on the following day.

As soon as Iain arrived home, Claire ran to him, as the possibility that she could have a malignancy was homing in on her. Worse yet, if the fluid was related, that meant it was far advanced. Claire had referred to one of her old medical books, where ovarian tumors were described from pages 374 to 386. The text started with those tumors of a benign nature and did indicate they could be a cause for fluid formation or ascites, as was the medical term. A wave of relief had come, but it ebbed with the next sentence, which read: "However, ascites is most commonly encountered with malignant neoplasms and must be considered indicative of stage IV disease." Claire didn't need to read further, for she well knew that stage IV was far advanced and essentially a numerical nuance for hopeless.

Iain was surprised and happy by the sudden embrace, and about to bend his head and bestow a kiss when it became apparent that Claire was clinging to him like a pillar she needed for support. "What's wrong, Claire?" he asked in alarm. Obviously, the gravity of the situation was portrayed on her uplifted face, and the tender tissues about her eyes had the dusky glow of a red rose's softest petals. Tears filled those dear blue eyes. They shimmered in the reflecting light until those newly formed gently pushed them down the ramparts of her cheeks.

Finally, Claire spoke, "I think I may have ovarian cancer, Iain, and it could be advanced." At the end of that most soulful sentence, she replaced her head on his chest.

Iain clasped Claire's head hard against himself and bent his face downward, allowing his nostrils to capture the sweet aroma of her still golden hair. In the solemn tones of a soldier, he said "It could be but a skirmish, Claire. Let us be optimistic until we determine for sure if we are locked in a mortal engagement."

Now seventy-five, Mary Cameron was informed of the situation. At dinner that night, speech was sparse and appetites sparing. Attempts were made to infuse optimism, and looks of love were omnipresent. In hope of generating a little bravado, Iain raised his wine glass and proposed a toast. "To a happy ending," were his words. True half-smiles were forthcoming, but none bore the imprint of conviction.

When Mary Cameron replaced her goblet on the white, starched linen, she stared into it, and the crystal glass was as empty as her own spirit. "Why not me dear God?" she asked. However, she knew full well that her Creator was not given to trades. Prayers would always be answered. But then she recalled the words the General had plagiarized from some good saint: "Prayers are always answered, but perhaps not in the way that you intended." Perhaps was the key, and the hope for it implied the answer might be just what you desired. At any rate, Mary decided that she would pray as fervently as she could and accept God's decision. She always had and was determined to continue.

Early the next morning, Iain and Claire left for Edinburgh. Their now ancient Austin Healey purred along, as nearly every part had been replaced and the body had been treated to several new coats of paint. *I wish, somehow, the human body parts could be replaced as easily,* Iain thought.

Meanwhile Claire was discerning and commenting on all the beauties of nature, as they passed through the countryside. Her hidden thought was, *Shall I ever experience this earthly beauty when autumn comes again?* However, Iain saw no captivating sights, for he could not extend his lucubrations beyond his fear for Claire. After the needs of the gear box were attended to, Iain's shifting hand would tighten gently on Claire's knee, and there were opportunities for loving smiles, as Claire placed her head on his brawny shoulder. Such simple gestures bespoke of their love for that emotion could be transmitted without verbal communication.

Chapter Thirty-Six

※ ※ ※

Upon their arrival at his office in Edinburgh, Dr. Chisholm examined Claire. His face maintained a pleasant countenance, though he had too much clinical acumen to be in any way sanguine. When his study was complete, the good doctor came to the side of the examination table and took Claire's hand. "You are correct, Claire. There is ascites and every reason to feel it is of ovarian origin. At this moment, I can't tell you whether the condition is benign or malignant. I'll draw off some fluid and send it to the pathologist. Cells are usually present, and they should be able to make a determination. You remember the drill, I'm sure. Pick a spot, paint it up with merthiolate, and then put in some lidocaine to deaden the area before the big needle goes in. While I'm there, I might as well aspirate all the fluid I can, for it doesn't do you any good, and you will be more comfortable." Shortly, when the big-bore needle was in place, it was connected to tubing, a three-way stopcock and a very large syringe. In color, the fluid, which flowed through the tubing was amber much like ale. When the flow stopped, 1500 ccs had been removed.

Iain was called in, and Dr. Chisholm explained in detail what had been done and what he needed to do. For Iain, there was acceptance without aggravation. Yes, they would stay at the Caledonian Hotel and return at the same time on the following day. When that hour came, they sat across from the physician's desk like two defendants awaiting the judge's decision. To Claire and Iain, Dr. Chisholm's face appeared resolute, and there seemed to be no reason for him to don the white lace cover as English jurists once did before announcing a death sentence. With compassion, Dr. Chisholm spoke, "The diagnosis is papillary cystadenocarcinoma, I'm afraid, and the fact fluid has formed indicates spread beyond the ovary to the peritoneum. Unfortunately, surgery would be of no avail," were his first solemn words. Then, he continued, "External radiation therapy has been utilized, and so has the injection of radioactive gold. However, there are side effects, and they could be severe. At best, they offer a reasonable chance at palliation, and a very slim hope of a five-year survival. I wish the news were different, Claire and Iain, but it isn't. Think it over tonight and if you decide to try I'll be proud, along with my colleagues, to do my best. God willing, we will be successful."

Iain held Claire's hand tightly. Obviously, there was no need to ask what could be expected without treatment. Allegorically, to the military mind, it would be Gordon at Khartoum, Goodwin Austin at Islawanda, and yes Geordie MacCallum on a ridge in Malay. Perhaps radiation therapy could be a relief column marching to save the detachment completely surrounded and vastly outnumbered. One could fight on harder, given the thought that help was on the way. Surrender wasn't worthy of consideration. The Camerons would battle on until death or victory came, and the first clash of arms would take place in the University Medical Center on the following day.

Oncologists and radiologists were selected to start Claire's therapy with the radioactive gold colloid Au 198. Claire's liquid theraputic isotope was far removed in color compared to the precious bars in Crosseus's hoard; in fact, it was colorless. First, a needle was inserted into her abdomen, as before. Then, the injection was made, with the instruction, "You'll have to roll around now, Mrs. Cameron. We have to mix it up well," said the radiologist pleasantly. Then, he said, "It's just a matter of staying in bed for a few days in keeping with the half-life of the isotope. Nuclear physicists are fussy fellows, and they don't wish you to go about bombarding other folks with gamma rays. However, in my opinion, you would really have to get very chummy with someone for several days to be of significance. But, then, I'm not a rule maker. Your nurse will give you special instructions about what to do when you tinkle." The radiologist's childish euphemism was followed by the doctor's smile, and Claire could not help but reciprocate.

"I'll see you tomorrow, and in the meantime, I'll let the Colonel in for a few minutes. He will be in less danger than he was in the past if he ever stepped into one of those old fluoroscopes, which they used to have at the shoe store to check to see if shoes fit your feet. I must confess that I enjoyed them immensely, probably why I went into radiology." Shortly after the doctor departed, Iain came in the room and stayed through to the last second of the mandated minutes. Again, Claire realized what an anchor he was; one that would hold her ship in place, in the face of the fiercest gale. Iain thought the first skirmish was being fought, and it was a comfort to know that his side was shooting back.

Ten days later, the fluid formation in Claire's abdomen had seemed to abate, and there was no sign of any fluid within her chest. Her doctors seemed very cautiously optimistic, leading to a proposal that more aggressive therapy be considered. With Iain present, the institution's leading radiotherapist suggested a course of intense radiation to the lower abdomen and pelvis might prove efficacious. A linear accelerator would be employed, thus permitting the delivery of what might possibly be a cancerocidal dose of high-energy electrons to the site of the ovarian primary cancer.

After delivering the lines that the prize of life might be obtained, the doctor went on to attest to the price that must be paid. "There will be skin changes, Mrs. Cameron, not unlike a bad sunburn. In addition, other things can happen deep inside. The intestine lies partially in the pelvic area, as well as the lower abdomen. Unfortunately, it's quite sensitive to radiation, so nausea, poor appetite, diarrhea, and cramping may ensue. As well, the urinary bladder becomes inflamed, so urination could be much more frequent and somewhat painful."

Then, the radiologist continued the medical mantra like a thespian in the final act of a play that had run too long. He had done it hundreds of times, after all. Also, the subject matter was not of the type that could be enlivened to enthrall a first-night audience. Then, he said, "The final side effect is ablation of the ovaries, resulting in sterilization, along with the rapid onset of menopause, and all that implies." No words were added to indicate that if the therapy was unsuccessful, the loss of ovarian function would have no meaning at all. No doubt, the patient had already reached that conclusion!

Their little conference was terminated with, "Think it over and in the event you want to proceed, we can start tomorrow." At this point, Iain could only surmise that it was like being trapped in a room on the third floor of a building enveloped in flames. When you looked out at the street far below, six firemen could be seen holding a net. One shouted up, "If you want to jump, best do it now!" He took Claire's hand and held it firmly, then softly said, "What do you wish to do, my love?"

"May I ask a question first?" she sweetly replied, and he responded, "of course." "When you graduated from Sandhurst, did anyone ever tell you that your leg might be blown off or your abdomen filled with shrapnel?"

"No, they never did," were Iain's words.

"Knowing you, my dear that would never have been a deterrent anyway," said Claire with a wan smile followed by a reach to take his other hand. "I'm sure you were well aware of those dangers, my love. But you went anyway. A

Cameron's wife will do no less, so let the doctor know he can commence firing, Colonel." Withdrawing her right hand, Claire brought it up in a brave little salute, and a grander but no more gallant one was returned by Iain.

Showing his love and extending support, Iain spent all possible hours at the hospital with Claire. Long nights alone in the Caledonian Hotel were fitful, but filled with prayers. Calls were made to young Iain in Baltimore, first to break the devastating news, then to keep him posted. Being a physician, his eldest son knew all the odds. He had his own life and a developing career, but his first words were, "I should come home!"

"No, Iain," his father replied. "Your mother wishes you to stay where you are. You know her well enough to accept the fact that she wants what is best for you. Should God decide that cure is not to be, surely He will give us all the opportunity to be together one last time in this world."

Jud was a different matter, for he was at sea. *Strange*, Iain thought, *For years, the Crown trusted me with the care of its soldiers. Now I'm not worthy to know the location of my son's ship.* However, a few terse wireless messages and replies were permitted. Someone somewhere had decided Flight Lieutenant Justin Cameron's need for shore leave could not be justified at this time, given the fact there was no medical evidence to indicate his mother was in eminent danger of death.

In regard to informing Geordie of Claire's condition, Iain decided that it was simply a matter of disclosing that she was ill. Iain knew that a teenager considered mortality the terminus reserved for the aged, apart from accidents, and these could be avoided. Colonel Cameron brought his youngest son to visit his mother each week since Geordie's school was very understanding, and Iain and Geordie's attention helped Claire maintain her resolve. In addition, Geordie's youthful humor was much in need.

Since Mary Cameron was not up to travel, she made up for her lack of physical presence with daily, light-hearted phone calls to Claire. Those calls took great resolve; however, she was a strong woman emotionally and up to the task. Her calls were always terminated with words meant to encourage. In the last call Claire received, Mary said, "I'm tending the fort, Claire, firing off my rosary every time I think of you, which is really all the time. A good rosary is worth fifty cannons, and I'm considered a fine shot!" These words, and the feeling they embodied were tonic for Claire's troubled mind and symptom racked body.

Often, radiation therapy was given on an outpatient basis. However, Claire had suffered a full measure of all the side effects and complications. In her own mind, as well as the those of the physician's witnessing her distress, the thought sometimes came that the treatment might be worse than the disease. Now, three-fourths of the way through the therapy, she had only ten more days to go. Even in her suffering, Claire could be impish. "St. Jude has probably never been told before that if his supplicant didn't feel better, she would consider him a loser!"

At last, the final day of therapy came. No evidence of residual fluid was found in Claire's abdomen, and her chest X-ray was clear. Other tests showed no likelihood of metastasis to her liver, or other organs to which cancer of the ovary was inclined to spread. Then, one week later, Claire was feeling stronger, able to take in more sustenance and hold it down. Christmas and New Year's had come and gone. Winter had lingered on and this year's spring seemed to possess little in the way of glory. Nonetheless, release from her antiseptic prison filled her heart with joy. Iain sensed a glimmer of hope and, perhaps, a new lease on life for his dearest one.

Although Iain had suggested an ambulance, Claire would have no part of it. "I want to sit in the front seat of the Jaguar and I'm going to do it," she said adamantly, and so she did. When the car arrived in the driveway leading to the manor house, a great surprise awaited them. Sandy MacPhee had recruited every piper in the region, it seemed, and they were playing "The Campbells Are Coming." Iain had never really liked the tune before, but now it was the sweetest he had ever heard. Continuing on, the piper's played "Annie Laurie" and, finally, "Auld Lang Syne." Claire was beaming for the first time in months, and she threw kisses as Iain carried her up the steps. They were thrown back a hundred times.

By April little waves of hope, perhaps kindled by the kind winds of wishful thinking, began to lap softly on the shores of the Cameron family's emotions. When Claire presented herself for a third month follow-up, her physician was immensely pleased. Her physical exam and laboratory studies looked excellent, apart from some mild residual anemia from the radiation therapy. "Mrs. Cameron, we'll see you back in another three months."

Then, toward the end of May, a five-pound weight gain had been realized, and it was flesh, not fluid. Unquestionably, her tolerance for physical activity was increasing, and Claire could be found out shopping and running errands on her own. Iain went back to business on a half-time basis. Matters were going sufficiently well that there was talk of going to Baltimore to see Iain Jr. Jud was destined for shore leave soon, and Geordie would be spending some time at home in July.

Midway through June, climatic conditions in the Highlands were terrible, even by the most apologetic assessment. However, for the Camerons, they could have been at the South Pole and radiant sunshine would have filled their days, such was the serenity that Claire's well-being generated. Then, along came that silly summer cold. At the beginning, only the irksome little cough was notable. *Surely, it will soon go away. For that matter, it might even be an allergy*, Claire thought.

However, July 1 found the cough to be worse, and there was the slightest hint of dyspnea.

On Claire's second post-therapy follow-up, the beam was gone from her physician's eyes. He frowned during the auscultation and percussion of his patient's chest. By the time his palpating fingers detected her liver to be slightly enlarged and nodular, the doctor's countenance had changed, becoming more distraught. Just as when you would look into the eyes of the captain of a floundering ship, the need to ask him if the vessel is sinking serves no purpose but to confirm the obvious. Claire knew the look, and Dr. Chisholm was aware of her perception. The doctor's voice faltered, as he gently said, "There are some suspicious findings, Claire. Let's do some tests and then we'll talk."

After the radiography, ultrasound, and other studies were performed and the reports were finalized, Claire and Iain were summoned. Dr. Chisholm was forthright and solemn. "Claire and Iain, this is very bad news, and there is really no decent way to deliver it. The cancer has spread widely and at a very fast rate. Your lungs and liver show signs of metastasis, Claire. Fluid is starting to reaccumulate in your abdomen, as well as forming in your chest."

After Dr. Chisholm finished speaking, with grave concern, Iain asked, "Is there any other form of treatment that might be efficacious?"

"I've discussed that with colleagues and consultants, here and in the United States," replied Dr. Chisholm. "Claire has had the maximum dose of radiation that she can tolerate, and surgery was always out of the question. There are chemicals, or so-called chemotherapy, but none are known to be really effective. Additionally, they act somewhat like radiation, or as we say they are radiomimetic, so there could be truly catastrophic side effects. I've talked with no one who would endorse their use." With sadness in his voice, Dr. Chisholm continued, "I'm, uh, afraid that medicine has nothing to offer but supportive care."

Given their nature, the devastated couple suppressed their emotions and thanked Dr. Chisholm for his candor, then departed. Claire and Iain walked hand in hand, though silent, until they reached their car. Iain held Claire tightly, and finally said, "I don't know what to say, Claire."

She replied "I do, my love. We always knew that we had to die sometime and thank God we only have to do it once. Unless we crashed in a car or an airplane, one of us had to go first, and I'm the one." Claire's tears started to flow. "I am afraid," she said. "I'll need all your love and support, as you will have mine."

Through clenched jaws, Iain could only whisper, "It will be an honor to give my all."

Iain suspended all his personal business. Fortunately, it was a luxury he could now afford. Boyd Walker, his longtime friend and past instructor had retired from Holland and Holland Shooting School. Walker's business skills, which he had never been able to use before, coupled with personal qualities and championship shooting abilities, made him a perfect choice to assume the chief executive office. Fortunately, Iain Jr., Jud, and Geordie saw their mother as often as duties would permit. For Iain Jr. it meant one trip home when the fateful news was learned, then a final one!

On one Sunday, Iain had just returned from Mass. Immediately, he went to Claire's bedside bearing little tokens of sustenance. Though she had no appetite, Claire would always try and eat just a little in response to her husband's encouragement. Since religion was on his mind, Iain asked Claire if he should arrange for Vicar Munro to drop by for a visit once a week. "No," Claire replied, "I would like to see Father Dalgity."

"Father Dalgity?" responded Iain. more than mildly surprised.

"Yes, Father Dalgity," Claire repeated. "Vicar Munroe is a dear person and I'm sure he is close to God, but I decided on Father Dalgity." Then, sensing that he needed an explanation, Claire continued, "I love my religion, Iain, but I've been thinking. This sounds silly, but I'm not delusional. I know that God loves me and wants me to be with Him, and I do believe I have a good chance to make it. Now, comes the silly part. I had a dream that we both ended up in heaven, but I was in the Anglican section and you were in the Roman Catholic one." She smiled and touched his cheek, then said "We wouldn't want that, would we?"

"I'd cross the fence," Iain replied.

"No, it's better to make all the arrangements here Iain. Besides, you Catholics have these extras that Henry gave up along with Catherine of Aragon. I really would like to go to Confession, even though I don't think that I've been very naughty and I especially desire Extreme Unction to help me over the hurdles." Father Dalgity came late that day, and Claire received her wish. In addition, the priest stopped by to give her Communion daily after he said his morning Mass.

Though Claire's body weakened rapidly, her spirit remained resilient. Finally, the most dreaded of all days came. Early in the day, a local doctor and old friend had visited Claire. As he took leave, emotion choked his speech and unabashed tears spoke volumes regarding his feelings. Finally, when words came, they were tortured. "Claire doesn't have long, Iain. She may not last the night. I've made her comfortable, and she is alert. I know that she has things to say to and hear from those she loves. I'll be at home. Call me at any hour!"

MacPhees and all the other staff came to say good-bye. They loved their lady, and that love was simple but pure. Their grief was profound. Mary Cameron was next. Stoic, though heartbroken, she wished to bolster Claire with her love and thanksgiving for the happiness she had given all of them and the care bestowed. For her sons, Claire conveyed her love, plus telling them of all the pride that she felt a mother could have for her children. At last, Iain Jr., realizing from his clinical acumen that little time was left, guided his brothers from the room, leaving their mother and father to share the minutes remaining.

Slowly, Iain walked to the bedside. As he drew close, he noted that Rory and Dougal were lying near by. "Come you two, your mistress needs to rest."

"No Iain, leave them be, for some of what I want to say pertains to them." Iain knelt at Claire's side. He was about to speak, but stopped to listen instead.

"I don't have much time, my dear. I've tried to be brave, and I hope you found me so, Iain."

Then, reaching into his pocket, Iain removed a miniature of his Victoria Cross and placed it on her neck. "This medal is given for an act of valor that may occur in seconds or over hours, Claire. You have been valorous for six months. I give it as a little reward on this earth, and a far greater one awaits you in heaven."

"I have a gift for you as well, Iain." Claire reached beneath her pillow and withdrew a small handkerchief. Slowly, she unrolled it, then held it open. "I did the lace and the needlepoint myself." The needlepoint said "Iain, with all my love, Claire." Her face was radiant, and though camellias had long since replaced the roses in her cheeks, she was never more beautiful.

"Now here is what I want the dogs to hear. I know you have your Rainbow Bridge. When you are old a long, long time from now and God calls you home, they will all be waiting there for you. Up the road a ways always will be a wee pink bridge, where I shall wait. This little cloth has my scent, and I'm sure that if you let them sniff it, they will help you find the way." Claire raised her hand to wipe away a tear that only a soldier could shed. Then, her hand fell away and lay still.

Rory and Dougal whined in unison. As surely as if it was a great white heron taking flight from the loch, they seemed to sense Claire's soul departing. Iain lingered long, and he hoped Claire's little bridge was not too far away. Half of his own spirit seemed dead, and it would be difficult to sustain the rest. Finally, realizing he still had three sons and a mother, Iain knew that somehow he must manage to fight on.

Only three days later, "Going Home, Going Home, Yes My Dear I'm Going Home." One of the Scots' most melancholy and heart-wrenching pieces of music was played on the bagpipes, and all of those assembled were deeply moved. In cadence with the mournful tune, Iain and Iain Jr., along with Jud and Geordie, stalwartly carried Claire's casket to the grave site. The Glorious Twelfth was only seven days away; however, no one thought of that now. When they did later, doubts arose and deeply troubled minds wondered if it would ever be glorious again. Now, life seemed like a fireplace in a dark, cold, and empty room and the crackling fire, which had emitted so much light and warmth, had been extinguished, leaving cold, gray ashes of gloom. Also, a cold wind born in the fjords of Norway had lost none of its sting by the time it came to prey on the mourners. The sun was totally in absentia, leaving the sky devoid of radiance or colors of white and blue. Shades of gray painted every cloud, and some shed their accumulated mist, adding volume to tears standing on every cheek.

Twin tartans of Campbell and Cameron covered the polished mahogany coffin top beneath the silver crucifix. All those present were reminded of how readily the tartan character could change, for fashioned in the form of a kilt, it came to life as it swirled in a reel or rippled in a fast march. Spirit, valor, and glory emerged from every thread. But, now, the blue, black, and muted yellow of the Campbell gave testimony to the gravest sorrows of life. No fire seemed to remain in the Cameron red, nor brightness persist in the fine yellow stripes. Seemingly, Iain could only see the black lines forming crosses. Previously, Father Dalgity had said Requiem Mass at the overflowing church. Now, it was time for the rites for Christian burial. All present were aware that in this life one is fortunate to find a man who stands between oneself and God and is bountifully endowed with the skills to help you find your way. Such was the priest who said the prayers. He could not erase their sorrow but did help soften the bearable proportions.

When all was over, and only the Cameron family remained, Iain sat among his mother, sons, sisters, and their families. All found the fortitude to let reminiscences from happy times flow forth. Then, gradually, all took their leave, and Iain found himself alone, apart from Rory and Dougal. They had no means of extending sympathy apart from wide and somber eyes and a paw or muzzle laid softly on Iain's knee. At last, Iain retired, and the little embroidered handkerchief that Claire had given him was holding all his tears.

Despite devastation, life went on for the Cameron family, as Iain Jr. returned to America, resuming his training. Jud returned to duty with the Naval Air Service, and young Geordie was in his first year at Sandhurst. As for Colonel Cameron, he plunged headlong into his business ventures in an effort to escape the great loss of Claire. Having Wilson and Boyd Walker on his team considerably lessened the need for him to be actively involved in daily activities in Scotland. Therefore, he had sought new horizons, and Africa seemed the brightest of all. Fortunately, Iain was well acquainted with the great gun houses of London, whose proprietors could introduce him to the type of man he sought. That man was Toby Drake, who was a legend even among the legendary. Iain was informed that Drake would be in London within a fortnight, as a celebrated speaker at the International Symposium and Exhibition sponsored by the leading sporting arms manufacturers of the world. Timing was propitious, so a dinner meeting was arranged.

Within minutes of their introduction and exchange of handshakes, it was obvious to both Drake and Cameron that they were simpatico to an extraordinary degree. Toby Drake, African hunter and guide, was a smallish man, though his sinews were cords of steel. Deeply bronzed by the African sun, a still handsome face hosted two of the brightest blue eyes Iain had ever seen. They were even more curious because Cameron could perceive that Drake's eyes were receptive to all the emotions man might encounter, and they would always reflect the proper aura. One thing was most certain they had often stared at danger and death without ever revealing fear. A caplet of lesser depth crowned Drake's head from the eyebrows and up, giving evidence that a proper safari hat had been in place more often than not. Topping Drake off was a carefully combed thatch of sun-bleached sandy hair.

As the pair moved off to occupy a quiet table reserved at the Savoy Grill, Iain readily noted that Toby moved with the same flowing grace of the great African cats he had pursued for more than thirty years. Colonel Cameron decided that Drake was the sensei he sought, but the question was, would Drake be impressed with him and his offer? By the time the second course of dinner was consumed, the great white hunter was equally impressed with his host. Iain had been forthright in admitting he had no experience in hunting dangerous game or in guiding others in their pursuit. *No, not four-legged ones Colonel Cameron,* Drake thought, *but plenty of two-legged ones who were out for your hide with guns and grenades, rather than fangs, claws, horns, tusks, trunks, and hooves.*

Midway through the solicitous savoring of their second after dinner cognac, a tentative agreement was reached. Drake would take Cameron on for a six-month trial and begin to teach him from his vast experience. If all went well, there would be a merger, then Drake and Cameron African Adventures would be formed. Iain could provide many new clients from his already established base of hunters plus contribute needed capital. Discussion and arrangements seemed perfect, as the African hunting season for the most part was in the six fallow months for bird hunting north of the Equator. Dates were set and much good advice passed from mentor to neophyte, which included everything from vaccinations and antimalarials to guns and cartridges. Their beginning appeared to be splendid. Now, there would be only a few months intervening before they could determine if satisfaction would meet expectations.

On his drive back to the manor house, Iain frequently sought out the little handkerchief Claire had given him. Feeling its softness, he could not help pondering why he was embarking on this course. Could it be because he was no longer able to court danger in a military career? Could he even be seeking the horn of a maddened rhino to provide an acceptable way to join his beloved? No, it would never be that, for such a decision could only be left to his Creator. By the time he had reached the gates of Capercaille, Iain was certain that he had made the choice solely in hope of finding a distraction that would help diminish the pain in his heart.

At dinner the next evening, Iain discussed his decision with his mother, and the fact that he would be away for six-month periods during the waning years of her life, which weighed heavily on his mind. Listening carefully to her son's announcement, Mary finished off the vestige of the single glass of wine that she allowed herself these days. Then, impetuously, she decided a second would do no harm on special occasions. Hesitantly, his mother took another sip, paused, and said, "You are ever so much your father's son, Iain! Oh! How I loved that man. Now that he is gone, I love him even more. I remember all the times he was gone off to war, and worry was my daily companion. When he finally returned, it was like being born again. I felt like a Lady Lazarus being awakened and brought forth from the tomb. I have less fear of the African plains than the trenches of France. I'm sure God will bring you back, and the joy of seeing you again will sustain me in your absence."

Pausing, while taking another sip of wine, she continued. "Also, your mother might find a challenge beneficial, for I could return to presiding over the estate. In the past, I used to do it very well when the General was gone, and frankly I don't think I've lost my touch. So Iain, go give this a try, and rest assured that mother will manage quite well. As my first official act, I shall pass on the remainder of this glass of claret, for it would be indecorous for the lady of the house to start out a little tipsy!" Then, Mary kissed her son tenderly and said, "If I know my men, you'll be going to the gun room to take stock. You'll find a few rifles that you'll want to take to Africa, but you'll also decide that several new purchases are in order. All your father's cherished brochures and catalogs remain in the left lower drawer under the stag's head, just where he left them. As I recall, he spent hours admiring the photos and description of the .470 Rigby Nitro Express but never got around to buying one." After these comments, Mary bid her son goodnight, and as she walked away, her face turned upward. "I'll bet you're smiling up there, Alexander." These words were followed by a sweet, little laugh embracing all her fondest memories.

As his mother had predicted, Iain headed for the gun room, and among the gun collection that he had inherited from his father was a fine Maurer Bolt Action Rifle in 10.75mm caliber, which had been made by one of the great gun makers in Ferlach, Austria. As he recalled, the General had purchased the gun on the recommendation of John Howard "Pandoro" Taylor, an acclaimed African hunter and writer who had guided his father on the first of several safaris in Africa. Also, there was a splendid bolt-action rifle in .375 Magnum caliber made by Holland and Holland, plus a .275 Rigby, which would be perfect for smaller game, though his father had used it in India to kill several tigers. Made by Purdey, the 450/400 double-barrel rifle was a beauty, but Iain knew cartridges were difficult to obtain. Then, thinking about what his mother had said, he decided she was correct, and he would coax himself into buying a double-barrel rifle in .470 Nitro Express, plus a Winchester Model 70 in the new .458 caliber. Also, there was a magnificent 600 Nitro Express in the rack. The diameter of its twin bores was awesome, but so was the weight and recoil. Perhaps, he should include it. Iain determined that he would need to bring at least one of his twelve-gauge double-barrel shotguns, which would be perfect for shooting the abundant game birds for the table, and the old pump action twelve-gauge Winchester trench gun would go as well. *Strange,* Iain thought. *This gun had saved his life from human adversaries in Malay! Now, Toby Drake had told him that loaded with buckshot it was probably the most desirable gun to use in defending oneself from the attack of a wounded, revenge-minded leopard springing out of the dense African bush.*

Soon, Colonel Cameron made another trip to London. He found that James Purdey and Sons on Audley Street would have a custom double-barrel .470 ready when needed. Also, the Winchester Model 70 in .458 caliber could be purchased over the counter, as it was largely machine made. Because Iain must of necessity shoot from the left side, that fact sadly precluded the use of his father's bolt-action rifles, all of which were made for right-handed hunters. Then, proper clothes were purchased and packed and the onerous vaccinations received.

Ready to go, Cameron was off to Africa in April. Noticeable to him was the fact that the throb of old reciprocating airplane engines was in the past; instead, the whine of jet engines was present. Still, if he tuned his mind, Iain could make them utter "Claire" repetitiously.

Arriving in Nairobi, Cameron found it was a bustling city with its own exclusive sights, sounds, and smells, and each was noted and filed by Iain's senses. Though he felt the experience was most interesting, he longed to be introduced to the bush, for it was to that destination his passions pulled him. As a flight had been arranged for six A.M. departure on the following day, his desires were not to be thwarted long. Fortunately, the sun had timed its arrival to greet their takeoff and, given the equatorial position of the capital of Kenya, seasonal variations were minimal. Quickly, Iain discerned that his pilot, Neville Blaire, was adverse to testing the twin-engine Cessna's altitude limits, preferring to cavort about with a ceiling locked at 300 feet or less.

Noting Iain's quick glance at the altimeter, which had followed immediately after his surveillance of the passing trees, the pilot grinned and said, "You infantry types always react the same, Colonel! For all the time you spend on the ground, one would think that you might like to fly close to it. Conversely, you probably wonder why I wouldn't want to be up as high as I could go? Two reasons, for I have no beacons to follow to Toby's camp, so I am what you might call a landmark flyer. Believe it or not, I can recognize half the trees of any stature, but rocks, rivers, and streams are my specialty. Secondly, much of my RAF time was spent in close support of you ground sloggers, so I got myself in a rut. Naturally, I would make exceptions if you want me to fly over Mount Kenya, but you can see all you want of it from camp."

Smiling broadly, Iain replied, "Really, I'm quite content if you remain above the tallest giraffe we are likely to encounter."

Blaire looked over and mirrored Cameron's smile. "You can count on that, Colonel. My first and only crash was the result of getting too intimate with a Kraut heavy machine gun on a strafing run. I made it back to the field, but the gear wouldn't come down, so scratch one Spitfire and a good left leg."

Relaxing, Iain took the pilot at his word and began to enjoy the great circus of teeming birds in myriad numbers passing below the Cessna's wings. "What a sight," he half-shouted.

"It's one that I never tire of seeing," Blaire replied.

Iain was entranced by the seeming endless herds of impalas, zebras, cape buffalo, kudus, gnus and elephants. However, some he didn't recognize, and that was to be expected for now, but shortly to be corrected.

When Blaire intoned, "There is old Moses," Cameron's enchantment was interrupted. Half expecting an old and bearded man holding his staff on high, Iain was puzzled at seeing a solitary tree of great dimension. "I told you I navigate by landmarks, Colonel, and that great baobab tree is named Moses, for he points to the promised land. Toby's camp is just ten miles ahead."

Their landing was rough, due to the surface of the makeshift strip, but Iain was free of apprehension. Off in the distance, he could see a column of dust played idly on the breeze, like the tail of a kite strung behind the approaching Land Rover. Colonel Iain Cameron had arrived in the heart of Kenya, and he would soon learn if it was to be a benevolent host.

Toby Drake was not a man prone to waste time or ammunition. As the camp attendants were unloading the Rover, he carefully set Iain's gun cases aside, then piled them on a sturdy table. "Mind if I have a look at the arsenal, Iain?" Already, the first gun case was halfway opened before Cameron's reply. Every gun delivered into the daylight brought an appreciative response, whether it was a spoken "beautiful," whistle, or a caress from his calloused hand. In turn, each gun was broken open, not only to ensure it was unloaded but also to assess the smoothness of the action and close tolerance of the components. Toby's less calloused and more sensitive little finger was run along the point of union between metal and wood, and this action was coupled with what his eye would relate as well. Three "splendids" emerged consecutively from his lips, and additional decibels of emphasis were added to the second and third. Bright blue eyes twinkled with merriment, as he stated with feigned solicitude, "Pity the stocks are too long for me. Otherwise, I would arrange to have you meet a crocodile of proper size and claim them for my own."

Continuing conversation, Drake said, "You arrived at a propitious time, my friend, as we find ourselves entirely depleted of fresh meat for the table. I've little to offer you for lunch, except for a generous serving of biltong and a cold Guinness to help wash it down."

Although Iain was not squeamish, biltong did not convey an apparition of a delectable dish. Iain's pursed lips and wrinkled brow preceded his quizzical utterance of the term "Biltong?"

"Just good dried meat made of the most tender cuts and cooked in the warm rays of that big, yellow fellow straight above us. It's quite like jerky, if you are a student of the American frontier folklore."

"It sounds delectable," Iain replied. "I had fears it might be akin to haggis, which I deplore despite my heritage. I should say, 'which I'm sure I would deplore,' since I've never gotten past reading the contents."

Smiling, Toby said, "Obviously, you have never learned the trick of imbibing sufficient Scotch whiskey to quell your dietary inhibitions before you taste it," accompanied by a boisterous laugh.

Iain countered with, "Should I drink that much Scotch, I would undoubtedly be unconscious." Fortunately, on tasting it, Cameron found biltong proved to be quite delicious and filling. Also, it went especially well with the Guinness.

Late afternoon found Drake and Cameron on the edge of a vast herd of grazing gazelles, and they were in the favorable downwind position. "Pick out a tasty one," whispered Drake. Iain selected a young buck slightly off to the side, aligned the gun sights to seek the area just behind the presenting shoulder, and squeezed off his shot. The .275 Rigby barked abruptly, signifying the departure of the projectile from the neck of the cartridge case. The bullet covered 150 yards in eighteen hundredths of a second, and it was placed exactly right. "Well done, Iain," were Drake's complimentary words. Coming from him, they were most congratulatory.

Later, fine gazelle steaks were prepared for dinner that night, and when the repast was complete, Toby introduced Iain to the charming ceremony of the sundowner. Cameron was appropriately seated, for his vista was westward. Now, the sun was surrendering Africa to the coming night and moving on to dazzle the southern Atlantic before awakening the parrots of Brazil, then warming the vast Amazon to create a steamy humidity. As Iain looked upward, he saw the pinnacle of Mount Kenya thrusting to 17,000 feet, appearing like a spear point of deepest rose, supported by a broad haft of purpled hue, made up of clefts and defiles, which added character to its image.

This was the time to relax, embellish experiences, sweeten reminiscences, enshrine the departed, and lay grandiose plans for the future. Always, there would be talk of the deadly animals; made up of the lion, elephant, cape buffalo, and leopard and why not throw in the hippo and crocodile as well! Epic charges along with last-second miraculous saving shots were not forgotten, nor would those compatriots who ran out of magic when they had come to face one lion or buffalo too many. Iain was engrossed by the sometimes melancholy but always exciting narratives. Because tradition was on display, he embraced it. Furthermore, he knew there were lessons taught that prudent students should embrace less they join the ranks of those mistaken or short on good fortune. As he looked up, Cameron noticed that stars were beginning to stipple the blackened heavens, for the sun was now long gone. New sounds were audible in the darkness, and all correctly categorized by Drake. "Just hungry hyenas, Iain," or "That lion doesn't sound as though she wishes to go to bed hungry!"

As he put it down for the night, Toby's empty glass weakly reflected the dying embers of their fire. "We'll be up early, Iain. Tomorrow could be an exciting day. We have no clients in for a week, and the Game Department wishes us to deal with a few marauders. In a near village, a pair of elephants are raising hell with the crops. One old lion has started eating the natives that he can catch instead of the zebra he can't. Finally, we are to try and dispose of a *Titanic*-size crocodile who has made it a hazardous occupation for the village women to wash their clothes in the big eddy along the river. You didn't think that you would become some sort of a jungle bobby, I suppose, but it goes with the territory!"

Replying, Iain said, "I don't mind a bit helping out as I hate to see some poor bastard who is struggling to get enough to eat getting eaten!" Later, while on his cot, Iain lay still for a moment and thought, *If I wanted to court danger, it sounds as though I've come to the right address.* However, danger had never deprived Cameron of sleep, nor would it on this night.

When Iain bounded from his cot, the sun was the sole sentinel in the eastern sky. Quickly donning some of the sartorial splendor acquired for safari life, he felt quite crisp until his hand idly brushed against his face, encountering a heavy stubble of beard. Crossing his mind was a transient consideration of a shave; however, outside his tent, Drake's voice was already growing strident, indicating that he was anxious to get on with the day's activities. Obviously, the men were a bit laggardly in following Drake's commands. Iain had little doubt that he was being regarded in the same vein. However, on his emergence, he found Drake far less laconic.

Turning his way, the white hunter in a half-shout exclaimed, "Iain slept well I hope! No black mambas came to share your cot?"

"If so, they slept as soundly as I did," Iain replied a bit apologetically.

"Grab the .470 and a dozen rounds of solids," were Drake's next words. Then, he continued, "We're after that pair of tuskers today, and solid is much preferable to the soft points in my experience. Whether it is a brain or a heart shot, Jumbo is pretty well protected, and you need all the penetration you can get. Breakfast is out I'm afraid, but there will be the ubiquitous biltong to save us from starvation!"

About an hour from camp, Drake slowed the Rover, as he noted the appearance of three natives standing in the long grass. One was Joro, Toby's chief tracker, and he was armed with a rifle. The other two men carried spears, and Iain judged that based on his regalia the larger one must be a chief or head man. When they dismounted and introductions were made, Iain's guesses were confirmed. Ten minutes of conversation followed, all in the local dialect, but Drake gave his pupil a running translation. Information given told them that the two rogue elephants were estimated to be about a mile ahead, rolling in the mud along a stream that wended its way through the area. The pair of pachyderms had feasted in the villagers' gardens that very morning and were only driven off when some of the braver warriors attacked with spears. Though the villagers' action was temporarily successful, it was not without grave cost. One of the elephants had charged his attacker, nabbed him with his trunk, then hurled him to the ground. With a badly broken body and unconscious, the man was stomped to death in the village dust in which he was born.

Drake's face mirrored concern, but fear was not to be found. Quietly, he said, "Load up, Iain, we'll walk from here!" During the early part of their stalk, there was still time for quiet conversation. Half whispering after a tug at Iain's sleeve, Toby said, "This may be a bit dicey since one of them is wounded and might be inclined to add to his list of victims. Perhaps, it is best that I go in first."

Replying, Iain whispered, "No, Toby, we discussed it last night. When you fly your first sortie, you never know if you are going to run into the Red Baron or some other fellow as green as you. I'll go in first, but I sure as hell want you backing me up."

Soon, Cameron and Drake were very near the stream bank, where advice and directions were limited to soft whispers and hand signals. For them, the grass and brush were too high to see their quarry, but sounds were more than enough to raise hackles. Drake paused, then slowly moved to Iain's side, where in a just audible whisper he indicated that it sounded as though the wounded elephant would be on the left. An extended left arm ending in a rigid index finger pointed the way. As they moved quietly and ever so cautiously forward, Iain brought the ten-and-a-half-pound Purdey to the ready with his left thumb poised on the safety and index finger intimately close to the most forward of the Purdey's double triggers. At last, Cameron had a clear line of sight; however, only a scant twenty-five yards separated the hunters and hunted! Perception of the intruders seemed to occur within a second from the time the elephant was perceived by the hunters. Toby had been correct—the wounded elephant was on the left. The spear had been dislodged from its flank, but a brownish-red swatch of dried blood divided by rivulets of vivid red from fresh bleeding attested to his wound. Instantaneously, the great trunk was held aloft, and the trumpet emitted was surely more fearsome than any Joshua could have sounded at Jericho.

Barely had the terrifying sound registered when Iain's single eye detected motion, for the beast was charging! Cameron knew that if he had found himself standing in the way of a speeding freight train, he could have always exercised his prerogative to step outside the tracks and let it pass. However, the elephant offered no such alternative. A shot to the brain was usually considered most effective, but the beast's great trunk would defy a midline shot. Would a bullet to the heart cause death in time to gain salvation? This was a deadly duel decided in seconds, not a chess game. Iain's feet were firmly planted; his body leaning forward to help absorb the recoil and prevent a fatal loss of balance. Suddenly, the Purdey roared as the first trigger was pulled.

So absorbed was Iain that he was barely conscious of the blast or recoil. He had chosen well, and the shot was perfect! While the elephant's frontal area was protected by the trunk, the beast's open mouth created an avenue to its brain stem, which was found with devastating effect by the 500-grain solid slug. Immediately, the mammoth faltered, and in so doing the trunk came down, and the great head turned to the side. Then, a second bullet entered just behind the eye and death came quickly!

Iain's heart was racing, and his breath held in check, while his thumb sought and found the top lever of the rifle, opening the massive action. Ejectors expelled the spent cartridges, which flew from the chambers. Two loaded rounds had been held in reserve between the lateral three fingers of his left hand. They looked like supernumerary, swollen brass digits; nearly the size of his own, as he slid them into the inner sanctum of the empty chambers and closed the action.

Only at that moment was Iain aware that Toby had killed the second elephant, which had retreated away to the right. Now, knowing the second elephant was no threat, Cameron let himself sag a bit, finally relenting to sucking in a badly needed deep breath. Words emitted by his mentor were starting to register. After struggling over them for a few seconds, Iain recognized, "Welcome to Africa Colonel Cameron!" This salutation was followed by a back slap, which produced no less recoil than the Purdey.

Joyous and relieved villagers (apart from the wife and children of the dead warrior) came en masse to salvage the hides and meat from the two slain pachyderms. To his delight, Iain was presented with a bracelet of woven hair from the tail of the elephant that he had killed. "What becomes of the tusks?" he inquired of Toby.

"Usually, they go to the Game Department," replied Drake. "That keeps them out of the illegal market, so they stand little chance of ending up as carved chess pieces in some Hong Kong tourist trap. However, the Chief Officer is a good bloke. I'll see if he might bestow the larger set on you, inasmuch as you did them a service, and it is your first one. They are a nice set, and probably would weigh in at ninety-plus pounds. I'll leave it to you to find out if Her Majesty's Customs will allow you to bring them home."

"No problem," replied Iain with a smile. "I'll fold them up in my suitcase and cover them with dirty underwear."

"Never underestimate the ingenuity of the canny Scot," Drake retorted.

As he consulted the abused Rolex that provided the only shade to a hairy forearm, Toby's eyes were in a full squint. Mahogany brown in color, Toby's skin had three linear scars bestowed by a lion; the marks bore no pigment and remained forever pink. After consulting his watch, Drake remarked, "The sun says 5:30 P.M., and my watch tells me 5:21 P.M. Which shall I believe, intuition based on timeless passage or a time piece packed with grime?" After Iain consulted his bright and shiny chronometer, he said, "Stick with the sun!"

On the following day after the elephant hunt, Cameron was first up, having decided that once late, forever on time! Masamba, the cook, was all smiles at Iain's appearance, despite the fact there were few front teeth left to embellish the gesture. In the pre-dawn period, the camp chickens had done their duty, and fresh eggs were present aplenty. Additionally, the cook had prepared an abundance of pao. Though the Portuguese may not readily have recognized it in the form served, Iain's taste buds relished the flatbread. However, Masamba, who was somewhat of a culinary alchemist, had transformed it into a most delicious pancake. Iain was on his twelfth, thinking that with proper filling these would surely rival Henri Carpentier's crêpes Suzette.

Shortly later, Drake emerged and settled for copious amounts of strong, black coffee. At the sundowner ceremony the night before he had only made it halfway through a marvelous tale, which included nearly every Hollywood celebrity who ever swatted a tsetse fly on safari or in movie locations. Deciding Scotch was not delivering him to his destination with the alacrity desired, he had switched to a rum of most potent proof. Consequently, each cup of coffee was an installment payment to the piper!

Within twenty minutes, Toby declared his mind to be clear, and he would be ready to roll after a trip to the latrine. Before departure, he announced that all tall tales to be told at this night's sundowner would be left to Iain. Toby would remain a passive listener, slowly sipping a single Scotch.

By the time the Land Rover reached the other village, some fifteen miles to the south, Drake had regained his vigor and literally sprang from the vehicle. After a short, lively conversation with the head man of the settlement, they were ready to pursue the man-eating leopard who had preyed on the village.

"Perhaps, I should have opted for the cat first, Iain," Toby said solemnly. "He returned last night and carried off a teenage girl."

"I suppose a girl of that age would put up quite a struggle," Cameron responded.

"Not usually," was the reply. "Generally a big cat takes its smaller prey by the head and the head of a human would fit that category. A big leopard has canine teeth a couple of inches in length. When they close their jaws down on your skull, it is very much like having two sets of ice tongs driven deeply into your brain. For a second or so, there is sheer terror, but your body surrenders fast. Then, the smart cat hauls you off to be devoured at leisure. Given their size, they are amazingly adroit at carrying off a pretty large parcel. A teenage girl would present no problem at all!"

Stopping about fifteen paces ahead of Drake and Cameron, Joro the tracker was intensely studying a muddy area created by a tiny spring. Joro had come in this direction as soon as he noted the flattened blades of grass compressed by leopard's paws. Paralleling the trail was a broader path of bent grass. Toby explained to Iain that this was was caused by the flaccid torso and extremities of the victim, which hung lifeless from the leopard's mouth. Pug marks in the muddy ground, which Joro was studying, were of even greater interest.

Drake went down on one knee. Then, he reached up to pull Cameron's wrist. "Look here, Iain," came Drake's words through clenched teeth with his finger pointing to obvious tracks in softened soil. Drake continued. "Pug marks can tell a story, and the depth of the impression confirms the cat was carrying a load. More interesting is the fact the right paw print is bigger than the rest. That paw is swollen to a considerable degree, and the leopard favors it, as you can determine from the fact the imprint edges are smudged! He doesn't want to put much weight on it."

Deep in the center of the distorted pug mark, Drake became aware of a new discovery. "Pus and blood," he said quite loudly. "This paw is badly infected. That explains the sudden appetite for humans. Probably, the poor bastard picked up a thorn, or possibly a bite wound from another cat or hyena. There isn't a four-legged creature out here that he can catch. To survive, there is no choice but to try and fight off the vultures for a putrid scrap from another cat's kill, or grab what you can catch! City folk, especially those unacquainted with sweat, are horrified to think they can become a part of the food chain. Doubtless, this leopard would have preferred an elan calf. But, circumstances left little alternative, and he possessed no conscience or intellect to guide him."

Drake continued, "Often, people come to think of man-eaters as being diabolically possessed. Perhaps a few are, God only knows, but the majority are just doing the only thing they can to survive. Otherwise, man might be considered the perfect meal since there is no thick hide nor hair to chew through. Perhaps to an animal we all taste like haggis!"

"Best leave the philosophy to Augustine and Aquinas," Iain said, "and get on with things."

"Given the cat's condition, I expect we'll find him or her in a tree not far away," was Drake's rejoinder. Continuing their tracking, only one mile ahead, a great baobab tree loomed above all the rest. When they were close enough to study it with binoculars, they saw that the leopard was there! Also, what remained of the young girl's body was draped across one of the tree's massive lower limbs. Lying intimately close, the cat was tearing a strip of flesh from the victim's thigh! Such a sight is horrific, but extremes of carnage were well known to the three who observed.

Because the wind was in their faces, they made it to within seventy-five yards of the leopard. No discussion had occurred regarding who would take the first shot. Drake raised his 375 Holland and Holland and fired with the bullet taking the animal in the heart, as was intended! Approaching, they found that only scant amounts of flesh remained on the girl's body. Tendons and fascia seemed to hold the skeleton together when it was solemnly removed from the tree. Then, producing a small, light tarp, Drake covered the remains while sending Joro ahead at a run to notify the head man, so the remnants of the girl's body could be returned to the village.

Before Drake and Cameron left, a few minutes were spent studying the leopard. Toby's analysis of the pug marks outside the village were right in every detail. Marked edema of the right front paw was most obvious. When Drake turned it over, a large abscess was present between the leopard's pads. "Pity the old fellow had no Androcles to pull the thorn out." Iain noted Drake's fingers touching the broken end of the large thorn, which was firmly embedded. "Had Androcles been there, this old fellow would be out on the savannah hunting, as he was meant to do, and three families in the village wouldn't be in mourning." Toby pulled on the leopard's pelt. "See how loose it is. Iain, like an old beggar in a cast-away coat six sizes too big? Starvation brought him to this point, pure and simple."

Soon the villagers arrived. Iain noted Toby going to the members of the victims' families and paying condolences in the local dialect. At what he perceived to be appropriate times, Cameron could do little more than nod his head. English, French, and Gurkhali had no place here. Therefore, Cameron resolved to acquire proficiency in as many African tongues as possible.

After Drake had further words with the head man, he beckoned Iain and Joro to remount the Rover. After they drove away, Toby seemed to have reclaimed his aplomb, as he glanced at his forsaken and banged-up Rolex. Suddenly, he exclaimed, "It's time to go bob for apples."

Iain wondered if he was the victim of auditory hallucinations, or Drake had uttered some sort of African aphorism. Rather than risk indication of ignorance, he replied "Fine with me."

Within minutes, the Rover had pulled up along the bank of a good-sized river. Drake gave it a name, which eluded Cameron. *Another thing to learn under light of the camp lantern,* he thought.

Leading the way to the river's edge, Drake pointed to a rocky section of bank containing a generous eddy. "One of thousands of African washing machines," he announced. "Village women come here nearly every day to clean their clothes. Don't ask me how they get them white in muddy, wash water, but they do! I never gave it much thought, but crocodiles seem smarter than myself or the washer women. My dear friend Peter Capstick pointed out the obvious to me between sundowners one evening. Incidentally, I have all the books he has written to date. Besides being a hell of a hunter, he is a marvelous writer. Believe me, no one has the ability to describe African catastrophes, wild animals, guides, and clients in such superb description and uproarious humor as Peter. You must read them after you have learned Swahili and all the local geography, Iain."

Cameron was surprised, for it seemed that he had aligned himself with a mind reader, who doubled as a fabled African hunter. "At any rate," continued Drake "what I meant by 'bobbing for apples' was trying to shot crocodiles in the brain. That's the only place they are really vulnerable, and their brain is about the size of an apple, hence the allegory. Now, if we sit here patiently and watch that protrusion from the bank, we might just be lucky enough to see the great saurian and get off a shot! Should an hour go by without success, I may ask you to go down and wash your shirt, Iain. Such a sight will surely arouse his interest."

"My nose tells me that my shirt is fresher than yours," Iain dourly replied. Joro laughed, while Toby simulated a crest-fallen demeanor.

Only one-half hour had passed when Toby pulled on Iain's sleeve, exclaiming, "There Iain! Take him!" Cameron followed Drake's pointing finger to what seemed to be a wake on the smooth river surface. Then, nostrils emerged in front of an enormously large snout surmounted by a pair of protruding, hooded eyes. Iain leveled the .375 H & H Winchester with his cheek firmly placed against the stock of the gun and sought the lens of the telescopic sight. With post and cross-hairs firmly placed in relation to the position of the monster's apple-sized brain, Iain fired, and 300 grains of copper-clad lead left the barrel of his rifle.

At the site of impact of the soft pointed slug, water erupted, and shorebirds flew in all directions, greatly alarmed by the noisy intrusion on their sanctuary. However, there was no thrashing crocodile in its death throes to be seen. Then, Drake's 375 thundered, and this time the placid water began to boil, as the saurian's great tail lashed convulsively before he died.

"Bloody hell," shouted Iain. "I missed him, and I was dead on! Well congratulations, Toby, you have proven to be the better man."

"Not better, Iain, just more crocodile-oriented. An old saying in the British Navy way back before Horatio Nelson was 'fire on the roll.' The old wooden ships would wallow in the waves. So, if the iron men who sailed them wanted to hit anything, they waited until the ship rolled. When the cannon were elevated, it was time to fire. Crocodiles tend to come up for a snort and look about them, then they submerge again. After counting to five, I saw him put up his periscope again, so to speak, and nailed him!" Shortly, Joro, covered by the two hunters, tied a rope fast to the dead crocodile, and they reeled it in with the Rover's winch. "He'll go twenty feet that old fellow," Drake intoned. When the villagers get around to opening him up, I imagine his stomach will contain some trinkets once worn by the women he consumed."

After returning to camp, sundowner time was on schedule that night. Though Toby did limit himself to one, Iain noted the glass Drake held was considerably taller than his own. Before turning in for the night, Cameron questioned his mentor. "Toby, if Peter Capstick has brought the dangers of washing in crocodile-infested waters to everyone's attention, why don't they take precautions?"

"Well he has certainly done his utmost," Drake replied. "He's suggested everything from using nets to building dikes. In the end, it's like warning people if they go to Monte Carlo, they'll lose money. Some folks seem not to mind taking chances."

Iain shrugged and replied, "Good analogy."

Toby arose and said, "No action tomorrow other than getting the camp ready for our next clients. All the usual things—try and make sure there are no cobras or black mambas in the latrine, and the camp crew should practice saying 'bwana.' New clients love that. In the event you are going to stay up a little longer, there is a finely detailed map with all the villages, streams, and river names over there on the table. Tomorrow, Joro and I will start you out on your introduction to Swahili."

Iain was gifted when it came to languages, and he wasted no time in attaching himself to Joro as a tutor. Patience on behalf of the native made him a good match for Cameron's enthusiasm to learn. Within two months, Iain could give rudimentary directions to the staff, plus carry on a disjointed though reasonably coherent conversation. When there were no clients to court, he approached Toby with the concept of carrying on at least part of the dinner conversation in Swahili. Toby agreed, but drew the line at dinner time.

"When I'm having my sundowners, Iain, I refuse to converse in anything but English. You must understand! I have hundreds of stories that I have to relate while John Barleycorn still grants me release from the grave. My innate sense of modesty usually prevents me from fully describing all my exploits and marvelous skills, even in my native tongue. Without a doubt, speaking in Swahili, I would be seriously handicapped, for despite my exhaustive knowledge of African dialects, I have found them rather deficient in the quality of adjectives that would do me justice."

"Very well," Iain replied. "It will be dinner only. However, I hasten to add that your self-depreciation regarding modesty sounds rather like an elephant's flatus."

Not one to surrender readily when it came to repartee, Toby countered with, "I'm surprised you haven't learned that an elephant's fart can be very meaningful. You'll not learn the reason from me, since my feelings have been deeply hurt."

"I'll remain forever downwind," Iain stated smugly. Clinking glasses, they both laughed. Then, Cameron went to work on local geography and topography.

By midsummer, the first of Iain's own customers were starting to appear. Toby felt his disciple had earned his spurs and thus the right to guide half the parties. With guarded enthusiasm, this promotion was welcomed, despite the fact that Cameron was not totally self-confident. After all, Drake had thirty successful years of postgraduate education. Regardless of how adroit the student might be, some pages of Iain's notebook remained blank in regard to both principles and nuances.

Sensing Iain's concern, Toby spoke up. "Your feelings are apparent to me. my friend, for I too confronted this dilemma once upon a time. Of course, we will always continue to consult when we are out of earshot of clients. But, oft times, we'll be separated by distance. Predictably, that's the time the feces hit the fan. Happily, Joro has enthusiastically agreed to accompany you and said something about enjoying the way you roll your r's. At any rate, he and I go back a good twenty years, and I'll wager he will remember all my tricks better than I do. When we face a dangerous animal, their response is instinctive and locked away in their genes. However, each and every species has its repertoire, so you can't expect the same tune on every occasion."

Continuing, Drake explained, "Joro has heard the whole song book on numerous occasions. Plus, he sees, hears, and smells things that we might pass by. I trust you with him, and him with you, so relax and enjoy yourself. Meanwhile, Tawali will be my number one man, so I'm well taken care of also. I feel fortunate you can communicate with Joro in a language none of the bwanas can understand. Believe me, when you are seeking advice on the best way to dispatch a wounded buff lurking out in the tall grass, the clients get skittish when you start discussing what to do next. I've been there, way back when I started out. One last bit of advice! During the discussion about whether or not the buffalo is intending to gore or stomp you to death, always maintain a pleasing and reassuring smile."

Iain's first big test alone was nearly his final exam. An oil tycoon, Jack Dalyrimple, had the fortune and desire to be a big game hunter who would add new entries into the record book. Unfortunately, his major impediment was the fact that he was a lousy marksman. Surely, the old adage of not being able to hit your ass with either hand, was created with him in mind. When Jack and his wife, Dorothy, arrived, Cameron had grave reservations. Jack was to hunt, while "Dot," as she liked to be called, would record it all on film.

As custom dictated, all new arrivals must spend some time sighting in their rifles. Two very cogent reasons predicated this routine. First, a rifle's sights could be knocked askew in transit, thus rendering any semblance of accuracy highly improbable. Should such a problem occur, the sights could be aligned during the practice session. Second, the guide could determine just how good a shot the client really was. Then, Iain or any other guide would have to extrapolate and estimate how the hunter might do on running game or against those in a charging mood! Further complexity was added to the equation by the fact some shooting might be done in what was known as the "off-hand position." Here the rifleman stood rifle to shoulder. Also, one could shoot in a kneeling, sitting or prone position. These had the advantage of adding stability in holding the gun.

Most stable of all was shooting from the a rest, which meant the gun rested on some object such as a lower tree branch, stump, or ant hill. Since a rifle weighing from seven and a half to twelve pounds didn't have to be held out straight by tiring arms, the gun barrel remained very stable. Though such a method was great for a shot at an essentially stationary target, it couldn't be used effectively on a fast-moving one, for an adequate traverse was not possible. When discussing this with his clients, Iain always drew laughs when he suggested, "Shooting prone with a rest was not generally employed for charging rhinos!"

Jack's gun sighting in session left Iain dismayed. Several proper targets of generous size were placed at intervals of 75, 125, and 200 yards. Ten shots at seventy-five yards did little to effect the pristine condition of target number one, apart from signs of impacted sand resulting from misses, which could be generously described as near! Dalyrimple did not seem dismayed, nor did Dot, who was fighting to keep it all in focus. Hoping against hope that the poor performance resulted from sight misalignment, Iain requested the opportunity to try Jack's weapon. After three shots, the spotting scope was employed to check the results. Three perforations were present in the bull's eye sufficiently close to be encompassed by a circle less than two inches in diameter.

Calling on all his reserves in tact, diplomacy, and optimism, Iain had real doubt that Jack would have a successful safari. No ethical guide would shoot trophies for a client, at least primarily. Should a wounded animal be running off, shooting it secondarily would be acceptable. Guides were expected to be solely responsible for dispatching wounded, dangerous game. Unfortunately, Cameron felt he couldn't tell Jack that he was considered hopeless, as one simply doesn't convey that verdict to an erstwhile hunter who had spent thousands of dollars to come to this nimrod's nirvana high in the hope of being a celebrity at next year's Safari Club Dinner. No, he would conduct the best hunt possible and take extra precautions to ensure safety. Meanwhile, Dot could enrich Kodak or Fuji in recording it all for posterity.

On Dalyrimple's list, zebras were first, and Iain pointed out a beauty. Jack got ready and took careful aim at a very large male grazing on the edge of the herd about ninety yards away. When the rifle fired, thundering hooves filled the air with sound and vibrated the earth. Iain noted the prize zebra passing the rest with every stride of his powerful legs. Jack had flinched when he had pulled the trigger, leaving the trophy unscathed! Glancing at the site where the beast once grazed, Iain was about to say, "Too bad, Jack, tomorrow we'll try again." However, words of condolence were cut short when a quite dead though much smaller zebra was noted lying a good ten paces to the rear of the intended target. Dalyrimple was ecstatic! Dot was depressed, as she was in the process of changing film when the great event occurred. Charm returned to her demeanor when she took pictures of Jack with his trophy. While posing and shaking the hero's hand, Iain and Joro tried to look excited in this trying situation.

At sundowner time, conversation was boisterous. Toby's clients had returned with real trophies in several species. Queried about the size of Jack's zebra, Iain described it as "just below record size." Cameron had an extra Scotch to help ease the discomfort from Dot's photo flash, but all went well. When the festivities were over, and the fading embers of exuberance gave way to fatigue, Iain smiled at Toby and said softly in Swahili, "I can hardly wait until tomorrow."

Chapter Thirty-Seven

※ ※ ※

After day ten of Jack's safari, only the undersized zebra had been bagged. Cameron was growing weary of inventing new alibis for lack of success at each subsequent sundowner session. Real doubt was in his mind that he could construe further innovative pretenses that would not totally challenge credibility. Additionally, Iain began to worry that the members of Toby's party, not being able to comprehend what a dismally poor shot Jack was, would conclude that Cameron was at fault. Word would spread: "Avoid Iain Cameron, that fellow doesn't seem able to find any game."

On day eleven, lions were on tap for the day, and Joro had located a magnificent male. *MGM would have done well to put this fellow in their animated logo,* Iain thought. Both he and Joro estimated the lion was somewhere between nine and nine and a half feet in length and approximately 750 pounds in weight. Careful observation of this awesome specimen of Felis leo was undertaken, and he appeared like a great tawny jewel set in the crown of a hillock. About him, in a crude circle, his pride made up of a dozen lionesses and numerous cubs was displayed. Rotund abdomens, when coupled with the sight of feeding vultures ravishing three wildebeest carcasses off in the distance attested to the fact the lions had feasted short moments before. Now, it was time for adult napping and cub cavorting.

Iain found it difficult to replace the spyglass in its holster, as there was so much to study and admire. Leo appeared to be asleep, but he was not. Two playful cubs, fascinated by the twitching tuft on his great tail, tried to pounce on it, as the very thick, flexible tail swayed lazily in an arc between them. Being more adventurous, one of the two cubs went so far as to try and nip it with his tiny teeth and finally attained his goal. Rather than roar and smash them with a massive paw, the lion simply raised a lid covering one great eye. Then, he proceeded to swing his tail over a wider area, sending both feline urchins rolling down the bank.

From his reading, Iain had learned that lions, especially sated ones, were among the most indulgent of parents, and the lesson was borne out by his observation. With his spyglass returning to the lion's head, Cameron noted the great cat's mane was of prodigious proportions. Colors ranged from amber to ebony with streaks of tan, toast brown, and auburn interspersed. Even while at rest, or nearly so, the lion's massive muscles rippled between the fascia, which bound the bundles in place. Thick as a weightlifter's thigh, a forearm came into play, seeking an ear that needed a rub.

Joro had indicated the lion to be approximately five years of age. However, it was unnecessary to stipulate since he was in his prime. Leo bore no scars of encounter, so Iain guessed that competitors seeking to claim his harem never got past the assessment stage! Twelve lionesses in the seraglio gave the appearance of leonine puppets bereft of strings. Some lay on their backs; legs relaxed and tongues lolling from cavernous canyons, guarded by pillars of ivory. Others lay akimbo; heads resting on pillowing paws. At least four could be seen in a mode of repose that permitted ample access to their nipples, much to the delight of a number of cubs intent on suckling.

Cameron thought, *Surely this lion, given all the gifts of heredity, would sire many more like himself.* Suddenly, the thought of Jack shooting this marvelous creature seemed totally anathema to Iain. "Bloody hell," he hissed. "Why couldn't Joro have found some senior with a decent mane, and no longer contributing to the gene pool, for good old Jack to blast away at?" Well he couldn't show a client a great trophy lion, then simply say, "Too bad, old fellow, but this lion is much too good for you." Then, Cameron took some solace in the fact that Dalyrimple would probably miss. "I have to be doubly sure that he aims at the king," he concluded. "Should Jack sight in on the lionesses, he might hit him by mistake."

Shortly thereafter, Ian found some new hope of achieving an unsuccessful outcome when he observed Jack trying to load the magazine of his .460 Weatherby. Half a dozen of the polished big-bore brass cartridges lay strewn in the sand. Dot had laid aside her Leica and was picking them up. Noticing that she had not bothered to wipe off the grit adherent to the brass, Joro came to the rescue. With his able, continued assistance, Jack was finally ready, and once the safety of the client's rifle was in a secure position, the stalk began. After making sure that no one was in Jack's line of fire, Iain was sometimes given to wondering what parameters might apply in that regard.

As they approached within eighty yards from the pride, most of the adult members were becoming alert and quite curious. However, the cubs remained at play or nipple. Iain mused, "This is the part of lion hunting that the uninitiated can never comprehend. Reviewing film of our approach, thus far, they would reach the ineluctable conclusion that our venture is akin to blasting Elsie the Borden cow. Most never seem to appreciate the fact that at any time one or all of these lions may put teeth into their decision that we are invading their domain, and would find it intolerable! No doubt, some film footage of thirteen mature lions devouring two hapless hunters and a shutter-bug would please our detractors."

Cameron had already calculated how long it would take a charging lion to cover fifty yards. Going from zero to twenty-eight or thirty mph could be achieved faster than a Ferrari with a maniacal Italian at the wheel. According to his math, an athletic lion (and most were) could travel thirty-five feet in a second. Iain did a little more computation, arriving at the alarming revelation that Leo could cover fifty yards in a hair past four seconds. Given the fact that a hunter has to work the bolt for each shot, plus they only have four to start with, or two in a double, the odds needn't always favor the group with the guns.

As they moved slowly forward, only fifty yards were all that separated them from the lions. Whispering to Jack, Iain said, "Take the big one with the mane! He's lying on top of the mound." Then, Joro hushed Dot into silence, as she exclaimed, "Aren't they cute!" Partly to ensure that he was aiming in the right direction, Cameron moved behind his client. Also, he wanted to place himself to intercept Mrs. Dalyrimple just in case she convinced herself that she had discovered a petting zoo. Jack took aim through a trembling sight. Then, he flinched as he pulled on the trigger, despite the fact that the safety was still on and the gun didn't discharge.

Cameron hissed, "Take off the bloody safety, Jack!"

Meanwhile, the king of beasts was getting perturbed, manifest by an ever widening maw flanked by fangs that looked like porcelain icicles Then, a roar was emitted that would curdle the blood of the most stalwart! While not nearly as loud, Dot's scream was just as unnerving. Reacting as professionals, Iain and Joro readied themselves and their guns for a possible charge. Dalyrimple's gun finally detonated. However, no sign of a stricken lion was noted. If some hapless monkey in the adjacent trees was felled, no one would ever know. Fortunately, there was no charge, and the lions retreated, hurling defiant roars over their front quarters as they departed. As the great lion was still a make able shot, Iain exhorted Jack to fire again. Though Dalyrimble was working the bolt feverishly, he neglected to pull the trigger as the potent .460 rounds were chambered. All three remaining cartridges fell to the earth with their potential never realized.

Again, sundowner time came, and Toby's clients had taken lions that very same day. *Just old dukes compared to the king,* Iain thought. However, he was inwardly happy at how today's story ended. Jack and Dot were as convivial as ever, and Mrs. Dalyrimple expressed her distress at the fact there was no darkroom facilities in which she might develop her film. "You could all see how big the lion was that got away," she exclaimed. After that statement, Iain grabbed her glass, added extra gin, and returned it with a smile. Within minutes, Dot was giddy and laughed at everything that was said, but spoke no more. On the way to his tent, Cameron thought, *Three more days, then its over!*

Sleep didn't come to Cameron as quickly as usual. Some nagging, mental discomfort assailed him, keeping the cloak of somnolence at bay. After three turns on the right side and two on the left, it finally came to him and he recognized it as a pang of conscience. Laughing Jack off or throwing up his hands in dismay, was an easy way out. Sure, the client was a bit of a buffoon, but deep down he was a nice guy. "Back in Malay, or at a training facility, I wouldn't act this way," he murmured. "Given a recruit, who couldn't shoot straight would have presented a challenge, and I would have a Sergeant drill him until he was perfect!" Well Jack was a client, not a raw soldier, so did he deserve less? A plan came to Cameron's mind, With its formation, sleep followed soon thereafter.

On the following morning, additional rifles were secured inside the Rover by the time set for sallying forth. At an apprpriate site far enough from camp to secure privacy, Iain braked the vehicle to a halt. As there was not a single animal in sight, Dalyrimple seemed curious about the stop.

Abruptly, Iain got to the point. "Jack," he said calmly, "I don't wish to offend you, but simply stated, you are a terrible shot."

To say that Dalyrimple appeared crestfallen would have been a gross understatement. However, no rebuttal or excuses were forthcoming, for the pronouncement scuttled such efforts and scrambled Jack's thoughts. Dot cleared her throat and squeezed the Leica close to her chest, as might a censured child seeking solace by embracing her doll.

"I don't want it to be this way, Jack, so I have a proposal. My next clients don't arrive for a week, so I would like to extend my services gratis for four more days. You in turn must listen attentively and do your utmost to respond to my directions."

"What do you want me to do Colonel?" finally emerged from Jack, while Dot's knuckles grew less white, as she relaxed her hands clutching the camera case.

"Joro is going to set up some targets, and you are going to practice until we find success or run out of ammunition. First of all, the heavy artillery will be set aside. You've never complained, but it's obvious that you flinch, so you either have a real or subconscious fear of recoil. Hopefully, we can overcome that with a combination of instruction and gradual accommodation to the kick of the gun. So, we start with a .22, which makes little noise and has no recoil at all. You can shoot hundreds of rounds without punishment, whereas ten or twenty with the .460 would be all that you would wish to endure."

Although the little Winchester Model 61 pump gun had seen hard service, its bore was as bright as a bride's ring. Iain loaded the tubular magazine with its full allotment of .22 long rifle cartridges, then he handed it to Jack with the safety on. "Your first target is out about twenty-five yards, Jack. We'll use the Rover's hood as a rest to lay the rifle on. Here, you can place the barrel on top of the pad, which Joro just laid out. For the first ten shots, I don't want you to even attempt to use the sights. Lesson number one is just try and keep your shooting eye open, and see if you can tell where the bullet strikes." Jack did exactly as he was told, and his right eye remained open for the first three rounds. A remission of his flinching affliction occurred on the fourth firing but did not resurface. Jack was beginning to say, "The bullet seemed to strike high and off to the left."

Pleased with initial results and portent of success, Iain decided to try stage 2. "You will use the sights now, Jack! Place the bead on the front sight in the little niche of the rear one. Then, aim directly at the bull's eye, and don't close your eyes." A hole appeared in the target—not in the center but comfortably close. Two hundred rounds later, the bull's-eye took on a sievelike appearance. Iain's words, "Good shooting, Jack, and now, its time for stage 3," was all the approbation needed to kindle expanded exuberance in the Dalyrimple duo. "Time for a break and some refreshments, then back to work."

Joro place the next target at 100 yards, and Iain produced a prim, little Winchester Model 70 .22 Hornet from a case. "A little more noise and just a hint of recoil from this sweet, little fellow," Iain said. Then, he added, "We'll try the telescopic sight. It's the same principle, but use the cross-hairs and place them right in the bull's eye." Jack readied himself, but just as he was about to pull the trigger Iain noted that he was starting to close his right eye. "Stop Jack!," he commanded. "You're not kissing Dot on your first date. You're shooting a gun, and you bloody well want to hit something!"

Dalyrimple raised his head and looked at Iain, appearing sheepish, then resolute. After some delay, the rifle barked, and the spotting scope recorded a hit. By late afternoon, Jack had graduated to a 30.06, and his performance was credible. Thereupon, Iain informed the Dalyrimples, "Tomorrow we will resume hunting once again," and all were of the opinion that a new day might result in fruition instead of frustration!

On the following day, a nice sized impala fell to Jack's second shot. Three rounds were needed for the sable. One was a clear miss, the next a disabling hit, and the third a well-placed lethal shot! Iain had let Jack utilize the 30.06 for the lighter animal, but moved him up to a more potent .340 Weatherby for the larger beast. Over the days remaining, a fine gazelle, greater and lesser kudu warthog, as well as a gnu were acquired by Jack Dalyrimple. Consequently, Iain's appreciation of his client's efforts grew in correspondence to Jack's determination and success. In size, several of his specimens exceeded those of Toby's clients, who began to show signs of camaraderie previously lacking with the Dalyrimples. On the final day, Cameron decided it was reasonable to give Jack a reward and try for a cape buffalo.

"Mbogo," as he was called in Swahili, was no Ferdinand, though he might graze as the cartoon bull would and he was in no way predisposed to bouquets of flowers. Any intruder on his domain was an enemy and to be treated as such. Joro had located a herd of about forty buffalo grazing near a water hole. Apart from one large bull, who had just put a duo of hungry lionesses to flight, the majority were the picture of pacifism. Certainly, the large bull's hormone titer was still running high and, if his bellicosity had subsided, Iain and Joro recognized no evidence of it.

This particular bull had a fine set of horns, and Cameron estimated the spread at forty-eight inches or possibly more. As always, a downwind approach was selected, and Iain was pleased to note that there was a clear avenue between them and the bull. Without any intervening cows, the line of sight would be unrestricted. Hopefully, it would stay that way. At 100 yards, several of the cows and a pair of young bulls began to show signs of wariness and agitation. However, their target, at least for the moment, stared at them with sullen indifference. Advancing steps of the hunting party became slower, and heart rates increased. After another twenty-five yards of cautiously measured paces, heart rates were at full race, and beads of perspiration were beginning to blossom. However, paradoxically, mouths and lips began to dry.

Iain had decided Jack should revert to the .460 Weatherby. Three finger-sized rounds were stowed in the magazine, while one was snugly entombed in the chamber, awaiting the strike of the firing pin to unleash all the fury the brass cartridge case held within.

"Jack," Iain whispered. "The old boy in the center is the one you want! Take off the safety and be at the ready! He may decide to run away from us or charge. Either way, you have to fire instantly and shoot for the chest! Should he give us the opportunity, we'll close in another twenty-five yards before you shoot. But if he moves, it's now or never! Are you ready, Jack?"

"Yes Colonel," were the only two words that passed Dalyrimple's lips.

Moving several feet to his client's left, Cameron had the thumb of his trigger hand caressing the safety of his double-barrel .470 Nitro Express Holland and Holland, while his index finger was a millisecond away from the front trigger. Stealthily, Joro moved forward to stand abreast of the other two, leaving Dot shakily holding her movie camera behind the three guns, which formed the thinnest of protective walls. *Times like this are no different than when you're crouched in a landing barge, waiting for the door to fall, or hooking up your static line when the light flashes on to jump,* Iain thought. *You should ask yourself 'what the hell am I doing here?' but, you don't.*

Sensing that the big buffalo's indifference was changing to pique, Iain knew that rage might not be far behind. Cameron felt Mbogo would not attempt to flee the field this day. Soon, battle would be joined, and no one was ever granted quarter by an enraged cape buffalo. Suddenly, the massive head of the bull came down, and at the same instant hardened hooves, propelled by the great muscular pistons of legs fore and hind, hurled him forward in a charge. "Shoot Jack!" Iain shouted, and the Weatherby bellowed in response. Just medial to the anterior angle of the beast's right shoulder, the 500-grain bullet struck, but did nothing to slow his charge. Dalyrimple's second shot was well placed but seemingly ineffectual. Death's distance was only thirty yards away when the third shot rang out, but the bull barely faltered.

Frantically, Jack was working his rifle's bolt, trying to chamber his fourth and final round, and Joro was bringing his .416 to the ready. Looking down the barrel of the 470 Nitro Express, Iain saw the tip of the Buffalo horns appearing like two burnished lances aimed right at Jack's chest! Flame shot from the right barrel of Iain's rifle; a fiery send-off to the nearly half inch in diameter bullet that streaked from the muzzle. After the gun bucked upward, Iain restored the level of the barrels, as fast as humanly possible, then pulled the second trigger. Finally, Mbogo's legs buckled, and the great body plowed into the earth a scant five yards from where Jack stood. Then, Joro's rifle fired, delivering a coup de grâce to as noble an adversary as one might hope to vanquish.

Quickly, the rest of the herd scattered. None took up the challenge, as had their leader. At last, the Doppler effect curtailed the sound of departing hooves, and Iain said, "Well done, Jack!"

"No," he replied "You had to save me."

Somberly, Iain replied. "You stood your ground, like Horatio at the bridge crossing the Tiber. Horatio faced the Etruscan Army, and you a charging buff! Three shots in quick succession, and all struck home! I backed you up, Jack, as I would any man. Despite one's finest efforts, there are days when it works out that way. May I add that if the situation were reversed, I would be proud to have you do the same for me." Iain extended his hand, and Jack accepted the honor.

Everyone had forgotten Dot. When they turned her way, she was still kneeling in the sand with hands covering her head, and the discarded camera's lens was pointing forlornly at the sky. Handing his rifle to Joro, Jack ran to his wife. Gently, Dot was helped to her feet, but her knees partially buckled when she viewed the dead buffalo and realized that their distance from eternity was no further than where the massive beast finally fell. After holding Jack close for the longest time, slowly, her tears began to dry. Finally, Dot turned to Colonel Cameron and said softly, "Colonel, are men crazy?"

"Yes," he replied. "But, so are some women, and we make a hell of a team!" All laughed, then decided it was time to pose for a photograph, handshakes, and pats on the back, which were now quite genuine.

On the following day, Iain viewed the departure of the Dalyrimples with mixed emotions. Both Jack and Dot promised to return. In addition, there was a solemn vow rendered that the male member would assiduously practice his marksmanship in the intervening months. Before leaving, Jack held Iain's hand tightly and also grasped his forearm for added emphasis. Any feeling of gratitude not conveyed verbally were transmitted by his eyes. Choking up a bit, Dot got a little weepy but did manage to bestow a grateful kiss on Cameron's weathered cheek.

Driving back to camp, Iain pondered Jack's confession that he had come to Africa because it was one of only a few places they had never been. Short of climbing Annapurna or Mount Everest, it was considered to be a real conversation stopper among their circle of friends. Dalyrimple had never given much thought to his own abilities, or lack thereof, and hadn't considered the expected, thrilling adventures might only be referred to in the small print of his obituary. Therefore, a valuable experience was realized by both men. For Jack, it meant he should never assume that he was capable of doing something just because it seemed exciting and he could afford it. On the other hand, Iain made a note that Dalyrimple might not be unique. Thus, presumption that clients were at least roughly similar to Robert Ruark or Ernest Hemingway was audacious.

That evening, Colonel Cameron had a lengthy discussion with Toby Drake He proposed that all prospective clients be sent a questionnaire, which would detail their prior hunting experience. At first, Toby thought it might be insulting, for in his opinion it was a one in a thousand experience, and Iain had handled it extremely well. However, after time for reflection and a second sundowner, he arrived at the ineluctable conclusion that it might occur again, and this time to him. Smiling broadly, Drake said "On second thought, it might be a god idea! I'll phrase it right." Iain responded "That way it will look like a list of attributes rather than defects."

At the conclusion of the African hunting season, Cameron was off to Scotland. In the overall picture, his experience in the African bush had been rewarding and had helped erase some of the hollowness in his life. Claire was and would always be the center of that vacuum, and that would never change. Nonetheless, seeing his sons, mother and friends, along with the manor house and Scotland did much to alleviate the emptiness. They had loved these together in life, and now they would be shared in spirit.

On his arrival, Sandy MacPhee was there to meet Iain at the Edinburgh Airport. His old Sergeant Major stood as stalwart as he had on the parade grounds and battle fields of his youth. However, his movements attested to the sequelae from old wounds, and it was obvious that what war had left intact was being slowly eroded by age. Despite aging, MacPhee's fiery spirit blazed brightly, and the meeting was mutually joyous.

As they drove to Capercaille Manor, Sandy briefed Iain on all the details of the estate, and all the news indicated it was doing very well. At the gatehouse, Molly rushed out. The bun of hair, residing above the nape of her neck, was composed entirely of silver strands, which harmonized with those covering the rest of her head. More wrinkles had been added, but they all seemed to point toward her smile, embellishing it. As Iain continued up the driveway, Molly called the manor house to alert all that the laird was on the way.

As Iain approached Capercaille, 100 yards from the doorway, the setting sun defied the clouds and found an egress for its rays, igniting the garden in color and the old house took on a new life. At the entry, Mary Cameron stood a pillar of grace and she greeted her only son with a measure of love that could not be exceeded. Then, Iain went from one faithful retainer to the next, steeling himself from dwelling on the vacant spots where Claire and the General once stood. Rory and Dougal abandoned all tenets of well-trained canine restraint and burst forward to welcome their master in the only way they knew. Devoid of words, they stood high on hind legs with paws pounding Iain's chest, and long, wet tongues slathering his hands with canine kisses. *Yes,* Iain thought. *It is good to be home, and good for all to have him there.*

Later, at dinner that night, Mary informed her son that Iain Jr. would be returning for a two-week visit. Coyly, she added, "I understand he will be bringing a surprise!"

Iain paused, then wrinkled his brow, indicating conjecture. "Don't tell me he got married and is bringing a wife," was his reply, issued through now pursed lips pulled slightly to the left, as was his habit when conjecture gave way to concern.

Mary smiled, and her dimples, unscathed by age, appeared as charming as in her youth. Not looking directly at her son, she appeared to be confiding in her claret. "No bride, Iain, but a bride to be! Miss Amy Anne MacGregor has become the target of your eldest son's adulation, and he's bringing her with him expecting our approval."

"Bloody hell!" spouted Iain. "He couldn't have known her long, and he's too young to take on that responsibility."

"You have a selective memory quite in keeping with your father," she replied. "As I recall, you were younger and had known Claire for a shorter time. Don't you remember?"

Not wishing to admit frailties of recollection, Iain countered with another possible impediment. "What about religion?" Gazing at his mother's deepening dimples, Iain realized he was plunging deeper into the abyss of maladroit arguments, after reflecting on his own courtship of Claire.

Choosing not to indulge in verbal volleying, his mother quietly replied "The MacGregors are said to be pillars of the Church, the Roman Catholic Church."

After her reply, Iain sat back in his chair, then felt his mother's hand on his wrist. "Go to the gun room, Iain," she said softly. "I've learned men's problems are best resolved in such a sacred place."

Fortunately, on his return to Scotland, hunting season was in full swing. Thanks to the excellent work of Walker and Wilson, business was burgeoning and uncomfortably close to capacity. Given the fine reputation of Cameron and Sons, Iain was able to sign agreements with several more prestigious estates, thus giving the business a more generous buffer. Personally, he had no desire to spend any length of time on the Continent guiding bird-shooting tours, so agreements were made with local purveyors of excellent reputation. However, as usual, the social swirl accompanying the hunting season in the Highlands was undiminished, and Cameron entered into it, although not with the enthusiasm of previous years.

After Claire's death, Iain was not so much regarded as a widower, but more as a very eligible re-created bachelor. Seemingly, many families of note in the Highlands were encumbered by an array of spinster daughters, divorcées, maiden cousins or aunts, and an occasional widow. Suggestions received and introductions proposed seemed of endless variety and degree of assertion. Batting eyes, fawning smiles, and even uncomely aggression seemed to surround him. However, Iain was the master of pleasant aloofness and kind rebuff; when necessary he could be a very dominant discourager. The pinnacle upon which Claire's memory stood was far too high for any other woman to climb.

With alacrity, November burst on Capercaillie and its occupants, and it was hard for Iain to realize the time had come to pick up Iain Jr. and Amy Ann MacGregor. Jud was at sea on the HMS *Hermes* and wouldn't be able to meet his brother's fiancée. However, some leave was imminent for Geordie, allowing him to size up his future sister-in-law, and Mary Cameron was looking forward to Miss MacGregor's arrival. Sometimes, it seemed to Iain that his mother was like an avid reader entranced by her own biography and barely able to wait for the next chapter. However, her wait would be short, as Iain was about to depart for Edinburgh Airport to collect Iain Jr. and his future spouse.

Iain's commute went swiftly and, on arrival at the airport, he was happy to see the old Spitfire fighter plane still clung tenaciously to its pylon at the entry to the terminal. A new generation had come into being since this noble old warbird and dashing young pilots had taken to the heavens in an effort to cleanse the skies of the Heinkels and Messerschmitts that once defiled them. Inexorably diminished were the number of those who remembered, while those not yet born appeared apathetic to one of history's finest hours. After his car was parked, Iain's reminiscence assailed him, fueled by a magnificent memory of the minutia of moments past. He remembered "mother and father had parked here when I returned from Malay the first time." Also, "Many welcoming kisses were bestowed by Claire just over there!"

As Iain entered the airport terminal, an announcement "Aer Lingus Flight 313 now arriving from Dublin at Gate 3," blared from the Public Address system, shattering Iain's sad soliloquy, and Amy Anne MacGregor was about to enter his life. Among the deplaning passengers, Iain Jr. was easy to spot, for at six feet, five inches he eclipsed the vast majority of others. Looking very vibrant, he had gained a few pounds, but carried it extremely well. Then, Colonel Cameron observed that given their closeness, intertwining hands, and character of looks exchanged, obviously Miss MacGregor had come into view. She was tall and slender, and when Iain subtracted the height of the heels on her stylish pumps, an estimate of five feet, ten inches seemed appropriate. Raven black, the young woman's hair was smartly coiffed. Sapphire-blue eyes were well set in a beautifully complexioned, oval face of ivory hue alighted by lips and cheeks of red (no doubt applied, but striking).

Suddenly, young Iain's eyes beheld his father, compelling him to dash ahead. Vice-like handshakes followed but were soon abandoned in favor of bear hugs. Amy MacGregor was close by and beaming, as her fiancé turned from his father for the introduction.

Cameron noted that her blue eyes had warmth, as well as luster, and inquisitiveness dwelt within. Graceful fingers were extended and, as their eyes met, Iain knew Amy was forming a first impression just as rapidly as he.

Customs was not a problem. Soon, they were at the car, and the luggage stowed. Young Iain opened the Jaguar's rear door and beckoned Amy to enter, but not before stopping to admire how well dear old Bobiecka had withstood the ravages of the road for so many years. A mental note was made to call the car by name and await the quizzical expression and inevitable talk that would follow. When Amy was seated, Iain Jr. began to fold his lanky form in an effort to conform to the constricting confinement of the rear seat. As his maneuver was barely started, Amy sang out, "Sit with your Dad, Iain. You will be more comfortable, and I'm sure he would like to have you close after all the months away. I'll just listen and learn, but I won't promise not to ask questions."

No one saw the Colonel cock his good eye, nor did they hear what he murmured, which was, "This young woman is either a very warm and caring one, or a polished actress with a major in psychology—time will tell."

True to her word, Amy's questions came faster than the miles passed by. Thus, Bobiecka was brought to a halt on the siding every time a good scenic vista was sighted. On arrival at the manor house, Mary Cameron was enchanted by Amy and captured all on film. By the time that Iain Jr. and bride-to-be had passed muster and received all the affection Sandy and Molly MacPhee could bestow, Colonel Cameron remained in a quandary but was starting to lean in Amy's favor. "Is she like a very sweet sponge bent on absorbing all that is possible, or just persevering in guile like a gifted enchantress?"

In moments, Mary Cameron's mind had been made up, and Amy was soon assimilated as a grandchild. Much joy returned to Capercaille at dinner that night, as Amy's conversational skills and interesting, self-depreciating humor were all well received. Also, the fact she played the piano very well and sang beautifully with a repertoire of Scotland's most cherished music didn't go unnoticed. Later, in the evening, when he caught sight of Amy sitting on the floor alternately rubbing the ears of Rory and Dougal most affectionately, Colonel Cameron surrendered nearly all his suspicions. At last, he decided, "No young woman could be so contriving that she would endure slobbering jowls, playful paws, and dog breath solely for the sake of appearances. My son has chosen well," he said softly. *Takes after his father*, was left unsaid, but it was self-evident and needn't be put in words. However, a little nagging question was not dispelled, but it could wait until tomorrow. Then he could ascertain if Amy MacGregor liked guns.

Suspense ended at breakfast when it was revealed that Amy did like firearms. Though Amy was one of four sisters, she was the only one who liked to shoot. Bereft of sons, Bruce MacGregor had studied his daughters assiduously and had been elated to find both talent and desire in the youngest of his children. Well coached in trap and skeet shooting, Amy had gone the limit even bearing the bitter breezes of winter crouched in an icy duck blind with her dad. "Yes, I would love to participate in shooting driven birds," she responded enthusiastically when queried.

On learning of Amy's interest, Colonel Cameron knew that proper hunting garb would be needed along with a pair of guns. No sooner had the meal been completed, when the senior Cameron rushed Amy and his son to the gun room. Passing up the long row of fine shotguns suited to the Cameron men, he moved to the corner, where a pair of Boss Best guns, in side-by-side configurations, stood at attention in the rack. *Guns can't be forlorn, but these had always seemed to display that attitude,* Cameron thought. The General had purchased them from an estate sale, but he had never got around to having them restocked to fit himself. Iain knew his father already had more guns than he could utilize and, finally, he had come to the conclusion that the General simply enjoyed looking at and handling them. Mary Cameron had come to the same affirmation in the first years of their marriage when the purchase of a much-needed washing machine had been postponed in the same month as one of those strange, heavy, leather rectangle cases had been delivered by messenger. "Oh that!" her husband had replied. "Field equipment of course. We are going on maneuvers next month. You do recall me mentioning it to you, don't you?"

Although Mary had never been overly curious and certainly wasn't a sneak, she finally succumbed to taking a peak. When opened, the case revealed a splendid pair of Dickinson double-barrel shotguns. She thought her husband had been secretive, but he hadn't really lied. Truth had been bent in a circle, though not really broken. After all, a grouse moor was a field of sorts, and a driven shoot could be loosely construed as a maneuver.

When Amy mounted the Boss guns in a convincing fashion, they decided the fit was quite satisfactory. "She'll need a proper ensemble to shoot in," Cameron said to his son. "Fortunately, we have a fine selection at Cameron and Sons. Since you are a son, you are welcome to whatever either of you need."

"I couldn't do that, Colonel. You are most generous, but I wouldn't feel right," was Amy's response.

Colonel Cameron smiled saying, "You'll soon be a part owner in the shop, and I see nothing wrong in taking a dividend in advance. Besides, if you don't accept, I won't let you play with the dogs. Is it a deal?"

Amy's hesitancy was brief, and a sweet smile swept reluctance from her face. "You drive a hard bargain, Colonel. I could never bring myself to leave Rory and Dougal with itchy ears."

On the next day, Iain Jr. requisitioned the Austin Healey. Soon, the happy couple were off to Perth. Iain watched from the window, as the car with the top down sped along the driveway, and raven tresses were pressed against his son's shoulder. For Colonel Cameron, the picture was a happy one, and he took joy in it until his thoughts became bittersweet. Leaving the window, Cameron progressed upstairs, seeking the bedroom he and Claire had shared. Upon opening the closet door, he peered sadly at all his love's clothes, still hanging there. "Such a paradox am I," he reflected. "Capable of taking a man's life in the heat of battle, but unable or unwilling to discard my darling's garments. Do I keep them like a candle in the window, somehow hoping for her return?"

Though incapable of sight, Iain's prosthetic eye still had the capacity to form tears. Joining the intact mate, it spawned a few slowly rolling down his cheeks, which had only known perspiration since Claire's death and seemed to welcome these little revisitations. In Iain's pocket, the little handkerchief Claire had given him was prim and snug, but it was not withdrawn. Instead, he tenderly lifted the lifeless sleeve of her old hunting jacket, which she had prized, and dabbed at his eyes. Tears were blotted, though the horrible emptiness was not eased. Plunging his face into the garment, Iain used his hands to press it close. A tiny residual of her sweet scent could still be perceived, prompting him to cry out, "Claire, Claire my darling! Oh! God how I miss you!" At last, composure came, and when Iain Jr. and Amy returned, a semblance of joy returned to his heart. Guests would be coming for dinner, and birds would be flying high tomorrow.

On the following day, introducing Amy MacGregor to joy of the hunt rekindled Colonel Cameron's spirits. Taking to the shooting with a fervor that was most gratifying, Amy comported herself very well, and Cameron vowed to relish every moment of his son's and Amy's visit. And so he did! When time for their departure came, solace was found in knowing he would attend their wedding, now just three months away. Rory and Dougal had no such opportunity, and they sulked for a good three days after their benefactress had gone. Iain became aware that his two previously devoted dogs had even decided to ignore him. Rankled, he finally issued a strong admonition, which got their attention. Sternly, his booming voice perked up their hang-dog appearance when he said, "Go scratch your own damn ears!" Soon, the contrite canines were beside his chair vying for his favors.

Wedding plans for Iain Jr. and Amy proved to be a logistical quagmire. So much had to be taken into account, starting with her parents and siblings' schedules. Also, when would Jud and Geordie be able to obtain leave, and what about the availability of the MacGregor's parish church? Then, there was the health of Mary Cameron and Iain's return to Africa, not to mention aunts and uncles. One cul-de-sac after another arose in the Byzantine labyrinth in which the engaged couple seemed to be trapped. Undoubtedly, some guardian angels and patron saints came to the conclusion the couple had done penance enough. Suddenly, a date emerged that would satisfy the needs of all the principals leaving the nitty-gritty to divine providence. On the first Saturday in March, Amy Ann MacGregor and Iain Alexander Cameron Jr. would be united in Holy Matrimony at the Basilica of the National Shrine of the Assumption of the Blessed Virgin Mary, Co-Cathedral of Baltimore.

One sept of the Cameron clan made the trip to Baltimore en masse. Also, seemingly invigorated by the opportunity to attend her grandson's wedding, Mary Cameron decided to discard her cane and rely on the strong arms of kith and kin should the need arise.

Camerons and MacGregors turned out to be well matched in temperament as well as faith. Men of the wedding party were all kilted, and no ear had to strain to detect the drone of the pipes. The two families were brought together for nuptials, but they emerged true friends, which all acknowledged as not being the most common of occurrences. In the future, the Camerons would be lovingly welcomed back at any time and without question the MacGregors would find their way to Capercaillie.

After the wedding celebrations, upon their return to Scotland, the Camerons for the most part scattered to whence they came. Now, it was time for Colonel Cameron to make ready for his return to Africa and Toby Drake. Plans called for departure April 2, which was later than desired, though necessary due to his visit to Baltimore. Iain could not think of anything that would delay him longer.

Packing wasn't much of a chore for Colonel Cameron, now African hunting guide, for he had left his safari garb and guns in the safekeeping of Toby Drake. However, while he was packing, the question arose of whether he should bring along another rifle or two. Then, Iain answered his own dilemma with, "Why present yourself with a question? You'll make a pretense of pondering when you know you will. Better to decide which ones."

While Iain was packing, there was a small radio playing in the corner of the gun room, which was proclaiming a live concert of the Scottish Fiddle Orchestra, a group that Iain greatly enjoyed. Intermission had come, and the announcer was carrying on about the SFO, much to Cameron's aggravation. "Bloody hell! Can't you say Scottish Fiddle Orchestra instead of always using acronyms? You make them sound like revolutionists instead of musicians!" Iain continued his private protesting, despite knowing full well the little radio had no two-way capability.

"SFO sneaks submachine guns into Edinburgh Opera House in fiddle cases and mows down audience," he retorted to the radio in mawkish unilateral repartee. Then, a different voice cut off his diatribe. "We interrupt this broadcast for a news alert. Talks between her Majesty's Government and Argentina appear to be breaking down. Prime Minister Margaret Thatcher has indicated that the Falkland Islands are a British possession, and any move by Argentina to occupy them would be dealt with harshly." Thereupon, Iain's mind decided to become recusant, resulting in immediate dismissal of the SFO, thereby permitting it to dwell on the Falklands.

Centuries ago, England had discovered the Falklands and laid claim to them. Spain took over the archipelago, way back when they were colonizing South

America and changed the name to Malvinas. When Spanish colonialism came to an end in the New World, Britannia took the islands back. Whaling and coaling gave the Falklands some importance in the nineteenth century. Then, sail had given way to steam, and masses of coal had been transported there by a stream of British colliers in an effort to ensure that none of Her Majesty's men of war would ever run out of steam. Close by the prime whaling grounds of the South Atlantic, the Falkland Islands proved to be a nearly ideal haven to process all the great leviathans that succumbed to a British harpoon. Then diesel fuel, electricity, petroleum-based lubricants, and ecology-minded folk left the whalers hoisted on their own harpoons, and Newcastle's black treasure was needed no more.

Continuing his reverie, Iain surmised that some long-gone resident, finally disgusted by feasting on the fruits of the sea, had imported some sheep onto the islands. Ovis had prospered there, finding sufficient fodder to fill their needs. Harsh winds, bred in the South Pole, crossed Drake's Strait, the Horn, and Tierra del Fuego before expending their fury on the Falklands, where the sheep exposed to their wrath responded by producing wool of luxurious length. *With those great bovine herds scattered throughout the pampas, what need would the Argies have for mutton?* Iain thought. *Maybe there is oil out there, or simply a political need to placate a restless populace faced with political and monetary uncertainty?*

Losing interest in the Scottish Fiddle Orchestra, Cameron turned off the radio and started to analyze the military implications. "Should General now President Leopaldo Galtiere continue to rattle his rusty saber, there was no doubt the Iron Lady, Margaret Thatcher, would increase her own bellicose rhetoric. War would come if the saber was brandished, and it would be a conflict between a power that never was and one that used to be." Iain needed no reference to conclude that "there was never a Tommy or Jock who could walk on water. The Navy would be needed, and that means Jud!"

Flight Lieutenant Justin Cameron had recently been given a billet ashore. His former ship, HMS *Hermes,* was just a few short steps removed from being a rusty hulk, soon to be drawn and quartered by a cutting torch in a salvage yard. "The same old British indifference to preparedness," Iain murmured. "Just like the old days of Nelson when brave men died, as men of war disintegrated due to 'robber' bolts used by some treasonous, murderous, shipbuilders of that time. Instead of a long and massive bolt of copper binding the great ribs of oak to the keel, only the bolt heads were pounded home, and the necessary shaft omitted. All to pocket a few dirty quid."

"Going to Paris to see Bonaparte's troops at drill was a merry diversion for London dandies before the war," he recalled. Next, Iain wondered how many of them died in it? "What of Malay which is now clenched tight in a dictator's fist?

Perhaps Kipling will always be right," Iain concluded, as he recited the poet's words written after the Crimean War. "For it's Tommy this and Tommy that, and throw him out the brute. But, he's the hero of his country when the guns begin to shoot!" Iain could only wonder, "How many citizens and especially politicians ever got on their knees to thank God that courageous men still answered their country's call? My family has and hopefully always will."

Colonel Cameron heard that Argentine units had invaded the Falklands (Malvinas Islands) and South Georgia in the first days of April. Mrs. Thatcher responded as predicted, and despite the well-intentioned diplomacy of the U.S. diplomat Alexander Haig, war was declared! HMS *Hermes* was reprieved from the wrecking yard, while oceanliners and container ships were rented to supplement Her Majesty's Fleet. Iain's heart went with the Scots Guards and Ghurka units, but his soul went with his son.

Shortly after war was declared, Colonel Cameron was back in Africa, and Jud's ship had cast off its hawsers. Having wondered if he should go back to Africa, Iain realized that as a father and colonel, now retired, he had only two options. One could stay home and fret, or go on with life and pray. God would listen just as well if the prayers came from Kenya, so that was his final decision.

With Justin on board, the HMS *Hermes* reached its position close to the Falklands in early May. Weather permitting training flights, gunnery and rocket firing practice were done along the way. Soon, it would all be for real! By superpower standards, the Argentine Air Force was a ragtag group largely flying hand-me-down Daggers, Skyhawks, and Mirages plus a few newer French Super Entendards. Some of the aviators were regulars; others were airline pilots called to serve their country. As a group, they were skilled, resolute, and brave. Despite the risks they took, the pilots were frequently frustrated by bombs and rockets that didn't explode. To the contrary, it was a blessing for the British, who would have suffered far more losses if their adversaries munitions were more effective. British ships were clustered some 300 miles from coastal Argentine air bases, close enough to strike while not leaving much time to linger.

Jud's aircraft was a FRSMKI Sea Harrier, originally designed for vertical take-off and landing. Since the U.S. Marines also favored the concept, the early models were the result of collaboration between British Aerospace and McDonnell Douglas. However, the desires of the different services quickly outstripped the designer's original concepts. Despite increasing the engine's thrust from 8,000 to 21,500 pounds, true vertical take-off of a fully fueled and armed aircraft could not be realized. At last, some bright fellow figured out the Harrier could be launched fully loaded from a deck curled upward on the end, much in the fashion of a ski jump. Landing was accomplished with relative ease in a vertical orientation once fuel had been expended. As a result, in the acronyms of aerospace, the Harrier became an STOVL, which stood for Short Take-Off Vertical Landing.

Flight Lieutenant Justin Cameron had been airborne a good part of the past few days. Two were pretty much spent in ground support operations and the others scouting for Argentine attack planes. One of Jud's Sidewinder missiles had detonated close to a Super Entendard, but to his dismay the damaged plane had managed to escape, at least to somewhere out of sight if not back to base. Consequently, there would be no white and blue flag to paint alongside his cockpit.

Then, early on May 6, Jud raced his Harrier on to the upturned deck. Full throttle, the wings caught the needed lift, and he was airborne. Being that his was the last plane out, Jud knew he would probably be the last one back. "Keep in mind that wolves are fond of laggard sheep," he murmured, as he surveyed his surroundings. Patrol time seemed to pass swiftly and before long fuel gauges were beginning to catch Jud's attention. "Looks like the Argies are taking time out for an Asada," was the flight leader's message to his group. "Hope the weather is better at Mar del Plata than it is here; otherwise, the steaks will get soggy," called another pilot. "At any rate, we'd best top off with petrol soon," responded the leader. "Let's head home to Mother!"

With Jud bringing up the rear, the four planes turned in unison. Once over HMS *Hermes,* the group leader radioed again, "Looks bloody rough down there, the old girl's flight deck is like a trampoline, so easy does it!" The third plane landed, just as the deck was heaving and somewhat canted, and a portion of the landing gear buckled. Consequently, some rearranging was necessary before Jud could land.

The Commanding Officer of the Air Group called over the radio, "I say, Cameron, it's a bit dicey here at the moment. How many minutes are you good for?"

"Another fifteen," replied Jud. "And then I'd better come home to roost. Do you advise I try Invincible?"

"No, we'll get all the birds arranged by then, so just cruise a bit until we call you in," came through his helmet's earphones.

Advancing the throttle just enough to gain some altitude, Jud kept it to a minimum to preserve his fuel supply. Then, at that very moment, he received an urgent message advising all ships and planes that six Argentine aircraft had been detected on radar. As several of the enemy were already within three miles, the disclosure was late, and the excited voice also exclaimed that several Exocet missiles were on the way.

Jud had been warned that he wasn't to attempt a landing. Additionally, he would be highly vulnerable in a hovering altitude. Furthermore, if he could launch a very quick attack on the intruders, British lives could be saved. Having seen the *Sheffield* sink just a few days earlier, he needed no further stimulus. Within seconds, he had a radar lock on a Dagger, and he immediately began to close. Preoccupied, the Argentine pilot was trying to precisely drop his bomb and was fatally inattentive. Quickly, securing a lock-up with his sighting mechanism, Jud launched a Sidewinder, which flew unerringly to the hot tail pipe of the enemy's plane. Like a comet entering the earth's atmosphere, the Dagger exploded! With no parachute deployed, the enemy died with his plane.

Quickly glancing at the fuel gauge, Jud noted it wasn't critical but soon would be. Further consideration of that problem ended when his missile warning system sent out its ominous message. Smoothly, he deployed chaff and flares, which delayed two heat-seeking missiles from a second Dagger. Next, the Harrier was placed in as steep a climb as Jud could accomplish without a fatal stall. Warning system now quiet, the plane was put in a roll followed by descent. Right below was the second Dagger. As Jud had done, the Argentine pilot released his decoys, saving him from the Sidewinder's wrath. However, he was not as fortunate when a second missile left the rail beneath the Harrier's wing. Since there had been no call to return to Hermes, but the fuel gauge revealed his supply to be just under precarious, he decided to look for a friendly deck.

Suddenly, Jud's missile warning system came back violently to life. "Oh God!" he exclaimed, as he thought of the choice between further evasive action or ejection when fuel was exhausted. Fortunately, his great peripheral vision granted a millisecond of relief, for the inbound missile was an Exocet targeted on a large container ship. Having seen the *Sheffield* turned into a burning hulk by the 652-kg warhead of a similar missile, Jud knew he must attempt to stop it. "Thank God the angle is right," he murmured, as he fired his fourth and last Sidewinder.

Since the Exocet had been deadly close to him at the time he fired, there was little opportunity to escape the tremendous explosion generated by the colliding rockets. Fragments from the Exocet ripped through the Harrier's fuselage, seeking the most vulnerable thing on board! Jud felt little pain and was still conscious, though aware that his wounds were severe. With powerless hands, he sought the trigger mechanism for the ejection seat, but they were not up to the task. Other shrapnel fragments had found the turbine blades and plenum chamber. When the great orange burst came, Justin Cameron didn't mind, for his soul had already gone to join his mother.

Sandy MacPhee finally reached Iain by shortwave radio. Despite the crackling interference and the old man's broken voice, the tragic message was clear and absolute. Flight Lieutenant Justin Cameron was missing in action and presumed dead. When the communication was received, Toby Drake was standing nearby, and there was no question as to how profound an impact it carried. Iain's face was a mask of absolute pain, and his body seemed to shrink in size. Although men often have difficulty in either expressing or receiving words of comfort, Toby did his best in the vernacular that seemed to fit his personal distress. "Dirty fookn' politicians! Good men sent 4,000 miles to die, for some shitty rock that none of them have set foot on!" Though Iain's thoughts were much the same, he set his jaw; he found Claire's little cloth and swept it across his eyes in a cursory movement.

Toby spoke again in a softer, calmer voice. "Sorry Iain, I guess I've always tried to solve my own sorrow with invective. Better than drink, I'm sure. But after you've exhausted your rage, you haven't eased the hurt one damn bit." Then, coming up behind Iain, Toby laid a gnarled, brown hand hard on his shoulder and said most solicitously, "Go home Iain. Take the time to comfort yourself and your family."

"I will Toby," Iain replied somberly. Luckily, a charter plane was in the vicinity. Knowing of Iain's loss, the pilot forsook all his usual cockpit banter to leave Colonel Cameron alone with his thoughts, while he reflected back on his own younger brother, whose Spitfire had disappeared over the English Channel. Having experienced air war, he knew full well how it would be to die out there alone and be trapped in a falling star!

At last, he landed at Edinburgh Airport and, for Iain, it seemed like the most God-forsaken place in all the world. As promised, Sandy MacPhee was there, making no attempt to greet Iain but only to console him. "I'm so sorry about Jud, Iain. No finer lad ever put on a uniform. He got two Argies in aerial combat, then intercepted an Exocet that was heading for a supply ship. As best anyone can figure out, the missile was so close that shrapnel from the explosion must have hit his Harrier and killed Jud. There's talk of a decoration, but I know medals don't erase misery. Unfortunately, Iain, I've more bad news to pile upon you. We tried to keep Jud's death from your mother, but it came over the television. I guess it was just one blow too many for even a stout old Scot. Mary suffered a stroke last night, and she's paralyzed on her right side. Dr. Grey wanted to call for an ambulance, but your mother perked up enough to scribble a note with her left hand. We could make out, 'No! Iain is coming. I must stay.' At first, Dr. Grey was reluctant, but he decided that trying to move her would be so upsetting that it might cause more harm than good. He said he would stop by morning and night, but at eighty the outcome would be largely up to God."

Iain thanked his old friend in word and expression. Having such a comrade at his side during this time of anguish was very similar to MacPhee's being beside him in time of battle. Their trip to the manor house seemed like a cortege; however, at last, they pulled up to the front door. Again, Sandy was thanked before Iain bolted for the entrance then dashed upstairs. Thoughts of boyhood days filled his mind. So many times he had sought his mother out, running up those same stairs, whether it was to seek a soothing kiss to erase an injury or a congratulation as a reward for some success.

When Iain entered his mother's bedroom, the nurse quietly withdrew to provide privacy for mother and son. Remembering what Sandy had said, Iain quickly moved to the unscathed side. Soon, Mary perceived his presence and produced an asymmetrical smile. Her loving son bestowed a tender kiss, then softly stroked back a strand of errant hair. Some comfort came from the fact that he had come in time for one last visit, as he suffered no delusion that recovery would occur.

Quietly, Iain remained at his mother's side as she drifted in and out of sleep. When wakefulness came, he never talked of Jud and only communicated his love for her. Fortunately, one last little period of alertness took place close to midnight. Mary's frail left hand touched her son's strong face, and a brave half-smile returned to her lips. This action prompted another kiss with whispered words of endearment. Then, the same dear hand sought and found her rosary. Although the beads were worn, the sterling silver links were bright, just like the soul that silently departed.

Three days later, the little church was spilling over when his eminence, the bishop, came to say the solemn Requiem Mass for Mary Cameron. Many stood, umbrellas raised, in pouring rain to pay their respects to a beloved mother and son. Mary's casket was covered in proud tartan, while Jud's symbolic one was draped with the Union Jack. When the sermon was intoned, Iain's thoughts drifted, and he could not help but wish that he had his son's body to bury in Scottish soil. As the Atlantic Ocean was nearly 32 million square miles, with depth ranging from 12 to 27,000 feet, the Falklands were the only stone that would mark where Jud was entombed somewhere in the black, cold depths. Gazing on the crucifix above the altar, Iain thought, *May Thy will and not mine be done.* Then, a prayer of thanksgiving followed, as Iain took solace in the promise of resurrection and knowledge that someday they would all be reunited.

At the family grave site, Mary Cameron was laid to rest beside General John Alexander Cameron. Jud would have no grave as such, though a granite stone carved as a Celtic cross told the world that he was once present. Deeply cut letters proclaimed Flight Lieutenant Justin Joseph Cameron, R.N. Killed in action, The Falklands 6 May 1983. Iain had decided to place the marker on one side of Claire. In time, he would be on the other side. Music played on the pipes had all been selected by Iain, knowing full well those tunes most loved by his mother and Jud. Her Majesty's Navy had seen fit to provide an Honor Guard and a chaplain, who solemnly recited the prescribed text for burial at sea, just before the salute was fired. Then, the bishop read the Catholic rite and blessed the grave.

When the final melancholy notes emitted from a piper's drone had left the ears of those assembled to be extinguished in the heather-covered hills, the mourners drifted away. As Iain decided to linger a while, his sister was left to attend to the reception, as he made his way to a great, gray granite stone suitable for sitting on. From that cold, hard vantage place, Iain's eye swept the somber, stone sentinels that stood as monuments to the loves he had lost. Halting words were addressed to each before he came to Claire.

"Well, my dearest, you shall soon have more with you in heaven than I have here. Please ask God to protect Iain and Geordie. As for me, I would like to abide for a time to see, God willing, what sort of grandchildren arise from us. Then, along with my pack of faithful hounds, I'll come to find you at your little pink bridge." Iain replaced Claire's small handkerchief, now dampened, into his pocket, for the time had come to mingle with and thank all those who had come to share his grief. Just four days later found Colonel Cameron shaking Toby's hand back in Africa.

In the ensuing two years, some clear skies with intermittent sunshine did come into Iain's life. Geordie graduated from Sandhurst very near the top of his class, and his duties to date had been domestic and danger-free. However, Geordie was involved in another type engagement, and that was to Alysse Mary Murray, youngest daughter of a retired colonel who had served with the Argyll and Southerland Highlanders. Like Geordie, Alysse had hair of red, though darker and more burnished in tone. She seemed an ideal mate for the Second Lieutenant, for she was just as beautiful inside, as out—thoughtful, loving, serious when needed, but a part-time pixie on occasions.

Coming from a Regimental family, Alysse was well aware of all that was entailed in marriage to a soldier, and religion would be no problem. When Colonel Cameron returned from his second season in Kenya, their gala Highland wedding took place. Iain Jr. and Amy came from America, proudly bearing an infant son, Daniel Alexander by name.

When Iain visited Claire's grave, he went on talking at length about the beautiful little rainbow that had come into his life after all the storms. "Did you conspire with St. Jude again, my love?" he asked. Then he added, "I know you can see it all from heaven, but how I wish we could share it here." Before Iain returned to Africa, Claire rewarded him with a dividend. Alysse was expecting and, God willing, another rainbow would be awaiting his return to Capercaillie. In the meantime, Cameron's sister Annie had agreed to manage the estate while he was away. She had a fine husband and family of her own, and Iain felt it would be nice to have kith and kin to lovingly look after things at the estate.

During these years, Cameron and Drake enjoyed full bookings and a waiting list of considerable length as their reputation expanded. However, from time to time, it was necessary to switch their country of operation, as dictators and guerrilla groups came and went. Frequently discussed over sundowners was the stability afforded in the days of colonialism; however, reminiscence carried little weight by comparison to political pragmatism. Danger enough was involved in hunting Africa's man-eaters and killers without adding marauding insurgents. Fortunately, sanity prevailed in sufficient capitals to make life relatively complacent.

Jack and Dot Dalyrimple returned on two occasions, and the experience was far different from the first one, though the original adventure was frequently recounted by Jack with self-depreciating humor. Also, Iain and Toby kept guests entertained with tales of who saved who last, and those exploits were sufficiently hair-raising as to defy embellishment.

Iain was currently one up on Toby in the contest by literally snatching him from the jaws of an enraged hippo that had upset Drake's pirogue, throwing him into the water. To entranced listeners, Cameron went on to explain that Drake was trying to hold on to his rifle, rendering him incapable of any meaningful mobility in the water. At that point, the hippo had decided that he might as well further exploit the advantage created and eat a morsel like Drake! As soon as the listeners' minds had seized on the lethal potential of the situation, Cameron would freely quote from hunter author Peter Capstick's description of *Hippopotamus amphibious,* which painted an entirely different picture than that of Disney's illustrations. Hippopotami were second only to elephants in mass for land mammals and certainly not given to playfully cavorting about in pink tutus. Primarily aquatic in regard to habitat, they still ventured on land when they so desired. As Iain explained, "They were herbivorous, though one has to realize hippos shared space with crocodiles and were quite capable of vanquishing the largest predator that favored protein over lilypads."

As Iain's narrative continued, his voice grew more intense. "The hippo surfaced and headed for Toby. Suddenly, his great jaws opened, and they looked like halves of two wheelbarrows, with the uppermost one inverted. Remember, the hippo has jaw muscles as big as a horse's thigh, and four ivory tusk-like teeth the size of marlin spikes. Were it not for my immediate accurate placement of two 470 Nitro Express solids into the monster's brain, my partner would have been history now being recalled in a requiem toast!"

Then Toby retorted that he could have easily saved himself, but chose to risk his life because he was holding one of Iain's favorite rifles, and that he would have sacrificed himself rather than lose it in the water. Arising, Drake continued. "Freshen up your drinks while you decide who was the more courageous?" At this juncture, the listeners were of a mind that they were being subjected to fantasy and an entertaining interlude until Joro started the projector, which recorded the footage that Dot Dalyrimple had captured of the actual event. Obviously, no fiction was involved!

For Colonel Cameron, these were good years. Hunting, guiding, and guns were the love of his life, after family, and he devoted himself to both. To promote his enterprise and hold greedy tax collectors at bay through the medium of business expenses, he made a number of trips to the United States. Iain Jr. was now in practice in Spokane, Washington, close to the beautiful lakes and rivers of northern Idaho. All richly blue, they were surrounded by verdant, pristine forests of pine, fir, and spruce, spiring upward from the mountains and were easily likened to a great necklace of sapphires surrounded by emeralds. After moving to Spokane, Amy Anne had given birth once again, this time to twins. Duncan and Douglas joined Daniel in the Cameron clan. However, Geordie and Alysse were not to be left at the starting gate, for George Alexander had been added to a growing stable of grandchildren, not long after their first wedding anniversary. Given the fact the parents' genes were so heavily loaded with red, the odds were far better than roulette that this little fellow would also sport a fiery mane and so it was!

Dutifully, Iain wrote letters once a month, following his father's faithful habit. Given his remote location in Africa, they seemed to arrive in clusters, which were always welcome and thoroughly read. When Colonel Cameron received Geordie's last letter of reply, he noted a return address attesting to his promotion to First Lieutenant Scots Guards. Initially pleased, Iain's pleasure gave way to concern when the folded pages of the envelope's contents indicated an upcoming transfer to Northern Ireland. "Ulster isn't the most dangerous spot in which a soldier could find himself," Iain concluded. "Certainly, not like Malay, the Falklands, or hundreds of other spots scattered about the world in the past 300 years of the British Empire. In fact, it was far less hazardous than being a Jacobite in Scotland in 1745." A little voice told him that Geordie would survive. Maybe, it was Claire whispering in his ear, or a concoction made up of two parts wishful thinking, and one part hope! Time would tell and prayers would help. With these thoughts in mind, Colonel Cameron reminded himself that his own occupation wasn't quite as safe as a banker's, at least one presiding over a solvent institution. "Best worry during leisure hours," Iain concluded. "Otherwise, you may find yourself ungainly deployed on some angry rhino's horn, or a low-calorie meal for a pride of lions."

Geordie Cameron's initial letters from Belfast indicated he was bored, terribly lonely, and missed Alysse and Geordie II, as the baby was now called. "We all feel like overtrained Bobbies, in Camos instead of blue uniforms, out on patrol trying to snare a few street toughs," he wrote to his father. "On occasion, some shout at us, while others sling rocks or petrol bombs. Our lads haven't suffered significant casualties to date. I suppose, though, that it's better this way. I'm sure you and grandfather would concur on that." Also, Geordie added a footnote indicating ten days' leave was coming up, and it would be spent at Capercaillie with Alysse, Geordie II, and his aunt and uncle. Like a camel's nose beneath the flap of a tent, complacency was beginning to assert itself, thus displacing Cameron's initial concern.

Geordie's next letter changed all the components of the equation. He did have a glorious holiday at the estate but upon return his group was engaged in a sizable street action. A private was killed, and a second man was paralyzed from a bullet that tore into his spine. Iain wrote back, "The Irish are not all punks or thugs. Many are dedicated, intelligent, proficient, and gallant. They view things far differently than we, probably more like our ancestors did from Wallace and Bruce all the way to Cuchulainn. Be kind, understanding and chivalrous to those deserving, but absolutely forceful with those who are not. Above all, protect your men and yourself as best you can, while still striving for victory with all the skill and ardor you possess." Colonel Cameron put down his pen and thought, *Four more months to go before Geordie rotates home. Thank God!*

Then came Toby's clamorous voice shouting, "For God's sake, it's sundowner time, Cameron, and you're keeping us all waiting," broke into his thoughts.

Iain shouted back, "From the sound of you, I don't think you waited at all. Pour me a double, and I'll catch up."

Chapter Thirty-Eight

✠   ✠   ✠

    In the Scottish Highlands, March 1983 found spring making only the most feeble of efforts to secure any foothold. Winter was so firmly entrenched that even the octogenarians were loathe to make any predictions beyond "I think spring has been postponed until September, and summer has been canceled!" Prospects for a good batch of grouse, pheasant, and partridge chicks seemed dismal. To provide new growth, along with the tender seeds needed by fledgling grouse that hatched in the spring, thousands of acres of heather had been burned at the appropriate time. Now, Iain doubted there would be sufficient chicks surviving the nesting and hatching process to live long enough to partake in the bounty the new growth should provide. After thinking over the situation, he decided, "Well, let Wilson and Walker, along with the gamekeepers and Game Conservancy anguish over that, for I am needed in Africa." Drake had decided it would be a good year to try their success in Mozambique, and to that end he had secured a permit for exclusive hunting rights in a large area teeming with game. As yet, Iain was uncertain just how to get to Maputo, the capital city; however, he felt surely his Travel Office could work out the details.

    Despite the deplorable weather, this year's Scottish sojourn had been most happy for Colonel Cameron. When the season's bird hunting was winding down, Iain had sufficient leisure time to visit Geordie twice in Belfast, Additionally, Geordie managed a four-day leave coinciding with the visit of Amy, Iain Jr., and their children. Alysse with young Geordie were living full-time at Capercaillie while Lieutenant Cameron remained on duty in Ulster. For Iain, both were a joy to have about, and the ability to be a devoted, doting grandfather helped fill in some of the ruts and potholes in life's highway. Colonel Cameron's sister, Annie, and her husband looked upon Alysse and her toddler as members of their own family; consequently, this made for a very harmonious relationship.

Apart from weather, the only unsettling circumstance Iain encountered was the extension of Geordie's assignment in Ulster. Scots Guards Administration had just as great a potential for maladroitness as any unit in any army. Somehow, their chess board had come up an officer shy, and Geordie was the necessary piece to continue the game. Orders issued were phrased in appropriate military parlance, but the basic message was, "Sorry old fellow, but there's been a bit of a foul-up, and we need you to stay in Ulster another four months. Dreadfully sorry and all that, but we'll make it up to you sometime." Iain reflected on the imaginary order he had concocted and added "maybe," with quotations and a pair of exclamation points!! Well his soldier son had remained unscathed so far, and God willing, he would stay safe. He felt the whole thing was like extending a ten-round boxing match another five rounds. A fighter, fortunate enough to have fended off his opponent's blows for ten rounds, could presumably continue on for five more. Always, there was the chance of getting smashed with a lucky punch, and that possibility lay just below the surface of Iain's thoughts. Also, he was aware that the roundhouse right that you failed to dodge didn't just result in the referee giving you a count of ten. Punches thrown in this fight could be lethal. However, in spite of Cameron's concern, it was time to return to Africa and business obligations there.

At last, Iain was airborne and enjoying the favors of British Airways first-class service to Johannesburg. Despite best-laid plans and cheerful reassurances of his travel office, there was no quick change of planes for the continued flight to Maputo or Lorenco Marques, if you wished to take on the challenge of the double-noun description for Mozambique's capital city. Little doubt was left in Iain's mind that if the end of colonialism had some benefits, they did not pertain to travel. After a frustrating hour at the desk of Air Whatever, no conclusive evidence was produced as to when the next flight to Maputo would occur, if ever! The desks of all the world's major air carriers were consulted, leaving Colonel Cameron with the feeling that agents were not entirely sure Mozambique even existed, much less how to get there!

Suddenly, feeling a hand touching his shoulder, the now angry Cameron pulled abruptly away and turned to confront whoever had accosted him. Instead of the ubiquitous purveyor of tours of delight for gentlemen he had expected, there stood a ramrod-straight chap who could be none else than an aviator. The uniform he wore was crisp and a combination of safari and first-rate airline pilot garb. Before the man's smile was firmly fixed, a deep baritone English accented voice proclaimed, "Colonel Cameron, I presume?"

Iain returned the smile, and quipped, "Now I know how Dr. Livingston felt."

"Archie Andrus, at your service, Colonel." Matching the intensity of the man's grip, Cameron accepted his proffered hand. Since the two men were of almost equal height, seeking the other man's eyes could be done on the horizontal plane. Archie's eyes were keen and green besides emanating confidence and experience. Eyebrows and visible hair beneath the classic pilot's cap were well matched in sun-bleached blond, while his deeply tanned skin blended well with his starched and pleated khaki shirt. Notably, a discoloration of the upper right cheek and pinna of the man's ear was due to an obvious burn scar, thus producing a more interesting face, rather than a distraction.

"I've come to take you to the camp, Colonel," said Archie. "As you've found out, airline service is a bit subpar and, frankly, it's rather dicey. To the contrary, Air Safari possesses a fine old Dakota, meticulously restored and refurbished in grandeur. She's the closest thing to a winged Rolls Royce that you'll encounter in this part of the world. Although rather slow by today's standards, the Dakota is guaranteed to get you where you want to go."

After Cameron's luggage was gathered and taken along with him to the promised plane, he discovered Archie's description was apt in all regards. Complete with azure blue sky, the aircraft's fuselage was painted to portray the Serengeti Plain. Inside, it was a flying gentleman's London Club with service to match. A handsome black African named Martin Tumba served as steward and baggage handler. Bertram "Buster" Crisp, the co-pilot, was an Aussie who only made it halfway back home after the big war. Quickly, Iain succumbed to Martin's entreaties and gladly devoured a tray of sandwiches chased down with a fine South African lager. After lunch, most of Cameron's time was spent in the cockpit's jump seat, swapping tales with Archie and Buster.

Having been named Alstair at birth, Archie hated the name as much as his co-pilot disliked Bertram. "When I joined the RAF, I tried to get my comrades to call me AA or at least by some palatable nickname. Since I was flying a Lancaster over Germany, we encountered lots of AA, or anti-aircraft fire. Pilots started calling it Archie, instead of AA, so the new designation became my nickname. Buster and I ended up as the last survivors of our squadron. Late in 1944, a Fock Wulfe put a cannon round into the cockpit; toasted my ear and face a bit, but nothing worse. Both of us, along with three of the crew, were able to bail out before the old Lancaster exploded. Unfortunately, the rest of the war was spent in one of Herman Goering's hotels, but we made it. When we got riffed after the war, we decided to stay together, so here we are. Strange thing is that he ended up marrying a girl from Piccadilly, and my bride was from Adelaide, so we can't complain about accents. Now, as to why Buster took that name over Bertram, both of which are abominable, I'll let him explain."

Iain enjoyed the entire journey immensely. He decided that Toby was a genius. What client wouldn't rave about being transported on Air Safari, for it was like taking the old Oriental Express off its rails and giving it wings. When they touched down, Drake was there to meet them at the newly fashioned air strip, complete with windsock and a reasonable supply of petrol. Standing together, Iain and Toby waved the Dakota off, then Toby turned to Iain and muttered, "Same old Cameron, always arrives with more guns than clothes."

Chapter Thirty-Nine

❈ ❈ ❈

For Mickey Moynihan, trips to Belfast to rendezvous with Alexis always held a certain degree of fascination. When it came to eluding surveillance, he assumed the Russian KGB agent was the quintessence of proficiency. *After all,* he thought, *one didn't achieve the rank of Colonel in the Fifth Directorate as a reward for ineptitude in a career directed to the covert.* Nonetheless, the Soviet agent had diplomatic immunity. While being caught by MI-6 might result in assignment to Upper Volta, the Soviet Russian would never languish in an English prison. Mickey Moynihan enjoyed no such immunity and, if apprehended, those little ridges on his fingertips would surely alert the Ulster authorities to the fact he was really Michael Manion, who had a previous record and was still being sought for murders occurring at the time of the old armored car heist, plus the shoot-out at the garage. Knowing all this, Mickey was always on guard. Therefore, he personally set all the criteria for clandestine meetings with Alexis.

Moynihan decided the old "come to the aid of the motorist with the flat tire and no jack" gambit was a good one, though too many trips to the well with that ruse could arouse suspicion. As of late, Mickey knew that Alexis had become an all-around sports fan, attending all manner of sporting events. Since Mickey had suggested the ploy, he knew beforehand where the Russian would park. In addition, he possessed a duplicate key to the boot of Alexis's Zil sedan. Moynihan figured that any surveillance crew who might be capable of trailing the spy would likely follow him into the stadium or grandstand rather than simply sit and stare at an empty automobile.

Now in need of restocking the tools of his trade, Mickey had made arrangements for his KGB supplier to attend a highly publicized rugby match between two of the leagues leading contenders. Contest time was to commence at one P.M., and Alexis was to park in the preordained area by 12:30. Allowance for traffic tie-ups was an established part of Moynihan's regimen, so his departure for Belfast was timed accordingly. Soon, he was heading north on a well-traveled two-lane highway looking forward especially to obtaining additional hand-loaded cartridges for the Draganov sniper rifle. Also, Semtex and a dozen rocket-propelled grenades were on his list.

One new wrinkle was to be added to the routine on this occasion. Just in case of need, Moynihan had decided a car would be rented in Belfast and used for the purpose of the pick-up. *Am I overly cautious?* he thought. *No,* was his decision, for he concluded it was better for a nondescript Vauxhall to cozy up to the Zil, rather than the ostentatious Aston Martin. "Why didn't I conclude that before?" he wondered. "So far, maybe I've just been lucky!"

As he drove along, it seemed that holding the Aston Martin to the posted, legal speed limit was akin to riding a racehorse at a canter. Nonetheless, his mind drifted back to the days at Sweeney's Garage. True, he had slain the men from MI-5, but the man responsible for tracking him down was probably still alive. "Maybe, I'll save one of these cartridges for him," he reflected. It had been so long ago that he'd forgotten the man's name. Consequently, Mickey searched his memory, and a few miles down the road he recalled that there was a connection with King Arthur. "No, it wasn't Lancelot, and surely not Guenivere! Merlin the magician? Yes! That's the clue." Now, with the first half of the puzzle solved, the second came more easily. "Merlin Spencer, that's the bastard!" As the Inspector's name reverberated through his mind, Moynihan began to dwell on how he could have postponed this particular revenge for so long. Finally, he thought, *It's a strange world where you have so much revenge to obtain that you have to prioritize it!*

With this thought still occupying his mind, Mickey noticed a large lorry was approaching from the opposite direction, and the driver seemed determined to occupy part of Mickey's lane. Aggravated, Mickey flashed his lights to warn the lousy driver of his trespass. Simultaneously, the shoulder on his side of the road was immediately scrutinized to see how far off he could safely go in the event evasive action was mandated.

Mickey's eyes returned to the errant lorry and to his shock, he noted a British Army Command Car attempting to pass the lorry and, thus, heading straight toward him. "Son of a bitch!" he screamed, as he twisted the Aston's steering wheel hard to the left. From observation, he knew a ditch and a number of massive oak trees were just beyond the road's narrow shoulder. *Better them, as they're stationary, rather than hitting head-on in a collision with a speeding car coming in the opposite direction,* flashed through his mind. With one last desperate turn of the wheel, he avoided the unyielding tree trunks, but the ditch awaited. When the Aston Martin's front wheels dropped into the defile, the bumper and grill smashed into the opposite bank. Thus, all the force of the impact was transmitted to Mickey's legs, then to his pelvis. Extreme pain seized him and exceeded the threshold that even Moynihan could tolerate.

Reflecting back later, Mickey could recall no near-death experience, or any experience at all. When his sensorium started to clear, he was conscious of a strange and unfriendly room with faces to match. Pondering long about where he was, other than to assure himself that it wasn't hell, he ceased to feel concern because of the resurgence of pain. No beatings at the Maze had ever been like this! Whoever was torturing him was a master. Could he bear it? Would he have to confess and involve others, even his sons? One of the interrogators seemed to be moving toward him. Would there be more beatings?" Surprise came when the imagined inquisitor's voice was soft and feminine. "Oh you're awake, Mr. Moynihan. Having a lot of pain, I see. The doctor ordered morphine, and I'll get you some right away." Mickey couldn't recall hearing sweeter words. *I'm finally going to meet old Morpheus,* he thought, then added *I hope he's all they say he is.*

When Moynihan awoke the next time, Sean was there with a grave look on his face. Bending over his father, he whispered, "As we used to say back in the States, you nearly bought the farm!"

Hesitatingly, Mickey responded, "Do you know if I said anything I shouldn't have while I was unconscious?"

At last, Sean smiled, then spoke, "Well you aren't shackled to the bed, and I'm not a bobby, so I presume you didn't give anything away."

Mickey fought to clear his head, then added, "The fookin' Brits tried to kill me! Was it a set-up?"

"No just an impatient officer and a stupid driver," Sean replied. "They ended up side-swiping the lorry before they rolled and burst into flames. The driver and two passengers were all cremated." Now, though the pain was starting to resurface, Mickey forced a small smile, then said, "Some good can be found in nearly everything."

On succeeding, more lucent days, orthopedic surgeons supplied Moynihan with the damage assessment. Fortunately, his ankle, knee, and hip joints were intact, but both femurs, along with the right and left tibias and fibulas were fractured, and so were portions of his pelvis. Intramedullary rods had already been inserted. Alignment appeared excellent, and healing was predicted in six weeks. As expected, the caveat "barring any complications," was part of the prognosis. "Given the success we've had with the rods, you could probably be up and about before six weeks, Mr. Moynihan." One doctor said that the pelvic fractures add another dimension, though. "You should think in terms of bed rest for at least a month. Of course, that can be done at home. We should be able to release you from hospital in ten days or so, we believe. Her Britannic Majesty's Solicitor was more than happy to replace the totaled Aston Martin with a new one, along with pound notes for pain and suffering."

In amount, the money wasn't overly generous; however, Mickey knew he wasn't well positioned to launch a publicized lawsuit against the Crown. Also, Sean had told his father that Alexis had been informed of what had happened, and why the munitions were never retrieved. Although the Russian sent his condolences, he never called on the patient. for obvious reasons. Whispering in his father's ear, Sean repeated Alexis's message that "if an accident was going to occur, far better it be on the way, rather than the return. Certainly, suspicion would be raised if the police found rocket-propelled grenades and Semtex in the boot."

Of course, I could have been lucky, and they all would have exploded, Mickey thought. After thinking about that for a while, he concluded, "Living in a Communist paradise does provoke a strange sense of humor." For Moynihan, some jocularity had begun to return, and once the pain had abated, the physicians found their patient pushing rehabilitation to the extreme. However, no ill effects were perceived and in fact callus formation at fracture sites seemed accelerated. They wondered just how long it would be until he tried to sit in a saddle atop his stallion Warlord! That would be a real test of stoicism.

Meanwhile, while Mickey was hospitalized, Liam sat across from Darby McKevitt in a smoke-filled room to which sunlight was granted only minimal intrusion. Two other high-ranking Provos were present, bringing the number of conspirators to a quartet. McKevitt was striving to gain acclamation for a plan to detonate a car bomb of hellish proportions in front of the Harris Department Store, which was Belfast's most fashionable emporium. Barely letting the ex-jockey complete the details of his plan, Kevin Lacey, Darby's most militant advisor, exploded in anger. "You're livin' in the fookin' 1920s McKevitt! The fookin' Brits and RUC watch the Harris like it was the fookin' Crown Jewels. Roll up there in some old wreck stuffed with Semtex, and they would be all over you like flies on a warm cow turd."

With Lacey's outburst, Corkery, one of the other men present apparently unwilling to exhale the cigarette smoke just inhaled, simply nodded in accord. Lacey continued his bombast. "Shit, I like to blow up Prods as much as the next man, but this idea is about as innovative as fartin' after eating beans."

Out of the corner of one eye, Darby, well versed in catching the movements of a closing horse, noted Liam's smile. "Let's hear from Moynihan," he said sternly. McKevitt's words were emphasized with an upraised hand, and Liam spoke on cue.

"I'm impressed, Lacey. I wouldn't even have thought you knew the meaning of *innovative*." On the verge of snarling out a full ration of expletives, the target of the insult observed there was something about Liam's eyes that insinuated he would rather outline his plan to a dead man than an irascible one. Therefore, setting his jaw, Lacey glared but remained silent. Knowing full well he had won the exchange and why, Liam kept his murderous eyes fixed on Lacey as he slowly revealed his plan.

"I concur," he said. "Putting an old junker in front of a posh store with a driver who looks like a Paddy then gets out and runs like hell is like a five-day-old fish left on the counter. However, a Trojan horse doesn't have to look like a horse. Complete with chauffeur, drive up a fine Mercedes sedan, and surveillance sees only what they expect to see. A splendidly dressed lady goes in the front door of the store, then out the back way."

While listening, Corkery had freshened his drink and was searching his coat pocket for a fresh pack of smokes. Suddenly, he exclaimed, "What about the fookin' driver? Is he supposed to be some fookin' martyr, who gets blown up along with the car?"

"You don't spend enough time up town," Liam replied in concert with a shift of his eyes to the new speaker. "Many chauffeurs take advantage of time spent waiting to make phone calls, and there are three pay phones on the corner. Armed with a clipboard, a chauffeur walks to a phone and makes it look like he is doing precisely that. However, instead of talking, he is looking about and when it seems apparent that no one is paying attention, the chauffeur's hat, clipboard, and gloves go in the trash bin by the phone booths. After all, a chauffeur only looks like a chauffeur mostly due to the hat and gloves. Once they're gone, he just looks like a gentleman in a dark suit. According to plans, that same gentleman links up with the lady, who came out the back door, and they're off for an afternoon of cocktails."

"Who in hell is the chauffeur?" rasped Lacey after finally recovering a modicum of aplomb.

"My plan is that I am the driver, and my woman will be the fine lady Rosie Carey. As for your part," Moynihan continued, "Lacey, your group will steal the car! Corkery you have the best bomb rigger, so you'll be in charge of that. However, I'll want full say in where the timing device will be located, and I want the boot wired to go off in case someone decides to open it before the blast occurs. Additionally, we'll need some of your lads along with ours to create diversion at the proper time. You know the drill—rock throwing, a petrol bomb or two, all at widely scattered areas, plus a dozen bomb scare phone calls for every place but Harris Department Store."

Finally, Lacey and Corkery got around to admitting the plan sounded good, though they didn't add that much of the appeal resided in the fact there was no danger to themselves. After approval of the plan, the date was set for April 13.

McKevitt and Moynihan determined the big Mercedes could handle 500 pounds of explosives without a sign of sagging. With proper wiring, all Liam had to do was turn on the radio, and that would start the timer.

After explaining to Rosie her part in the plan, Liam's longtime live-in lover was thrilled to have 500 Irish pounds to spend on a wardrobe, plus a total make-over at a very upscale beauty salon. She was tired of old blonde tresses, and this would be an exciting change. However, one final vexing question was posed to Liam: "Can I shop some more while I'm in Harris?" Rosie queried from beneath pleading eyes. "Are you out of your fookin' mind?" was Liam's seething response.

Liam had gone over the positioning of the explosives, wiring, and timing device three times with Lacey's top bomb maker, and all seemed ready. As a chauffeur, Moynihan looked quite dapper. Although slightly risqué, Rosie was splendidly decked out in the latest haute couture, and she looked to be quite appropriate for a young socialite of considerable means. Unfortunately, the impeccable make-up applied by none other than the owner of Caesar's Salon was starting to streak by virtue of Rosie's predisposition to perspiring in what she deemed to be a precarious situation. When the defect was called to her attention, a tantrum arose, and it was made quite clear that she was not at fault. "Why wouldn't I sweat with a bloody big bomb right under me arse!" Then to Liam's chagrin, she cried. But Rosie recovered and, always a quick study, she repaired the damage by immediate application of some of the treasures in her oversized Gucci purse. Actually, her deft strokes improved on Caesar's original painting.

Finally, they were ready, and Rosie started to get in the front seat. Quickly, she was reprimanded and told the location for a lady of leisure was definitely in the rear. Then, at exactly two o'clock, the highly polished black Mercedes took leave of the garage with destination Harris Department Store!

Earlier in the day, First Lieutenant George Cameron had consulted with the Duty Sergeant regarding details relevant to the rest of the afternoon. Overall, it had been an unexciting morning, and the lunch was as drab as an Army cook could concoct. "All the action will be tomorrow, Lieutenant," the Sergeant related. "Things look dead for the rest of the afternoon up until the briefing session at 1700 hours."

Pausing, Geordie thought, *Alysse's birthday is just ten days away, and I haven't gotten her a gift.* Consequently, he asked, "Sergeant, if you wanted to get your wife a special gift, where would you go, and how long would it take?"

"Harris Department Store, Lieutenant, no question there. You can make it in about twenty minutes each way. However, the big problem is parking, but then that's life in the city. I'll cover for you if you want a go at it, Lieutenant, but remember, the briefing is at 1700!" Grinning broadly, the raw boned man added, "A good Sergeant will give his life for his CO, but there's a limit to how much of his ass he is willing to have chewed."

"Count on me to protect your most valuable asset, Sergeant," Cameron replied in a manner that caused the Sergeant to erupt in a broad grin.

Geordie entered his office to retrieve the ignition key for an old but still spry MGA roadster that he named Willie for no special reason he could recall. Suddenly, it occurred to him that it would be a good idea to change into civvies. Since Alysse loved lingerie, he was determined to find her something gorgeous. Geordie knew this would be a daunting and embarrassing task even in a blazer, shirt and tie; nevertheless, camos, combat boots, and a Balmoral bonnet were entirely out of the question. Little imagination was needed to picture a saleslady's response in trying to sell a peignoir to a commando, so no further hesitation in changing clothes occurred. Willie was on the road at 2:00 P.M. with the canvas top down and sunshine filling the unroofed roadster.

Until proximity to the Harris Department Store had been achieved, the traffic was light, then it slowed to a crawl. Just ahead, Geordie took note of a liveried doorman smugly motioning a Mercedes limo to the curb. As soon as the big black car stopped, a chauffeur popped out and opened the rear passenger door. Geordie was expecting a dowager, but was surprised to see a rich looker emerge enveloped in the best that beau monde had to offer. "I'm out of tune with the times," he reflected. "One would imagine that the husband of a wife who looked like that would have some sedate, gray-haired, grandfatherly type to drive her around." Then, suddenly it occurred to him. "Maybe, that's how the husband looks, and she selected her own driver for more obvious reasons." As Willie inched forward, Geordie noticed a conference was occurring between the chauffeur and the doorman, while the blonde bombshell was giving the latter a smile that would melt brass buttons, along with the promise of a major tip should he prove resourceful.

Success was obvious when the doorman proudly directed the Mercedes to a snug harbor at the far end of the area designated for picking up and discharging passengers. Belfast's answer to Marilyn Monroe had already entered the store, but the afteraffects of the seductive smile to the doorman remained pervasive. Although still incarcerated in the creeping traffic, as Geordie drew abreast of the store, he studied the pantomime unfolding between the doorman and the chauffeur. The latter was holding a small clipboard and gesturing to a row of phone boxes nearby. Obviously, any request made was being granted, as telegraphed by the doorman's mannerisms. Soon, Cameron found himself silently adding dialogue. "Sure, make your calls, don't worry about the car. I'll take care of everything." "Thanks mate," the driver responded. "I'll see that gorgeous slips you another five-pound note."

Something about the driver galled Geordie, and it wasn't jealousy. *Too flippant or too smug—what was it?* Debate ended, as the red light gave way to green. Ahead, only one-half block, Geordie observed a Jaguar moving out of a parking spot. "Damn," he said when he noticed another car was insinuated between himself and the one vacating the precious parking space. Then, elation came when the intervening vehicle showed no interest in claiming it. Willie rushed in like a hound after a cornered fox and claimed the prize.

Since it was no longer needed, before exiting the Mercedes, Liam had removed the red tag, which he had placed on the car's radio on-and-off switch, as a reminder to prevent absentmindedly turning it on, thus irrevocably starting the bomb's timer. Though inaudible, the radio had come to life, and somewhere in the car's boot a timer commenced its relentless passage to detonation. *Thirty minutes before hell erupts,* Liam thought, before quickly correcting it to *twenty-eight minutes.* After exiting the car, he locked it and moved toward the pay phones. A quick check of his watch reflected passage of sixty more seconds. As planned, a maximum of ten minutes would be spent at the phone, then he had to get the hell out of there! As the doorman was fully occupied, getting passengers in and out of cars, a task somewhat aggravated due to the presence of the Mercedes, Liam decided it would be no problem.

Carefully, Liam scanned 360 degrees and saw nothing to alert suspicion. Things were looking good. "Oh wait, that fellow coming this way. He walks like a fookin' soldier and observes everything as he goes. I can't stash this fookin' hat and gloves with him looking at me!"

Coincidentally, Geordie was developing more interest in Liam. He thought that the chauffeur seemed to be doing a lot more looking than talking, and the searching motions seemed purposeful with a full sweep up and down the streets, then a look at his watch. "That guy is like a bloody lighthouse, and every time he makes a full circle, he seems more agitated." Preoccupied by suspicion, Geordie nearly collided with a woman carrying a bouquet of roses who had just emerged from a florist shop. "Flowers! I should order some for Alysse." As the topic of his thoughts turned, so did his direction, and he headed toward the door from which the woman had just emerged. Looking in the flower shop, he noted the place was jammed with customers, so he quickly decided to call the florist in Dunkeld rather than wait in a queue.

Meanwhile, Liam was just completing his last sweep, and everything was clear "except for that damn soldier. Wait, he's not there must have gone into some store." Relieved, Moynihan tossed the clipboard into the trash and quickly moved to doff the cap. However, this was caught by Geordie, who was once more out on the sidewalk. Immediately, a five-alarm fire of suspicion burst on Cameron! Dashing down the street with identification already displayed, he called out, "You there! I want to talk to you!" Simultaneously, Geordie's right hand located the butt of the Browning Hi-Power tucked in a holster and nestled snugly in his waistband, where it had been hidden by his blazer. Immediately, with his hand seeking a similar gun, Liam started to sprint toward the cab stand.

Now, Geordie, soldier turned policeman, faced a new dilemma. He couldn't simply shoot a man on a crowded street because he had discarded his chauffeur's cap and gloves and started to run. Conversely, it was going to be a problem to tackle or grapple with him holding a pistol in one hand and a military ID badge in the other. For Liam, the rules of engagement differed sharply, for he was free to shoot, then try to escape. However, he had caught sight of his pursuer reaching for what he presumed to be a weapon when the chase started. Indeed, should his antagonist have a weapon at the ready, then all the advantage would be in his favor since Liam knew he would have to turn to get off a telling shot.

To some degree, both men's problems were undone simultaneously by a teenage girl, who seemed to materialize out of nowhere. Quickly, Liam threw out his left arm and caught the shocked girl around the neck. Twisting his own body behind her back, he pulled her close to form a perfect shield interspaced between him and his adversary. Immediately, Geordie stopped after sizing up the situation, which was greatly magnified as Liam placed the muzzle of his Browning hard against the terrified girl's right temple.

"Drop your gun, fooker, or I'll blow this bitch's brains out!" Liam shouted. However, Geordie stood firm, with his pistol aimed squarely at the other man's head, and maintained it steadily in a two-handed grip. Unfortunately, the girl was tall, thus screening much of the other man's body and head. Lieutenant Cameron was an excellent marksman, but there was no way he could risk firing at half a terrorist's head when the rest was hidden behind an innocent one. Geordie knew that laying down his gun would be a fool's play, for the terrorist would surely kill him and still have the use of his hostage. *Maintain the stalemate*, Geordie thought. *People are starting to notice and soon help should be coming!* Buying time, he called to the terrorist, "Shoot the girl, and I'll kill you. Soon, help is coming, and you'll be surrounded. Drop your gun, and it will go a hell of a lot easier on you!"

With murderous eyes, Liam stared fully into Geordie's, which flashed steely determination and confidence. Liam recognized the red-headed man's accent was unequivocally Scots. Impelled by hatred and wrath, Liam responded instantaneously, "Fook you, Scotty!" he shouted, as he pulled his gun from the girl's head and leveled it at Geordie. This motion caused the horrified teenager to flinch violently, partially breaking her captor's hold. Two pistols fired in unison, and 115-grain bullets erupted from each gun then passed each other in opposite directions somewhere along their flight.

From the searing pain in the left side of his chest, Geordie knew that he had been hit in a vital area. Symptoms of shock seized him, and he started to falter. *I'm conscious,* he thought. *Best say an Act of Contrition, while I can.* No sooner had, "Oh my God, I am heartily sorry for having offended Thee," crossed his mind when the prayer was interrupted by burly arms wrapped about his chest. "What the hell is going on here?" boomed in his ears, and it was followed by "and who the hell are you?" As Geordie was being eased to a sitting position on the side walk, a hand came from somewhere, snatching the pistol from his feeble grip.

Still in possession of his military ID, Geordie did his best to display it, while saying softly, "First Lieutenant Cameron, Scots Guards." His badge was next to be pulled away, and another strange voice exclaimed, "That's what the badge says." Becoming aware that consciousness would soon elude him, Geordie wanted to complete the prayer he had started when a picture of the Mercedes flashed into his mind. "Black Mercedes in front of Harris Store. I'm sure it's rigged with a bomb!" Further lucid thoughts and speech were not forthcoming. Only vaguely aware of clamorous sounds, though no longer able to ascertain if they were coming from an ambulance or Gabriel's horn, Geordie lapsed into unconsciousness.

Just as she exited the rear of Harris Department Store, Rosie heard what sounded like a single shot. Approaching the cab stand where she was to meet Liam, she first noted a number of policemen gathered about a young man with red hair sitting on the sidewalk. Several other officers were tending to a young girl, who was obviously hysterical. Then, Rosie noted that an unattended body was laid out full length on the sidewalk with a pistol lying near his right hand. "Liam! Oh Jesus, it's Liam!" she screamed.

To Rosie and all the world, it appeared there was a grotesque, purplish, small-bodied spider in the middle of his forehead. Long spider legs of congealing crimson ran spoke-like across and down his face. His gaping mouth appeared, as though it wished to protest, but no words came. Pupils, beginning to fix, stared off as though trying to focus on eternity. In shock, Rosie ran as fast as she could, hobbled by the too-high heels of her ultra-fashionable shoes. Only a block away, one of those heels caught in a grate and tore off, causing a headlong fall, which badly bruised and abraded her face, hands, and knees. Finally, she reached the fashionable flat she had shared with Liam. Looking into a full-length mirror, Rosie confronted a face so recently beautifully painted, which now looked more like a painter's palette, smudged and streaked! The dress, which she had coveted so very much, hung like a torn, dirty shroud. Totally overcome, Rosie began to rend the garment with her hands, rendering it to shreds of silk. Her expensive lingerie was ripped off in a similar fashion. Finally reduced to nudity, Rosie confronted the blonde tresses, so recently acquired. She sheared them off, as best she could, before huddling in a vacant corner from which she didn't emerge until well into the next day.

Meanwhile, Geordie's final words before the ambulance came did not go unheeded. Since the Bomb Squad of the RUC was headquartered nearby, it reached the Mercedes in record time. Sergeant Russel was Ulster's best, and his evaluation of the situation was calm but feverish. While he started his work, the entire two blocks was being evacuated. When facing a bomb, Russel always remembered all those hollow feelings in the pit of his stomach at the start of a rugby match. At this moment, it was as though all the hundreds of professional games that he had played were all compounded into one. He remembered, doctors called it "the fight or flight reflex," which was used in an effort to help laymen understand the physiology of the sympathetic and parasympathetic nervous systems. He knew he couldn't flee, so he had better try and fight and do it fast for if there was a bomb, maybe only minutes or seconds were left before its fury would be unleashed!

Instead of trying to open the door, which could be booby-trapped, a window was smashed out. Once the Sergeant's head was inside the car, he became aware the radio was on, though barely audible. "Probably used that to start the timer," he decided, as he recalled, "the Basque separatists had been said to employ that means." Quickly, Russel crawled through the window. "So far so good." Then, an assistant called out, "Shall we pry the boot open Sergeant?"

"I wouldn't," he shouted back, "or you may leave this world as a vapor trail." Russel found wires running from under the dashboard, then beneath the carpeted floor to the back seat. "Bingo," he murmured. Then, calling out, Russel asked, "Has Smokey said anything yet?" His reference was to a large Alsatian dog with a nose dedicated to ferreting out explosives. His assistant responded, "He's acting like he wants to bite a hole in the boot!"

"Proves great minds think alike," responded Russel. Having no concept of how many seconds were available, the Sergeant tore at the back of the rear seat and pulled it away from the frame. As expected in a quality car, a metal plate barred access to the boot, though it did have an aperture of reasonable size, and he noted two wires extended through it. At this point, Russel was perspiring profusely, but his hands were steady. *Hopefully, the bastards were lazy and left the timer in sight,* was his next thought, as he shined the light of his torch through the hole in the steel dividers. If it was not visible, it would infer a time-consuming cutting away of the metal shield.

Suddenly, a digital device came into view. "Oh shit," he hissed when it became clear to him there was one minute and thirty-seven seconds before his world came to an end. At this point, as a bomb disposal expert, Russel came face to face with a host of deadly possibilities. Was the digital timer a decoy? Did some sadistic son-of-a-bitch wire it in some complex way that clipping the wires, or stopping the clock would result in instant death? However, this was not a drill, and the changing seconds left no room for further study or analysis. Because Russel's arm filled nearly the entire area of the aperture, he was allowed only minimal illumination from his torch. Expertly, he guided the wire cutters to the point selected. All that was left was to close the jaws of the pliers-like device and hope a clicking sound was audible. Then, "click click," was discernible in the deadly quiet, and the clock stopped at forty-one seconds.

Exhausted, Russel wasn't quite sure whether he was going to faint, vomit, soil his pants, or all three! However, a degree of equanimity slowly returned, and he was able to exit the Mercedes looking pale and limp, but with all his molecules still bound together. Smokey led the congratulatory contingent and made a spectacle out of licking the sweat from Russel's face, as the Sergeant sat on the pavement with his head resting on his knees.

Soon after, reporters arrived, and the bomb disposal expert did his best to appear nonchalant to the photographers and video men. When asked, "How does it feel to be trying to disarm a bomb when you don't know how much time is left?" Russel looked askance at the reporters. Finally, he said, "Picture yourself in a room with a thick pile carpet. You hear a voice that says your heart may stop at sometime in the next thirty minutes unless you find a pill that will save you hidden in the rug. Not knowing whether you have one second or 1800 seconds, you sure as hell start looking. Every time a second passes, you know your heart didn't stop yet, but it might in the next one. Really makes for an exciting afternoon. Now, if you'll excuse me, I would like to go home and hold my wife and children."

Because of Sergeant Russel's heroic deed, Harris Department Store and the surrounding area, plus many lives and limbs had been saved. Liam was dead and an autopsy would soon be under way. Chastened by a nearness of a great calamity, the authorities pulled out all stops in leading an investigation. Meanwhile, Geordie was in surgery, anesthetized and intubated, while surgeons were removing a small portion of his left lung and repairing the damage to his chest wall.

While Geordie was recuperating, Rosey Carrie was self-destructing. Since she shared the flat with Liam, Rosie hadn't touched hard drugs; however, now the urge was unquenchable. Heroin became her master, lover, and god. Each time she came to worship at its altar, the narcotic embraced her more fully, and finally, it enveloped her totally. "Another junkie," said the autopsy surgeon, who was called to dissect out Rosie's secrets. Seeing the needle tracks on the pale, emaciated, and now stiffened arms, he had little doubt what killed her. However, the ritual was carried out nonetheless. When the scalp of the once pretty corpse was pulled back to permit access to the skull and finally the brain, there was conjecture about the shorn hair. Then, upon opening the uterus, a fetus was found. "Just as well for you little fellow," the pathologist said. "You wouldn't have wanted a damn junkie for your mother." No one came to claim the body, which finally found a place in Potter's Field.

Chapter Forty

Word of Liam's death was conveyed to Mickey by Darby McKevitt. On this occasion, the former jockey came directly, rather than surreptitiously. Since the housekeeper was out, the elder Moynihan limped to the door, and only a glance at McKevitt's solemn face was needed for Mickey to ascertain that any information the messenger brought was grave. Moynihan's initial word was "Liam?" McKevitt replied, "Perhaps we should go inside and grab a seat before we talk."

Mickey turned and led the caller into a parlor, directed McKevitt to a chair, though remained standing. Then, turning to face Darby, he asked "Is he injured or dead?"

"Dead, I'm afraid," McKevitt replied somberly, and went on to explain in detail all that had transpired.

"So, it was some Brit who killed my son," Moynihan said in a voice reflecting deepening anger and hatred, which was beginning to consume him.

McKevitt answered, "A Scot, to be precise and an Officer in the Scots Guards named Cameron."

Mickey queried, "They don't usually divulge the names of the mercenary murderers. How did you get it?" Answering, McKevitt explained, "A reporter was standing nearby, and heard him give his name and rank to a RUC Officer before they carted him off in an ambulance."

Moynihan asked "Did Liam get a shot in then? Too bad he didn't kill the bastard!" he stated harshly.

"Liam's shot caught him in the left lung, but it wasn't fatal. Word we received from several of our sources indicated they were able to patch him up. He'll be in the Military Hospital for a couple of weeks. We're not sure, after that, if he will return to duty, or they'll provide him with time for rehabilitation. Research done by the reporter who picked up on the name indicates that this Cameron comes from a long line of military officers, and the family has an estate over around Dunkeld in Perthshire."

Mickey needed no more information to know who to kill in reprisal; however, there was still the question of Liam's body, which led him to inquire, "What about my son's remains?"

Replying, Darby said, "I'll give you my plan and see what you think." Continuing, he said, "They haven't been able to identify Liam, as he was carrying no papers, and he never had a record of any sort. For now, they are holding his body as a John Doe, waiting to see if any claimants show up. There is a widow named Corey, who had a son near Liam's age and description, and he disappeared. She is willing to identify his body and claim that he is her son. A mortician we can trust will arrange for a quiet funeral."

Mickey interrupted with "Can this same man stage the funeral and not bury Liam in a stranger's plot?"

"I'm not following you, I'm afraid," replied McKevitt.

Looking the small man hard in the eye, Mickey said, "McKevitt, I want Liam cremated and the ashes given to me. Put a couple of sandbags in the coffin if need be, or I'll find another body to fill it!"

"I'm sure we can work it out," Darby replied. "Now, I'd best take my leave. I'm sure you want to be alone with your thoughts. I'll keep you posted."

"Oh one last thing, McKevitt. I want to be there for the cremation to be sure that I'm getting Liam's ashes. I've never really trusted you."

Once alone, Mickey slumped in a chair with fists tightened and eyes closed. He felt blind and helpless, like Sampson chained between the pillars of the Philistine temple, wishing for all the world that he could topple the supporting columns and bring it all down on the heads of the British Empire. However, since that wasn't possible, he could certainly make the Cameron family pay a horrific price, which would be their extermination. Then aloud, though in muted tones, he cried out "Oh Bernie, Bernie, Bernie! I'll bring Liam's ashes to your sacred island, and I'll avenge him, as I did you!"

Then Mickey thought, *Strange, I feel the loss of this son more than I could have imagined. My prodigal son,* he said, as his thoughts continued. *All the years of never speaking and never giving a hug. For some reason, there was always hope in my heart that we would reconcile and have some good years together you, Sean, Michael, and me. Now, my last vision of you will be a cold corpse going into an oven.* Simultaneously, a third tear came into Moynihan's eye. The first had been for his little brother, Sean; the second for Bernie; and this one was for Liam.

When his son Sean returned home some hours later, Mickey solemnly related all that had transpired. Devastated by the death of his younger brother, the young man was just as adamant about revenge as his father. Obviously, the slaying of Liam's murderer would have to wait, as the prize was unattainable at the moment due to security at the hospital on a well-guarded Army Base. "Revenge delayed is just as sweet," Mickey concluded. "We'll bide our time and research the Cameron Family. Then, when we're ready, we'll cut them down one by one!"

Just two days later, McKevitt called back to say all the arrangements had been made according to Mickey's desire. He added that the authorities were enraged due to the fact the widow was unable to shed any light on her "son's" activities or compatriots, leaving their hot pursuit at the terminus of a dead-end street.

Later, on arrival at the mortuary, Mickey and Sean steeled themselves, then proceeded to say good-bye to son and brother. Unfortunately, the undertaker had not bothered to apply his skill in any type of cosmetic effort, so the grotesque wound in Liam's forehead stood out even more hideously than it had at the time of death. Knowing all about bullets and their effects, Mickey and Sean had no desire to inspect the back of Liam's head. Granted privacy, their final words were said, in hopes that Liam's spirit would hear them. At last, the ashes were gathered and placed in an urn, where they would remain until such time as they could be mingled with those of his mother on Skellig Island.

Meanwhile, news of Geordie's wound and heroic action had reached Iain in Africa by shortwave radio. At first, he was deeply skeptical that the doctor's description of his son's true condition was entirely forthright. Just as the worried father was about to decide that a prompt return to the United Kingdom should be undertaken, Geordie's voice came over the speaker. "My chest hurts like hell, Dad, so don't say anything humorous that would cause me to laugh." They had a good talk, and Iain was much relieved. Finally, the surgeon came back on, and indicated Lieutenant Cameron would be retained in hospital at Belfast for three weeks, then returned to Edinburgh for convalescent care. Conversation was closed after the physician disclosed that there seemed to be no impediment to Geordie's return to full duty. A very grateful father returned to his anxious partner and clients, and they were quick to join in a celebration over the splendid news. Before bedtime, Colonel Cameron thanked God and a host of patron saints for the great favor that had been bestowed.

While Iain was talking to his son via radio, Mickey and Sean's return to Grey Abbey with Liam's ashes was a trip of torment. Words were sparse, though thoughts ran rampant. Devastation of spirit was a heavy enough load for Mickey to carry, but coupled with physical debility it seemed insufferable. For the first time in his life, the senior Moynihan ws feeling old and tired. Not even the new Aston Martin, which the Crown had provided to replace the one their careless minion destroyed, did anything to restore his vigor. Given his physical and emotional state, Mickey had no desire to drive, so Sean was in command of the car. Then, once inside the house, Liam's ashes were placed within a vault in the study, and both men consigned themselves to chairs.

Minutes passed, and since Sean found the silence depressing and pervasive, he finally spoke. "Where do we start?" he asked in a somber tone.

"With the foundation," his father answered in like voice.

"You're losing me," came back Sean's reply.

Mickey hesitated before speaking. "This Cameron, who killed Liam is but the spawn of an older one, and it is he who I hold as most responsible, and in greatest contempt. Also, this Colonel Cameron is no doubt of considerable experience, craft, and wile. Kill him first, and the others will come easily. Kill him last, and we may find ourselves up against a foe whose skill may match or exceed our own."

Suddenly with anguish distorting his face, Mickey exclaimed, "Damn it all to hell! I want to kill all of them myself, but I'm not up to it at the moment. Sean I need you now like I need my right hand. Go to Scotland, and see if you can find this fookin' bastard. Scout him out completely, to the last detail, but take no action! The last thing I need is to lose another son due to the wrong decision, This must be planned exactly, so bring back the information, and we'll perfect a plan. Forced rehabilitation is what I'll undertake, for I wish to pull the trigger on Colonel Cameron myself!"

Knowing further discussion, let alone argument was futile, Sean agreed to his father's proposal. "I'll leave in the morning," he said, then continued. "No more than a week should be needed, as I've learned my lessons from the best." Father and son shook hands, and the looks exchanged left no doubt they were one in purpose and intent. Liam would be avenged in the fullest possible measure!

Once in Dunkeld, Sean resurrected his Yankee-accented English and made a direct inquiry at a small tea shop. Obviously, Colonel Cameron was very well known and directions to his estate were forthcoming, though to his dismay he was subject to a lengthy description of how to get to Capercaillie manor in the Highland dialect, which could only be interpreted with difficulty. After carefully giving directions, which took Sean a number of frustrating minutes to copy down, his informant smiled and added "However, The Colonel isn't at home, as he goes to Africa every year about this time." The young lady who gave the information was quite attractive, and Sean sensed she might be more interested in him than in merely providing assistance to a stranger.

Forsaking offers of more tea very solicitously given, Moynihan arose, smiled, and left a very generous tip in hopes it would make up for his lack of personal interest. "Oh sir," the young waitress called, as he walked to the door. "You can probably get more information on the Colonel's whereabouts if you go to his shop in Perth. I'll be happy to give you directions." Patiently, Sean suffered through another lengthy verbal tour of Perthshire, then added to his map. With his hand on the shop's door, he was interrupted once again by the young woman's plaintive call, "We're open until seven this evening sir, and we'll have duck soup and fine finnan haddie or brisket, should you have need of a place for dinner."

"I'll try," Sean replied, hoping to finally to secure sanctuary in the street.

Half an hour later, Sean nosed the rental car into a parking spot, just a short distance from the shop heralding a large, tasteful sign that proclaimed CAMERON AND SONS. After entering, he wended his way through displays of clothing, equipment, accessories, and guns, and observed all were meant for the discerning, well-to-do shooting sportsman.

Shortly, a cheerful, helpful-sounding half-baritone and half-base voice resonated from a desk in the rear. "Good afternoon, sir, may I be of assistance?" Seconds later, a tall man emerged with right hand extended. Nattily garbed in well-tailored attire, *No doubt from the store's stock,* thought Sean, the man appeared initially as the quintessential sportsman turned salesman.

However, something about his bearing spoke of prior military service, and when carefully observed Sean noticed a slight list to the side, along with a degree of motion limitations. Consequently, he thought it was possible to sum up the man as a retired officer wounded in action.

Firmly, Sean took the other man's hand, smiled, and responded, "Bob Murphy, a Boston Yankee, touring about your beautiful country. I heard that if you were interested in hunting, this was the place to come."

Retired Major Wilson further broadened his smile and responded, "Indeed it is! Are you primarily interested in birds or big game, Scotland or Africa?"

"Well I love to hunt anything and anywhere, but an African safari is top priority at the moment," said Sean.

"All of this year's space is already booked, I'm afraid, both big game and birds. Some few openings are available for next year. How anxious are you?" replied Wilson.

"Actually, I always place quality and reputation before temporal considerations, so I can wait a year for the best bet," Sean said with a smile.

"I'll show you dates available, and we can proceed from there," was the former Major's response. Soon, Sean was seated across a desk from the agent, and Wilson passed a large album featuring Colonel Iain Cameron and Toby Drake with their camp, staff, and a host of obviously happy hunters posing alongside a very wide range of big game trophies.

"Where are they hunting now?" queried Sean

"This year, it's Mozambique, and from all the reports I've received the hunting has been fabulous! No doubt they'll remain there for another season or more," was Wilson's response.

"How does one go about getting to some remote location like that out in the bush?" asked Moynihan, head shaking in feigned interest.

"Here's how," came the reply, followed by turning pages and placement of a pointing finger directing attention to photos of Safari Airline complete with inside shots of the DC-3 Dakota's skillful-appearing pilots and a smiling African steward.

In his appraisal, Sean was most complimentary and ended by asking, "From which African City does Safari Airlines fly out?"

"Johannesburg currently," came the response. "Subject to change next year, as airline service to Africa expands, but for now only Johannesburg." Then, more business ensued and, when it was done, Sean was given a packet of brochures, along with application forms.

Slowly showing the assumed customer out, Wilson stopped at the door and gave all the proper pronouncements for a departing client. Then, he ended by suggesting a booking if desired should be made as soon as possible. "I'll be in Boston in two days," responded Sean and, as soon as I arrive, I'll discuss it all with my father. He is also greatly interested in Cameron and Sons and, if possible, I'm sure he will wish to join me." After handshakes of departure were completed, Sean turned to leave.

"One last thing," Wilson called out. "You and your father have had big game experience and are proficient marksmen, I assume, as the Colonel is a stickler for that."

"Right on both accounts," Sean called back, while thinking, "I assume Prods and Brits would qualify as big game of sorts."

Looking at the clock with disappointment, the young waitress removed her apron and prepared to depart, for the handsome young Yank had failed to return. After leaving Cameron and Sons, Sean had driven immediately from Perth to Edinburgh and taken the first flight available to Belfast. Alone with his thoughts during these several hours of travel, he came up with a plan much to his liking. However, whether or not it would be accepted by his father was open to question, but soon that would be clear.

Finally arriving at Grey Abbey just past ten o'clock, Sean found his father astride an exercise bicycle. Mickey's jaw was clenched with beads of perspiration, induced by pain and exertion stippling his face, while the gray sweatshirt was very damp. After calling out a third time, "He's in Africa," the younger Moynihan finally got his father's attention. While toweling off the excess sweat, Mickey poured some tea for both of them before he sat down to hear the full report.

When the preliminaries were completed, Sean took the offensive. "Let me tell you my plan, Dad, and see what you think. First off, I don't really think you are up to a trip to Africa, much less heading to some hunting camp out in the boonies."

Mickey looked quizzical, then recalled that was the American slang word for "somewhere out in nowhere."

"Don't tell me you're planning on taking on this Colonel by yourself?" his angry father snapped.

"Hell no!," Sean shot back. "I'm smart enough to know that I don't know a damn thing about Africa, but hear me out! As you well know, we have our friends in Libya and the Becca Valley, and they have contacts with Arabs everywhere else in Africa. I can go to Paris and contact Mustafa. and Haji, without fear of an intercept on the phone. There's no doubt in my mind they'll agree to give me all the help I need," said Sean.

"I suppose you'll just go to bloody Mozambique and hike around until you locate this Scot son of a bitch," Mickey snarled.

"Of course not," his son retorted with equal intensity. Then, Sean tossed a brochure on his father's lap and pointed to the photo exhibited. "This is how I'll find him," he exclaimed.

For many years, Mickey had made many perfect plans, and he was reluctant to admit his son might be as proficient. Then, his mind flashed back to several NFL Super Bowls that he had enjoyed on TV when he was in Boston. Now, he felt like the star quarterback injured in the early part of the fourth quarter, then forced to sit on the bench, while an understudy won the game. Was it possible for him to be a team player? Winning was all that was important wasn't it? "Sean did have the plays," was his grudging admission. After a period of quiet, finally he said aloud, "You've a good plan, Sean. I like it! Get started in the morning."

Early the next day, Sean was on his way to carrying out their plan. Then, as soon as he was settled in the French capital, a line of communication to his Moslem allies was established. All conversation was in Arabic and sufficiently vague so as to defy any meaningful interpretations by interlopers in the event any were listening. Mustafa and Haji understood his needs and intentions perfectly. Plans would be put in motion for his expected African arrival in seven to ten days. Their communication ended with "Insha Allah," (translated from Arabic to English "Allah be praised"). Sean took it as a promising sign of ultimate success, aided by allies entirely sympathetic to the desires of him and his father.

For certain, he knew Arabs were no strangers to revenge, and he knew they wouldn't hesitate to join him in a personal jihad!

After returning to Ulster, Sean made his way back to Grey Abbey to hold one last discussion with his father. Together, they pored over the plans. Sean was quite satisfied that all was in place, but his father had reservations and became somewhat irascible.

"You're not dealing with a bunch of shutterbugs trying to catch lions at play, Sean. We know Cameron will be there, along with this Drake fellow. How many hunters will be there is just a guess. Additionally, do they have any trackers or other auxiliary help that might aid in defense? I figure you might run into eight or ten, who would have rifles accessible, and you can be damn sure they know how to use them."

"Look," exclaimed Sean. "Our arrival should be a surprise, and that's a definite plus. Besides, Haji and I will have four well-trained PLO commandos who are veterans of dozens of firefights, plus two Africans we will pick up in Johannesburg. According to Haji, they are also veterans of various struggles down there. So, we add up to eight." In a serious tone, Sean added, "On the other side, we can assume this Colonel Cameron is an experienced soldier and unless the Victoria Cross was a gift, he damn well knows what a skirmish is all about. Drake is a question mark and, apart from that fact, we can assume he knows how to shoot straight. As far as the clients are concerned, it is likely they are overweight bankers from Chicago who won't be particularly prone to taking on someone who is shooting at them, rather than some beast that is trying to save himself from being mounted on a wall. Sure, they'll have bolt-action rifles, but we'll have AK-47s, plus the Draganov. While they're getting off one shot, we can empty a thirty-round magazine!"

Momentarily Sean's rationalization stifled Mickey's objections, reducing him to silence at the same time. Affecting an unusual attitude, Sean's father let his head sag slightly, then decided to support it with his hands. Seconds later, Mickey straightened up and stared intently at Sean saying, "I worry that we're not understanding the opposition. Could we be dealing with something inscrutable?" Once again, silence prevailed, and during this round, thoughts not to be spoken came to both men. Pondering his own personality, Mickey confronted self-doubt. Had he somehow lost his nerve, becoming unable to take hazards and have someone else do it instead?

Sean's thoughts were not dissimilar, and he began to think his father was on the brink of a meltdown. Maybe death and uncertainty had been faced too many times resulting in a culmination of courage. Speaking out once more, in softer tones, Sean advanced an added argument, "Look, Dad, we both agree, we need revenge for Liam. Risk is involved in killing Cameron, whether it be in

Africa, Scotland, or anywhere else! Attack him in Dunkeld or Perth, and who knows how many gamekeepers or clients might be around with shotguns. Added to that, you have to find your way through a maze of country roads and policemen. How many witnesses would you have to stiff in order to make a clear get away? With my plan, all the dirty work is done miles from anybody. Hell, it could be weeks before anyone even finds out he's dead!"

At last, Mickey was able to scrape away the mental asbestos that had started to insulate his passion. As Sean looked at him, Mickey's brightening face heralded the return of the father he knew, and he said, "Maybe, I was starting to get a little soft in the brain or the balls, but I'm over it now. You've convinced me that your plan is best, Sean, so go do it! I wish that I could be with you for this one, but I am getting stronger. We'll go together to get the rest of them!"

Following his father's instructions, as in past occasions, Sean took a circuitous route to the rendezvous, which would take place in Benghazi, Libya's second largest city. Meanwhile, Haji and his men would make their way to the seaport by water. Arrangements had been made for a long range Lear jet to be at their disposal. Certain there would be sufficient baksheesh coming their way to make it personally profitable, Libyan officials were happy to supply the aircraft. Compared to the output of the oil fields, the amount of fuel used would be miniscule.

In the Arab fashion, Sean and Haji greeted each other as loving brothers. When introduced to the other four men, Sean was very impressed. None had the appearance of a ragtag nomad—they were dressed in finely tailored suits and could have easily been mistaken for a quartet of sheiks out for a night of indulgence in a foreign city, entirely free of Mohammad's morality. Three pilots, all first-rate men, would also be on board the jet.

Despite prodigious planning, Sean was surprised to learn of the distance to be traveled. Considering the fact they wished to avoid nosy inquiries by ground controllers, radar, and interceptor planes where they existed, no straight line flight plan was applicable. "Approximately 6,500 miles," the Chief Pilot related, thus answering speculation about the need for a third man in the cockpit. Specifics of the flight plan were given next. From Benghazi, they would proceed to El Fasher in the Sudan, a distance of approximately 1,250 miles, then continue on to Addis Ababa in Ethiopia, total distance 2,250 miles. Day two would call for flying from Addis Ababa to Antonio Enes in Mozambique via Mogadishu in Somalia, distance approximately 1,900 miles. On the third day, they would fly over Maputo in Mozambique, then on to Johannesburg, South Africa, an 1,100-mile-long leg.

When the pilot finished describing the flight plan, Sean let out a whistle, as he realized this one-way trip was longer than a round-trip from Belfast to

Boston. After integrating the acquired details into his plan, Sean was quick to conclude, "What real difference did the distance make?!" Looking at it another way, Sean calculated the Lear could make 500 miles per hour, so actual flight time was close to twelve hours and not really so bad. Of course, they couldn't keep flying continuously, and fairly long layovers might need to be made at certain stops. After all, some end-of-the-world place like Antonio Enes in Mozambique would be fortunate to have an airfield and a petrol pump, much less landing lights and a competent manned control tower." Next, flashing into Sean's mind was, "When we get to Mozambique, we might be flying right over this Cameron. Too bad, we don't know exactly where the hell he is because it would be a lot easier just to drop a bomb on him." Instead, they would pass over on the way to Johannesburg and, then, fly back into Mozambique. "Well at least this way I'll get to see him die!," he concluded.

Plans made, and finally on the way, Sean was thankful for his proficiency in Arabic, as it would be hell to spend all those hours in an airplane cabin unable to converse with fellow passengers. As it was, time passed quickly, as Haji, his men, and the pilots were filled with captivating stories ranging from fighting Israelis to seducing belly dancers. Also, desert terrain and cities seen were of great interest to Sean, as were the endless variety of bribery schemes encountered. Thankfully, the supply of greenbacks, which he carried in a satchel, were still in ample supply. *Yankee dollars,* he thought, *are Uncle Sam's gift to greed, whether you call it baksheesh, as the Arabs or fragrant grease, like the Chinese for they are, surely, the lubricant that keeps the unscrupulous in motion.* In the midst of Sean's musings, he realized that they were finally touching down in Johannesburg, and an opportunity to spend a night in a real bed awaited him. Tomorrow would be reconnoitering day, while the one to follow would be filled with action and the sweet taste of revenge!

As a result of prior arrangements conducted through the auspices of the Arab brotherhood, inspection of papers, plane, and luggage were less than cursory. Customs and immigration officials would probably have not bothered to stop by at all, apart from the fact it provided privacy for the purpose of bestowing a large wad of currency to the security of their uniform pockets. Once the formal exchange of money for smiles was complete, the Lear was serviced, then put in the hanger out of sight.

Checking in at a four-star hotel went smoothly for the Libyan "Oil Men" and their pilots. After dinner, Haji and Sean left the others and made their way to a nondescript bar named Sinbads, a twenty-minute cab ride from the hotel. Once inside, Haji satisfied himself with tea in attendance to Mohammad's dictates. Heeding no approbation from any God or prophet, Sean ordered a double Bushmill's. Since they were seated at the bar, it was difficult for Moynihan to scan the depths of the darkened room in an effort to discern whom they might be meeting. Leaning close to his associate, he whispered, "I presume you know whom we are looking for."

"Not exactly," was the reply. "But I will when I finish counting coins." Baffled by the response, Sean stared into the amber depths of his whiskey, as though it might be a crystal ball and possibly provide a revelation. When he turned to seek further enlightenment from Haji, he was confronted by an empty bar stool, and the PLO sergeant was now standing near the end of the bar conversing with a tantalizing cocktail waitress. Before Sean could speculate as to whether or not his friend had spoken of coins in reference to purchase of the beauty's favors, Haji returned. Given the universal signal for "follow me," Sean arose and took up the tail end of a procession led by the waitress, which ended in a private room far in the rear of the establishment. Seductively dressed in the mode of the harem, the guide provided entry to the room, then departed out not obsequiously. Brushing a bare shoulder against Sean's covered one, she caught his attention, causing him to turn his face to meet hers. Kohl-enhanced eyes of darkest brown were flashed in such a way as to mean only one thing. Up close, Sean became aware that the gossamer veil she was wearing was so transparent that painted red lips were absolutely not obscured. Shifting his eyes slightly, he noticed gossamer cloth covering other areas was no more protective. *Tempting*, he thought. *But I have no desire for diversion now, and even less for Cupid's catarrh, or worse.* From Sean, the local version of Scheherezade received no more than a smile, for business was business, and his was more important than hers!

Another hour was spent on earnest discussion with the two African mercenaries Sean and Haji had come to see. For sure, they were very tough men, though most likely reliable. Yes, they had spent time in Mozambique, and explained most of poaching was for game in areas where Cameron would likely be found. Both were conversant in English and Arabic, so conversation between them and Sean's group should present no problem. "What about the local dialects of Mozambique natives? Can you handle that?" queried Sean. Affirmation came quickly, and it was outwardly convincing, though obviously not subject to verification. Finally both parties ended in agreement with more dollars forthcoming to cement the bond. However, caution dictated that it was 50 percent now, and the rest on return. Plans were that the two hirelings would make their way to the airport and designated place of rendezvous the day after next. As soon as the meeting concluded, they all took their leave. Sean was pleased that Scheherezade was off in a corner when they departed. Once in the cab, he turned to Haji and inquired in Arabic, "What did all the camel shit about counting coins mean?"

"I thought you were wise to our ways, Sean. Did you not notice all the waitresses wore necklaces of gold coins? Our contact wore thirteen, and all the rest had twelve or less."

Rest in a comfortable bed did much to ameliorate Sean's fatigue, brought on by the long journey. Nonetheless, he was awake by the time that the sun's tendrils began to seek the city of Johannesburg. Shortly, from in front of the hanger housing their plane, he had a sweeping view of the tarmac and all it held. On the opposite extreme of the airfield stood the pride of Safari Airlines, just as perfect as the picture he had seen in Perth. Careful study of the aircraft with high-powered binoculars provided no hint of activity. Moments later, Haji and his men arrived, and one was dispatched to seek the service of a previously bribed official. For a few dollars more, he should be able to ascertain if the pilot of Safari Air had filed any flight plans or if anyone had any idea when its departure might occur. Word came back about two hours later that the plane was slated to leave the following day at 0800 to pick up some cargo at the Port of Durban.

"Perfect," murmured Sean. "Going to pick up freight, so it would be unlikely anyone but the crew would be on board. Now, I must think of a plausible way to approach them." By noon, assiduity paid off with what Sean considered an entirely new, nonsuspicious plan. Consequently, more bribes were offered, and the use of a cartage lorry was promised with availability ensured by 0600 the next day. Then, the remainder of the day was spent coaching his team on the fine points of the plan he had devised. Assertion was quickly forthcoming and unanimous. Sean determined the Africans could be briefed in the morning, as they had no need to know until then.

By 0600, the following day, all was in readiness. Dressed in coveralls, Sean and a procured driver were ensconced in the lorry's cab, while Haji and four PLO compatriots plus two local Africans and one of the Libyan pilots occupied the lorry's box-like cargo compartment. Wishing to leave nothing to chance, Sean had elected to be certain that at least one pilot was certified in the DC-3 Dakota just in case. All the men were armed with the ubiquitous AK-47 assault rifles, along with whatever sidearms suited their fancy. Hidden in the pocket of his coveralls, Scan had a Browning Hi-Power pistol. Also, his Draganov sniper rifle and camo fatigues were stored in the rear of the lorry.

Quickly scrutinizing the Safari Airlines plane with binoculars, Moynihan noted there were men approaching it. Observing them, Sean thought that no doubt about it, they were the same pilot, copilot, and steward, whose pictures he had been shown. After being given the command to go, the lorry driver carefully maneuvered the vehicle across the tarmac to their target. Arrival was timed perfectly, as Archie, Buster, and Martin were all standing together talking, just behind the port wing and close to the plane's open cabin door. Curious looks were played on the now-stopped lorry, but no suspicion arose.

Sean opened his door and emerged with a smile, "I understand you are heading for Durban. Could I entice you to deliver some machine parts, as they need them in a hurry?"

Now, Archie and Buster were getting curious enough to border on suspicion. "May I ask you how you showed up here?" Archie inquired warily. Buster piped up with, "We don't advertise, you know." Then, he added, "At least for freight. Our regular customers are business enough." Archie chimed in with, "We prefer to haul only small loads of provisions. A bunch of crates filled with machinery wouldn't even make it through the door."

Sean smiled, but the three other men saw no humor in it, nor did they watch it fade. By that time, their attention was focused on the pistol leveled at Archie's chest!

Still holding the trio at gunpoint, Moynihan motioned to the driver, who responded to the "Pssst!" arranged signal by moving to the rear of the lorry to open the cargo door. To Archie, Buster, and Martin's surprise and apprehension, heavily armed men dressed in battle gear emerged. The hijacking of their plane was obvious; however, the motive was obscure. Seeing that the leader was probably Irish, two were black, and the rest Arab was yet more confusing. Both Safari pilots were attempting to decipher what sort of operation such a racial mix would indicate when their thoughts were interrupted.

With his pistol at the ready, and an AK-47 slung over his shoulder, one of the Arabs ran up the steps of the plane, which were an integral part of the fold-down door. After completing what they assumed was a search of the aircraft's interior, he returned to the doorway and silently signaled the others, whereupon Moynihan moved the muzzle of his pistol in a manner to indicate it was time for his captives to board. As no viable alternative seemed possible, Archie, Buster, and Martin complied. Once inside, the two pilots were directed to the cockpit and to their proper seats by Sean. Martin's hands were roughly bound behind him, then he was forced into a passenger seat and tightly restrained by the seat belt. Within seconds, all the hijackers were on board, and the door secured. Snarling, "Crank it up!" Moynihan pushed the Browning Hi-Power against Archie's head.

Archie was mad as hell, but remained cool and under control, as he replied softly, "Look whoever you are. We'll do our best to comply with your wishes, but you just don't roar down the runway without an okay from the tower." Sean looked at his watch, then said, "Tell them you are a bit early, but you would like to leave. Don't try to be cute, or I'll kill you. One of your passengers is qualified in multi-engine aircraft, so we don't really need you."

"Just as you say," Archie replied. The tower was receptive to his request. "Start them up, Buster," were the pilot's next words.

"Not much choice to do otherwise mate," Crisp replied.

Both engines were perfectly tuned, and the starboard one coughed only once before it sprang to life, followed quickly by the port side. Brakes released, the engines responded to the throttles, and the taxi run across the tarmac commenced. Just like its American cognomen, "Gooney Bird," the DC-3 Dakota took its time before seeking release from the gravitational grasp of the earth.

Archie was in the process of contemplating a deliberate crash at the time of liftoff, if such an act could be completed before the Arab, assumed to be a pilot, could react. Mentally, he sized up the situation. He and Buster were belted in, while the other three crammed in the cockpit were crouched behind them and would be violently thrown off balance and probably injured. In the cabin of the plane, they would be belted in their seats; therefore, having as much a chance to survive as he and Buster. What would their response be? Get out and run or start shooting? Also, the man pushing the pistol against his head could size up the situation and fire into the back of his head, just as he was being thrown off balance.

Only two seconds before lift off, Archie was about to commit to crashing. Then, he heard from the man holding the pistol, "I know what you are thinking." Moynihan's voice seethed. "Surviving a crash by a dead pilot will be no harder than if he were alive!" Synapses between Archie's brain and his hand directing that appendage to cut power to the engines aborted in route. Air Safari left terra firma in its accustomed manner.

At 1,500 feet, the Dakota banked and headed southeast. "We are going to Durban, aren't we?" asked Archie haltingly, still shaken by the interruption of his destructive decision. No direct reply was forthcoming, just a rapid discussion in Arabic, which Archie couldn't comprehend. Finally, English commands followed, "Take it up to 6,000 feet and hold it steady on your present course," Sean instructed, as he concomitantly eased the pressure of his pistol from Archie's head. "You! Copilot! Out of your seat!"

Anxiously, Buster looked to Archie, who granted a nod of affirmation. Once unbuckled, Crisp arose hesitatingly. Haji grabbed him, bound his hands with cord, and propelled him aft, where he was secured in a seat beside Martin. Just as swiftly, the Arab pilot assumed Buster's vacated position. With his confederate now ready to assume control, if necessary, Sean was slightly more relaxed. "Take us to see Colonel Cameron," was Moynihan's next command.

"I don't know any Colonel Cameron," Archie replied in an unconvincing manner.

Reaching inside his jacket, Sean pulled out a wrinkled brochure from a pocket and tossed it in the pilot's lap. "Maybe, this will refresh your memory," he threatened.

Archie now appreciated that pretense was of no avail but elected to ask one more question. "What do you want with the Colonel?"

"You'll find out when you get there," was the stinging reply.

Placing a little steel in his voice, Archie shot back, "Fine, you can let King Faisal here fly around until we run out of petrol," pointing to the Libyan pilot.

"Some people need a lot of convincing," Sean responded before issuing further commands in Arabic. Minutes later, Martin, with hands still bound, was hustled into the cockpit. Upon his arrival, Sean kicked the steward's legs out from beneath him, thus forcing him into a kneeling position. Sensing the commotion, Archie turned in his seat, just as Haji was slipping a wire garrote around Martin's neck. As the wire slowly tightened, a grimace of horror appeared on Martin's face. Blood started to seep from the edges of the deep indentation caused by the ever tightening ligature. Speech was impossible and unneeded, as the bulging eyes and pervading facial cyanosis were more convincing than words.

"For God's sake, stop!" Archie screamed, hoping the reprieve was in time. Horrified, he knew Martin was either dead or unconscious, as evidenced by the limpness of his body as it was dragged to the rear.

Turning his plane toward Colonel Cameron's camp, Andrus was a man in turmoil. Though long separated from his boyhood religious upbringing in the Church of England, all had not been forgotten. One particular quotation burned into his mind: "No greater love hath any man than to lay down his life for a friend." Could he still contrive to crash the plane on landing and thus save Iain Cameron, Toby Drake, and perhaps others? Martin and Buster would be making the same sacrifice, though they would be denied approbation. Wouldn't the ring leader be clever enough to insist the Libyan land the plane, thereby ensuring that no further chance of a crash were possible? Then, again, Cameron and Drake might be suspicious at seeing Arab commandos emerging from the aircraft. Perhaps, since both were superb marksmen, they could annihilate the terrorists, given the chance! Archie's mind seemed on the verge of imploding, as all the "what ifs" ricocheted about his brain. Finally, he concluded that it was best to wait for an opening. "Surely, one would come! After all, they were still alive and with life comes hope." Gravely, Archie spoke for the first time since Martin was dragged off. "Cameron's Camp is about seventy miles ahead. I'm going to drop down if it meets with your approval?"

Reacting to tension, Sean pressed his gun harder against Archie's head, then said, "Not yet! When you reach the camp, bring the plane down to 200 feet and make a circle about the camp!"

Soon, they were within easy vision, and saw three Land Rovers were parked in a row beside a cluster of tents. Several Africans came into view, but no Caucasians were evident. All looked quite orderly and peaceful. Approximately a half mile from the camp lay an obvious air strip, which the Libyan pilot scrutinized carefully. Sean noted the Arab's nod and smile, and in recognition of the signal he brought the heavy steel barrel housing of the Browning Pistol down hard against Archie's head. Slumping forward, Archie was rendered unconscious by the blow, though his restraining harness prevented him from impinging on the plane's controls.

Meanwhile Buster had not been inactive during his confinement in the passenger compartment. Surreptitiously, he had worked his wrists to and fro, causing some relaxation in the rope that tightly bound them together. Sufficient abrasion of his skin had occurred to cause bleeding, but the blood acted as a lubricant, and finally his hands slid free.

Responding to the plane's descent and slow banking, the terrorists in the cabin became preoccupied with peering out the plane's windows. Rather than have his position and vision encumbered, one of the Arabs had carelessly leaned his AK-47 against the seat next to the one he occupied. Hands free, Buster unsnapped his seat belt and grabbed the rifle. Since the weapon had a folded stock, it was easy for him to bring it into position. However, rapid movements bring notice, and the errant terrorist made a desperate lunge to regain his gun. Immediately, Buster got off a short burst, which shredded the African's chest. Swinging the gun's muzzle to bear on another antagonist still seated, Crisp was unaware that Haji had sprung from the cockpit with his own AK-47 leveled. Reality seemed to rush from Buster's recognition, as four of the slugs impacted on his own chest. Senses dulled, he felt no pain, only a pervading hollowness and stunned wonderment with Tillie, his wife, visualized, as his last thought. Buster knew there was something he wanted to tell her, but the words wouldn't come.

Haji's burst of fire was very sweeping; unfortunately, before the traverse stopped, Martin was caught in the line of fire. Barely alive and unconscious, he was oblivious to death's arrival.

Chapter Forty-One

A siesta was not normally part of Toby Drake's agenda; however, since clients were in absentia, he made an exception. Secure in the surrounding mosquito netting, Drake was about to succumb to a combination of hangover, noon heat, and fatigue. Just as he was starting to cross the threshold into somnolence, the sound of droning engines intruded. One eye cocked open abruptly, as his mind scrambled to put the calendar into orderly array. Finally, reaching a conclusion, just short of philosophical certitude, Toby declared to himself it was Tuesday not Thursday. "Why the hell are Archie and Buster buzzing us today?" emerged from his lips. Readily recognizing the timbre of Gertie's engines, the DC-3's lovingly bestowed appellation precluded any need to ask "Who the hell is that flying around?" Now, in a sitting position, Toby reached out to put on a pair of terribly abused Chukka boots. Halfway through the effort, he paused, deciding that a cautious massage of two angry temples was what he needed at the moment. Unfortunately, Toby's fingers were unable to extract any of the vengeance from the preceding night's reverie, now residing in his head amid throbbing pain.

Boots on, Drake finally emerged from his tent, just in time to witness Gertie's touchdown. "Damn, Archie must be more hung over than I am," he exclaimed, while noting the plane going through a series of bounces. Thankfully, they appeared to be of diminishing amplitude, and finally all three wheels were down. Quickly sliding behind the Land Rover's steering wheel, Toby started the engine and headed for the landing strip. Halfway there, it became apparent that Gertie's engines had stopped. *That's peculiar,* Drake thought. *Safari Air had come in here a hundred times, and they never parked the plane with the door facing away from the camp*. Suddenly, 200 yards from the aircraft, Drake braked the Rover to a halt. Instinct, intuition, or simple curiosity may have been the cause, while the effect was to ponder the situation. Barely visible, disembodied legs clad in what seemed to be camo fabric were starting to appear just under the lower edge of the plane's fuselage. Drake's field glasses were sought and found. Once focused, the binoculars confirmed the presence of multiple legs all similarly covered.

Now, Toby was perplexed. Could this be some native police contingent? Just like a production line, going ever faster, new questions kept coming at an increasing rate. "Have they come looking for poachers? Has someone started a revolution, and the camp was last to get the word? Why didn't Archie, Buster, or some governmental agency call them on the radio? All of Toby's questions were succinctly answered when a small squad of men came around the tail of the plane and formed an obvious skirmish line. All had AK-47s, and they were heading straight for him.

Meanwhile, Andrus, Crisp, and Martin were nowhere in sight. Toby's first impulse was to put the Rover in gear and race back to camp; however, it was foolishly overruled by the engrained code of the hunter. No more able to retreat from men than a charging rhino, Drake elected to take a stand. Grabbing a .243-caliber Mauser rifle from a rack inside the vehicle, he was pleased to note a full complement of five cartridges divided between the chamber and the magazine. Also, a nearby cartridge box contained an additional fifteen rounds. Next, Drake sought security behind the Rover. Now, binoculars were no longer needed, as the four-power telescope sight on the rifle would provide all the visual information necessary. Strangely at ease, Drake felt ready. However, he felt before he could open fire, overt aggressive action by the approaching band would be necessary. Only a few more moments would pass before that occurred.

In similar fashion, Sean had used his own field glasses, and was fully cognizant that his group was facing only a single man. From prior scrutiny of the Cameron and Sons brochure, it was readily apparent that the individual was Toby Drake and not Iain Cameron. Quickly, Moynihan's tactical acumen produced a list of positives and negatives in regard to the situation. Having decided to leave the pilot behind in the plane, they were now seven in number. Safari Airlines copilot was now dead, while the pilot was unconscious and, possibly incapable of any flying in the near future. Should the Libyan aviator be killed or wounded in a fire fight, they could well end up stranded. Seven to one were excellent odds. Additionally, Sean knew his own men were all armed with automatic weapons, while their opponent had a bolt-action rifle incapable of matching their fire power. On the negative side was the fact that he and his men were in the open, while Drake was shielded by the Land Rover. Most pervasive in deciding a pragmatic strategy, Moynihan decided, was the knowledge that the opponent had guts. Also, he was a crack shot and quite used to precarious situations. Turning to Haji, Sean spoke in a quiet voice, "Spread the men out and get them down in a prone position. Utilize whatever cover they can find. No one fires before I do!" One second later, Moynihan dove for the ground, just behind a small boulder, which offered only minimal cover. Nonetheless, it was far better than none at all.

As soon as he hit the ground, Sean laid his AK-47 aside and unlimbered the Draganov sniper rifle from off his shoulder. All the Palestinians retained their assault rifles and sought cover. However, the sole remaining African mercenary they had acquired in Johannesburg was of a different mind. Having seen his fellow African friend killed aboard the plane by the copilot, he was left unnerved. No doubt, his mental state was responsible for the burst of automatic weapon fire unleashed at Toby. All thirty rounds in the mercenary's Kalishnikov's magazine were expended before Sean and the Libyans were fully prepared.

Behind the Rover, where Toby crouched, spraying dirt, sand, and shreds of foliage erupted. Above the staccato chant of the gun, Drake was able to hear the sharp ping followed by the siren-like sound of bullets ricocheting off rocks and the steel body of his vehicular shield. Interspersed were a handful of dull thuds, indicating some of the projectiles had burrowed in the vehicle. Still unscathed, Drake popped up within a second after the firing stopped. Still standing, the African presented the most attractive target. Just as Sean found the center of Toby's head in the crosshairs of his telescopic sight, Toby touched off the trigger of his rifle. Unerring was his aim, and the bullet flew its deadly path without deviation. First, the soft-point projectile evacuated the African's right orbit before mushrooming to do indescribable damage to the brain and back of the skull. Then, all hell broke loose, as the dead man pitched forward!

Now Drake was facing a barrage of hundreds of rounds unleashed by the six adversaries remaining. Most were fired in haste and fortunately went astray. Nonetheless, a sufficient number impacted the Rover, so it was starting to be blown to shreds. Engine block, front wheels, axles and transfer case were the only areas of concentrated steel, which could any longer provide Drake the slightest degree of protection.

To himself, Toby screamed a scathing denunciation, "You bloody fucking fool! Why didn't you drive off when you could?!" At any time, a lucky shot, ricochet, or even a piece of shrapnel from the disintegrating Rover could do him in, and gas was leaking out all over. Any second, it could ignite and turn into an inferno. "Try and run for it, and you won't last a second," he murmured. "Well, I won't let them turn me into a torch or riddle my back, so I'll die facing them," Drake decided.

Suddenly, there was a microsecond lull in the firing. Instantaneously, Toby peered around at what remained of the Rover's front bumper. Glancing, he observed one of the killers at the far edge of their right flank, who was changing the magazine of his rifle, leaving him relatively exposed. Drake had never made a quicker shot, or a more telling one in his life. Acting as an agent for the Angel of Death, the bullet took out one of the Palestinians, hitting him in the neck and cleaving his spine, leaving him with less than ten seconds of life.

An instant after Toby fired his gun, one other rifle fired a single shot, as Sean with his Draganov at the ready had been waiting for Drake to expose himself. Though only a split second of consciousness remained for Toby, somehow he was able to recall a similar incident when thrown hurdling from his bicycle against a stone wall. Beyond that, there was total blackness. Moynihan and most of his men saw Drake's body fall. By the time their approach was complete, a large halo of blood had spread into the sand beyond the margins of Toby's head, and signs of life were imperceptible in the still form. No movement occurred, apart from response to a savage kick rendered by Haji and accompanied by an Arabic curse, beseeching Allah to deliver the man's soul to the deepest regions of Hell. One of the other Palestinians had his pistol out, and he was about to fire several more rounds into Drake's flaccid body. However, sensing a coup de grâce was "gilding the lily," Moynihan stilled the other man's hand. Then, reforming their skirmish line, the group moved inexorably forward toward the camp.

After entering the camp. Colonel Cameron was nowhere to be found. Therefore, Sean ordered his men to spread out around the perimeter of the camp and, after an hour of searching, they managed to find only two of the staff, who had hidden in some adjacent tall grass. At first, the pair of prisoners refused to indicate they understood the questions hurled at them. Finally, when a trench knife was produced, and they were threatened with severance of their virility, one admitted knowledge of English. Some meager information was forthcoming. "Colonel Cameron was in the camp, but he left early this morning to scout for game because new clients were coming." In answer to further questioning, "He was not alone. Joro, one of the trackers, was with him." After being asked when Cameron was to return, no answer came until the gleaming knife blade was unsheathed once more. "He should return before sundown."

Two intact Range Rovers remained at the camp; however, after discussion, neither Sean nor Haji could see any reason to start searching for Cameron. "Better to wait, and let him come to us," they concluded. Not long after, a column of dust was discernible off to the west and Sean decided that in all probability the vehicle producing it should arrive soon, and Colonel Cameron's welcome would not be what he usually received.

Quickly, Sean and Haji stationed their men at vantage points that offered good firing positions, as well as concealment. Then, orders were given to the captured pair, from the camp's retinue, to remain in the open and act busy, as though they were performing camp duties. When all camp preparation seemed complete, Sean and Haji sought their own positions.

From Moynihan's vantage point, it appeared that Colonel Cameron would be driving into the camp in a straight line, making a continuum of the dust column previously observed. Having not taken the opportunity to scout the enclave's perimeter, his ignorance was vincible, due to the fact there was a narrow but deep rift just beyond the hill, which he expected the Colonel to come over. When no vehicle appeared within Sean's estimated time, he began to feel puzzled, but not as yet dismayed.

Meanwhile, as usual, Iain drove to the edge of the rift and then turned south. Thoroughly familiar with the cleft and its topography, he was well aware that it was necessary to drive an extra half mile to the point where the crevice flattened out, making an easy crossing possible. Once the passage was finished, it was a straight drive north and back to camp. While out scouting, Cameron had seen and heard the familiar drone and silhouette of Gertie. Just as Toby did, he had wondered what had brought Safari Air to this vicinity two days early. Seconds later, after spotting and marking the location of two very large bull elephants, the question about the aircraft became quickly sublimated. Now, it was resurrected, as the DC-3 Dakota, sitting on the air strip, came suddenly into Cameron's view. Also, something was parked several hundred yards away, but if Toby had driven down to the plane, why would he have parked so far away?

Cameron realized that he was growing uneasy, and an inner sense of wariness was developing, compelling him to stop. Two seconds later, a ten-power telescope was positioned to his good left eye. After Iain focused the lens, it was now apparent why the Rover looked odd. Rather than manifesting the sharply square outline that was so classic, the Rover seemed almost amorphous. Portions of the body were nearly torn away, and bullet holes were everywhere. "Bloody hell," hissed Iain, then continued, "Something is terribly wrong at camp, Joro!"

Had Cameron continued to study the wreck, he might have caught sight of Toby's legs projecting out behind the right front tire. Instead, he turned the telescope toward camp. Two of his men were visible out in front, both armed with rakes and seemingly tidying up the grounds. Cameron knew "pecking orders" existed in all African hunting camps, and talented skinners were near the top. No good man possessing that skill would degrade himself performing a menial task unless forced. Now, Iain was sure the camp was under hostile control, and whoever it might be, they were waiting for him!

While Colonel Cameron had stopped to survey the situation, Moynihan kept screening the hillock to the west, and there was still no sign of a vehicle crossing over it. Sean wondered, "Could the dust trail have been made by a herd of running animals?" However, he really didn't know enough about Africa to do more than speculate. Had it not been for the fact that Sean was so concentrated on expecting the vehicle, presumably raising the dust and traveling in a straight line, Moynihan might have concluded the Rover had turned or was crossing a surface that did not give rise to airborne particulate matter. Agitated, Sean cursed under his breath, and began to sweep his binoculars in a wide arc. Suddenly, he observed over there to the south was a stopped Land Rover, with a white man standing in the front and scanning the camp with a spy glass. Also, though not as clearly visible, there was an African in the passenger seat. "Cameron," he hissed, "and he's suspicious." Quickly, Moynihan decided no butterfly would come to the spider's web, so it would be up to the spider to chase his prey! Immediately, an Arabic command was shouted, and Sean, Haji, and the three remaining terrorists ran to the nearest Rover. Earlier, Moynihan had made sure the ignition keys were in hand, and that was a positive.

However, he realized that leaving the Draganov at a distance and relying on the AK-47 was a mistake. His target was out of effective range for the assault weapons, but he could have been hit with the long-range gun.

Still studying the camp through the telescope, Cameron became immediately aware of the frantic movements of his would-be killers, so with clutch in, the gears were shifted. Then, with clutch released and accelerator depressed, Iain turned the Rover in a full circle, heading back south. Ordinarily, driving around scouting was not more dangerous than a camera safari, so Iain wasn't concerned with having only one gun when they had left camp. However, anger engulfed him, as he realized one of his personal commandments had been broken by no other than himself. "Always expect the unexpected" was the rule he had violated. Given his principal duty as a tracker, Joro was frequently unarmed, and such was the occasion today. However, much experienced in the practice of strategic withdrawal, Cameron was free of Toby's folly. "Get the hell away and, then, figure out what to do next!" was the only rational course of action.

Careening across the savanna at the highest possible speed didn't provide opportunity for a well-conceived strategy, but some thought was possible. Defensively, there was only a single firearm at his disposal. Toby always called it the insurance cannon. Wesley Richards had created it, and the gun now lay safely strapped in a rack, just behind him. Two of the thumb-sized 600 Nitro Express cartridges were chambered, with one in each of the massive double barrels. Another four should be in a leather cartridge holder, but it hadn't been replenished, and only two remained. *Unless I wreck the Rover, or they kill me first, I've got only four shots,* Iain thought, and it wasn't reassuring. Fortunately, Joro had filled the petrol tank, so at least they would be able to travel as far as their pursuers.

Looking into the rearview mirror, Cameron noted the distance between the other Rover and his was static. Initially, he had hoped to increase their lead, but it wasn't happening. Even worse, Iain knew that their escape route would soon take him into an area where his speed had to be reduced, and that would allow the pursuers to at least partially close the gap before they also had to slow down. Joro and he would gain advantage on the other side of the boulder-strewn dry river bed, although only if they made it across without being shot. Whoever was chasing could get closer if they were able to keep up the same pace. At that distance, the AK47s he saw them carrying out of the camp, while not precisely accurate, were still very lethal.

As Colonel Cameron and Joro were fleeing for their lives, Moynihan and his men were in hot pursuit. Among his many skills, Haji was an excellent driver in rough terrain, thus explaining Cameron's inability to outdistance them. Sean became aware the fleeing vehicle was forced to slow down, as it veered between the large rocks it was now encountering. *Temporarily,* Moynihan thought, *this could be a real advantage.* Having regained the Draganov on the way to the river, Sean made a decision to stop when they had closed to about 500 yards from the fleeing vehicle. Five shots would be possible, and some might disable the other Land Rover or kill its occupants. Haji had been apprised of the plan, and he jammed on the brakes at Moynihan's command. Immediately, Sean ejected, and soon had the sniper rifle firing. Hitting a zig-zagging target at such a distance was enhanced by skill, but was still a matter of luck. Rifle empty, Moynihan jumped back in the Rover, and Haji roared off again in hot pursuit. Sean had no reason to think any of his shots had scored, and he was angered by that.

Having witnessed their pursuers stopping, Ian and Joro were aware they were being fired upon. One bullet had struck the right front fender, but had missed the tire or anything else of importance. Another sound was of more concern, a heavy metallic *thunk*, which had seemed to emanate from near the rear bumper. Iain murmured, "Well the Rover is still running and full of petrol, and hopefully no damage of consequence occurred." Soon, Iain and Joro were in better terrain, while the pursuers were still negotiating the boulders. Sighting a small ridge ahead, Iain quickly decided to cross the front edge and then stop! Minimal cover would be present, temporarily hiding them and their Rover, and allowing them some safety from return fire. At the same time, it would be possible to let his attackers come within 200 yards before he fired two of the only four cartridges he had at his disposal.

Immediately, Sean and Haji were aware their quarry had gone to ground. "Shall I stop?" Haji screamed.

"No! Pour it on, but keep swerving," Moynihan shouted back. They were closing fast, and the engine was at full throttle when the first bullet from the 600

Nitro Express tore through the grill. Some 7,600 foot-pounds of energy, which the projectile possessed when it left the barrel, was diminished in flight, but much remained. After smashing its way through the radiator, it hit the fan like the Hammer of Thor and finally embedded itself in the engine block. From flying fan blades, clattering noise filled the air with gut-wrenching sound.

"Fook it all," screamed Sean. Haji made no reply, as the second monster slug exploded the windshield before splitting his head like an overripe pumpkin dropped from high up. Then, after impacting on a large ant hill, the devastated Rover finally stopped, allowing Sean and the other three survivors to emerge unscathed, apart from cuts and bruises.

Although such an occurrence would have unnerved most men, Sean and the other three were far from ordinary, so no time was wasted in mourning, though all revered Haji. Unbothered by the shreds of Haji's brain splattered on their fatigues, they charged forward, hoping to deliver fire into the once again fleeing Rover. At the top of the ridge, they stopped, badly winded and desperate but still determined. Realizing Cameron's Rover was now a good half-mile away and out of range, all the cruel facts now fell on Sean with full force. They were miles away from the plane and on foot. Worse yet, Cameron had eluded them, and he could double back, secure reinforcements, and pick them off one at a time. "I've failed," Sean screamed inwardly. "Well, better off dead than having to face my father."

Dejectedly, Sean looked at the hot African sand between his boots. At the same time, his nostrils detected a familiar odor. Petrol, and lots of it. One of his shots must have hit the tank on Cameron's lorry. How far could they go? After retrieving the Draganov and his field glasses, Sean intently studied the landscape ahead. Just a mile away, a Land Rover was stopped, and two men were walking away, and only one was carrying a rifle. Since Cameron was older, they should easily be able to catch up. *Maybe victory can be snatched from the jaws of defeat,* he thought. Then, four desperate men proceeded forward at a fast march, and victory seemed possible!

Direction wise, the pair of men Sean was studying seemed headed toward what appeared to be a cluster of trees and brush, which were about a quarter of a mile ahead of them. Obviously, they were seeking cover, but in so doing the yards separating him from them were actually decreasing, an advantage Sean intended to capitalize on. Sweeping his binoculars in an arc to the right, Moynihan noted there was a large herd of very big, blackish-brown animals interposed between his present position, and where he intended to intercept Cameron. They weren't elephants or rhinos, he wasn't sure what they were; however, he was sure that the herd of whatever it was, would surely ran off. Should the beasts continue to graze, as he and his men approached, they certainly looked large enough to provide good cover. Conversely, if they ran off, that could provide an advantageous distraction. Since there were no cape buffalo in Palestine or Lebanon, Sean's three remaining men had no reason to question his plan. Therefore, after quickly refreshing themselves with water from canteens they had obtained from the stolen Rover, they spread out to form what had become an abbreviated skirmish line. Opportunity for revenge was not far away, and this reflection accelerated their advance.

What Sean had seen could be explained by what had occurred to Cameron and Joro. As they were trying to make their escape, Colonel Cameron had spotted the same herd of buffalo. Purposefully, he drove around them, knowing full well that no more capricious and ill-tempered beast dwelt on the planet. Though the term was derived from the mannerisms of goats, mbogo possessed it in spades! Far better to give them a wide berth, rather than being trapped in the middle of the herd, where a great bull might decide that even a Land Rover was an adversary deserving of confrontation. Although circumventing the herd had cost them dearly in consumption of petrol, Cameron still felt it had been the wisest course of action.

Shortly after having avoided the cape buffalo, the last drop of fuel had either leaked out or been consumed by the engine, so the Rover coughed and died. Further retreat would now have to occur on foot. However, before departing the stalled vehicle, Iain and Joro grabbed two full canteens of water, plus the double-barrel rifle. Sliding the last two precious rounds into its chambers, he could only think that carrying the canteens was a futile gesture, inasmuch as he and Joro might not live long enough to drink. Also, Joro stuck two razor-sharp skinning knives into his belt, even though he knew they were not much defense against a gun. At least it freed him from a feeling of impotence against their enemies. "We'd best get on our way," Joro said to Iain in a tone of confidence he really didn't feel.

Suddenly, Joro exclaimed, "Colonel there is one jerry can of petrol that is still full. Perhaps, we could drive on further."

"Afraid not," replied Cameron. "We would lose time pouring it in the Rover, and more time would be lost trying to prime the carburetor, then, most of it would have drained out the hole in the tank before we got started." Desperate to go, Iain knew they had already lost precious seconds, and these translated into decreasing yards separating them from their enemy.

Although anxious as Colonel Cameron was, the hunter's instincts were still alive. As far as breezes went, there wasn't much of one, but what there was came from the east. As a result, their scent would be softly wafted toward the buffalo herd.

Entirely wrong if we were stalking them, but possibly advantageous in this situation,

Iain thought. Suddenly, he shouted, "Bring the jerry can, Joro!" Then they took off. Sixty-year-old lower limbs, even those constantly used, lacked the stamina of youth. However, such was not apparent in Colonel Cameron, as the pair moved off toward the patch of trees and thorn bushes. Even the twelve-pound rifle, canteens, and jerry can did little to impede their progress.

As Cameron and Joro headed for cover, Moynihan, while snatching a glance through his binoculars, was impressed by the alacrity of movement in Cameron and the African. Now, he was close enough to determine that the man he lusted to kill was bearing a double-barreled rifle. *Good,* he thought. *Only two shots before he has to reload.* No telescopic sight was obvious, and that would mean iron sights with all their inherent inaccuracy. Sean and his three remaining men could easily saturate any cover they tried to hide in with automatic fire. Even better, they all had a minimum of eight spare magazines, each holding thirty rounds. Last, the Draganov was his ace in the hole! Using its optic sight, it was deadly at 500 yards or more. Pushing himself even harder, Sean increased his pace, and the Palestinians matched him step for step.

Looming ever larger was the herd of animals that Moynihan had perceived before starting the chase. "Buffalo of some sort," he concluded, for they looked much like pictures of water buffalo that he had seen in his school books. Recalling that they were usually hooked to some sort of cultivating device in a rice paddy, he continued to assume these were similar and possibly semi-domesticated. Should that not be the case, a burst of fire would surely run them off, and any dissenters would be easily cut down, like a bunch of cows with a few rounds from their AK-47s. As the quartet progressed, the herd indeed took notice of their coming, and a few started moving slowly away, much to the satisfaction of Sean and his men.

Despite heroic efforts, Iain and Joro were reaching the point of exhaustion. Forty some pounds of petrol in a ten pound jerry can and the cumbersome rifle were wearing them down, even though they had traded loads on several occasions. Hope of reaching shelter of the trees and thorn bushes was fading fast. Soon, the enemy would encounter the buffalo and, if the animals scattered, Iain knew he and Joro would be within range of the enemy's guns. Sooner yet, they would be in danger if the tall European who appeared to lead them was able to use the rifle with the telescope sight, which he carried over his shoulder. Immediately, Cameron decided, *Now or never, the time has come.*

Opening the jerry can, Iain proceeded to slosh its contents along a twenty-five-yard stretch of dried grass. Along with the match, which he threw in the grass, went a short prayer. Ignition took place, but no conflagration occurred, as the breeze was weak, and the grass was not tinder dry. Nonetheless, a small quantity of smoke was produced, and the compliant breeze saw fit to slowly waft it toward the herd. Seconds later, many buffalo heads began to disdain the grass on which they grazed, as they were raised to sample the air. Mbogo infrequently encountered fire; however, for those that had, the acrid odor was forever stored in whatever memory capacity they possessed. Well past her prime, one old cow wrinkled her great black nostrils and showed signs of agitation. Soon, others followed suit; some not knowing why. Finally, the massive bull, who led the herd, caught the scent and knew immediately it was time to flee, even for an animal that seldom fled! Given the great olfactory sense that nature had provided, he was well aware of the area from which the noxious odor came, and true security was the opposite direction. Some other animals he may have recognized and avoided; however, only men stood in the path of flight, and instinct dictated they would be no impediment.

As a hundred massive beasts commenced their stampede, Sean and his men were stunned, horrified, and fascinated all at the same time. Curved, burnished horns arose from the massive bosses on their foreheads, and the points were as deadly as a cavalry man's lance. Four flint-hard hooves, as threatening as a hard-swung mace, were borne by each of the beasts. As the distance narrowed, flared nostrils and great demon eyes became ever more apparent. Sure they were witnessing the opening of the Gates of Hell, two of the Palestinians dropped their guns and turned to flee. However, Sean and one Palestinian stood their ground and opened fire. Multiple hits were observed, for it was nearly impossible to miss. However, their magazines now empty, there was not time to reload. Hoping the more powerful weapon would serve him better, Moynihan ripped the Draganov from his shoulder. Immediately, he realized the ten-power scope was a fatal impediment at a distance of twenty yards and closing. Hurled into the air by the tremendous impact from the great bull's head, Sean nearly lost consciousness, but that gift was denied. When he was back on the ground, the cape buffalo's horn pierced his chest. However, death only came from the ravages of four stone-hard hooves. For the fleeing Palestinians, fate decreed that they fared no better, for although normal bovines usually try to avoid a fallen man, even while stampeding, the cape buffalo subscribed to no such convention.

Slowly, Iain and Joro walked to the scene. Even though these were enemies, it was devastating to see other humans destroyed in such a manner. Obviously, one was a European, but he now lay grotesquely distorted and featureless. As for the others, they appeared to have come from somewhere in the Middle East. None carried any obvious identification. Although Christian culture would call for an attempt to bury them; however, stones were few, and shovels nonexistent. Also, their physical reserve was entirely depleted. Iain did say a prayer for them, realizing only God knew how responsible they were for their actions. Future investigation would probably be forthcoming if and when the proper authorities could be notified. Forensics could be forgotten, for the jackals, hyenas, and vultures would have digested all the evidence by then.

Close to a nearby body, one intact AK-47 was found, and Iain picked it up along with some magazines and handed those to Joro. Obviously, he knew it wasn't the gun of choice for cape buffalo, but it might be of some use if trouble remained at camp. Undoubtedly, there were many wounded mbogo ahead of them. However, being used to their wiles, they hoped the wounded beasts could be avoided. Two rounds remained in Toby's insurance cannon, just in case they were needed. Still, as soon as possible, they would have to return and cull any injured animals that might still survive, as they would be a grave danger to any men they might encounter. *Probably, they would be few if any*, Iain thought, *as the lions would seize on the situation and feast accordingly.*

Before departing, Iain turned for one last look at his fire line. Fortunately, the breeze had abated, and the flames had died. Then, while trudging back to camp, they passed the Rover, which had been put out of commission, and a nearly headless driver was slumped behind the wheel, still safe from the scavengers until they lost their fear of the vehicle. When the rays of the sun at last touched their backs, the camp was in sight. Still to be discovered was what lie in wait for them.

Chapter Forty-Two

✦ ✦ ✦

At about the time Iain and Joro were preparing for the final encounter with their adversaries, miles to the west, Archie Andrus's sensorium started to clear. Process wise, it was far from smooth. Instead, it occurred in little irregular steps, with the first being a vague recognition of pain emanating primarily from the right side of his head. Perceiving recognizable features inside Gertie's compartment, Archie slowly concluded that he wasn't dead! Just one little ragged step further, and the pilot realized he hadn't crashed the plane. No, he had been struck in the head by the hijackers just as power to the engines was cut. Other memories started to drift back into place. "Buster and Martin? There were shots back here in the cabin. I must look around. Got to look around! Something's holding me." Finally, Archie realized his wrists and ankles were tightly bound.

Grimacing from pain as he tried to work his hands free, Archie felt as though the right side of his face was covered with some sort of adhesive. "Dried blood," he concluded. "Anyone else on the plane? Did they leave guards? They did talk about having an extra pilot with them. Yes, he took Buster's seat after they dragged him off. Somehow I've got to shift my position so I can look around, but I'm bound up tighter than hell, and they've got me wedged between the seats. Gotta get loose, so I can see!" Working strenuously against the rope that held his wrists, Archie produced no hint of release, just more pain that added to the agony associated with his head wound.

Suddenly, another memory surfaced; a very propitious one if only he could reach his pocket. Therein was a clasp knife, small but sharp. Exerting himself to the maximum, Archie was finally able to secure one index finger in his pocket's opening. Like the legs of a slowly moving spider, another finger crawled in, followed by the third. Bolstered by the fact that the tip of his middle finger had palpated the end of the knife's base, Archie made one last thrust of his hands.

Finally, the knife was between his index and middle fingers; however, withdrawal was unsuccessful. "Oh shit," he softly murmured. Then, he forced himself to try again. Pressing the opposing surfaces of his fingers as tightly together as possible, Archie tried the knife retrieval a second time. *Careful!* he thought. *For God's sake, don't let it drop.* Millimeter by millimeter, the knife emerged.

Finally, the knife was out and locked securely in the flexed fingers of Archie's left hand. Grasping with the right hand, he was able to direct his thumbnail into the small indentation on the knife blade's top surface. Then, burning pain in his left wrist alerted Archie to the fact that the first thrust of the blade was misdirected. Concentrating intently and moving the blade slightly, another attempt was made. Something was being cut, and thank God it didn't hurt.

Very gradually, the ligature relaxed until at last Archie's hands came free! Now, able to use the power of his arms to aid in movement, he methodically shifted his position. Finally able to look about, he slowly turned his head aft. "Oh good Jesus," he whispered, as soon as his eyes caught sight of the crumpled, blood-drenched bodies of Martin and Buster. Eyes fixed, with rigor mortis already appearing and swarming of flies around, Andrus knew they were already dead. Swelling like a tsunami, Archie's wrath and hatred became his all-consuming thought, as he whispered ,"Those dirty fuckers will pay for this!"

Trying to dispel madness and recoup reason, Archie brought his eyes to bear on the forward section. More buzzing flies brought his attention to the body of the African mercenary, also obviously dead. Next, Archie's gaze was riveted on the cockpit. Just visible, was the Arab pilot, no doubt left in what was assumed to be a place of safety. "They're expecting you to fly them back aren't they? Well, you son of a bitch, it will be over my dead body!"

With concern, Archie noted, "The bastard's got a Makarov in his hand." Immediately, he began to work out a stratagem. Obviously, there was no chance to rush him before the Arab could open fire. "Groans from the victim always worked in the movies and on TV, but this sod might just come back partway and shoot me!" Pondering the situation, suddenly Archie thought, *Keys!* Immediately, he reached for the heavily laden key ring in his pocket, now easily accessible since his hands were free. "Surely, the Arab would hear the keys striking metal in the rear of the fuselage and come to investigate." Then, Archie realized his ankles must first be free. When the rope was cut, he moved his feet as much as possible. After deciding his lower extremities would be dependable, Archie lofted the key ring to the rear of the compartment. Immediate alertness was the Arab pilot's response. Arising, he came to the cockpit door with his pistol at the ready, and dark eyes searching for the source of the sound. Slowly the terrorist proceeded down the narrow aisle with pistol-holding hands outstretched.

After glancing at Archie's inert form, he continued aft. Just as the man passed, Archie's right fist smashed out and impacted on the Arab's groin. Experiencing excruciating pain from traumatized testicles, the man screamed out as he doubled over. Then, Archie's knife was plunged into the right side of the terrorist's neck. Though the blade was short, the distance to the carotid artery was even less. While the pilot's scream died on his lips, the mortally wounded man was able to turn his head, and Archie watched as vitality fled the hard, dark eyes. After whipping the Makarov pistol from the Arab's relaxing hand, he was prepared to shoot. However, bullets were not needed, for the four-inch blade had sent the man to Allah for judgment!

Standing, at last, Andrus staggered to the plane's door. Having seen no obvious guards, he committed to descending the steps to the ground. After half staggering to the wheel strut on the starboard side of the plane, he grabbed it for support. Then, off at a short distance he recognized a number of the camp staff, and they were clustered about the front of a shot-up Rover. Seeing no sign of any terrorists, Archie called out, and two of the men came running over. Anxious eyes peered down at the pilot, as he sank to a sitting position. Though not a linguist, Archie had a sufficient command of pidgin English to understand "Mr. Toby was over there—was much bad but still alive."

Knowing both he and Drake needed medical care urgently, he said, "Radio, Mr. Toby's radio work?" After noting their faces, Archie searched for the word he needed. "Wayiles?" Finally, he had remembered the Fangalo word derived from the English *wireless*.

"Wayiles no work," they replied, shaking their heads for emphasis. "Chital and Zomba go get Sampson," Archie murmured, while still just barely able to remain sitting upright. Soon, Sampson appeared. As the camp cook, he was slightly conversant in ten languages, especially English.

Knowing he was growing weaker, Archie had to explain to someone what had to be done in the shortest possible time, and the cook was his man. Helped to the cockpit, Archie was depressed but not surprised to find that Gertie's radio was inoperable. "Dirty bastards," he hissed, too exhausted to shout. The radio wasn't smashed; however, a number of essential tubes and parts had been removed. Trying to jury rig something even if there were intact parts available in the camp radio could take hours, and they had none to spare. Desperation loomed, as Archie tried the engines. Fortunately, they had been left inviolate by the terrorists, assuming they would be needed to take them wherever they planned to go. Meanwhile, Sampson had responded to Archie's orders, and soon

Drake's limp body, borne on a makeshift stretcher, was placed in the plane and secured with straps. As best the cook could determine, a single bullet had glanced along Drake's skull. There was no sign that it had penetrated, but Toby still appeared critical.

Being a realist, Archie was sufficiently conscious of his own condition to know that he would never make it back to Johannesburg or a city of any size. However, medical care of some sort would be available in Maputo, but he wasn't known there. Little imagination was needed to figure out that he and Toby would probably both be dead before the authorities in Mozambique decided what to do with four dead bodies, and two more that were halfway there. All of them would be arriving in a South African plane exhibiting numerous bullet holes. Certainly, a first-class international incident by anyone's estimation!

Mbabone was their best chance, since it was just across the border in South Africa, and had a decent landing strip and a radio would be available. With luck, there might be another plane and pilot there who could ferry them on to a better medical facility. Realizing he could die or pass out at any time, Archie knew that Sampson was needed to go with them; however, the cook couldn't fly the plane. Was it fair to put the man at such risk when he and Toby were the only ones, who had anything to gain? This was a Gordian knot for sure, and one Archie hadn't time to cut or untie. "I'll fly low," he decided and, if I feel that I'm going to pass out, I'll try and crash-land Gertie for Sampson's sake."

Archie wasn't a particularly religious man, but he said a prayer to God to lend a hand. While he was doing this, it came to his mind that during all of his hair-raising flying career, God had already been watching over him. While releasing the brakes and advancing the throttles, Archie felt remorse for never having said thanks.

Skimming tree tops and cavorting like a drunken dove, Gertie did make it to Mbabone. As they approached, Archie realized that he was close to losing all strength and coordination in his left side. With barely any consciousness remaining, he gave mumbled instructions to Sampson to pull the throttles back as soon as they touched down.

As stalwart, as he was talented, the cook was terrified during the journey to Mbabone; however, he wasn't a man to waver. Many times during the flight he thought that he would be better off facing a pride of hungry lions. After the landing, and rolling halfway down the runway, Archie became totally unconscious. Though Gertie's props were feathered, she seized on new-found freedom to go her own way. Fortunately, the ground beside the strip was relatively smooth, apart from one hole, into which she wandered. As Safari Airlines' pride and joy came to a stop, the right front tire was flattened and supporting gear bent. However, otherwise, the Dakota was unscathed.

Bewildered by what they found, the local police and town doctor could offer no help. Fortunately, a twin engine Lockheed Lodestar had arrived only minutes before Gertie and would be able to transport Andrus and Drake still alive to Johannesburg. They would depart immediately. Police inspectors were summoned from Johannesburg and would arrive in Mbabone shortly to inspect the disabled plane. Although Sampson was anxious to relate his impressions on his first airplane ride, the police had greater interest in the facts. Succinctly, Sampson related these with a recommendation that someone should fly to the camp site at first light to check on Joro and Colonel Cameron. For that purpose, contact was made with Mozambique. Though not pleased, they agreed to go out to the camp and see what was happening. Also, permission was given for a few South African officials to visit the site. Sampson agreed to fly along, if they would promise to stay high above the ground until it was time to land.

Meanwhile, though foot sore and bone weary, Iain and Joro didn't collapse into a cot after finally reaching camp. Finding out what had happened to Toby, Archie, Buster, Martin, and the camp staff was their first priority. Responses to questions were cataclysmic and heart-rending. Hope remained for Drake and Andrus, and that helped greatly when it came to facing the finality of Martin's and Buster's murders. Already appraised of the short-wave radio's destruction, Iain was trying to decide in which direction he should drive to find another accessible wireless. However, exhausted, filled with anxiety, and facing impending darkness, Iain knew his only recourse was some rest in order to restore his faculties. Therefore, he was barely recumbent when sleep totally enveloped him.

Upon awakening early the next morning, Iain sensed an air of excitement developing among his men. Cameron looked about in an effort to ascertain what the source might be. Most of his staff had been spared the sequelae of cordite ear malady, common to soldiers and big game hunters and named after the powder responsible, as ears were not meant to bear the insults and shockwaves of innumerable explosions. Increasing deafness was an insidious complication, and Cameron had already noted an auditory deficit in himself. However, the Africans' pristine ears had heard the approach of an airplane, thus explaining the prevalent mood of the men. While looking skyward, and pointing their index fingers, they repeatedly used the term for an aircraft.

Once burned, twice cautious, was an old canard, but an applicable one after yesterday's experience, thought Iain. Therefore, spare rifles and ammunition were passed around, and any invaders arriving today would be greeted far differently. Pleased that he had encouraged his staff to learn to shoot, he knew all of them were reasonably proficient, and a few were quite good. Vigilance was maintained until the plane was on the ground, and a South African insignia was obviously displayed. Shortly, four men emerged from the cabin door, and all were appropriately uniformed.

"Joro," Iain called out. "I'll drive down and pick them up, as I assume they are what they appear to be. However, keep the lads on the alert. We don't need any more surprises, and if this group turns out to be phonies, blow them away with my blessings!"

While smiling broadly, the tracker exhibited some gold between the ivory, as he replied, "My pleasure, Colonel sir." These words were followed by a pantomime of a Gunga Din–like salute, which evoked further smiles from the rest of the staff.

Smiling back, Iain said, "I see you have read your Kipling, Joro, but don't forget I want you to shoot, not blow some bloody bugle."

As the four-man contingent were genuine government officials, shooting did not occur. However, as Iain would soon find out, the head man was utterly unlikable. Introduction consisted of "I'm Chief Inspector Vandermoot, and I assume you are Cameron."

Replying "Yes," Iain proffered his right hand, and when unaccepted, it was withdrawn. No attempt was made to give names to the three men accompanying Vandermoot. All were younger, and they stood by awkwardly like gawky adolescents at their first dance. The Inspector's lack of manners informed Cameron that the man came equipped with a self-assessment that proclaimed "very superior" in every category. Iain's one good eye appeared steely, as he coldly responded, "I'm Colonel Iain Cameron. I trust you have a radio in your plane. Unless you are able to give me information on the condition of my two good friends from personal knowledge, I insist on placing a call before I do anything else."

"Look here, Cameron," the Chief Inspector retorted. "I'm here to ask questions and get answers. An airplane licensed in South Africa has been involved in a hijacking. Two citizens of South Africa are dead, along with a couple of others from God knows where. I ask questions. You provide answers! Is that clear?"

Drawing himself up rigidly, Cameron stared at Vandermoot, with his appearance taking on that of an officer in charge of a firing squad. Then, three harsh, unmistakable words were uttered by Cameron, and they weren't "Ready, aim, fire," but given the response of the four men, they could have been. "Go to hell," was what Iain actually said. Brushing aside the startled Inspector, he entered the Cessna and proceeded to the cockpit. Now smiling and very personable, Colonel Cameron established immediate rapport with the pilot. Soon, a radio link was opened with the proper hospital.

"Mr. Drake and Mr. Andrus are both alive, but semi-comatose. Similar surgery had been performed on each late last night. We call it 'placing burr holes,'" the nurse responded. "They are made in the skull to permit evacuation of a subdural hematoma." Then, she added "Oh, excuse me. I didn't mean to sound too medical. What I mean is the doctor drills holes in the skull to drain a blood clot."

Iain was about to say "It sounds like you mean a trephination procedure," but the young lady seemed very sweet and doing her best. Iain remembered dear Claire had frequently reminded him that wry humor was not always appreciated, so he abstained from the remark. After asking the young nurse to wish his friends well as soon as they were alert, Cameron informed her that he would stay in touch. Sincere gratitude was expressed before ringing off. Now, he felt better, for he knew Egyptians had done trephination with bronze instruments centuries before Christ.

Outside the plane, Vandermoot had regained his demeanor and was bristling with hostility. "How dare you go stalking off?" he shouted.

Again, Iain was in charge of the firing squad, and his words were intense. "Chief Inspector Vandermoot, I shall now endeavor to answer your questions. However, I should like to remind you that the sand beneath your feet is soil I have leased from Mozambique. You have as much jurisdiction here as a zebra's turd. Now let us go to my camp. I'm sure your men would welcome some shade and a cool drink." From their expressions, Iain wasn't sure what made them happier, the invitation just extended or the Chief Inspector's dressing down.

After a fine lunch whipped up by the assistant cook and three frosty brews, in the early afternoon Vandermoot had approached within an elephant's trunk length of being a reasonable, decent chap. As for the three underlings, they soon became loquacious and showed signs of being better cops than their boss. Multiple theories were forthcoming, but all were shot through with conjecture. In the midst of their discussions, they heard above them a helicopter, which was a noisy beast now arriving and bearing Mozambique insignia. Captain Bwanda was in charge of a squad of five. Fortunately, the man was most unofficious and freely joined in a constructive dialogue which although good for international relations, shed no light on the mystery.

Finally, abandoning discussion of the invaders, Iain and Joro plus Vandermoot and Bwanda, with one aide each, crawled into the last intact Rover. Before too long, their journey took them to the site where the lorry used by the terrorists had come to rest. Again, Iain recounted in detail what had happened. As predicted, Haji's body had been removed by emboldened predators. Only scattered, sometimes splintered bones, and the remnants of his shattered skull remained. Jackals or hyenas had devoured much of the body. Then, savoring the marrow, they had crunched the bones with their rock-crusher jaws. No doubt, vultures had been next in line. Naturally equipped with pointed beaks, they had stripped away whatever flesh the jackals may have left, including the eyes and tongue. Finally, ants would have come for whatever sparse shreds remained. Such was the effectiveness of the three-tiered African cleanup squads. Two unlucky assistants had the grisly task of logging all the tissue and bones that could be found.

On the second site, where four men had died, their AK-47s along with a Draganov rifle lay inert in the hot sand. Again, they found scattered, splintered bones and skulls. Still encased in combat boots were several amputated feet, adding further horror to the macabre scene. Apparently, whatever scavengers had passed this way were sufficiently sated that they were not compelled to rip away the hard, rubber soles for the sparse amount of flesh on the feet, so ants and beetles could fight for that. Crossing past the area where the Draganov was found, Iain noted a skull still largely intact apart from the missing jaw. Larger than the others, it was likely the skull of the solitary European. Some straight, white teeth remained. Interestingly, there were a few dental fillings, Iain noted.

Finally, back at camp, Cameron let the representatives of the two nations decide how the artifacts and meager clues would be apportioned. Then, as darkness fell, the Cessna and helicopter took off in two different directions. With the coming of night, it seemed fitting, for after all the discussion and evidence they had gathered had shed no light on who these people were, and why they had come. Meanwhile, parallel events were unfolding back in Johannesburg while the police were investigating the Cameron and Drake camp terrorist invasion.

Twenty-four hours had passed since Sean, along with the Arabs, African mercenaries, and the spare pilot had departed in the hijacked plane. Apprehension had now pervaded the spirits of the two remaining Libyan pilots, still ensconced in a hotel in Johannesburg. Unsure of what Sean's mission was, they had been told a little which indicated it would be only a one- or two-day operation, so something had to have gone terribly wrong. Maybe the targets had turned the tables, and some of their colleagues could have been captured and were now being interrogated. Regardless of how determined and stoic, they could be induced to talk. Confessions would certainly lead back to them. Quickly dressing, the pair made for their embassy in hopes of garnering information. Coded messages were sent to Benghazi, but they provided no help. However, the last response ordered their recall on the following morning with or without Sean Moynihan and the others. Therefore, at 0800 hours on the next day, the two pilots boarded the Libyan jet and lifted off the runway at Johannesburg International Airport heading east, then turning north for the long trip home. Before departure, the two men had carefully removed all the luggage and any personal gear from the rooms the group had occupied.

Satisfaction of the bill had come from residual cash left in Sean's money belt, and the remainder of a goodly sum was split between them. Dead men—and the pilots presumed Moynihan and his group now fit that description—had no need for money. Who better to make use of it than themselves?

Back in Benghazi, the two pilots were debriefed. Their leader was happy to have his plane back. In time, Libyan intelligence pieced together what had happened, at least to their own satisfaction. Since Sean Moynihan and his group had never returned and intercepted police communications in Johannesburg had spoken of body parts found near a safari campsite in Mozambique, when all added together, it pointed to a failed mission and death of the participants.

Slowly, the information filtered its way to Mustapha in the Becca Valley of Lebanon. Next, it went to Moscow and, then, on to Alexis at the Russian embassy in Belfast. KGB agent though he was, Colonel Zellanova was capable of feelings, and now he directed them toward his friend Mickey Moynihan. Much of the "cat and mouse" folderol was forsaken when the two met personally. Though not given to embracing other men, apart from family, Mickey did accept the Russian's hug. Perceptive as he was and given the time elapsed, Mickey had already concluded that Sean's mission had been a failure, and his son was dead. Alexis's embrace just constituted the final verdict. At least, he had ashes for Liam; for Sean there would be none. Most of his son's body had already become part of Africa, and the rest was consigned to some laboratory, from whence it would finally be disposed, as no more than garbage.

Once alone, Mickey's mind tore at his heart. *You did it! You might as well have shot him yourself.* As days passed, his despondency deepened. Finally, once again able to sit astride Warlord, Mickey spurred the thoroughbred into a furious gallop. On and on they went until the numbness passed from Mickey's mind, and he noted how heavily lathered the stallion was. Stopping immediately, he dismounted and caressed the horse's head gently. "I'll not kill you, too," he whispered softly to the animal before leading him off on a slow walk home.

Trudging along, Mickey became aware that a montage of images were forming in his mind. Little Sean, his long dead younger brother, was first. Then came his Ma and Da, followed by Mickey's sons, Liam and Sean. Bernie was last, and her visage remained the longest. Try as he might, Mickey was unable to picture any of them smiling, though he had experienced many happy times with most of them. Instead, their faces were all in deathly repose.

By now, Warlord was well cooled, so he mounted again, and proceeded home at a slow canter. Motions transmitted by the stallion's gait started to help clear the depressing images from his mind. Always a romantic, Mickey began to picture himself mounted on a charger centuries ago with a great sword hung at his side. Ahead was Iain Cameron similarly mounted and armed for a duel to the death! Mickey's shield bore an Irish harp in brightest gold on a field of green.

Cameron's shield was emblazoned with a red, rampant Scottish lion surrounded by vibrant yellow.

At that moment, Mickey decided, duel to the death must take place between him and the Scot! Modern weapons would be employed, but the outcome would be the same. Hopefully, Cameron wouldn't die quickly, for Mickey wished to tell him it was his intention to slay all the Scot's male heirs, and that no Cameron of his blood would ever walk the earth again! For Mickey, depression departed, as its icy grasp was melted away by flames of revenge. "So it had been in the past, and so it was now! Plans must be made for the battle between the Lion and the Harp."

Meanwhile, back in Africa, Colonel Iain Cameron was a busy man. As frequently as possible, trips to hospital in Johannesburg were made. Toby and Archie were mending well, as physician's skills were augmented by indomitable spirits. Due to the tragedy, temporary air service to the camp was provided by a friendly competitor and, among their peers, other professional hunters filled in Toby's spot, so all clients of Cameron and Drake were well satisfied.

Iain's most irksome task was what to do with the wrecked Rovers. New ones had been procured, and some parts from the wrecks had been cannibalized. Still, the shot-up hulk of Toby's Rover sat, as a very sad reminder of that fateful day. Many times, Colonel Cameron thought how nice it would be if hyenas ate old lorries. Knowing that would never happen, he ordered a cutting torch and tanks be flown into the camp, and, finally, the landscape was restored. However, vigilance was not abandoned, and defenders were always at the ready when a plane or vehicle came into sight. Unfortunately, determination of the names and origin of those who had come to murder, or a reasonable motive, could not be found. Still, Cameron was haunted by the fact that the terrorists must have primarily wanted *him* dead! He felt that Toby, Archie, Martin, and Buster were simply pawns that got in the way.

Fortunately, before the season ended, Toby was back in camp, good as ever and entertaining clients with stories of how he got the new part in his hair. Archie was cleared to fly again in a restored Gertie by the Civil Aviation Authorities and now had a very skilled young Afrikaner in the copilot's seat. Buster would always be missed, but Tillie, his widow, was made a nonflying partner in Safari Air, preserving at least that part of continuity. As for a new steward, Joshua, Martin's cousin, made a fine replacement, and he would see to providing for Martin's widowed mother. Iain thought, *All the ducks were now in a row. Some were new and most welcome, while the fallen would always be missed!*

Soon, fall came, and brought with it Iain's annual migration to the Highlands. Strapped snugly in one of Gertie's refurbished seats, Iain gazed from his window at the fascinating panorama passing by him. On the ground below, though not far below, for Archie was flying at 500 feet, stood or ran examples of all Africa's fabled animals. Drake frequently referred to it as "a Continental menagerie." Well tutored by Toby, Iain could recognize and name in English, Fangalo, Afrikaans, and even Latin all the species seen. Elephants, giraffes, rhinos, hippos, buffalo, and zebras were easy, but it got tougher when it came to kudu, wildebeest, impala, duikee, steinbuck, tressebe, eland, klipapringa, sable, gemsbok, roan, dik dik, springbok, and hartebeest, just to name a few.

For Iain, Africa had become a second home, though the Scottish Highlands would always be his true home. Now, as he sat back and savored the single-malt Scotch whiskey, which Joshua had served, Iain began to reflect on the mystery of the marauders who had invaded their camp. When nothing new came to mind, he decided to set it aside until presented with the opportunity to discuss it with an old friend still working among the Intelligence Spooks at MI-5. Just as he had made this decision, an enthusiastic voice interrupted further contemplation on the matter. "It's fun to fly isn't it Colonel?"

"Yes Sampson, but more fun when you aren't flying between the trees."

"I understand," the cook replied. Now addicted to flying, Sampson had missed no opportunity to take to the skies, and Archie was pleased to accommodate him.

Chapter Forty-Three

As ever, Heathrow Airport was a mad house when Iain disembarked the flight from Johannesburg to London. After Her Majesty's Customs was cleared, he grabbed the nearest public phone and dialed the number from memory. "Cahill here," resounded in the receiver.

"Rodney, Iain Cameron calling. Did I ring you up at a good time?"

"Iain, where in hell are you? I don't hear any elephants trumpeting in the background. Are you at home?"

"At Heathrow," came the reply, to which was added "I don't hear any secretaries giggling. I assume you are alone."

"Unfortunately yes," responded Cahill, who then added, "Budget cuts being what they are, the luscious gigglers have gone on to greener pastures. At MI-5, I'm fortunate to have a superannuated spinster who sighs periodically, then raises an eyebrow above the rim of her pince-nez glasses."

"You needn't feed me some of your implausible disinformation," was Iain's retort. "Would you consider dinner at the Savoy Grill this evening at eight sharp?"

"Should I bring my wallet?" Cahill asked, tongue in cheek.

"I don't see why. You've never opened it in my presence yet. I'll gladly foot the bill," jested Iain.

"Music to my ears," responded Cahill, who added, "Eight sharp, Savoy Grill."

Before hanging up, Cameron added, "One more thing—try and wear something subdued. That jacket you wore last time was rather ostentatious. I felt like I was seated across from a strobe light," said Cameron with a chuckle.

Cahill shot back, "It was the height of fashion and I know you relish being in the lime light. Besides that, my jacket was Cahill tartan, as I recall."

"Cahill tartan my arse. It looked more like a table cloth from a low-budget Italian restaurant," was Cameron's rejoinder.

"Very well, I'll wear something funereal, and you'll end up acting like some poor bastard forced to take a winter holiday in Scapa Flow," came Cahill's response. Both men laughed, and knew it would be a pleasure to see each other again.

Ex-Army Rodney Cahill was a former Captain in the Special Air Service, better known as SAS. After Iain had returned from his second tour in Malay, they had met for the first time and liked each other immediately, remaining stalwart friends. Rodney was a Senior Operative in British Intelligence, or MI-5, as it was known.

While dining together at the Savoy Grill, recollection of shared memories, exploits, and hunting parties was the initial topic of conversation. Bringing each other up to date on all that had transpired since they saw last each other was next. Tastebuds having savored with great relish very generous servings of the Savoy Grill's featured venison and a bottle of delectable Margaux, they sat back, sated. Warm snifters of an exquisite cognac and hand-rolled fine Havana cigars carefully cut were ignited, and Iain was ready to pick Rodney's brain in reference to the commando attack on his camp.

Intently, Cahill listened to the briefing, then meticulously delivered a small amount of cognac to his mouth to be savored before swallowing. Next, he drew in smoke from the smoldering cigar and finally exhaled before speaking. "Five or six Arabs; exact nationality unknown, and one possible Irishman, who appeared very much in charge. Of course, I would assume the Irishman to be the leader. As my surname indicates, a bit of green is in my own blood lines. For good or bad, my branch of the Cahill shed the popery early on, as they no doubt wished to avoid dangling offensively from some gibbet, as I'm sure some Camerons managed to do. You indicate these men were obviously intent on killing you and had no compunction in killing others. Have you had any run in with our Arab brethren, Iain?"

"Absolutely not! There have been some Arab princes who have been clients either in Scotland or Africa, but I can't imagine them wanting to do me in permanently," Iain replied.

"How about our Fenian cousins?" was Rodney's next question. "I never served in Ireland. However, there have been some hunting parties I have booked there. Lots of birds and great accommodations at some of the estates in the Republic. All of the negotiations were entirely affable. They have all expressed considerable desire to have my company book more hunting time," was Iain's reply.

"Since General Cameron passed away years ago, I can't imagine some hangfire vendetta developing now over anything he might have done." Cahill mused.

"Unlikely," Iain responded. "One might really consider the General almost pro-Irish, given the history of England's domination over both Scotland and Ireland. Besides, there was that bond that papists share, as you well know."

"Yes, but soldiers must also do their duty as long as it is moral, and sometimes duty can conflict with sentiment," was Rodney's response. Then, he continued, "Now, as I understand it, these fine furry, feathered, and creepy friends of yours out there in the Veldt or wherever, managed to devour anything of forensic importance from the corpses left strewn about, and the Johannesburg Medical Examiner came up with a gigantic goose egg. Skeletal remains of the tall one who you thought was likely Irish, showed no signs of old fractures, pins, or any other devices the orthopedic carpenters are prone to install."

"Some teeth were salvaged and in remarkably good condition. These were shopped around by Interpol, and not a single dentist, descendants of the old barber surgeons, recognized any of the fillings found as being their handiwork."

After a shrug, Cahill continued. "We wouldn't be much worse off if you had vaporized all your attackers with a nuclear device." After a pause for cognac refills, the two men coaxed the last bit of satisfying smoke from greatly shortened cigars. While frowning, Cahill spoke again. "Could we be in the wrong generation, Iain? Geordie, your soldier son, did kill a young Irishman in Belfast, as I recall. Wasn't it at a time fairly close to when the gang tried to kill you?" Immediately, Iain's attention was caught.

"You're right," he said "You might have hit on something!"

"Best lead we have," responded Cahill. "At least, it's a fox we can chase. In the meantime, you had best look over your shoulder while you're back home. Might not be a bad idea for the whole family to be cautious."

Before departing, there was the last vestige of repartee and a feigned fight over the dinner check. "Consider it a retainer for sleuthing service," Iain said with a smile.

Cahill shot back "I'd rather regard it as payment or fine for insulting my jacket. I'll be in touch, Iain, keep safe."

On the next morning, Cameron left for Edinburgh with hope that the mystery might be solvable. As usual, Sandy MacPhee was at Edinburgh Airport to welcome Iain home. Still straight as a ramrod, though less agile and a bit more gimpy, the old soldier barked out a greeting in a barracks barro cantante strong enough to send shivers down a recruit's spine. Luggage gathered, they were soon on their way to Capercaillie. Iain did note that Sandy was now driving a Rover with automatic transmission. Obviously, the old war wounds had made use of a clutch intolerable. While en route, Cameron fully briefed MacPhee on all the details of the raid and his meeting with Cahill.

When they were near the gate, Sandy explained, "I'll have a proper talk with the gamekeepers, ghillies, and gardeners, as well as the household help. We'll have a strong picket line in place, you can depend on that!"

Quickly, Iain picked up on the fact that MacPhee had braced himself even while driving and sharply added the title of respect. Automatically, Cameron straightened himself up, and answered smartly, "I know I can rely on you Sergeant Major," with extra rolls given to every "r" as was proper in the Highland dialect.

Homecoming for Iain would not be the same without a stop at the gatehouse to receive a hug, kiss, and torrent of happy tears from Molly MacPhee. After the crying stopped and sniffles ended, dear Mollie would admonish herself for being a silly, sentimental old woman. Then, straightening to her full five feet, four inches, she would always cast inspecting eyes on Iain and declare him "thin as a rail." Next, some of Scotland's finest scones, just out of the oven, were placed on the table, along with three cups of freshly steeped Darjeeling tea. Indeed, though Iain was famished, he remained standing, as he fully anticipated the next order of the day, which was ,"Take a seat Colonel. I expect you to eat at least five, but I'll be more pleased with six." Immediately, Iain sat down, and his conduct left no displeasure in his hostess.

Finally, at the steps of the manor house, "the laird" greeted all assembled there to welcome him home. Ancient was the tradition, and Iain could not help pondering how many times, and at how many manor houses, it had been repeated over the centuries. Doubtlessly, it was the same that greeted those who had fought with Wallace, Robert the Bruce, and Bonny Prince Charlie, as well as dozens of expeditions and scores of wars. Seeing his daughter-in-law and a toddler grandson hiding in the folds of her skirt and a wee granddaughter held in her arms, it brought back memories. Sweet was the temporary apparition of himself standing beside his own mother and welcoming a father, long at duty far away, that he really didn't know but would soon come to love.

Formalities now ended, Colonel Cameron showered and donned a kilt and a fine Shetland sweater, since there was a chill in the late afternoon air. Then, the first stop was the kennels, where there were many heads to pet and muzzles to rub. Raucous barking erupted from the older dogs, as their master's scent heralded his coming well before he came into view. Puppies whelped in Iain's absence joined the canine chorus, as they wished to participate in the excitement. After sufficient attention was given the older dogs, they were quieted by the handlers, so the pups could be introduced to their master and, immediately, they were vying for his attention. Soon, Tighe and Feather, now the canine seneschals of the kennel, were placed on leads, and Iain headed for the little bridge where he and Claire had spent so many beautiful hours together. Next was the cemetery for all the beloved dogs and even some horses. Finally, Iain came to the family graves, starting with ancestors that he had only heard about or noted in paintings on the wall of the great hall. Though prayers were said for all, Iain spoke only to his parents, Jud, his son, and Claire. Personal thoughts were expressed to each; however, a whole conversation was reserved for his beloved wife. Over the ensuing months, the little pilgrimages were repeated as often as Iain's busy schedule would allow.

Right in the midst of the gala shooting season, Cahill called, just before dinner. "Iain, Rodney here. I want to fill you in on information that I've gleaned since our meeting."

"I am all ears," Cameron responded.

"Much better in person," was Cahill's response. "You know how it is in the spy world, safe lines and all of that. Besides, I'll be much more prolix drinking your whiskey, shooting your birds, and flirting with those rich widows who chase you, despite your disdain."

"How can I pass up such a proposal from the world's friendliest freeloader?" was Iain's reply.

"I'll be there in time for dinner; set aside one of your finest rooms, old socks," came over the telephone line from Rodney's end.

"I trust you'll bring your own game," Iain responded, then continued, "That way you can't blame me for your singular lack of success."

"Of course," responded Rodney. "That pair of guns with the bent barrels you lent me last time severely injured my reputation as a crack shot."

Iain snorted and said, "Did I hear crack shot or crack pot?"

Cahill laughed, then he laughed harder when Iain added, "Bring a tuxedo to wear for dinner. You looked trollopy in that kilt you wore last year."

"I need a referee to keep you from hitting below the belt," was Rodney's rejoinder, and he ended with "See you on Thursday."

Iain added "I'll be anxious to greet you and hear what you found out. Thanks, Rodney, and see you Thursday!"

Soon, Capercaillie began to swell with arriving members of the Cameron clan. Eldest son, Iain Jr. the cardiologist, having arrived from the States was already ensconced with his wife, Amy, and their children. Now, a first Lieutenant, Geordie, who had been off on a training mission, was due back on the morrow to join Alysse and their children, who were already at hand.

Due to the severe and inclement weather of the spring, it had been a relatively poor season for Scottish red grouse, and a toll on the chicks was to be expected. Anticipating this, a large number of Chinese pheasants and partridges had been secured in pens and then released. Quickly reverting to a wild state, the birds would be hardy and high flyers and surely a test for any shooting sportsmen. Purposefully, Iain had limited the number of estates that he was supervising in the last week of August and first two weeks of September. Business was business, but kith and kin took precedence. Much as he loved the sport and camaraderie, it couldn't match cradling a grandchild in his arms or holding a wee hand as he led a little fellow or granddaughter, out in the glen to share the mystery and wonder found there. Besides, Major Wilson and Boyd Walker had become superb managers, and probably could run the enterprise just as well without him. However, pride and personal love of participation were hurdles over which Colonel Cameron chose not to jump. He would remain in control for all the foreseeable future, he had decided. Even so, Iain was a man who dealt with reality and the certainty that he wasn't immortal. While walking across a moor with a grandchild's hand warmly held in his own, conjecture would arise. *Will I live to see this toddler become an adolescent; anxious to learn how to safely handle a firearm, and use it with great proficiency? All up to God,* he would conclude.

On Thursday afternoon, just after one of Iain's pilgrimages, Rodney Cahill arrived punctually, as promised and expected. Fortunately, he was a favorite of all the family, so his visits were never intrusive. With charm, Cahill had the marvelous ability to convince all the guests who had never met him that he was indeed a super spy. Somehow, this was accomplished without him ever disclosing his employer, and certainly, Rodney never revealed any secrets. Just as some people have a Satanic aura, Cahill had one that proclaimed "spook." Especially, women were often spellbound, though to his credit Rodney only charmed the single, especially if wealthy and stunning.

Finally able to tear Cahill away from the circle of the newly entranced, Iain led him to his study and privacy. Conversation never commenced between the two great friends without a few verbal broadsides, and this occasion was no exception. "Damn it, Cameron! You always interrupt at the worst possible time," blurted out Rodney, feigning high dudgeon. "That luscious blonde with the cornflower blue eyes matching the nabob-sized sapphire highlighting her necklace was enchanted with me. Then, out of the blue, you butt in like some black cloud and rain on my parade!"

"That luscious blonde is living proof that a lady can give birth to five without losing her figure," was Iain's returning salvo. He continued, "Concentrate on the tall, slender matron with the black gown."

"You mean the one with the lace that comes up to her chin?" replied Rodney with glum inflection.

Iain smiled. "She is still in mourning, but the year will end soon and then she'll have to find ways to spend all those pounds that Sir Percy made in his massive, multinational empire," he responded, smiling.

"Good God! She's older than my aunt and not as good-looking. Even an impoverished professional bachelors have standards, old fellow! Well you have bested me for the moment, Cameron, but I won't sulk. Fill my glass with some of your private reserve, and we'll get down to business."

Having been served his whiskey neat, near golden in color, Cahill sat back while savoring the flavor unadulterated by icy water or soda, just as he preferred it. The drink brought a smile to his face and a smack to Rodney's lips. "Fantastic," he sighed. "All your outrageous barbs and arrows are forgiven." Then, with his countenance growing serious, Cahill continued. "I'm convinced, after a lot of sniffing around, that Geordie's gunfight in Belfast is absolutely linked to the attack on your camp. Byzantine labyrinths are said to be the most complex of all, but even they have an exit, if you can find it. However, none exists in this Irish maze, as far as I can determine. Geordie killed a man dressed as a chauffeur, as he probably told you. Furthermore, the deceased had driven up in front of Harris Department Store in a large Mercedes with a well-dressed and well-stacked young woman as the sole passenger. Later, massive amounts of Semtex were found in the car and deactivated. Unfortunately, the woman vanished. Not a shred of ID was found on the phony chauffeur, apart from a counterfeit driver's license with an obvious alias for a name and a nonexistent address. Despite the fact there was an intact body, it provided no more information to the Medical Examiner than the meager remains from Africa. No match for prints or dental records was found. In short, no one has the foggiest idea who he was. Oh yes, there was a round-up of Provos and, despite some heavy-handed interrogation, no helpful information was gleaned. Somewhat later on, another corpse turned up—a young woman dead as a result of a drug overdose, presumably self-administered. She was thought to fit the description of the passenger in the Mercedes, though no one was really sure. More interrogations took place, but no more information was gained. Of course, dead tartlets tell no tales!"

Thus far, as Cahill shared his recently acquired information, Cameron had remained silent. However, noting that crystal was starting to show in the bottom of Rodney's glass, he rose to refill it, knowing Cahill's engine always ran best on a full tank. After a sip, Cahill raised his glass in a tipster's salute, then continued.

"I got the bright idea that it might be possible to scientifically connect the Belfast body to the African one. My reading revealed that deep thinkers in the white lab coats have been playing with a substance called DNA, which is an acronym for some polysyllabic monstrosity that I cannot recall. At any rate, it's part of the makeup of the cells or tissues of all living things, and there are specific characteristics that allow one to say with considerable assurances that Chap A was related to Chap B, if you follow me?"

"I'm not totally lost yet," responded Iain, while in the process of refilling his own glass.

Cahill continued, "I was beginning to think I could find the egress in the labyrinth. My next step was to have the Belfast body disinterred, on the q.t. of course. When we opened the cheap pine coffin, it contained sand bags. The genius behind this must have been obsessive compulsive, for the bags weighed exactly 182 pounds, which was the weight of the corpse recorded by the Medical Examiner at the time of autopsy. Things get even better! Some old lady, who signed for the body saying it was that of her son is now reported to have something called Alzheimer's disease, which as best I can determine is a sort of end-stage dementia. Her relatives claim she can't even tell them what she is currently eating, much less what she had for breakfast. To make matters worse, she has moved to America. Perhaps, she's faking it, but rubber truncheons are not the favorite tool of the Yanks, especially on Grandma Moses. American relatives were of no help and, again, you can't beat it out of them!"

While slowly continuing to sip his drink, Cahill said, "Now, back to Belfast. The supposed embalmer who picked up the body is nonexistent. Apparently, those working in the morbid confines of the morgue are not prone to checking authenticity. Church services were never held, or at least admitted to being performed. An anonymous donor paid for the plot and opening of the grave, and six nondescript pallbearers carried the box to the grave site, then vanished. Obviously, there was once a body, and someone made damn sure we would never see it again. Provos have an affinity for peat bogs in which to bury problems. Perhaps, it may turn up sometime in the fourth millennium as the new Piltdown Man. Cremation or burial in the depths of the sea would have the same result. So, my friend, I'm still in the labyrinth, with no clear way out. I'll keep looking, but I don't expect to find the exit!"

Looking grave, Iain said, "We kid a bit Rodney, but you are one hell of a friend. I can't say how much I appreciate all you have done."

While cocking his head, Cahill smiled, replying, "Another dram of your private reserve would be a fine start."

A bit later, Iain and Rodney retired. Both were anticipating a wonderful weekend of shooting and friendship, and the following two days were exciting in the extreme; however, they passed all too quickly. Suddenly, it seemed, Sunday had arrived and it was a day committed to church and rest, with a generally accepted prohibition on hunting.

Returning from Catholic Mass with the rest of the Cameron clan and a few guests, Iain was surprised to see Rodney busily packing up for his return to London. Even more unusual was the fact that several of the household staff recalled having seen Cahill leaving for the Episcopal services in the Rover, in which the Roffeys were riding.

"I've heard of born-again Christians, but not evolving Episcopalians," muttered Iain to no one in particular. When Cahill returned, he brushed by Cameron with a smile, and said, "I've got to load up the Jag, Iain. Give me a hand, will you?"

When the luggage was secured, Rodney turned to his host and said, "I've thought a lot about the labyrinth, Iain. I figure there is someone with cunning connections and a big sack of pound notes behind what happened in Africa. No run-of-the-mill Provo soldier or even a cell leader could pull enough strings to get Quadafi to lend him a plane and recruit a squad from the Becca Valley. My working hypothesis at the moment is that Geordie killed one of the sons of a very influential Fenian, who probably sent a second son to obtain retribution."

"Why me and not Geordie?" asked Iain.

"Geordie was in an Army Hospital, so it was very hard to get to him. Additionally, in some cultures, slaying the patriarch is the first step in the vendetta."

"That is very incisive intuition, Rodney," intoned Cameron, while firmly setting his face, as the logic of the deductions took hold.

"Maybe so," responded Cahill. "But, we are still light years away from knowing who such a father might be, and how many sons he might have to send out as knights errant." After pausing and reflecting, Rodney continued the conversation. "Your enemy might be out of sons to send after you, at least older ones up to the job. Therefore, he might come after you himself. We already know that Mr. X has the money and connections to do that. At any rate, *en garde* old friend. This goes for all the family as well. While it isn't good news, I would rather leave you all very concerned and especially cautious!"

"Again, Rodney, I'm profoundly grateful," Cameron said somberly.

"Not nearly as grateful, as I am," responded Cahill, "for I have soiled your finest linen, eaten the most delectable food on the planet, depleted your reserve of distinguished potables, and shot your birds."

"I'll give you a high score on the first three," jested Iain. "But I think it more accurate to say you shot at my birds."

"All in the name of conservation, old fellow," replied Cahill.

Smiling, Iain said, "You forget that the fine restaurants of London pay handsomely for our downed birds, my dear fellow."

Cahill winked, then responded, "That will be foremost in my mind when I take aim on my next invitation." This brought a laugh from Iain, who was about to extend his hand, and wish his friend a safe trip back.

Before departing, Rodney Cahill had one last question to ask, "Iain, I must know. Were you responsible for the seating assignments at dinner the past three nights?"

"That is left to my daughters-in-law," responded Cameron, with a quizzical look.

"Please convey my affectionate thanks," replied Rodney. "Either by guile or good fortune, I was placed alongside Miss Abigail Roffey, who came from Australia in the company of her parents. Perhaps, it may have occurred because she and I, apart from yourself, were the only singles present at dinner. Of course, you as host would be at the head of the table. Abby is a beautiful young lady in all respects and, quite frankly, I've fallen in love with her, and I believe she might have an interest in me."

"Does this perhaps explain your sudden religious fervor?" quipped Iain.

"Oh I should have known the keen-eyed, ever observant hunter would have noted that." Then, Cahill continued. "I was up early, and happened to encounter Abby, and she asked me if I would like to go to church with her and her parents. Perhaps, she saw enough good in me that she assumed I was a church-goer. Immediately, I blurted out that I'd love to go. During my whole life, I can never remember wanting to go to church, but at that moment I really desired to go. No doubt, God was aware that I went to impress her, rather than Him. But at the service while He and I were getting reacquainted, I suggested I was ready to change. Fortunately, I was able to recall enough of the rubrics to pass myself off reasonably well." As Rodney continued, Iain remained quietly listening. "You probably think of me as a rake, as well as a raconteur my friend, but I'm really not. During the early years with SAS, I never could be sure I would return from an operation, and I had no desire to leave a widow and children behind. Problem wise, it was the same during my stint, as the Scarlet Pimpernel. When

I met you and Claire, I was filled with admiration, and also envy, though still I wasn't at ease seeking a spouse. Now, I've met Abby, and I'm desk bound and reasonably safe from getting killed. Best news is that she is a nurse like Claire and is taking a six-month postgraduate course at Guy's Hospital in London starting next week. Her parents will stay on for a fortnight to get her settled, then she'll be on her own. They even asked me to look after her, and I intend to do so in a very proper way. However, there is a ten-year difference in our ages, still, as you know, I'm young at heart." While seeming to pour his personal secrets out, Cahill said, "Better still, she is young enough to have children, and I would very much like that."

Iain smiled broadly and crushed Rodney's hand. "Blessings, my friend, and I am sure you will be able to aim your heart much better than your pair of Purdys."

Just then, the topic of their one-sided conversation came running down the stairs. "Oh Rod, I'm so happy you haven't left! Daddy said we would be staying at the Connaught and will arrive a week from today. He insists on another week of shooting with the Colonel, but then we'll come."

"I would never have left without bidding adieu," Rod said gallantly.

Feeling much the supernumerary, Iain said his good-bye to Cahill once again along with profound gratitude. Turning, as he reached the door, Cameron noted Cahill bestowing a light kiss on Abby Roffey's cheek. "Quite proper indeed," he said to the closing door. Then, despite concern over the warning words Cahill had issued, Cameron was elated at his friend's happiness. Perhaps, he might be called on to serve as best man before Africa beckoned.

After Rodney's departure, Colonel Cameron held a conference with Iain Jr. and Geordie, along with Sandy MacPhee, Wilson, and Walker. Speaking to his sons, their concerned father remarked, "You two can discuss this matter with Amy and Alysse in the manner you see fit, as we don't want to frighten them unduly, but forewarned is forearmed. They are calm, resourceful ladies, and I'm sure they will take it in stride." Then, Sandy MacPhee reiterated all the actions he had already put in place, then broached the subject of new ones that had come to mind. All agreed that his ideas were solid and well worth the undertaking. Gamekeepers, long skilled in surveillance, could just as easily spot a two-legged wolf as a four-legged fox. Wilson and Walker averred that special care would be taken at Cameron and Sons shop and office in Perth in regard to phone calls or customers that did not fit the profile of their usual clients.

When the meeting concluded, a couple of drams of good Scot's whiskey was downed, and talk shifted to lighter subjects. Ever wary and ever prudent, Colonel Cameron took on the task of passing along warnings to his sisters and their husbands, though Jane and her family were unlikely targets. Annie and her family commuted between their country home and Capercaillie, depending on the season. Annie's husband, Bruce McKay, was not ex-military, but he had many of their attributes and was a crack shot, so as far as Colonel Cameron was concerned, they had done all that was reasonable for safety's sake. He thought, *One couldn't live in a vault and if and when trouble came, they would face it! Sinister, as the assailants might be, they were nothing compared to the raiding Norsemen that his ancestors had dealt with centuries ago.* Soon, another gala shooting season was swiftly drawing to a close, and not a single threat was perceived. For some, that was welcome, though security remained a high priority. Others felt it a great relief, with resultant relaxation.

Chapter Forty-Four

On Colonel Cameron's calendar, Christmas and New Year's were pivotal points. Packing up duffel and kit would soon follow hard on the heels of Christmas shopping and yule logs, plus setting up Claire's beloved crèche, midnight Mass, and the Christmas feast. Then, five days after the last toast of New Year's Eve, and the final verse of "Auld Lang Syne," it would be back to Africa.

At least once every week, Toby Drake could be counted on to ring Iain up, and he seemed to be unusually talkative. Iain attributed this to the fact that nearly all the news was good. Bookings were described as fantastic, game was as plentiful as Drake had ever seen, and a high proportion had horn, tusks, or manes of trophy proportions. *Fortunately,* thought Iain, *Toby has to fly back to Johannesburg to call me. If there were a telephone in camp, I'd probably hear from him twice a day.* After closing off the latest call, Iain chuckled and thought, *Sure, old Toby is verbose to a fault, but he's a champion in all other respects. How would I make it with some silent sneak and swindler? Far better to have your ear talked off than your fortune wiped out.*

Shortly, the Christmas holiday had arrived, and for Colonel Cameron and growing clan, the birth of the Christ child's celebration was filled with love and remembrances. Intermittent sadness occurred for Iain, when reflecting on the wonderfully soft touch of Claire's delicate hands, protruding from the sleeves of her favorite fur coat and seeking the encompassing warmth of his hands. Iain remembered Claire had never lost the childlike wonderment of opening her gifts. Now, the presence of his grandchildren and time had eased the loss, partially atoning for her absence. Still, there were voids that could never be filled.

Also, New Year's had always been difficult for Iain. Ever since boyhood, it had struck him as a somewhat melancholy day.

Recently, he had felt it might be better spent on inventorying and reflection on the past twelve months a munificent God had bestowed on him. This he did in quiet moments that came his way; yet in the assembly of dear friends and loved ones, Cameron would strive to be the ever gracious, charming host.

With holidays over, according to ritual established and expected, Sandy MacPhee would drive Iain to the airport for departure back to Africa. On the way down the A-9 highway his old Sergeant Major brought into their conversation consideration of "the Threat," as he called Cahill's hypothesis. "I've been thinking, Colonel. Young Doctor Iain and his family are off in America and reasonably safe. Also, your sister Jane and family are out of the country while Annie and family live either at Capercaillie or nearby, which increases their risk. Geordie, Alysse, and their children are at the greatest peril, especially since Geordie started the whole thing, if Captain Cahill is correct." So ingrained in the military was the retired Sergeant Major that he would always use a title of rank, if he could find a way to make it appropriate. "Would it not be best if Alysse and the children stayed at the manor house full time, until no further threat is thought possible?"

"You're right, Sergeant Major," replied Iain, who also felt more comfortable using military titles when strategy was being discussed. "However, as we both know, Army life demands much sacrifice in the separations of men and wives already. While I wholeheartedly agree with you, I'm not sure that I should try and impose my will, despite how prudent that choice might be. As you know, Geordie will be stationed in London the next two years, and it would be hell to have Alysse 300 miles away. On this one, I think we'll just have to rely on their good judgment and God's protection. However, you've given me a good idea. I'll call Captain Cahill while I'm in London and tell him to line up any aid he can to help keep an eye on my dear ones."

During the rest of the trip, small talk, mutual memories, and future plans were discussed. Then, before parting handshakes, Iain reassured MacPhee that the dozen scones sent along by Molly were safely secured, though readily accessible. Dear Mrs. MacPhee had been certain the Colonel would be on half rations all the way to Johannesburg. She was not the type of lady who could bear to think of her husband's savior facing starvation.

When the flight's last call resounded, Colonel Cameron was happy to note that his Sergeant Major had finally accepted a handshake as the means for gentlemen to say good-bye! For several years, people nearby had been mildly alarmed and then amused to hear the ritual resonation of Sergeant MacPhee's leather heels on the terminal tile followed by a resounding "SIRrrr!," which could be heard far out on the tarmac.

When Cameron arrived at Heathrow, he did ring up Cahill. Being as the time was after six P.M. he tried the phone number for Rodney's Kensington flat. After two rings, the familiar "Cahill here," was intoned into Iain's receiver.

"I do believe this is the first time I have ever called your flat and got an answer. Are you ill?" asked Cameron without giving his name.

"Colonel Cameron I presume," was Rodney's reply. "I suppose you are on the way back to Africa to help the super-rich make rugs out of all those huggable, defenseless creatures. May I add that you are wrong about never reaching me at my flat. As I recall, you did reach me one morning at 0500 hours!"

"I'm dreadfully sorry, you are right of course," replied Iain with feigned condolence. "If memory serves me right, you had just come in and were terribly hungover, so our conversation was punctuated by repeated acts of emesis on your part. Hopefully, you are not nauseated at the moment."

"No I'm not, but I can't take long, as I have much to do," Rodney responded in an assertive tone.

"Don't tell me you are falling on hard times, and MI-5 has you working the night shift," was Iain's response.

"My dear fellow if you must know, I'm in the throes of preparing pheasant under glass, plus crêpes Suzette, Caesar salad, and lobster bisque all from the original recipes of Henri Carpentier, Caesar Cardini and Escoffier."

Amazed, Cameron retorted "You must be trying to get a merit badge in cooking, so you can rise to the rank of Eagle Scout!"

After a slight pause, Cahill reiterated. "Sorry, but I don't have time for guffaws, Iain, as I am in the process of preparing a candlelight dinner for two. Furthermore, I intend to propose to Miss Abigail Roffey sometime between crêpes and cognac. Instead of a new Jag, which I surely need, my entire savings has been spent on one of DeBeers' sparkly pieces of carbon. You are now up to date on the life and times of Rodney Cahill, hopefully husband to be! However, I trust I have time before the birds burn, and the romaine wilts to tell you I'm still very serious about the labyrinth, and I devote all the time and resources I can to solving the threat."

Quickly, Iain told his friend about Geordie and his family living in London. "No fox will invade that hen house while this old hound is on guard," was Cahill's assurance.

With all sincerity, Cameron thanked his friend and bestowed his blessings on the proposal. "Let me know when you set the date," Iain continued. "I assume you won't elope."

"Elope indeed!" Cahill shot back. "I told you this was to be a very proper courtship, and I assume against all urges that I'll patiently await the publishing of bands and observe all the proprieties."

"Well I'll let you go now, Monsieur le Chef," said Iain happily. "But, I must ask one last question. Where did you buy the pheasants? I'm damn sure that you didn't shoot them."

After laughing, Cahill added, "I have only four words for you, sir, and they are: Good-bye you clever bastard."

After hanging up the phone, within ten hours, Colonel Cameron would be in Johannesburg. Safari Air would be there to take him on the final leg, and Toby Drake welcome him back to Cameron's second home. Despite first-class accommodations, Iain had managed to eat all the scones Molly had prepared.

If anyone could have comprehended how close his analysis paralleled actuality, Cahill would have been heralded as a clairvoyant. Indeed, there was an older man on the western side of the Irish Sea who very much wished revenge for the killing of his two sons. Lack of desire had played no role in the surcease the Camerons had enjoyed these past few months. Instead, they had been spared by Mickey Moynihan's need for convalescence and rehabilitation, necessitated by the devastating injuries he had received in the auto accident. His partial recovery having been achieved, Mickey was involved in further rehabilitation with reckless abandonment. There was still pain with strenuous exercise, but he conquered it by willpower alone. Although Moynihan knew he could never run again, he could walk long and hard. Most important, Mickey was able to climb the steepest trails. Exuberant callous formations, uniting the fragments of his fractured pelvis, made sitting a saddle an ordeal. Though Mickey fancied it the same as sitting on top of a pocket full of rocks, extreme stoicism and begrudging addition of a little padding to the seat of his saddle, made it endurable. Warlord, Moynihan's great stallion, now raced and jumped to his noble heart's content and the fullness of his master's fervor. For Mickey, all manners of exercise equipment filled in the moments between riding, walking, and climbing. Also, time was taken to revisit the areas of his Provo youth to sharpen his skills with rifles and pistols. While in the vicinity of the cliffs, bordering the Atlantic, Moynihan took advantage of the opportunity to climb steep trails, which most would consider the purview of goats.

At almost the exact time Iain left for Africa, Mickey decided the time had come for reprisal. Along with the recapture of much of his physical prowess, Mickey had continued a mental metamorphosis. Confrontation with Colonel Cameron was what he desired, along with recognition that he, too, was a soldier of equal courage. As in the days of dueling, satisfaction was what Mickey demanded and what he expected to receive! Nonetheless, that far-off time, when hurling your gauntlet at an opponent's feet would precede a duel, was long past. Moynihan felt some way must be found to force a man-to-man meeting, with a duel to the death! Colonel Cameron and his sons had killed Sean and Liam, in what Mickey could only construe as fair fights. Even though he lacked details of what exactly had transpired in Africa, Moynihan was well aware that the Colonel could not possibly have had advantage in men, firepower, or foreknowledge. Therefore, Moynihan had decided he had killed from ambush in the past, but to do so now would forever mark him as less the man than Cameron and lacking in chivalry. Finally, time had come to flesh out the bare skeleton of revenge with what he hoped would be a cunning plan.

Having no idea that Rodney Cahill even existed, Moynihan was ignorant of his brilliant hypothesis and the faith that Cameron had in it. Nonetheless, Mickey had decided he was not dealing with fools, thus, he should make no concessions to chance. Made while he had reconnoitered in Scotland, Sean's notes were scattered atop the desk in front of him. An entry, under "Cameron and Sons, Perth," indicated that his son had visited Cameron's shop and headquarters. Underlined on the next page was Colonel Cameron in Africa. *Could someone have been astute enough to make a connection between Sean conducting inquiries, and a man of similar description showing up soon afterward at Cameron's camp? Probably not, but safer to assume they did.* Suddenly, Mickey smashed the desktop. "Foolish Arabs!" he shouted. "I didn't get one stinkin' bit of information from them regarding Sean's remains. All they cared about was getting their fookin' airplane back. Duplicitous, scheming bastards," Mickey murmured, as he quieted down, then concluded that cursing Arabs didn't bring Sean back to life.

Besides, the plan had been Sean's. "Best I see to my own preparations," he decided, only to discover his mind seemed locked and he was incapable of shifting to another gear. Arising from his chair, Moynihan decided that he needed sleep, a precious physiologic commodity of which he had deprived himself during his arduous rehabilitation phase.

Six hours later, upon arising, Moynihan was much sharper and came to the immediate conclusion that he would catch an afternoon flight from Belfast to Manchester, England. While there, he would obtain another good night's repose. Then, driving from Manchester to Scotland would provide him with an opportunity for planning, as Mickey often thought that perspectives became clearer when he was in motion. Upon arrival in the English city, Mickey proceeded to a four-star Hotel, and the suite reserved under the appellation of Patrick Broderick, which was one name from the list of a dozen aliases he maintained.

Using the right clandestine services, he knew all too well that it was easy to keep passports and driver's licenses updated. However, Moynihan always used alias names that he could easily remember. Patrick Broderick was the shopkeeper who had thrashed him soundly when he had tried to snatch a candy so many years ago. Mickey was six at that time and had never even tasted a candy. However, fortunes had greatly changed for him and when it came to payment of bills, traveler's cheques were used rather than cash, as they always came across as more touristy. Besides, it would be impossible to maintain a stable of credit cards on twelve people who didn't really exist. Hotels with all the stars were booked out of habit only. Since Bernie's death, a hotel was no more than a place of privacy, with the necessity of bed and bathroom. However, the presence of a conscientious and capable concierge was a plus found only in pricey places.

When Mickey arrived at the hotel, to the young female at the reception desk, Mr. Broderick seemed to fit the expected mold of a well-to-do New Yorker. Obviously, he looked Irish, and there was a hint of a brogue in his speech. After checking into the hotel and having a good night's rest, at nine o'clock on the next morning, a rented Jaguar sedan was parked beneath the hotel marquee thanks to the action of the concierge. Deftly, Mickey guided the car through the last vestige of the morning traffic rush and was soon on the way north to Blackburn, where he would turn northeast to Skipton, then on to Harrogate. Though travel wise, it was longer and slower, this route was much less used than the more direct way via Leeds. After Harrogate would come Consett, New Castle upon Tyne, and finally Edinburgh. Welcomed to the Caledonian Hotel in the late afternoon, Mr. Patrick Broderick was booked for one night only, with departure the next morning, for the city of Aberdeen was Mickey's final destination. Geographically, Aberdeen was close enough to Perth and Dunkeld; the site of Cameron's headquarters and home so as to make them reasonably accessible. Also, most beneficial, was the fact Aberdeen was large enough to grant anonymity. Mickey had decided long ago that small town's accommodations always came with overly inquisitive or friendly folk, who seemed desirous of sharing the highlights of one's life, so best avoid them. Since North Sea petroleum deposits had turned Aberdeen into a bustling commercial city, if asked what your business might be, one could simply reply "oil." Immediately, black gold conjured up elements of secrecy and excitement, which seemed to dissuade all but the most resolute to inquire no further.

Driving from Aberdeen down to Dundee on the following day, Moynihan was pleased to find the City Library. Deciding that "oil" was inappropriate as an explanation to the inquisitive gray-haired librarian, Mickey found "genealogy" followed by a smile worked very well. Mickey's research proved relatively simple and rewarding, as the Camerons were frequently written about and their comings and goings to wars, or whatever synonym deemed politically correct at the time, were prominent and easily accessible. Since important people are given much greater coverage in regard to births, deaths, and marriages, Mickey faced no mind-numbing task in gleaning all the information he needed. Even obituaries were sources of necessary information that he desired, since the city and town of residence for surviving next of kin were dutifully provided. Back at his hotel room, after a reasonably satisfying dinner of Scottish salmon, Mickey consulted his notes, and the highlights read as follows:

"Lt. Colonel Iain Cameron departed for Africa on 5 January, wife is deceased. Lt. Justin Cameron middle son Naval Aviator killed in combat, Falkland Islands. Dr. Iain Jr. eldest son Cardiologist trained in USA now practicing in Spokane, Washington, USA. Lt. George youngest son stationed Scots Guards Hdq. London. HE KILLED LIAM. Annie Cameron youngest sister of Col. Cameron husband Bruce McKay sometimes stays at Capercaillie Manor, but most often at Country Home outside Blairgowrie 2 children, late teens."

Lying back on the bed in his underwear, Mickey began to arrange all the information in the neat files of his mind. "It's the soldiers I want most of all, but I'll also take the oldest son of the Colonel in time. Women and children are out of the question. That kind of killing is for Provos and Prods without conscience, and probably those drug lords who are sprouting up like poisonous mushrooms. However, I could use a woman or child as bait and still do them no harm. Unless I wait for Colonel Cameron to return when he plans to come, I'll need a means to lure him back to the place where I intend to kill him. Forced to return hurriedly from Africa would leave him at a disadvantage, and deprived of the resources he would have here."

Sometime back, Mickey had decided the duel that he desired would take place on Skellig Michael. Now, he must determine what pawn to move, so as to force the knight to the predetermined jousting ground. At that moment in his planning, sleep overcame Mickey. His plan's completion would be contemplated again when further information was at hand.

On the following morning, Aberdeen was left behind and soon Mickey closed in on Blairgowrie. In the phone directory, Annie's husband, Bruce McKay, was listed, though the address shown was meaningless without a map. Fortunately, resolution came quickly because finding homes in the Highlands was an arduous, frustrating task for nearly everyone, and maps were made with tiny labeled dots scattered about, indicating just where everything was located. Furthermore, there was one on display in the post office, making access easy and anonymous. Easter Cairn, the McKay home, was no exception; soon, Mickey was driving past it, then, stopping later to add to his notes.

Before returning to Edinburgh, Mickey had a compulsion to see Cameron's shop and office in Perth, perhaps because Sean had once stopped there. "I'll just walk by," he decided. "No going in, as Sean did." While passing the shop's window, Mickey noted an older man looking out. He had the appearance of a proprietor waiting for a customer to enter. Though not looking directly at the former Major Wilson, and not knowing that he was the man who Sean had talked with, Mickey could see enough of his face to tell a puzzled look was developing.

Immediately, Mickey recognized it was the countenance of a man, who is trying to decide if they have recognized a person of interest. Indeed, Wilson was coming to the conclusion that the man passing by the window bore a striking resemblance to the younger man that he had talked with about Colonel Cameron months before. Countless reflections on that meeting, and all of Cahill's speculations, spurred his imagination and suspicions. The man was nearing the door. *Would he come in?* wondered Wilson.

Meanwhile, suspecting what might be going through the other man's mind, Mickey cast a disparaging look at a mounted grouse in the shop window, and muttered loud enough to be heard on the inside, "Despoilers of nature!" Although Wilson was somewhat disarmed by the epithet, he was still consumed by the association he had postulated. Moynihan passed the entry and proceeded down the street. Nonetheless, he was aware that a man had come out of the shop, probably to question him. *Similarity proves nothing,* Mickey thought. *But I can't be sure this fellow might not have some pull with the constables, and I don't need anyone checking into me.* As the other man drew near, Mickey spied a place of possible sanctuary and entered. Wilson stopped short. He didn't have to read the sign as he passed the shop each day, and knew it well. Wilson mumbled in a half-loud voice, "Monique's Uni-Sex Hair Styling, terrorist indeed," he lectured himself. "As any Army man would know, only a fop would enter such a place."

Wilson returned to Cameron and Sons, apologized to his customer and immediately proceeded to find the fly rod in which he was interested. As for Mickey, he made an appointment for a permanent wave one week hence. Having noted the sign saying "Parking in the rear" when he had entered, Moynihan left through the back door. "Sometimes the little unexpected things one does may be their salvation," he muttered. Then, he added, "How small the hinges upon which fate swings."

Soon, the Jaguar was under way, with one more stop in Edinburgh, then a return to Manchester and, finally, Belfast. *Now*, he thought, *All the pieces were on the chessboard*, and Moynihan would figure which to move and when!

Once back in his home in Grey Abby, Mickey forced himself to return to the rigors of his exercise routine during the day. Evenings were left for planning how to lure Iain Cameron to Skellig Michael. Force was the only real option, and that must take the form of presenting the Colonel with a hostage situation. Someone very near and dear to him had to be kidnapped. Then, it had to be made clear to Cameron that the only way to spare the life of a loved one was to accept the proposal of a duel. Win or lose, that particular hostage would be set free. However, Mickey didn't expect to lose, and he would let Annie Cameron McKay go unharmed. Sparing the lives of Cameron's two living sons would not, of course, be part of the bargain. Annie was not only the logical choice to snatch, she was the only one. Consequently, copious notes on other family members were set aside, and Moynihan's entire focus centered in hard on the sister's file.

Knowing that virtually every human being has some kind of routine, and this was a fact that assassins and kidnappers had relied on for centuries, Mickey began a search for opportunity. Mickey noted that being gentry and generous of time and money, the Camerons had piled up an enviable record of philanthropy and community service. Annie was no exception, and this was verified by the numerous Society Column activities which Mickey had poured over in Dundee. Shuffling through the file's papers, Moynihan came across one article that had particularly caught his attention at the time of his note taking. "Mrs. Annie Cameron McKay was presented the Lady of the Year Award by members of the Women's Guild of Perthshire." Among the young woman's attributes, which the award mentioned, was perfect attendance at the bimonthly meetings for the past five years. Fortunately, the article was of recent vintage and also mentioned that any ladies interested in joining the guild need only come to the ten A.M. meetings, held on the first and third Tuesdays of every month at St. Andrew's Episcopal Parish Hall. Knowing the Camerons were Catholic from his survey of births, deaths, and marriages, Mickey chuckled, as he thought, *The Camerons certainly are broad mindedly ecumenical.*

Having discerned the location of the guild's meetings were in Perth, Mickey knew Annie would have to drive. Since a woman's guild was exclusionary, there was no need to think her husband would attend, nor would her teenage children. "Snatching ACM," as Mickey began to call her, "wouldn't be smart in the church parking lot," he decided. "However, I must grab her before or after the meeting," was his conclusion. Taking up a pencil, Mickey wrote "BEFORE," in large letters atop the page of a clean sheet of paper, Below, he wrote "Not inside or outside her house—domestic help might be present. Road into Perth poor as this would be too conspicuous." Then, looking over the few lines written, it was obvious to Mickey that the snatch was not to be before the meeting.

After crumpling the paper in a tightly clutched hand, Moynihan threw it in a wastepaper basket and grabbed a new sheet, which he labeled "AFTER." Below, he wrote, "Highway and home out for same reason, as before." While laying down his pencil, Mickey started to concentrate on what a woman would likely do after the meeting? *No doubt, she would probably go to lunch with some friends,* he concluded. *Then what?* he pondered. *Well, if Bernie were still alive and she were going to such a meeting, then afterward, she would probably save an hour or so to shop.* Picking up the pencil, he wrote, "Best time after presumed lunch." Then he added heavy underlining.

Chapter Forty-Five

When Moynihan left Belfast on the following week, his destination was Glasgow. Now he was traveling under the alias of Harry Crosby, an easy name to remember, as it was the true given and surname for the legendary singer. However, only a rare individual knew of him by any other name than Bing Crosby, thus, no attention was given it. Mr. Crosby went from the Glasgow Airport to a downtown car rental agency and secured the use of a large van for a two-week period. Several advantages could be found in a conveyance of that nature. First, it was associated with commerce and not particularly suspicious. Best, however, was the fact that the closed cargo compartment afforded considerable privacy. One could easily change clothes or hide a kidnapped victim without detection. While proffering a bogus business card, Moynihan said to the agency's clerk, "Antique furniture dealer from the States," with a smile. "If you find something good, then you need a conveyance to haul it away. I'm mostly into smaller things though—lamps, clocks, armor, vases, and stuff like that. If I can't carry it, I don't buy it." Finding Mr. Crosby's patter what she would expect from a Yank, the young clerk was mildly entertained and asked no questions.

Edinburgh wasn't a long drive from Glasgow, and Mickey arrived in late afternoon. On this occasion, a modest hotel was selected on the northern fringe of Edinburgh and close to the Firth of Forth bridge. Prior to signing the register, Mr. Crosby asked the clerk if there was adequate space to park his van, and he received a cordial, "Of course. We take pride in watching over our guests."

After a good night's sleep, Mickey was on the road early the next morning for Perth. An old bed cover, which he had brought along, was spread over the driver's seat. As soon as they had a look at it, anyone observing would understand the purpose, after they had a glimpse at the driver. "Very practical thing for a mechanic in those grease-covered overalls," would immediately come to mind.

While driving north, Moynihan was having some misgivings. Plan-wise, it was far from a sure thing. Yes, ACM had won the award for perfect attendance, but maybe she had decided to rest on her laurels, and let someone else gain whatever glory the Woman's Guild was capable of bestowing. "Hell," he snorted, "she could be sick in bed." Mickey's ire with himself grew with each mile. Had he ever set off on such a cockamamie mission with so many unanswered questions? Rebuffing the riddles inside his psyche, Moynihan took hold of the situation. "Look, you fool, you aren't committed to anything. Any time it looks like a loser, just back away. You haven't put yourself in any danger until you actually grab her!"

Only a short time later, Annie Cameron McKay didn't notice the white van parked about 100 feet from her driveway and, if she had, she would only have seen a rather greasy chap studying a road map. That man must have found what he wanted, for he pulled on to the highway behind her, just seconds after she passed. *ACM is going for another perfect attendance record,* thought Mickey, when he saw her Jaguar sedan pull into St. Andrew's parking lot. "Not only a perfect attendee but punctual as hell," Mickey murmured.

Carefully, Moynihan parked his van in the periphery of the church's parking lot, then moved into the van's rear compartment. Always wary and highly intuitive, Mickey knew women were suspicious if a man was sitting behind a wheel of any car and giving the appearance he was checking things out. "Could that man be some kind of predator?" they would warn themselves. Conversely, vehicles that appeared empty yet clean and in good repair seldom even registered, especially when white in color. Also, knowing women were frequently late for meetings; waiting for nails to dry, dropping off laundry, or trying to decide what ensemble to wear, he elected to bide his time, so one and a half hours after the meeting was convened, he chose to move into action. Waiting longer would have increased risk by one of the ladies leaving early.

After starting the van, Moynihan moved it into a vacant space closest to ACM's car. When the driver's side door opened, a coverall-clad man emerged with a mechanic's cap pulled well down on his head. Sufficient grease was deployed on his coveralls and exposed skin to make a convincing pictorial representation of a hard-working mechanic out on a call. Suddenly, he was prone on the asphalt and, just as quickly, he slid beneath the Jaguar, then, immediately brought his arms under the radiator. Having gained considerable mechanical experience back in the old days at Sweeney's, in addition, Mickey was a car buff.

Thus, he was well acquainted with some of the proclivities of the Jaguar XJ-6 sedan.

Unlike Achilles, who had only one vulnerable spot, the 1974 Jaguar had a number of them, and Mickey intended to attack the soft underbelly of the sedan. British Motor Car was obsessive when it came to radiator hoses, and nothing would do but the use of natural gum rubber, fashioned in sigmoid configurations. One of these was attached to the top and bottom of the radiator. After quickly spying the lower hose, Moynihan slid a stiletto out of his sleeve. In a second, the razor-sharp tip had pierced the rubber hose, destroying its integrity. Without any pressure building up in the cooling system of the automobile, the leak for the moment at least, would remain imperceptible. However, when the engine was running, loss of coolant would occur in significant volume, and engine overheating would take place. At that point in time, steam emerging from under the bonnet would be obvious to the driver, as would the dramatic change in the temperature gauge. Any prudent motorist would pull to the side of the road and turn off the ignition. For those who didn't, seizure of the overheated engine parts would force the car to a halt.

Deftly, Moynihan pulled himself from beneath the sabotaged Jaguar and returned to his van unobserved. Settling back in the driver's seat, Mickey soon had the van under way, returning back to the spot it had originally occupied in the church's parking lot. Ensconced in the van's rear compartment once again, Moynihan was essentially undetectable. Nonetheless, he could see Annie's car and, thus, he waited.

Fifteen minutes after the meeting was supposed to end, women in singles, pairs, trios, and an occasional quartet began to emerge. In the tail end of those departing, Mickey recognized from a newspaper photo ACM engaged in conversation with two other women of similar age. All were dressed stylishly in garb of obvious quality. Pausing next to a BMW sedan, the trio appeared to have some plan under discussion. Shortly, breakup came, and each entered their individual cars, heading off in a little convoy.

Following discreetly in the van, Mickey began to note a little trail of antifreeze-tinted water beneath his quarry's car. Fortunately, for Mickey's plans, the ladies did not have far to travel and, soon, all were parked at the quaint Inn of the White Hackle. One hour and forty minutes passed without a sign of their emergence. Now, hidden again, in the rear of his van, Mickey took time to have his own lunch and relieve his full bladder in a little bag brought for that purpose. Finally, a trio of young women, including Annie Cameron McKay, emerged to Moynihan's relief. However, consternation followed quickly, when they all stopped to chatter. "Blasted women can't pull themselves away from mindless conversation," he fumed. "You'd think they hadn't seen each other since grade school. They can bleed a topic until it's exsanguinated." As if in answer to his mutterings, the ladies started to pull away from each other, though they still called back with their faces turned in the other's direction.

Finally, ACM was in her car. First, the brake lights illuminated, then the back-up lights. Emerging from the parking lot, she turned in the direction of home, while the other two ladies left in opposite directions. Following in the van, Mickey perceived an increasing volume of fluid, leaving a narrow trail behind the Jag. Two miles further on, a vapor cloud of steam was being emitted from beneath the car's bonnet. Meanwhile, inside the car, ACM noted the noxious smell, first compelling her eyes to seek the temperature gauge, only to note the dial had already achieved the H, for hot. Then came the steam, and as an experienced driver, she knew there was no recourse except to pull over and turn off the engine lest she cause its ruin. Fortunately, the street was wide, with ample space between the large, stately homes that lined it. Easing to the curb, Annie quickly turned off the engine, which was now beginning to sputter. "Preventive maintenance indeed!" she said. "Two weeks out of the shop and this happens."

Quickly glancing at the dashboard clock, Annie noted there were only fifteen minutes before her hair appointment. Punctual as she was, her next thought was the need to alert her hairdresser regarding the car problem. Next, she would call her husband to come pick her up and arrange for her car to be towed. She remembered that Carrie Anderson lived only two blocks down the street and, surely if she wasn't home, the maid would let her in to use the phone. With the car door open, and her right foot on the ground, Annie turned to emerge. Just then, she noted a man approaching from a white van, which had pulled up behind her. "My lucky day," she happily murmured. "A mechanic to the rescue. There is nothing else that he could be, looking like that."

Although purposefully grubby, Moynihan was absolutely gallant. Turning on a disarming, utterly charming smile, enhanced by the grease paint deftly deployed about the corners of his mouth, he approached Annie's car like a smudged guardian angel. Knuckling the brim of his hat, in a fashion long dated but surely welcome, he said softly, "May I be of assistance ma'am? I couldn't help noticing the steam emerging from under the bonnet when I came along behind you. Oh! look here," he continued, as he bent over to inspect the last stream of antifreeze flowing past the stalled sedan's right front tire.

"Just as I thought," replied Annie. Then, she continued, "I would be most appreciative if you could do anything to help me get under way, as I have an appointment to keep."

"If you could pull the latch for the bonnet, I'll grab a quick look," was Mickey's smile-reinforced response. After feigning an inspection, Moynihan returned to the driver's open door. "Radiator looks fine ma'am, but there's a leak coming off the bottom of the radiator. Old British Motor Car, bless their hearts, put that hose in a tight spot. Unfortunately, you need a large jack or a lift to get at it. I'm on the way to my garage, and I can pick up a new hose, water, antifreeze, and a jack and be back in twenty minutes, if that would help. Of course, if you want to have it serviced by the dealer, I could give them a call and request they send a tow lorry."

Forming a few frown lines commensurate with her dilemma, Annie pursed her lips and responded. "I would like very much to have you fix it, sir, especially since I just had the car into the dealership, and they obviously didn't bother to check the hoses." Now, Annie having taken care of one problem, she remembered the matter of her hair appointment. Softening her countenance to a wan damsel in distress smile, Annie continued "Would Eighth and Trafalgar be out of your way sir?"

Politely, Mickey cut in, and said, "It's Freddy ma'am, from Freddy's Garage." whereupon, he pointed to the embroidered print above his coverall pocket. Annie's smile deepened as the result of Freddy's gesture.

She continued on. "I have a hair appointment in five minutes, and I'm afraid I'm a bit silly about being punctual. If you could drop me off at Eighth and Trafalgar, I would be more than happy to pay you extra for the service."

As Annie unwittingly had made her abduction infinitely more simple, this request brought a broad smile to Mickey's face. "No need for that ma'am, as I wouldn't be driving an inch out of my way. In fact, if you know when you'll be done, I can even pick you up and bring you back to your car."

"That's very kind of you sir, er Freddy, but that would really be an imposition."

"Not at all," Mickey replied. "I'm the new kid on the block just out of twenty years service with the Army, as a mechanic, and I want to establish Freddy's as a business of service; therefore, it will be my pleasure. Now, if you want to hop in the van, I'll get you to your appointment before the curlers get cold."

As Annie exited her Jaguar, she thought, *This is too good to be true.*

Meanwhile, Moynihan was carefully scrutinizing the street and nearby houses. "Not a soul anywhere in sight," was Mickey's summation of his rapid recon. Moving smartly, Freddy opened the van door for his unsuspecting customer, and just as quickly closed the driver's door of the Jaguar. As Annie was getting into the van, Mickey quipped, "No grease on the passenger's side ma'am. I'm meticulous about that."

When both were seated, Moynihan started the van and called out softly, "Next stop Eighth and Trafalgar."

After a few short blocks, the grateful and relaxed passenger was startled.

Suddenly, her benefactor pulled off into a narrow, tree-lined road without a visible house or automobile. When the van pulled to the side, and "Freddy" produced the sinister stiletto, Annie's startled countenance turned to one of terror! Since Mickey knew that razors or knives were more abhorrent to most females than guns, especially when the blade was near their face, his choice of the weapon was predecided.

Once, Mickey had read a study indicating that a woman shooting herself in the head or face was a rare event, as they found the thought of facial disfigurement either in life or death as unthinkable, and the damage that could be inflicted by a blade was far greater than that of a bullet. Consequently, he had chosen the weapon most likely to frighten her, since he knew she came from a family of courageous women.

So stunned was Annie that she could only stammer, "Oh dear God what have I done?! Take my money please, but for God's sake, please don't hurt me."

With menace in his voice, Moynihan replied. "That's the least thing I intend, provided you do exactly as you are told! Now, get in the back of the van and make it quick." Even for the abducted, in fear of rape or death, hope springs eternal, so Moynihan's prisoner arose as fast as her nearly flaccid legs would allow, and she proceeded to the rear compartment. "I'm happy to see you are complying," Mickey said in a hoarse whisper. "Now lay down on that sheet of sponge rubber!" Immediately, Annie did as she was told, though she was certain that she was about to be sexually assaulted. No sooner had she stretched out than her abductor wrapped her ankles and knees in several layers of duct tape. Next, came her wrists and, finally, two pieces of the tape were placed across her mouth. "I trust you can breathe through your nose," said her abductor in a matter-of-fact manner. Annie's response was in the form of a few gurgled sounds barely perceptible and, certainly, unintelligible. "Just shake your head," was her captor's response, and Annie did so, in an affirmative fashion.

Previously, Mickey had placed a number of ropes beneath the foam rubber pad. Quickly, drawing out the ends, he fashioned figure eight knots and proceeded to tighten the spongy material about her body like a cocoon, leaving only Annie's face exposed. Before pulling the last slip knot tight, Moynihan removed his victim's high-heeled pumps, then said, "I'm trying to make you as comfortable as possible. I'm sorry that you have to be wrapped up like a mummy, but I can't have you thumping or kicking back here. Again, I mean you no harm. You're being used as a hostage and, as long as you do what you are told, you'll come out entirely unscathed."

Shortly, as the van picked up speed, after returning to the main road, Annie was thankful that she was still alive and, as yet not violated or disfigured. Nonetheless, she remained too terrified to do anything but pray.

Soon, Mickey was on the open highway, with his destination the town of Oban in Argyllshire. Though he had read in his research that it was the former home of Claire Campbell Cameron, now deceased, wife of Colonel Iain Cameron, that was not the reason it was selected. Instead, Moynihan was well aware there were several sheltered coves near the town. According to his plan, one of these was to be his point of rendezvous with his yacht *Sargasso,* now temporarily under the command of his old friend Seamus O'Neil and crewed by a couple of men from his recently inactive squad, whom he had personally trained. Mickey had estimated his own arrival at two in the morning, In the meantime, the *Sargasso* would lazily cruise the Irish Sea under partial sail until the appointed hour. At that time, they would "hove to," just outside the breakers, rolling into the cove. Once the signal light on shore was recognized, a Zodiac would be launched to pick up Moynihan and the hostage; then all sail would be made for the return to Grey Abbey.

As for Annie, though she could see nothing apart from the ceiling of the van, it came to her realization that the vehicle was on the open road to somewhere. Given the fact her abductor was up front and occupied with driving, at last her thoughts turned from prayer to those of escape. However, absolute frustration was fast to follow. Beside her wrists, the abductor had taped her hands and fingers, thus denying her any opportunity to pick at the tape or foam rubber shroud in which she was encased. With considerable effort, she did manage to raise her heels slightly, but they made absolutely no sound when she brought them down, only to impact on the foam.

After three hours into her captivity and journey, a filled bladder was the cause of increasing distress to the point of agony. For the first time since infancy, finally, she gave way to wetting herself. Feeling soiled and ashamed, tears seemed Annie's only recourse, and these were produced in abundance. Before long, she began to think she must comport herself as the model prisoner. Then, realizing how quickly she had succumbed to what hostage negotiators referred to as Stockholm syndrome, Annie's thoughts gave way to despair.

At one A.M., Mickey caught sight of the sign proclaiming that Oban was one mile away, and he knew there would be a side road one-half mile ahead, which would deliver him and his hostage to the chosen cove. Apart from futile attempts to shift her position, Cameron's captured younger sister had been quiescent for much of the way. Despite the cushioning effects of the sponge rubber, Moynihan knew she was no doubt uncomfortable. Indeed, Annie was suffering from physical discomfiture, although it did not compare with the mental anguish and fear that pervaded her completely. Due to the circumstances preceding her abduction, there were many details about her captor that had failed to register. Now, these were beginning to seep into her sensorium.

Slowly, Annie began to reconstruct details about the man who called himself "Freddy." He was tall, muscular in build, even beneath the coveralls. *What about his hair and face? Freddy's cap covered much of his hair, but the visible part was nearly coal black, wasn't it?* Mentally answering her question, Annie remembered, *No there was a silvery fringe, wasn't there?* Though confused, she continued, with recollections regarding her abduction. *Facially, he seemed handsome, initially friendly and smiling, although all of that changed once he had me in the van.* Could she really describe him, assuming she was to live, and the opportunity would someday come? Mentally, Annie pictured a clown, whose face was covered with grease paint, then, the same person with their face clean in a line up next to men of similar appearance. *Never,* she speculated. *I couldn't be sure.* Next, she thought, *Those eyes, wouldn't they be recognizable, even when the makeup was removed? So bright, so blue, and penetrating. Tender and honest one minute, then, fierce and unrelenting the next!*

Suddenly, Annie reflected back to before her marriage when she had been a language major at the University in Edinburgh, and she had won praise from her professors for her ability to detect regional accents and dialects even in foreign languages. Why hadn't it dawned on her? Freddy had come across as having a convincing Scot's brogue, but thinking back on it she had never discerned a particular dialect. While remaining in retrospect, suddenly a horrible truth burst on Annie's memory. After he had pulled the knife, Freddy's accent had changed! It had become Irish, Ulster Irish, and Catholic not Protestant! *Oh my God, he is IRA, and part of the plot Rodney Cahill had theorized and warned us about!* Mentally, she began to berate herself, feeling guilty for her own stupidity.

After sensing the van was slowing, suddenly Annie appreciated the fact that it was actually stopping. Immediately, a new terror seized the totally helpless victim. She realized Freddy was getting out of the van, and fresh air rushed into the vehicle, carrying the distinctive aroma of salty sea air. *He's taken me to the coast,* was the thought coming to Annie's mind, like a scream in the dark. Knowing that she had been in the van for hours, she knew she must be on the west coast of Scotland. Dark images exploded in her brain, and Annie wished she could dispel them by issuing a primordial scream from her own mouth, but the heavy layers of tape defied her efforts. First, she imagined being lowered into the cold, black sea weighted down, so her body would never surface. How long could she hold her breath? What would it feel like, when the desperate need to breathe forced her to gasp sea water, which would pour in to fill her lungs, and life would vanish in seconds? Family forever gone, and final judgment for all her deeds and misdeeds awaited her!

Next, came the horrible apparition of being taken to Ireland, and being forced to face the Kangaroo Court of the IRA. Soon, she conjured up images of torture, knee-capping, and the final ignominy—her nude, tortured body hanging by the neck from a lamp post and covered only by a crudely lettered sign proclaiming "Scottish Slut." So engulfed by terror and her own imagery, Annie was unaware of her captor's return until he spoke. "Sorry, this may smart a bit," he said. Then, the tape was quickly pulled from her mouth.

Struggling to conform numb lips into a configuration compatible with speech, the Colonel's sister finally blurted out, "Please, Freddy, please don't hurt me. I have children and a husband. I'm a Catholic, just like you. You believe in God, don't you Freddy? He'll reward you if you spare me."

Somberly replying, Mickey said, "He hasn't sent any blessings my way, so far."

Hearing that, Annie started to scream, but a large hand placed across her mouth sealed off the sound. "This antique locket you are wearing, is it a family heirloom that your brother would recognize? Just shake your head yes or no," Moynihan asked, while holding his hand firmly in place. Once his captive's nodding chin gave the answer, Mickey applied fresh tape to Annie's mouth, then gently unfastened her locket's clasp. Once more, Annie was alone and her stark terror unabated.

As Moynihan looked at his Rolex, it indicated exactly two, and time to send his signal. Held in his hand, light from the torch flashed out the proper sequence in Morse code for the letters MOY. Thirty seconds later, the signal was repeated. Out in the blackness of the Firth of Lorn, an answer was flashed, also in Morse code, representing the letters SO for Seamus O'Neil. Moments later, the sound of a powerful outboard motor was audible and, following Doppler's law, it grew increasingly louder. Soon, the phosphorescence of spray, arising from the bow's incision of the sea, was discernible. St. Elmo's fire, the ancient mariners called it, Mickey reflected. With landfall near, the Zodiac's motor had been cut, and the inflated boat proceeded by its own momentum, augmented by a soft push from the gentle surf playing atop a rising tide. Grabbing a line thrown from the bow, Moynihan pulled the boat sufficiently up on the sand to fix it in place.

"Need any help?" said a muffled voice from the boat.

"No she's a weight watcher," Mickey replied before returning to the van.

Immediately, Annie was aware of his return. Soon, she felt Freddy's strong arms scooping her up in her bondage. Next, she felt the slight jolt of fifty-four steps leading toward sounds of the sea. Looking up, Annie's eyes caught sight of stars, and she wondered if they would be the last ones she would see, at least from this side of heaven, where she hoped to go, if she was to die. Next, Annie saw a boat, and soon her body was nestled therein and it shifted slightly, when the craft gained inertia from a powerful shove. Then, a motor came to life, bestowing the sensation of ever increasing momentum.

Somehow, Annie was beginning to sense some security inside her cocoon. *If they throw me in the water, perhaps, I could float wrapped up like this and they can't hurt me.* At this stage in her ordeal, Annie's wrappings were becoming a security blanket, like the one she used to trail behind her as a toddler. Suddenly, the smaller boat in which she was being carried nudged against a much larger one, and strong arms carried her below its deck to an unlit cabin. Audible noises told Annie the small boat was being stowed and the big one, her prison ship, was now underway. All the terrifying images returned, and she was once more in agony over what her fate might be.

Back in Perth, not long after Annie's abduction, a pair of policemen out on patrol passed the deserted Jaguar, but paid it no heed. Two hours later, they became more mindful and pulled in behind it. Unfortunately, fate decreed their tires passed over and effaced the tracks left by Mickey's van. "The bloody rich for you," snorted the Sergeant.

His junior officer added, "If I had a toy like this, I sure as hell wouldn't leave it like a stray cat!"

"Good analogy," the Sergeant responded to the younger officer, who continued. "In fact, it is a cat—a Jaguar." Ignoring his junior's pun, the Sergeant said gruffly, "Call in the license number and see who owns this jewel. You can tell Miss MacKendry to call the owners, and tell them to come fetch it, or we'll have it towed off and impounded."

Although the car was reported as seemingly abandoned, due to shift changes which leave cracks for information to fall through, Miss MacKendry never made the call or passed on the information to her relief.

Meanwhile, Heather MacEachron, Annie's hair stylist, had wondered why the punctual Mrs. McKay was late. However, worried about a sick child at home, she gave her client an extra thirty minutes to appear, then left for the day. Approximately an hour later, Bruce McKay returned home from work and found his youngest daughter snacking in the kitchen. Their oldest child was away at college, and Mrs. Hendry the cook and housekeeper was busy preparing dinner. Noting the absence of his wife, Bruce inquired of the cook, "Where is Mrs. McKay, Dorothy?"

"She's not come home, nor has she called Mr. McKay. I assume she had errands to run after her hair appointment. Miss MacEachron didn't ring up, so she must have been there." Despite her scone-filled mouth, young Betsy managed to mumble, "Maybe mother had car trouble."

"Not likely, said her father. "We had mother's car all checked out a couple of weeks ago. One more thing, young lady, you shouldn't talk with your mouth full, and you shouldn't be snacking before dinner."

"Yes father" came, after a last sip of milk and a long sigh.

"Well I'll go change into something more comfortable. I'm sure she will be home soon," announced Bruce before leaving for the bedroom.

Since Annie did not return as predicted, at 6:30 a concerned husband left in his own car to see if he could find her. Already, Annie's friends who would have been at the meeting had been called. "Yes she had been there, and we went together for lunch at the White Hackle," they reported with voices steeped in curiosity. Very worried, Bruce McKay wished he had called the beauty shop earlier, as it was now closed. Mrs. MacEachron didn't have a residence number and he hadn't the foggiest notion where she lived, so his search began at the White Hackle, then ended when he found his wife's Jaguar along the route to the salon.

Sliding his car in behind the Jaguar, he unwittingly added to the despoliation of any remaining former evidence. On his approach to the sedan, he noticed a small puddle of residual antifreeze. Then, after opening the car, he looked for a purse, a note, or any other tangible sign of what had happened to Annie. Next, he pulled on the bonnet latch, and exited the car to look inside the front compartment. Feeling the cold radiator, Bruce knew the sedan had not been driven recently, and after he had inserted a finger into the radiator opening, he discovered that it was bone dry. Concern swiftly turned to alarm, and he raced his car for home. Ignoring the cook and his daughter, who were still in the kitchen, he propelled himself to the nearest phone. Anxious fingers flicked the pages of their personal phone and address book, until the sought-for phone number was found.

Three rings, then, "Thank God an answer!"

"Cahill here."

"Rodney it's Bruce McKay. Annie's disappeared! I think she may have been abducted!"

"Give me every bit of information that you can, Bruce. I'll be taking notes, and I may interrupt you from time to time. Let's get started."

As requested, McKay related every detail in a purposeful manner, though the anguish in his voice was unmistakable.

"Alright, we know when she left the luncheon, and she had a hair appointment at 2:30, which we presume she didn't keep. It's now after seven, so there's approximately a five-hour window in which she hasn't been heard from. Annie's a smart woman, so she obviously pulled over when the engine overheated. I presume there are no public phones close to where the car was stopped. Perhaps, there could be some friend's house nearby. Can you think of any place she might go to make a call?"

"Yes," came the response. "The Andersons live just up the street. Carrie Anderson is one of Annie's best friends."

"Have you called her?" Cahill flashed back.

"No, I didn't think about that possibility, but if she had gone there, why wouldn't she have called me, or got Carrie to give her a lift?"

Pausing for a moment, then, speaking with a serious tone to his voice, Cahill said, "Bruce I must ask has Annie ever done anything like this before. Foolish question, perhaps, but one that has to be asked."

"Never," was the reply.

"Call the Andersons just in case," stipulated Cahill. Then, he continued, "Bruce I'm not an alarmist, but this event troubles me deeply."

"Should I call the police?" Bruce responded with more of a tremor in his voice after hearing Cahill's pronouncement.

"No, I'll do that," said the MI-5 man, and he continued. "Most police departments, especially the more professional ones, tend to be lackadaisical about missing person's reports. Often, they assume the missing are either lushes out on a toot or a bored spouse engaging in a tryst with a paramour, so they tell you to come back in forty-eight hours. Then, they smile gratuitously, and add that in all probability the lost sheep will return home, wagging their tails behind them. However, a blast from London will get an immediate response, and that is just what they are about to receive!"

Continuing with his plan, Cahill announced, "As soon as I make the call, I'll catch a late flight to Edinburgh. Once there, official transportation will be available, and I should arrive in Perth shortly after midnight. In the meantime, hang tough, my friend. We'll sort this all out."

With emotion in his voice, McKay replied, "Fine Rodney, I'll do that, and thank you! Oh one more thing. Should I try and notify Iain?"

Pausing for a moment, Cahill answered, "Believe me Bruce. Everything that can be done will be done! I would rather wait for at least twenty-four hours before we confront him with this. He will have a million questions, and I want to have the best answers available. I'll see you soon, there is work to be done."

Then, Cahill cut off that call, only to place another immediately. At MI-5 headquarters, Betty Tinsdale adroitly answered the call coming in on a special line. According to protocol, she didn't announce the name of the organization for which she worked. Before she managed the first syllable of her name, her salutation was interrupted. "Betty, this is Cahill, patch me through to the Chief Inspector in Perth. I'll give you three minutes, no more," he said in a jovial voice, which really didn't reflect his mood.

"Worth a lunch," she replied, while her fingers and eyes had already begun the search for the number.

"A small bouquet, maybe, but this is the newly engaged Cahill on good behavior forever more," Rodney added.

Betty laughed appreciatively, then she said, "Ringing, sir."

Picking up his phone, Chief Inspector Harold Munro was about to protest interruption of a fine dinner, smack in the middle of the main course, when it became readily apparent that this was an urgent matter made all the more so due to the origin of the call. Cahill's instructions were all answered by a mantra, made up of "yes sirs."

Mrs. McKay's car would be guarded in place. Examination of logs of all garages, towing companies, and taxi cabs would commence immediately. Individual drivers should be brought in for questioning, given the slightest provocation. Then, Cahill announced he would personally arrive on scene around midnight.

Before his leaving for the London airport to catch the last commuter flight to Edinburgh, a second phone call was made by Cahill, and a third contemplated. With Betty Tinsdale back on the line, she was instructed to find Perry Devon. Fortunately, the man was a homebody, and at the moment of her call, he was playing Scrabble with his three adolescent children. Immediately, Betty patched Rodney through.

"Perry, Rodney Cahill here. Drop whatever you are doing, and run a check on the location of every IRA, Provo, or whatever else they are calling themselves, and safehouses in the U.K.! Bend some arms and have them placed under surveillance. My present interest is in finding an abducted lady named Annie Cameron McKay, age forty-six, with blonde hair cut moderately short, but stylish. She's five seven tall, and approximately 125 pounds, last seen wearing a light blue knit suit. Should anyone like that show up, have the place surrounded. I'm on the way to Perth, and you can reach me via their police department."

"Big order, Rodney, old chap! Who shall I say pulled all the strings, when the official inquiry starts over who authorized all this?"

"Send them all to see Cahill over at the Russian embassy," was the reply. Then, the line went dead.

With discouragement, Devon looked at the Scrabble board and, then, the upturned faces of his three progeny, thinking, *Will there ever be another chance to complete a word worth more than 125 points? Probably not!* After giving his wife a quick explanation, he kissed them all good-bye. He wouldn't be back until the wee hours.

On the way to Heathrow, Cahill wracked his mind. Safe havens, at least the ones they knew about, were presumably covered. Would they try and get Annie out of Scotland? If so to where? Their own back yard was the reasonable answer. "How would they do that?" was the next question. Flying her out was a possibility, but there was no Paddy air force, and to the best of his knowledge, it wasn't a modus operandi associated with their activities. Surely, transport by sea was the most likely, but that could be done from a hundred places, and on a reasonably calm day, even a whale boat and eight good men at the oars would suffice to achieve a crossing. Searching the sea and all the coastline, even if limited to the west coast, would be a vast undertaking. Perhaps, if it were the Prime Minister or the Queen, authority would be granted, but for Annie McKay, missing only about seven hours, not a chance!

Having arrived at Heathrow to take the last flight out, Cahill was thinking back to Devon's remarks, and murmured, "Those dear chaps who hold the reins of power would no doubt roast my ass for the activities I've already taken. I will surely be cremated in totality for suggesting more." Contemplating what he had already done, and what he couldn't possibly do, Cahill frowned, pursed his lips, and quietly said "Oh shit!" Vulgar though it was, there were times when no other words seemed appropriate.

Cahill managed catching a cat nap while on the flight to Edinburgh, then at last Perth was reached, and so was the site of Annie's abandoned car. Under the illumination of police officers' torches, remnants of multiple tire tracks were seen. Chief Inspector Munro's car, now parked behind Annie's Jaguar, had made the last set. Cahill knew this would undoubtedly prove to be a hopeless morass. However, multiple fingerprints were lifted from many surfaces and taken to forensics. Most interesting of all were finger smudges on the bonnet and driver's side door. Obviously, someone's fingers had left the greasy streaks, as they had slid across the surface. No actual prints were evident; however, it was a sign that someone, presumably a mechanic, had been there. Annie's own fingers would never leave such signs; inasmuch as she always kept her car in impeccable condition, they must have been recently placed there. Number one suspect must be a mechanic, or a person posing as one.

Rodney concluded, "Let's tow the car into the Police Garage," he ordered, addressing a very tired Chief Inspector whose stomach was constantly protesting the interrupted dinner of curried lamb that he had looked forward to digesting. While doing his best to stifle a much-needed yawn, the Chief Inspector mumbled, "Yes sir! Of course sir."

Once in the confines of the garage, Rodney immediately started to search for the cause of the coolant fluid leak. No clues were found looking into the engine compartment. Having no desire to soil his Savile Row suit, Cahill ordered the car placed on a hoist. Now, easily seen with the car elevated, the lower radiator hose came under his close scrutiny. "Take off this hose," was Rodney's next command. Immediately, a standby mechanic followed his order. Once under bright lights, on top of a work bench, a telltale hole was easily found. "Cut it in half, along the long axis," Rodney told the mechanic. Peering into the bottom half of the dissected hose, Cahill was quick to note that edges of the hole were slightly turned upward. Apart from this one small violation, the rubber was in pristine condition. "Some bastard stuck a knife into it!" he exclaimed, while in the process of slamming the hose against the bench, as an exclamation to his conclusion.

Wishing to please the man from London, Chief Inspector Munro now proffered a list of all the garages and towing companies that had so far been contacted. "One of the tow lorry drivers has a past history of sexual assault," the Inspector averred, in a manner suggestive of a man seeking a commendation for work well done.

Not wishing to appear haughty or dismissive, Cahill produced a wan smile before saying, "Fine work, Chief Inspector Munro. Bring him in and sweat him a bit, for it might possibly lead to something. However, I'm certain this car was sabotaged by some quasi-mechanic with an ingratiating manner, whose immediate motive wasn't rape. Now, if I could get a lift to the McKay house, I'd be most grateful. Thank you and all your lads and lassies, Chief Inspector. You have all done your duties well, and I am most grateful, as will be reflected in my official report." Immediately, Cahill thought, *Official report, hell I'll probably get sacked when Lord Dithers finds out I've gone walkabout!* After having issued commands and running up expenses without his Lordship's blessing, phony or not, Cahill was pleased to leave Chief Inspector Munro and his crew basking in imagined glory.

Upon arrival at the McKay home, Rodney was let in by an exhausted and most anxious appearing Mrs. Hendry. Bruce and his daughter were seated at the kitchen table, and young Betsy was toying with a long-turned-cold cup of cocoa, even though Mrs. Hendry had offered to warm it up a bit. Bruce's hands were folded about a teacup, as empty as his spirits. As Cahill entered, they both looked up with their faces displaying the same anxiety as relatives peering toward the face of a surgeon who had embarked on a potentially life-saving operation on one of their dearest. However, judging from the look on Cahill's face, Bruce knew the operation wasn't a success.

Though he would much rather have had a full eight ounces of single malt, not to be sipped but gulped, Rodney did accept the proffered cup of strong, hot tea. When the two men's eyes met across the table, Cahill's eyes suddenly shifted to Betsy, with a quick flick of his hand, indicating the discussion should be in private. Immediately, Bruce said, "Betsy, Mr. Cahill and I need to talk, and I think it best for you to get ready for bed. It's very late, and you need some rest."

"But Daddy, I want to hear about Mummy," Betsy replied, as tears began to form. "In the morning, Betsy. Go to bed, and say some special prayers for your mother." Quickly, Mrs. Hendry caught the implication and moved to the girl's chair. "Come along now, Betsy. I haven't tucked you in since you were a wee one. I would like to say some prayers for your mother, as well. We can say them together. You know what the good Lord says, 'When two or more are gathered in my name, I shall be among them.'" Reluctantly, Betsy rose, kissed her father goodnight, turned tear-strained eyes toward Cahill, then departed in the shelter of Mrs. Hendry's hovering form. Now alone, the two men sat silently for a moment. "Bad news," sighed McKay at last.

"Maybe the worst possible," was Cahill's reply. Then continuing, he said, "Annie's car was sabotaged by stabbing a hole in the bottom radiator hose. Whoever did it knew she would be forced to stop and, then, she could be abducted by guile or force."

"What do you mean by guile?" queried her distraught husband.

"While posing as a mechanic, the saboteur would follow Annie, knowing her car would stall. Then, she would see him coming, as the cavalry to the rescue. 'Give you a lift ma'am?' Not hard to see how she might be taken in by this ruse."

"She knew about the threat! Why would she do something so stupid?" replied McKay.

"Sure it seems that way now, but picture yourself in the same situation. Would you have sat in the car leaning on the horn with the car windows rolled up, and the car doors locked? I doubt it!"

"You're right, Rodney. I would have been just as unsuspecting. What do we do now?"

"I've placed a watch on every IRA safe house in the U.K. that we know about, and I'm sure I've exceeded my authority, but I will face that later on." After sipping his tea, Cahill continued. "In the event they plan to keep Annie in Scotland or England, we may get a break. If they decided to take her to Ireland, it would probably be by sea. Unfortunately, at this point, one of Her Majesty's humble servants can't order any land, sea, or air surveillance. However, I have called in some favors from old friends in a few likely west coast cities to give us a hand and check those areas out as close as possible."

After a further pause, Cahill spoke again. "I have every hope that Annie is still alive. If the bastards wanted to kill her, you would have found her in the car with a bullet in her head."

Although McKay was not in any way comforted by Cahill's words, they did convey the slimmest ray of hope. "What about Iain?" McKay asked once again.

"I still think it is best to wait a little longer before bringing him back, if necessary, under controlled conditions. Perhaps, having him come storming back, under their terms, is just what they want. Annie could be the bait, but Iain is the real target," was Cahill's somber summation.

Meanwhile, at nearly the same hour Cahill and McKay were soul searching in the kitchen at Perth, Moynihan was progressing southward toward Holy Loch. Alexis would be awaiting him there, all part of a preformed plan, which they had agreed on the previous week. Historically, the town was well named, but from the Russian perspective there was nothing holy about three U.S. nuclear submarines that used the loch as their base. Thus, it was important for Russian intelligence to know when the missile launching behemoths, or "boomers," as they were called, either put to sea or returned from their strategic locations in the Gulf of Finland.

Located with a sweeping view of the harbor, there was a rustic cottage owned by a man sympathetic to the Communist cause. Beside that man, Alexis Zellanova sat at a small table drinking strong tea from an authentic samovar, while waiting for Moynihan's arrival.

Just after dawn, Mickey's rented van pulled into the drive. Leaning over, Alexis separated a curtain, just to be certain it was Moynihan. Indeed, it was Mickey, looking tired and covered with grease. Springing up from the table, Alexis opened the door and bade Moynihan to enter. "No Russian bear hugs for you my friend," he said in jocular tone. "I have no desire to wear any of that lubricant you are sporting. Did all go well, Tovarich?"

"Better than I could have hoped for," replied Mickey. "As far as I know, no one witnessed the snatch, and I didn't leave any clues behind." Turning toward the KGB sympathizer, Alexis bestowed a "get lost" look on the man, which was immediately heeded. "I've got some work to do outside," he said defensively, then departed.

"Here is the clincher," said Mickey dangling Annie's locket and chain before the Russian. "Now all is complete," replied Alexis. "Your letter to Colonel Cameron is tucked away in the lining of my coat. Please go and take a shower my friend. Then, you can drive me to the Glasgow Airport."

"I was beginning to like this stuff," Mickey said, regarding the grease on his hands and face, "but I do suppose it would look unseemly for a Yankee antique dealer to return the van looking like a grease monkey. Where's the shower?" Moynihan asked, while in the process of divesting himself of the coveralls.

"Down that hall and to the right," answered the Russian.

Then, halfway down the hall, Mickey called back, "Do have Olaf or whatever his name is burn the coveralls and the old spread covering the driver's seat. Oh yes, he can also wipe off the steering wheel and the gear shift, or any other grease spots!"

"At once my friend," replied Alexis. "I'll supervise the job, myself. Comrades from this country are useful, but not entirely reliable. I assume you have some clothes in the van that you neglected to bring inside," he said with humor. "Otherwise, showing up at Avis in your underwear would look even more unseemly."

"It's been a long night," Mickey replied before entering the bathroom.

Shortly, before exiting the van at the airport, Alexis addressed Mickey one last time. "I'll meet one of my comrades at Heathrow, and place the letters and locket in the diplomatic pouch. Certainly, there will be adequate time to get it on the nonstop to Johannesburg, where our people will pick it up. Then, early in the morning, someone will deliver the first letter to Safari Airlines, with instructions that it be given to Colonel Cameron as a matter of the utmost urgency! Letter number two will be taken to the Star of Africa Hotel to be given to the Colonel on his arrival."

"Favorable treatment fit for a czar," said Mickey with a smile.

"That word is no longer in my vocabulary," responded Alexis, also with a smile.

"Dosvedanya," was Mickey's parting remark, which was answered by "Spasiva."

On the next morning, when delivering the van back to the rental agency, Mickey was surprised to see the same clerk on duty. "Good morning, Mr. Crosby," she said emphasizing the "r" with a roll of her tongue.

"You've a good memory, miss," Mickey replied.

"Same name as the singer," she replied. "Hasn't anyone ever called you 'Bing'?"

"Not after they heard me sing," Mickey responded. Outwardly, Moynihan remained affable, but people remembering too much were always a bit disturbing. But, why should he worry? There was no reason to assume the van had ever been used except to haul antiques, and Mickey was careful to point out to the clerk that he had been very successful finding some fine ones. Closing off the conversation, he related that it was too bad he couldn't let her see the treasures he had found. Unfortunately, they were already crated and delivered to the docks for shipment home.

"Glad you brought it back so soon, Mr. Crosby. Some other party has been trying to rent one to move auto parts all the way to the Orkneys."

"Tell them not to get it dirty," Mickey responded. "I may want to rent it again sometime." At last, Mickey was out on the street and quickly hailed a cab. Soon, he was back at the Glasgow Airport, in time to catch the next flight to Belfast.

Upon arrival back at his home, Mickey was absorbed by the quiet of the place. Mrs. Hennessey, the cook, had been sent on vacation with full pay. Memories made no sound, so there was only the emptiness to remind him of Bernie, Sean, and Liam, all now gone and Michael off in America. Arrival of the *Sargasso*, bearing the hostage, was not expected until late evening or perhaps sometime into the night. *Best I check out the captive's accommodations,* Mickey thought, leading him to descend the stairs into the basement.

Roughly ten by twelve feet, the room previously used for storage seemed ideal from the jailer's standpoint. Windowless, with walls made of concrete and a heavy, reinforced, wooden door, made it quite soundproof and inescapable. However, amenities had been allowed, including a sink, shower and toilet recently plumbed. Small though adequate was a refrigerator containing a variety of juices. Fresh perishables would be added later upon Annie McKay's arrival. "Milk—I must get some. She might want it for the dry cereal in the cupboard."

Laid out on the bed was a touch of Mickey's irony. Three dresses, and three sets of underclothes in all ways similar to those issued to Paddy Colleens, unfortunate enough, to qualify as guests of the Queen, in one of Ulster's Women's Prisons. *Scratchy and rough but quite modest,* he reflected. *No harsher on a Scotty's skin than one of our own.*

Standing in the doorway, Mickey began to think about the letters that he had consigned to be delivered to the Colonel. *Should Colonel Iain Cameron not present himself for the duel, or conspire to send the police in his stead, will I have her killed? He will have brought in on himself,* Mickey decided. *Shameless men deserve no quarter, nor do their kin.*

When the *Sargasso,* devoid of sail and running on her powerful diesel auxiliary found the sanctuary of her quay, darkness had fallen. Once tethered by her mooring lines, the sleek yacht was ready to discharge her cargo. Still mummified in the sponge rubber and bindings, Annie could sense the transition. Perhaps, she was now safe from being consigned to the cold depths of the sea. Conversely, whatever fate awaited her, in what she presumed to be Ireland, could possibly be for the worse—"time for more prayer!" Though Annie's field of vision was limited, due to the deployment of her wrappings, she could see that the men approaching the bunk on which she lay were hooded. Lifted off by reasonably gentle hands, she was carried across a dock and up a path past a large house, the features of which were not discernible in the dark. Next, they passed through several rooms before descending a stairway, which must lead to the basement.

Immediately, Annie's terror-filled mind switched to thoughts of a dungeon. For her, dungeons were places of torture, where the victim's screams would be shielded from any rescuer's ears by walls of stone. Now, came a voice; this time undisguised and certainly that of Freddy.

"Lay her on the floor and release her bindings," he said. Seconds later, the sound and sensation of tape being cut was obvious to Annie. Again, she heard Freddy say, "This may smart a bit," and the tape across her mouth was pulled away. Next, came the bindings from her hands and legs, and Annie's arms fell to her sides, where they began to quiver like the rest of her body.

Finally, finding speech, she cried out again, "Please Freddy don't hurt me!"

"You're safe for now, Mrs. McKay." Again, the voice was that of her abductor, but it came from a face now masked. *Of course,* she thought, *Free of all the grease, Freddy did not want to be recognized.* With some relief, Annie searched for solace, grasping at the fact that if they intended to kill her, there would be no need to hide their faces.

Once again, Freddy spoke, "We'll leave you alone for now, Mrs. McKay. When you loosen up a bit, you can get up and take a shower. As I'm sure you realize, you are a bit aromatic from your confinement. There's some clean clothes on the bed. You needn't worry about your privacy, as there are no windows, peek holes, or hidden cameras. I'll be back to talk to you later. Help yourself to the food and drink. Not what you are used to, I'm sure, but you won't starve."

For about fifteen minutes, after the door was closed, Annie lay still. Finally, she arose and made sure the promise of privacy was true, then, she undressed and showered. After feeling clean and, somewhat refreshed, she toweled herself dry. Although the clean garments left for her were crude and chafed her skin, they were a covering. Suddenly, as it might in any lady, vanity came to mind. Yes her jailers had provided essentials, but nothing like a hairbrush or even basic cosmetics. Looking into the little mirror above the sink, she pictured herself as a hag, but at least for the time being, she was alive.

Later, Freddy returned as promised and knocked before entering. Again, he spoke through a mask. "Mrs. McKay I told you in Perth that you were taken as a hostage. Your brother owes me satisfaction for the death of two of my sons. Colonel Cameron will be told your life will be spared, and you will be released unharmed, if he agrees to a duel under my conditions, which is the right of the offended. My intention is to kill him, but if he should prevail, you will still be set free. However, should he prove to be cowardly and dishonorable, I have no recourse but to follow through with my threat to have you executed. For your sake, I hope your brother is the man I expect him to be. All of this will be decided within a week. In the meantime, you have my word of honor that you are safe in your confinement. You will be left entirely to yourself, unless you need something, in which case you can push the buzzer above the bed." Eyes blue, like the flame of an acetylene torch flashed outward from the openings in his mask. Then, no more was said, as he turned and left.

For Annie, her personal dread was now compounded by the possible death of her brother. Once again, a prayer, "Dear God don't let my sentence be commuted by the death of Iain." Now, Annie the prisoner knew this dungeon was not one where the rack and hot irons were employed, though she wondered if the anguish was any less.

Although Mickey had been extremely reticent to recall Seamus O'Neil to duty, the old man was eager, not reluctant, to be back at what he always referred to as "Ireland's work." "You'll be the lady's jailer until I return," Moynihan had told him. "Should Cameron prevail without any indication of outside interference, then, you are to set her free and unharmed. Many sets of good eyes will be watching from Valentia Island and, if there is any sign of treachery on behalf of the Colonel, you will be notified at once."

Mickey was about to continue when O'Neil interrupted. "Yes Mick, I know. If the Colonel doesn't show up alone, or in the event of any sign of police or military involvement by sea or air, I'm to stiff her and bury her at sea."

"Can you do it Seamus?" queried Mickey his voice firm. "I know you have sisters and daughters aplenty. Shooting a woman won't go down easy."

"I was doing dirty work for the Cause before you were even conceived," O'Neil retorted. "I've never done a woman or child, as God is my judge, but I would feel it justified and deservin' if Cameron shows no honor. However, you and I have pulled off some good ones over the years, and I think you will come out on top."

"Well that's taken care of, and now I must see about getting my gear together," said Mickey. "Probably, there isn't any hurry, seeing as I won't hear from Colonel Cameron until he gets to London, and that won't be for several days. Nonetheless, I want to check and recheck everything, so I know it's all in perfect shape for the duel at Skellig Michael. Best I limber up as well, and give Warlord a couple of hard runs. There's plenty of fixins in the kitchen. Why don't you whip up a big pot of O'Neil's famous Irish stew, enough for three days at least. Oh Seamus! You might give Mrs. McKay a bowl, as well. Never let it be said that the Irish aren't one step ahead of the Geneva Convention." Mickey started to laugh at his own joke, then stopped and added, "Should it come to her having a last meal, you can't beat Irish stew." Though it was meant in humor, no mirth registered on the face of either man.

Seamus said, "I'll get started," and Mickey went off to his den.

Chapter Forty-Six

As Alexis had promised, the Russian diplomatic pouch was delivered in Johannesburg late on the same day that it was dispatched from London. Even though it passed through the hands of the curious and before the eyes of MI-6 watchers, its contents remained unknown. *One of the international niceties,* a British agent thought. *We and they sneak people in and out, tap each other's phone lines, compromise the other's guy's citizens and operatives, along with murder, blackmail, and all that's unholy. Yet we and probably they would never think of peeking inside a diplomatic pouch, although we sure as hell might fluoroscope the bloody thing.* In fact, he was doing just that at the moment, and so the locket and chain was recognized. *Some Ivan must have got his sweetie a trinket,* thought the agent, who never bothered to record the item.

After the pouch was collected at the Johannesburg airport, the courier brought it immediately to Major Yuri Zhadanov, who was Alexis's counterpart in South Africa. Within the pouch was one letter from Alexis addressed to him and bound by a rubber band with two other letters. Though he was curious about the other two, the Major opened only the personal one. Zhadanov smirked over the banter of the first paragraph, inquiring as to how he was doing in the land of the zebras, monkeys, and apartheid? Was there adequate vodka to quench his thirst and free him from his inhibitions? Finally, he got to the meat of the matter, the one Zhadanov was most curious about.

"I know you would like to peek inside the other two envelopes, but that is forbidden, Tovarich. Suffice it to say, they have to do with a favor I'm bestowing on a good friend, who has done much to indirectly aid the Rodina. Please have one of your most capable aides deliver them. Number one contains an item of jewelry, which I am sure you have already palpated. This envelope, addressed to Colonel Iain Cameron, should be taken immediately to a man named Archie Andrus, who is the owner of Safari Airlines. Have your man stress the urgency! Andrus will know where this Cameron is to be found. Letter number 2 goes to the Star of Africa Hotel to be given to the same Colonel Cameron on his arrival. Keep both the Safari Airlines and the hotel under surveillance. Should Colonel Cameron fail to return with the airplane, send a coded dispatch immediately. Explanation in full will be given when next we meet. I'm assuming you are buying my dinner. Hopefully, it won't be in Moscow." It was signed "Alexis." Then, a P.S. was added: "I'm sure I can trust that the whole matter will be attended to with the utmost discretion, as there must be no hint of involvement by the U.S.S.R."

Early, the next morning KGB Lieutenant Pioter Stravinsky was at the site of operation for Safari Airlines, where he promptly handed the first letter to Archie Andrus. Still suspicious after the harrowing incident months earlier, Andrus was readily emboldened to ask, "What's this all about?"

"I am only a humble messenger, who does as requested and delves no deeper," responded Stravinsky. All of the man's speech had been in perfect Afrikaans; a language Archie understood well. If asked to give the man's nationality, Russian would have been at the bottom of the list. Having no grounds to question the man further, Andrus said he was flying out to the camp later in the day anyway, and the letter's delivery was guaranteed. For a response, and this time in English straight out of Eton, the messenger said with a smile, "Be sure and wait for a decision from Colonel Cameron." Then, he was gone, and Archie was left with a bigger mystery than when he had appeared.

Later that same afternoon, Archie touched old Gertie down at Cameron's camp with his usual feather-like perfection, despite the heaviness he felt inside. His greeting to Toby Drake was rather brusque, and he did little more than to inquire where Iain might be found. Being somewhat perturbed, Drake responded in a similar form and pointed toward the mess tent, then set about his own routine.

When Archie entered, Iain was seated at a table poring over some letters from booking agents and making notes. "What's up Archie?"

"A mysterious letter given by God knows who, to be delivered to you, as a matter of utmost urgency." While looking perplexed, Iain extended his hand to grasp the proffered envelope. As he did, Iain was alerted by the sound and feel of something metallic on the inside. "Not a letter bomb, I hope," was voiced as one eyebrow raised and the other depressed, with lines of concern interspaced across his broad forehead.

"Well, we can soak it in a bucket of water and hope the ink doesn't run," was Archie halfhearted quip.

With sheath knife in hand, Iain carefully slit the envelope along the bottom edges, signifying to Archie that his earlier comment wasn't made in jest. No sooner had his knife completed its task than Annie's locket fell forthwith into the palm of Iain's hand. Only a millisecond was needed for recognition and, now, the locket and fragile gold chain felt like a molten ingot. His sister had received it from their Grandmother Cameron, as a gift on her twelfth birthday. Cherished from that day forward, Annie was rarely seen without it.

Archie had noted the locket dropping out, and had followed the closure of Iain's great fist about it. Traversing from Cameron's hand to his face, he was not surprised by the anguished look that developed. Like a distress flare or SOS from a sinking ship, it told of instant devastation.

Wordless, Iain ripped the letter from inside the envelope. Already appreciating that the presence of Annie's precious amulet signified her death or hostage taking, he opened the folded paper with a vengeance that increased in magnitude with every word he read, as follows.

Colonel Cameron,

I am an Irish patriot, and I consider myself a soldier of honor equal to yourself. Two of my sons have been killed, either by your hand or that of your kin. Though you may reject my considering myself as your equal, in being both an officer and gentleman, I hold it to be true. As the offended and aggrieved in the matter of the murder of my sons, I do sir demand satisfaction on a field of honor between just you and myself. Therefore, I ask that you return immediately to Johannesburg. A second letter of instructions awaits you at the Star of Africa Hotel.

In order to secure your compliance, I have taken your sister, Annie Cameron McKay, as my hostage, confirmed by the locket enclosed, which you no doubt recognize. She is unharmed and will remain so if you meet my demands with compliance.

It is recommended in the strongest terms that you do not divulge the contents of this letter to anyone. Despite your intentions, others may try to interfere, and this would be fatal for your sister. On the other hand, if you have no honor and do not come along, Annie has no hope.

Be advised to bring a single rifle of your choice, and I will be armed the same. Our duel will be to the death; no quarter to be given or expected.

Signature wise, there was only a flowery Spenserian script decipherable as the initials MM.

With a face of chiseled stone, Iain looked up at Archie and said, "I'll return to Johannesburg with you, as soon as I gather some gear."

"What the hell is going on?" replied the pilot.

"Family emergency," was all that Iain disclosed. Furthermore, his face implied that absolutely nothing further would be divulged as he left for his tent.

Within minutes, Iain emerged with a duffel bag in one hand and a rifle case in the other. As he emerged from the tent, Toby Drake caught his partner by the shoulder. "Archie said you have to leave immediately?"

"That's right. There's a family emergency of some sort." Then, Cameron said no more.

Bewildered, Drake shot back, "What about the party from Argentina that you are expecting?"

"Everyone can appreciate a family emergency, and I've got a real one," Iain responded tersely, then continued. "Peter Boyce has been with us since the season started, and he had five solid years of experience with the Game Department in Tanzania before that, as you know. Peter will do fine filling in for me."

"There is something bloody strange about this, Iain," Drake retorted.

"Accept my word, and leave it be," was Cameron's response.

Even more bewildered by Iain's behavior, Toby inquired in a tone iced with indignation, "Why the hell do you need to take a rifle for a family emergency?"

"I'm going to see a gunsmith while I'm home. The claw extractor isn't working as it should. I'll get back as soon as I can, Toby. However, I'm not sure how long that will be." Iain didn't add "if I survive." Turning away, he left Toby stammering and sputtering profanities, punctuated with vulgarities.

Soon airborne, Iain declined the hospitality and verbal exchanges of the cockpit and sat in singular silence in the rear. Uncharacteristic behavior by Colonel Cameron caused bewilderment in the new steward, Joshua, as he was only able to serve him a brace of single malt and received only token recognition in response. Realizing they were carrying an angry lion on their flight, the crew knew that angry lions are best left alone.

As he had been directed, immediately on his arrival in Johannesburg, Iain took a cab to the Star of Africa Hotel. Archie offered to give Iain a lift, which he had declined. His actions had caused some further dismay in Archie. However, far from being a fool Cameron was fully cognizant of the fact that he might be falling into an ambush.

On the way into town, he wondered who in hell this Irishman, identified only as MM was, "since he now controls me like a bloody puppet!" Turning in his seat, Cameron surveyed the street behind him, and there was no sign of a trailing car or one closing swiftly on the taxi. Though his rifle was stowed in the boot, along with his luggage, Iain did have a Walther PPK .380 caliber, sometimes referred to as a 9mm Kurtz, readily accessible. *Certainly, not a lot of fire power,* he thought, but he knew he was deadly accurate with the weapon, and it might suffice if needed. No suspicious incident occurred during his trip, although Cameron was just as cautious when exiting the cab and entering the spacious, baroque lobby of the grand old hotel.

"Yes, sir, may I be of assistance?" asked the desk clerk, who was statuesque, ebony in color, and well educated in English. "I am Colonel Cameron." Iain replied. "I haven't a reservation, but I need a room for the night. I assume I'll be flying out in the morning."

"We do have a nice room on the fifth floor available, and we can give you a commercial rate, if applicable," the young woman responded.

"I'm with Cameron and Drake, Limited," Iain said.

"Very well, Colonel. If you would be so kind as to sign the register, we'll get you right to your room." After signing, Iain looked at the young lady and asked if she might check to see if there were any messages for him.

"Certainly, sir. I will be back in a moment." Upon return, the clerk handed Iain an envelope identical with the one Archie had delivered to the safari camp, but without the palpable sign of anything except paper in the contents. "Have a nice stay, Colonel. Oh! I forgot to mention the dining room is open until eleven, and breakfast is available from six onward. Also, there is a twenty-four-hour room service."

"I'm much obliged," responded Iain before turning to follow the summoned porter. Having observed there was no one suspicious in the lobby, Cameron continued following the porter, and they caught the next lift. After getting off on the fifth floor, Iain noted only two small children in the company of what must certainly be their nanny. No other people were visible in the hallway.

On approach to Room 507, Iain took the key from the porter and turned it in the lock Although Cameron's voice was low and would not be audible inside the room, he said, with a smile, "Please go in first, as you know where all the light switches are located." Surprised by the role reversal, the porter smiled back and preceded Cameron into the room. Meanwhile, Iain fiddled with the key until the man was well inside the room, assuming that if he were walking into a set-up, some action would have already occurred. However, there was none, so he entered and dismissed the man with words of appreciation and a generous tip. Still most vigilant, he secured the door, checked the windows, and looked behind the drapes and under the bed.

Am I being overly cautious and becoming childish? he thought, recalling days as a child when fear of the dark and the bogeyman very much pervaded his thoughts. With safety concerns dispelled, at last, it was time to open the envelope. Again, it was done from the bottom, revealing only a single, neatly folded sheet of fine linen paper. Once unfolded, the letter read:

Colonel Cameron,

Obviously, you have made it safely to your room without incident. A fact that should indicate that I am, as previously indicated, a man of honor. I do, sir, trust that you can obtain a flight to London in the morning. From my research, I have determined that you have a fondness for the Savoy Hotel. A third letter, with detailed instructions, will await you there.

Just as I am sure that you are taking precautions, so must I. Hopefully, this will explain why you are being informed in increments. This is in no way some type of scavenger hunt, only a necessary prelude to our duel, and attainment of the satisfaction that I demand. Your sister's life remains based on your full compliance.

Again, the missive was signed only by the letters MM in broad script, identical to the first letter.

After refolding the letter, Cameron placed it in the envelope, then, he sat on the side of the bed in a pose of contemplation. *Can I really believe all this? He tells of honor and a duel. Perhaps this MM is just a viper, leading me ever closer to his lair, thus making it far easier to kill me on his own terms. Help could readily be beckoned, but doing so might result in Annie's murder. Regardless of risk, sometimes you have to go at it alone.* Then, Cameron reflected that back in Malay, he had led a few men to face greater odds. Also, in Africa, as a guide, he had gone single-handed against many very dangerous, wounded beasts. *If this MM is as honorable as he claims, I'll face him and kill him if necessary. Should he be dishonorable and waiting to spring a trap in surprise, then, as always, I'll give a good account of myself.*

Rising up, Iain decided he had never let imminent danger ruin his appetite, so he departed for the dining room where he allowed himself the pleasure of fine food and drink, though he was still wary of his surroundings. On the following morning, space was available for a flight to London on British Airways. Knowing full well that he could not carry the PPK on his person, Iain secreted it in a compartment within his rifle case. Sandwiched between two rows of rifle cartridges, it would not be apparent to any observer, in the event that checked luggage was examined fluoroscopically. Then, once at Heathrow Airport, Cameron was well known to Customs personnel and, in addition, as a licensed hunt operator and sporting goods store owner, he possessed a surfeit of proper papers making entry with sporting firearms an easy matter. Also, since he managed hunts on Irish estates, it made entry there, if summoned to do so, equally simple. Remaining cautious on arrival at Heathrow Airport in London, Iain passed Customs readily.

Soon after, he was in the lobby of the Savoy Hotel. At the reception desk, Jeffrey Cook was the clerk on duty, and he greeted Cameron loquaciously. "Well Colonel! We weren't originally expecting you at this time of year, but, on the other hand, we were, since we have a letter to be given you on arrival. This was delivered yesterday by messenger, so I assumed you would be coming and took the liberty of reserving your favorite room. How long will we have the pleasure of your stay, Colonel?"

"Probably only for the night, Jeffrey. But, I'll know for sure once I've read this," Cameron replied, accompanied by a small wave of the envelope, which he was now holding.

"A day or a month, always our pleasure, sir," responded Jeffery, with a simultaneous sharp tap on the desk bell to summon a ready porter. After Iain registered his name, along with his appreciation, he followed his luggage to a familiar room.

Alexis Zellanova had seen to the delivery of Mickey's third letter. In fact, anticipating the arrival of the man that Mickey was so interested in, he was sitting in the lobby looking not at all suspicious. Of course, he hadn't personally delivered the letter. That was done by an unassuming underling. Knowing to whom all three letters were addressed, the KGB agent had no trouble finding Cameron's photo in their files. As he saw his quest board the lift, he was debating whether to follow this any further. *No*, he decided wistfully. *Irish men do crazy things and certainly Moynihan is capable of such. Curiosity killed the cat, and this cat doesn't want to end up sitting on the wrong side of the bars back in Moscow at Lubyanka Prison. Best I do the Rodena's work, and let Mickey do his.* As he was passing out of the lobby, he made one last observation, *Whatever my friend is planning, by the looks of this Colonel Cameron, he has a very worthy opponent.*

As for Iain, opening puzzles was becoming tiresome and an irksome routine. Nonetheless, he did so, following the mode previously adopted. Letter three consisted of three pages.

Colonel Cameron,

Once again, you have arrived at your destination, without any threat to your life. Your safety will continue to be assured, until we meet in combat on the fourteenth day of this month. Tomorrow please proceed to Dublin, then on to Killarney in County Kerry. Rest there for the night, but plan to arrive at Port Magee at noon the following day. Make inquiry about a boat called Denny's Destiny. *Captain Dennis Kilpatrick will take you on board, and he will sail immediately for the Isle of Skellig Michael. Upon landing, he will give you explicit instructions on how to reach the old monastic site. After proceeding, according to his instructions, you should arrive at your station on the west side of the ruins before dark. I shall be on the east side, but make no attempt to call out to me. Each of us will spend the night in what shelter we can find. Dawn of the following day shall herald the commencement of our duel. Again, I consider it a duel to the death!*

Please be aware that Captain Kilpatrick has no knowledge of what we are about, and he is therefore guilty of nothing. Also, he has been instructed to return at noon on the following day after the duel to pick up whoever is leaving. Thus, he does not know that one of us will remain behind forever.

There is a chance the sea will be so tempestuous that landing will not be possible on the day that I have chosen. Your captain will know and, thus, inform you. I will be able to sense the weather, as well. Therefore, I can ascertain if your failure to appear is based on conditions or cowardice. In case of inclement weather, further instructions will be given.

Again, it was signed, MM.

The other two pages contained hand-drawn maps. One gave details for getting from Killarney to Port Magee, while the other was a sketch of the monastery ruins of Skellig Michael.

After having received the third letter on arrival at the Savoy Hotel, that night Cameron was more restless, no doubt due to the proximity and time of a duel, which would decide not only Annie's fate but his own. Iain had faced death before, either alongside military comrades in the past or in the present with a nearby tracker or gun-bearing client. However, he was concerned about the outcome. What if he was not successful in "the duel," as the mysterious MM called it? No one in the world, apart from the Irishman and possibly the skipper of the boat taking him to this Skellig Michael, would have any idea of what had become of him.

Surely, this MM won't be displaying my body as some sort of trophy. I'd probably be buried on the Island, or tossed in the sea. Dear Annie—would they tell her that her brother tried to save her, but he died in the effort? Can I truly be sure that he will set Annie free, whatever way this duel comes out? Concerned, given all the imponderables, Iain decided to write a letter to Rodney Cahill to be delivered in seventy-two hours if he didn't return. *That way, someone will at least know where I died, and for what reason. Also, it would immediately cause a search for Annie and alert my sons to be ever on their guard.* Once the details were inscribed on paper, Iain sealed it in an envelope, to which he affixed Cahill's address and telephone number. Now, more at ease, he returned to bed and was soon deeply asleep.

Early the next morning, on the way to breakfast, Cameron gave the envelope to one of the just-arrived managers that he knew quite well. While his instructions were circumspect, Iain knew from experience they would be followed precisely. "Kendall," he said. "I tried to ring up my old friend Rodney Cahill last night, but he wasn't available. I'll be out of London for a few days, and possibly I might return to Africa from Paris. If I do not come back by the evening of the sixteenth, then, please see Mr. Cahill receives this letter first thing on the morning of the seventeenth. His telephone numbers are on the front!"

"I'll certainly attend to it, Colonel," Kendall replied.

"One more thing Kendall." Is there a book shop nearby? One that would have information for travelers?"

"Gillman's Book Store just two easy blocks away. We would be happy to try and secure any title you might like, Colonel. What is your pleasure?"

"Just wanted to browse," replied Cameron, who continued, "I'm not sure at the moment, as to exactly what I want."

"Gillman's is the perfect place to do so, and from my experience, I know that Mr. Moody, the owner, has nearly encyclopedic knowledge."

"I'm most appreciative," said Iain, breaking off the conversation.

Certainly, Mr. Moody was on par with what had been promised, and Iain left Gillman's Book Store with two titles containing all the information about Skellig Michael Island that he needed. One more stop was necessary, and that would be at Cantrell's, outfitters for sportsmen and trekkers. Rapidly completed was the purchase of a lightweight waterproof sleeping bag with a thin mattress, as well as waterproof, hooded jacket and pants, plus woolen underwear. Purposely, slate gray was the color of the outer clothes, so as to blend with Skellig Island's aged granite. Drawing the hood close about his face would result in the lowest possible silhouette.

Shortly later, after checking out of the Savoy Hotel, Iain was back at Heathrow Airport by noon, and arrived in Dublin within an hour. Other than a little chiding from an Irish Customs official, he knew from the past, that agency provided no hurdle. "Rushing the season, are you Colonel? I thought we shot our stags in the autumn."

"You know Scotsmen, Inspector," laughed Iain. "Never miss a chance to poach in or out of season. Actually, one of your landowners that I lease from had the great misfortune to miss three grand stags last fall. I'm going to see him on business and brought this rifle along, so I could coach him for a couple of days."

Explanation combined with humor, sufficed to quell the inspector's need to examine further. After patting the rifle case, he handed it back unopened, then quipped, "The only Irishmen who can hit anything seem to be in the IRA, Colonel."

Broadening his smile to match the Inspector's, Iain nodded in assent and departed. Once inside the rental car, Cameron removed the Walther PPK from the rifle case and slid it inside his coat, from where it bestowed at least a promise of security. MM had specified, or perhaps suggested was the better term, that he spend the night in Killarney. However, no mention of a particular place of lodging was given in the third letter, which Iain had opened the previous evening. Arrival at Port Magee before noon tomorrow was the only condition. Since Iain had to adhere to smoothly accelerating the rental car through its four available gears, he decided to spend the night in Bantry instead of Killarney. *Go to hell MM,* he thought. *This Scot is going to spend this night where he damn well chooses.*

Chapter Forty-Seven

In Perth, at police headquarters and most specifically at the McKay household were sites of confusion. Also, London and MI-5 headquarters could easily be added to the mix. Under threats from higher-ups, Cahill's immediate superior had called several times, demanding to know what Cahill was up to.

"Are you daft, man?" the indignant voice had screamed on the last call. "You can't just go walkabout on a whim. Sir Douglas wants to know what the hell you are doing up in Perth! If you can't come up with some explanation, he intends to have you picked up, placed in one of those jackets with the wrap around sleeves, and sent off for psychiatric examination, as the first step before sacking you and recommending a prolonged stay at some loony farm!"

Realizing some rational explanation was now necessary, Rodney did reveal that he was working on a kidnapping case involving the sister of Colonel Iain Cameron, a quite distinguished personage and holder of the Victoria Cross. Departure from London's consultation had been necessitated by emergency! Yes, he was working with local officials. Soon, it would be possible to return to London for greater explanation. "However, in the meantime, Sidney old fellow, please concentrate on crime rather than condemnation, and call some of our chaps in Ulster and the Garde in the Republic to look around for Annie Cameron McKay."

"Come, as quickly as you can, Rodney," came over the line, "and be sure you drive straight east!"

"You mean right into the English Channel," retorted Cahill. "I would be happy to do that. But, in the meantime, Sidney, have a bad day!"

Unflustered, as usual, Rodney turned his face toward Bruce McKay, who looked haggard, and appeared all the more so underneath a two-day growth of beard. "I've got to return to London, Bruce, but I think I can convince the moguls at headquarters to broaden the search. Probably, there's no more to be done here anyway."

"What about Iain?" Bruce responded in a voice more like a groan.

"Yes. It's time that we contact him," replied Cahill. "Do you have the contact number in Johannesburg?"

While letting his body lurch back to the right, finally, McKay commanded an arm overly tired from supporting a distraught head to grope for his phone book. However, Cahill, also tired and distressed, was unable to decipher the mumbled numbers, causing him to snatch the phone book from McKay's hands in an act of exasperation. After apologizing, Rodney ran his finger down the open page and stopped at Safari Airlines. After four rings, Cahill began to calculate the difference in time zones. "Not yet three in the afternoon there," he said. "Come on! Come on! Answer the bloody phone!"

After the tenth ring, a voice just as irritable responded. Nothing irked Archie more than having to crawl down a ladder placed for work on Gertie's engines with grease-covered hands. Rather than pleasantly announce the name of his concern, Archie spit out his "Hello!"

"Is this Safari Airlines?" a voice curtly asked.

"No, it's Noah's Arc," said Andrus. "Did you want to talk to one of the animals?"

"Look," said Cahill, with increasing ire. "I want to reach Colonel Cameron! Can you help or not?"

"Who are you, and why are you calling?" was Archie's harsh response.

"I am Rodney Cahill, friend of Iain Cameron, and an Inspector in MI-5. I need to get a message to him, as soon as possible, and I was told he could be reached through this number."

"Where are you calling from?" asked Andrus with a little moderation creeping into his voice.

"I'm calling from Perth," was the response.

Thinking, *This is weird,* Archie stopped short of announcing it to the caller. Softening his voice, he said, "Iain left for home three days ago. He should be there by now, especially since he said that he was returning because of a family emergency."

Suddenly, both men's moods changed. Archie was bewildered, Cahill deeply perplexed. All Rodney could say was, "Thank you," before replacing the receiver, whereupon he sat in stunned silence. Cahill needed time to think before he tried to explain what he had just learned.

Slowly, he said, "Bruce, I understand Iain has left for home."

"Why? We haven't called him," gasped Bruce.

"Possibly, someone at the Police Department did," responded Cahill, unconvincingly. "At any rate, I must return to London immediately. You hold down the fort here. I'll call you as soon as I have anything new, or by tomorrow morning at the latest." Again, Cahill picked up the phone, rang up police headquarters, and requested immediate transport to the Edinburgh Airport. Before departing the McKay home, Rodney did his best to bestow hope in a convincing manner to Annie's husband. However, his words seemed to bounce off the thick shell of despair in which Bruce had encased himself.

Finally, on the flight to London, and free of the banality of the police headquarters chatter, Cahill was able to think. *Iain had left Africa for a family emergency. Only one person could have contacted him three days ago, and that would be the kidnapper. Furthermore, only the father or a close relative of the man killed would be likely to know how to contact him. "Come alone, or your sister will be killed," was undoubtedly the message that Cameron had received, and he unquestionably responded in the fashion that one would expect from him. Well, it would be easy enough to check Customs Records at Heathrow Airport and find out if and when Cameron had arrived.* As to defusing the imminent explosion of his superiors, on the next morning, Cahill proceeded to do just that.

Records showed that Colonel Cameron had arrived in London on the thirteenth, and departed for Dublin the following day. Not thinking of checking on where his friend had stayed in London kept Rodney from receiving Cameron's letter, which he might have obtained prematurely. Hair-trigger minds quickly focus on the next move, leaving the last one to bob about in the wake of their intuition; instead, Cahill decided Iain must have gone to the northern part of the Republic, possibly Ulster. Therefore, after pleading his convincing case, and exhibiting sufficient contrition to satisfy his superiors, Cahill was allowed to go to Belfast and launch an operation to locate Iain, Annie, or both!

When it came to matters of deduction, Rodney would probably have surprised Dr. Watson. However, carrying out the comparison, it would seem improbable that even Sherlock Holmes would have surmised Colonel Cameron was headed south, not north. Also, his destination was at the very edge of Europe, a desolate isle called Skellig Michael.

While Rodney Cahill was trying to unravel the mystery, Iain spent a night in solitude at a quaint little inn on the outskirts of Bantree, rather than in

Killarney. Tomorrow, he would set foot on Skellig Michael for the first time in his life, and Iain thought, *Perhaps it would be the last place on earth on which my feet will tread.* Similar moods and reflections went concurrently with such thoughts, and Cameron's mind was besieged. Remembering that it is said that a dying man sees his entire life flash before him during his last mortal moment, Iain Cameron's images lingered, then languished. Unique in his life was the experience soon to befall him. Going on a sortie with other soldiers, especially those under one's command, made myriad preparations necessary. Thus, his mind had been focused on details, and alleviated by virtue of the fact that, if he was to die, it wouldn't be alone. *Going into a thorn thicket, after a wounded lion, was an act of spontaneity. Situation recognized, you did immediately what was needed, without dwelling upon it. Almost the same thing, as plunging into the water to save a drowning man. Here, in this lonely room, there was no one else in which to try and temper my spirit with conviction and courage.* Such actions in the past had served to assuage Iain's own fear. One rifle and sixty cartridges needed little in the way of preparation. Therefore, Cameron decided, "Whatever minutes remained before sleep came, should best be devoted to an examination of my own conscience. Could I defend this coming action, before an omnipotent God, all merciful? Yes, but He is all just as well? Am I presumptuous, in feeling God would accept my arguments before His tribunal?" Then, he thought, *If I really knew the mind of God, I would be God myself. However, the conscience he gave me, and the one that I have tried to form in His ways, tells me that I'm doing right!*

Decision made, Iain was released from his turmoil, and a deep sleep followed. Meanwhile, barely fifty miles away, Mickey Moynihan lay on a similar bed in a comparable room, though with dissimilar meditation. Revenge had long ago replaced his conscience and, at the moment, there were no thoughts of heaven or hell. However, some of his self-confidence was starting to ebb, which gave rise to the possibility of his own demise. *What's it like out there in the void?* he began to wonder, recalling it was a term atheists like to employ. He himself had employed the word frequently on many occasions. In memory, Mickey pictured himself waving his hands in emphasis, as he proclaimed, "there is no heaven or hell, just a big, black void." Now, the word began to accost his intelligence. Buried deep in his psyche was the thought that when he died there would somehow be a reunion with Bernie, Sean, and Liam; also, maybe his Ma, Da, and little brother Sean might be there. "Hell," he muttered, "void is void and void means empty." Upset by the definition, Mickey slammed the door on his thoughts by adamantly declaring aloud that "Cameron should be sent to the void!" Consoling himself with "Should it turn out to be nothing, at least he will be there before I am!" Relieved by this one last vengeful thought, Mickey fell asleep.

Shortly after sunrise, Moynihan was at the quay where he met Dennis Kilpatrick. His rifle and kit were soon stored aboard, and the boat *Denny's Destiny* put to sea. Mickey shared the wheel house with the skipper, while two crewmen busied themselves with chores on the deck. They wondered why there were two runs scheduled to Skellig Island on the same day, for it wasn't tourist season, and why couldn't both passengers have gone at the same time? "What the hell," they whispered to one another, while out on the fan tail, where the wind whisked their words away. "There's an extra five punts in it for each of us, and the weather is not half bad. Why should we care?" Had they known their passenger was in possession of a high-powered rifle, they might have cared.

In the wheel house, while handing an envelope to Dennis Kilpatrick, Moynihan said "Here's for your trouble." Taking the proffered envelope, the skipper used his fingers as cash-counting calipers and estimated the thickness was consistent with £500, in £10 notes. *No point in angering this man by counting it or looking inside,* he thought. Five thousand had been their agreement, and he could count it later, in private. Besides, if the money was short, Moynihan couldn't get back by himself, and it would be a hell of a swim unless he could walk on water. Kilpatrick figured there was something dirty going on, but he didn't want to know what it was. In case there was ever an inquiry, ignorance was a good wall to hide behind during the inquisition.

Little more was said between the two men, apart from Mickey asking Kilpatrick if he were certain that he could get back to Port Magee before noon, and if the captain felt the weather would hold. After being reassured on both accounts, Mickey handed Kilpatrick a photo of Cameron. "Here is who you will be hauling next, if he shows up. Don't forget that unless the weather is fierce, you are to return early the day after tomorrow to pick up whomever is standing on the dock. The other person will be staying on, so you needn't worry about their arrangements."

After landing, Moynihan watched from where he stood on the south landing of Skellig Michael, as *Denny's Destiny* left for its return trip to pick up the boat's next passenger. Moments later, he began the steep ascent of steps hewn from granite by the hands of monks ages ago. Despite his arduous training program, Moynihan felt tired when he crested the final step and was able to visualize the ancient monastic site. Sitting for a while, Mickey was quick to remember that he and Bernie once sat upon this very step. *Oh! If I could pull her tight against me, thrill to the warmth of her, and smell the delicate scent of her hair. What wouldn't I give for that!* Warm thoughts of their honeymoon happiness returned, then gave way to the horror of her murder! How many months ago had it been? Time was ever so strange. Joy was fleeting, while sorrow could stretch to infinity. *What difference does it make now, anyway? One hollow month is the same as another. So why bother to count, for it makes no more sense than multiplying by zero.* Abruptly, Mickey wondered, "Are you calling to me, Bernie, trying to tell me something? Well, I can't listen now. I've got an important thing to do." Then, he added the words, "Same as when you were here. Is that what you're saying?"

With strong emotions evident on his face, Mickey murmured, "I listened on the little things, then did what I wanted on the big things. You know, Bernie, I figured out why you wanted to name the last boat *Sargasso*. You were trying to tell me that our lives were becoming ensnarled in a sea of weeds, from which there was no escape!" Though Mickey's eyes displayed no tears, he swiped harshly at a dab of moisture on his nose. Quickly looking at his watch's hands, he saw that it was fifteen minutes past noon.

Far distant was the speck outside Port Magee, but it inexorably grew in size. No doubt it was *Denny's Destiny*, and perhaps his own as well. Rising, Mickey began to subordinate all other thoughts but one. Cameron was coming, and it was time for final preparations. Sunrise was eighteen hours away. *Everyone faces a final dawn,* he thought, *and tomorrow will be the last dawn that one of us will ever see.*

Soon, Moynihan was moving among the ruins of the crumbling oratories of the monks' cells, and a tiny cemetery in which the former occupants' remains had reposed for a thousand years. Minutes later, Mickey found the lair he would occupy when dusk commenced. After all his gear had been placed in position, Moynihan surveyed his space, then he pondered, *Will it serve as a spring board to victory or a tomb?*

While Mickey was reminiscing and pondering his fate, exactly as he had surmised, Iain was aboard *Denny's Destiny* and headed toward culmination of the vendetta Moynihan had decreed. On arrival at Port Magee, Iain had surveyed the little harbor with a powerful spy glass, most useful to his single eye. Approaching the boat at precisely noon, he noted the captain to be a sullen man, solid in stature, textured and weathered by the elements inherent in his calling. Only two words were uttered at their meeting. Kilpatrick said, "Cameron," and Iain responded, "Aye." Furtive behavior was observed in the manner of the two deckhands; however, the Colonel paid them little heed.

After stowing his cased rifle and gear in a well behind the wheelhouse, Iain sat down on an adjacent hatch cover from which he could keep captain and crew in sight. His action preempted a need for words, prompting Kilpatrick to start the engine while the crew cast off the hawsers.

Soon at sea, Skellig Michael began to loom ever larger. After drawing closer, the great, gray, craggy monolith seemed to emit an aura most eerie. Finally, the sturdy old craft was made fast to the jetty, and Kilpatrick's head tilted in the right direction, leading to Cameron's affirmative nod. Minutes later, the last of the two combatants stood staring out at the wake of a departing craft. At that moment, Iain felt as though he was on some far, distant planet occupied only by himself and his deadly adversary.

After looking around, Cameron decided that his position was one of total exposure. Furthermore, as he surveyed the steps he must climb to the place of the duel, he realized the precarious situation would not change during his ascent. Voicing his concern, he murmured "You are either an intuitive genius, basing presumptions on paper promises, given by MM, or one of the greatest fools who ever lived. He could be up there anywhere, and here I am, just like a duck in a shooting gallery of his design."

Seeking what minimal shelter he could find, Iain uncased his rifle, fingered four rounds into the magazine, and chambered a fifth. *Should this MM prove to be craven, then I surely hope he is no marksman.* Cautiously climbing the same granite stairway which his adversary had so recently mounted, Iain started up. At last he attained the final flight of steps, which he recognized from his reading as those leading past what was called Christ's Saddle, surely an allegorical description for the two giant granite outcroppings, which projected upward, having much the appearance of fractured, cavitated shark's teeth.

During his climb, sometimes Iain had been startled by seabirds taking flight or rabbits darting for cover. Always the consummate hunter, he recognized these for what they were and remained steadfast. Finally, arriving unscathed on the top, ancient ruins lay spread before him, appearing like a diorama with a background painted by God. Sensing the sacredness of these ruins, Iain could not help but wonder if he had come to a place of sanctuary or sacrilege? Well he had decided that matter on the preceding night, in what he considered good conscience and, now, he would abide by it. To this moment, MM had been a man of his word, so Cameron settled down to await the night on the southwest corner of the ruins directly opposite from his opponent. This was the position MM's letter had decreed. Here, there would be trial by combat.

MM had described the site, as being the size of a soccer field; however, there was no expanse of grass between them. Rather, there were beehive-shaped monks' cells, made of slabs of chiseled stone, plus two boat-shaped oratories, constructed in a similar manner. One wall remained of a medieval church, while the other walls had long ago crumbled away. A single window remained in the standing wall, looking like a doorway to eternity. With the layout now locked in Cameron's mind, he began to plot his campaign, knowing full well that 100 yards away, MM was doing the same. Tomorrow would be a game of chess, when all the pieces but one might be swept from the board, with a single move.

As daylight began to dwindle, the pair of duelists sat huddled in their private parapets, with attention focused primarily on their rifles. Iain had come with a Winchester Model 70 in 30 06 caliber, while Mickey relied on his Draganov chambered for 762 x 54 caliber cartridges. Ballistically, there was no significant difference in performance and, if one converted fractions of an inch to the metric system, bullet diameter was much the same. Colonel Cameron had employed the Winchester extensively for taking light game, such as elans on the African plains, and was totally familiar with the weapon. Conversely, Moynihan had great success with the Russian rifle and had practiced shooting it on hundreds of occasions. Thus, there was little to separate them, either in skill or weaponry. Mickey's cartridges had been hand-loaded with great care, where Iain chose factory loads of premium quality. Nonetheless, there would be a difference when it came to the type of sights on their guns employed by each man. For Moynihan, it would be a Russian made PSO telescopic sight with four-power magnification. Cameron had considered employing similar optics, though he had finally decided on more conventional iron sights, as they were called. No cross-hairs or posts were involved. He simply placed the gold bead on the front sight in alignment with a notch in the rear one, and pointed at the target.

Westward moving, the sun was about to embrace the new world, leaving only a faint yellow-gray wake tailing behind to weakly illuminate Skellig Michael. Soon, the last vestige of light was gone. Fully insulated from the light of the moon and stars by a quilt of clouds, the island was cloaked in total darkness. Wind sounds and the chatter of a restless sea, scrapes of clothing on stone, along with one's own breathing, were all that remained to stimulate senses. Tired bodies called out in supplication for sleep; however, tightly strung minds forbade its coming. Situation-wise, it was rather bizarre for each man realized that he was the only available picket on guard, as no one else was there to spell him and share the watch. Falling asleep and missing the call of dawn, could be a final and fatal error. Each man lay huddled, wanting to get the duel over, and both shared fear about what that phase might portend. Surely, it would have been a relief to hear the sound of another human voice, but only two men were present on Skellig Michael that night. In either case, each man was possibly the other's executioner. As hours passed, with steadfast determination, each man awaited the dawn.

Hours later, after both Mickey and Iain began to wonder if mind or heart would be the first to burst, subtle environmental changes were experienced. Where blackness alone had previously existed, there was now the faintest perception of form. Off in the distance, gulls, terns, and other birds gave voice to a morning song. Raucous, strident calls would come later, though for now, the sound was sweet, as if they were wooing the sunrise. From that time onward, each succeeding second added a single lumen of light to the island crest.

Soon, the sun began to release rays, though most were absorbed by gray clouds, acting like a fluffy filter of lead. Only the most energetic penetrated, but these numbers were sufficient to proclaim the dawn. Adrenaline began to surge in the veins of both men, as it had every time circumstances proclaimed one should try and kill the other. Abruptly, realization came to both Moynihan's and Cameron's minds simultaneously that dawn was battling darkness, and the latter was succumbing.

Slowly, two pair of hands opened rifle bolts, just far enough to recognize there was a burnished brass cartridge held tightly in the claw of their rifle's extractor. Then, soundlessly, the bolts were allowed to close, reseating the cartridges in their respective chambers. Like spawn of Vulcan, they would rest in their steel wombs until a thrusting firing pin indented their primers, releasing the pent-up fury of the powder nestled inside. When fully ignited, the propellant would form expanding gases, which would challenge the chamber walls with pressure of nearly 50,000 pounds per square inch. By design, the chambers and bolts of the rifles would hold firm. The projectile, like a pointed steel stopper wedged in the neck of a small brass bottle, would be freed of its tether by the rapidly expanding gas. Then, the bullet would rocket down the barrel, achieving a speed of 3,600 feet per second. A journey of 100 yards would take little more than 0.08 of a second. Small as it was, the projectile would impact like a massive sledge hammer. Slowly, sound waves generated by the cartridge's discharge would follow the bullet's flight and, if the projectile traversed a brain, the tardy sound would never be heard by the victim.

While relying on the profile of his snug-fitting, blending, gray anorak hood, Cameron cautiously peeked around the edge of one of the monks' cells. Noticing that a tiny opening had developed in the cloud cover and using it like a loophole or fining portal, the sun shot forth a golden ray that momentarily brightened MM's expected position. Carefully, Iain was studying the rocky profiles, and a tiny reflection flashed on his retina. Undoubtedly, it resulted from a sunbeam striking the front lens of a telescopic sight. Cameron responded, as if his radar had suddenly detected a missile homing in on him.

Iain had been fully correct, for no sooner had he contracted his head when a bullet whistled by, which preceded the report of MM's rifle by nearly a second. Since one eye was always a disadvantage compared to two, even more so at this time in this situation, Iain mumbled, "I'll always have to look around any upright shield from the left side. I wonder if he knows that?"

Realizing that he was pinned down where he was currently located, Cameron looked to his left without exposing himself. Six feet away, there was a low wall, perhaps four feet in height. Along its top, some stones has fallen away, giving the wall a crenellated appearance. *Far better place than this,* he thought. *But how do I get there?*

Meanwhile, Moynihan was sure his first shot had drawn no blood; however, his confidence was beginning to build. Old newspaper clippings he had received alerted him to the fact that Cameron had lost his right eye in Malay years ago. *You'll always have to peek around the left side Scotty, and I'll be waiting.* Zeroing in on the spot where he was expecting his opponent to look around, Mickey slowed his breathing and tensed his fingers in anticipation, but nothing happened. Suddenly, it dawned on Moynihan that he could be the victim of his first failed shot. *What if the bastard just stays where he is? He can't shoot at me, but I can't shoot at him either, while hidden behind that cell.* Agitated, Mickey began to look about for another vantage space. *Perhaps, I can gradually move to the right or left, until some part of him is in view. Five more minutes, and I'll move to my left, which will be to his blind side. Maybe I'll be able to see some part of him sticking out. Even if I hit him in the leg, he might be disabled. Then I can move in for the kill! Five more minutes, Scotty. Come on, take a peek, and I can save myself the trouble of moving.*

While Moynihan was planning his next move, Cameron's thoughts were still on the adjacent stone wall, and how to get there safely. *Think, man, think! What have I learned so far? MM has a scope sighted rifle, possibly with the powerful optics that snipers like to employ.* Fully knowledgeable about such weapons, Iain knew that when held steady on a rest, the detail they gave and accuracy provided was superb. Nevertheless, nearly everything has some inherent disadvantage, and such may surely be the case in regard to his opponent. Iain thought about the fact that when a high-powered rifle fires, it recoils momentarily, so the shooter's eye is not perfectly aligned with the optics. Thus, the chance of his immediately getting off an unerring second shot is greatly diminished. *Obviously, I can't stick my head out, so how about trying a decoy?*

Quickly, Iain grasped his telescope and extended it to full length. Next, he whipped off his left glove, and affixed it over the small end of the instrument. Gingerly, the glove was elevated, just into his adversary's line of fire. Instantaneously, the bullet from Mickey's gun tore through the dangling leather, and even before the sound of the report reached his ears, Cameron dashed for the safety of the wall. Moynihan did get off a rapid second shot, but as Iain had predicted, it wasn't accurate. Impacting on a stone above and behind his right leg, the projectile departed, leaving only the eerie whistle of a ricochet to mark its passage.

Once safely behind the wall, Iain moved to one of crenellation and, from this new vantage point, he risked taking a look. MM''s rifle muzzle was traversing the stone wall, and soon the sight would find Cameron's portal. Consequently, Iain's initial shot was hurried and not as accurate as he wished. Nonetheless, it did remove Moynihan's hat when the bullet cut its way through the visor, less than an inch from his head. Now, both men were in the agonizing position of placing themselves in jeopardy, just in the process of trying to snatch a glance and possibly get off a quick shot.

Next, Mickey decided that he could safely crawl over to his left and perhaps eke out an advantage. At the same instant, Cameron moved to his right. Finding themselves in a stalemate, they changed positions repeatedly each time it seemed safe. However, they both found that what seemed secure was not necessarily true, as Cameron's left ear pinna had been nicked by one bullet, and another that impacted close by had peppered the left side of his neck with tiny shards of granite. After a minute of profuse bleeding, soon, it was stanched. *Fortunately,* he thought, *my one good eye was spared*.

Perhaps, Mickey was slightly the worse off, as pieces of rocky shrapnel had torn into his left fifth finger and fractured one of his metacarpals. Painful though it was, when tightly bandaged, the finger was still partially functional, and he could continue to grip the forearm of his rifle tightly to ensure accuracy. However, that was a feat he found agonizingly difficult, as he had only a millisecond to look, and a second one to fire, then a third to duck.

Dodging between the rocks, the two men were getting ever closer to each other. By noon, they were only fifty paces apart. Each man was nearing exhaustion from the stress, and both mouths were beginning to agonize over obtaining a sip of water. Strategy-wise, it had become cell-to-cell or wall-to-wall fighting, and any second could bring victory or defeat. Iain and Mickey had become much like a pair of gladiators fighting in an ancient colseum, nearly as old as that of Rome, though bereft of the Roman sun and frenzied crowd. Also, no emperor was present to raise or lower his thumb. That privilege would belong to the victor.

After reaching a new position, hopefully relatively safe, Cameron rolled partially on his back in order to facilitate a swift inventory of his cartridge belt. Eighteen remaining rounds were estimated. Then, flashing a look at the sky, Iain beheld a sun that appeared like a single yellowish, baleful eye trying to peer through a thick layer of cloudy exudate. Next, he noted that blood from the wounds to the left side of his face had congealed. Running his fingers over the forming scab, Cameron needed no micrometer to gauge how close the cuts were to his single remaining eye. Just a few millimeters difference and blindness would have been immediate, with death scant seconds later when the foe became aware of his advantage.

Mickey also had a few seconds for reflection and assessment of his cartridge supply. "Thirteen rounds," he concluded, murmuring "an unlucky number." Then, suddenly, the haunting lyrics of "The Minstrel Boy" flashed into his mind and froze on the phrase "In the ranks of death, you'll find him." Vainly, Moynihan tried to exorcise the memory with a silent curse, though to little avail. Both combatants were keenly aware of their perilous situation.

Slowly but inexorably, both Moynihan and Cameron continued to expend the supply of cartridges held in their belts. Each had additional rounds, but these were stored safely in less accessible pouches, fearing they might be lost from an open pocket. Should they not obtain victory soon, taking time to tap the additional supply might prove disadvantageous. More shots were fired, as Mickey and Iain continued to change positions while always seeking an advantage. Bullets whizzed by so closely that the combatants were sure they could feel each projectile's hot breath, as friction was generated by their passage through the moisture laden air, scant millimeters from their heads. Ricochets sang out a soul-searing song. Fragments of stony shrapnel buzzed by like hornets from hell. Both men were aware that should one or more of these missiles strike eyes or have sufficient mass and velocity to pierce a vital organ, they would be just as devastating as a bullet. Death would thus define the defeated duelist.

Two events occurred in rapid succession, which terrifyingly reminded each man of his opponent's prowess and his own vulnerability. Sensing an opportunity to move to a more advantageous position, Mickey slipped in the effort and fell. Immediately, he rolled to the right only a millisecond before Cameron's bullet impacted where his head had been, and tiny slivers of stone cut into his scalp. Bleeding ensued, though fortunately it was not disabling. Now, in a safer position, Moynihan returned fire. An arrowhead shaped fragment of granite was dislodged by the impact of Mickey's bullet and imbedded itself in the dense walnut of Iain's gunstock. He was sure that had its course been altered a few degrees, it might now be lodged in his brain.

As distance closed, Mickey became more aware of a crucial mistake he had made. No longer an advantage, his telescopic sight was increasingly hard to use. An object fifty yards away and moving rapidly was easily seen with the naked eye but very hard to focus on with magnification. Resourceful Russians had endowed Mickey's Draganov rifle with iron sights as a backup. These were attached to the top of the gun's receiver below the scope and the barrel's end.

Predicting such a predicament as Mickey now faced, the telescopic sight was secured in place by a readily detachable mount. However, Moynihan had replaced the original stock with one having a higher comb to aid alignment of his eye with the eye piece of the optical sight. Even if he removed the scope, his shooting eye would not align properly with the iron sights. He decided that perhaps it would be best to try and ignore the sights altogether, and simply shoot instinctively. Mickey used to practice with the concept of instinctive shooting in the past. This was with a .22-caliber rifle, and he had become able to hit tossed coins in the air. Well, he would try the scope when he could; otherwise, he must resort to the other method. Glimpses he had caught revealed that Cameron had no telescopic sight. *Thought he might outsmart me, did he? Well I can punch a hole in him, just like I did to a penny!*

Moments later, both men chose the same, singular second to peek, then fire. Just as the reverberations of their shots had resounded from the stones surrounding them, the obvious sound of a rifle clattering on rock as it fell was heard. One man waited, then, with his rifle at the ready, he began to slowly and very cautiously approach the site where the weapon landed. Silently, he moved closer and soon he was standing over the fallen gun. With his rifle muzzle leveled and pointing forward, he chanced a quick look over the low wall, which his adversary had so recently utilized for protection. Lying there obviously wounded but still alive was his opponent.

"Have you come to gloat over the vanquished, Scotty?" hissed Moynihan, through teeth clenched tightly in pain.

"No," was Cameron's somber response.

"Then, finish me off damn you! Don't just stand there; put a bullet in my brain."

"I've no intention of doing that either," Iain replied, as he visually surveyed his opponent's right shoulder area. Like ripples from a rock, tossed in a pacific pond, a circle of crimson was forming on the cloth of Mickey's coat with an increasing circumference. Centrally, a tiny spurt timed to the contractions of a heart fighting shock, was discernible. Laying his rifle aside, Iain bent over the stricken man, and softly said, "I've got a small pack with some dressings. Let me see if I can attend to your wound." Iain was not quite the type of man that Mickey had expected.

Dropping his ferocious attitude several degrees, Mickey spoke, saying, "I've a pistol in a shoulder holster under my left arm. Best you take it, Colonel Cameron. That's the way it's done, isn't it? The conquered surrender their arms to the victor."

"If you could have got at it, I suspect you would have tried to use it," replied Iain with what bordered on a fraction of a smile.

"You've got me pretty well figured out, haven't you Colonel?" replied Moynihan.

"Call me Iain," was Cameron's response. "While we're at it, I assume you have a name, other than MM."

"Michael Moynihan," came back the reply. "But Mickey will do."

Shortly, after procuring his kit, Iain said, "Well Mickey, let me cut away your jacket, and see what I can do for you." Slicing deftly through Moynihan's garment, the cloth was retracted away, and an operative field of sorts was exposed. Peripheral edges of an obvious bullet entry wound were readily discernible, right over the mid-portion of Mickey's clavicle, or collar bone. Knowing the velocity and steel-jacketed characteristics of the bullet responsible for the wound, Iain expected a slightly larger exit wound should be discernible on the opposite side. Then, Cameron noted an elliptical, jagged laceration, just an inch or so below that of the bullet hole. Quickly, he surmised that it must be secondary to a fragment of granite with a razor-sharp edge. He thought, *No doubt the slug had grazed the rock, dislocated the sliver of stone, and turned it into a primordial piece of shrapnel.* Also, he noted about the wounds that the soft tissues were becoming increasingly swollen and outwardly convex, attesting to the presence of subcutaneous hemorrhage. Tiny red geysers continued to erupt from both wounds, indicative of severed small arteries and arterioles. Quickly Cameron applied pressure dressings, front and back; then, he bound them tightly in place with a elastic bandage.

Despite the pain associated with the first-aid measures, Mickey remained as stoic as any soldier so distressed. Cameron had made no preemptive remarks, regarding the fact that what he was about to do would cause more pain, for he was certain Mickey would tough it out. Observing the dressings for a few minutes, it was obvious to Cameron that they were having a beneficial effect regarding the superficial bleeding. However, he wondered about hemorrhage that might be deeper. One glance at Mickey's face provided an answer that Iain did not want to see. Mickey's skin, which had such a sort time ago conveyed every sign of vigor was now a visage of deadly white, causing his one-day dark growth of beard to appear even blacker. Meanwhile, drops of perspiration dappling his forehead showed no sign of the warmth of arduous sweat, but rather the cold feel of body systems on the brink of surrender.

Though he felt none himself, Iain tried to induce hope in Mickey. "We seem to have stopped some bleeding on the outside, but I'm not sure how we are doing on the inside."

Looking into Cameron's eyes, Mickey replied, "Iain, I'm grateful to you. As a soldier, you may never have lost a battle, but you are losing this one. I feel like a human hourglass. Instead of sand running from top to bottom, deep inside, there is blood moving from where it should be to where it shouldn't be. I don't suppose either of us know enough anatomy to tell what got destroyed. However, the nerves in my arm must be shredded because I can't move it at all. In all probability, there are big arteries and veins in there that are pumping me out, and I suspect the blood is going into the right side of my chest. Look close and you can see that when I breathe, the left side expands, while the right barely changes. I'm drowning in my own juice."

Iain wiped away some of the cold beads on Moynihan's brow, then looked Mickey straight in the eyes. "Mickey, you may be right. I know there's a lighthouse on this island. No people are stationed there, as it is fully automatic. However, perhaps, there could be a radio or phone still operative. Also, sometimes, even large arteries contract when shock deepens, and the bleeding could slow down or even stop. Let me make you as warm as I can, then, I'll go to the lighthouse. Perhaps, I can get an helicopter here in time."

Mickey looked at Iain with the countenance of a dying soldier beholding the visage of his comrade trying to help in any way he could. "Sound reasons to say no, Iain. First, I don't think you would make it in time. Secondly what explanation could you give? Two rabbit hunters looking for rabbits with oversized rifles, and one victim of a tragic hunting accident. Lastly, if I were to survive, I have a past history of what the courts would call murder, though I truly looked upon it as war. Far better that I go here, rather than rot in prison."

Suddenly, there seemed to be a transformation in Mickey's face, signifying the pain was lessening, along with his life. Wan was his smile, though genuine. "You know, Iain. I spent sometime in the States, and I developed a keen interest in the Old West, as they like to refer to it. I remember there was a song of lament of which I was especially fond. They called it "The Streets of Laredo," and one of the verses went:

> *One day, as I walked on the Streets of Laredo*
> *I spied a young cowpoke, all wrapped in white linen,*
> *All wrapped in white linen as cold as the clay.*
> *I see by your outfit that you are a cowboy,*
> *He said to me, as I boldly stopped by.*
> *Come sit down beside me and hear my sad story,*
> *For I'm a young cowboy, and I know I must die.*

In a weakening voice, with the sad smile still remaining, Mickey added, "I suppose, I should have changed the words from 'young cowboy' to 'old rebel,' but I'm sure you get the gist of it."

Sitting down beside him, Cameron listened as Mickey continued. "I spent sometime in prison for planting a bomb. When I finally got out, I wanted to even the score and wage war on those I considered the enemy and oppressors of Ireland. There is no time for all the details, but suffice it to say that I've killed many men in various ways, but never a woman or child, as far as know. I think of myself as a soldier, much like yourself. You could return a hero. I was always a hunted felon.

"Along the way, I married a fine woman, Bernadette Donahue. Oh how I loved my Bernie, but sadly, I guess that I thought I could have her and the Cause at the same time. Bernie bore me three fine sons; two of whom are now dead, as you have no doubt surmised. Dear Bernie was mutilated and killed by a bomb. Not a Sassenach one, but a Provo bomb, mind you, one of my own! That score was evened, then I turned my attention, again to the Brits. More and more violence continued, and two of my sons were swept up into it and died!"

With his voice growing weaker, Moynihan said, "You are probably wondering why I chose this place, this big rock called Skellig Michael. Well, dear Bernie and I came here on our honeymoon. She loved it like no place else on earth. Her ashes are here, and so are those of my son Liam. I could have tried to kill you from a distance, like I have others in the past. However, the more I read about you, the more something inside me cried out, 'If you are going to try and kill a soldier of honor, do it in an honorable way. Kidnapping your sister wasn't honorable, I agree, but she is well treated and will be set free when you return. No doubt, this all seems childish—some poor Paddy imagining himself a soldier and, somehow, the equal of a gentleman such as yourself."

"No Mickey, it doesn't," responded Iain somberly, with a slight nod of his head. "Change history a little, and I could have been you. Four hundred years ago, there was a Battle of Boyne with Cromwell's forces, and Ireland has known some degree of oppression ever since. Also, Scotland's woes started centuries before, when Wallace and Bruce battled the far greater masses of the English, under Edward I. We kept on until Culloden in 1745, when we were finally conquered once and for all. Both of our people relinquished much. Your green, our tartan; all of our weapons, music, much of our religion, and even our freedoms. Irish died during the potato famines. Some survived, and many migrated. Scots' Celts were torn from their land to make way for sheep. Some of them survived, and many suffered forced migration as well. I guess those that stayed on finally decided that if you couldn't defeat your enemy—and God knows that many tried—then perhaps it is best you join them."

Using the Celtic term for the English, Iain continued on, "Over the years since Culloden, the Sassenach came to learn they needed us for cannon fodder, if nothing else. Always very clever, they gave us back our tartans and our pipes, knowing full well that we would fight all the harder, and this we did. In Ireland, many who stayed on accepted the English yoke. However, others like yourself fought on for freedom. Yes, it was guerrilla warfare, and those who fought it bravely in the way of a true soldier have my admiration. I truly believe that you were one of these. However, there were and are many who have acted as craven killers, indiscriminately murdering or maiming the innocent. For them, I have no compassion."

Replying, Mickey said, "I thank you for that, Iain. I agree with all you have said." Now, Mickey's words were becoming halting, and his breathing extremely labored. Raising his left arm, he extended his hand, seeking Iain's. When it was received, the grip was firm, though telling on Mickey's final reserve. "I'm going Iain," said Mickey between gasping breaths. "Bernie's trying to tell me something. She wants me to come to her, and I want so much to do so, but I can't. For years, I've mocked God, and I feel now that I'm damned to Hell, and Bernie is in Heaven. She confessed and had absolution, so I know she's there, and I never will be with her."

"Do you want to be with God, as well?" queried Iain softly.

"I don't know Him. I only know Bernie," sighed Mickey. Now beads of sweat were joined by the first tears Mickey had shed in years.

Cameron bent close to the dying man, with his lips only an inch from Moynihan's ear. "Mickey, listen. The reason you want to be with Bernie is because she was the finest thing you ever knew in this life. Everything you loved about her were the embodiments of God. If you love Bernie, you must love God and wish to be with Him as well. Do you understand, and do you truly believe that?"

"I do, Iain," Moynihan gasped.

"Mickey, I'm no more a shriver than a surgeon. But I am Catholic, as you once were. I can't give you absolution, as only a priest can do that, as you know. Repeat the perfect Act of Contrition after me, and it will do the same." Now, with his lips pressed to Mickey's ear, Iain fervently and strongly said the words: "Oh my God, I am heartily sorry for having offended you . . ."

With the very last vestige of his strength, Mickey repeated the prayer. Then, his last five words followed, and they were "Oh Bernie! Thank you God"

Iain carried Mickey's body to a place just outside the ancient monastic site. Carefully, he laid it out in repose. Surrounded by beautiful blossoms, somehow, Iain thought it would be what Bernie, Mickey's beloved, would have chosen. Next, all of Moynihan's personal effects were removed, apart from the weapons that Iain now laid beside him. Then, building a cairn from nearby debris, Iain took care to try and keep it from looking like a grave.

Finished, at last, near the time when day would also die, Iain stood back and picked up his rifle. After saying the proper prayers for a comrade in arms, Cameron brought the rifle up smartly to his shoulder. Three shots were fired, at rapid though equal intervals, bringing to Iain's mind words of the American poet that had been penned for fallen comrades, before he was also killed. Kilmer's words seemed appropriate, with a minor modification. "Over his grave abrupt and clear three volleys ring. Perhaps his brave spirit hears the bugle sing, Go to sleep, go to sleep dangers past. Now at last go to sleep."

Iain stood at attention and held his salute, for it was for a man that he had come to understand. He had no uniform, rank, or even an army, as such. But Mickey had been a soldier, and he deserved no less. Obviously, there were no bugles or pipes to play Taps as a final lament. However, soft calls of Skellig Michael's birds would surely do as well.

Turning to look at Mickey's grave for one last time, Iain recited the Memorare, as he had done for his dear friend Geordie in Malay so long ago. Additionally, he asked that dear lady whom he felt surely to be the mother of God to mediate for Michael Moynihan before her almighty son. Hopefully, even now, Mickey's guardian angel and perhaps even the Archangel Michael for whom he might have been named had already borne his soul from Skellig Michael to Heaven's ramparts, there to await judgment by an all just and all merciful Creator.